BLACK SABBATH

... Beijing's deadly quest

JASON DENARO

Avid Readers Publishing Group
Lakewood, California

i

Avid Readers Publishing Group

http://www.avidreaderspg.com

ISBN-13: 978-1-935105-75-6

Printed in the United States

Author's Note

"The creation of 'Black Sabbath' has spanned a period covering 2006-2010. References were obtained through extensive research, including declassified CIA files.

The Chinese Operation Compass/Beidou, and the Miracl satellite program are fact. The Myanmar junta, and its incarceration of that nation's democratically elected leader, Aung San Suu Kyi, is fact. Reference to MK ULTRA and WWII interrogation methods, as well as the termination of CIA Agent, Frank Olson is also fact. US military bases are fact. Catalina is . . . hmm?

The time frame is the George W. Bush era.

The characters, Drew Blake, Carson Dallas and their associates, are 'fictional.' Their mannerisms, humor, and language exist for entertainment value. Many political Heads-of-State are fact. Some remain in 'positions of influence' today, perhaps in anticipation of plutocratic osmosis.

It will be a lengthy wait."

******

ACKNOWLEDGEMENTS

A special thanks to Carolyn Royer for her ceaseless editing, her enthusiasm, and her welcome encouragement.

To Steve Fanter (Ret. Federal Agent) for his technical expertise, and guidance.

To Captain Leland Ozawa (Ret.) for his technical guidance with regards all aspects of aviation specifications.

To retired CIA agent (name withheld) for her eye opening tales of classified assignments that Fox News would give its left nut to get hold of!

To Whea Chang for her informative contribution pertaining to China and Myanmar, the locations, topography and descriptive accuracy throughout this work are precise, thanks to her careful cross referencing.

To "Dominic Broski," you know who you are. Great job, mate! Stay safe!

*****

Tribute

"What kind of a peace do we seek? I am talking about genuine peace, the kind of peace that makes life on Earth worth living. Not merely peace in our time, peace in all times. Our problems are man-made, therefore they can be solved by man, for in the final analysis our most basic common link is that we all inhabit this small planet, we all breathe the same air, we all cherish our children's future, and we are all mortal."

President John F. Kennedy

PROLOGUE

THE OLD PLANE WAS HEAVY when asked to perform steep turns and quick maneuvers, veering sideways in the black sky as the pilot pulled it into a steep climb, losing his struggle with the controls, the Chinese chopper now less than three thousand feet off their tail.

The chopper sent another burst of gunfire into the Antonov's fuselage causing Harry Ching and Paul Slade to instinctively lowered their heads. Drew Blake, shouting, stormed into the cockpit, the impact of the hits ripping into the rear of the Antonov. But his shouts were wasted on the two men in the cockpit, their intercom headsets blocking out external sound, the positioning of the plane's exhaust just two feet from Slade's right foot rendered conversation useless other than through the headsets. Blake shouted again, but Paul Slade and Harry Ching couldn't hear a word. He reached forward, grabbed at Harry's headset, ripping it off and shouted directly into the aviator's ear, "Come on Harry, for Christ's sake! Do somethin' different. Think outside the fuckin' box."

Ignoring Blake's shouting, the aviator continued pushing the Antonov to a height of thirty-eight hundred meters. "We're over twelve thousand feet, that chopper can't go much higher," he yelled, his message barely audible above the noise of the engine, smoke billowing along the length of the fuselage and Harry shouting even louder with a terrifying tenacity, "I'm gonna try pushing her a bit higher!"

He pointed at the gauges, leaned forward and tapping in an unnerving way, while attempting to appear in control. "We've lost some of our horses. This little girl has a thousand of 'em; right now she feels more like eight hundred. If we can maintain this ceiling, that chopper can't stay with us. If I'm right, that chopper's ceiling has gotta be around thirteen thousand feet, that's just over four thousand meters." He looked about, straining to see the chopper, and flipped a thumb in its direction. "He can make one ninety miles an hour." Then, pointing straight up, "We gotta go higher, get above those clouds. If we can get to fourteen thousand, enough to stay above him, we can give him the slip." He waved a hand at the clouds and said with a pessimistic shrug, "If the cloud layers don't break."

Gardner Hunter thought about joining Blake in the cockpit; felt he needed to be where the controls were being worked, but like a flame to a moth, the chopper held his gaze., its automatic firing at the undercarriage of the Antonov, hitting the tail section and taking a section off the tip of one wing. Hunter stared down, subconsciously questioning the sudden glow inside the chopper. *What the fuck*, he thought, *their faces are so clear, like their bein' lit up.* The chopper's gunner made panicked *take it down gestures* with his hands, over and over; panic worsening with each passing moment. The glow illuminated his features, his face contorting as he shouted, jabbing at the man controlling the chopper as it began to invert. And then, in the nanosecond it took Gardner Hunter to figure what was going on, in the nanosecond it took him to blink, to focus, in that absolutely miniscule nanosecond the chopper ignited in a blinding ball of flame, lighting the night sky with an eerie orange flash.

Harry shielded his eyes, instinctively looked about and shouted, "They've blown the tip off the starboard wing!"

Slade turned in the direction Harry pointed; saw

the meter long section missing from the wingtip, shouted a jumble of panicked words, then realized he had headset communication, and continued in a normal tone, "That's what took the chopper out. I saw it getting blown off with that last big hit we took, blew it clean down into their rotor. Lucky we were above 'em or it would've missed."

The Antonov shuddered and Slade gave Harry a worried look. "Can you still control her?"

"Yeah, but it doesn't feel good. The motor's been hit, were losing oil pressure fast. Our air speed's dropped to one forty; if we drop to ninety, she'll stall."

Harry Ching tapped on the gauge showing one twenty-five and dropping.

Blake shouted, "How far to the border town?"

"Thirty minutes."

Blake's eyes took on a viscosity of hope as he squatted behind Harry, raised the pilot's headset, and shouted even louder, "We are gonna make it, right?"

The aviator stared at the array of gauges. "Look at this," and he tapped on the fuel gauge, and shouted over the engine's roar, "This should be showing three quarters full. It's dropped below half in a few minutes." He flicked a thumb. "Go aft, see if you can smell gas."

Blake scrambled into the cabin area, was greeted by Dal waving his arms and shouting, "What the fuck's this smell back here!"

Hunter and Slade followed Blake to the rear of the Antonov and peered from the windows at the gasoline spray in the plane's wake as Harry rolled his girl into a vertical descent, an uncomfortable feeling with only the stars to indicate which way was up. Blake stumbled back into the cockpit as the plane refused to respond to her master's effort, regardless of several procedures to get her back on track. Accepting the inevitable, Harry decided it was time to share with his passengers.

"Go back," the pilot shouted, leaning into Blake. "Have the guys hand out the chutes!"

This piece of joyous news hit Drew Blake like a desolating storm, *hand out the fuckin' chutes!* The last time he had reason to jump from a plane was on a mission over South America, and this was déjà vu. He let out a deep breath, moved into the cabin and made demonic eye contact with Dal.

Sung waved at Blake, making finger jabbing motions at the tail, placing his hands around his mouth to form a megaphone, and yelling, "The tail, it's been hit!"

Blake shouted to Dal and pointed to the parachutes. Dal, being absolutely reluctant to jump from a solid aircraft, called, "Are you sure Harry correctly assessed the fuckin' situation?"

Blake nodded *yes*. He was a good liar, always had been. He moved closer to Dal, placed a reassuring hand on his shoulder and said, "Where's that calm demeanor you show in stressful situations?"

"Fuck you, I ain't seein' you in no rush to jump."

Harry considered his options; fly the aircraft over a possible safe area and parachute out, or attempt to land the disabled Antonov. Slade shrugged his shoulders in a *'what are we going to do?'* gesture.

"I can do one of two things, try to land a plane that's broke, or jump. I got no yearning to do the latter."

Blake re-entered the cockpit, his parachute strapped on, gave Harry his *what the fuck's happening* shrug, slipped between him and Slade, gesturing for Slade's headset, took it, pulled it on, was about to speak when Harry said, "I guess it's my call about whether we all jump, or try to land this baby."

In the next minute, the Antonov dropped another hundred meters and Harry again tapping on the gas gauge showing empty. "We're running on fumes. If we can stay up here a little longer, until first light, I might be able to put her down." He lowered the starboard wing, looking toward the ground. "Down there someplace," and he pointed. "It'd be guesswork in this darkness. Just can't risk it."

The passengers sat in silence, feeling each vibration, gagging at the odor of gasoline. Billie and Sung straining to catch a glimpse of anything as Patrice Bellinger reached across the aisle, tightly grasping Gardner Hunter's hand. The aviator waved across at Blake who'd commandeered the co-pilot's seat from Slade. "Shit man," Harry said, perspiring. "Don't remember being this wet since I put a Cessna down on the Hoover Dam."

"Gimme it straight," Blake exclaimed with a nervous tremor. "What are our chances? It's your call, no one's gonna hold you to blame for the outcome. Wha'dya say?"

"There's plan 'A'," Harry replied. "I could stay up here long enough to see what's down there. My money says I can put her down."

"And plan 'B'?"

"If we run out of gas, and it's still dark, we jump."

"Fuck! That's it? That's plan 'B'? I say we keep flyin' until she splutters."

"Splutters?"

"Come on Harry, fuckin' humor me here."

"Don't know what to tell you," and he gave another quick look at the gauge. "What can I say to give you a little hope?"

"Can you glide her?"

"Oh yeah, she'll glide all right. She'll glide like a rock."

He made a diving motion with his hand, didn't look at Blake. "Yeah, she'll glide . . . straight down. If you hear me yell, jump, jump, jump - the last two will be echoes. If you stop to ask why, you'll be talking to yourself, at that point you'll be the pilot."

Blake, wet and white, returned to the bullet riddled cabin, discussed what he and Harry had figured to be their best chance.

"So, we wait until the gas goes and jump?" Dal muttered. "It's pitch fuckin' black out there, nothin' but jungle."

"Yeah, helps to break your fall," Blake said. "Harry'll keep her as high as possible. When he runs outa gas he'll see if he can make out the horizon. If he can see the ground, he'll figure our chances. If not . . . we jump. So, with that in mind let's all be clear on *how* we fuckin' jump."

Slade offered to go through the jump procedure and Bell began sobbing.

"Hey, hey, hey! What the fuck? Come on, take it like a man," Dal said, and gave her a thumbs up.

"Yeah sweetie, I'll take care of you," Hunter said, reaching over his seat and squeezing her shoulder.

Ten minutes later the Antonov was still airborne.

"Get ready to go," Harry shouted, straining to be heard above the scream of the engine. "We're losing altitude fast!" And in the next breath he shouted, "Go! Go! Go!"

CHAPTER 1

THREE WEEKS EARLIER

THE ROOM WAS MUSTY, rank, and for this president, held superlative memories of another time, of a bygone era.

Eisenhower had sat in this very room, and Nixon had held many an incognito briefing between these walls. Of course, following Richard Nixon, one was assured any possible listening devices had been removed from the building.

This president understood why the cardinal requested the meeting be held in '*the shelter,*' as it had come to be known. Access was by way of a White House elevator, a door hidden away behind a floor-to-ceiling library wall, descending into a rabbit's warren of tunnels. The complex was the size of a shopping mall, an area of twenty acres, with military personnel at each turn and at every doorway.

The president made his way down a poorly lit tunnel, the confines of which earned his deepest appreciation for the countless therapy sessions on claustrophobia, tax dollars at work as they say, money not wasted.

Two uniformed guards snapped a salute, and the president, hearing an elbow crack, cocked his head and grinned at the man. The sentry grimaced, biting hard on his lower lip.

"Mornin' gentlemen," the Commander in Chief said. "Doin' a splendid job as always."

The two men smiled and held their salute. The president, reciprocating with a halfhearted salutation, turned to face his entourage, consisting of Captain Manning, Senator Wilson and Admiral Bates standing behind him, the president's face projected a look of, *'Okay, deep breath.'*

They walked through the open door, where a well-dressed man rose to meet the Commander-in-Chief, extending a welcoming hand as he stepped forward.

"Dominic Broski, it's good to see ya again," the president said with a warm smile. "It's been a long time since you visited the ranch. Laura says to say howdy," and he released the handshake. "How was the flight from Vienna?"

The reply was delivered in a heavy, perfunctory tone, tinged with a curious accent, part Russian, part Polish, with an over abundance of rolled 'r's.

"It went well, Mr. President, thank you so much. It is good to see you again, and please, pass my warmest regards on to your lovely wife, Laura. I cannot tell you what fond memories I have of my stay at your wonderful ranch."

The president and Broski comfortably positioned themselves opposite each other at an oval table, as six other men began taking up seats; the three who accompanied the president, and the other three, an ever present support team, accompanying Dominic Broski. With introductory formalities over, a serious atmosphere filled the room. Dom Broski studied his old friend closely, drummed his fingers on the table for a few long moments and gestured to one of his aides.

The aide opened an attaché case and passed a file to his boss. Broski removed an eight-inch by ten-inch black and white photograph and slid it across the table toward the president. "This is Paul Slade. He is on an extremely esoteric assignment involving . . ." and he paused, his eyes moving from one person to the next, hesitating, assessing.

The president sensed the hesitation, the look of uncertainty. "Dom, have no doubt my friend, all of the men in this room can be trusted with our lives, as well as the safety of your man. They're briefed on our past operations. No matter how delicate the matter, you can confidently discuss it in front of 'em." He chuckled, "We're all on the same team here."

Broski coughed, a nonplused clearing of the throat and said in a grunting rumble, "Gentlemen, I am a member of a group known as cardinals. The term was chosen to signify their, hmm . . ." and he thought for a few moments, "to signify rank, their level of respect. The powers in our organization felt that the words president and general were far too eh, too governmental, too militaristic. No offense my friends," he said, smiling at the president and Admiral Bates. "But we are empowered with unique decision making responsibilities, and eh . . . unlike you, we answer to no one." He nodded to the president, making a grin that lasted several long seconds, then, pointing at the ceiling, "We answer to no one, except our conscience, and eh, our God."

The president grinned, swiveled in his chair and said, "Congress'd cramp ya style, Broski."

"Another reason to voraciously thank my God, I do not suffer the indignity of prostration before messy oversight committees."

A short laugh spread about the room.

Dom Broski smiled.

The man had people skills. He knew exactly what his curiosity value was among his American hosts, knew it kept those around the table intrigued with whatever he had to say; each realizing Broski's power, but yet to estimate its magnitude.

Broski exhaled. "Our organization is similar to a private Board of Directors, a watchdog, striving toward maintaining a balance between super powers. We have been compared to the Bilderbergers Society; however unlike the Bilderbergers, we draw the line at New World Order aspirations."

"Sir, we've been minimally briefed on the purpose of your visit," Bates said leaning forward. "What we've been told is that one of your operatives is in a situation in China, that his exit's been blocked." Bates frowned with a look of uncertainty. "Can you expand on this?"

"We have suffered an unfortunate incident," Broski said exhaling slowly as he tilted back in his chair, "which involves our computer-programming specialist. He was carrying a substitute computer flash drive, a virus known as 'Black Sabbath.' He was to install the drive into the Chinese mother-unit, in Penghu."

Pouring a glass of water, he smiled and swallowed a good deal of the contents, feeling their eyes on him, making an apologetic shrug and a saddened face.

A Khrushchev touch.

"Not good, not good at all. During the crossing to the mainland they encountered a . . ." He stopped, carefully thinking over his next words. "It was after midnight, they were crossing the East China Sea, almost to the mainland. A Chinese gunboat fired on them, hitting their boat. It went down. All on board perished with exception of our one man, Paul Slade, who was able to swim the four miles to shore. However, we lost the substitute flash drive. The plan was to switch flash drives without the Penghu facility realizing the switch." He paused.

Bates hung back, and gave a calculated look. "This eh, Black Sabbath," he said in an unsure way. "What precisely . . ."

Broski ran his fingers delicately through his graying hair, cutting Bates short. "Black Sabbath will shut down Beijing's satellite system for quite some time. But equally as

4

important, we would have their program; we could integrate their technology with ours. Slade obtained access to the Chinese facility but unfortunately there was a skirmish. There were casualties at the facility. Slade secured the flash drive that holds the program for their satellite strategic defense system, as well as launch configuration and flight data for three new satellites. Our intelligence network has revealed Beijing's plan to launch three super satellites into their Operation Compass program."

The president interrupted, "Operation Compass? We're up to date with what Beijing's doin' with its satellites, surely there's nothin' in their pipeline that our guys aren't already aware of? If there's any kinda Beijing bullshit goin' on, our guys would be onto it."

He gestured to the captain. Manning reached into an attaché case, began flipping through the contents, and moments later passed a notepad to his chief.

"Mr. President," Broski said, "I do not wish to sound like an oracle of doom. Beijing, it eh, has plans to send up satellites that your people definitely have no knowledge of. Their plan is known as Operation Compass/Beidou. One of their units, an advanced Climatrol, has weather pattern manipulation capacity. With such a satellite they can affect weather patterns at coordinates any place on the globe. China has launched ten Compass satellites giving Beijing regional positioning, navigation, and timing capability in the Asia-Pacific region. Operation Compass/Beidou is a fully-fledged GNSS. Fortunately for us, Mr. President, they have been developing their system on a 'step-by-step' basis, and based on the economic downturn . . . their technology budget has applied the brakes somewhat."

"Sir," the captain said giving an emphatic nod, "the China Satellite Navigation Engineering Center has been responsible for building the system with five geosynchronous satellites and thirty MEO spacecraft."

Bates lifted an interjecting hand. "Whoa, whoa, Manning. I heard they launched a more advanced communication unit just recently. Is that somewhat similar to eh . . ."

Bates was lost.

"Yes, Admiral," Manning said interrupting. "Three GEOs were launched in their Compass navigation demonstration system."

Bates and Manning continued the discussion on the satellite issue, until the latter, scouring through his notes, said, "Beijing put on quite a good show for the world at the recent Hefei China Forum on Compass Navigation Technology and Industrial Development." And Manning turned a page around so that it faced Bates. "Speaking in his role as Director of the Compass/Beidou Civil Application Market and Industrialization Expert Committee," he said, tapping on the page, "this spokesperson announced the total output of China's satellite navigation industry will be 300 billion Yuan. Admiral, that's around US$50 billion by the year 2015."

"My people have briefed me on that budget statement," Bates said with a wry smile. "But I gotta think, in light of the recessionary climate, the figure will come down some." He gestured to Broski. "If they cut their expenditure, they won't be able to implement that program. Am I right, Mr. Broski?"

"Perhaps, Admiral," Broski said, seriously rolling the r's in *perhaps*, sitting more erect, more composed. "According to the Navi Biz newsletter from the Shanghai Navigation Forum, Shao Liqin, the executive deputy director of the National Remote Sensing Center of China has stated that the positioning accuracy of Operation Compass has, in fact, been improved to five meters, that the construction of Beidou 2 is nearing completion as we speak. By 2020, according to Shao, Operation Compass is expected to have a positioning accuracy of less than one meter. Do you realize the vulnerability of your west coast aqua duct, of your power grid system? These are such easy targets, easily contaminated by an accurately placed beam from a Compass Beidou. Can you see Mount Rushmore's sculptures reduced to dust?"

"I'm sorry to hear that," Bates said sliding a compassionate glance at Broski. "My knowledge of Operation Compass is, umm, well, I gotta say, I've no knowledge of this climate control technology, and I doubt the Chinese possess the sophistication to contaminate our power grids. It's news to me. Hypothetically speaking, do you think Beijing's plan to send up this satellite is realistic?"

Broski glanced at Bates, frowning with an expression of amusement. "Hypothetically speaking, Admiral? Let us not become comfortable with anything hypothetical regarding the technology of Climatrol."

Senator Wilson took a long moment considering the gravity of Broski's statement. "If Slade had no flash drive replacement, if like you say, he just took *their* flash drive, they'd know immediately, wouldn't they? Seein' how he had no replacement."

"Correct, Senator," Broski replied, with a bobbing of his head. "That is why they are out in force, why Slade is struggling to make it out of China."

The senator, a little perplexed, gave a look of confusion to Bates, then slid back into an overly relaxed position.

"Gentlemen," Broski said. "In the past weeks, Beijing has fired high-powered lasers at American spy satellites with flight paths over their territory. A blatant case of Beijing flexing its muscles, showing the world they are capable of blinding any satellite a foreign force moves over them. They destroyed one of your satellites, but of course, in order to avoid a confrontation, the news release claimed the cause of your loss was a defunct Russian satellite colliding with your unit." And he allowed the moment to drag a little, chuckling at his inference. "How amusing, the news media has such creative juices."

Senator Wilson straightened himself, looking some-what uncomfortable with Broski's comment. "We're aware of Beijing struttin' about with their dicks in their hands, flauntin' their laser technology," Wilson said, "but we can implement shieldin' that'll block their lasers." He glanced at the president, and got a succinct 'yes' nod, to which he quickly returned an acknowledging eyebrow lift. "It ain't that we don't know how to handle China's space threat. Frankly, and I know I have your consent to say this sir," and he nodded again at his boss, "we can do the shieldin', but eh, we just don't have the funds in our space budget to send up new satellites. Beijing knows this. They're aware of the trillions of dollars goin' into the Iraq and Afghanistan campaigns, of our presses printin' out more dollars than the National Depository can back up." He made a disgusted noise and waved a dismissing hand. "Our Air Force's plans for fieldin' airborne and orbital reconnaissance systems are comin' unhinged in the budget process. There just ain't the funds to suitably upgrade the Space Program from missile warnin' to future radar planes. We got jets grounded, unsafe to fly, and we can't dish out a few billion for each of the latest models." Wilson flashed a look of tenacity; felt his point had been very nicely driven home. With an added burst of adrenalin, he pressed on. "The Canadians are gonna be workin' overtime coverin' our asses, coverin' U.S airspace. The Russians are gettin' a real kick out of it. We got so many of our guys flyin' around Afghanistan we've left ourselves undermanned here at home."

When the adrenalin had subsided, he stretched his neck uncomfortably, throwing an apologetic nod to the president, the silence forcing an uncomfortable cough from Wilson. "We've a major concern here," he said.

No one spoke.

Wilson looked around the room for awhile, glanced

at Bates, and then gave an even longer glance to Broski. The floor was still his and he threw another smile at the president. "The whole mission area's meltin' down. The shields' are gonna hafta do," Wilson groaned in a pathetic and apologetic way. "They'll just hafta do the job."

"Yes Senator," Broski replied with a grin. "Your country is spending far more than its annual income. But your shields are only sufficient when the laser beam originates from an earth-based source. It will be very different if Beijing is able to instigate the launch of Operation Compass. They will have super-satellites capable of stalking foreign units; they will have beams that will go through other nations' units like hot knives through butter."

Broski switched his attention to Admiral Bates. "Admiral, a synergistic program between Russia and China has created the capability to jam your space networks. This shuts down the U.S. Air Force's ability to move forward with the development of space architecture as well as highly classified deep space technology. Your Keyhole spacecraft can easily be blinded. The new more powerful Chinese units have sufficient power to hit them hard. Once Operation Compass is in full gear and with its far tighter dispersion, the advanced software will not only allow Beijing to easily blind any electro-optical and radar satellites like your Onyx and Lacrosse units, their units will be capable of totally disabling any of your satellites they so choose. They are looking at both symmetrical and asymmetrical means to offset your space dominance. Your units, Admiral, will become useless space junk."

The president made a feeble attempt to put a little shine on his team.

Failed.

Moments later, realizing he'd failed, he gestured at the man sitting across from him. "Dom, our Air Force encountered Russian jammin' systems back in '03. The

Russians supplied it to Iraq. Our GPS bombs had no trouble takin' the Iraqi system out."

His head bobbed slightly to confirm his arrogance, and Bates threw him a *so what* look.

"Please, Mr. President, gentlemen," Broski said shrugging, dismissing the comment. "Your administration's efforts to avoid aggravating Beijing obviously have taken precedence over the implementation of advanced space technology. Meanwhile autonomous China continues to re-affirm its position as the number one world power."

He stood, took several paces around the table, stopped, raised a hand as though to speak, then made an emphatic nod. "American presidents have shaped the future of this planet in ways many have not realized. Do you understand the implications of President Reagan's famous words, 'Mr. Gorbachev, tear down this wall!' Beijing was jubilant when the wall fell; this effectively initiated the destruction of the Soviet Union, removing the nearest threat to Chinese expansion. There is now nothing stopping China from conquering Europe. There is no longer any resistance on the European continent. Do you see a Eurasia in your not too distant future?

"Mr. President, your CIA functions behind closed doors, yet maintains contact with their comrades at the State Department, with the Pentagon and the National Security Council." He shrugged, a dismissing gesture, "all of whom loyally support Administration policies. They showed disre-gard for information we supplied regarding locations within your country of several al Qaida cells."

Admiral Bates cleared his throat as Senator Wilson grumbled incoherent words that could have been *fuckin' asshole* or *wise ass*, like that.

Broski knew better than to immediately react, instead he gestured somewhat apologetically, hesitating a few moments. Time enough for his gesture to further aggravate

Wilson's red-faced stare.

"Admiral, Senator, perhaps a reevaluation of your CIA's poorly made decisions, along with more centralized compliance may work to reduce dissonance within their ranks," Broski said with a shrug. "On the other hand, perhaps they were hoping for bureaucratic osmosis.

"Your administration, Mr. President, is allowing policy to influence Intelligence. In this case, unless there is intervention, U.S. policy will work in favor of the Chinese. Your Intelligence . . ." and he leaned on the word, *intelligence*, "is still suffering heartburn from the Clinton era. They deny knowledge of . . ."

"Goddamnit," Wilson growled. "That's bullshit! We had the truth! We knew what was goin' on. It was the timin'. We were caught out in New York. Period. End of fuckin' story!"

Broski stayed out of Wilson's minefield . . . almost. "Your CIA wallows in dissidence, Senator," Broski said in a mild mannered way, "historically suffering inability to come up with clear answers, turning a deaf ear to unpalatable intelligence of foreign threats, threats that raise congressional demands for military action. Truth is not the issue. The agency suffers blindness in its estimates of the threats ever present to the United States. The CIA's ideological trappings will not go away, such ideology is the agency's DNA. One could hypothesize over its reinvention, who knows, somewhere in time." He nodded in turn to Wilson, to Bates, then for the longest time . . . to the president. "Perhaps food for thought, Mr. President, for hmm, for another day." He turned to Wilson with a quick flick of his eyes. "You see Senator; truth is far from manifest, unlike Beijing's intentions."

The president cleared his throat, not that the clearing was necessary mind you, more a clearing of the air. "Beijing's intentions, huh?" he said with lowered eyes. "You made your point, Broski. But it ain't as easy as you make out, ya know

, keepin' policy and politics separate from intelligence. That ain't so easy."

Silence, accompanied by an uncomfortable drop in room temperature.

Broski allowed the silence its fifteen seconds of fame, time for blood pressures to stabilize somewhat. "Mr. President, with respect, we thought we had seen the end of pampering Beijing when your predecessor vacated the White House. Apparently we were mistaken. Your fear of incurring China's wrath is eh, hmm, well documented."

The president didn't take time to think out his reply, ignoring the Eurasia reference. "Dom, I think it best we maintain the highest possible tradin' relationship with the motherfuckers. It's better than 'em partnerin' with Iran and the North Koreans, and ya know they'd do that for goddamn sure if we slammed the door on 'em."

Broski wasn't fazed by the colorful outburst, his voice rising with his reply, "Really? What if Beijing should liquidate its vast holdings of United States treasuries? If you move toward imposing trade sanctions on China as a protest against their burgeoning space program, as threatening as it is, Beijing will most certainly send the U.S. into an even worsening recession. Mr. President, Beijing holds in excess of nine hundred billion dollars in United States bonds. They are about to release a large part of that holding, as the Swiss, Russians, and many others have already done. This is China's alternate option to defeating the United States by nuclear means. Beijing is the United States' biggest foreign creditor, and could very soon be holding a trillion dollars of federal U.S. debt. This will give China astonishing power over the United States. And of course, Mr. President, Beijing realizes it has earned its leadership of the financial world in light of the global recession, which it clearly blames on your nation, with its financial industry excesses and poor management."

They have the ability to devalue the dollar to the point

where a truckload of dollars might not buy you a happy meal at McDonalds. Beijing holds the ace card. It has the perfect nuclear option."

Manning made a timely cough as the senator interjected, wagging a finger at Broski, "What are you implyin'?" Wilson asked. "Protectionist legislation won't work?"

Broski shook his head. "Senator, trade sanctions by your people against China would be suicidal."

The room fell quiet for a long minute, after which Admiral Bates and Senator Wilson began chatting quietly. Broski allowed the time to pass. *Time for wounds to be licked,* he thought, *for egos to slink back into their shells.* When he felt ample time had passed, he shifted in his seat, and the president, seeing his discomfort, raised a finger to the still chatting Bates and Wilson, and nodded at Broski.

"So you see gentlemen, we cannot allow them to complete Operation Compass," Broski said. "They already have the ability to very quickly bring down your economy. If they complete Operation Compass, it will be checkmate to Beijing; they will drive the last nail into your coffin."

"That's a pretty dauntin' scenario," the president said, looking at the notes he'd scribbled during Broski's briefing. He tapped on the photograph. "So we get this guy out of China. It still leaves Beijing holdin' the ace card, they'll replace their program, and Operation Compass will go ahead. Ain't that correct?"

More silence.

"We have no alternative," Broski replied. "We must get Slade out. However, we cannot slap Beijing in the face while it holds that ace card. Before taking such action, we need to level the playing field."

"Level the playin' field, huh?" Wilson grunted with a questioning smirk. "Sounds like you have a plan."

"We need to proceed with the original operation," Broski answered. "Beijing must believe they have re-acquired their original flash drive. Meanwhile, any attempt by them to take retaliatory action could possibly backfire."

"Backfire?" the senator asked with a screwed up face.

"Yes, if Beijing suspects something is amiss and conducts tests from its current satellites, I am told that transmissions could go astray, blanket China in a death shroud of ice, a horrendous winter. But this, of course," and he made a dismissing shrug, "this is pure conjecture, nothing but hearsay."

"Ya make it sound like we're one move from extinction," the president said in a grave voice.

"You lost me," the senator said to Broski, in a condescending, almost mocking tone, his red Texan face glowing.

Broski spoke through nearly clenched teeth. "Gentlemen, we need to give Beijing the Black Sabbath drive. But they need to believe it is the original flash drive, the drive my man took from Penghu."

The veins in Wilson's forehead expanded. "And how might you be plannin' on doin' that? Divine fuckin' intervention!"

The president threw a cold, punishing stare at the senator, making a few air stabs with his finger in Broski's direction. "I'm all ears," he said. "What've you got in mind, Dom?"

Before Broski could respond, Bates pushed his chair from the table, stood, and walked a few paces, turned, and jabbed an angry finger at absolutely nothing at all. "Lemme get this straight, you're gonna get this flash drive back to 'em without 'em realizing it's a fake? Can you expand on eh, how exactly?"

"We need Beijing to believe they have caught the cat with the canary in its mouth. If they come by the drive too easily, it will arouse their suspicion. Our work would be a little easier if not for an unfortunate incident involving

Slade. One of the Chinese soldiers Slade eliminated was the son of General Cheng. This has brought about a tightening of all routes leading out of China. General Cheng has turned this into a personal vendetta, placing our man in an even worse predicament." Broski nodded at the president, making solid eye contact. "In view of the many times we have cooperated with the United States, I am here to request immediate assistance in getting Paul Slade out of China. We must do so to intervene in Beijing's systemic plan for world dominance."

Bates moved alongside the president, leaning down and quietly whispering into his boss's ear. "Sir, if Slade can reach Datong, we've got a guy in place who just might be able to fly him out."

The president entered thought mode for a minute, but said nothing, pondering the suggestion, looking at Broski whose face had an expression of hope, a look of anticipation, a look searching for a positive response. "Dom, d'ya think you can get your man as far as Datong on his own, you know, without outside help?"

"Mr. President, I believe he will require assistance to get even that far. He was wounded in his skirmish with the general's son. I cannot impress on you the seriousness of the situation. We must get the computer flash drive out, at any cost."

Admiral Bates gestured at the president: "If I may, sir?"

"Sure, go ahead Steve."

"Where's Slade headed right now, what I mean to say is, where exactly in China is he?"

"He is heading to meet with our Asian based man, in Beijing, at the Xishiku Cathedral."

"At a cathedral?" Bates asked with a curious look. "What's a cathedral doing in Beijing?"

"It is a pittance of kinds. The Chinese acquiesce

to avoid showing the world their prejudices at work. It is a Catholic cathedral, run by Bishop Bolin of the Salesian order. Bolin is my counterpart, just as I am the cardinal in Europe; Bishop Bolin holds the equivalent position in Asia. The plan was for him to help get our man out, but the death of General Cheng's son has placed the Chinese 13th Chuan Army on alert. They are relentless in their efforts to find the killer of Captain David Cheng."

"Okay, bottom line," the president said, clearing his throat. "How d'ya see us helpin' with this situation?"

"We would greatly appreciate you sending in some of your people to get Slade out," Broski said. "We know you have operatives positioned throughout Asia; we also know some of these operatives have the means to fly Slade to a safe port. As you mentioned, you have a man in Datong. Perhaps he can get Slade to, hmm . . ."

A timely pause.

He gave his chin a slow massage, didn't need to procrastinate. "Burma might be a consideration," he said. "Can you help with this, Mr. President?"

The president nervously drummed his fingers on the table. "Burma, Myanmar? They got major issues goin' on with their military junta. We are eh, whatcha might call, persona non grata. But ya know that already, don'tcha Dom?"

"Of course Mr. President, all the more reason we would not be taking that route to get our man out. Sir, with respect, we informed your CIA well in advance regarding terrorist activity. Our information was passed to your National Security Adviser, who passed it on to his subordinates, who thought the whole thing was merely a contrived and remote possibility at best. Even though our sources are reliable, our information was again wasted on deaf CIA and NSA ears."

An air of resentment swelled in the room, but Broski hung tough, his body language signaling his dissatisfaction. "That was one of several attempts by our organization to pass on information to your people. Then we informed your CIA of the precise coordinates for the whereabouts of Bin Laden, and what do you suppose happened?" He threw a sharp look at Bates. "How did your CIA handle that information?" He paused, and those about him remained silent. He ran the question a little further. "What did your people do? Allow me to answer, if I may. Your people again hesitated and eventually passed it on to their chain of command, who in time instructed shelling of the coordinates. By that time, the cat was out of the bag."

"That's enough!" the president said abruptly switching his gaze from the sullen Broski to Bates, then just as quickly flicking it back to Broski. "I know your organization supplied us with intelligence and much appreciated information." He stopped, looked for respite in the faces of Bates, then Wilson. Both men kept their eyes down, avoiding any association. The president swallowed hard, moistened his lips, and forced an apologetic grin. "I admit in some cases we've had our problems coordinatin' our people to act in a timely manner. But Dom, it ain't just a matter of gettin' this information from you and immediately dispatchin' forces to act on it. Shit like that takes time; we have channels to go through and . . ."

The big man stood, enraged by the president's excuses for the inefficiency of his CIA and NSA.

"Mr. President, with respect, my intellect is not in need of massaging. It is clear our sources have been far better informed than those of the United States. As in the past, we have accessed information that will prevent China's threats from being unleashed on the world. Are you again going to pass this on to your incompetent CIA people, who will sit, have lengthy discussions over coffee about the possibilities, taking too long to authenticate the information we provide? Are you going to wait until another terrorist plot succeeds, until planes strike the Towers before the finger pointing commences?"

Set back by Broski's displeasure over America's snail's pace call-to-action, the president glanced at Admiral Bates, whose blood pressure was now testing its limit.

"Mr. President," Broski growled, "we did inform your people, and we do have the appropriate contacts in the United States. It is not as though we do not get our information through to the right channels." Broski waved a hand, a complacent gesture. "For God's sake, we informed your Central Intelligence Agency of North Korean underground nuclear tests. They conducted several small-sized nuclear tests that clearly showed up in the abnormal radioactivity count along the shared border. They have enough weaponized plutonium for at least a half-dozen nuclear weapons. U.N. sanctions are in place, but these do little to dissuade the North Koreans from continuing their nuclear activity.

"Back in 2003, we supplied the CIA with information on activities taking place during the visit by Russia's Konstantin Pulikovsky to Kim Il Sung. We even had advance knowledge of what was being offered on the menu for their train journey. We have people so close to Kim we know which eighteen year old girl he is bedding each night."

"I understand how reliable your people are," the president said in exasperation. "And off the record, yes I agree, your information regardin' terrorist activity was correct. I'm sorry for the CIA's inaction, and as far as the information on Bin Laden is concerned, what can I tell ya? We gave it our best goddamn shot. We missed. However . . ." and he held up an index finger, emphasizing his point, "with regards Saddam, we did go directly to the location your people supplied and we thank you for that, a job well done by your sources." He turned to Admiral Bates and Senator Wilson. "Sounds like we need to kick some ass, a job for Sam Ridkin's boys. Wha'dya think, Steve?"

"Yes Mr. President, I agree, Ridkin's team. We need

to get the Interpol Division in there and get Slade out, on condition of course."

"On condition!" Broski snapped defensively.

He reached across, placing a hand on the man to his right, his Russian grating. "Теперь они хотят условия, всегда играя игры. Politics," he said directly to Bates, "It always comes down to politics, of which there are no morals, only expedience. What conditions are you after, Admiral?"

"We'll work on a plan for our guys to get this Black Sabbath program back into Beijing's hands, make them think they've taken back the real deal, but we get the flash drive as soon as Slade's out."

He glared at Broski, and Broski felt the eyes, pausing several seconds before responding. The man by his side tapped his finger a few times, getting Broski's ear, and quietly murmuring, "Независимо от того, что они хотят сэра, мы должны согласиться с их условиями."

Dominic Broski nodded, drumming his fingers on the tabletop for a few long moments, then lifting heavy eyes to meet Admiral Bates'. "Of course, that is our intention." And his eyes shifted to the president. "As you said, Mr. President, we are after all . . . on the same team."

CHAPTER 2

THE DAY BEGAN EARLY for Adam McDowell, arriving at the Wilshire Boulevard office of the American Interpol Division at five minutes before seven, feeling uncomfortable with Sam scheduling such an impromptu meeting. His chief's email was brief, *Morning meeting, usual place, seven o'clock.*

McDowell found Sam waiting, coffee cup in hand. Looking up at McDowell and inhaling deeply, he half raised his cup in a salutary gesture.

He grunted, followed by McDowell responding, "Morning, Sam. Early start, gotta be something special."

Ridkin placed his cup on the table, leaned over a stack of paperwork. "Had a call last night requesting I set up a meeting in two hours, so eh, don't need to tell you I had a . . ."

"Yeah, you had a late night," mused McDowell.

Frustrated and sleep deprived, Sam forced the words while suppressing a yawn. "Yeah, yeah, yeah, and it didn't end. I came here straight from the goddamn meeting."

"Christ, with who?"

"Steve Bates."

After a few long moments of looking into Sam's heavy eyes, McDowell sighed, "*Admiral* Steve Bates?"

"Yeah, he stayed until four, him and a Captain Manning."

"I know Manning. He works at the Pentagon, pretty

impressive. So what . . ."

"You're not gonna believe this," Sam interrupted, gesturing toward the small kitchen. "Coffee's on, go get yourself a mug, a big mug, gonna need it."

With brows bunched in consternation, and looking like a man set to throw himself from the twelfth story window, Sam took an hour going through the events involving Paul Slade and laying out the information passed on by Dominic Broski.

"Steve Bates has a proposal. The president's given consent to what I'm about to tell you." He jabbed a slow, tired finger at McDowell, "Off the record of course."

Sniggering, McDowell faked a sagging gesture, as though weighed down by the comment. "Off the record, huh Sam? No big surprise."

"Yeah, yeah, I know, so predictable," and he took a pull on the coffee. "I've eleven donuts in the box by the percolator. Be my guest."

Picking through the donuts, McDowell settled on his favorite, pink icing with sprinkles, jamming most of it into his mouth, then making his way back to the table.

Sam was standing by the window, his back to McDowell, looking down on early morning traffic edging along Wilshire Boulevard, and asked without turning, "How do you feel about working for the commies?"

Inhaling most of the donut, McDowell dashed across the room to the kitchen, and coughed uncontrollably into the sink.

"You okay, Adam?" Sam asked with a grin. "Go get another; the chocolate ones aren't too bad."

"Join the commies!" McDowell snapped, staring hard at his boss. "What the fuck are you talkin' about? This is some kind of test, right Sam?"

"What I just told you about getting the Black Sabbath flash drive back into Chinese hands, well, you're gonna be a big part of pulling that off."

McDowell closed his eyes, restraining a feeling of nausea, holding an expressionless gaze as Sam continued, "The Chinese are being spoon fed information. They're out in force, trying to catch this guy, Slade. Our people are directing him to an antique shop over there. The owner, a guy named Yidui, is going to solder the flash drive into the base of a statue. I hear it's some kind of Chinese idol, something called a Tara, a golden Tara."

There was a twenty second pause before McDowell spoke. "Oh yeah, I definitely wanna be a part of that - a clusterfuck in the making."

Sam eyed him with a touch of uncertainty, sensing a note of insincerity in McDowell's body language, made a mental note of it. "It gets better," Sam said. "A duplicate statue will be ready to go to another player. You'll be sending it to him in Hong Kong, together with a few other items, including a preprogrammed cell phone, and we'll be eavesdropping on all conversations on that phone."

While listening intently, McDowell washed down his third donut with a gulp of coffee. "Eavesdropping huh?" he grunted in a sharp and unyielding tone. "I see nothing much has changed with the Republican administration."

Sam hesitated. He needed to spoon feed McDowell, but at the same time not risk putting him on information overload. "There are these two guys coming in from Taiwan. They're with the TIB, the Taiwanese Intelligence Bureau." He pulled a small note pad from his jacket pocket. "Names are Wang Jingwei and Sung Chiao. Taipei's known for a while one of the two has been feeding information to Beijing, getting some of his stuff from a discontented former CIA operative. The guy was based in New York; was under surveillance for fifteen months."

His pause was timely, allowing himself sufficient time to absorb McDowell's body language.

Got none.

Sam remained stoic, no wiser for lack of a reaction. "The agency was onto him," he said convincingly. "They made certain the information given was always slightly flawed. The other Taiwanese guy is clean, has no clue his friend's a double agent."

There was guarded hesitation in McDowell's voice. "Which eh, which of the two is the bad boy?"

Sam could feel his blood rising, but his dark complexion provided camouflage. He lowered his eyes to avoid showing any adverse reaction. "Bad boy's Wang."

Adam McDowell was beyond cool.

Was frigid.

His reaction was expressionless. "So then, what's the plan?"

Sam cursed to himself, cleared his throat, and said in a subdued voice, "Wang's never met with his CIA informant, he just has a name, Sellers. They each have Swiss accounts, courtesy of Beijing."

McDowell didn't reply immediately, and Sam wondered if it was his acting skill or stupidity that stoked his courage. Twirling the empty coffee cup side to side, then finally, with an inquisitive face said, "He's been buying for China, this eh, this guy, Sellers. That's his name right, Sellers?"

Sam lit up a Marlboro, and taking a deep breath thought, *you're good, you're very fucking good*. He looked away, lest his expression betray his distrust. Then he faked a grin, making light of it. "Better than the Pink Panther, don'tcha think?"

"Yeah really," McDowell said in indifferently. "So how do we do this?"

"You'll introduce yourself to Wang, tell him you're Sellers. He won't know any different. Take this folder. It contains CIA classified information. Read it, bring it back.

No copies, understand? If Wang gets chatty, you'll need to know what he's talking about. You have the answers all here," he pointed at the folder, "all in this folder."

McDowell nodded, took the folder and flipped through the two inch thick file. Sam leaned back in his chair, most relaxed, taking a few long drags on the Marlboro and exhaling a set of perfectly interspaced smoke rings. "As Sellers, you're to contact the guy with the antique store, the one who has the Tara."

Opening a drawer, he removed a cellular phone and slid it across to McDowell. "We'll see that this phone is delivered to our antiquities friend, along with a note from Sellers. It'll be the only way you're to communicate with the guy. We have a listening device installed."

He wrote a number on a small note page, folded it, and slid it across the desk. "Here's the number. Memorize it. It's your only means of two-way discussion with the store owner, Yidui. It'll take forty-eight hours to get the guys here from Taiwan. One of our cars will collect them at LAX, take them to the Wilshire Grand, across from Seventh Street Marketplace."

"Got it. Good choice," McDowell said absentmindedly, his eyes unblinking at the sound of his cohort's name. "Two miles from Little Tokyo, good food there."

"Yeah right," Sam replied with a note of sarcasm. "Japanese food, very diplomatic. It'll take me two days to get things in place. We'll meet here day after tomorrow, at ten. I'll get Blake and the guys for an early breakfast, give them a preliminary briefing on our guests. Remember, as far as anyone's concerned, you're gonna turn into the bad guy. I understand that you eh . . . that you did some amateur theater, correct?"

McDowell looked perplexed. He raised his eyes from the file, nodding as Sam refilled both cups.

"This is gonna take all of your acting skills," Sam

said. "Stay in character. The mission will depend on it. None of our guys will know you're working a scheme. As far as Blake and his crew are concerned, you switched to eh, to the dark side. If things go bad, we don't want your name coming up."

Sam raised his coffee mug, and gave an uncomfortable smile. McDowell felt his chief's discomfort, didn't like the plan, didn't like it one bit. He gave his mug a reciprocal lift. "You're the boss, whatever you say. Just make sure I can get back home. Don't wanna be using fuckin' chopsticks the rest of my life."

"And Adam," Sam said dropping his voice to a whisper. "That cell number, you memorize it. Got it?"

CHAPTER 3

THE INTERPOL OFFICE WAS on the twelfth floor of the Radisson Wilshire Plaza Hotel. The door displayed the words, SoCal Exports, neatly etched into a beveled glass plate hanging at eye level on the wall. As they entered, an almost attractive, dark-haired receptionist greeted them, her blue-speckled aquamarine eyes smiling.

"Good morning, Sam."

He said nothing for several seconds, held the door open, standing to one side as the entourage streamed on through. When they'd passed, he gave a head shake to the smiling eyes and said softly, in an almost apologetic tone, "Morning Marcie."

Adam McDowell, with two serious faced Asian men following closely behind, made his way into the conference room, where he gestured to chairs spread around a table, chatting to the two for a few minutes until another four entered, Interpol Special Agents Drew Blake, Patrice Bellinger, Gardner Hunter and Carson Dallas. Hunter and Bellinger were recent acquisitions of the Interpol Division, lured, you might say, from the ranks of the CIA. Their recent South American sortie had won each of them, as well as Carson Dallas and Drew Blake, the highest praise from Washington.

McDowell was acting chief under Sam Ridkin, a position giving him access to most top-level information, without being spoon fed the more delicate items accessed only by his chief.

He was on a 'need to know' basis, the way Sam preferred it stay. Waving a hand toward the heavy steel framed chairs neatly placed around the large oval table, Sam gave a nod to his team as they sauntered into familiar surroundings. Carson Dallas's eyes immediately fell on the two Asian guests. He half nodded to Bellinger, then to Hunter, and flashed a quick grin at McDowell.

Blake smiled at those seated around the table, reached into his jacket, peeled the silver wrapper from a stick of cinnamon gum and asked, "Anyone?"

Drew Blake had a commanding presence, an occasional air of arrogance enhanced by a near athletic body that over recent years, much to his disdain, developed love handles. He managed to disguise the added weight beneath his standard attire, an Armani sport coat. He was six feet two inches tall, two hundred pounds, plus or take a few, his dark wavy hair sporting a sprinkling of silvery gray at the temples, his turquoise eyes the color of the summer sky reflected in a crystal lake.

Cool.

Ice blue.

Somewhere, someplace way back, way inside of those eyes, someone had ingeniously installed a luminescence. His eyes cast a magnetic glow, a beaming aura that attracted women like moths to a candle; some, those who had flown a little too close to his glow, had crashed and burned. The casualty list, according to Dal who considered himself the unofficial scorekeeper, was extensive. Not that Blake placed much credence on Dal's scorekeeping; he was of the opinion that Dal's *aspirations reverberated far beyond the boundaries of his domain.* In light of Dal's own rather short *casualty list*, Blake would occasionally remind him of his disability, that in fact, he was an emotional retard. Over the years, the joke had grown weary.

Blake had a close resemblance to an early-fortyish-years-of-age Michael Madsen, and on many an occasion he had been approached for his autograph by fans of Madsen.

He'd made the cover of GQ, an accomplishment his fellow collegiate members hadn't let him live down too soon.

He drove Porsches, Lamborghinis; nothing less would suffice, although he once test-drove a Pagani Zoned Roadster F, prior to its debut, found its 7.3-liter AMG V12 motor 'a challenge,' the 650 horses offering more thrust than his trusty Porsche. With only twenty-five Pagani Roadsters slated for manufacture, Blake scored his loaner as a special favor for 'a job well done.'

When the CEO of Pagani needed a man 'on the inside,' Blake came through, off the record of course. But this was his style, and he carried it well, the man most wanted at your side in any tight spot. Knowing Drew Blake, well, it was a virtual 'get out of jail free card'.

The Porsche seemed sluggish after the Pagani, and Blake, almost losing sleep over the drop in horsepower, sent it off to the workshop to have the motor revamped. His philosophy was "*be prepared.*" He believed luck would figure a way to find him.

Maybe.

Sometimes, when luck *did* smile on him, it'd plant a kiss on his ass. But then there were those times it didn't. He was always prepared, anticipating the less memorable occasions on which that kiss went astray. But Blake was dogged in his belief that with appropriate preparation, opportunity would always create luck.

A liaison between the Taiwanese Embassy and Washington set up the meeting, absolutely *off the record*, and not involving the government agencies of either nation. The Asian man, the one wearing the finely tailored silver flecked silk suit, began to nervously tap a pencil on the table, leaned toward his companion, smiled, whispered, and after a few moments had passed, both men cracked slight grins. They each eyed Dallas, and allowed slightly suppressed chuckles to gain momentum. Dal glanced down at his jacket to see if he could pinpoint the cause of their amusement. Blake took in the scene, coughed a subdued signal to catch Dal's attention. Dal picked up on the body language, looked down, realized his shirt-tail was protruding from his zipper. He abruptly crossed his legs, sliding the chair further beneath the table, away from prying eyes, blushing a little under his blonde surfer tussled hair.

Sam Ridkin opened his attaché case, wriggled about in his chair and gestured toward the two Asian men. "I'd like to introduce our two guests from Taipei. This is Wang Jingwei, and Sung Chiao; they're with the TIB, the Taiwanese Intelligence Bureau," he said, nodding at each. "I hope I got the names right, gentlemen. My Chinese is a little rusty."

He smiled.

The only smile in the room.

But they nodded *yes* at Sam, as Blake threw his chief an inquisitive look, an obvious question mark above his head. Blake asked curiously, "Taiwanese Intelligence Bureau?"

The AID chief thought for awhile before replying, "Similar to ourselves. It eh, it exists, but it's not acknowledged to exist. It's a kind of unofficial CIA."

Blake's gaze was unblinking.

Dal whispered, "Ain't this just what the world needs - another alphabetized fuckin' agency."

"Acronymic," Blake said. "It's an *acronymic* fuckin' agency."

Sam looked uneasy, an unusual trait from the Interpol chief. More so when strangers were present, he was generally a stoic figure with a confident aura. After a long ten seconds, he stood, walked toward a window, raised a hand and separated two wooden louver slats. He peeked down on

Wilshire Boulevard and shook his head at the heavy traffic grinding along at a snail's pace. He turned back to face the seven pairs of eyes following him, his demeanor promising a revelation of sorts.

"I've been contacted by the White House about a guy with a problem; he's on an assignment in China." He opened a folder and began reading from notes. "We've been asked by the governments of Taiwan and the United States, to prepare further intelligence on what I'm about to discuss, to come up with a suggested course of action regarding the events, as well as getting this guy out of China. Our plan needs the optimum chance of diffusing what's developing as a possible precursor to a war."

Blake lowered his face into his palms and groaned, "Aw Christ!"

Sam passed him a disapproving glare, scratching at his three day beard growth and continuing, "I'm about to open a can of worms that's been hushed up by most of the networks, swept under the carpet by the politicians, something that looks like it could lead to a major international showdown."

He passed a paper to each of those around the table. "Ten days back, a fleet of coast guard and naval vessels chased after a spy ship of, hmm, of Chinese origin. It was cruising along the southern Taiwanese coast, the ship was the eh . . ." He paused, struggling to pronounce the word.

One of the Taiwanese, the one named Sung, raised a hand.

"If I may?"

Sung traced a finger down the note page, reading through until he found the word. "Let me see, let me see, hmm, the ship in question, the ship in question, ah yes, here it is, it's the Xiangyanghung. It says here it was spotted twenty-five miles off the Taiwanese military base, *our military base*, at Chiupeng."

Looking up from the notes, he nodded, making his

point. "Yes, extremely dangerous indeed."

When he'd finished making his point, Sam said, "This is the site where the majority of Taiwanese missile tests have been conducted. In fact, in recent weeks several Chinese spy ships've been detected off the northern part of Taiwan, and a Chinese ship called the Yuanwang, one of four reconnaissance ships being run around Taiwanese waters by the Chinese, was clearly spying on Taiwanese operations." He moved across the room and retrieved a file containing a collection of maps, books and papers, uncurled a map and said, "These ships, they're armed with state of the art equipment for observation and communications."

"Yeah," Blake said, coughing and giving a sarcastic shrug, "let's keep it all politically fuckin' correct."

"You know the sensitivity of these types of situations," Sam said with a wry smile. "They're hmm, carefully scrutinizing, and I use that word loosely, yes, *scrutinizing* the island, collecting information."

Reaching across the table, he pulled the pitcher of water closer, poured a glass, and slowly consumed half of the contents. The two Taiwanese men chatted quietly, then Sung asked, in an impressive Americanized accent, "Do you mind if we smoke?"

"Not at all," Sam replied. "Go ahead."

Blake raised his hand to draw Sam's attention.

"Yeah, Drew, fire away."

"I've heard a bit about the growin' tension around the Taiwan islets. Is that where you're headin' with this?"

"Yeah, there are islets, plenty of 'em, enough in fact that the Chinese have actually built on them, creating new land masses right at Taiwan's front door. They're sending in civilians to populate them. In this way, it doesn't blatantly resemble a military advance; they're doing this as a means to test out Taipei's patience."

Blake commented halfheartedly to Dal, "Jesus, I ain't

game to ask where *we* come into this scenario. The whole rigmarole sounds like bullshit, just another case of Beijing doin' whatever it wants, and fuck everyone else."

Leaning in close, Dal whispered, "I got a feelin' we're gonna enjoy plenty of kung pao."

Blake cleared his throat, letting out a disguised laugh, hoping the two men from Taipei hadn't caught the comment. Sam Ridkin however, had caught sufficient to quickly move ahead with the briefing.

"Beijing's been collecting environmental research information in the waters around the islets. They're pushing toward sovereignty claims on the islets and reefs near the Taiwanese island known as Penghu. There've been continual conflicts between Taipei and Beijing over territorial claims for hundreds of islets, shoals and reefs scattered around the South China Sea."

"Isn't there some international law?" McDowell asked. "You know, one the United Nations enforces, something to do with territorial claims in international waters?"

"Yeah there is," Sam said. "The United Nations has the Law of the Sea, says Beijing can't touch anything within Taiwan's territorial boundary."

"How far is that?" Blake asked.

"The boundary reaches out twelve miles from the coast of Taiwan. You'd think Beijing'd be smart enough to stay just a whisker outside of the twelve mile boundary, right?" He stopped, took another drink, eyeballing each person at the table, shaking his head, then silently answering his own question with, "Of course not, they started jumping on islets; jumping on shoals and building ramps across reefs, whatever you want to call them. Some are encroaching on the twelve mile limit. They commandeered small shoals off Penghu Island in international waters, right in front of the whole goddamn world." Sam gazed at the eyes intently focused on him, realizing his delivery bordered on over-emotional. "The building up of a land mass system with the use of ramps is just one small step."

"How can they take land and not break the, what'd you call it?" Dal asked, "The Law of the what?"

"Law of the Sea. They get away with it because the land is underwater at high tide," Sam said with a shrug, his palms turning upward in a frustrated gesture. "It only pops up above water when the tide's out."

"It's not considered as land per say?" Patrice Bellinger asked.

"Correct. It isn't technically classified as dry land. It's a loophole Beijing is taking advantage of, The Law of the Sea, International Law. We can't touch 'em on this issue."

"How many of these islets are involved?" Gardner Hunter asked. "Are there just a few, are they big, what's the deal?"

"They're called the Pescadores, made up of over sixty islets in the Taiwan Straight, half way between Taiwan and the Chinese mainland."

"Half way?" Blake asked.

"Half way across; choose a point between Taiwan and China. It'd fall on the Pescadores."

Sam stopped, using the eraser on the end of a yellow pencil to point on a map. "Hmm, 'bout right there, separating the South and East China Seas."

"Why are they so strategic to China?" Blake asked, looking toward the two Taiwanese men. "Either of you guys wanna tell me?"

Wang moved as though about to answer Blake, but Sung placed a hand on his arm. "These islands are connected by a bridging system, and the Chinese are living on the islands," Sung said. "The three main islands of Paisha, Yuweng and Penghu have over eighty percent Chinese occupancy. They have cleverly constructed a series of bridges running from one island to the next, thus joining the islands." And he made a meshing move with his fingers. "They have more than seventy spans joining over one hundred and twenty square miles of islands. It's the longest island hopping bridge system in the East, a growing cobweb of Chinese development. It is waving an antagonistic red flag at Taiwan."

Raising a solitary finger, Blake said sighing, "Point well made, Mr. Sung, thanks."

Sam said, "Washington's received intelligence that Beijing's been using spy ships, as well as satellites, monitoring the area around Penghu. Their ships are buzzing around those waters like a bunch of kids on an Easter egg hunt, and what the hell is being done about it?"

"Anyone?" Sam asked, inviting a response.

Got none.

Dal leaned forward as though to speak, opened his mouth, but got no further as Sam frowned scornfully at his contemplation. Dal shrugged, his eyes shifting about the room.

"Beijing's messing with a technicality here," Sam said. "They're after something unique, can't openly take over an actual island because that'd contravene international law," and he bobbed his head at the two Asian men. "That'd really piss off our Taiwanese friends now, wouldn't it?" He leaned heavily on the word *really*, allowed a timely pause, then nodded at Sung and Wang. "My apology gentlemen," he said. "No offense intended."

Wang leaned toward him, and spoke in a less than believable, *friendly* tone. "We are eternally grateful to you for alerting your team of our need of assistance. It is a fear with which we in Taipei have become accustomed in our daily lives. We have such powerful adversaries in China, and in the North Koreans." He tapped on his stomach and grinned. "They are far too hungry." He glanced about the table and waved a hand. "They have an insatiable hunger for additional territory. As far as the North Koreans are concerned, they have developed sufficient nuclear weaponry to warn the rest of the world that they are able to play with the big boys. Seventy percent of the North Korean Army of eight million troops . . ."

A timely pause.

Time for facts to sink in.

Blake thought, *fuckin' thespian.*

Wang made a self indulgent nod. "They have over eight thousand artillery systems and two thousand tanks based within eighty-five miles of the DMZ. And these are being continually reinforced. Without moving any of its more than twelve thousand artillery pieces, Pyongyang could sustain up to half a million rounds per hour on Combined Forces Command defenses and Seoul for several hours. They have the world's third largest ground force with in excess of one million active-duty soldiers, an air force of almost two thousand planes, and an eight hundred and twenty ship navy including the largest submarine fleet on the planet.

"North Korea's special operations force is the largest in the world. It exceeds one hundred thousand men. Over the past twenty-five years, in spite of struggling through a nearly collapsed economy, the Democratic People's Republic of Korea has relentlessly continued to re-equip, restructure and redeploy the North Korean People's Army. These military initiatives directly support North Korea's national objectives to reunify the Korean peninsula under Communism, apply military force to achieve reunification, and ensure the survival of North Korea's regime.

"By 1992, the NKPA had increased its army to approximately one million active duty personnel, and as the world witnessed the fall of North Korea's once powerful ally, the former Soviet Union, the NKPA diligently continued its initiatives to reposition ten corps, that is seventy percent of their active duty ground forces. They relocated them to within ninety miles of the demilitarized zone. During this same time-period, they restructured their Special Purpose Forces into the largest special operations force in the world.

"The world needs to look into its crystal ball, Agent Blake," Wang said. "The threat is only now emerging from its embryonic stage in the form of a 'Young General.' Few have heard of him, aside from those among North Korea's Pyongyang elite; his name is Kim Jong Un, the 21 year old son of the 'Dear Leader.' He is being groomed to succeed Kim Jong Il. This will create what will be the first hereditary communist dictatorship in history."

"You're right," Blake said. "I ain't heard of the guy."

"You ain't that elite," Dal quipped beneath his breath.

"To outsiders," Wang continued, "North Korea often appears an unchanging place, a paradise for socialism."

"A result of that guy, Kim whatever?" asked Blake.

"Yes, stemming from Kim Il Sung," Wang responded, "who solved the conundrums of governance, the father who founded North Korea."

"But we all see the changes goin' on in North Korea; don't the people livin' there know what's goin' on?" Dal asked. "I mean, aside from the people in the military?"

Wang waved a finger at Sung, stopping him from replying. Wang stood and said, "The North Koreans are the last to learn what is happening behind the scenes. These days, in Pyongyang however, even *they* feel change in the air. It is a place of tension, of anticipation, both of which are fueled by propaganda and lies." Wang gave his comrade a nod, seeking approval. He lit a fresh cigarette, tilted his head back and blew an egotistical smoke stream. "North Korea," he said in an annoyed tone, "is an anachronism, Agent Blake. It is not only bankrupt economically, but also politically and intellectually. Popular thinking deems it should have collapsed many years back under the weight of its own contradictions." And his annoyance was reflected in his stubbing out of a just lit cigarette.

"But the capital," Blake said quizzically. "When you see it in newscasts, in the media, it looks so . . ."

"Of course, it is an impressive city, but Pyongyang's cleanliness is superficial," Wang replied. "The orderliness and majesty can be attributed to the oppression at the heart of North Korean life."

"So eh, their satellite program," Sam said, "are they up to scale with their technology?"

"North Korea will soon launch its satellite. We are aware this so called '*satellite*' will have intercontinental ballistic missile capacity. We also have intelligence of pending underground nuclear tests scheduled to take place within the next two years."

Blake asked Wang, "What do they say to back up their nuclear presence?"

"That they are proud their country has become a nuclear power."

"Proud . . . how so?"

"The North Koreans, they believe they must develop nuclear power so they can defend their country against the impending threats from the west."

"So this new guy, the son, what's the South Korean take on him?"

"The mention of his name has been banned in South Korea," Wang said. "It minimally surfaces in times of his father's ill health. But then, with recovery, it ceases to be a matter of urgency."

"They got a time frame for this new leader?" Blake asked. "When is he takin' over from his father?"

"They expect Kim Jong-Un to take over between 2011 and 2013," Sung Chiao said. "He will soon receive a deputy director-level position in the party, a stepping stone. His Swiss education in Berne has groomed him well in the ways of the West."

Blake interrupted with, "He went to a Swiss University in . . ."

"Not under the name Jong-Un," Sung said. "Under a pseudonym of course, to them he was nothing more than a Korean student."

Sam drummed a yellow pencil, then shifted his eyes to the other Taiwanese agent. "Do you feel, Mr. Wang, that the North Koreans represent a greater threat than Beijing?"

Wang stood, slid the chair back and paced for a few long moments, as though he were about to disclose something special, something unbeknownst to those in the room. "Mr. Ridkin, North Korea's armed forces are capable of carrying viral and bacterial weaponry, the range of their biological weapons arsenal is growing annually. Our Taiwanese intelligence has heard estimates exceeding a dozen strains of bacteria."

Sam Ridkin interjected. "Like what?"

"Off the top of my head, and I do have files that regrettably I did not bring to this meeting, they have biological agents that include, hmm," and he paused as though searching. "The North Koreans have biological agents. They have cholera, yellow fever, dysentery, smallpox, typhoid fever, and typhus as well as sarin, mustard gas and phosgene."

Blake nodded, "Hmm, off the top of your head Mr. Wang? That's very fuckin' impressive!"

"Yes," Wang replied. "In fact there are around 5000 tons of chemical weapons stored in North Korea. Indeed, Beijing had a more than worthy adversary in its neighbor to the northeast. For Beijing, the acquisition of Hong Kong was a minuscule start; Hong Kong was nothing more than an hors d' oeuvre, an inheritance of the British lease. Beijing believes Taiwan is also its legal right, and China is planning a domino theory that will streamline its creeping into Taiwan's backyard. The Chinese have an eye on Taiwan, and another on their North Korean adversaries."

Blake made a coughing sound. "And one on us," he grunted. "Ouch!"

Pulling the pack of gum from his side pocket, he stripped the foil wrapper from another stick, tossed the pack on the table, and said, "Still no one?" He chewed the gum for a few seconds, then with a gentle finger pointing at Wang, asked, "Sounds like a race between the North Koreans and Beijing to grab territory. How long have they been movin' people onto these islands?"

"Beijing has been moving civilians onto the reefs throughout the South China Sea over several years. They believe Taiwan will not be aggressive toward civilians. They are of the opinion that any show of aggression would add fuel to the already elevated tension between us and them. It would make Taipei appear to be the aggressor."

Sam puckered his lips, popping them in a whop, whop sound as he quickly responded to Wang's delivery. "You express yourself eloquently, Mr. Wang. I commend you on your English language skills."

"The result of six years studying law in San Diego," Wang replied, "six very long years. It helped a great deal in my interpreting of the United Nations Law of the Sea, the very law that cannot come forward with a clear policy on the right to claim land that is submerged at high tide. This raises many questions."

Sam, smoothing his hands across the map, began tapping on one small region. "This is the area where we know the Chinese occupy a number of reefs." He placed the tip of the pencil on a small group of islands, moving it about a little, and coming to rest in one area. "These right here, the Shuan Tzu Chao reefs. Did I say that correctly?"

Wang nodded and leaned forward, gesturing toward the map, tilting his head for a better view of the area around the eraser. He placed his finger on the map alongside the pencil, and then turned to face those around the table. "Taiwan has the right to repel any Chinese occupation if the islets lie within our waters. We cannot touch them if the islets are outside the twelve-mile limit. Our government has made it clear that any occupation by Beijing will be considered a hostile act and Taipei will be forced into retaliatory action." He placed heavy emphasis on the words *retaliatory action*. "It violates an understanding between Taipei and Beijing, an understanding that the imaginary middle line of the Strait will be honored by both nations."

Sam moved the pencil from the map, sitting back with arms folded. The two Asians mimicked his position, each leaning back in his chair. For a full minute there was a piercing silence, time to assess the potential severity of the situation, a staring match as Sam rapped his fingers impatiently on the table, passed a warm grin to Wang and Sung, and thought *motherfuckers*.

"Retaliatory action, huh, now that does concern me," Sam said. "What exactly do you believe Taipei would do in the way of *retaliatory action*?"

"Our Defense Minister, Tang Yao-ming, has pledged to fortify our armed forces. Our forces may be small, but they are elite and lethal. We are prepared to defend our island in the event of Beijing trespassing in Taiwanese waters. We have been most tolerant, but they are testing our patience. It is common knowledge that Beijing has been sending in fishing fleets, supposedly civilians. We have recently apprehended some of these vessels on Taiwan's side of the middle line, and interrogated the occupants." Wang folded his arms, allowing a few moments for curiosity to swell. "They are not civilians; they are spy ships entering Taiwanese waters on missions of espionage."

"That's quite a . . ." Sam began to say, but was cut short as Wang rose to his feet with one hand extended, leaned

40

toward Sam, stubbed his cigarette into an empty coffee cup, and spoke in a condescending tone.

"It is clear to the Taiwanese government that your people are aware of what is happening in the South China Sea. Financial interests have kept your American government from raising objections in the appropriate quarters."

Wang smiled, bowed slightly, acknowledging his delivery of a body blow to Ridkin. Blake placed a hand over his mouth, hiding the grin. He thought, *round one to the man from Taiwan.*

Wang said, "Your country is, how is it you Americans put it, kissing Beijing ass? American money is deep into Chinese coffers, is that the word, coffers? Yes, I like that word . . . coffers."

He paused again, gave a half-bow, smiling at Ridkin. Sung, head in hands, appeared embarrassed by his comrade's delivery.

"In fact," Wang said, "very deep into Beijing coffers. So deep in fact, your politicians are not brave enough to upset the orange cart."

"Apple cart," Dal said in a soft tone.

"The financial men in America would have, what is it you say, Agent Dallas?" Wang asked glaring at Dal. "They would have their testacies for ear-rings?"

"Balls," Dal chuckled, and caught another glare from Sam.

Blake flicked a quick scowl to Dal and mumbled, "Jerk off."

Momentarily set back by Wang's delivery, Sam glared at Wang. "That's totally uncalled for, Mr. Wang!"

Wang smiled calmly, relishing Sam's loss of cool. "Forgive me for not putting the integrity of your United States ahead of my personal opinion, Mr. Ridkin, and of course, no offense intended."

Hmm, Blake thought . . .

Wang placed another cigarette between his lips, nodded toward McDowell, who in turn reached across and smiled as he acknowledged the man from Taiwan's point scoring, and lit the cigarette and Wang slowly resumed a seated position.

The posturing of an Asian Napoleon.

A victory pose.

Again, from Blake, the thought, *motherfucker*.

Tapping his cigarette on the rim of his coffee cup, Wang leaned toward Sam Ridkin, using the cigarette as a pointer, jabbing it in Sam's direction and speaking with revelry. "Furthermore, when the Chinese believe they have spread the American economy sufficiently thin, believe that they have created a strangle hold on your economy, do you know what they will do? They will sever all supplies, all finance. The United States will tumble like a falling tree. The American economy, which is so strongly entwined with China, will fall to its knees within months."

Brazen little prick, Hunter thought, nudging Blake.

Wang stubbed the cigarette, took another from its pack as all eyes stayed on him, lit it, blew an opaque stream of smoke and said in a snide tone, "Strange bedmates, do you not agree?" There was deathly silence as he eyed each of the Americans. "Let me ask you again, do you not agree?"

Ridkin replied in a concerned tone, "If what you're saying is true, the action of Chinese takeovers in this country is a well laid plan to defeat the United States without firing a shot. May I assume this correct?"

Wang nodded *yes*, and Sung concurred.

"A Chinese company recently attempted to put into play its little piece of the puzzle," Wang said. "It was the takeover of a California based company named Unocal, a direct threat to American security. It would give Beijing great political leverage within the United States, great control of a strategic commodity, control of energy."

"How would this affect Taiwan?" Sam asked.

"Very cleverly, the newly acquired Chinese company, Unocal, would hold the drilling rights and exploratory capabilities in regions surrounding Taiwan, as well as elsewhere. So you see, it would affect not only the United States but Taiwan and other nations. The Chinese acquisition of established giants such as Unocal would place Beijing in total control of the world's energy distribution; enlightenment cannot be rushed, nor can world dominance. Make no mistake, Beijing would have its finger firmly in place on the off switch."

"I believe our country has any such takeover possibility stymied by the interjection of our House Armed Services Committee," Blake said. "You aware of that?"

Wang grinned. "Yes, Agent Blake. I am well aware of their interjection. They, in fact, stopped the Chinese company, Gnooc, from acquiring Unocal. That is merely a bump in the road. Gnooc is over seventy percent owned by the Chinese government and offered $18.5 billion for Unocal. That is how badly Beijing needs to position itself in the world's energy cockpit."

"So eh, where exactly are you headin' with this? And you can drop the formalities, no more of the agent shit. You say the rejection is, what was it, *a bump in the road?* What exactly do you mean, *a bump in the road?*"

Sung began to reply. Wang again placed a hand on his arm, stood, and walked to the far end of the table. He reached a spot between Hunter and Bellinger, looked down at Patrice Bellinger, smiled. "You are a very beautiful woman, if I may say so. Western women do hold a fascination for me. I am sure the over-populated Chinese male majority would dearly love access to the flowers of the United States."

"Really, I must object!" Ridkin shouted, pounding a fist on the table.

Wang turned, stared directly into Sam's eyes.

43

"Object, Mr. Ridkin . . . object! You cannot see the reality of the future. You have a boiling cauldron hanging over your head and you are offended at my inference that Chinese men are desirous of deflowering your excess women? Do you realize . . ." He paused, slowly moved his hand around the table, pointing at each. "Do any of you realize the gravity of the situation? It is not just a selfish motive that causes us to express concern, not singularly a Taiwanese concern. It is of international concern. The Chinese have a male population explosion. China has over twenty million more marriageable-aged men than women. What are they going to do with such a surplus?

"We believe they lean toward a militaristic solution. Beijing realizes this many young men, when left to their own devices, will only increase the crime rate, even add to the rise in the ever-growing AIDS epidemic. The logical answer is the military. They can afford military losses, they are adding to their already over-population at the rate of one child every thirty seconds. They were able to increase their military strength dramatically while your White House was under the misguidance of Clinton. In China, they see your president, maybe not this current leader, but certainly some future Democratic president, destroying the American way of life."

"How so?" Blake asked.

"Quite simple, Agent Blake. He will simply fill the ballot boxes with the votes from illegal immigrants. This will give him unlimited power." He glanced around the table, took in the curious looks, and continued, "With one time illegal immigrants able to vote, naturally they will all support the president who handed them citizenship. This of course would set up a president with the power to eliminate term limits. Your United States would fall under the control of a dictator for life."

Dal tilted toward Blake, speaking as though it were

for Blake alone to hear, yet sufficiently audible to be shared with all present. He said, "Hola! That's very hypothetical, right?"

"No, not hypothetical, predictable. With your printing presses in the hands of such a president, he will create a false economy by printing trillions of dollars, thus eroding your currency. What you have in your pocket will be nothing more than Monopoly money."

"Okay," Dal said in a dismissive way. "Enough of the economics lesson, what about all those guys they have over there, what'll they arm these twenty million Chinese guys with, fuckin' knock off golf clubs?"

"Oh, Agent Dallas, excuse me, Mr. Dallas," leaning on the *Mr*. "You underestimate the many bedmates of China. Do not, for a moment, believe the United States has acquired immunity by consummating a 'Clintonesque' relationship with Beijing. On the contrary, Taipei has been aware for many years of the support Beijing has been receiving from the Russians. China walks with one foot on either side of the fence. Many say this is a dangerous position." He let out a lighthearted laugh. "China can be likened to a prodigious whore, with legs well spread. The degree of danger is minimized, but have no doubt; China has thousands of spies in place in your country. They have access to email in and out of your Pentagon. Beijing receives immediate reports on everything your people stamp as eh, *top secret*."

Sam Ridkin exhaled loudly, interlocking his fingers and cracking his knuckles.

"Ouch," Blake said smiling, then addressing Wang, "Mr. Wang, please enlighten me here. Gimme your opinion of what the Russian view is of territorial infringement by Beijing?"

Wang rolled his head from side to side as though his neck was stiffening. "The Russians consider the stand by Taiwan for independence from China as a secessionist move. In appreciation, the Chinese recognize Russia's right over Chechnya. It is hmm, what is it you say, tit for tat? This strategic partnership between Russia and China is a prequel to new world order, one nation scratching the back of the other."

"I recall, back in 2000," Blake said. "I believe it was 2000, Mr. Wang, when Putin went on about the importance of China, how China was a Russian foreign policy priority. If you ask me, what he was really doin' was shorin' up his weaknesses after the big split up of the Soviet Union. All he did was leave one sleazy relationship and fall into bed with an even bigger whore, Beijing."

Wang nodded agreement. "Quite correct. Russia feels alienated since the destruction of the Soviet Union; it sees the United States spreading its influence across the world. It sees the North Atlantic Treaty Organization also expanding its influence. This image America has of being an unmatched world power delivers a message of caution to Russia as well as China. Moscow has relinquished its position as a world power. Russia views the Americans as a threat they can no longer handle alone, and Russia has also been further alienated from the west by the NATO expansion into the Baltic States."

"You sayin' the Russians feel they need China to regain some respect, is that the case?"

"Indeed, a balance of sorts, Mr. Blake. Only too fair, would you not say? China has developed their new-concept energy weapons. They clearly possess the ability to utilize nuclear technology, high-powered microwave technology and ultra high-powered laser weaponry. The bear is already sleeping with the dragon. If the world attempts to interject, perhaps by employing the United Nations as a sheriff, well, needless to say, we will all sit back and have a jolly old chuckle at that feeble tactic."

Sam stared at Wang, as he considered Wang's use

of the colloquial *jolly old chuckle,* amused by his attempt to add a touch of colonial school jargon to his delivery. *No point commenting on his inference of having personal pro-communist sympathy,* Sam thought.

But Dal jumped right on in. "Wha'dya mean *a balance of sorts?*"

"You cannot make an omelet without first breaking the egg, Agent Dallas."

"Me too," Dal interjected, "and no more *agent* shit, okay?"

"My apology, we do respect protocol in Taiwan."

"So," Dal said with a forced grin. "What about the omelet?"

"China is determined to become a major power, not that this is news to anyone, but Beijing feels stifled because America has far too strong a military presence in Asia. It also fears the challenge of the North Koreans; they are too close for comfort. This places China in a dilemma; it would mean Beijing allying itself with former enemies such as Japan against the West, a pseudo group of deputized nations waiting to slap the North Koreans on the wrist. They would become sheriffs, doing the United Nations job, but independent to that organization." Wang chuckled, "Though I do use the word *united* very, very loosely."

Sam's eyes impatiently raked the room. "The friendly alliance between the United States, Japan, South Korea and Taiwan has really shoved a bug up Beijing's ass," he said in a frustrated tone. "This alliance has in effect stymied any chance Beijing has of regional expansion." He paused, looked at his watch. "This's been a deep briefing. Let's wrap it up for now. How about we meet in the morning, say around ten?"

There was a note of agreement around the table, with some shuffling about, and chairs sliding back from the table as each gathered up personal effects. Sam nodded at his two top men. "Drew, Dal, you guys hang back a few minutes, okay?"

Hunter, Bellinger, and McDowell headed for the door, and as they left the room they nodded to the security guard standing rigidly in the hallway. The man smiled, held the door open, tipped his hat with his right index finger. As they passed the guard, the two Asian men gave a thank you nod.

"Damnit, Sam, what's this all about?" Blake asked in a disgruntled manner. "And don't start back with all that political bullshit. I don't go along with a lot of the crap this Wang guy's dishin' out."

"Yeah, Sam," Dal said, ruffling his blonde hair. "About as big a bunch of bullshit I've heard from anyone since *'if the glove don't fit, you gotta . . . '* Ya know the rest."

"I had to keep on the up and up," Sam said, avoiding their annoyed stares. "Those guys, Wang and Sung, they're a bit of an unknown quantity. The Department wants us to play both sides for now, them and us. It goes a lot deeper; you'll hear more from me on this as we move forward. Sorry guys. One more thing, Beijing's treating us as though we're kids in a candy store while they drive forward at warp speed, making their products available to the world's consumers. Lead paint, dry wall, rape date chemicals, all that shit included, we can't begin to guess what else China's exported to world markets. They've no check of contaminates. The imitation leather you're both sitting on could be impregnated with a contagion.

"They're not about to stop selling contaminated products, but even if that were a consideration, do you know what'd happen if they stopped the flow of goods and spare parts to the States, you know how long we'd be able to carry on before total meltdown? Three months, just twelve weeks, we'd have no replacement parts, no stock on the shelves. How do you think that'd affect our economy? It'd be absolute panic. Shops'd be looted in the rush for all types of shit. If your television broke down you'd have to replace the whole set, but with what? There'd be no more television sets out there, no computers, not too many cell phones either, they're all back in China, and so it goes. The world would grind to a halt if Beijing pushes the stop button, they needn't fire a shot. And for a grand finale, they need only flick the cyber space switch."

"Cyber space switch?" asked Blake with a confused expression.

"I kinda hate to tell you this, knowing how you and Dal here like to visit those matchmaker sites, but Beijing'll shut down all internet services within the U.S. Can you imagine how it'd be here if all computer communication stopped dead?"

"Yeah, yeah, yeah," Blake said groaning and scrubbing his scalp. "No more fuckin' eBay. So where do we fit in?"

Sam pulled a cigarette, took a little longer than usual to light it, additional seconds to draw on it, then exhaled. "Last year we reported China was building its capability to strike Taiwan. Beijing has more than eight hundred missiles pointed in its direction, and can use new technology to create a large magnitude earthquake right under Taiwan. This'd effectively immobilize Taipei's military capability. The Chinese are continually staging war games simulating attacks on Taiwan." He gave a knowing look at Blake, then at Dal. "An earthquake or tsunami would be a perfect excuse for Beijing to send troops into Taiwan, you know, as a humanitarian rescue force." He gave Blake a sarcastic wink. "Once in, they'd be most reluctant to get out. I'll tell you right now, Beijing's rehearsing for the inevitable. It recently placed Taiwanese-type fighter jets on the island of Dahuo. You know what they did next? Staged an attack on the island, that's what they did. A blatant dress rehearsal!

"The ballistic missiles deployed in Yingan, Ganzhou, Leping and Jiangxi provinces are a direct threat to Taiwan. If this leads to World War III, there's one thing we can say for sure, a World War IV will be fought with sticks and stones." He paused, allowed the image to sink in. "My personal opinion doesn't count for much here, but as I see it, Beijing's threatening us with dumping Treasury Notes on the floor, and we're into China for trillions. So long as we promise to keep buying from 'em, they'll keep lending. If they dump those notes, Uncle Sam goes belly up. They'll demand more commerce, more trade relations; those orders Beijing's placed for planes, they'll cancel 'em and go with Airbus. Our military complexes will be flying different stars on their flags. They've got us by the balls. Next thing, they'll be after some kind of insurance, they'll want control over their stake in the U.S."

Blake laced his fingers, placed them under his chin, and took on a look of confusion. "Just wha'dya mean, control?"

"Well, think about it. If they can force the G20 guys to convene a summit and replace all world currencies with one currency, they'll put the dollar into equal parity with the Yen, the Yuan, and the Euro. If the U.S. tries to devalue or print out trillions to cover bad debt and devalue China's treasury notes, well, that little scenario just got stymied. Ya see, Beijing sees its idea of a world currency as a means to stabilize the international monetary markets. What we risk here is in reality, a World War without the firing of a single weapon, a victory via manipulation. These one time Third World Nations are looting our resources. And our people just keep allowing outsourcing. Job losses are equivalent to casualties, and all that our people do is acquiesce to the machinery that now supplies us with our needs. India, China, nations that once looked up to us are now pulling the strings, while our president dances about like a puppet, smiling, shaking God knows whose hand, everything short of sucking dick."

Dal chuckled and caught a cold stare from Blake.

"We're losing this new struggle to foreign powers that are sitting back and enjoying the show," Sam said, "Just watching as '*the home of the brave*' slides deeper into a financial maelstrom." He pulled another Marlboro, lit up. "Whereas we're always helping out struggling nations," and he blew out a thick pall of smoke, tapping the non-existent ash on the edge of a Cinzano ashtray. "We've got no one throwing *us* a lifeline. They all just sit back jealously sniggering at those darned Yankee capitalists getting '*what they deserve.*'"

"Sounds a lot like science fiction," Blake said, sighing dismissively.

"Yeah well, so did Around the World in Eighty Days*,*" Sam said. "How long do you think it'll be before they acquire U.S. companies, like Microsoft and Motorola? Our National Securities Administration can't get near enough bugs out there to keep an ear to the ground. As far as Taiwan's concerned, well I hate to say it, but with China squeezing our balls, they can tell us to go pound sand. If Beijing tells our government that we have to support one China, well, I gotta say, our president will absolutely support a one China policy, and you can take that one to the bank."

"Goddamn," Blake said with a shrug. "That sounds defeatist."

The corners of Sam's mouth turned downward ever so slightly. "Maybe, and of course what I just said is off the record, but if this country wants to avoid a major depression and a real combatant World War Three, we gotta kiss Taiwan's ass goodbye, no doubt about that. If Beijing gets those super satellites in place . . ."

Sam's expression retained the dispassionate look; shaking his head for a few long seconds. "We can kiss our ass's goodbye. Tension at the present time is at a fever pitch. Whatever the day-to-day situation is, Beijing and Washington are inextricably intertwined in each other's embrace. Difference is China's now wearing the trousers. We've been placed on preparation alert, this mission's now officially tagged, 'Black Sabbath'."

He pointed at Dal, then at Blake. "You two see a trip to China in your near future?"

"Ah Christ," Blake said looking at the ceiling.

"Yup, kung pao chicken," Dal added. "Sometimes '*I told ya so*' just don't cut it."

CHAPTER 4

THE FOLLOWING MORNING, BLAKE relaxed on the hotel room sofa, humming Queen's, '*Another One Bites the Dust.*'

The tune lingered in Dal's mind for a long haunting minute. Finally relenting, he said, "You seem mighty relaxed for a guy who's got no clue what he'll be doin' this time next week, and you're hummin' that song again. Worries me when ya do that. Means ya thinkin' at a deep level." Receiving no reply, he nonchalantly browsed through pages of a women's golf magazine called Tee Time left in the room by a former guest. He held the magazine toward Blake. "Look at these New England courses," he said. "We need to get out and hit a few. How long's it been?"

Blake had *never* beaten Dal at golf, just didn't have the game. He avoided involving himself in any activity presenting the remotest probability of his finishing second. His football days with the Minnesota Vikings had left him with injuries stifling flexibility necessary for an acceptable golf swing. "Over a year back," he replied. "Last time I played was at Mauna Lani," and he lowered his head in a self-pitying gesture. "I need to get out, work on my short game before I inflict immeasurable damage on another groomed fairway, and on myself."

Dal ignored his pathetic search for sympathy for a short while, then tossed the magazine on the bed. "Aw, spare me your self pityin' indignation," he said. "Ya wanna little

53

cheese to go along with the wine?"

Blake gave him the stink eye, was about to respond defensively, heard the buzzing, reached for the remote and picked up the phone on the first ring. "Yeah," he answered in an abrupt tone, still eyeing Dal with annoyance.

"You guys well rested?" Sam asked. "All set for the morning?"

Blake gave Dal a dismissive glance. "Yeah, we're rested," he said, switching to speakerphone. "We still set for ten? What's on the agenda?"

"I called the other guys, moved 'em back to later. We've got some serious issues to chew over."

Blake caught the inquisitive look on Dal's face. He covered the phone, and mouthed, "Fuck!"

"Just you two, no others," Sam said, in a perfunctory way. "We've some serious shit to talk over before Wang and Sung join us. Meet you in the Tulip Garden Restaurant, say at twelve. Okay with you guys?"

They shook their heads. "Yeah, sure Sam," muttered Blake.

"How about Hunter and Bellinger," Dal broke in, with a querying voice, "they joinin' us?"

"Not necessary. You'll understand why after we meet. The less they know at this point, the higher the probability things'll work out."

"And eh, what about Adam?" Dal asked with a look of uncertainty.

There was a momentary pause. "McDowell will be joining us a little later."

Click.

In the hotel's Tulip Garden Restaurant, Sam ordered for all three, handing the menus back to the waiter. "Home made pasta all round, okay guys?" he said. "I know you're all fine with that."

Blake replied, "Thanks, and a bottle of Merlot to go

along with it."

The waiter gave a nod and walked quickly toward the rear of the restaurant.

"Okay boys, here's the scoop; we need to get two of our guys into Beijing. Just flying in isn't an option, we need to get in under the radar."

"We were expectin' to hear somethin' like that," Blake said. "Why's it a problem? Seems it'd be straight forward. Ya know, just makin' a regular entry."

The waiter returned and showed Sam the bottle, got a nod of approval, opened the wine and poured a small amount. Dal passed his glass across, winked at the waiter and said, "Think I'd like a little more than that."

The waiter ignored the comment as Sam sipped, nodded, and all three glasses were filled.

"Problem's this," Sam said swallowing slowly. "Whoever we send will be under full surveillance by Beijing every minute of the time they're there. Our government's got no connection with the operation, so when you're in, you're on your own. If you're apprehended, no one knows you, and no one knows what you're doing there."

There was a moment's silence, then Dal asked, "What exactly is it we're supposed to be after?"

"There's a guy in Beijing. We need to get him back home. He's been gathering information on a Chinese satellite system known as Operation Compass."

There was a microflicker of confusion, then Blake added, "So what was all the bullshit about Taiwan?"

"You caught onto that, huh," Sam said grinning. "Well, that's actually part of the problem. Beijing's threatening to endanger stability in the region. It's not just the issue of the South China Sea and Tibet. We believe the Chinese are gonna make a unilateral move, one *we* can't buy into, partly because we're already spread too goddamn thin with the Middle East conflict, particularly Afghanistan, and we haven't seen the half of that one. The Russians are fully backing and arming millions of young Chinese men." He paused, nodding at Dal. "You know the ones, *those* guys you mentioned earlier, the ones carrying the knock-off golf clubs."

Blake turned to Dal and made a *duh* gesture.

"The Chinese People's Liberation Army acquired massive supplies of arms from Russia," Sam said, swiveling his chair, reaching into his attaché and pulling a file from the case and placing a series of satellite photographs on the table. "They've developed new weapons systems, including over one hundred short-range missiles." He tapped a finger on one location. "You see this place southeast of Beijing, right here. These missiles are aimed at Taiwan. Beijing's got nearly a thousand in place throughout China, so it's just a matter of time before we end up in a confrontation. If China's able to continue with its militaristic attitude, it'll always be there as a buyer for whatever the ex-Soviets shovel in their direction. Russia's continually supplying Beijing with the newest mobile intercontinental missile, the DF 31. Moscow's also supplied the Chinese with the submarine-based ballistic missile, the JL2, as well as advanced fighter aircraft. Not to mention Beijing has launched its own J10, a multi-role single-engine and single-seat tactical fighter."

He read the specifics, losing Dal and Blake for a few minutes.

It all sounded like madness and Dal put his confused face on and snapped his fingers, a habit Sam despised. "Aw shit," he said, eyes lowered. "Sorry Chief." His Maxwell Smart impersonation failed to amuse. He removed a notebook from the inside pocket of his jacket, and added in an apologetic way, "Eh Chief, can you run through those specifics again? I think I need to jot 'em down. What was it, a DF 10 and a J31? Jesus H. Christ, where do the guys upstairs come up with all this shit?"

Sam took a breath and went through his mantra.

He nearly smiled, but relented and gave Dal his best frigid glance. "Beijing isn't messing about," he growled. "The *guys upstairs,* as you put it, pass it to me exactly the way they get it. If you have to take notes, Dallas, eat 'em before you leave the fucking room."

"Ouch," Blake groaned, suppressing the urge to chuckle. *Warned you often enough*, he thought. *Don't go rufflin' the chief's feathers.*

Sam spent a few moments raking both their faces with his best frigid stare, then said to Blake, "You okay with all this?"

"Yeah Sam, I'm cool, I'm always cool. Ya know that, right Chief?"

"Good, stay cool. This isn't a novena you're going on." He paused, gave another glare at Dal. "You got that, Dallas?"

"Sorry, Sam," Dal said finally raising his eyes. "I got kinda lost in all that shit; I know we won't be gettin' tourist brochures, just thought . . ." Then, mumbling to Blake, "*Excusez fuckin' moi.*"

Sam closed his eyes, the look of a man running short on tolerance. "Can I continue?" he grunted.

Neither man replied.

"I want you both to remember this. While we go about planning this operation, there are people sitting in another room someplace on the planet, just planning every possible way to fuck with you. They're commies, and pretty darned good at what they do, so we have to be better than *just good*. We have to be stealth." Another glance passed between them. "The acquisition and development of precision strike weapons by Beijing is going on so fast, it can only be described as pandemonium. Its fleet of unmanned aircraft is continually being increased, and they've just acquired four new Russian-built guided missile destroyers. And you can add two new classes of diesel subs, one that carries submerged-launch missiles."

"Sounds like alert status," Blake said, disbelievingly.

"If you consider all of this, you've gotta believe China's got a plan in motion." Sam narrowed his eyes, and adopted more intense body language. "The Communist Party can't tolerate any hint of authority from outsiders, whether it's the Vatican, Taiwan, Tibet or any one of its own internal dissenters. Posturing by Beijing is nothing more than a selfish manipulation by China to achieve its own goddamn end.

"They've got themselves a bunch of satellite launch sites we know about, as well as a whole bunch more of them we don't know about. They've got the North Koreans armed to the nuts, just frothing at the mouth to take on the South. They're strong enough to defy anyone who stands in their way."

He took a break, cutting Blake and Dal equal eye contact.

"Forget the kung pao," Blake groaned to Dal. "Is it too late to order pizza, Venice is startin' to look extra good."

Dal lowered his eyes, hoping Blake wouldn't catch his amusement. When he looked back, he grinned at the inference, and asked, "Has China made any recent direct threats against us?"

"They have," Sam replied. "A Chinese general named Cheng. He threatened us with nuclear war over Taiwan back in '05. This General Cheng left no doubt the Taiwan issue is looked upon by Beijing as having *no room* for negotiation. They'll give no margin; leave no room for compromise. Sovereignty over Taiwan isn't up for a nanosecond of discussion. Period! Analysis of Beijing's military acquisitions suggests that the Chinese military, the People's Liberation Army, is generating far greater military capabilities than those required for a rather straight forward Taiwanese take over." He added in obvious disgust, "The sons of bitches. The word's getting around that this General Cheng is paranoid, got delusions of grandeur, a goddamn psycho."

Blake took a sharp breath. "I thought North Korea and the Middle East, ya know, Afghanistan and Pakistan, the Iranians, I thought *they* were the powder kegs."

"They're volatile," Sam said. "But their value to Beijing's mostly as a convenient distraction, offering opportunity for China to redirect international attention from the real issues by making the Middle East and North Korea the draw cards, making them into appropriate diversions. The world's eyeballing Iraq, Iran and North Korea, while the Chinese roll along skipping through the meadows hand in hand with Russia, each being just as fucking conniving and two faced as the other.

"The Russians have sold the Chinese dozens of their obsolete pieces-of-shit diesel subs. Not so obsolete now, those clever buggers have installed sophisticated silencing technology, all but eliminating the diesel engine clatter. They're now able to get under the West's listening devices. If North Korea wants to expand its fleet of subs, Beijing'll be only too willing to oblige. The quieter subs represent the biggest threat in the South China Sea."

"And they're specifically for . . .?" Blake asked with a shrug.

"They're *directly* developed for a move on Taiwan or South Korea. They're even shadowing our destroyers, there's hardly a move our Navy makes where one of Beijing's subs isn't following close by. We don't hear about it, but that's what subs do, they shadow the enemy. Who knows how many of our destroyers have 'ex-Soviet' Chinese subs in their wake, following their every move, watching their exercises, timing their actions?"

Glancing at Sam, Dal asked uneasily, "So why doesn't our Commander-in-Chief pull Medvedev and Putin aside and lay it out for 'em?"

Sam's voice took on a steely tone. "Putin met with his Chinese counterpart just a bit back, tried to further strengthen relationships between them, arranged a strategic accord on cooperation and solved both countries' border issues. Russia and China are actively cooperating in the international arena. Their meeting discussed tripling trade between Russia and China. Beijing and Moscow are doing over twenty billion each year in trade."

"Is that Yuan or Rubles?" Dal asked.

"Greenbacks," Sam chuckled.

"Didn't they just have a meetin'?" Blake asked.

"They did."

"And?"

"The two formed quite a relationship," Sam said.

"Putin and what's his name, huh?"

"Hu Jintao," Sam replied. "He traveled to meet with Putin and his boys, had four days with 'em."

"Was probably teachin' Putin and Medvedev how to use fuckin' chopsticks?" Dal responded with a facetious shrug.

The waiter returned to the table and placed a serving stand alongside. Sam took a break, a well-earned respite from the non-stop barrage of bad news. Blake ignored the food, his mind preoccupied. He rested both elbows on the table, and placing the balls of his hands deep into his eye sockets, rubbed for awhile. He squinted, gave Sam a blurred look, and asked, "Why hasn't the American public heard about all of this bullshit?"

Sam smiled at the waiter, pausing until he had moved off. Blake forced a smile of his own, leaned over his plate, twirling the pasta around his fork and inhaling it in one hungry bite. He looked about, gave the empty fork a few calm jabs toward Sam, and said with sauce trickling down his chin, "Why are they bein' kept in the fuckin' dark?"

He waited ten seconds for a reply while Sam washed down his first fork full of pasta with Merlot. "Same reason they don't hear about genuine UFO findings," Sam mumbled. "It'd shake Wall Street, cause panic food hoarding, and throw the economy into one big tailspin. If they heard the truth about Roswell, it'd mean a whole re-classifying; you'd be seeing the show on the History Channel."

Blake peripherally observed Dal sliding a very full fork of pasta into his mouth.

He nodded, catching Dal fully loaded, "Hey Dal, whatcha make of all this?"

With both cheeks bulging, Dal slowly raised his eyes toward Blake and glared.

Blake gave a teasing wink. He said, "Enjoyin' that, huh Dallas?"

Sam was making very little headway with his pasta. Dal wiped his plate with a fresh Italian bread roll, while Blake, taking in his friend's eating habits, said, "Just love watchin' a man enjoyin' his food."

Dal placed his fork on the edge of the plate, rubbed the side of his nose with a middle finger, caught the waiter's eye and ordered up another plate.

Sam finished his second glass of Merlot, placing the glass alongside his almost untouched plate, and folded his arms. "We remain allies with Moscow in the war against terror," he said, dabbing at his mouth with a checkered napkin. "But the Russians, well, they're grumbling about Washington's open objection to Putin, to his going into reverse gear on the issue of democracy. Some officials and law makers in Moscow are accusing us of instigating a regime change in the Ukraine, in Georgia and Kyrgyzstan."

Blake raised his glass in a toast. "I'll drink to that, and eh, Sam, *that* of course is a crock of shit, right?"

He winked at Sam and Dal, but the chief neither agreed with Blake's inference nor denied it.

Blake allowed the question to float, waiting for the reply.

Got none.

"Why even bother?" he said in utter frustration. "Whichever way we turn there's some asshole waitin' for us to bend over. Fuck 'em all, the Chinese, the Russians, the North Koreans, the Muslims, the Jews, and the Arabs. Let 'em all go at it. Every time there's a problem it costs the American tax-payer. And if we do help solve their problems, they go burn our flag and kill the guys who were sent to help 'em. Fuck 'em all, I say. Let 'em all go at each other."

Blake's losing it, Sam thought, sniggering. "Whoa, whoa, whoa," he said. "You don't mean all that. I've a bunch more stuff to talk over, but best for now if we just go with what I've told you, plus this . . ." He paused as Adam McDowell approached the table. "Hey Adam, I've been bringing our boys up to speed. Hope you don't mind us starting lunch without you. Are Sung and Wang joining us soon?"

"I called 'em in their suite," McDowell said, pulling up a chair. "They're getting set to head this way."

Noticing Dal devouring his food, McDowell waited until he had a mouthful, and then in a teasing manner said, "Hey Dal. How's the pasta?"

Dal rolled his eyes, made an *'aw shit-not again'* gesture, and gave a thumbs-up.

Ridkin grinned at Mc Dowell, then shifted his gaze back to his two agents. "We need to get you two guys into Beijing." Another pause, this time a little longer as he tried reading their body language. They sat unmoved. *Hmm, no reaction, not yet*, he thought. *Good*. "I see you're both okay on that," he said. "The quandary we face is this, there've been too many recent incidents involving American citizens of Chinese ethnicity going into China and ending up staying there as permanent guests of the Beijing government, *supposedly* spying, of course."

They talked for a further fifteen minutes, about spies, about espionage, good ol' boys exchanging stories - bragging rights. Sam sensed McDowell *'thinking in his dark side'* role, and hoped it was not obvious to Blake and Dal.

Blake leaned forward, poured more wine, and took a long drink. "I followed that one a bit, about that guy. The guy who was a business executive from Hillsborough," Blake said with a remorseful shrug. "Was arrested in Western China, and he *was* a fuckin' Chinaman, right?"

McDowell nodded, "Yeah, he was Chinese. He flew into Sichuan Province via a connecting flight from Beijing. Stood out like balls on a bull. Our entry's gotta be less conspicuous."

Tipping his head in agreement, Sam signaled the waiter, ordered coffee, and had his almost untouched plate of pasta taken from the table.

"Fuckin' waste," Dal said, watching the plate leaving the scene.

Sam grinned at Blake who was shaking his head at Dal's comment. They chatted and ate breadsticks for ten more minutes, most of the discussion bouncing between Blake and Sam, while the others picked away at a fresh plate of olives and salami that arrived just in time to satisfy Dal's ravenous appetite.

Sam's coffee arrived, with Blake waving off the invitation to have the same. "Nope, thanks Sam," he said. "Starbucks has spoiled me."

"China's conducting an ever-deepening investigation into Taiwanese espionage on the mainland," Sam murmured. "That executive from Hillsborough, he's under residential surveillance for suspicion of espionage."

"What are they officially sayin' about the guy?" Blake asked.

"That he's working for Taiwan. China recently announced expanded cooperation with Taiwan's two main opposition parties, the Nationalists and the People First Party. The leaders of both parties made recent ice-breaking visits to the mainland."

"Are they clampin' down?" Dal asked. "Ya know, all that armed security at the airport."

"The Chinese are super sensitive about foreigners going in," Sam said. "They're touchier than ever. Security cops are ignoring the regular channels. Their so-called *residential surveillance* is actually a state security-run guest-house in Chengdu."

"Chengdu?" Blake asked.

"Capital of Sichuan."

"Does this mean he's eh, free to come and go?" Dal asked. "Is the only issue the fact he ain't got a passport?"

"Not really," Sam replied. "Officially, they can keep him under isolated detention for six months. Like being under house arrest, but you're kept in *their* house instead of yours. Doing it this way, instead of criminal detention, they aren't limited to the *regular period* of just over a month to prosecute. They just bought themselves an extra five months."

"Clever fucks," said Blake, watching Sam stir his coffee, sipping at it, and letting out a satisfied, "Ahhh."

"Not too bad, huh?"

"Not exactly Starbucks, but it'll do."

Blake turned, caught the waiter's attention and held up three fingers.

"Other than the guy from Jersey," Dal said, "have they jumped on anyone else enterin' the place?"

"There've been plenty of recent detentions," Sam said, "a Hong Kong reporter, a Beijing scholar, anyone who so much as offers advice to the Chinese leaders."

"How'd this guy from Jersey get into China?" Blake asked with a petulant look. "What I mean to say is . . . what was his reason for visitin'? How often was he in and out of the fuckin' place?"

"Good question." And Sam shunted it off to McDowell. "You care to answer that one, Adam?"

McDowell lowered his fully wound fork, placed it on the plate, and wiped his mouth with a napkin. "The guy's got this vitamin supply business in Hillsborough," he said. "He sells pills and shit to China. He was traveling there on a regular basis, up to five visits each year. Last time he went they lost his luggage, so the guy calls up someone in a place called . . ." He paused, picked up the fork, slid the food into his mouth, gazing at the ceiling for a few long moments, chewed, then took a few extra seconds trying to recall the city. "I think the place was, yeah, it was Chengdu. So he tells 'em he's going back to Beijing to find his bags. Next thing you know, whammy, he's being held on espionage charges."

"Sweet Jesus," Dal said. "How old's the dude?"

"In his fifties," McDowell replied, slipping Sam a wry smile, and holding the grin. "Just a young *dude*, and smart enough to know what's going on. He'd made that trip enough times, and he was fluent with the language too. Like you said, he was a *Chinaman*." He pointed a sharp finger at Dal, then at Blake. "So, you see, he had a huge advantage over you two turkeys." Then with a jab of his fork, "And he ain't *ever* coming back."

"Lovely, just fuckin' lovely," Blake said stretching out. "So give us the good news. How the fuck do ya get us in?" He half nodded and flicked a thumb at Dal, "Especially the blonde guy here."

Sam nodded at Dal, who bore a close resemblance to actor, Owen Wilson. "You boys," Sam asked, "you both went to Catholic colleges, right?"

"Sure we did," Blake said turning to Dal, who was making a sketchy attempt at blessing himself. "So?"

"Well boys, how good's your Latin?"

Both men hung their heads, no one spoke for awhile, then raising one hand, Blake said, "In nominee Patris, et Filii, et Spiritus Sancti . . ."

Dal added, "Amen."

Sam stayed on the serious side of the discussion, ignoring their comical performance. "Stop shaving, you've some beard growing to do. Hair coloring and new credentials will be in the works as well."

"Why are just Dal and me in on this discussion and Adam here? What about Bellinger and Hunter, and where do the two Chinese, eh sorry, the Taiwanese guys fit in?"

"This is where we're at right now, but plans can change in a heartbeat when we're dealing with someone as unpredictable as Beijing."

We're all ears," Blake said, shaking his head. "Fire away."

Dal nodded agreement.

"There's a guy someplace in China," Sam said. "We've been asked to get him back to the States. He's got information on Beijing's strategic satellite weapons program. China's developed a star-wars type program known as Operation Compass. This guy's got proof that China's planning a unilateral move to expand militarily into Taiwan and Tibet. We're not exactly certain what they've planned, but we've a few guesses in place. We know it involves star-wars technology previously unheard of, something to do with world weather manipulation, thus the name Operation Compass."

Dal nodded, as though he knew what the fuck Sam was talking about.

"Ya don't really believe they'd use that star-wars shit, do ya?" asked Blake.

"Sure I do, in time. That's their intent, with possible plans for a total takeover of neighboring countries, including Japan, Singapore, Malaysia, The Philippines, Indonesia,

North and South Korea, and possibly Australia and New Zealand. It's Beijing's new world order.

"They'll make a move north, swarm through Russia and pick tulips in Holland. Europe will become a Chinese playground. This will leave two other powers, the Americas and the Middle East. This is the reason North Korea has stepped up its nuclear program, not because they're scared of the United States. It's China they're keeping a close eye on."

"Ya mean they ain't scared of us?" Dal asked mockingly.

"We're no threat to the North Koreans," Sam said with a chuckle. "We're an international sheriff for sure, but not belligerent like the North Koreans, but China, now *there* lies the catalyst. China knows its neighbor to the south would dearly love to move up the food chain."

"Don't need to switch to a knife and fork when they get there either, huh?" Dal quipped.

Blake smirked, twisting his mouth sideways to Sam. "Now wouldn't *that* be a war to top all fuckin' wars."

Sam gave them time to refocus on what he'd said. "We know China has neutron bombs stockpiled. The technology to build them came from, and you're not gonna believe, of all places, the good old US of A."

"What about the Russians?" Blake asked.

"They're sitting on huge ordnance, not to mention the world's largest arsenal of nuclear missiles, and China's got the strength and ability to storm into Russia and take that arsenal. Can you imagine the Chinese flag draped across the entire European continent? If I had to name any major threat to world peace, that'd be it."

He studied their faces, each baring a serious expression.

No sniggering.

No head shaking.

"And as far as the Middle East goes, Israel has hundreds of neutron weapons," Sam said. "The neutron bombs would allow Israel to stop Arab armies and tank columns in their tracks, even on Israeli soil, without permanently contaminating the land. South Africa constructed a cache of neutron weapons before the end of white rule."

"But I heard they got rid of all that shit," Dal said.

"The South Africans claim they'd dismantled theirs before handing over power to the Nelson Mandela government, but our sources assure us that's a load of bullshit, the South African stockpile's still there."

He paused, looking around, then leaned toward the two men as though about to place more emphasis on his next morsel of information. McDowell moved in too, pulling his chair closer to the three, just as Bellinger and Hunter walked toward their table.

"Hope we haven't missed much," Hunter said, pulling a chair across from an unoccupied table.

"Nope, the waiter will be back shortly," Sam replied, tongue in cheek. "And eh, Dal recommends the bucatini."

Sam turned his attention back to Blake. "The guy in China's name is Paul Slade. He's the best chance we've got of getting our hands on the surveillance history and satellite technology from Beijing. With the information he has, the U.N. can take a solid stand and expose the complicity of the relationship between China and Russia, bring it all out before any moves can be instigated by a Sino Soviet partnership."

"Slade huh, so what's the problem with him?" Blake asked with an inquiring head cock. "Where exactly is he hidin'? I assume he's gone to ground."

"Underground," Sam said. Beijing knows about Slade, so they've been grabbing every non-Asian traveling in China to root him out."

"Thus the fuckup for Mr. Vitamins," Dal said.

"For the guy from Hillsborough," Sam replied.

"Yeah, and he *was* Chinese!"

"But on a U.S. passport," McDowell added.

"Why hasn't this Slade guy been able to communicate back with, well, whoever the fuck he's supposed to be workin' with?" Blake asked, leaning back in his chair.

Sam shook his head unenthusiastically. "Way too risky. The Chinese threw a blanket over transmissions. It's airtight. No one can get shit in or out of the place, short of it being carried in person. What with the ever increasing tourism trade, the goddamn Chinese are paranoid about who's an innocent tourist and who's in their country doing shit they shouldn't be doing."

Blake winced a little, washing down the last of a breadstick. "So eh, dare I ask, what's with the not shavin'?"

Dal chimed in, "And the Latin?"

"Wondered when you'd get around to that," Sam said with a look of resignation. "You two boys are gonna join the priesthood."

Silence.

"Halle-fuckin'-lujah," Blake groaned. "Ya gotta be shittin' me."

"Nope, I'm not shitting you. Salesian priests, in fact. We'll get your paperwork in order. You can start harvesting those beards. We're having you both made over, your appearance is gonna need a little work."

Dal, more than comfortable with his current look, said in a vinegary tone, "A little work, wha'dya have in mind?"

"You'll have your hair darkened, Mr. Billabong, your beard too, can't have that blonde hair standing out like a guiding light." Sam angled his head toward Blake. "And you'll have more grays added, maybe add on ten years. We can only hope."

Blake stared at Dal in disbelief, nodded his head toward Hunter and Bellinger who worked hard at suppressing their smiles.

"Why us?" Dal asked. "Why not these two?" and he flicked a thumb at Bellinger and Hunter. "Why not Father Hunter and Sister fuckin' Bellinger?"

"We're holding back with these two," Sam grinned. "If we need to send in backup, they'll be there for you. We've sort of a plan in the works."

"Sort of a plan!" Blake snapped, rolling his head, "Sort of a fuckin' plan! That sounds comfortin'," and he flipped a finger at Bellinger and Hunter, both struggling to restrain their mirth. Mid-flip he threw in, "Will these two be brushin' up on *their* Latin?"

Sam gestured at McDowell, who said, "Man, I gotta pee like a racehorse and you ain't helping. Time to drain the weasel."

McDowell took the easy way out, excused himself from the table, and headed to the restroom. As he disappeared from view, Sam leaned in closer to his four agents. "This bit I'll share with you, and it *doesn't go any further*." He was staring hard from one to the other, cutting into their eyes. "Do you read what I'm saying?"

Puzzled by his placing such weight on *'does not go any further'*, Blake leaned nearer to Sam and said in a mimicking tone, "Sam, please tell me there's a backup plan?"

"There's a plan 'B', but it's not a done deal yet."

"Done deal?" Dal asked.

"Hunter's a scratch golfer."

"So am I," Dal replied sharply.

"Listen to me! We're considering his golf skills as a possible angle. If necessary, we'll send him over for an Asian Tour event in Beijing, the Volvo Open, in April. If all goes to plan, this'll coincide with the arrival of yourself and Drew in China."

Sam's eyes locked onto Dal. "With appropriate credentials, and some adequate brushing up of his current golf game, Hunter will be quite believable."

"That's it," Blake groaned. "That's your backup plan?"

"Jesus, Chief. I suppose Bellinger here's the caddy?" Dal asked, shaking his head in disgust.

"Perceptive, Dal," Blake added, "very perceptive." Then, scrubbing his fingers through his hair, "Dal's right, huh Chief? She's the fuckin' caddy, ain't she?"

Bellinger rubbed her hands together, grinning at Dal, savored the few long moments, twisting the knife a little deeper into his wound.

"Aw shit," Dal whined. "Ya know I play scratch golf, why can't I be the golfer, let Hunter be the priest. He looks pious enough." He passed a slow hand by Hunter's face. "How can ya look at this face and not wanna say *bless me father?*"

Sam didn't smile, just stared at Dal as he bit off the end of another breadstick. The expression on the chief's face left little room for negotiation over the so called *plan 'B'*. A few chilled moments slipped on by, then Sam, who rarely cussed, used a breadstick as a pointer, jabbing it toward Dal. "Because fucking Hunter has a much lower fucking profile and can move into China without raising suspicion, whereas *you,* Dal, well, they'd whip that golf bag off of you, jam your driver up your ass and nail you to the fucking wall," and Sam had reached the end of his tether.

"Ah, gee, thanks Chief," Dal said, grimacing at the outburst, "In view of my low pain tolerance, point well taken."

There was a long-drawn-out silence. Bellinger let out a slight snigger, only to receive a quick ankle tap from Hunter.

"Remember, plan 'B' is for you four only," Sam said in a somewhat acquiescing tone, ". . . for you four, no one else. And one more little crumb, we're arranging for a special cell phone to get into the hands of a problematic operative in China, his name's Yidui. The phone's carrying a small charge of C4, enough to wreak one mother of all headaches."

"Problematic operative?" Blake asked in a perplexed way.

Sam glanced about, pursed his lips and said, "Dominic Broski's people have the guy under surveillance. That's all I've been officially told. But I had our people dig a little deeper into this Yidui character." He pulled his cell phone, placed it on the table. "He'll have Franco Brantini's little gem." He tapped on the phone. "When the moment's right, I dial in a sequence of digits, just like this," and he punched 6-6-6. "Then whammy, no more problematic operative."

"Damnit," Dal said. "Don't go upgradin' *my* service anytime soon."

Sam spent a few long moments staring at each of his team. "None of this can be discussed with anyone outside this group."

"Adam knows about all this shit, right?" Blake asked.

"What part of what I just said didn't you get? I said *no one*, that includes McDowell. The information's just for you four."

"Hey, hey, hey, that's pretty non-departmental shit," Blake retorted. "Adam's a part of the team; why not share it with him?"

"I've learned one thing heading up this Interpol Division," Sam snapped. "What we do here stays with us, and in this case, us, being the four of you and yours fucking truly."

Dal sighed, "Jeeesus!"

Ridkin looked about, smiled as McDowell returned, accompanied by Wang and Sung, who pulled over chairs from a nearby table, and McDowell signaled the waiter as Wang made a half bowing gesture. "Good afternoon, Mr.

Ridkin, Miss Bellinger, gentlemen," Wang said. "It is good to see you all. Are we late?"

Sung reached across the table and shook hands with each of the group.

Sam tried to appear relaxed, leaning back, stretching. "Not at all," he said. "We arrived a little early; you haven't missed anything, just a minor briefing, so please, go ahead, order." He nodded at Wang and Sung, then gave a short head-nod to the others. "You guys won't be going into Beijing directly; that'd be way too high a risk. We're taking you in through Nepal."

He paused, looking again at each of the group. *Wang's very attentive,* he thought, swallowing hard. Blake caught the body language, felt Sam looked uncomfortable. *Somethin's wrong with how he's dishin' this out, too much bullshit. He's coverin' up somethin'.* He kept the thought to himself.

"You'll be accompanied by Mr. Wang and Mr. Sung, so translation won't be an issue. They've both been briefed on the procedure and are getting their identities in order. The four of you will enter as Salesian missionaries. You'll be visiting a Catholic cathedral in Beijing, the Xishiku."

"A Catholic church in Beijing," Blake ventured skeptically.

"It's not a Roman Catholic Church. It's called a patriotic Catholic church. Because the Vatican supports Taiwanese independence, the Catholic Church is persecuted, that's why it's underground. Even though the cathedral isn't Catholic, it's the largest church in China. Actually, I hear the Sunday mass there attracts about a thousand Catholic Chinese at each one of its four Sunday Masses."

"Aw shit," Blake groaned with a roll of his head. "So how do we get involved if we're priests?"

"We'll leak propaganda you're part of a breakaway group wanting to support the patriotic movement," Sam said, "As well as supporting the move to pull Taiwan into the Chinese fold."

"So we go in as *disgruntled priests*," Blake said. "Hmm, not too bad, Sam, it sounds kinda believable. Will Sung and Wang be able to pull this off, 'cause we ain't gonna be doin' any conversin'. What if we're separated?"

"If the Chinese want to interrogate you, they'll use English, but you better pray it never comes to that. I strongly suggest you all keep your hoods up, your heads down, and your rosary beads in hand."

"Oh sweet Jesus," Blake groaned.

"Amen to that," Dal added as Sam leaked a smirk.

Blake bit on his bottom lip and slid a sideways glance at Dal. "That's good, Dal. Ya got that *Amen* bit pretty well nailed. Yes siree Bob, you've got that fuckin' *Amen* part down." Then, with a look of discontent, he added, "I'm still starvin', I need some real food. Ya fancy a burger, some fries? Let's go eat."

CHAPTER 5

RADISSON JAPANESE RESTAURANT, later that day.

The Teppan-yaki bar.

Over Sushi and Tempura.

Sung and Wang met with the AID team, and loosely discussed plans for the journey that lay ahead, one that'd take them through the northern region of India and Nepal, across the Himalayas, culminating in Beijing. With sufficient Sake under his belt, Dal's eyes bore down on the two men from Taiwan. "You guys," . . . burp . . . "ya gonna be, Father S S Sung, and F Father Wang?"

The two men from Taiwan balked at the question.

Sam absorbed the exchange, and any hope that the four were establishing good rapport began developing reservations. During their time over rice wine, he occasionally nudged McDowell, giving him a wink; a tenuous sign that things were looking good, that the '*team*' was bonding. But Sam sensed doubt, sensed animosity raising its head.

"Bonding?" McDowell asked, whispering as he leaned into Sam.

"I'd like to think we've moved past the bonding part of this assignment," Sam replied. "What's your first impression, you think they aren't?"

"I'm not disputing it," McDowell said in a defensive way, his eyes darting across the restaurant. There was a lengthy pause as Sam waited, expecting McDowell to add a

75

little more. When nothing further came, he cast an eye across the room.

"You see that painting over there," and he pointed to a large framed canvas hanging above a leather sofa. "I think it's a . . ." He gestured to the artwork. "Come on over, let's take a look at it."

McDowell grinned at the four, shook his head and he and Sam slid their chairs out from the table.

Sam placed a hand on Dal's shoulder. "You guys'll be spending a hell of a lot of time together," and he brushed non-existent *whatever* from his jacket. "You're gonna need tolerance and a shitload of luck. Crossing the Himalayas is no easy task. Coordination between the four of you is mandatory, can't have any confusion."

He dwelled on Blake and Dal, then smiled at the two Asian men, both stony faced. "If you've any reservations," he said in a near surreptitious way, "speak now or forever hold your . . ." and he grinned at Dal. "Well, whatever it is that the two of you hold." He tapered off, leaving them sitting in silence as he and McDowell excused themselves, and moved off toward the artwork.

"What's up, Adam?" Sam asked as he tried to appear interested in the artwork. "I was waiting for a call from you earlier. Everything on track?"

"Wang's been hitting me up with so much shit. Wants more info about a few of the deals he and this Sellers character had going. I'm just lucky I memorized most the agency's file. I know Beijing's deposited a payment into both his and Seller's Swiss accounts. I told Wang I'm expecting instructions from Beijing."

"And?"

"Seems he's a buddy of that general, the guy whose son was killed."

"Cheng?"

McDowell was anxious. It showed. "Yeah, that's the

guy, the eh, the general."

"I can see you're uncomfortable and that's okay. I understand that." He turned, looked back at their table. "Take it easy, they're looking this way."

Sam turned his back to the group, his mind wandering, not wanting to allow too much time to slip by. Not wanting to push his luck, thinking, *can't risk McDowell pushing the panic button.* "Stay calm, Adam," he said. "Stick with the plan, play the part." He needed to ask the question, and did. "You're not getting cold feet, are you?"

McDowell looked away, took a deep breath.

Didn't answer.

Sam knew too well how Blake would suspect something was amiss should they have stayed away too long. They returned to the group at the table. They were discussing the Himalayas, with Blake contributing the least to the dialogue. His encounters with reactive depression in years gone by, had left him with an awareness of the chemical imbalance that signaled an oncoming bout - the familiar dry mouth, the slight hint of shakiness that swelled and grew from deep in his nervous system. His eyes rose to meet Sam's as he fought off the gremlins of depression.

"Okay then," Sam said, taking on a buoyant tone. "I assume it's a definite go for you guys."

A supposition on Sam's part, Blake thought, *more so than a question.*

Wang, Sung, and Dal looked at Blake who was staring mindlessly at a far wall. He felt one of the gremlins slip on through, mentally pounced on it, blinked it away and regrouped. Sam recognized Blake's *off with the pixies* stare. He'd seen the familiar glazed look, seen it during times when stress resulted in Drew Blake's withdrawal, a turtle retracting its head.

"Drew! You with us?"

The reply was slow to come. Blake replied somewhat

unconvincingly to the questioning gaze, giving a slow nod. "Yeah, sure Sam, I'm with ya."

And he caught the warning glance.

Swift.

Cutting.

Recognized the look.

Adam McDowell and Sam Ridkin leaned back, each absorbing the body language as Blake reached to the center of the table, placing his right hand palm down. Dal, knowing the routine, smiled, reached across and placed his hand on top of Blake's. They turned to Sung and Wang. Sung caught onto their gesture and placed his hand on top of Dal's. Wang followed suit, and all four stayed in that position for a few soldering moments.

"So we've got ourselves a team then?" Sam asked, disguising his doubt as all four hands vacated the table.

"I ain't heard of this *Salesian* order of priests," Blake said. "What's the deal with 'em?"

Divine guidance eluded Sam, but he gave it his best shot. "It was in 1939, a priest, Father Cowhig, he was forced out of China, settled in Los Angeles, and established a mission in Chinatown. Began with a Chinese school, a church and a recreation center. Around 1954 I think it was, another priest kicked it along a bit more, and around 1980 another priest emigrated from Hong Kong. He became the first bilingual guy to head up the church."

"What's the name of this place?" asked Blake.

"St. Bridget's Catholic Chinese Center," Sam said, in an all business way.

Adam McDowell came in on cue, the hint of a smile on his face. "You four will be staying at the pastor's quarters for two weeks. You'll see two guys, Father Francis and his assistant, Father Paul. Francis is going to give you a crash course in how to act like priests. You know, what to say, how to serve mass, to bear up as priests if you're unlucky enough

78

to go under interrogation." He gave Sam an okay wink, and his smile widened.

"They'll be your guardian angels," Sam said. "If you mess up, you won't be going to Starbucks any time soon." Then he chuckled sympathetically and added, "Good job guys, time to move forward." He placed his attaché case in the center of the table, opened it, and pulled out a folder. "Some years ago, an organization came to our attention, a secret organization with a global political agenda. The government has had past exchanges with these people, at least when we have matching agendas. I heard they had advance notice on nine eleven. Our boys at the CIA thought it was a load of bullshit."

"Yeah . . . big fuckin' surprise," Blake groaned.

Dal peeked between fingers that had quickly covered his face, could feel the vibration in the air, bit his top lip as Sam gave Blake a cold, icy stare.

"I guess we all think that, and thanks for your eh, your candor." He made allowances for Blake's tactless displays of sarcasm. "I know that a group of trustees was formed, ten people in positions of trust. These ten were known as cardinals. The word 'cardinal' kind of indicated the level the guy was at."

Dal asked, "Kinda, huh? Kinda like a general."

"Yeah, you know, like a general, kinda," Sam said, falling into Dal's syntax. After a few chuckles from Blake and McDowell, Sam opened the file. "If what I've got here ever leaks out, it'd tumble governments and put people into jail cells for life. I'll tell you as much as you need to know at this time, will pass on more as needed, but that'll be my call."

Their eyes remained fixed on the folder.

"Drew. I wanna see you aside for a few minutes, over by the bar."

He excused himself from the table, as McDowell continued a conversation with Wang and Sung. Fifteen seconds after making their way to the bar, Blake asked, "What's goin' on, Sam?"

"Drew, you need to know how powerful the movement is that we're up against."

"Ah jeez," Blake blurted with cynicism. "Don't like the sound of this one bit."

Sam said, "Back in '55, the cardinals named two tribunes, one for safeguarding information regarding operatives in the Soviet Union, another for China. One of these tribunes was a bishop, his name was Albino Luciani."

"Can't say the name rings a bell," Blake said, shaking his head. "What happened to this eh, this bishop?"

The barman sidled up, a damp cloth in hand, wiping the area in front of the two, and gave a questioning face.

"Gimme a Jim Beam, lots of ice," Sam said with a short smile.

The drink man shifted his eyes to Blake.

"Me too, plenty of ice, but make mine milk."

"Milk?"

Blake flashed the man his *'ya got a fuckin' problem with that?'* glare. The barman nodded, looked at Sam, shrugged and moved away. Sam resumed the discussion. "How about the name, Pope John Paul, does that ring your bell?"

Blake pulled on his lower lip for a few seconds, and then said with a penetrating glare, "Jesus Christ, the guy who died after about a month as pope?"

"Same guy, the whole show was fixed, rigged. There was a short conclave. It ended in record time; the white smoke blew from the chimney, telling the world that the guys in the Vatican had their man. They had him all right; they had Cardinal Sergio Pignedoli on a crash diet so he'd fit into the white cassock when elected."

Letting out a long breath, Blake grunted. "Aw fuck!

I'm readin' between the lines here, so correct me if I'm wrong. Don't wanna hear that old cliché, if I tell ya, I'll have to . . . ya know the rest, Sam."

Silence.

"Sam?"

Avoiding Blake's stare, Sam scoffed, "So much of the shit that went down's based on unfounded speculation. Best I can tell you is you'll know all that the privileged few know. You catching my drift here?"

"Sure, but I'll ask anyway, take my chances."

"What the hell," Sam chuckled, shaking his head. "Fire away."

"As I see it, John Paul was sharin' the information with just one other cardinal. Each of 'em knew the identity of the operative in China, right?"

"Hmm, yeah, okay so far, go on."

"While he was bishop, he wasn't in a position that worried anyone. So eh, he was pretty safe." He paused, looked at Sam's expression. "How am I doin', chief, still okay?"

The waiter arrived, placed the bourbon in front of Sam, winked at Blake and slid the milk across as though the glass were contagious. Half a minute passed by. It gave Sam time to run Blake's words through his mental computer. He took a pull on the Jim Beam. "Go on," he said, his finger circumnavigating the rim of the glass, his eyes closed in anticipation.

Blake, avoiding the waiter's dissing, raised his glass and clinked it against Sam's bourbon. "So he gets handed the papacy on a platter, 'cause he's got this reputation of bein' easy goin', a push over, a regular type guy," Blake said taking a gulp of milk. "Had no power aspirations, someone who'd easily be coaxed into givin' out information, an easy puppet compared to the more favored candidates." He looked deep into Sam's eyes, and returned his stare. "Someone knew he was one of the tribunes." He paused, took another swallow of milk, and wiped his chin with the back of his hand. "They figured that as pope, he'd be a great pawn, could be easily screwed for information."

"That sounds good," Sam said eyes down, rattling ice about in his near empty glass. He said in a morose tone, "They figured he'd sooner give them a name than risk losing his crown. They were wrong. He had a short reign."

Blake shook his head incredulously. "Was hopin' I was barkin' up the wrong tree, can't believe it, the pope!"

Sam's reply was sharp. "He was a good man, had the papacy for thirty-three days, a short term lease." He started back to the table, pausing, turning for Blake, but Blake hung back.

The group at the table was scouring over a map, watching McDowell as he traced a finger across the Himalayas, explaining unimaginable routes into China.

"I think we can call it a night," Sam yawned. "We can meet back in one of the suites in the morning?"

He glanced around, looking back for Blake.

A solitary figure at the bar.

Patrice Bellinger asked, "Usual suite, twelfth floor?"

"Nah, here in the lounge," McDowell replied. "We'll grab a quick breakfast. Won't know in advance what room we'll be using. But it won't be the usual twelfth floor suite, so we can be sure of one thing; any bugging attempt will need a shitload of gadgets to cover the entire Radisson."

"Can't take chances," Sam said, giving a curious glance back at Blake. "See you here, nine sharp."

Bellinger and Hunter sat for awhile, chatting with Sung and Wang, as Blake, now joined by Dal, bid goodnight to the rest of the group. Sam and McDowell retired to the bar area for a nightcap. The nightcap lasted three hours.

Dal made the elevator ride to the tenth floor in silence, as Blake attempted to whistle a few bars of something resembling Queen's, *Another One Bites The Dust.* They stepped from the elevator and walked to their room where Blake slid the entry card into the lock. Dal flopped on the bed, kicked off his loafers. "So what's the deal with Sam?" he asked. "Ya know, the private side-bar 'n all?"

"He talked about the pope," Blake said, letting out a long sigh. "Not too sure I followed much of it, I got this gut feelin' he's got a shit load more to tell us. So uh, let *him* tell ya 'bout the pope."

"Pope?"

*****

At eight o'clock the radio alarm by the bedside played Faith Hill singing *Breathless.* Blake stretched out, switched the music off and grunted in disgust, "Country fuckin' music. So this's how the day's gonna be. Lord spare me."

The meeting got underway on time, in a room chosen at random from three offered by the desk clerk. Sam selected the second of the three, entering with an air of distrust. He walked about, gave it a once over, checking under lampshades, under tables, and running his fingers under edges. Then, moving to the bedroom, he kneeled, raised the skirt and peered beneath the bed.

"Christ, Sam, you watch too many movies," Hunter said, stretching out on a sofa and getting a supportive nod from Patrice Bellinger.

"You think, huh?" Sam replied, attempting to peek behind a picture frame, trying to look cool as he realized it was screwed to the fucking wall.

"Can't trust anyone these days," Blake said, flipping through pages of a hotel directory, pretending not to notice Sam as he continued running a final methodical scan across the room, eyes searching, feeling out all possibilities until totally satisfied, at which point, he sat at a small table and began punching buttons on the remote. He found The Golf Channel, turned the volume up, and let the mundane monotone voice of the British commentator float about the room.

"I'm gonna run two names by you," Sam said. "Pope John Paul, and Australian Prime Minister, Harold Holt. Those two guys had a common denominator; they were Tribunes, chosen by the cardinals in the '50s. Each was an up-and-comer in his field, and each was based on a different continent."

Gardner Hunter, feeling a little left out of the discussion, asked, "How and why were those two selected to be tribunes?"

"The pope was nobody when the tribunes picked him, just a bishop," Sam answered, nodding despondently. "Holt was an Australian Member of Parliament, but each of these guys had information relevant to world security."

"So they had access to shit," Hunter said. "How'd that make 'em candidates?"

"Their access to *shit* . . ." and he threw Hunter a dagger-like glare, "as you so eloquently put it, assured each of them success in their respective fields once elected to the position of tribunes."

Bellinger made a shrugging gesture. "They were promoted because of their . . .?"

Sam cut her short. "Promoted? Yeah, that's one hell of a promotion, one made pope, the other made Prime Minister. Yeah, *promoted* would be an understatement. Like they say, it ain't *what* you know. The cardinals have ways of getting their guys to the top. Each of these had their covers exposed to Beijing and Moscow. When John Paul refused to capitulate to the Russians, they got rid of him. He was dead in just over one month of moving house into the Vatican."

"And the reason he was killed?" Bell asked.

"He was set to do some serious ass kicking; get rid

of the Masonic faction, the crooks, as well as cleaning up the messy Vatican Bank scandal," Sam said shaking his head. "The Vatican loaned money for projects worldwide, was involved in some shaky, illegal schemes. Money laundering, speculative investing, ties to the mafia, stuff like that was common knowledge. They were funneling funds through our CIA to finance the Solidarity movement in Poland, and eh, well . . . the new pope, he was planning to change all of that."

Blake asked, "I heard stories of poison being to blame for the pope's death. What about that?"

Sam smiled ruefully, "Theorists say he was overdosed on digitalis."

"Aha," Blake grinned. "Efficient little fucks too."

"Clean too," Dal added.

"The poison theory, it's supported by the lack of a post-mortem," Sam said, and he quickly scanned their reactions.

"Fuckin' Vatican," Blake said, rolling his eyes. "Don't tell me they didn't . . ."

"They didn't," Sam said. "His body was embalmed within a day of his death."

"The next day? That's bullshit."

"Nope, that's power," Sam said with a grin. "They move fast in the Holy See, they go by their own rules. The speed of his embalming raised suspicions that it was rushed to prevent any autopsy. The Vatican insisted a papal autopsy was prohibited under Vatican law, ignoring the fact that one had been performed on the remains of Pius VIII, back in 1830." He pulled a file from his attaché case, and read from notes. "Oh yeah, it's also interesting to note that two visiting priests also died from drinking poisoned coffee."

Hunter gave him a questioning gaze. "Why take out those guys?"

"It was unintentional. The coffee, it eh, it'd been

brewed for the pope."

Dal looked up from a file that Sam had placed in the center of the small table. "Sam, I'm sure it's bullshit, but I recall hearing the Masons played a part in the pope's death."

This caught the attention of all in the room.

"There's a law in the Catholic church," Sam said, "one of which I assume you and Drew are aware of," and he paused, put on an overstated smile, "being the good Catholic boys you two are." The line was delivered with irreverent sarcasm. "That law relates to Freemasons, how they're not accepted as Catholic."

"Are ya sayin' there are priests who are Masons?" Dal ventured with a querulous look.

"Absolutely," Sam nodded. "There are more than a hundred Masonic priests and cardinals spread throughout the Vatican. Forbidden under Canon Law, they would've been excommunicated if the pope had time enough to have his way."

"They killed him over that?" Bell asked.

"Not just that. He was about to give birth control the go ahead."

"Whoa, he was gonna kick the church on its ass. Darn shame," Dal said. "The guy sounds like a breath of fresh air."

"The smiling pope, that's what he was tagged. Didn't do him any good, trying to make changes. The Freemasons won out as they always have, probably always will. Some things, well, some things never change," Sam said curtly.

"Who's the other guy, the Australian guy?" Blake asked.

"Harold Holt, the Prime Minister," Sam replied. "He decided to go swimming. The surf was heavy, and the beach, Cheviot Beach, had dangerous rips and strong currents. The guy was an excellent swimmer and a highly regarded skin diver. He'd recently suffered a shoulder injury and wasn't in the best of health. He dived into the surf, disappeared from sight. His friends raised the alert, but no trace of him was found. Two days later on December 19 of 1967, the government made an official announcement that Holt was presumed dead. Word got around that a Chinese submarine kidnapped him. In 1983 a British journalist, Anthony Grey, published a book claiming Holt had been an agent for the People's Republic of China, claimed he'd been picked up by a Chinese sub.

"If there were so called Chinese threats to his family, and maybe also to the Australian nation, then Holt's action might've been his only choice. Some said he actually passed on secrets to the Chinese because of threats by Beijing. Of course, it could be propaganda, but that's conjecture. You see, the tribunes are not only privy to highly classified information, their anonymity must be maintained. When it's not, they invariably end up as puppets . . . or dead."

No one spoke.

"There are three names you'll need to remember. I don't want them written down, you get that, Dallas? One's in Beijing, name's David Leung. I'll give you directions to his home; again you'll memorize, not notate." He nodded at Dal. "I'm not seeing a nod from you. You clear on that, Dal?"

Dal grunted.

"We've got two contacts in Datong, that's about eight hours drive from Beijing. One guy owns an antique shop and goes by the name, Yidui. The other's quite a character, Harry Ching. He operates a crop duster; the guy's a bi-plane freak. He'll be on stand-by in the event you need his services. You're gonna know exactly how to find these guys, where to find 'em. They're your insurance if things, hmm . . ." Sam swallowed hard, didn't like the thought, hated saying the words. "In the event of any unforeseen problems, or . . ."

and he squeezed his lips tight, making an apologetic face, "in the event of a change in plans."

No reaction.

He analyzed their faces as Patrice Bellinger stared at Hunter, Blake at Dal.

Sam gave it ten long seconds, looking from one to the other.

Waited for comments.

Sam's demeanor was indifferent. Blake, sensing his indifference, searched for a more appropriate word . . . settling on, *evasive*. The chief gathered up papers that had been spread about the table, stacked them into the attaché, mumbling as he went, "It's time to get this baby rolling." A minute later he buzzed through to Marcie. "Call Pirelli, tell him to get his ass up here, and get Franco Brantini on the line."

*****

Franco Brantini was a genius with a lifetime of Central Intelligence Agency work behind him. And, as is the way with many in his field, Franco chose to live an introvert lifestyle. Brantini's compound sat on acreage tucked away in the hills of Fallbrook, a two hour drive south of Los Angeles, close enough to the city, but insular enough to add a nuisance factor for anyone attempting to access his hideaway. Sam Ridkin and Pete Pirelli arrived in the Suburban, in time for a typical Italian lunch.

"Been awhile, Franco," Sam said, giving the older man a too firm handshake. "It's good to see you, sorry about the short notice."

Brantini, although expecting them, was not too keen over the visit. He grunted, massaging his hand after the greeting.

It was all Franco had. This spread in the back of

bum-fuck-Fallbrook, his side-kick, Mr. Snoops, and his joy of Italian cooking. And he laid out a traditional spread for his two guests.

"Old family recipe," he said, watching Pirelli polish off the last of the braciole."

Pirelli reached for a napkin, dabbed at the corners of his mouth, eying the pastries and settling on the cannoli. "Goddamn great stuff," he said appreciatively, devouring the sugar coated pastry. "Best I've had. Not like those at . . .

"I make my shells extra crispy," Franco said proudly, his chin raised. "Flour, butter, sugar and hmm, other ingredients, fill 'em with a special eh, *un vecchio segreto di famiglia*," and he made some kind of Italian gesture with a waving of his hands. "It's an old family secret recipe."

"You get into town much? I mean, throwing together this kind of food. You go to Little Italy, downtown San Diego, right?" Pirelli asked, passing a hand over the remaining pastries.

"Yeah, but not too often, don't trust the guys in LA. Not since I quit the agency. They think I know too much, and I think they know that I know too much."

"Sons of bitches, huh," Pirelli said, shaking his head consolingly.

Brantini's eyes were glazed as he stared lifelessly into the nearby brush surrounding the compound. "Yeah, something like that. But yeah, yeah, yeah, you're right, you gotta go to Little Italy."

"Dispense with the niceties," Sam said, displaying a touch of impatience. "Can you do it; you still got the touch, Franco?"

"Been doing it awhile now, have it perfected," he said in an excited tone. "You know what they say, you do it too many times and you go blind." He sniggered.

"Yeah, I heard rumors to that affect. So, how *are* your eyes?"

"Can still hit a melon from three hundred paces. Okay for my age."

"And the C4, the phone device?"

"Got it down to the size of a dime."

"A dime huh?" Pirelli said with a doubting shrug. "You've got it down quite a bit since that Marlboro pack."

Brantini gave a hurt look to Pirelli. "That ain't nice. The plastic binder wasn't quite perfected." He gave a less pained look to Sam. "Got a coating over the explosive material, makes it less sensitive to heat, to shock." He raised a hand missing two digits. "Makes it relatively safe to handle," he said, chuckling. "Relatively."

"Jeez," Pirelli groaned, "Better late than never."

"No big deal," Franco grinned, holding out both palms, "Got eight more. Now-a-days the explosive material's malleable. I can mold it into different shapes; amplify the direction of the explosion." He pulled his cell phone, passed it to Pirelli. "When it's placed into a guy's cell phone, its force is directed into the head by using a blast blanket, compressing the explosion. Stops it from spreading about. The polyisobutylene binder and the sebacate plasticizer are combined in just the right proportions."

Pirelli sneaked a sideways glance to Sam. "I knew that," he said in a hushed tone, and gingerly slid the cell phone back across the table.

Franco looked about, whistled, and a golden retriever bounded from a nearby paddock. "This is Mr. Snoops. We're partners. Best sniffer dog Jesus put breath into. Snoopsy here's my boy."

They took turns meeting Mr. Snoops as Franco fed the dog kibbles from a Tupperware container. "Don't ever feed him human food, no table scraps. This stuff keeps him sharp. Keeps his nose working."

"So then," Sam said, "you've got the blast regulated, huh?"

"Yeah, after distillation, with the water removed, I end up with slurry, then I add binder, wave my magic wand, and alakazam, I got modeling clay with a real kick."

"As I understand," Sam said, "past tests have had eh . . . a problem triggering the explosive."

"Well kind of, yeah. It takes a detonator."

"A blasting cap?" Pirelli asked.

"Precisely, a brief charge to set off the very small wad of C4."

"How'd you fit all of that into the cell phone?" Sam inquired. "How do you fit it all in there without someone spotting it?"

"Carefully."

"What's it like?" Pirelli asked. "Is it a spark, an impact?

"When the chemical reaction gets going, the C-4 decomposes releasing gases expanding at over 26,000 feet per second. That's a lot of force. The explosion's instantaneous. One second everything's fine, the next . . . we got us a body missing a head."

"If the guy's in a car, will it take the car apart?" Pirelli asked, waiting several seconds for his answer, as Franco reached for a bottle of Chianti, rattled the bottle, and gave his visitors an asking expression.

They declined.

He topped up his glass, and half turned to Pete Pirelli. "A small amount packs a big punch. Less than a pound will demolish a truck. I've just enough to take off your guy's head, nothing more, nothing less." He passed the cell phone to Sam, along with a note page on which were written the numbers, 666. "When you call, you punch in these numbers, then bam, no more headaches."

Pirelli shuddered.

CHAPTER 6

THEY CAME TO A STOP alongside the white church in Cottage Home Street, its aqua colored roof tiles adding a distinct Asian flavor to the architecture, the words St. Bridget on the left side of a cross, and Chinese Catholic Center to its right. Beneath the cross were five Chinese characters denoting the name of the church.

They'd packed meagerly, jeans, a tracksuit, comfortable sneakers, a sweater, and rudimentary bathroom items, but no razors or colognes. A Chinese bespectacled priest, wearing a high-buttoned white-necked shirt greeted Sam with a half-bow, and Sam placed a hand on each of the man's shoulders.

"It is good to see you once again," the priest said, the way that pious people do.

"Father, I'd like you to meet two special boys, both devoted Catholics," Sam said turning and nodding at his *two boys*. "Both tormented products of the Catholic school system."

Yeah, De La Salle Brothers of Perversion and Sadism, Blake thought, nodding at the priest.

"This is Carson Dallas and Drew Blake."

The *two special boys* stepped forward, each shaking hands with the priest.

"Dal, Drew, this is Father John. He's going to put you on the path to salvation, isn't that right, Father?"

The priest gave an amused look at the pair. "These

are your travelers to the cathedral?"

There was a protracted silence, sufficient for the priest to regain composure. He gave the two a more thorough looking over, cocked his head at Sam in an almost apologetic way, and said, "Hmm, they certainly appear to be city slickers." And then motioning at the pair, "I see I have my work cut out."

He grinned at Dal and Blake, crinkling his face, and nodding his head like a bobble doll, which caused his glasses to slide farther down the bridge of his nose. Just as Blake was about to lunge forward and catch the spectacles, they came to a stop on the tip of the priest's proboscis.

"Come along," Father John said, motioning toward the rear of the church, "this way."

They followed behind the bespectacled man, entered a room, and came to a halt just feet from another priest kneeling at a pew, rosary beads in hand.

"Gentlemen, this is Father Paul. He has come to us from Taiwan. He and Father Francis, whom you'll meet later, each have a single task for the next two weeks, transforming you into hardened priests."

Dal coughed a muffled, *bullshit*, followed immediately by Blake delivering a succinct elbow jab to his ribcage.

"You should see to that cough, Mr. Dallas," said the priest taking it in stride. "Where you are going, a cough can prove . . ." and he paused just long enough for his smile to widen, adding in an emphatic tone, "A cough such as yours can prove deadly."

Dal slid a look to Blake, whose reaction could best be described as morose.

"Once we begin your training," the priest said, restraining a grin, "we *will* see it through. Of that, have no doubt."

This guy has made this welcome speech a few times, Blake thought, catching Sam's grin, and the pained expression lingering on Dal's face as he recovered from the nudge to his rib cage.

Blake seldom felt discomfort, not to the point of becoming fearful of an upcoming assignment, but someplace in the deepest recess of his mind, a small red light was flashing. *I can live with this*, he thought, until the small red light became a fireworks display. He gave Sam a long look of dismay, followed by a partially disguised whisper, "Did ya throw those anxiety pills into the bathroom bag?"

"Don't like this," Dal cowered, wagging a sad finger. "Don't like it one bit."

"All right then," Sam said with a self satisfied look. "I'll leave you boys with Father John and Father Paul."

Blake's eyes tracked each of Sam's steps as he moved toward the exit. He resembled a three year old on his first day at pre-school, a kid watching his mom leave. "Sam!" he called with a pleading ring. "Leave your cell phone!"

Sam paused as he eased the door open, standing for a moment as though giving the request a smidgeon of consideration. Without turning, he called, "I'll check on you two novices in about a week. And by the way, we've a hair specialist coming in to see you both, something I thought you'd like to hear at this time, about twelve days off, time to ponder your new look."

"Total bullshit," Dal groaned, still clutching at his side.

"And eh," Sam called, "no cell phone."

The door closed.

Blake sensed Sam's departing chuckle as Dal slid onto the pew, his small travel bag between his feet. He mumbled beneath his breath, loud enough for Blake to hear. "Goddamn Hunter, out there hittin' golf balls!"

"Yeah, yeah, yeah," Blake muttered, "Fuckin' Hunter!"

CHAPTER 7

GARDNER HUNTER WAS ON his third bucket of range balls, sending one after another toward the eighty yard flag, each landing within feet of the target.

Hunter was good.

The Beijing Open was scheduled for April and his game was ready. Although his exemption status was nearing expiration, his entry was assured by the skin of his teeth, with his most recent posted rounds being in the high sixties to low seventies. As a matter of interest, he'd checked out the long range betting sheets, found Ladbrokes had him at odds of five hundred to one.

Being the self-assured gambler that he was, he placed a substantial bet and stood to win an amount that could be described as nothing less than obscene. When it came to backing himself in any venture, Hunter was compulsive. Considered a sandbagger by most, he took their consideration in stride. He'd seek out big hitting driving range golfers, look for the man with the one iron in his kit, take up a spot alongside, engage in conversation, then set about hitting a few good shots, but not *too* good. And when the inevitable challenge came about, he'd showed a reluctance to give strokes, but he'd relent for a press, always did, always relenting after a minute or so of objection. Hunter rarely lost. He once considered playing as a full time professional; in fact he had played on the Californian Golden State tour for two years. He'd also worked for a short time as an assistant at a private country club, but realized that booking tee times, folding golf sweaters and vacuuming the pro shop floor for a miserly sum of eight and a quarter bucks an hour were tasks he considered far too menial, tasks that made *no* contribution to the betterment of his game. So here he was, hitting balls in front of his pseudo caddy.

For Uncle Sam.

For Interpol.

"Pass me the nine," he said to Bellinger.

She reached to the bag, passed him the club.

"This is a six. The nine's got a line under the number; ya can't make a slip like that in Beijing."

Bellinger kicked at the tire on the golf cart parked alongside. Although she'd often accompanied Hunter on the course, her golfing skills were limited to riding as a passenger, and ordering from the snack bar menu. They'd once, as Hunter often said in a bragging way, had a hot and heavy relationship. But *hot and heavy* had undergone a metamorphosis, it had become cool and light. The flotsam and jettison was a great friendship.

Although they had their own private lives, they'd always confided in one another, had discussed problems of the heart. Bellinger advised Hunter on his many romantic escapades, and Hunter played the role of big brother, offering cautious advice to Bell on her romantic involvements.

"Gard, you ever think about that weekend we spent in Monterey and Carmel?"

He ignored the comment, hitting a few more lob wedges.

She persisted. "We toured the art galleries, made out on the beach." She pouted her lips, forced an almost inaudible giggle.

Got no reaction.

She pressed on. "The moon was full," she said, placing a hand on his hip. "What happened to us, Gard? Where'd it all break down?"

He lowered the club, exhaled loud enough to make his point, and slipped the wedge back in the bag. "I guess we made better friends than lovers. Yeah, I think about it plenty. You danced that slow swayin' way that you do, wherever did you learn to dance like that, kiddo?"

She pouted a little more prominently, let out a long sigh, and he caught the aroma of her lipstick. "I've got four brothers," she said. "I learned to dance waiting at the bathroom door." And she ignored his *better friends than lovers* comment.

Hunter chuckled, kicked another ball into position. "That's it huh, *that's* your answer? What a crock of shit. Gimme the eight iron!"

"More like you wanted another victory," she said, jabbing a finger into his shoulder, ignoring the request for the club. "You wanted another feather in your cap, another trophy for the weekend's play."

"Ya *know* that ain't true," he said staring down the range. "C'mon sweetie, lemme have the club."

He reached across and stroked her blonde hair. "I remember how great ya looked, ya know, wearin' nothin' except that white satin sheet draped around your shoulders. I still see ya standin' in the darkness, the sheet slidin' down, lower, lower. Man, my heart was poundin' just waitin' for ya to turn and face me, the shape of your ass, your hips, your perfect body. I swear to God, ya were all that mattered to me from that day on. I ain't been able to go near Monterey or Carmel since."

"In your dreams," she laughed. "And don't go bringing God into it. I don't need a sermon from you." She looked away, avoiding his eye. "And it's not even a good sermon."

"Ya wanna sermon?" he said, raising his voice in an indignant tone. "Ya wanna fuckin' sermon?"

"Yeah, go ahead, give it your best shot, but remember,

a *really* good sermon needs a great beginning and a really good ending, the latter of which you're unfamiliar, but you did succeed in keeping the beginning and ending as close together as possible. You men! You're all the same." She reached for a club. "Here, hit your eight iron!"

It was as though the conversation didn't happen. She passed him the club and he played the shot toward the one hundred and sixty-yard marker, watching as the ball climbed on the stiff ocean breeze. "Darn wind, does it ever stop blowin' here? Trump really picked a tough spot to build this baby."

Bell moved to the cart, sat, and pointed to the drifting ball. She said, "Look at that," nodding toward a struggling lady golfer taking her third swing at a ball embedded in a deep, white sand trap. "That thing's deep enough to swallow someone. Look how the wind's blowing that sand about, she won't need dermabrasion anytime soon."

Hunter watched the sand flying. "Gettin' the ball outa that bunker's like goin' through Congress," he said with a quick laugh, "gonna take forever." Three swings later, the ball remained in the bunker.

Oblivious to the comment, and suddenly in a world far away, Bell kicked at the brake pedal of the cart. Her tone was hushed. "What do you suppose the guys are doing?"

Hunter replaced the eight iron, went back to playing a high lob shot with his sixty-degree wedge, struck the seventy-yard pin, dropping the ball within inches of the cup. "You see that? What a shot!" His eyes slid back to her as he replied, "Guess they're brushin' up on their Latin. Dunno. Maybe they're gettin' their heads shaved . . . or gettin' fitted for Armani robes. One thing's for sure, they ain't gettin' their other heads worked on any time soon." He nudged her, winked, made a clicking sound with his tongue. "No siree Bob, they ain't getting none, neither of 'em, maybe they're gettin' tailored robes, Blake for sure. I'll bet he's gettin' custom fitted with an Armani triple pleated robe, side-cut pockets 'n all."

"Gard," Bell said soulfully, as she slid across the seat of the cart, "do *you* think they're gonna be able to play their parts convincingly? I mean to say, Sam seems to have us under wraps, this is pretty much *his* personal baby, you know, what with him not sharing with McDowell and all."

Hunter hesitated, walked to the cart, slipped the lob wedge into the bag, and sat by Bellinger. "Honey, I spent quite a bit of time talkin' this over with Sam," he said in his most consoling voice. "He was pretty chatty about the whole thing."

Bell crossed her legs and reached for the Pepsi in the cart's drink holder, sipped at it and passed the drink across. "Want some?"

"Nah, I'm fine. What Sam told me kinda scared me a bit. Those two guys, Sung and Wang, they're kinda like Navy SEALs. They've done all the trainin', ya know, all the serious shit. Each of 'em holds the highest level in Karate. They're both among the world's top mountaineers; in fact, three years back they led an expedition on K2. Climbin' don't get any tougher than that."

"That's good for our guys, right?" she asked, sounding both impressed and relieved.

"Sure, but it makes me wonder why Drew and Dal need two heavies goin' with 'em on a mission that ain't lookin' quite that dangerous."

The two moved to the snack bar area alongside a sumptuous dining room. It was lavishly decorated, wood paneling, spectacular ceiling frescoes.

"Jesus, take a look at this place," Hunter said in a bemused tone. "When The Donald does it, he does it with style."

Three monitors featured a PGA event, a celebrity golf tournament, and a pre-recorded baseball game, minus commentary.

The waiter arrived and passed a menu to Hunter.

"The sashimi sounds just too good," Hunter said. "This'll work for me, same for you, kiddo?"

"You remember, huh?"

"What I really remember," he whispered leaning into her, "is snackin' from a very, *very* perfect navel."

The look on his face had a certain appeal, as did his tone. The moment lingered, and just as Bell gave him her somewhat alluring look, he shot it down by jokingly asking, "Ya wanna do room service?"

She froze mid expression, somewhere between, *how about it*, and, *maybe we could try again*. Her defensive mode kicked in, an attribute possessed by domineering women. She edged ever so slightly back from him, needing to focus on his grinning face, the near-hopeful yet self-doubting, Gardner Hunter.

"In your dreams," she snapped. "You, m' dear, are out of luck in the sexual gratification department."

If he'd only known.

Sooo close!

Wistfully, he said, "With my sex life the way it is, if I fell into a barrel of nipples I'd come up suckin' my thumb."

She thought, *such an old line*, and dismissed it with a contemptuous shrug. She sniggered, "You . . . are pathetic!"

"My mom's fault."

"Oh? And how's that ?"

"She never nursed me. I've grown up with an obsession for lactating women."

"Well then," she smirked, "looks like your thumb's the only thing you'll be sucking on tonight."

He winked at her, while simultaneously smiling at the attractive waitress who might have just overheard the comment, throwing him an insidious glance and grimacing. *Was worth a try*, he thought. *Am I losin' my touch or what!*

Refocusing he said, "Back to business. Those two dudes, Wang and Sung, pretty heavy shit, don'tcha think?" He reached across the table, took her hand.

Never the quitter, she thought, *the eternal optimist.*

He gazed hard into her eyes, his best John Belushi *Blues Brothers* pleading look, but Patrice Bellinger wasn't there. She was drifting in thought, her mind someplace far off.

"Hey, kiddo . . . a penny?"

"I'm sorry. I was thinking about those two Chinese guys. I've a good feeling about them, you know, having Wang and Sung along with our guys. If I was making that trek to China, I'd want them along." She refocused, squeezing his hand and forcing a smile. "But on the other hand, surely it can't be *that* difficult."

"Oh baby, just one thing to add," Hunter grimaced. "They're goin' in through Nepal. And ya know what that means? It means they'll be hikin' over the fuckin' Himalayas." He shook his head, groaning, "Hootchie mamma!"

Bell bobbed her head and said in a worried tone, "Over the Himalayas? Our two aren't in shape for that."

"Not yet they ain't. But they're gonna be . . . real fuckin' fast."

CHAPTER 8

BLAKE GOT A ONCE over from the priest, he could feel the man's eyes scanning his six foot two frame. When the priest had finished the scan, he moved back a few paces, looked at Dal, then gave a slow rub to his chin as though about to deliver a summation. "Hmm," he said reverently, as he moved off to a closet where an assortment of robes hung. He pulled a dark brown robe, passed it to Dal, then switched his attention back to Blake, nodded with a dubious look, and then removed what was, beyond doubt, be the longest of the robes.

"You are taller than most who visit us," he said, holding the garment at arm's length. "This will be far too short, but will have to suffice for now."

Blake turned, saw the snigger on Dal's face and mouthed the words, *fuck you*. Then, turning back to the young priest, "Father Paul, where are ya from, what I mean to say is, where are you uh, *originally* from?"

"Please, call me Paul. I was raised in Taiwan. My family is still there, well, most of them are." He saddened at the mention of his family. "We had an incident you need be aware of. It will give you insight as to my involvement with the struggles within my country. My younger brother and I went to Penghu, do you know of it?"

"Yeah, we've been briefed on the islets, the bridges; all that stuff."

Paul wiped his eyes, and took a few seconds to

102

swallow, to get the words out with minimum emotion. "I had a brother, his name was Samuel. He traveled to Penghu to work on the bridges, the ones you mentioned. He was sent there to gather intelligence on Chinese plans for Taiwan. I followed six months after he had left. When I arrived . . ."

Tears.

He was losing it, and Dal turned away not wanting to add to the priest's discomfort. Blake pulled up a wooden chair, sat, crossed his legs and neatly placed the gown over his lap. Paul pulled a handkerchief and dabbed at his eyes, his voice quivering, "I am sorry. It is difficult to speak of the death of a loved one."

"Death?" Dal asked, with a questioning face.

"Go ahead," Blake said sympathetically. "Take your time. We got no place to go."

"I searched, but I could not find him. I spoke with many of the workers, being most careful not to raise suspicion. The last anyone had seen of him was . . ." Again, he lowered his eyes, and wiped away tears. "My brother had a confrontation with a Chinese officer."

"What happened?" asked Dal.

"I have been a Salesian priest for ten years. The taking of a person's life is not my belief, but I searched for that officer."

"This ain't a confession, is it, Paul?" Dal inquired.

"Perhaps I need to remove this from my soul," he said with a grief-stricken smile. "I made inquiries among friends, found the barracks where this man was stationed. I dressed as one of the local people, and I waited. I did not know he was out on patrol, my wait was several days long. When he returned, I stalked him. My colleagues told me of a place the soldiers frequented, a place where women offer services, a house of ill repute."

He said *ill repute* with a touch of embarrassment.

"What'd ya do?" Dal asked, shaking his head.

JASON DENARO

"When he came from the house, I confronted him. I questioned him about Samuel."

"What'd he say?" Blake asked.

"He told me he would rot in hell before he would apologize."

"Apologize?" Blake asked. "Apologize for what?"

"I asked him that very question. He said he had interrogated Samuel, that he was aware my brother was working for the Taiwanese, working as a spy. He told me where I could . . ." Swallowing deeply, Paul choked a little as he searched for the words, taking a few long moments to re-gather. When he'd found the words, he raised his eyes to meet Blake's. "He told me where I could visit Samuel's grave."

"Jesus Christ," Dal whispered, his eyes sliding away from the priest.

"So, eh, what'd ya do?" Blake asked despondently.

"I granted his request."

"Request?"

"He is rotting in hell."

Blake and Dal were silent, each with a look of disorientation, neither able to do anything but stare at the priest, their mouths agape, their expressions further adding to Paul's guilt. It took the young priest several long seconds to clear his throat, to settle his emotions. "Forgiveness has always been my feeble quality," he said. "It leaves me doubting my worthiness as a priest. It is just that I sometimes lose control." He gave each man a begging smile. "Please, I am a good man, a decent man, but I have always acquiesced when the weak are subjugated by those such as that soldier."

Still mildly startled, Dal reached out a hand. Paul took it, shook it firmly, and smiled. Blake followed suit and said with comforting chagrin, "You *are* a good man, things are okay, everythin's okay. Ya should've been given a Papal medal for doin' it."

104

There was a half-minute of silence, then Dal said, "So then, what's our next move?"

The young priest led them through the sacristy and into the rear alley where he motioned toward an SUV, a black Ford Expedition with tinted glass so dark it blocked the gaze of anyone trying to see the occupants. It sat on off-road tires and a suspension several inches higher than standard. The rear hitch was fitted with some type of winching system, and the front was more than amply protected by a monstrous black crash bar, the type you see on police cruisers. Paul was still working on Dal's question as he stepped up to the vehicle, and then waving a slow hand along the side of the Expedition, he said proudly, "This is our next move. We have some miles to cover and must be underway. Oh, and by the way . . ." He reached into the rear of the truck and handed a pair of Roman style sandals to each of the unbelieving agents. "You will need to wear these leather sandals."

"What's the deal?" Blake asked, nodding at his comfortable Reeboks. "We got perfectly comfortable sneakers."

Paul swallowed hard, knowing what he was about to say wouldn't sit well with either man. "When I was in Penghu, there were three Salesian missionaries who arrived to speak to the faithful."

"Missionaries?" Dal asked. "The Chinese, they're okay with that? Ya know, I mean like, with 'em preachin' out in the open."

"They tolerate us Salesians because we appear more along the lines of the non-Roman Catholic Church. It is an illusionary perception, Mr. Dallas, one we Salesians work on most assiduously."

"*Assiduously*, huh," Dal said with a grin.

"And the reason is?" Blake asked.

"To win more tolerance from Beijing. The Chinese want so badly for the Vatican to denounce Taiwan, they feel we might be able to sway Rome's attitude toward the ludicrous Chinese claims over the island."

"*Ludicrous*, huh?" Dal repeated, again with a snide grin.

"What's up, Dallas?" Blake snapped. "Ya need a dictionary or what?"

The priest paused, then after a moment of thought, turned to face the two passengers. "The Chinese officer, the one who is rotting in hell . . ." He slipped into a repentant demeanor, sighing, "When the priests arrived in Penghu, that officer had them taken to his quarters for interrogation."

"Those guys were the real deal then?" Blake asked. "Like eh . . . they weren't like me and Dal, they were actually real priests?"

"Yes, your predecessors were priests, and they had been thoroughly prepared."

Blake feared the answer, but asked anyway. "So eh, please, for Christ's sake, tell me it all went well."

Paul sighed, lowered his eyes and added even more sadness to his voice. "Oh, Mr. Blake, if only I could, but they failed to pass the test."

Dal pulled a face. "The test, what test?"

"They were asked to remove their shoes."

Blake and Dal exchanged glances.

"You see," Paul continued, "their feet were smooth, no calluses, they had no toughened skin on the soles of their feet. They were priests from a city Parish; a most grievous mistake. The Chinese recognized it immediately."

"Wha'dya mean?" Dal groaned, "*A most grievous mistake?*"

Blake's interest in the sandals heightened as Paul explained, "Salesian missionaries have hardened feet, whereas city priests from Taiwan, well, they simply do not. You will each need to wear the sandals from time to time," and he gave a knowing nod. "Wear them often, you must toughen your soles."

"What happened to the three guys?" Dal asked with a grimace.

"The officer had them crucified in Penghu. He left them hanging for all to see," Paul replied, glancing at their disbelieving faces. "If they catch you, you may as well tell them everything. They will extract a confession regardless, telling them is far preferable to hanging on a cross. So you see, the sandals are most important. The prospect of death is indeed a great motivator, Mr. Dallas."

"Gotcha," Dal said swallowing hard, "Just gimme the goddamn things."

Paul held out two pair. "Which pair would *you* like?" he asked Blake, lowering those in his left hand. "These appear to be your size."

"Yeah, yeah, yeah, pass 'em over, damnit!"

The drive began in silence, the Expedition winding its way out of Chinatown, through Los Angeles and toward distant mountains.

"Where're we headed?" Blake asked inquisitively.

Paul reached to the glove compartment, removed a small stack of tour brochures, and passed them to the two men comfortably seated in the rear. "We are going to Mount Whitney."

"Mount Whitney? We're goin' to Mount Whitney!" Dal reiterated as Blake glanced through a folder.

"Yes, it most replicates Himalayan conditions."

"So this's our prep for the crossin', huh?" Blake grumbled, shaking his head. "I've been wondering when this'd kick in."

"You will be going into China via a less suspect route, a route that will take you through Nepal." He gave a peripheral glance, and allowed an ever so slight grin to slip on through, "And it will be cold, very, *very* cold."

"Aw shit," Blake mumbled, and then, catching himself as well as Paul's eyes in the rear view mirror, added apologetically, "Uh, sorry Father."

"No apology necessary. I was expecting far worse profanity from each of you."

"Fuck," Dal chuckled softly as he blessed himself, "Wouldn't wanna disappoint ya, Father."

CHAPTER 9

BLAKE THOUGHT ABOUT THE cold for awhile as they began the three hundred mile, six hour drive along route 395, the Expedition edging its way north, a little east of the Sequoia National Forest, and Kings Canyon National Park. When they entered the town of Lone Pine, Paul pointed ahead. "There it is. The snow covered peak of Mt. Whitney, almost 15,000 feet, the tallest mountain in the contiguous United States, a fair training ground for you, don't you agree?"

Dal groaned, pressed his nose to the glass, said, "That's a mighty high hill," and his eyes squinted at the distant snow-capped peak.

"That is very good," Paul said, letting out a faint laugh. "A hill, Everest is a 29,000 foot hill, give or take a few feet. K2 is often said to be the taller of the two." He took both hands off of the wheel and shrugged, "But that depends on who measures the *hill*; they are very close to each other in height." He leaned on the word *hill*, amused by Dal's narrative.

They passed through Lone Pine, winding into a small village set away from the tourist areas, with snowdrifts dispersed in patches, insufficient to attract cross country skiers yet enough to maintain a noticeable chill in the mountain air. Paul maneuvered the truck toward a vacation cottage tucked away among huge pines. It had welcoming smoke billowing from a chimney, dancing into the early evening air like a snake performing a sensual dance to an unheard melody. Blake tilted his head to one side, straining to catch a glimpse of the white stream as it dissipated among overhead branches.

Paul steered the Expedition toward a garage attached to the dwelling, pressed a control clipped on the sunshade, and one side of the garage began rolling open, as a bearded man beaming a welcome smile stepped from a rear door of the house and moved toward them. Paul nodded at the figure in the black track suit, a narrow man, willowy, similar to a pine that'd taken on a permanent lean through years of resisting the west wind. The willowy man smiled, his nose twitching like a ferret sensing food.

Paul gestured toward the man. "That is Father Francis."

"Another fuckin' trainer," Dal groaned, his eyes cutting to Blake, "one for each of us."

Paul heard the comment. "No, no," he giggled. "Francis is your night time coach." He smiled eloquently at Blake, and added with a reassuring expression, "During the days, you will have me."

"Night time," Blake said with a stony glare, then pressing just a little, "ain't that when we sleep?"

Dal's foot nudged Blake. He reached forward, placed a hand on the priest's shoulder, and said, "Don't suppose you're plannin' on lettin' us sleep, huh?"

The priest ignored Dal's question. Unwavering, he turned off the engine, stepped from the truck, and with arms outstretched walked briskly to the willowy man in the track suit. "Francis, it has been a long time. It is good to see you," and the two men embraced. Dal gave Blake a sly nudge.

"Nah," Blake groaned. "Spare me."

"I heard of the three in Penghu," the track suit man said. "I am very sorry. I could not believe it."

"I did not personally work with that mission," Paul

said, bowing his head in a repentant way. "They would almost certainly be alive today had I done so."

He shook his head, made a remorseful shrug. "I was away on retreat. Their preparation was handled by another Parish, yet I feel accountable. If only they had been with me."

"You cannot hold yourself responsible. I am sure they were aptly trained." Francis gave a consoling shrug, pausing as though reflecting. "Sometimes the most difficult thing in life is to know which bridge to cross, and which to burn. Their deaths are one that you must burn." Then after a few long moments of reflection, "I heard it was their feet, is that so?"

"A sad oversight," Paul said, making a sorrowful face at Blake and Dal. "It will not happen with these two." He placed a hand on the willowy man's shoulder. "Mr. Blake, Mr. Dallas, this is Father Francis. He will conduct your Latin instruction."

"Welcome," the willowy man said, taking a step forward, reaching and offering his hand to Blake.

"Thank you, Father," Blake said with a respectful nod. "Pleasure to meet ya; I ain't too much on pyromaniacs. I eh, hope this'll be a bridge we can just cross."

"And so it shall be."

Blake assumed his reference to pyromaniacs had shot over the priest's head.

"Francis will school you both," Paul said. "You will learn as much Latin as he deems necessary for you each to partake in a regular mass, and for the administering of last rites, blessings, etcetera, etcetera."

"*Meus latin est valde bonus , Abbas,*" Blake said. "My Latin's very good, Father."

Both priests raised their eyebrows, and Francis bounced up and down a few times, enthusiastically clapping. "Oh my goodness," he laughed, "and you are able to say the mass, *vos can narro plebis?*"

"*Ego sum validus addo a bona . . .*" Blake replied pausing, getting stuck on the rest of the phrase, then stuttering, "*L l lego V V Vulgus, est ut bonus uh - satis?*"

"What exactly was that?" Dal asked with a smirk. "Ya lost me after, *I'm able*, then somethin' about bein' good."

"I said I can read the fuckin' mass," Blake whispered, hand over his mouth, then chortled, "ya moron."

With a wagging finger at Blake, Francis issued a lighthearted warning, "*Talis blasthemy mos terra vos in Abyssus , meus filius.*"

Staring at the ceiling of the garage, Dal chuckled almost to himself. "I think he said somethin' about your language, and eh, somethin' about goin' to hell."

"And that's where the pyromaniacs gather," Francis added, with a self ingratiating nod.

"So then, Father Blake," Dal said with a snide look, "Ya wanna converse a bit more with the teacher?"

Francis led them from the garage to the house; warm, comfortable, with a fire crackling below a heavy wood mantel, it was a room filled with an astonishing array of medieval furniture. "My humble, yet somewhat eclectic taste leaves many wondering," the priest said. "I am a simple man; these items originate from a bygone era. The hands that carved them are now with Our Lord, but their memory will live on forever in these, their creations. Please, be seated."

They sat on a carved bench with arms of solid mahogany, each depicting a different animal's head. Blake slid a hand along the length of the arm, his fingers sensing the shape of the lion's head decoration, as Dal leaned in for a closer inspection of a wolf's head, perfectly detailed, with sharp, bared teeth. "This is some workmanship all right, Father, it's beautiful carvin'. I'm a bit of a collector myself. This type of work, well, ya just *don't* find this kinda stuff at Macy's."

Blake coughed.

Dal remained deadly serious, causing Blake to roll back a little more in his seat, as Francis let the comment go unnoticed; instead, prodding the fire with a long metal rod, sending sparks drifting upward in a frantic attempt to escape the disturbed fire.

"May I call you by your first names?" Francis asked.

"Call me Blake, only the ladies call me Drew." He flicked a thumb toward Dal. "Stupid here, well, he's Dal."

Dal grumbled, "Back at ya!"

"Gentlemen, we are going to become very good friends during the next two weeks," Paul said primly. "You will have all of the necessary comforts; however there are certain requirements to which you must adhere." He smiled as he spoke; putting Dal and Blake at ease, while clearly inferring that worse lay ahead. "You will be staying in your own rooms at the rear of this building. They are spartan, and for that I apologize, however, this unfortunately must be. At times you will be afforded the comforts of this room." He said it with a smile, sweeping a hand from one end of the room to the other. "The warmth of this fire, a pleasure you will learn to appreciate more with each passing day, the feel of carpet underfoot, and the comfort of sitting on a real chair. Simple pleasures you will come to appreciate more than you have ever imagined."

Blake's face contorted, didn't like where the discussion was heading. Dal sat with his face locked in a probing gaze; every so often switching his eyes to Francis then back to Blake, a questioning look, borderline idiotic.

"Would you like a drink?" Paul asked, sensing the tension, his offer slowing the downhill slide, a brief respite from implied bad news.

"Sure," Dal quipped. "A dyin' man usually gets a last drink."

"Let's get on with it," Blake said abruptly, not wanting to delay the inevitable.

"Please gentlemen, follow me. This way."

The solid wooden door had a small metal grated opening, similar to those found in old castles, an eight inch square window that allowed the observation of occupants without the need for opening the door. Paul took hold of a large bar that acted as a locking device, sliding it to one side and pulling hard on the door, which creaked as it opened. It was an eerie sound, inferring the door had not been unlocked in quite some time. He reached in, felt about for a switch, found it. The light flickered as they stepped into another time, another century, a sparsely decorated, for want of a better description . . . dungeon.

"This will be the quarters in which you stay," Paul said in an apologetic tone. "Mr. Sung and Mr. Wang will arrive shortly. They are no longer novices, and as such, they will share quarters somewhat less spartan."

The floor was rough aged concrete with two bunks off to one side; there was no padding, no mattresses. Dal ran a hand across the back of a hickory chair that rested by a wooden table that rocked on uneven legs exacerbated by an equally uneven floor. *On its last legs,* he thought but refrained from using the line. A second door led into more luxury accommodation, or so Blake was hoping as they stepped through it.

"This is your bathing facility," Paul said, "Not exactly the Palace of Versailles." He raised his hand to cover his mouth, hunching his shoulders and letting out a sinister cackle. "But you are not preparing for a European vacation gentlemen, now are you?"

Dal shot a worried glance at Blake, and thought, *facetious little prick.*

A rust-covered tap sat at the end of an old iron pipe that hung precariously over a stained metal wash basin, the drain pipe appearing attached to absolutely nothing at all. Blake turned the handle, and gave a relieved smile as the tap coughed a few times and water finally found its way to the spout. He passed a sarcastic smile to Dal, who said, "For a while I was thinkin' we'd be goin' outside for a shower."

Paul chuckled, "It is not quite that bad. As you see, you do have running cold water and a squat." He pointed off to his left. "This is your squat-room."

Dal turned to Blake and shrugged, "A squat?" He placed a hand over his mouth. He asked, "What the fuck's a squat?"

"Come along," Paul said with a self-satisfied grin.

It was a small room set to the side of the bathing area, and their eyes were immediately drawn to a hole in the floor. On either side of the hole, a raised concrete pad had been constructed for the positioning of the user's feet. A tap supplied running water, which in turn wound its way downhill.

"Aw shit," Dal groaned.

"Yes, Mr. Dallas," Paul smiled, "quite so."

A wooden bucket with a stick protruding from it and half filled with brown water of dubious origin, sat by the hole. Father Paul reached, pulled the stick and extended it at arm's length, the pungent smelling sponge attached to one end causing Dal and Blake to take a few quick steps back.

"Do you know how this is used?" he asked, slowly passing it before the two men.

"Can only imagine," Dal said in an uncomfortable way.

The dank smelling sponge leaked water, each drop splashing onto the cold concrete floor. Dal's eyes tracked the fall of the water drops; all in slow motion, the drop landing, splashing, his eyes taking in the dissipating watermark on the stone floor. Everything about the moment was . . . cold.

Very cold.

"Yeah, can only imagine," Blake reiterated with a grimace.

Paul dunked the sponge back in the bucket. "It is an old Roman hygiene ritual. The soldiers of Rome did not have the luxury of toilet paper; to this day neither do many people in the rural areas of China, through which you will be passing."

He led them out of the squat-room and pointed to uncomfortable wooden chairs. "Please be seated," he said. "It is time for Francis to commence your Latin class."

Francis, acknowledging the young priest's class introduction, pulled a large chalkboard across from a corner, and spoke as he began writing. "Each of you will take notes," and he pointed to a nearby storage chest. "You will find note pads in the chest by the bunk."

It was not the Hilton, as the priest had said, more a replica of medieval confinement. Blake and Dal sat staring at each other, looking like two bears, cornered, backs to the wall, on the first day of hunting season.

An hour passed and the Latin lesson had grown tiresome. A soft tapping on the door gave the slimmest hope of reprieve, hope perhaps, that someone had arrived to wake them from the nightmare. A second series of taps, not unlike a drum roll, as though the person was rolling his knuckles across the door. The hope of reprieve quickly faded as Sung stepped in the room. His arrival added impetus to the Latin class, as Francis, feeling rejuvenated, handed more tutorial folders to his two novices. Blake opened a drawer, pulled out old writing blocks and pencils with erasers, as Francis wrote a verse in Latin, and repeated the line in English below. *In nomine Patris, et Filii, et Spiritus Sancti, Amen. In the name of the Father, and of the Son, and of the Holy Spirit, Amen.*

"Please write this on your pad three times. You also, Mr. Sung. We cannot assume your Latin is *too* perfect."

Sung walked forward, took up a seat by the chalkboard, and within moments began to work on his note pad. Francis tilted his head toward Dal, who avoided his nod. "Mr. Dallas, could you please read the Latin?"

Dal cleared his throat, an intentional stall that bought him a few seconds, then to the priest's amazement, he performed. The ability to learn parrot fashion had always worked for him, not only did he understand what it was he was saying, but he knew when to correctly use the phrasing. Feeling somewhat defeated, Francis shifted his attention to the other two.

"Mr. Blake, Mr. Sung, please do likewise, and eh, Mr. Dallas, please join in one more time."

At six in the morning, two cold figures huddled in the corner of the room, one in a fetal position, the other on its back, staring at the ceiling.

"Drew, you awake?" Dal groaned.

"Nah, I'm sleepin'. Don't even think of wakin' me. I was dreamin' that I was in a very warm place. Leave me alone, go to sleep."

A little later, "I'm dyin' here, dude. Is it daylight yet?"

The knock on the door startled them. Filled with frustration and shivering from the sub-human temperature, Blake made his way to the door, opened it with a little apprehension, and Francis leaned in, poking his smiling face toward them. "Rise and shine, gentlemen. It is time for mass."

Blake, Dal, Sung, and Father Paul kneeled on the hard ground while Francis completed a shortened version of the Latin mass. Paul handed out notes to Blake, as Francis moved along at a rambling pace, pointing from time to time at sections of the transcript. Sung, far more accustomed to the procedure, grinned at the two men, thoroughly relishing their sufferance. He knew what lay ahead.

Both the Latin mass and benediction is indelibly

imprinted in the minds of all Catholic boys, subsequently Father Paul was adequately impressed with his guest's ability to fall in with necessary responses, even though sections of the dialogue were too fast for them to truly follow. Francis had the paraphernalia, had the incense, candles and '*a neat fuckin' gong,*' as Dal called it, never failing to get an appreciative nod from Dal each time it was struck, cocking his head toward Blake and whispering, "I never get tired of that fuckin' sound."

"You're an idiot," Blake rasped.

The aroma of incense floated about the small room, a fresh puff escaping each time Francis rocked the urn from one side to the other. Dal whispered, "That smell sure takes me back a few years."

Considering not succumbing to Dal's banter, but wilting, Blake asked, "Wha'dya mean?" then immediately knew he'd regret it.

"Those girls, the ones from The Blessed Virgin Mary Convent, sittin' across the aisle from us at benediction each Friday, sniggerin' and flirtin'. Man, those were the days."

"What are ya talkin' about?" Blake groaned back, intrigued with the direction Dal was heading.

"They had this young nun, hot lookin' number, big blue eyes, the best pair of hooters under that gown. Us guys, well, we knew. We all knew what she was hidin'."

Blake exhaled, then whispered emphatically, "You're a jerk off. Shut up and follow the priest."

Dal persisted. "Those young priests, yeah, they all knew too. The straight ones did. Most of those guys were feelin' up the boys, hands up their shorts; that's what they were doin', in our class anyway, more interested in feelin' a young hard-on than the nun's tits." He nudged Blake, and sniggered. "Those De La Salle Brothers, they always had their hands in their pockets, inside their robes, ya know, a bunch of fuckin' deviates."

"Shhh," Paul hissed, glaring at Dal with a finger over his lips.

At the conclusion of the service, Francis sat beside the four men. "Should you be invited to participate, we must pray your involvement will be minimal. The services at the cathedral are rarely performed in anything other than Latin. If you learn what you have just seen, you should get by. If however, you cannot deliver the minimum Latin verse . . ." He placed a hand over his mouth, again hunching his shoulders, sniggering, "Well then, in that case, you may never return from China." He gestured at the sandals, drawing a slow finger across his throat, and nodding repeatedly as he drove home the point. "And you both understand the consequence of neglecting these."

Dal turned his face away from the priest, rubbing his hands briskly as he spoke, and exhaling breath that shot from his lips like steam from a locomotive. He leaned into Blake and groaned, "You'd think the Vatican would spring for a fuckin' heater." He wrapped his arms around himself and savored a small sense of satisfaction as Father Paul gave a brief shudder. *Feelin' the cold too, huh?* It was a satisfying thing to see. Not that it made him feel any the warmer, but it was - satisfying.

Francis continued, "Tonight at seven, we will reconvene for your first lesson in survival Latin. Until then gentlemen, I bid you good day."

"Breakfast waits," Paul said pointing to the larger room. "Mr. Blake, Mr. Dallas, please follow me."

Sung stood aside, gave a warm smile as they passed by, and murmured with a disingenuous delivery, "Bon appetite, gentlemen."

The bowl of watery gruel was displeasing to both men.

"Ya suppose this is a sample, Emeril?" Dal asked sardonically.

Blake ignored the remark.

"Hey!" Dal laughed, "Mr. Lagasse?"

"Eat and shut the fuck up," Blake growled. "Wait 'til I get my hands on Sam. This's the last time, the absolute last fuckin' time. I'm gettin' too old for this shit."

Dal scooped up a spoonful, placed the glue-like mix in his mouth as Blake watched curiously. He rolled the food around, forced it down and squirmed, "Aw, sweet Jesus," his face contorting and becoming near unrecognizable.

Blake didn't want to think about it, tried focusing on anything else, but after several long moments, lowered his eyes from Dal to his bowl, and said, "Ya want mine?" But Dal was distracted by the aroma of bacon and eggs drifting from beneath the door. Blake slid the grate open, looked through at Paul and Francis, and called through the opening, "Hey, Fathers, ya got enough of that stuff to share?" with only his nose and mouth visible from the other side. There was no reply, so a few seconds later, he added, "Hey we ain't too thrilled with the menu in this wing of the Vatican Hilton."

Paul walked to the open grate, looked into Blake's eyes, and gave a woeful look as he said, "It is a part of your mental strengthening. I believe it is called, *Pavlov's dog*." Blake sensed a touch of mirth in the delivery. The priest continued, "When you are able to achieve a certain goal, you will each move to the next item on the menu, but for now, that porridge, well, that *is* your level."

"Okay, I'm ready," Blake replied, snarling. "What's the next level?"

"Patience, Mr. Blake. Allow me to finish my breakfast and we will get underway. Meanwhile, please, shower and dress. You will then appreciate those heavy warm robes, and remember to wear the sandals."

Blake grumbled incoherently, something to the effect that when he next saw Sam Ridkin, he'd need surgery to have something-or-other surgically removed from his ass.

"What the fuck's all that about?" Dal asked as he finished the last of Blake's breakfast.

"Never mind," Blake snapped in an abrupt tone. "Ya don't need to know. We gotta shower, get ready for our day with Father fuckin' Paul."

The shower was fully enclosed and Dal offered to go first. Blake stayed seated, head in hands, still cussing at Sam, rolling his head from side to side, the balls of his palms rubbing deep into his eye sockets in frustration. Dal stepped into the cold stone recess, reached for the tap, stood to one side, turned it, waiting for the water to warm, waiting - waiting for the water to warm . . .

He stood shivering for a long minute, then called to Blake, "Buzz room service, ask 'em to turn the fuckin' water heater on." His voice grew louder. "Jesus, ya ain't gonna believe this!"

As the pads of his hands aggressively massaged his eye sockets, Blake didn't bother to turn toward the shower. He called to Dal, "You're shittin' me, right?"

The high pitched crescendo of the scream rattled the windows, raising Blake's head from its position of despair. His voice trembled, a blend of anger and sheer cold. He called aloud, "You okay, Dal?"

CHAPTER 10

THEY STOOD TRANSFIXED, STARING into darkness, a ghostly morning mist enshrouding the surrounding slopes.

"You okay, Dal?" Blake asked.

"Don't understand why we can't wear track suits."

Blake ignored the comment and continued rearranging his backpack.

"You need to not only acclimatize to the conditions," Paul said, "but also to the attire."

They appeared very Vatican-like, dressed in heavy dark brown woolen gowns. Dal, with his hood covering most of his golden hair, was fortunate enough to receive a gown more tailored than Blake's frame permitted.

Paul glanced at his watch, checked up and down the track leading to the house, a look of concern creeping into his body language.

"What's up, Paul?" Dal asked. "You're lookin' worried."

"It's Wang, huh?" Blake asked. "Wasn't *he* supposed to join us for this?"

Paul tapped on his watch face as Sung also checked the time.

"I cannot understand where he could be," Sung said with an anxious look. "It is unlike Wang to be late; he calls whenever there is a problem. I spoke to Sam earlier, he is also concerned. He tried to call Mr. McDowell, to have him look into it, but Mr. McDowell's cell phone was not picking up."

"But he'll catch up when he *does* arrive, right?" Blake asked nodding.

"Yes, of that I am sure," Sung said unconvincingly. "He will most certainly join us." He rubbed his hands together briskly, but the anxious look hung there.

"Tighten up those backpacks," Paul said. "They will annoy you if they are not tight." He hitched Dal's straps a little tighter, and said with a grunt, "Are you sure you have brought all the equipment I laid out for you?"

"Seems like a load of unnecessary shit," Dal said wincing.

"The two prayer books are essential," Paul said in a disciplined tone. "You will each work on your blessings and last rites, all of the usual more common Latin phrases. The reading is *all* that you will have to whittle away the cold evening hours."

A Police Patrol SUV came into view, its light bar flashing, the four turned as one and faced the vehicle as the car pulled alongside, its windows fogged from the cold air. They waited for the occupant to step out, and when the window slowly lowered, a black cop smiled at the priests. "Mornin', Father Paul, Fathers," he said nodding to Sung, Dal and Blake. "Gettin' an early start on the day, huh?" He stepped from the SUV and eyed their back packs. "Looks like you're doin' some *serious* hikin', those back packs must be totin' a week's worth of provisions."

Paul stepped forward and greeted the cop. "Good morning, Leroy. It is nice to see you up here. Allow me to introduce you to these three novices; this is Fathers John, Bond and Dominic."

They stepped forward, shook the cop's hand.

"A little out of your area," the cop said. "What brings ya up this way?"

He reached into his pocket, pulled a pack of cig-arettes, placed one between his lips, burned the tip with a Zippo, closed the lighter and leaned back against the roof of the truck. The powdery snow crunched under his feet as he slowly moved from one foot to the other in a dancing sway, fighting off the chilled air, blowing into cupped hands, and his eyes taking in the three hooded figures. He took a long suck on the cigarette, and nodded toward the mist. "We got us some kinda lunatic," he said pointing. "Someone runnin' about up there," and he fumbled as the cigarette stuck to his lower lip, trying to maintain a semblance of coolness, squinting, Dirty Harry style, the smoke stinging his eyes, causing a tear to trickle down his cheek. He wiped his shirt-sleeve across his face. He coughed and used the cigarette as a pointer, jabbing it toward the slopes, pointing to the Mount Whitney Trail.

"See up yonder?" he growled like a three pack per day smoker. "Well, we been keepin' this under the rug; ya know how the Tourist Bureau is about puttin' a scare into folks, kinda like that there movie, Jaws. Don't want any Amity Beach thing goin' on here, that's for dang sure." He paused, turned away, and spat in the snow. "Seems we got us a killer on the loose up there, and he's pickin' off hikers. Got us two bodies."

He waited for a reaction.

Looked at each of their faces. Nothing.

"Yup, we got us two stiffs, one over Whitney Portal, another yesterday, outside of Outpost Camp."

Blake glanced at Dal who tried not to let his police background click into interrogation mode.

"Oh, sweet Jesus, that is terrible," Father Paul said in shock. "Are they anyone we know?"

"Tourists, two guys, ID says they're from Europe. Ain't good for business if it leaks out, ain't good at all. Some guy saw this nut case runnin' from the dead guy at Outpost

Camp," the cop said, shuffling his feet in the powdery snow, slowly looking about with suspicious eyes, like cops do. "The witness ran to the body, seen the guy was dead, chased after the killer, got a couple of shots off with a varmint gun." He drew deep down from his throat, pulling phlegm and spitting again. "Thought he hit him he did, but ain't sure. I'm guessin' he did. Our guys found plenty of deep red blood on the snow."

Blake couldn't hold back any longer, so wanting to look priestly, wagged a finger at the cop. "Is there a search underway, Officer?"

"Been a chopper buzzin' about, and some suits from L.A. askin' a shit load of fuckin' questions." He caught himself, said, "Whoa, sorry Fathers. They were tryin' not to look conspicuous, like that's easy in a suit when everyone else up here's wearin' snow gear, except you guys of course, stand out like beacons they do. I figure the media'll get onto it sooner than later, there'll be TV crews swarmin' *all* over this goshdarn place by mornin'."

Dal sneaked a peek at Blake, had never heard a cop use the word *goshdarn*. Knew he really wanted to say *fuckin.* " Sung rolled his eyes, all three men thinking, *unwanted exposure*.

Dal had to ask, and he did. "Any leads on the suspect?"

"Hey," the black man chuckled, "you're soundin' just like a cop."

Blake slapped Dal on the back, harder than Dal was prepared for. Sung almost choked, holding back a near burst of laughter as Blake quickly chimed in, "Father Dominic's from Hawaii. He grew up surfin' and watchin' police shows on television. We joke with him about his, eh, what show was that, oh yeah, his Hawaii Five 0 vocabulary."

The black man laughed as Dal forced the words, "Ten-four, Dano."

"So where are y'all headin' with that equipment you're haulin' there?" the cop said pointing skyward, "Up yonder?"

Paul gestured with a wave at the mountain now blanketed in heavy snow-bearing cloud. "We are doing a retreat. Father Dominic, Father Bond and Father John will be staying at the rescue sheds; you know, the ones close to the summit."

"Hope ya got plenty of blankets in those packs. Weather man says we're in for one hell of a fuckin' storm." He placed a quick hand over his mouth, said, "Oops, sorry Fathers." The black man opened the door of the SUV, dusted the fresh snowflakes from his shoulders and smiled at each of the priests. "Happy trails. Keep a sharp eye out for anything that doesn't seem normal. That lunatic probably ain't around these parts anymore, most likely in Nevada by now. Stay alert anyways, can't be too safe." He dropped the cigarette, swiveling his toe on it until it became a brown stain on the icy white powder. "Good luck," he said. "Nice meetin' y'all."

He sat in the truck, started the motor, turned to Dal, nodded and said, "Book 'em, Dano."

His laugh echoed about as he drove into the white mist now spreading its ghostly fingers down the slopes, an eerie slow motion white lava flow, consuming all before it as it crept toward them at sixty frames per minute. Sung grinned at Blake and let out a long, slow breath, glaring at Dal who wisely refused eye contact with either man. He pulled the brown hood further over his face, hiding from their stare and blessing himself. Paul ignored the moment, gesturing ahead at the pre-dawn highlights, an artist's pallet tinting normally white clouds now cloaking Whitney.

"This might take a day or so longer than planned," Sung said with a look of consternation.

"Lovely, just fuckin' lovely," Blake whispered.

And the trek began.

*****

Ahead of them lay a climb of twelve thousand feet to reach Trail Camp, after which they faced a push to the fourteen thousand five hundred foot summit of Mt. Whitney, although the trail head was eight thousand three hundred and sixty feet. Paul moved at an easy pace, allowing his novices to catch their breath when needed. On day one they'd covered the four miles to Outpost camp, a mere ten thousand three hundred feet above sea level. They came across several heavy-duty all season tents belonging to other climbers, tents spread about the edge of a frozen waterfall. Exhausted, Dal and Blake welcomed Paul's next words, "We have reached the first camp. It is time to rest."

Blake inspected a jagged toenail, carefully ripped off the tip, placed it in his palm and displayed it to Dal.

He got no sympathy at all.

He pulled a Marlboro, lit it, and whined to Paul. But again, all complaints of numb toes and ripped nails went unheeded.

Camp consisted of two tents, with Paul and Sung sharing one, Blake and Dal the other. Blake's Boy Scout experience was put to immediate use, with him and Dal assigned campfire duty, gathering sufficient wood to get them through a long, cold night. Father Paul and Sung took on kitchen duties, preparing a dinner consisting of Spam and beans, followed by freshly brewed coffee.

After a few minutes annihilating his serving of beans, and wiping the plate clean with a bread roll, Dal's ears pricked up when Paul announced, "We have plenty of beans remaining."

"I'll have 'em," Dal snapped, passing his empty plate.

Blake reached for the leftovers, took the handle, and tipped the beans into the fire. Dal, arm still outstretched holding his empty plate, stared in disbelief.

"I've seen Blazin' Saddles," Blake said with a defiant stare at Dal. "And you and me are sharin' a tent." He lowered his voice, and whispered through clenched teeth. "Don't say a fuckin' word."

The wind howled, whipping up embers from the dying fire, adding an orange glow to the outside air, sparks shooting skyward with each strong gust that swept over. Blake turned and faced Dal, as thoughts of Wang ran through his mind. "I've been runnin' all this shit through my head, and I still ain't been able to figure what's goin' on. There's somethin' that ain't kosher about Wang not makin' the climb."

"How d'ya figure?"

"Wang and Sung are pretty tight. I'd have thought Wang would've contacted him, explained why he couldn't make it. Gotta be more to this than meets the eye."

"Gotta wait and see, I guess."

The morning brought a light drizzle that made the ground even more uncomfortable, more dangerous, and as they broke camp and resumed the climb, the two struggled, slipping about with each step in the '*motherfuckin' flip flops*,' as Dal referred to them.

"Christ, my feet are . . ." Dal began to say.

"Don't go there," Blake snapped in a wooden perfunctory tone.

They trudged on, Sung chatting away with Father Paul as though on a casual Sunday stroll.

"They've done it all before, hey?" Dal grumbled quietly, tripping over a snow covered log. He tripped, cast a sideways glance at Blake and spat out the words, "Fuckin' log!"

"Shut up and walk," Blake snarled not looking back, managing a stumbling pace a few yards ahead of Dal.

When noon arrived they'd reached a switchback overlooking a panoramic view of alpine meadows far below.

"We will rest here for a while, then eat," Paul said, pointing at the heavy clouds accumulating toward the peak. "We must make good progress ahead of that weather."

Blake and Dal immediately removed their sandals, and Dal, taking a few long moments to furiously massage his feet, groaned at their near blue color. "I'm freezin' under this robe. How'd the Scottish handle it? It's freezin' in fuckin' Scotland ain't it?"

Blake peered at him for a moment. "The Scottish?"

"Yeah, ya know, the kilts, the short checkered skirts, ya know, what with 'em havin' nothin' underneath."

Blake struggled to restrain the grin. "Yeah, poor bastards havin' to live there, must be freezin', good thing we're wearin' these long johns," and he caught Dal's blank expression, his thighs pressed together as he shivered uncontrollably. His body language announced, *but I ain't wearin' long johns.*

*****

Paul and Sung were first to stand and gather their packs. Within minutes all four were trudging onward in single file, passing eleven thousand feet as the light faded. Paul sighted a sprinkling of small fires belonging to Trail Camp hikers perched precariously at twelve thousand feet. "We'll camp here tonight," he said. "Tomorrow we will make a push for the summit. Break out the tents; we have some Latin lessons to take care of before we call it a day."

At midnight, with the battery lantern in each tent extinguished, Paul said goodnight to his trainees who were now relatively warm, their tents positioned to capture heat from the fire. Dal's lack of undergarment protection had taken its toll; he turned toward Blake and groaned, "I'll be glad to get into a house again, one with carpet, a heatin' system, and a real bed."

"Ain't gonna happen up here," Blake sniggered. "I know we've some kind of shack waitin' ahead, but nothin' like you're describin' for sure. On the other hand, maybe I shouldn't assume," and he briskly rubbed his hands together and blew into them. "Paul could have a surprise in store; ya know how he likes springin' these little gems on us."

The assumption fed Dal a morsel of hope, allowing a smile to creep onto his face. The smile hung there for a few seconds, until a cold blast catapulted him back to reality. "Wha'dya suppose Hunter and Bellinger are doin'?"

Blake rolled on his side, and after a moment grunted, "Fore."

*****

The temperature at sunrise was a few degrees warmer, a fine misted drizzle made its presence felt, just enough to keep a man's face damp, just enough to keep it chilled.

"Morning, gentlemen," Paul said, poking his head in the tent. "I trust you each had a good night's sleep."

Dal shrugged with an air of indifference. Paul felt the chill and feigned a look of concern. "Mr. Dallas," he asked, "you did not sleep well?"

Dal brushed on by him, stepped from the tent and moved toward a covered area, a make-shift bathroom. Blake yawned and flicked a thumb toward Dal. "Don't mind him, Father," he said grinning. "he's travellin' a little light."

A faint, *fuck you*, came from the distant bushes. Paul missed the comment. It didn't matter. Dal called a second time, this time louder. "Fuck you!"

"Sorry about that, Father. Think he might be needin' a doctor," Blake said grinning.

"We must break camp," the priest said in a mellow voice. "We need to move forward, we must make the top before dusk."

*****

When they arrived at Guitar Lake, Paul pointed to a clearing and suggested they stop for a food break. "We have just six miles remaining to the top," he said, pointing toward a distant ridge. "That ridge, it will take us up to the Whitney summit shelter. There are two sheds not far from the shelter; we will spend our time in the sheds." He gave a nod to Blake. "Are you up to it?"

No one spoke as they dislodged their back packs, the packs landing with a thud on the powdery snow followed by each man slumping to the ground and laying his head on his pseudo pillow.

"This is not a good sign," Paul said. "What we have done is a mere stroll compared to the passage from Nepal into China. You need to be more driven, you must be more positive."

"I'm positive, all right," Dal said, propping himself on one elbow. "Positive I'm gonna . . ."

"We'll be fine," Blake interjected. "Just takes a bit of gettin' used to." He raised a slow index finger to Dal and grinned saying, "And some warm long johns."

Paul allowed what he described as 'ample rest time.' Just fifteen minutes. "We have about a two hour trek to the sheds," he said loftily. "Once there, we can heat water, and take well-earned warm baths."

Blake gave a condescending smirk to Dal, who was still shivering, but managed to smile back, each thinking *warm bath*.

CHAPTER 11

"SO WHERE'S THE WARM water?" Dal enthusiastically inquired as he entered the shed. "Lemme at that
bath."

"You thought I was serious?" Paul replied, faking an
apologetic shrug.

"Sonofabitch, I'll k k k kill him," Dal cried to Blake,
as he quickly stepped between the two.

"Sorry Father," Blake laughed. "Ya gotta excuse
him; he's got this slight speech impediment . . . sometimes
he stops to breathe."

Paul laughed as he looked about the shack. "Not
too bad, there have just been a few critters in here looking
for food I suspect. No major damage." Then pointing to the
bathing area, "That way, Mr. Dallas, there is a tub. Allow me
to start the fire beneath it and run the tap."

"I was just messin' with ya, Paul," Dal said, feeling
somewhat embarrassed. "I knew ya were jerkin' my chain."

The priest smiled discreetly at Blake, shook his head
and gave Dal a disconcerting look. Dal went on for a while
about the unacceptable conditions, until Sung interrupted in
a comforting voice. "Give me a few minutes, I will get some
food underway and try to warm the other shed as well."

"Very good, and I will join you," Paul said still
smiling, "as soon as we are able to stimulate blood flow for
Mr. Dallas."

"God bless America," Dal groaned.

Blake nodded.

The cabins consisted of two small sheds divided by a breezeway, with one bedroom in each shed, each with its own bathing area and small kitchen. The priest unfolded a map of the Himalayas and began discussing plans for the climb.

"You see," he said, tapping on the map, "this is Kaytu. We will stay away from this one, there is an easier passage not too many people know about, and Mr. Sung knows it as well as he knows his own neighborhood. Right, Mr. Sung?"

"Yes, the passage," Sung said affirmatively. "I have used it many times, but Wang has made this crossing more than *any* person, and could probably travel through it blind-folded."

"Speakin' of Wang, wha'dya suppose held him up?" Blake asked as he removed a can of Spam from his pack. "Where's Wang?"

"I called Mr. Ridkin before we set out and briefed him on your progress," Father Paul said. "He said to give you both his *very best.*"

Dal whispered, "Bullshit," and glared at Blake. "Mr. Ridkin sends his *very best*, good ol' Mr. Ridkin."

"So where's Wang?" Blake repeated.

The question was up for grabs. It hung there . . . in the cold mountain air.

Paul poked the fire a few times and stared trance-like into the embers. "Mr. Wang has not been seen for three days," he said in a melancholy tone. "A car was found at the Los Angeles Airport. It had been there for days. Security was suspicious of the license plate, being out of state. It raised a red flag."

"Ain't soundin' good," Dal said.

"Don't go jumpin' to conclusions," Blake replied. "You've seen too many movies."

"The car was left unlocked," Paul said. "Or someone

had opened it. They found a few fingerprints, other than Wang's of course."

"Okay, so now ya *definitely* have my attention," Blake said, "Go on."

Paul glanced at Sung, who remained expressionless, his eyes staring coldly into the dancing flames.

"It is very difficult," Sung said in a hushed tone, "when you have a close friend with whom you have years of building a strong relationship. You know what I am saying, right, Mr. Blake?" And he waved his hand at Blake and Dal as he spoke.

Paul coughed and broke the moment. He reached across and passed a can opener to Blake who was holding the Spam, his eyes fixed on Sung.

"The fingerprints from the vehicle are at the laboratory," Paul added shrugging. "Mr. Ridkin had computer matching done. The computer results are eh, well, not quite what we expected."

"Yeah, to err is human," Dal sighed. "But to really fuck up, ya gotta have a computer."

Blake shot a censorious look at Dal, and asked, "What were the results?"

"They never made it back from the laboratory," Paul said. "The technician was found dead. The fingerprint sheet was missing, gone. There are no records."

Blake turned the opener, his eyes following the gyrating can. "So eh, the CSI guys, they took another set of prints from the vehicle?" He said *vee hickle*, mimicking Paul.

Dal poured a drink, looked up at Paul, and gave an affirmative nod in anticipation of a positive response.

"I asked Mr. Ridkin that very question," Paul replied. "He said they tried to get a second set. Could not understand how the prints disappeared. They were under lock and key."

"If it was, someone had the key."

"The vehicle was clean," the priest said shrugging, shaking his head, "there were no prints, nothing at all."

Blake gave up on the can, stared down at his reddened thumb, sighing in frustration, "Aw Christ, let's leave this until mornin'. I gotta digest it." He shot a look of disdain at the half-opened can. "Fuckin' Korean can opener."

"Yeah, we gotta digest it," Dal added, eying the can. He leaned across and commandeered the Spam.

*****

Blake tugged the blanket tightly around his shoulders. *How'd the lab guys fuck up? Who wants this hushed up so badly they'd kill the lab tech to get the prints? Why's Wang gone missin'? Fuck breakin' the 'no contact' part of the program, gotta speak with Sam.* As they grouped around the fire, Blake asked, "Ya got that cell phone with ya, Paul?"

"The cellular telephone is not part of the plan; in fact, it is back at the house. I have made this trek so many times and look forward to the escape. Bringing a telephone, well, that would be similar to bringing my troubles along with me." He let out a friendly giggle, hunching his shoulders and nodding at Dal. "Besides, as you said, Mr. Dallas, this is a mere hill, not Everest."

"Might as well be," Dal said shrugging, then jabbed a thumb toward the snow covered window pane and grumbled, "If we get our asses stuck up here."

"That will not happen," Paul said, losing the merriment, hesitating for a few moments. "We will start back early, shorten the exercise if necessary." He turned his eyes away and Blake picked up on the priest's discomfort. "Yes, in view of Wang's disappearance, and the death at the laboratory," Sung said, "I feel we should head back at first light. I need to know what has happened to Wang."

The wind had grown stronger, shooting horizontal sparks from the small chimney across the snow-covered landscape. Father Paul and Sung Chiao pulled their hoods in tighter around their faces, bidding goodnight to Blake and Dal, and made the short dash to the second shed.

"Not a good night," Blake said, staring through the doorway at the sky overhead. "The weather's turnin' bad."

"And why not turn fuckin' bad?" Dal asked. "It ain't meant to be easy."

"Wha'dya make of the fingerprint mess?" asked Blake.

"Someone at the Division's got reasons for us to blow this whole mission. Someone don't want this guy Slade leavin' China alive."

"Been thinkin' the same thing, ever since Paul broke the news on the lab killin'." Blake said. "What I can't figure is why Father Paul didn't tell us before we left the house?" He hesitated, swallowing hard as his old ankle injury sent pain up his leg. He grimaced, bent down and massaged the shinbone.

"Yeah, thought crossed my mind too," Dal said. "Maybe we should hit him with that."

"Wait 'til we're down the mountain," Blake groaned, wanting a little sympathy. "Don't wanna rock the boat. Don't want our asses stuck up here."

Dal cupped his hands against the frigid window pane, pressed his face to the glass, and squinted at the whiteout as the wind intensified. "You're right, let's get back down. Then we can quiz the motherfucker." Then a half-minute later, "Drew, ya don't really feel Father Paul has any bullshit reasons for not mentionin' this whole mess sooner, do ya?"

"Nah, I'm tryin' to believe he's okay," Blake said, still working on the ankle. "But I felt uneasy with Wang's body language ever since we met the guy."

"What about Paul?"

"Sam probably told him to go ahead with the climb; maybe Paul fucked up a bit by tellin' us about the fingerprints."

"Kinda put himself in a spot, don'tcha think?"

No reply. Then from Dal, after a half-minute, "Glad ya mentioned how ya feel about Wang, my sentiments too."

"Sure, Wang's a mystery," Blake said staring at the wind gusting outside the window. "But I'm okay with Paul. He just opened up a bit with us, not really spillin' the beans, so to speak. *Sharin'* would be more what he did."

"Yeah," Dal said, scratching his bearded chin, "that's gotta be the answer, that's gotta be it. He was *sharin'*."

They stretched out on the inadequate substitutes for beds, blankets that could've doubled as mattresses, except for the temperature, which definitely made them more valuable as covers, rather than beneath the shivering campers.

"Jesus Christ," Dal said, tugging at the too short blanket, struggling to pull it up around his neck. "Almost all the comforts of home."

"Yeah, all the fuckin' comforts."

After a few minutes of silence, Blake could hear Dal chuckling to himself.

The sniggering stopped and Blake lazily half opened his eyes in anticipation of something . . . knowing Dal's modus operandi.

He wasn't disappointed.

Twenty seconds later, "Just thinkin' about this Chinese doctor back home. Did I ever tell ya 'bout Doctor Chin?"

"Aw man, I'm tryin' to sleep here."

Dal sulked for a full minute, tossing and turning. "So ya don't wanna hear about Chin?"

"Aw, for Christ's sake, if it means I'll get some peace, what about him?"

Propping himself up Dal said, "There's this woman

who lived next door to me, she asks me to show her how to get onto a datin' site on the net. So I go and hook her up with one of those matchmaker places, ya know."

"Good. Can I go to sleep now?"

"No, no. I'm not done. Ya see, she goes and meets up with about fifteen different guys over about a month. Starbucks loved her for it. I guess she didn't have any luck. So I see her one day sittin' on a bench in the park, ask her about how the datin' scene is doin'. She says she ain't had a date in a year. No sex for a fuckin' year."

"Really, huh," Blake said with disinterest.

"She says she went to see this Chinese doctor, the doctor tells her she's got Ed Zachary Syndrome."

Silence.

After a minute of sniggering, "Ya heard of it?" Dal asked.

"No! Can't say I have. Ed Zachary, huh, nope, never heard of it. How'd he analyze that one?"

"Well, he says to her . . ."

And right there, Blake realized he should've *never asked the fucking question.*

"So he says to her, '*Take all your croes off.*' Tells her to get on all fours, he says, '*Get down and craw reery, reery fass to odderside of room.*' So this woman, she crawls across, just like the doc says. So then the doc says, '*Okay, now ya craw reery, reery fass ower here to me.*' So the doc shakes his head and scribbles notes in his pad. The woman, still wearin' nothin, sits back in a chair. The doc says, '*Put your croes back on.*' So the woman starts dressin', and she says, '*So, what do ya think is the problem?*' He says, '*Ya haf Ed Zachary Syndrome. Dat why ya no have dates, or sex.*' By this time my neighbor's havin' a fuckin' conniption. She says, '*Oh my God, I've never heard of such a thing. Ed Zachary Syndrome, what exactly is that?*' Dal grinned, struggled to remain serious. "So the doc says, '*Probrem vewy bad, worse case I ever see.'*

He paused, thought he heard Blake snoring, but Blake grumbled, "So ya gonna finish, or what?"

"Yeah, yeah. So the doc tells her, '*Ed Zachary Syndrome. It when your face looks Ed Zachary like your ass.*"

"Go to sleep, ya fuckin' retard!"

A few silent minutes lapsed, and Dal whispered, "There's somethin' out there. Ya hear it?"

"Go to sleep," Blake said, tugging the blanket over his head. "Leave me alone."

"G'night, grandpa," Dal said.

Blake replied, smiling to himself, "G'night, John-Boy."

Although faint, the sound was audible enough to once again attract Dal's attention. He raised his head, turning his stronger ear in the direction of the door, waiting for the sound to return.

"Drew, ya hear that?"

"Go to sleep!"

Again, the distinct scratching sound at the door fol-lowed by a loud growl and Dal leaped to his feet and stood frozen, staring at the door.

"Ah shit, it's a bear. What'll we do?"

"Jeeesus!" Blake whined in a disbelieving tone, trying to salvage his diminishing level of sleep.

Dal moved to the window, peeked through, and watched as a large bear waddled off into the thick tree cover that surrounded the sheds. He mumbled quietly, "Thank you God, thank you, thank you, thank you." Then, blessing himself repeatedly, he said, "Ya see, good livin' pays off, Drew."

But again, Blake was not there.

Blake was in another place.

Dal mumbled, fell back into bed, pulled the blanket

around his ears and began to drift. As he lay there he heard the noise again, more scratching.

This time, not as loud.

It was a softer tapping, followed by a faint voice whimpering, "Hello, someone in there?"

"Drew," Dal said quietly, as though wanting Blake's attention, yet at the same time, hoping to not incur his anger.

Then again louder, "Drew!"

"What!" Blake groaned. "What now?"

"There's' someone at the door."

"You're dreamin'. Go t' sleep."

"No, there's someone out there I tell ya."

"Go open it, invite 'em in. It'll give ya someone to talk to. Lemme get some sleep!"

The scratching and faint tapping continued.

Dal sat up.

Rigid.

Listening intently, heard the voice again, and called, "Drew." Then again, a great deal louder, "DREW!"

Blake didn't answer.

"Drew, wake up, for Christ's sake!"

Blake grumbled, rolled away and pressed a pillow over his ear. Dal moved to the door, raised the rusty bar that acted as a lock of sorts, and stepped back as the man kneeling outside the door collapsed into the shed.

He stood looking at the pathetic figure for a few long moments, then dragged him toward the fire and called to Blake, "Get on over, help me here."

Blake, now alert to the situation, sprung from his almost warm bunk.

"Look at this guy," Dal said. "He's near frozen to death."

His clothes were tattered, and blood from a head wound trickled down the edge of matted hair. Blake squatted alongside, thought, gave three quick taps on the man's face, and said, "Fuck him. He's gonna screw up our plan."

Dal hung a small cauldron over the fire, heated water, and began to clean off the wound. Fifteen minutes later the stranger regained consciousness, and gazed at the two hooded figures. "Thank you, Fathers," he said, in a raspy voice. "Thank you."

Blake looked to see if Father Paul was standing behind him, then realized the man was speaking to him, and said in a somewhat priestly way, "What happened to ya, my son?"

Dal cut Blake a look, caught a quick jab, and went along with the role play.

"Father Dominic," Blake said half turning to Dal. "Maybe ya can put some coffee on for this poor soul?" He thought *why waste an opportunity to try out the priest shit*, and the two moved their patient to the bunk nearest to the fire.

"Wha'dya think?" Dal whispered.

"Gunshot wound, slug's grazed his temple." He took the man's hand, turning it palm down, touching the knuckles. "Ya see this tattoo; this is the kind ya see on ex cons . . . the triple six."

"Ya think we're bein' a bit paranoid?" Dal asked. "I mean, more paranoid than usual?"

"Yeah."

"Father," the man said faintly. "There's a guy still out there, couldn't make it here, he can't have been too far behind me."

Blake made a face at Dal, motioning with a tilt of his head toward the door. Dal touched his leg, shuddered and said, "Nah, ya got the warm underwear, I'll stay here with this one." And he turned to the man and said, "Father Bond here'll go out and find your friend."

There was a sense of achievement in Dal's *making*

of a priest. He thought, *a fuckin' Kodak moment. I'm in the warm shed. Blake's out there in a snow blizzard, wonderful.* He chuckled as he gazed through the near opaque window at the horizontal snow whipping into Blake's face, his hood ballooning from his head. He mumbled with relish. "Good one, God!" as Blake's hood took on the appearance of a spinnaker on a twelve meter yacht.

Dal's chuckle turned to laughter.

Blake studied the direction of the tracks, and followed them back toward nearby boulders. He slipped, stumbled, and regained his footing. He scampered a further twenty yards and stumbled right on top of the second man who was tattered, bleeding, *maybe dead,* Blake thought. "Hey, can ya hear me? Come on!" He shook the man and his head flopped from side to side like a rag-doll. *We can't get involved with local cops. They'll want a report filed. We'll need to make statements. They'll wanna see I.D. It'll blow the mission.* He quickly assessed his options. *I can leave him here, get the other guy back on his feet and get him off tomorrow. No, can't do that either, fuck it!* Minutes later, Blake called from outside the door, "Dal, Dal, get your ass out here, NOW!"

Sung and Father Paul slept soundly, their shed being just far enough away to not hear the imbroglio as the wounded man was dragged into Blake's shack.

"How's he doin'?" a concerned Dal asked.

"Unconscious. Nearly fuckin' dead from the cold," Blake panted, his hands on his hips, struggling to regain his breath, and pointing to the man by the fire. "How's that guy doin'?"

"The dude's in shock, delusional. Keeps wakin' up and ramblin'."

"I ain't too sure what we should do here," Blake groaned, scratching at his chin. "We can't get involved with the local cops, can't show 'em I.D."

"You're right. Sam'll have our balls if we blow this

over some local clusterfuck."

Blake moved nearer the fire, held out both hands, searched for warmth. The first man reached toward Blake, tugged at his robe, and pulled his ear down to his mouth. "Father, I need to tell you something. Need to have you hear my confession."

Dal shook his head frantically and mouthed, '*Fuck no, not me.*'

Blake's eyes flashed from Dal to the pleading man, and he piously replied, "I cannot do that."

"I'm gone," the man said. "Need to make peace with The Lord."

The cover, Blake thought, *can't blow the fuckin' cover. Need to see this thing through.*

Dal reached into his backpack, pulled the purple confessional sash, and whispered into Blake's ear. "Ya could do with the practice, ain't gonna do no harm. Nothin' bad can come of it. If it helps the fucker feel better . . . do it!"

Blake kissed the sash, placed it around his neck, and leaned toward the man. "In nomine Patris, et Filii, et Spiritus Sancti. Tell me your sins, my son."

"Father, I killed two guys. They tried to pick me up in a bar over in Bishop. I followed 'em down to Lone Pine, then up the mountain path, killed 'em both."

Dal stared at Blake, his eyes opened wider. Again, he mouthed, "*What the fuck!*"

Blake said nothing.

The words were faint. "Father, forgive me."

"Yes my son, but this man who's with ya?" And he gestured to the unconscious man. "Did he help with the killings?"

Dal made a *keep going* gesture with his hands.

The man slurred his words, "Nah, he was gonna be my, my, my next victim. Please, gimme absolution, Father . . . Father?"

Blake was unsure why Dal was grinning like an idiot. He turned and flashed a look of annoyance that shouted, *Idiot!* Then, back to the stranger. "My son, God forgives ya, but ya cannot continue to commit such sins."

Dal, somewhat put out, nudged Blake, who figured he'd best not push his luck. He raised a hand in a blessing position. "God, the Father of mercies," Blake said in a pious way, "Through the death and resurrection of his Son has reconciled the world to Himself, and sent the Holy Spirit among us for the forgiveness of sins through the ministry of the Church. May God give ya pardon and peace, and I absolve ya from your sins in the name of the Father, and of the Son, and of the Holy Spirit."

The man breathed a sigh of relief. "Thank you, Father."

"Rest my son," Blake said with one hand on the man's head, "rest."

Unable to contain his amusement, Dal whispered, "Impressive, very fuckin' impressive."

They sat silently for minutes, mentally searching for a solution as the man slipped into a deep sleep, or maybe a coma.

"Okay," Blake said, "I've figured out a plan. Gonna go with plan 'A'."

"Fire away, this is gonna be somethin'. I'm all ears."

Blake pushed his hood back, and paced the room. "This guy needs to be taken into custody."

"Okay."

"We ain't gonna be involved in makin' an arrest. Neither of these guys has seen our faces clearly." He gave Dal a quick look. "Ya with me so far?"

"Okay."

He walked back to the sleeping man, whose head wound was now bleeding more profusely, his face reddened as blood ran down onto the stained pillow casing.

"We gotta get outa here, get back to Francis; get out real fuckin' fast. We'll have Sung and Paul stay here with these two. As far as these guys'll remember, they were rescued by two priests, by Sung and Paul. They won't remember anythin' about us. Wha'dya think?"

"Okay."

Blake gave an annoyed stare. "Okay? But wha'dya fuckin' think?"

"That's it? That's your plan 'A'? That's all ya got?" A few seconds of bewildered silence, after which Dal nodded, his expression belying his intake of plan 'A'. He really had no clue what the fuck had been said, but nodded enthusiastically just the same, catching Blake's twitching right eye. *Best to go along*, he thought, knowing full well the early warning sign of that *right eye twitch*. "Ah yeah, okay," Dal nodded. "Got it, could just work."

"With these hoods up," Blake said, "and what with the beards and the bad light and all, they wouldn't know the difference between shit and shinola."

"Brilliant, I like it. Go on."

And Dal had convinced himself.

"We'll leave 'em here, go back down the mountain and leave an anonymous message with the local cops, sayin' there's a suspect up here bein' watched over by two priests." He paused, drew air, thought out his next words. "We'll tell 'em there's one guy up here who could be a witness against the nutcase. Tell 'em he needs medical attention, and for 'em to get a medic chopper up here fast."

Dal chewed over the whole scenario, then raised a finger and said, "*Uno problemo.*"

"Okay, chuck it at me; we gotta sort it all out right now, no time to change the story once we call in the report."

"That cop, the patrolman, the black dude, he knows four of us trekked up the mountain. He'll know you and me were here, knows Paul and Sung aren't up here on their lonesome."

"Good point." He looked at Dal who'd begun dabbing at the blood now running freely from their unconscious guest. He thought for two minutes, then paced from the fire to the window, hands behind his back, looking very priestly. "How's this scenario?" he said. "We started back down at mid-day yesterday. We camped close to Trail Camp, that's around 12,000 feet. When we left the sheds, these two still hadn't arrived here. We know nothin' about it, and can move straight back to LA and leave the *clusterfuck* for Paul to figure out."

"Hmm," Dal mused. "Sounds good, could work fine, as long as we get our asses back down fast enough to fit the time frame."

"Yeah, when we get down, I'll make a short call, report the whole fuckin' thing, and whammy, we're home free. Sung'll catch up with us after Paul's done with this pair."

They gave one another a look, assessing the believability of the story. Blake exhaled loudly, "Would *you* buy that crock o' shit?"

"Dunno. Maybe . . . maybe not."

"*Maybe not,* ain't exactly the words I need to be hearin'," Blake said letting out a groan. "What a mess. It's Murphy's fuckin' Law."

It wasn't perfect, but it'd have to do. Blake bundled up, pulled the hood over his head, and made a dash to the adjoining shed.

The wind had kicked up and was howling with such intensity that Blake shouted to the point of hoarseness, pounding, pushing on the shed door.

"Hey, hey, hey!" Paul shouted, waking Sung.

"Open up. Come over to our place, we got a huge problem here!"

Back in the shack, Sung and Paul stood in disbelief as they stared down at the two strangers.

"Pull up a log," Blake said. "Make yourselves comfortable, it's gonna be a long-ass night."

He went through the events of the evening, as Father Paul and Sung Chiao sat in silence like two children enthralled by a storyteller. Dal had moved to the provisions, found the Oreo cookies, split one, and licked at the cream, giving an intermittent nod in support of Blake's explanation. Neither Paul nor Sung interrupted, each hanging on every word.

"So, wha'dya think," Blake asked them. "Would ya buy it?"

Paul sat with his head in his hands, face hidden.

"Good news is . . ." Sung said, "you performed believably with the priest routine."

"Yeah," Dal said, wiping the back of one hand across his mouth, "Father Bond here handled his first confession like a pro."

"Let's get this straight," Blake scowled. "Dal and me are headin' back down the mountain at first light. You two keep these guys under wraps. The unconscious guy ain't a problem. We'll secure the other guy, tie his hands." He held Sung's eyes for a few long moments. "Ya know how to handle the situation, we'll leave the explainin' shit in your hands, okay Sung?"

"No problem, Mr. Blake. They will be well cared for."

"Just remember, Sung, you're a priest. Don't go ballistic on me. We gotta keep the cover goin'."

He directed his focus to Paul. "Let Sung here take care of these two, understand?"

"Yes, I understand fully; I will stay calm and wait for help from the local police, and yes, I understand, neither of you were here this evening."

When the two had scurried back to their shed, Dal

sat by the dying fire and asked, "Aw Christ, dare I ask about plan 'B'?"

Blake, staring into the embers, said, "Ain't no plan 'B'."

*****

The mountain descent went smoothly, barring a few slips and slides, both men emerged none the worse for wear.

"That might qualify for a record descent," Dal panted as he scuffled along the track leading to the house.

Blake knocked firmly on the door, heard the hurried footsteps and the click of the lock as Father Francis opened it, stared at the two men, and gave them each a blank stare as though they were strangers. "Oh, sweet Jesus, what happened? You are both looking absolutely horrid."

Blake pushed past the priest and made his way to the bathroom, as Dal stepped into the room, dropped his backpack, and immediately began briefing the priest on what had taken place on Whitney. An ear-piercing scream came from the bathroom, and Dal dashed by Francis and stormed to where Blake stood staring into the mirror.

"Jesus Christ! Oh Jesus!"

"What's up?"

"The mirror, look at my face."

Dal took four quick steps to the mirror, and stood staring at his own image.

They hadn't looked in a mirror for over a week. The faces staring back were weather beaten, bearded, and snow burnt, close to foreign. Father Francis stood at the door and took in the scene. "Mirror shock," he said with a subdued grin. "I have seen it before. After you wash up and trim the beards a little, you will both feel much better." It did little to ease their anxiety. He added, "I have medication for your faces and feet."

Blake said with a snarl, "Father, lemme have your phone!"

The voice on the other end sounded lazy, and Blake thought, *nothin' much happenin' up this way, huh buddy? So lemme totally fuck with your day!*

"I just came down from the sheds on the mountain, about an hour's hike beyond Trail Crest. Ya know where I mean?"

"Yeah, I know the sheds," the unconcerned cop said, "the priest's place."

"Yeah, the priest's place! Well, I was up there and there are these two guys. One of 'em could be some kind of fruit cake, he's sufferin' from exposure, has a wound, could be from a gun, was ravin' on about killin' a couple of hikers."

Silence.

"Are ya gettin' all of this or what?"

"Yeah, go on, I'm writin' as fast as I can," the cop said. "What's ya name?"

"Name don't matter. Listen t' me, the other guy's sufferin' hypothermia, needs urgent medical help. There're a couple of priests up there with 'em. They're waitin' for ya. Ya got a chopper?"

"Sure we do, but . . ."

"Better get it up there real fast."

He punched the power button.

Snarled.

Punched in new numbers.

"Marcie? Drew. Put fuckin' Sam on."

CHAPTER 12

SLADE CRINGED, STAGGERED A little, and slipped a hand inside his jacket as pain shot along one arm. He felt the vomit rising, leaned against a wall, bent forward and threw up and saw blood in the vomit, blinked, and looked closer. Bracing himself, he regained composure, dwelt on the pain momentarily and wondered when *enough is enough*, questioned himself and quickly decided this wasn't that moment. He wiped his chin and pressed on. And there it was, one hundred yards ahead, The Temple of Heaven. *I'm heading in the right direction, the Xishiku has to be close.* He staggered, tried to steady himself, looked about, and realized how suspicious he appeared to passers by. *I don't see soldiers, no one watching me. Gotta recompose, breathe deep, I feel like shit. I'm disoriented. I've travelled how far? Can't recall, gotta reach the cathedral, get there without raising suspicion. How long've I been walking, two hours, three, maybe four?*

A tall withered man with a long braided ponytail and thick lens glasses stepped from an alley, nearly stumbling into Slade. They held each other's gaze momentarily, and then with no change of expression, the withered man stared ahead as though looking beyond Slade, his eyes cold, lifeless, his white cane tapping a steady beat as Slade stepped aside, and the withered man simply passed on by.

A blind man.

He waited for his heart to slow a little, and thought,

has eyes like mine, empty, lost.

He felt damp, looked down at his saturated trouser leg, groaned in a peripherally embarrassed way. *I've pissed myself, aw Jesus, I've pissed myself.* He lifted heavy eyes and searched down the way for the withered man, spotted him some twenty paces further on tapping his cane on the door of a shop. The door opened and took him in.

Old newspapers abandoned by a previous occupant littered a bench ahead. He sat, gathered the loose pages, he thought *maybe there's something about the killings*, and felt a rush of panic, *maybe a description of me, or an artist's composite, what are the odds?*

A fine drizzle added to the grayness of the day, and Slade raised his collar at the sound of approaching footsteps. Five troops, men on a mission striding in his direction caused a sudden tightness to sweep through him.

Chatter passed from one to the other, as Slade hid his look of paralyzed intensity behind the newspaper, holding it high to cover his face, listening to the chatter, getting nearer, nearer, then slowing, slowing - on top of him.

Stopped.

His heart raced and he continued to make out as though reading, thinking *oh Jesus, they're standing right here. Dare I . . .?*

Shouting came from maybe a hundred yards off, a distant disturbance causing the footsteps to scurry away. He raised his eyes skyward and offered silent thanks. He clutched at his arm as he lowered the paper, felt nothing. *Shit, it's numb, not good. Gotta get up; get to the cathedral.* Twelve minutes further on, he stood in silence as the drizzle added a shine to his five day stubble, settling on his beard like dew drops. He staggered as he rounded a corner . . . and it was there, the Xishiku, in all its splendor.

The sight of the magnificent architecture momentarily blocked his pain, bringing temporary relief, then the warmth of blood seeping from the wound ripped him back to reality. *All these people, black umbrellas, sheltering in twos and threes, all huddling together, funneling in the one direction, escaping the drizzle. Where's my umbrella?* And the demons set in. *Momma, where's my umbrella?*

Hallucinations.

He hung back, sought refuge in the doorway of a shop.

Cowering, he slipped a hand inside his jacket and felt the warm stickiness. When he removed the hand, it was saturated with blood - deep, deep purple blood. *Not good,* he thought. *Not good at all, momma. What day is it? How long has it been? Momma, please help me . . . momma?*

He moved backward until he bumped a wall, then with clear visions of his mother, his knees buckled and he slid to the ground.

Jimmy, the sea is rough tonight. Don't like the look of it. Mike? Mike? Momma?

Blackness.

He came to in a dim and confused way, attempted a count, rubbing at his beard, trying to measure time by the length of its the growth. *I smell like shit. Was I dreaming? My beard's long, gotta be a few days.*

The Sunday Mass at the Xishiku attracted hundreds of Chinese Catholics. Each Sunday they'd gather outside the cathedral, and at precisely fifteen minutes before six, the doors would swing open. On this day, at ten minutes before six, Paul Slade would attempt to enter with the throng. Operated by the patriotic Catholic church of China, it was constructed in 1890 by a French mission. Because of Vatican diplomatic recognition of Taiwan, the actual Roman Catholic Church had been forced to operate underground in mainland China, an ironic situation subjecting it to persecution for a position similar to that of the reformation era. The patriotic church of China did however, follow Pope Benedict XV.

Sunday, it's gotta be Sunday, he thought as he limped half dazed toward the enormous doorway. *Gotta stay in the present, gotta know what I'm doing.* He conjured up thoughts of the bishop. *Have to concentrate on contacting the guy.* More fear, negative possibilities. *What if it's the wrong guy? If I show my cards to the wrong bishop I'm done for sure.* Regardless of mental reconnoitering, his orders were simple. *Get to Xishiku; our man will be expecting you.* He made an audible groan, stopping abruptly as bells began a Pied Piper call and the faithful walked trance-like through Gothic doors. *Safest place is in with the crowd, gotta find my contact.* He huddled among a group of men all shorter than himself, had to stoop to keep his head lower than those around him. Summoning what little remained of his strength, he picked up his pace, and threaded through the congregation, avoiding the three soldiers carrying automatic weapons and working their way through the crowd. A priest approached one of the soldiers, spoke quietly and motioned at the M16 with a head shake. The soldier smiled, lowered the weapon, and continued bumping his way forward.

A shoulder blocked his passage. As the soldier's elbow bumped hard into Slade, he grunted, grabbed at his shoulder fearing the wound had re-opened, feeling panic as his body temperature rose and blood began seeping, and, and . . . He thought, *oh Jesus, oh Jesus, I'm so close. If they're searching for me, surely that guy would've spotted me.*

Two priests made their way toward him. The taller of the two whispered with a distinct lisp in his voice, "I am Father Lee, we are here to help you. Uncle Tham thent uth, pleath walk to the door at corner of cathedral." He was tall for an Asian, thinly built and attractive in an effeminate way, with short buzzed hair and an extreme lisp, but the combination gave him added appeal, a puppy-like quality.

"Oh, you do thmell bad," the tall priest said turning his face away. He took a hold of Slade's arm, led him through

153

a concealed door at the rear of the cathedral and into a round chamber, pointing to a settee as Slade staggered, swaying, his knees turning to jelly as he was lowered into a reclining position. He stared at the ceiling, with only peripheral awareness of the two priests as they began to fade, fading, fading, and they were gone.

The blackness returned.

If this is death, he thought, *it ain't so bad.*

The drifting aroma of incense filtered through the room as Slade re-entered the world. A few minutes passed and he realized he was actually enjoying the warmth and secure ambience of this religious enclave. He raised his head, groaned inwardly as the pain pounded like a drum. "I'm not dead," he grimaced as one of the priests placed a gentle hand beneath his back. The door opened, and an older priest, a portly man who was sweating profusely, floated toward Slade. He wore a red cassock and a matching hat that typically indicated a high position. The portly man waved at the two young men, dismissing them from the room. The red cassocked man pulled a chair to the bed, sat alongside, and said in a soft voice, "Welcome, Mr. Slade. My goodness, you certainly do need bathing and clothing."

"Who are you? You know my name."

"I have been aware of your existence for some time. I know we are working toward the same end. In fact, I could say I have actually involved myself in, hmm, how do you Westerners put it? Ah yes, extra curricular activity. Living my life to help others makes my life worthwhile. I live by this philosophy." He looked toward the door, and then leaned to Slade's ear. "I can tell you this because each of us has no choice but to trust the other. I am Bishop Bolin. I am one of the two tribunes."

"The tribunes, you're one of the tribunes? I was told to meet my contact here, but . . ."

He hesitated, thought *could be a set-up. No choice,*

the guy knows my name, he's gotta be the contact. "How do I know this isn't a set up, if you're really a tribune? You're supposed to remain anonymous, you and the other guy."

"This is not a set up, Mr. Slade. The cardinals were able to get a message through to me, and as no one could reach you, I became involved."

Slade raised himself on one shoulder. "I think I'm gonna throw up. Have you got a bucket?"

The bishop called out, and a priest returned to the room, carrying towels, clothing, shaving equipment, and a bowl of water. Two hours later, Slade squinted, focused on the ceiling, then down at his boots. He glanced slowly across the room at two figures; the bishop was standing in the far corner speaking with a man dressed in tattered street clothing. The man caught Slade's stare, nodded, and gave an acknowledging wave. After a few minutes the man gestured goodbye, and left the room. The bishop returned to the edge of the bed, placed a gentle hand on Slade's forehead, and said, "Ah, Mr. Slade, welcome back. Feeling a little better are we?"

"How long . . . how long have I been here?"

They looked at each other for a few moments, neither saying a word, their thoughts crossing within a nanosecond of eye contact.

Slade: *Can I trust this guy?*

Bolin: *I am not sure I can trust this American.*

"Everything is in hand, we are preparing to move you to a safer place. This is not the best location for you to recover from your injury. The increased activities of the general's troops suggest that something is suspected, so we must get you to a village where you will be far safer."

Slade shook his head, still harboring doubt. "I'm still not convinced you're who you say you are."

"If I tell you the two words, Mr. Slade, just two, will that convince you of my trustworthiness?"

He nodded like he knew what the bishop was talking about. "How could two words make a difference?"

The bishop grinned widely, helping to lessen the tension.

"What two words?" Slade asked.

"Black Sabbath."

CHAPTER 13

A WHITE HAIRED MAN, alongside a makeshift shanty . . . the village of Houniugang, a mile from the Xiaotangshan hospital, hobbled forward, and greeted the young priest accompanying Paul Slade.

"Father Lee! It is so good to see you. Please . . ." and he stood to one side, sweeping his hand in an 'enter' gesture. He and Lee bowed, and Lee made a reassuring gesture to Slade who momentarily hung back, uncertain. They stepped into a cramped living space, a family sitting around a makeshift table, a bowl of soup in front of each, and an elderly woman nodding at the new arrivals, beckoning for them to sit at the table. The white haired man opened a medical bag and motioned for Slade to remove his shirt. Lee, sensing Slade's hesitation, leaned forward with an assuring nod, and said, "He ith doctor."

The bullet had made a clean exit, passing through the soft underside of his upper arm. With poor English, impeded further by his speech impediment, the priest attempted to translate what the doctor was saying. "My Englith ith not good. My name ith Lee Hua. Thith doctor, he they you very lucky that bullet not break bone. You okay."

Slade nodded and grinned at the priest.

"We thtay here and retht. Tomorrow we go to village, we go to thafe houth. What your name?"

The priest extended a hand.

"Good to meet you, my name's Slade."

JASON DENARO

While they ate, the young priest attempted a steady stream of banter, his lisp making heavy going of the chatter. He passed a slow hand around the room. "Earthquake hit thith land, many hurt, houth fall down. Thith family hath lotht their houth, build thith from old dwelling. Their thon killed, tholdierth take daughter. Thith doctor, he born in Taiwan."

Slade knew where Lee was going, understanding too well why the doctor sympathized with the priest's cause. His brow furrowed momentarily and his face took on a smile as he wondered whether or not to dig a little deeper into the demise of the village. Just when he'd found the words, Lee shrugged, "The Lord workth in thtrange wayth."

When the dressing of the wound was done, Lee smiled across at the doctor, then gave a gentle touch to Slade. "We go thoon," and he slid a bowl nearer to his new friend. "You eat thoop, will feel better, pleath . . . eat."

CHAPTER 14

SAM RIDKIN'S OFFICE WAS an interior designer's worst nightmare, made up of a mish mash of Swift Store non-collectibles with no charm added by the splattering of gifts from overseas dignitaries. The worn carpet square stretched from one baseboard to the other, and featured a history of questionable stains, a forensic team's wet dream.

Preoccupied with the caller, Sam missed the Cinzano ashtray as he ashed the cigarette. He spoke softly, a quivering reply, eyes down, avoiding McDowell sitting opposite, guessing at each piece of Sam's body language, trying to read between his boss's words.

"How badly?" Sam said into the phone, then after a few moments of listening to the caller, "Okay, okay, do they know where?"

McDowell mouthed, "What?" and shrugged.

Ridkin raised a hand, stopping him, and continuing with the conversation. "Jesus Christ! They sent him *where*? I can't believe it, that's way too risky." His face sunk into a grave expression. "You're fucking with me, right?" His expression of morbidity lingered as he listened to the caller's closing comments, then shutting the phone he groaned as he rested his head in his hands.

"What's going on?" McDowell asked.

"Awhile back, Slade was trying to help some local kid. He got into a skirmish, he . . ." Sam paused, waved a hand in a frustrated way and went about explaining the death of Cheng's eldest son. "A bunch of soldiers were trying to molest her. Our boy wrestled an M16 off one of them, ended up killing two." He scrubbed anxious fingers through his gray streaked Afro hair, then slid the anxious fingers down his face, dragging his cheeks as they went. "Slade's been hit. You realize the complications this can cause?"

"That's bad, means we need to . . ." McDowell hesitated, realizing the magnitude of the words '*been hit,*' and asked, "Jesus, is he okay?"

"The cardinals . . ." Sam began, avoiding McDowell's stare, "they eh, they heard he made it away."

"Christ, rule number one for these guys, don't get involved in domestic shit. Don't risk the mission."

"I'd have done the same. You too."

"Where's he at?"

"Goddamn Chinese are stepping up the search. One of the dead guys was the son of Zhu Cheng."

"Major General Zhu Cheng?" McDowell exclaimed. "Jesus Christ, that guy's serious bad news."

"Yeah, he already threatened to use nuclear weapons if they're attacked over Taiwan," Sam said flashing a worried expression across the desk. "He told the world press if we aim missiles at any target, he'd respond with nuclear weapons. Not a man whose son you go killing."

"Was this called in by the bishop?"

Sam looked puzzled. He allowed the question to hang there, not liking the way McDowell's eyes flickered about the room as he waited for a reply.

This is gonna compromise the situation, too much military getting stirred up, Sam thought. *Time to get Wang over there, gotta get the plan underway immediately.* "I'll arrange for Wang's brother's hospitalization," Sam said. "I'll see that his flight's booked, and his hotel in Hong Kong. I've been in touch with our guy in China." He hesitated, stretching his neck just a little, an old nervous trait. "He'll have two statues. One'll go to Wang's hotel room."

McDowell shook his head but Sam cut him short, couldn't risk McDowell throwing him a curve ball. "You know what you need to do? Let your nasty side come out." He held McDowell's stare. "Set up a meeting with Wang tomorrow, maybe a restaurant, someplace quiet." He shot his eyes to the right, nodding in that direction. "Someplace downtown, take him to the airport from there. Sell yourself; he's gotta believe he's still dealing with Sellers. Stay in character. You know what I'm saying."

McDowell's face hardened, and an unscrupulous grin settled on his face as a tenebrous voice echoed from within, *You're fucking with me. God help me.* He had further to say.

*****

It was a secluded section of Los Angeles, a restaurant away from popular eateries, reducing the chance of crossing paths with associates of either man. Background music played Eric Burdon's, *House of the Rising Sun,* as McDowell picked through his plate in a finicky way. Szechwan Plum Beef, his favorite. Nodding stonily, he threw a suspicious glance about the restaurant.

Wang said, "I do not feel good about this change in plans. I cannot understand why you pulled me from the Mount Whitney assignment."

No response.

"I am sure Sung will be concerned over my absence."

Again, silence.

"Why must I leave so abruptly?"

McDowell answered without raising his eyes. "Beijing's more than just concerned about this mission. They know Blake and Dallas are coming in. They'll be expecting 'em to cross from Nepal." He reached for his glass, washing down some beef. "Cheng'll have his men covering the entry route, shadowing Ridkin's guys; probably wait until they meet up with Slade.

"Sam hasn't been as open as usual, makes me think there might be a back up plan. I've been feeling uncomfortable around him lately, can't put my finger on any one thing that I said or did. I just sense he's being too guarded."

Wang's eyes continued scouring the patrons as he peripherally moved food about on his plate. For two long minutes neither spoke nor made eye contact. Wang glanced across the far side of the restaurant and made a half nodding gesture, causing McDowell to turn, then quickly realized he'd been distracted by Wang's curiosity, realized he'd allowed Wang to distract him from his *bad guy* character. Thought, *idiot!*

He slipped back into his role.

Darker . . . even more uncouth.

Wang refocused on his food. "I cannot imagine how a second plan could be in the making. Certainly we would be aware of this, if it were true. Your Interpol intelligence would have that knowledge on file for yourself, and for Sam Ridkin, would it not?" His voice lowered to a whisper.

McDowell shot him a dubious look as Wang leaned forward, staring hard into his face. "You disappoint me, Mr. McDowell. I think I much preferred working with you when you were only known to me as Mr. Sellers, merely a voice over the telephone. In person, I find you a most incorrigible human being."

McDowell didn't bite.

"Sam can be shifty," he replied unmoving, staying in character. "He's playing his cards close to his chest. He . . ."

Wang's cell phone beeped.

"Shut the goddamn thing off. Don't want any interruptions."

Wang reached into his coat pocket, took out the cell, and punched the off button. He looked at McDowell, a look of disappointment, shaking his head as he spoke. "Why is it you feel uncomfortable with Sam Ridkin?" He tinkered with his food, eyes low. "Does he have reason to distrust *you*?"

"No reason," McDowell replied, with a look of disdain. "Like I said, lately I've had this feeling there's more going on than I'm being told." He jabbed at a lump of beef. "And I don't like it. This guy Paul Slade, the real kick-in-the-ass is that he's probably getting help from locals. And that, my friend," he said, lifting the jabbed lump of beef and pointing it at Wang, "is more than a minor fuckin' impediment."

He feigned annoyance, stuffed the beef in his mouth, and banged his fork angrily on the plate. "I tried to pry his whereabouts from Ridkin but he avoided the question."

Wang, feeling adrift, leaned toward McDowell. "It seems strange to me your own bureaucratic system disallows you access to information. I would think you would be privy to such."

"I ain't gonna speculate on the hypothetical. My job's to see that the mission's carried out. There are times Ridkin's tighter than a fish's asshole."

Wang weighed up McDowell's delivery, narrowing his eyes. "In my world, we are given relevant information. I fail to see . . ."

McDowell let out an impatient snarl, his voice rising. "Listen goddamnit. Slade should've been caught by now. Beijing has hundreds of guys looking for him. There's no way he can move toward the coast without passing through a checkpoint."

Wang once again eyed McDowell's *avoidance* with suspicion. "So you are saying there very well may be a second plan, and if there is, you are unable access such information?" He fidgeted about, like a child playing with his meal, while consuming very little. "If that is the case, it certainly appears Sam Ridkin *does* doubt your trustworthiness."

They glared at each other as McDowell pulled a deep breath, his blood pressure nearing boiling point, struggling to remain calm, and choosing to remain silent. *Don't need to share any more with you,* he thought, *gotta cut the interrogation right off.*

"Yeah well," McDowell said pressing. "If he does doubt me, you're eating with a dead man." He felt a sweat weaving its way along his scalp. "On the other hand," he said, "maybe I'm just paranoid. Let's forget about it."

"Forget about it?" Wang snapped in an aggressive tone, attracting attention of nearby diners. "Do not dismiss Beijing lightly. If you fail with your supply of reliable information, neither you nor I will see those Swiss deposits. Beijing rewards well, but its punishment is swift and merciless."

There was a noticeable hush as other diners glanced at the noisy pair. Wang ceased his rant, allowed a few seconds to pass, then placed a hand on either side of his face and raised his eyes to McDowell. "Beijing will eliminate us before ever admitting involvement," he whispered. "They are growing impatient with your inability to supply relevant information concerning Slade's whereabouts."

McDowell's agitation required little in the way of acting, the limit of his patience was genuinely being tested.

"If you suspect an alternate plan, a plan 'B' for entry into China, you must report the possibility. I intend to make it clear to Beijing that I have no choice other than to base my actions entirely on the intelligence I receive from Sellers." He gestured at McDowell with a nod, "From you, *Mr. Sellers.* From nobody else, just you, I believe Sung will lead them through the Nepal pass." He pointed an accusing finger, driving his point home. "If you suspect otherwise, Beijing needs to hear of it. Not from me, they need to hear it from you. If you are wrong, Beijing must know that it is *you* who is solely responsible. I pass on information that *you* deem reliable. Beijing is patient, but that patience is not a bottomless pit."

"Fuck you Wang, and the horse you rode in on. Why'd they be growing impatient with me? To hell with you and Beijing, I stick my neck on the chopping block each day for their fuckin' cause . . ."

Wang raised a hand in protest. "Yes, for their cause as well as their most generous rewards, do not forget the money."

"You think . . ." McDowell growled, "that I want to retire in three years with a handshake from Uncle Sam, a gold watch, and a fuckin' pension?"

Wang glanced quickly about the restaurant. "Please," he said softly. "people are staring."

Glancing about, McDowell thought, *I gotta look nasty.* He sneered at the diners staring at the disturbance. "This is none of your concern!" he snorted, glaring angrily at nearby tables, as a panicked waiter made a dash to resolve the problem.

"Please gentlemen," he said in a pleading tone, with a nod toward tables behind him. "we are getting complaints from other diners."

"Aw shit, I'm sorry," McDowell said turning toward the *other diners.* "Sorry folks," he called in a patronizing way. "It's been a motherfucker of a day. We all have 'em now, don't we?" He nodded as though begging approval, gave an apologetic wave, one that resembled the British royal salute, a condescending, emotionless gesture.

They left the restaurant amidst elation from patrons relieved to see the two depart. McDowell, embarrassed at his conduct, wanted to sneak back, explain his uncharacteristic behavior. *Hope I never see any of 'em again,* he thought. *Have to grow a mustache.*

They made their way to the parking lot, where a young Hispanic man reached for McDowell's valet ticket, and soon returned with the vehicle. He opened the passenger door and McDowell slid in. The valet ran around, opened the driver's door for Wang, as McDowell reached across, and passed a twenty-dollar bill.

"Gracias, I did as you said, senor. I wiped down every place."

"That is an unusually large tip," Wang said. "I have heard you Americans are very gratuitous, but I could not help notice you gave him a large amount."

"He wiped over the car, can't have my prints . . ." He paused, caught himself, said, "Just a precaution."

"Can I go by my hotel and gather my belongings?" Wang asked.

"No time."

Wang began driving in the direction of Los Angeles International Airport, under navigational guidance from McDowell.

"No time to pack. Pick up what you need at the other end. Do Duty Free, they'll have enough shit for you for now."

Wang stared at him in disbelief.

"Watch the road," McDowell grunted. "Don't fuck up at this point."

"You speak so coldly, are you sure you have never been an attorney?"

McDowell paid no heed to Wang's sarcasm.

"How will you explain my disappearance to the others? Sung is expecting me to attend the Mount Whitney exercise."

"Got it all organized. We got a call from Hong Kong, *and we did* just in case anyone pulls the records at the office. Your brother was taken to hospital, a medical emergency. My secretary took the message saying . . ."

Wang interrupted with, "Knowing how you do not leave loose ends, I must assume my brother is truly in a hospital, correct?"

McDowell smiled, realizing Wang didn't underestimate his modus operandi. Sam had called Adam earlier and confirmed the hospitalization of Wang's brother.

"Yeah, he's at the Queen Mary Hospital. Consider it a brotherly vacation. He'll be fine. Once you're back there, give it a few days, we'll have him discharged. I know what I'm doing, needed it to be on the level, in case there's any checking on things at headquarters. We can't have any loose ends."

"This is not good, involving my family in our business, not good at all."

"I get orders. Beijing says send Wang back urgently. They don't give a fuck how I handle the mess at this end." McDowell pointed ahead and snapped, "Watch the road, and don't go giving me no *good guy* attitude. I don't get a road map sent me by Beijing to get this job done; they say do it, I do it. You wanna lodge a complaint, go ahead. But you lodge it from fuckin' Hong Kong. Don't go lodging it from my backyard. My job's to get you on a plane. What you do when you get there, well, that's on your head, not mine. Make a left at the traffic light."

For the next block, Wang drove in silence. After a lengthy wait at a red light, he let out a long breath. "It is impossible for me to contact Beijing, but if it were possible, I would certainly not lodge a complaint." He glanced at McDowell. "I am sorry I have aggravated you with this." His tone was sincere, apologetic.

McDowell nodded, accepted his acquiescence, and allowed a little of the 'nice guy' to slip out. "Let me put you in the loop a little more. I wasn't planning on giving you this information until . . ."

A taxi swerved across the path of their car. Wang

blasted the horn and quickly switched lanes. McDowell lowered the passenger window, shouted at the taxi. Wang was shaken; he slowed, took a half-minute to settle. "You were saying, about giving me some information?"

"Yeah, wasn't gonna give you this until you reached China. I heard Slade had a skirmish with some of General Cheng's men outside of Beijing. He killed two of the troops. One was Cheng's eldest kid, David."

Wang's knuckles turned white as his grip on the wheel tightened. He flashed a sideways look at McDowell.

"The heat's on more than ever to get this guy. They want him dead more than alive, but we need to get him out alive, you're clear on that, right? He must get out in one piece," and he pointed ahead. "Up there, up ahead, swing in, right there."

Wang swung the car into the parking area across from the Bradley terminal. As he pulled into a tight space, McDowell reached into his jacket and passed an envelope. "You'll fly direct to Hong Kong. Ticket's here with travel papers, everything's arranged. Contact me from Kowloon. You'll be staying at the Langham Hotel on Peking Road, arriving around eight in the morning. The hotel's expecting you, so early check-in won't be a problem. No doubt you'll want to shower and freshen up. After you're done, at around nine thirty or so, you'll go to Sun's Café on the hotel's upper lobby level. There'll be a young lady sitting alone at the table nearest the buffet. You carry a newspaper under your arm, she'll recognize you."

"What is her involvement in this?"

"This girl had a brief affair with a eh, a *person of interest,* as they say."

Wang's attention peaked. "It's not . . ." He paused, searched for the name.

"Yeah, the very same. Paul Slade."

Wang grinned, "How did they locate this girl?"

"A disgruntled lover," McDowell chuckled. "And the motivational power of a Swiss bank account."

"Ah yes, the Swiss account, a marvelous motivator. Can you tell me more about this woman?"

"She was born in Beijing. Her father was a military man but she was born out of wedlock. She gets pretty pissed off when it comes to her homeland. Feels jilted, what with being born a bastard and all. Story goes she was turned out at birth, left by a pile of trash, and lucky the dogs didn't get her in the first hour. Anyway, a part of the funds have been deposited in her account. She won't get the balance until she produces Slade. She's got no pictures of him. If she had photos, she'd probably be dead. Slade would already be a guest of the Beijing Government, so it's her eyes that we need."

"Do you have a name for this woman?"

"Lisa Ling. She'll have a statue, a golden Tara. Slade has an identical piece. Your job is to exchange the Tara she has for you with Slade's. We have it from our sources that he'll be attempting to take a small flash drive out of China; it's inside his statue. The statue you'll be carrying contains a duplicate drive except for one difference. The data has an embedded virus, code named *Black Sabbath*. When it's uploaded into Beijing's motherboard, well, it'll be lights out for China's satellite system for a long, long, very long time. When you exchange your statue with Slade's, the U.S. will get quite a kick out of their acquisition. The paltry sum that Beijing's paying into those accounts will be tripled by Uncle Sam, plenty enough for us to safely retire out of the reach of both government's bullshit threats."

Wang was confused, made a face. "I do not follow."

McDowell had kept Yidui hidden away in the darkest recess of his mind. It was a name he seldom mentioned, *Yidui. That motherfucker would sell his mother for a price*, subsequently, McDowell's trust in Yidui was marginal. He mulled it over, wanted to say, *we've got this guy in China who's a cheap piece of shit with as much trustworthiness as a fuckin' Judas*, but he said, "We've got a guy in China, he owns an antique store. The plan is for Slade to go to the store with the stolen flash drive. The owner's a Taiwanese guy, his name's Yidui. He's gonna place the flash drive into a Tara statue, he's gonna contact me when Slade shows up.

"The woman you're meeting, Lisa Ling, she has a duplicate Tara containing a contaminated drive. She'll have the Tara when you meet up with her, and she'll hand it over to you. Like I said, you've gotta cross paths with Slade. You gotta switch your statue, the statue you get from Lisa Ling, with the one the antiques guy gives Slade. His will have Beijing's satellite program"

"Why not just have Cheng's men lay in wait for Slade at Yidui's premises?" Wang asked. "Should we not have better intelligence in place? I expected a smoother operation from Beijing." He gave the steering wheel an annoyed thump. "My return should not have been necessary."

McDowell paused, looked about, keeping his voice low. "Listen to me, Wang; we needed to get Lisa Ling involved with our plans for several reasons, but primarily because so much has changed in China. Christ man, we find lead in toys they manufacture and some toy company president gets himself executed. They ain't got time for losers, ain't no three strike rule in Beijing."

Wang discontentedly weighed the comment, mentally testing it, found it wanting.

McDowell said, "Our communication with China would be a lot better if we had a self serving left wing president in the White House, like when Clinton was in. Clinton tolerated China's bullshit, turned a blind eye to their military modernization and their transferring of weapons to questionable areas." He pointed a finger at the clouds. "Their space program boomed without question during his presidency, Clinton's administration didn't query Jack shit. He was a weak fluctuating negotiator, always open to China's bribes, oblivious to our weakening military position. China's problem is that America has replaced that liberal humanitarian globetrotting leftist with a president who hasn't sucked Beijing's dick. Clinton was too hesitant when it came to acting decisively, unless of course it was dropping his zipper, or taking action against some nation that was too weak to resist."

Wang cracked a smile. "I can see you are not a fan of the Democrats."

"Fuck the two party system. Disgruntled voters don't have a real choice. It's not a matter of my being a supporter of one party or the other; it's all to do with the bucks and the guts. Clinton was reluctant to carry out any threats and the major powers knew that. Unfortunately for us, it cost this country dearly. Now we need to work our asses a lot harder to get what we want from the Chinese. We want that flash drive, Wang. We need to be certain our additional funds are transferred to those Swiss accounts; your arriving in Beijing is like insurance, it's the only way the Chinese funds will transfer. Once the flash drive gets back here to the States, the rest of the payoff, the big bucks from Uncle Sam, all U.S. dollars, will go into our accounts."

McDowell showed discomfort as they stepped from the car. "I'll say goodbye here. Don't wanna bump into familiar faces at the terminal."

"The car," Wang enquired, "does it stay here; are you driving it back to the office?"

"It'll be collected later today; I've a ride standing by." He pointed to the door. "Leave it unlocked."

"And these keys?"

"Toss 'em on the floor."

McDowell nodded toward a black Lincoln Town Car. The driver's window slid down a few inches and the man behind the wheel signaled by jiggling two fingers in his direction through a gap above dark tinted glass. As they walked from the white car, the driver of the Lincoln, wearing white gloves and carrying a yellow dust cloth and spray can, walked quickly to the white car, opened the door, and began spraying and wiping over the doors, the handles, and the seats. It would remain where Wang had parked it - with no fingerprints.

Curious, Wang thought. "Very thorough of you, but then, why would I expect anything less," he said with a wry grin. "I assume you will act surprised when you receive news of my unexpected departure?"

"Of course, my secretary's already called your cell and left you a message." He pointed at Wang's coat pocket. "You really should keep that cell phone switched on. Shame you eh, missed the call."

Wang reached into his jacket, pulled the cell phone, realizing he'd turned it off back at the restaurant. He powered it up, got the battery warning light, and groaned, "Korean technology, not good."

"Yeah, Korea, land of the almost right," McDowell chuckled. "Just like their missiles. When news gets out you've flown home, I'm gonna act surprised. As far as the AID is concerned, I'd've shoved you in a cab and kissed your ass goodbye. Sam knows we wouldn't have made this drive together, it's just not my form. They've got me well and truly profiled."

"I do not follow. It does not sound believable."

"Wang, last time my family was in town I put them in a cab for their trip to the airport. I don't do taxi duty. I can't change the pattern, it would be out of character. If I don't drive family, I sure as hell wouldn't be driving *you.*"

He placed a firm hand on Wang's shoulder, and got a nervous eye from Wang.

Grinning at Wang's discomfort, McDowell sneered,

"You drove yourself to the airport, were in such a rush to get back to see your sick brother, you left the car right here and flew off into the sunset." He scribbled on a note pad, removed the page, folded it twice, and handed it to Wang. "When you're in the terminal, wait twenty minutes then call this number. Leave a message, our answering machine will take your call. Leave clear instructions for them. Apologize for having to leave in a rush, tell 'em where to collect the car. When they open in the morning and hear your message, everything'll work itself out. Your leaving unexpectedly will be explained, and the car will be collected. I'll be just as surprised to hear of your sudden departure as everyone else."

Wang gave a hateful stare. "You have it well thought out. You are truly a devious fuckermother."

"Motherfucker," the reply came with a smile. "And that, my friend, is why I get paid the big bucks."

The handshake came with reluctance. As Wang made his way to the terminal, and still within hearing range, McDowell called, "Just get back there and locate the guy. We'll celebrate together when we visit the land of the cuckoo clocks!"

Wang grinned back.

"And Wang, when you get the information from Slade, you'll be able to reach me. I've arranged for a preprogrammed cell phone to be delivered to your hotel room in Hong Kong, together with a few other items."

Wang entered the Bradley terminal, found his way to Starbucks, ordered a latte, began sipping the coffee, and opened the notepaper. He looked at the number, allowed a minute to pass as he watched travelers scurrying about. Deep in thought, he felt something was wrong, felt things were happening too quickly. He finished the coffee, pulled the ticket from its pouch, read it. *Cathay Pacific Flight 883, departs just before midnight, arrive in Hong Kong around seven o'clock tomorrow morning.* He strolled to the duty free store, *plenty of time to kill,* he thought.

Time to think.

McDowell returned to his office, found the answering machine light flashing, the digital counter showing six messages. With a look of self-satisfaction he pressed the retrieval button.

"Adam? Dave here, are ya able to make it on Sunday? Lemme know, thanks."

Delete.

"Hello Adam. Don't forget to get that card for Louis's birthday, give me a call."

Delete.

Four calls remained.

Wang's probably the last caller, he thought.

"Hey Adam, can't locate that McKenzie file. If you can find it, leave it with Marcie and I'll call by in the morning."

Delete.

"Mr. McDowell, your next appointment . . ."

Delete.

"Are you paying more than 4.75% for your mortgage? If so . . ."

Delete.

The last message was a hang-up.

He stretched his neck to the left, cracked it.

Looked at the ceiling.

Christ, what are you doing, Wang; you'll be boarding in a couple of hours. You've had plenty of time to call.

He punched a rapid dial button. Waited.

"Come on, come on, pick up the fuckin'phone."

The call-tone continued.

Four rings.

Five.

Six.

Seven . . . then a voice.
"Yeah?"
"Sam? Our boy's on his way."

CHAPTER 15

SPECULATION OVER THE KILLING of the lab technician centered on insider involvement, and Sam discussed the incident with David Rogers, Chief Inspector of Los Angeles homicide.

"Let's go over this again," Rogers said. "I'm sorry but you know how it is, we have this departmental procedure we need to follow."

Two uniformed cops sat across from Sam, one readying himself to take notes, the other placed a recorder on the table, and sat with one finger on the record button.

"We're aware of two Taiwanese guys flying in eleven days back," Rogers said. "We're also aware they're both connected with your field operatives, Dallas and Blake, correct?"

Sam drummed a pencil on the table. "Yeah, correct so far."

"Our records show 'em as Wang Jingwei and Sung Chiao; our sources say they're with the Taiwanese Intelligence Agency."

"Bureau, Taiwanese Intelligence *Bureau*. You've been doing your homework, Rogers. Well done. When you quit this kindergarten call me, we could use . . ."

"When did you last hear from either of these guys?"

"They were scheduled to go on a training exercise nine days back. Wang was a no show."

"Sung showed?"

"Yeah, he showed. He's on the exercise right now. Wang's not been heard from."

"Did you run a missing persons?"

"Missing persons? He's under fucking cover. If I ran a check on every agent who didn't report in, you'd fit me for a white jacket. Wang should've been on the exercise nine days back."

"So eh, he's been missing nine days?"

"Yeah, guess you could technically say that."

"You guess huh? Where do *you* think he is?"

"Shit happens, I truly can't say."

"The car at LAX was a loaner, a departmental backup car. Did you know that?"

"Of course I knew. We arranged the vehicle for him, a government car."

"So then, his car gets left at the terminal. I gotta assume he took a flight, you agree?"

"That's how it looks," Sam said. "Yeah, he could've taken a flight."

"Sam, this ain't root canal. Why do I have to squeeze you to get any help here? You're playing cat and mouse with me."

"For Christ's sake, Rogers, you know how Interpol operates; most of our shit's classified." He jabbed a finger at the cop sitting opposite. "You got fucking Billie Bob here with his finger on the button, recording this interrogation. I can claim immunity to any of this questioning." He leaked a dissident smile at the cop with his finger on the button. "You know that, right?"

Rogers sighed, slid the chair back, stood, paced around the room, turned and growled at the recorder cop, "Shut that fuckin' thing off!"

The cop pressed the button, turned the recorder face down.

"Sam, I appreciate your cooperation, and yes, I know

you've got immunity. I just hope you'll pitch in whatever you can."

He gave Rogers a long, unemotional look. *Just a cop doing his job*, he thought, not about to disclose information that might jeopardize the mission. This halted any further discussion regarding Sung and Wang.

Rogers stayed silent for so long Sam's ears began to ring. He eventually continued, "Forensics has given the thumbs-down on finding any prints, the car's been cleaned," Rogers said, shaking his head. "Whoever wanted that car cleaned did a near perfect job of it."

The room began to fill with negative uncooperative vibes as Sam took in the words, and watched as Rogers poured a glass of water from a decanter.

"A near perfect job," he said looking up, raising his glass. "except for one print, one print, Sam, on top of the passenger's door."

Again the pause. He took a long, slow drink, speaking with eyes down, "If you were to suspect . . ."

Another pause.

He placed a cigarette in his mouth, lit it. "Sam, if you were to suspect one person in your department of involvement, who would it be? And eh, of course, this is *off the record*."

Long pause.

Sam studied Rogers as he moved about the room, knew better than be drawn into a typical cop trap. He looked down for a moment, leaned forward and said in a sarcastic tone, "Off the record, yeah, right!"

Rogers sat on the table's edge immediately in front of Sam, leaned forward and jabbed a finger into Sam's chest. "Now you listen and you listen fuckin' good. I've had as much of your immunity bullshit as I can handle; you, the FBI, the CIA, and all of those *heads-up-their-ass* acronymic fuckin' departments."

Sam backed away from the finger, outstretched both hands with palms facing Rogers. "Hey, hey, hey, I know you're just doing your job, and no, I haven't any suspicions at this time, and sure there are some unanswered questions out there. If I give you a few names and you follow procedure, you'll pull them in for questioning. If you do that, a very important mission will be totally ruined; you won't need worry about the CIA, the FBI or our AID. Let me tell you why, Rogers," Sam snarled. "because you'll be directing fucking traffic downtown, that's why! And that'll be after Washington's done chewing off your balls."

Rogers concealed his resentment, a frigid moment that ended as the desk phone buzzed. "Yeah, yeah, when? Okay, be right there. Have the guys dust the table, there's gotta be prints." He disconnected the call, and dismissed the two cops. "Gotta get going," he said, "there's a possible lead on the car. Some diners at a restaurant in Chinatown reported overhearing an argument between two guys. One was Asian. I've a hunch it's your guy, Wang."

As Sam walked from the office and passed the desk sergeant, Rogers cocked his head, business-like. He placed a hand to his mouth, as though shielding what he was about to say from all but Sam. "For the record, that one small print they found, it belongs to your man, Adam McDowell."

Sam stared at the door ahead, said nothing. He digested the situation as he walked slowly to his car, buckled the seat belt, and pondered how he'd call off the dogs, just how far Rogers would push the inquiry. His cell phone buzzed, snapping him back to the present. "Yeah, this is Sam."

Blake's voice was angry, loud. "Sam!"

"Drew, what's up? You're supposed to be on Whitney. Is everything okay? You sound angry."

"Angry, Sam? I'm not sure where to start, but eh, yeah, ya could say I'm angry. In fact me and Dal are both very fuckin' angry."

"Okay, okay, steady down. Start at the top, what's put a bug up your ass?"

"A bug up my ass? If it were just a bug I'd be smilin'. Wang was a no show, Sung has no fuckin' idea why his buddy *is* a no show, and to top it all off, we ran into a little problem with some fuckin' lunatic up on Whitney. Sung and Paul are back up there waitin' for the local cops to sort out the whole clusterfuck."

"Take it easy. Where're you calling from?"

"At the house, in the foothills, at Francis's place."

*****

As Sam began the drive toward Chinatown, he briefed Blake over his cell, filling him in on the situation with Wang. "There's been a problem regarding Wang's disappearance," he said. "His car was found at LAX, was towed to impound and dusted. To cut a long story short . . ."

Five minutes later, "You're shittin' me, right?" Blake said. "The print was Adam's?"

"Possible scenario," Sam said, "Wang drove to the airport, Adam followed him, suspected he was meeting with someone, stumbled across something he wasn't meant to see, and then things got screwed up."

Blake exhaled into the phone. "Okay, my turn. Possible scenario, Adam drove Wang to the airport, him and Wang were forced, or agreed, whatever, to depart. One or the other, ain't sure yet which one. Anyway, they got on a plane and eh . . ." He paused, and Sam heard the shrug. "Then he just flew off."

"Okay, I'll buy that," Sam sighed, "but why?"

"I've no fuckin' idea, but it's just as crazy as your scenario. So where do we go from here?"

"You and Dal get back here pronto. Can you make it

here by tonight?"

"It'll take Francis six hours to get us there. Yeah, guess so, around ten."

"Jot this down, 6254 Wilshire. It's a coffee shop, the Café Latte. See you there at ten. If you get hung up, call me. And Drew, for God's sake, calm down."

"Sure Sam, we'll see you then. And eh, don't worry . . . we'll both be real fuckin' calm."

Father Francis laid out clean black hooded robes for both men and stood back admiring his protégés. "My goodness," he said, "you both look so much better after showering and trimming up those beards. I had quite a scare when you arrived back from the mountain."

Blake and Dal, still stiff from their record-setting descent of Whitney, appeared quite dapper in their black cassocks, hoods peaking on top of their heads, each with the prowess of Jedi Knights.

"Are we all set then, gentlemen?" Francis asked, as Blake and Dal took one last look at St. Bridget's through the back window of the jeep. "I am very proud of you both," he said looking in his rear view mirror. "Father Paul and Mr. Sung have done splendid work with your training. It is a sad thing that your predecessors were not as well prepared as yourselves." He took his right hand off the wheel and quickly blessed himself. "Yes, a most horribly sad thing," he added in a sorrowful tone.

Dal sensed his sadness and nudged Blake's arm. Blake peripherally caught the priest's eyes in the rear view mirror. He replied, "Yeah, a most horribly sad fuckin' thing."

"Right," Dal added, in a dull tone.

The priest asked, "Do I detect a note of dissatisfaction?"

"Aw, I wouldn't say a *note*," Blake said, "How about a symphony?"

"Yep," Dal said as he yawned and continued staring

out the window. "I'd go along with that, a cacophony."

The city blurred by, luminous hues, neon signage in the colors of an artist's palette as Dal began singing, "It's A Small World." The infectious melody replayed over and over in Blake's head until, unable to handle Dal's repetitious verses a moment longer, he said to the driver, "Can ya get us some decent music there, Padre?"

Francis punched the seek button and the radio finally settled on a soft jazz station. A few miles on it fell away to static, leaving the only sounds the occasional passing vehicle . . . and Dal's snoring.

The priest made one too many comments on the priesthood, then realizing this from the sound of Dal's snoring and Blake's grunting, accepted that it was time to drive rather than discuss their induction into the cloth. At twenty minutes after nine, the Cherokee pulled alongside the Café Latte.

"I will say goodbye to you here. I assume you will be in Mr. Ridkin's capable hands from this point on?"

"Yeah," Blake grunted, giving Dal a shake, "In Sam's capable hands."

Francis shook their hands, and Blake and Dal stepped from the jeep.

"Thanks, Francis, you've all been outstandin'," Blake said. "Can't say it was a pleasure, but it sure was memorable."

"Yeah, memorable stuff, Father," Dal added stretching, and making a face. "Take it easy, and have a safe drive home." Then in a whisper, "And say a few rosaries for us."

They entered the coffee shop to the sound of soft music, the chatter of diners, and the hiss of a steaming coffee machine. Silence hit the place as all eyes turned to analyze the two hooded figures, one with a dark groomed beard, the other a beard of golden blonde. The waiter sashayed between tables, gazing in disbelief at the two priests, his hair resembling a Mohawk headdress, a disheveled concoction that must have taken considerable time to create.

"Yes, Fathers, can I help you?" the young man with the spiked coif asked.

Dal whispered, "It ain't Halloween is it? We been gone that long, or what?"

He fought off the smile, avoided raising his eyes to the hairstyle. "A table for three," Blake said. "someplace quiet."

The Mohawk looked past the two priests, and said curiously, "Three?"

Dal half turned, glanced at Blake, who in turn looked back toward the entrance, sarcastically raising three fingers.

The waiter gave an unconcerned shrug. "Very well, follow me please."

They made their way to a table set back in the rear of the coffee shop; with lighting too dim for comfort, a darkness that increased the element of mystery accompanying the two hooded figures. Dal looked at the people seated about the café, nodding to those still staring. A few returned his nod, a show of respect for the two priests. Dal made a few quick blessings, reveling in the moment until Blake gave a quick jab to his side.

Once seated, the waiter nodded his head to Blake. "Would you like to order, Father?"

"Two cappuccinos."

"Of course, why not, two cappuccinos it is."

Dal leaned toward Blake. "Pretty cool, huh. Kinda feel like celebrity material."

"You got your hands in your pockets again," Blake said grinning. "Ya worry me when ya do that."

Sam Ridkin arrived at ten sharp. He strolled into the café, and was escorted to a table not far from where the two priests were seated, each working through coffee and biscotti. Dal placed a hand to his cheek, and without raising his eyes, whispered, "Sam just walked in."

En route to a table, Sam passed right by the two priests, nodded at them, but showed no sign of recognition.

"Can ya believe that?" Dal said quietly to Blake.

Blake chuckled, "Give him a few minutes."

Sam sneaked a quick glance at his watch, then at the door, and allowed five minutes to pass. He stood, left the table, walked to the front of the café and spoke to the Mohawk. "Have you had a couple of guys arrive in the past half hour or so?"

The Mohawk thought for a few seconds. "Mostly couples. Oh yeah, and the two priests."

Sam's eyes widened, "Two priests?"

Without turning, the waiter flicked a thumb over his shoulder. "Those two guys back there. We don't often attract the ecumenical council."

Sam thought, *smart-ass little fuck*, but said, "Point well taken," and made his way to the rear. He pulled a chair, shifting his gaze from one to the other, then exclaimed, "Jesus Christ!"

"Close," Blake snarled. "very fuckin' close!"

CHAPTER 16

DAL PLACED A RESTRAINING hand on Blake's arm, and shot a penetrating stare at Sam.

"Hope the adventure wasn't too harrowing for the two of you."

"Harrowin'?" Dal replied sardonically. "Harrowin'?" He flicked his eyes to Blake, repeated, "Harrowin? Would *you* call it that, Father Bond . . . *harrowin'*?"

Sam cleared his throat, placed his index finger inside the neck of his shirt, and stretched the collar as though the tie were a hangman's noose. "Listen guys, I'm sorry it went a bit tougher than expected, what with the killings on the mountain, and Sung having to hang back to take care of the mess."

They shook their heads and muttered a few *fucks* and *bullshit*, meaningful words to that effect.

"Really!" Blake said softly. "Yeah, I'd say it was harrowin'. We're lucky we're not back there as accessories."

Sam placed his head in his hands, shook it slowly from side to side.

Blake leaned in closer. "What happened to Wang?"

Sam's eyes scanned the coffee shop, uncomfortable with the close proximity of other patrons. Blake leaned even nearer, giving an abbreviated compact blessing. "That make ya feel any better, Chief?" Aware of the quieter atmosphere, he jabbed a thumb over his shoulder, gesturing at curious customers. "Ya see 'em? They all think I've been hearin' your confession." And he leaned just a little more into Sam, leaned to his ear and whispered, "You cocksucker!"

Sam stammered, "Look guys, I had you meet me here because I wasn't real sure your cover was safe."

It was a poor attempt.

Failed miserably.

"There's been a problem with Adam and Wang; it seems there might be collusion, a mole in the Division."

"Who?" Blake asked.

"Mc Dowell might be playing both sides."

And this put a few points on Sam's side of the balance sheet.

The darker complexioned of the two priests relaxed his demeanor a little, showing less aggression, backing off from Sam and glancing at Dal, then back at Sam. "I ain't sure how to take that," Blake said. "Adam's been your man for so long, involved with all the operations, could've sold us out a shitload of times, why wait 'til now?"

"I don't have the answer, could've been solidifying his credibility in the Division, waiting for the really big fish to go for the hook."

The two Jedi Knights stared with incredulity at the Morgan Freeman look-a-like. Sam had missed shaving for a few days and his wiry salt and pepper beard added to his wild Afro-American rugged good looks. Little else was said for several minutes. Sam gestured toward the door, left a bill on the table and the three departed.

*****

The drive from the café passed with little conversation. Sam drove to a Holiday Inn Express just off the I-405, in close proximity to Van Nuys Airport. "Think about this," he said, "the Chinese have advanced methods to make a man spill his guts. The Nazis had nothing compared to Beijing. The less any of you guys know, the less Beijing can get out of you if they get their hands on you."

"Ya mean like MK-ULTRA," Dal said, "the shit the CIA used on that Frank Olsen guy in Manhattan?"

"Yeah, the Chinese have ways to get you talking; ways that make MK- ULTRA feel like a day at Disneyland."

They pulled into the hotel.

"I've a room registered here under SoCal Exports," Sam said, pointing toward the lobby. "I've extra clothing for both of you, and eh, a bunch of other stuff you'll need."

They waited in the car as Sam checked them in. A few minutes later he returned. "Father Francis called me after you got underway with your climb, briefed me on your progress. He said your Latin had gone really well."

They dragged the luggage from the trunk and headed through the lobby.

"All the necessary documentation's done," Sam said, "we just need passports. We'll take care of those in the morning."

"Can't wait to get to the hot shower," Dal said, "and have some room service."

Sam called a nearby restaurant, ordered dinner. Forty-five minutes later a pizza arrived, and Sam watched in amusement as the two, well versed in etiquette and protocol, unleashed voracious appetites . . . with etiquette and protocol dying a swift death.

*****

The morning marked the beginning of a long day in Van Nuys. At nine o'clock, a Chinese interviewer from the American Interpol Division's security section grilled both priests mercilessly. Sam absorbed the inquisition with much satisfaction as both men went through a non-stop barrage of questions, similar, Sam mused, to what they might encounter in China . . . if they were interrogated. At four o'clock, the interviewer smiled broadly at Sam. "They're absolutely convincing," he said. "Congratulations, good luck."

He gave a thumbs up to the two priests, and as he stepped from the room Dal couldn't resist calling, "God bless ya, my son."

Two minutes after he'd gone another knock had Blake and Dal's attention. Sam opened the door and a bulbous man wearing a priest's collar and a poorly fitted black suit entered. He flashed a satirical glance at the two cloaked men. "So then, these are your Salesians?"

Blake stiffened as the priest made his way to a table and opened a brown leather carry bag.

"Who's this clown?" Blake whispered, still eyeing the bulbous man.

"Please gentlemen, be seated."

Another knock.

A tall thin man stood beaming at Sam, a stark contrast to the priest seated inside.

"I'm meetin' more people here than at a Kiwanis fuckin' convention," Blake said. "What's goin' on?"

"Hello Sam, been a while," the thin man said.

"Louis. Come on in, this won't take long."

The thin man tripped into the room, and nodded to the dark suited priest seated at the table. His eyes remained on the priest as he said, "Hello Fathers," and he whispered, "Hey Sam, it's a conclave. It's like, where's the white smoke?" Then pointing at Dal, "Okay, so who'm I shootin' first?"

Dal and Blake sat for their photographs, and within five minutes, Louis said goodbye, and left the room.

"Next time, Louis," Sam said, and closed the door behind him.

"Let's get underway," the solemn priest said, looking

at his watch in a business-like manner. He pulled a book from his bag, faced the two bearded men and said, "Each in turn will reply in Latin." He raised his eyes to each, adding in a consoling tone, "If you don't mind, of course." The priest quizzed the two men for forty-five minutes, after which he accepted their Latin skills. "They're acceptable, their knowledge appears adequate."

He shook hands with each man, bidding Sam farewell. As he stepped toward the door, Blake called, "Father, please, one thing before ya leave, can we have a blessin'?"

Facing the two and slotting into a most solemn demeanor, he gave an inspiring Latin blessing.

"Well done guys," Sam said. "Impressive, to say the least."

"Yeah well," Dal said with a portentous smirk, "we really worked hard at it."

"I'll second that," Blake added. "But I feel a bit lucky. He picked the verses I really worked on."

"I hope your luck holds up," Sam said with a sardonic grin. "I'll see you boys at nine in the morning. I'll have the final documents, we'll go over the game plan."

"Sam," Blake said, "have ya heard from Sung?"

"He'll join us tomorrow. Paul stayed back to tidy up a few formalities. He and Sung are entitled to a reward for holding that guy on the mountain."

Dal groaned, "Aw shit."

"Murphy's Law," Blake grumbled.

Sam's eyes took on a self-satisfied smirk. He stood in the doorway and spoke without turning. "And the guy that just blessed you, he ain't a priest."

CHAPTER 17

AN ABILITY TO RECALL the minutest detail was among Slade's most valuable assets. But now, the nightmares, the horror of the past two weeks, the loss of Mike Carver, the killings at Penghu had turned his prodigious memory to one of torment.

On his arrival in Houniugang, a murmur of astonishment crept into his demeanor. He didn't need look far to realize the increase in troop activity.

Struggling to keep his breathing and heart rate in check as a splash of blood seeped through his dressing, Slade's cognizance of the wound contributed to a slight limping gait. Lee Hua turned out to be more than just a young priest, he and the doctor had created a hideaway even the best eyes couldn't find, unless of course they brought along sniffer dogs. But there were no dogs. Poverty and the number of mouths to feed was bad news for the dog population of rural China.

Lee asked, "Thlade, can you try to walk?"

Slade was beginning to feel weak and despite self affirmation, his psychiatric self talk was spreading thin.

"I'll have to walk. Can you get me a stick?"

"A thtick?"

"To help me walk."

"Oh yeth, a clutch, you need a clutch?"

Slade looked gaunt and weary but managed a grin, "Yeah, Lee, a crutch."

The doctor brought a basin of hot water and began changing the dressing, carefully sponging the wound, and when the hole around the entry point resembled a small pencil sized opening, he leaned back and admired his work, his smile exuding self-satisfaction. "It looks much better," he said, giving a gentle pat to Slade's head.

Lee returned, carrying an antique walking crutch that could've belonged to Moses. He leaned over Slade, placing the stick alongside the red tinged water bowl. "When it dark, we go that way," he said, pointing in a southerly direction.

"Where exactly do we go?"

"We go to Xi'an."

"Xi'an?"

"Bithop Bolin, he hath plan for you, you have help in Xi'an."

"What help, Lee?"

"Help from uncle."

"Uncle?"

"Your uncle Tham, he thent help for you."

Slade propped himself up, raising a weary pair of eyes. "Tham?" he groaned. "You mean, Sam, Uncle Sam, like U.S.A.?"

"That what I thay, your uncle Tham."

Slade went quiet for a moment, wondering who was coming, how experienced they'd be.

"It get dark thoon," Lee said, pointing at the window. "When dark, we go."

The young priest changed his outfit, slipped into a black robe, a hood covering his head, and in his hands was a neatly folded black outfit. "Bithop Bolin tell me it better you wear robe."

Inspired by the young man's support and guidance, the inspiration was quickly eroded by the thought of having to dress as a priest. But then he thought, *what the hell, whatever works*, and changed into the cassock. There was a micro flicker of embarrassment as he tenuously viewed himself in a wall-mirror. "I'll wear the gown, Lee, but the boots stay on," Slade grunted, gesturing at a pair of Roman sandals, and wagging a finger. "I'm not wearing those sandals."

Sometime after sunset, it began to rain. They bid farewell to the doctor and headed off south as heavy drops saturated their hoods, causing discomfort to Slade's injury. Lee avoided the regular route, suspecting military or Chinese Police could very likely be randomly patrolling main roads in search of drug runners. They hiked for three hours until Slade needed rest. Lee suggested a covered slope beneath an overpass, and it was here both men eventually drifted into sleep, under the Chinese sky.

By the rice fields.

*****

The sound of a crowing rooster was welcomed by Slade; he rolled to one side, groaned as he propped himself up and turned toward where the priest had been sleeping.

Lee was gone.

He felt a sense of urgency, and called softly, "Lee, Lee?"

When there was no response, with a heightened sense of caution, he called a little louder, "Lee!"

But Lee was nowhere to be seen and Slade didn't feel safe calling any louder. He listened for sounds, heard running water, and limped in the direction of the sound.

The voice came from beyond a slope directly ahead. "Morning to you. I have food."

"Lee. Thank the Lord! Where'd you get this?"

Lee crouched down and spread a checkered cloth. "I am a prietht, village people give me food."

Slade hesitated as Lee laid out the food, thought he heard a voice in the distance, paused, heard nothing, and began demolishing the chicken.

The young boy on the bicycle was shouting as he approached from the north, "Father Lee, Father Lee!"

When he'd regained his breath, the two chatted for a few minutes while Slade finished off the last of the food.

"Thlade, we go from here, thith boy come from Bithop. Tholdierth come here, they looking for you, we go back to Beijing, we mutht go around them. Go back to thafe houth, near Beijing."

The return journey to Beijing covered rough terrain and Slade struggled to stay with Lee as he moved along like a man on a mission.

"Lee! How much further?"

"Not far, we go to houth not far from Bithop Bolin."

A well-dressed man in his forties welcomed them, quickly closed the door and escorted them to a rear room where two children sat at a Play Station console. They were totally absorbed playing Onimura, Dawn of Dreams. The screen showed a Japanese warrior fighting the evil Hideyoshi and Genma forces. Slade recognized the game because his own son had spent hours fighting the same evil forces.

He nodded at the players, gave a friendly smile, pointing at the monitor as the boy gave a peripheral glance sideways, reluctant to move his concentration from the action. The boy said, "Me, Hideyashu."

He nodded at the warrior. "Me, Ohatsu," said the small girl, her eyes not moving from the screen.

Their father laughed and nodded graciously toward a settee opposite the large TV screen. "Please, make yourselves comfortable. My children play this game very well."

Impressed with his English language skill, Slade commented, "Your English is outstanding."

"Thank you. My name is David Leung."

"Your English is excellent. Where'd you study?"

"I was a professor in California for three years, I taught Chinese at UCLA."

"What are you doing here?"

"I came for the food."

Slade acknowledged the man's attempt at humor. "Yeah me too, beats Panda Express."

"Panda Express?"

Slade locked his fingers and looked amused, realizing his humor had failed to register. But Leung nodded confirmation. "You'll rest here tonight. Tomorrow, Father Lee will accompany you to the rail station in Beijing where you'll board a train to Datong."

"How far off's that? And eh . . . why Datong?"

"Would you like tea?" Leung asked, pouring a cup for himself and Lee.

"Yeah sure, thanks."

Leung stepped to an old record player, selected a 45 RPM recording and placed it on the revolving rubber surface. "This is my favorite aria, Madame Butterfly," and he lowered the needle, one track across, turned about and smiled in a melancholy way. "I adore the work of Giacomo Puccini. Butterfly is so different, so intimate, not far removed from my own life, Mr. Slade. Devoid of spectacle, in the same way my work confines me to this house, Butterfly is completely confined to a similar house . . . but in Nagasaki of course." He stopped, waved a flowing hand to the music, then sipped on his tea. "As Captain Pinkerton pursued the fifteen year old Butterfly, I too must pursue a successful end to my mission here in China. My dream is to return with my family to America, and as with Pinkerton pursuing the young geisha, Cio-Cio San, I must pursue my dream even though I may damage my own wings."

The music filled the room, capturing the feelings of love, of yearning, of pain. Slade sat with eyes closed, inhaling the ambiance as the aria raised the entire experience to the realm of unimaginable art, becoming transcendently moving.

Leung raised his voice above the soprano. "There's a man in Datong who's expecting you; he has a small antiquities business, specializing in rare Chinese statuary. When you arrive, the reason for your visit will be clear. You and Father Lee each have a duffel bag containing all the clothing and personal effects you'll require for your journey. You've a room reserved in the names of Fathers Lee and Mathew, and in the morning I'll have your travel documents with your photographs. You'll be Salesian priests, and Mr. Slade, be sure to keep your head bowed and covered." Leung moved a teacup to Slade. "Once you arrive, take a taxi from the station to the Garden Hotel at 59 Danang Street. They're accustomed to Salesian guests, you'll not raise suspicion."

He reached into a cupboard, brought out a Polaroid camera.

His smile was not unlike that of the Mona Lisa, a smile that left Slade wondering what passed through Leung's mind.

"Please, Father Mathew," Leung said. "Smile at the camera."

He took the photos, placing them to one side as the images materialized on the white Polaroid background. Lee had remained with the children, fascinated at their game skills.

"Father Lee, please, time for your photograph."

"Am I permitted to know the rest of this eh, plan?" Paul Slade asked.

"The information you've taken from Chengdu must leave China at any price. I've been instructed to provide certain items in order to get you to Datong. Once you arrive at the Garden Hotel, you'll find you are registered as Fathers Mathew and Lee." He poured more tea into his cup, looked at Lee, who nodded, and he topped up the young priest's cup. "You'll then visit Wei Yidui's antiquities shop in Datong."

It had been thought best that information regarding

Yidui's skullduggery be kept from David Leung. That was a
card best kept for bigger fish. Yidui, Broski's team believed,
may be part of a far larger picture. For now, best Leung
remain oblivious to any sting operation on Yidui, lest it
compromise Sam's team . . . as well as Slade's extraction.

"More tea, Mr. Slade?"

Slade placed a hand over his cup, waving away the
top-up. "Go on, I need to hear all of this."

"In Datong you'll collect an exquisite statue known
as a Tara. A replica of this Tara has been sent to an associate
who'll carry out her part of this mission. She'll deliver it into
the hands of a Beijing double-agent."

"The agent's a woman?"

"Her name's Lisa Ling. That's all that I'm able
to divulge. I'm only fed one mouthful at a time. If I'm
interrogated, I've no knowledge of the operation for authorities to extract. But I'll add this; we do have a backup plan
operating at a location near Datong."

"A backup plan, hmm . . . I darn well hope so. Would
you expand on that?"

"Not at this time. Best you have as little information
as possible. If we have any hiccups along the way, we'll
attempt to implement that plan."

"What am I doing with the statue?"

"It's a game of crisscross, similar to the parlor trick,
knowing which cup the pea is under. You'll get the statue
back to your country at any cost. If you're apprehended and
searched, or even robbed, it's highly unlikely this particular
statue would be considered valuable to thieves."

Slade glanced at David Leung, nodded in a pensive
way, appreciating the risk the man was taking, the danger his
family was placed due to his 'tenure.' With the pensive look,
Slade said, "Stay safe, David. Good luck, huh."

"We make our own luck, Mr. Slade."

The following day, Lee and Slade boarded the train.

CHAPTER 18

THE OVERNIGHT TRAIN DEPARTED Beijing at ten after eleven. It would travel a distance of two hundred and sixty kilometers, arriving in Datong a little before eight o'clock the following morning. Lee passed Slade an apologetic look, finding a hard wooden seat by a window for what would be a most uncomfortable eight hour journey, passing through the Juyong Pass and Badaling Grottoes in the inner Great Wall, and winding its way slowly through the Yanmen Pass.

An acrid odor caught Slade's attention as he peered from the window. He looked about, slyly sniffed at his armpit and found the source. "Lee, I'm going to the bathroom."

Lee nodded, pointing to the doorway at the end of the carriage. The walk to the bathroom gave Slade a chance to stretch his legs, and offered a welcome reprieve from the hard wooden seat. He weaved his way between sleeping passengers, bare feet extending beyond the ends of the seats, the longer legs impeding his passage. He reached the men's toilet, pushed the door open, found the stench totally unbearable and quickly jerked away. Better prepared, he took a deep breath, dashed in, held his breath long enough to get through a very forced pee, stepped out of the small lavatory, and walked right into the arms of the soldier waiting to enter. Slade instinctively dropped his eyes, and turned his face away, hoping the hood would amply disguise his Caucasian looks.

His attempt failed.

The soldier jabbed his automatic weapon into Slade's stomach, demanding, "Papers!"

He ignored the demand, keeping his eyes lowered, and tried to pass on by. Aggravated by his silence, the man became more vigilant. He repeated, "Papers!"

In an inaudible tone, "I don't understand."

This added to the soldier's displeasure. He grabbed hold of Slade's shoulder, spinning him around and shoving him hard against the toilet door. With his forearm pressed across the priest's throat, he propped his weapon on the opposite wall, kicking Slade's feet apart, and grinned like a Cheshire cat, running his hands under the priest's robe. He edged them up the priest's bare legs, not stopping until he reached his crotch. Slade flinched, feeling violated as the soldier's hands lingered a little too long. "You fuck!" he snapped. "Hey, hey, hey, cut it out!"

The shock at such an aggressive reaction from a priest sent the soldier stumbling backward. He reached for the M16 and Slade reached for the man's head and placed one arm around his face and quickly whipped his head to the right and there was a cracking noise and the soldier was deceased.

He shuffled the man into the rest room, propping him on the seat. Looking each way along the passageway, he scooped up the M16, placed it alongside the soldier and closed the door. *I can't leave the body. If anyone comes to use the toilet they'll raise hell. I gotta stay at the door, make out like I'm waiting to use the toilet. It can't be too long before Lee comes looking for me.*

Lee's concern over Slade's absence eventually prompted him into making the walk to the far end of the carriage.

"Well it's about time," Slade said leaning against the door. "We've got a big fucking problem."

Lee grinned at the profanity and quickly dismissed it, assuming the toilet was occupied. He pointed further along, toward the preceding carriage. "There ith another toilet in next carriage. Why you wait here, why you not go there?"

Slade opened the door a few inches, sufficient for Lee to see the man slumped on the seat. Confused and wondering why Slade was spying on the man, Lee took a second look, said, "He having a problem?"

"*Him having a problem?* Yeah . . . him fucking dead."

"Him dead? How him dead?"

"Don't ask," Slade said, as Lee held onto his '*what happened*' expression, shrugging with both hands palms up.

"We need to get him off the train, and quickly."

Lee raised a hand. "I muth remove hith name and paperth."

He opened the door, and quickly stepped into the small space.

While Lee attended to the occupant, another soldier made his way toward Slade, still leaning against the door as though waiting his turn. Slade tapped on the door with his boot, he whispered, "Soldier's coming. Stay quiet."

The soldier looked at his watch, and pointed to the toilet. Slade shrugged as though annoyed at the long wait. The soldier shook his head and returned in the direction from which he'd come. Slade cracked the door, "Jesus, Lee, how much longer?"

Lee groaned, "Ith it thafe for me to come out?"

Slade opened the door, and Lee, gasping for fresh air, leaped from the small room.

"Oh," Lee gasped, rolling his eyes and waving his hands about. "It very bad," and he furiously nodded his head toward the toilet.

"Yeah, an air freshener wouldn't even be a winner."

Lee made a quizzical expression. "No, not thmell.

Thith tholdier, he belong to 13th Army, General Cheng, he ith the one who ith looking hard for you. The tholdier you killed back in village wath the thon of general, he wath Captain David Cheng."

"Cheng's son was one of those guys? I don't believe it. Aw shit!"

The young priest blessed himself, groaning, "Yeth . . . thit."

Slade slid down the wall, staring at the door of the lavatory, deep in thought for many seconds. "Okay. We need to get him off the train. Can you open that window? There's nothing but rocks and fields, can't do it near any villages. We'll wait until the moon's behind the clouds."

He sat with the M16 straddled across his knees and remained in a pensive mood for a long minute, gesturing with his chin in the direction the train was heading.

"Yeth, we mutht wait, there ith a bridge coming thoon."

"A bridge, how far?"

"Thoon."

"How soon?"

"Very thoon."

Lee unlatched the window, gave it a firm tug and raised it a few feet. The chilled night air ripped at his face as he stretched his head out, staring into the darkness, wind billowing the hood back until it flapped about like an angry spinnaker. He turned, made certain the carriageway was clear, and opened the toilet door. They dragged the soldier from the toilet, lifted him, and positioned him with his upper body hanging from the train.

Slade's eyes alighted on a woman who'd turned the corner. They stood frozen, Slade's eyes zapping to the left, to the right. She was moving quickly, striding toward the lavatory, was right there, right on top of them before Slade had time to assess the situation. Lee turned to the woman, gesturing at the soldier. "He ate thomething that did not agree with him. He not well," and then turning away, making out like he was comforting the poor soul hanging from the window, he added, "He ith a very thick man."

The woman surveyed the scene and Slade recognized the body language, caught the disbelief in her eyes. *If she goes into the lavatory,* he thought*, she lives. If not . . .*

She chose poorly.

She turned and began a shuffling sprint back to the passenger cabin. Slade released his grip on the soldier, took a few leaping steps, reached the woman's head, grabbed it, snapped it.

She didn't see death coming.

Her train ride had ended.

Lee was oblivious to the woman's demise. He hung from the window, the wind flapping his cheeks. He squinted ahead, searching out the bridge, then shouted, "Bridge!" The interior noise of the carriage intensified as the train rattled over loose tracks ahead of the suspension bridge.

Slade thought, *show time*, and shouted at Lee, "Now!"

They pushed the man over the ledge, watching as he disappeared into the darkness, maybe into water far below. Lee's eyes followed the body as Slade tugged on the priest's shoulder, flicking a thumb and saying, "Now her."

Lee swiveled about, surprised to see the woman propped against the wall. He asked, "Why ith woman there?"

"Had to do it, she saw our faces, had no choice, I'm sorry, Lee."

Lee blessed himself, then gave the woman a blessing in Latin. "May God forgive uth."

"Yeah, amen," Slade added in a rushed and not too solemn tone.

They hoisted the woman, and in one action shoved

her body, head first, from the train and into the dark beyond the bridge. Lee allowed three minutes to pass, and then threw the soldier's tags into the night. Slade glanced over his shoulder at Lee, wondering if the young priest could ever salvage sufficient Godliness to move beyond the trauma of that evening. He placed a hand on Lee's shoulder. "Forget it happened," he said to Lee. " We need to get our asses off this train real quick."

"Yeth, very thoon."

They returned to their seats, collected their duffel bags and began a slow self-conscious trek toward the rear carriage. As the train raced down a slight incline, a sudden jolt threw Lee against a pair of bootless feet hanging obstructively over the walkway. The owner of the feet grunted, raised his head at the priest, and gave him a look of discontent. Lee nodded apologetically, but his concern was quickly overruled by a sharp jab to his lower back as Slade leaned into his ear.

"I forgot the M16, left it back at the lavatory."

Lee's eyes locked on Slade's, frozen as each imagined the worst, *shouts from troops with weapons jabbing menacingly at all non-military passengers. The two priests, legs spread.* When the frozen moment had passed, they made a quick turnabout and moved back to retrieve the M16.

"Thank Christ," Slade said as he opened the door and found the weapon standing where he'd left it. He checked the carriageway, no one coming.

Checked the clip.

Full.

Lee gave a questioning look as Slade went through the weapon check, got a reassuring nod as Slade slipped the M16 under his robe and the two priests began their brisk walk toward the rear of the train. They slowed their pace, slower, slower, appearing priestly, nodding, smiling, looking calm. They passed more soldiers trying to grab some sleep, stretched out on hard wooden seats, their boots kicked into the aisle, toes protruding through socks long past their expiration date. Lee's pace was a model of how a priest should walk; it was a reverent stroll with a certain relaxed holy demeanor, as he freely nodded to the occasional passenger, throwing out a sporadic, *In nominee Patris.*

When they arrived at the rear of the train, Slade leaned out the final window, tucked back his hood, and called to Lee, "Jesus Christ, I'm dying here. I worked up a sweat while you blessed your way through fifteen fucking carriages."

They stared at the wooden rail-ties; mesmerized by the clickety-clack sound of the train passing over and Slade timed the sound. *If only the speed were slower.* After several worrying minutes, he realized the counting had in fact become slower, the intensity of the wind against his face gentler, the train was indeed slowing.

"Now!" Slade shouted, "Jump!"

And it all happened so quickly.

Slade threw the M16 and duffel bag, and both men leaped from the train, with Slade landing on a slope to the right of the track and Lee crashing down behind him, each going into a seemingly endless roll, both finally coming to a stop in a soft field alongside a near-dry creek. Some minutes later, Slade came out of a daze and laid motionless, listening to the raspy voice a few yards from him.

"We very lucky," Lee said, gazing at the stars.

Slade caught the gaze, felt his boot and checked for damage. "Yeah, very, *very* lucky," he said in a pained way.

Lee collected the two duffel bags as Slade retrieved the M16, holding the weapon up to Lee with a self-gratifying smile.

And the walk began.

"You know where we're going?"

"Datong. We go on buth."

Slade walked along behind, unsure what Lee had said, stumbling in the darkness as clouds rolled across the moon, causing the light to cut in and out. He pressed the button on his Casio, illuminating the dial, almost four o'clock. *Daylight in two hours*, he thought. *Shit! When the guy on the train is reported missing, they'll start searching the track.*

Lee picked up the pace. "The buth path thith way at ten o'clock."

"Buth . . . you mean *a bus*?"

"Yeth!" He snapped in a frustrated way. "The buth to Datong."

The fucker does have a plan, Slade thought with a grin. *We're getting onto a bus, great!*

They continued along the side of a long dirt road, and Slade felt as though he'd walked twenty miles as the sun broke above the horizon.

Lee pointed toward the southeast, "That ith way to Datong."

Slade threw the M16 into scrub by the roadside, and caught the appreciative smile on Lee's face. He was about to suggest a rest break when Lee jubilantly pointed to a slow vehicle topping the rise. He waved it down and the two stepped aboard. Passengers nodded at the hooded men as they made their way to a seat in the rear – swathing a path through a cloud of cigarette smoke.

It was cramped, hot, and the stench of body odor added a fine patina of steam to the windows. The smell of feathers provided a unique touch to the interior ambiance of the bus. A cackling woman, suspicious of the two cloaked figures, secured her hold on a red and black feathered rooster. A well dressed man, *a touritht*, Lee thought, *maybe thome offithial with the Thtate Department*, handed Lee a bank note, and the priest graciously bowed his head, accepting the donation. It was local currency known as renminbi, and both men knew this would be the most common type of currency they'd encounter in Datong.

They took a seat in the rear of the bus, across from a

round faced, cigar smoking man. The round faced man made it a point to ignore the two arrivals. Slade leaned into Lee and gestured at a copy of a newspaper that lay in the aisle. Lee whispered, "You pretend to read newthpaper."

The bureaucratic looking man had now shifted his attention to the two priests. He stood and walked to the rear, sidling alongside Lee. "Father, I am Lieu. I have a favor to ask. I have a business near the cathedral. I have seen you at the Xishiku and have heard Bishop Bolin has been apprehended, that he was injured. Do you have word of him?"

Slade kept his face in the newspaper, wondering where the discussion was heading, didn't have a long wait long for the answer. When the bus pulled into a cluster of buildings, the man stood, gave a half-bow and exited.

"What's all that about?"

"He ith Mr. Lieu, local bithneth man, thay bithop taken to General Cheng headquarterth, he thay bithop injured, that many troop looking for an American."

"You think he'll have troops outside of the city area?"

"I not think," Lee said yawning. "He thay many are on way to Chengdu, they think American will ethcape to Taiwan."

"Good, they went for it."

David Leung had given each of the priests five hundred Yuan in foreign exchange certificates, the equivalent to one thousand American dollars, which would work fine in the hotel, and most tourist spots, but not on the street. The renminbi would be more accepted by the average person, many of whom had never seen nor heard of a foreign exchange certificate.

"He gave you renminbi," Slade said. "He must be leaving China."

Lee nodded *yes*, impressed that Slade knew the street money could only be used in provincial areas. If a traveler had renminbi remaining when leaving China, the currency would make a great bookmark.

On arrival at the Garden Hotel on Danang Street, Lee stood at the desk and spoke with the clerk who looked at them briefly and scanned a monitor. "Ah yes, welcome, Father Mathew and Father Lee. Check-in time is not until two o'clock.

"Pleath, can we have the room thooner?" Lee asked smiling reverently, then turned to Slade and whispered, "Room, it ith not ready."

Mildly set back, Slade had to think for a moment, strolling away from the desk, head bowed as though in prayer. After a minute, he moved his eyes across the wall, to the corners of the ceiling, scanning, searching out cameras, paranoid that perhaps they were being monitored. He moved back to the reception desk, again with eyes down, head bowed, his hood totally obscuring his face. Although unable to understand the discussion, he followed the body language, and assumed the tapping on the watch by Lee indicated the discussion rotated around the check in problem.

The man hesitated, caught Slade's eyes as the hood momentarily slipped back enough to reveal the ruggedly handsome Westerner. His expression showed mild surprise as Slade subtly pulled the hood back into place. Without further conversation the clerk passed a key card across the desk. "For the church, Father, I will give you the room early."

When they closed their room door, Slade threw himself onto the bed, and shouted into the pillow, "Thank you Jesus!"

Lee moved to the bathroom, closed the door, and mumbled, "Amen."

Early the following morning they headed off to meet with the antique dealer whose store was in a busy area on the outskirts of the city, surrounded by similar furniture shops and curio stores, a sign in Chinese, English, and French hanging above the door. Lee tapped on the leaded window and within seconds a diminutive, insecure looking man in his mid thirties unlocked the door and extended a warm greeting to the two priests. His hair appeared to be lacquered black, with a center part, his oak brown eyes sat above a sharp nose and a mouth that looked like it could double for a storage room. Slade saw him as an Asian Joe. E. Brown.

"Fathers, I am Wei Yidui. Welcome, I have been expecting you."

"I am Father Lee, and thith ith Father Mathew."

Yidui's English was surprisingly good, and Lee kept the conversation in English, which pleased Slade.

"Please, come this way," he said in a gracious manner, and gestured to a room at the rear of the overly stocked antique store. Slade took a minute to take in the intriguing statuary, carvings, and fine antique furniture. He nodded to Lee, showing his appreciation of the inventory.

Yidui tipped his head toward a church pew. "Be seated."

He pointed to Slade's boot and turned to a small tool kit. "Please remove your boot."

Slade contemplated the request. "My boot, why?"

Lee attempted to explain. "It ith thafe. Bithop Bolin hath order from your Uncle, take Thlade to Yidui, the Bithop ith aware of what you carry in your boot, he thed you must have it in thafer plath, Uncle Tham and Bithop planned thith."

Slade felt a sense of relief at no longer needing to continually check the status of his heel. "Okay," he said. "What's he gonna do with the flash drive?"

"You will thee."

Wei Yidui opened the tool kit, removed a metal ring that held several keys. He chose one, walked to a deep red cabinet, removed an object in a sealed box and placed the box on the table. Slade was intrigued by the manner in which

Yidui handled the content, inferring it was something special, an item of great value. He gently unwound the red velvet, removed the golden statue and placed it on the cloth.

Slade stared at the exquisite eight-inch tall work of art. He reached across, turned the statue to face him. "That's one great looking piece." He noticed the base had been neatly removed, and the missing section had been separately wrapped in tissue. He pointed at the hole in the base. "Be a lot better if it wasn't mutilated. What is it?"

Yidui leaned back in his chair and motioned at the statue. There was a brief silence during which he gave the crown of the figure a caressing rub with a polishing cloth. "It is a golden Tara, a very important piece of Chinese history. There are many duplicates for the tourist market, but serious collectors look for the artisan's skillful hand." He raised the Tara, fondled it, treating it with respect. "The better reproductions bring a hefty premium," Yidui said. "This is an exquisite example. I am going to remove the flash drive from your heel, and seal it inside the statue. This is why the base has been removed. I will place it into the Tara and replace the original base in such a way it will be undetectable."

The golden Tara was a collector's piece, and from the moment Paul Slade laid eyes on it, he knew that by mission's end the Tara would be added to his collection. Yidui removed the heel from Slade's boot, extracted the flash drive and rested it on a porcelain plate. He placed a jeweler's loupe to his eye, showing concern as he inspected a slight stain on the drive's metallic casing.

Slade restrained himself during the inspection, then after a protracted pause, asked Yidui, "What's up?"

"This stain . . ." And he gently pinpointed it with a needle like tool, "I believe it is blood."

Slade tightened up, bit his lower lip. "I was in a rush," he said. "These two guards jumped me. Guess there was a bit of blood flying. Not a problem though, right?"

Yidui passed a look to Slade, then glanced at Lee. "No, not a problem at all." Slade gave an apologetic shrug as Yidui refocused on the drive. "I will clean it a little." Yidui carefully removed the stain and sealed the flash drive into the base of the statue. Twenty-five minutes later, he handed the Tara to Slade with the base carefully welded and scuffed so that it appeared aged.

"Looks like new."

Yidui's reply came with a self-satisfied smile. "For your sake," he grinned, "I hope not."

CHAPTER 19

CATHAY PACIFIC ANNOUNCED ITS final boarding call. With forty minutes to spare, Wang again opened McDowell's note, stared at the number, walked to the nearest pay phone, and punched in the digits. He got as far as the middle number, slowed, and stared at the paper. *Something isn't right*, he thought. *Why is the number scribbled on notepaper, why not a business card?* The thought passed through his mind repeatedly, but the relevance of McDowell's scribbled note eluded him. *He gave me a scrap of paper?* He stopped punching buttons, placed the hand-piece back on the wall set, backed away from the phone, picked up his one piece of carry-on luggage and began walking to the security checkpoint. As he passed a trashcan he crumpled the paper, threw it in.

He liked airports; enjoyed the atmosphere, the people, the faces, savored the aroma of jet fuel wafting through the air, the uncertainty of delays adding a touch of anticipation, of gambling. Betting was in his genes, he was born with a desire to play the odds. If the flight is on time you win, if not . . .

Four security personnel stood in a line and cast suspicious eyes on luggage sliding through the x-ray unit. Wang passed inspection, collected his bag, and proceeded to the gate designated for flight 883. It was now eleven o'clock. In fifteen hours and thirty minutes his Cathay Pacific jet would touch down in China. He placed a pillow against the headrest and stared mindlessly from the window of the plane, pondered McDowell's reaction to not receiving the phone call. As passengers filled seats, he unbuckled, walked to the lavatory, washed his hands, and leaned into the mirror. "Wang, something does not feel good," he said to himself. "You have forfeited control over your destiny. Where do you go from here?"

His self analysis was cut short by a soft tapping on the door. "Please return to your seat. We're preparing for departure."

The flight attendant was young and far more attractive than most. He stared each time she passed by, imagining the many ways he could join the mile-high club. *In the grand scheme of things such a club does not exist,* he thought dismissively. But he indulged in the fantasy, and when she passed by again, he nodded, wanting her to stop, wanting to touch her.

Softly.

The attendant didn't smile, and Wang didn't get his feel. He wanted to ask her, to ask anything, to just engage in meaningless conversation, but as she drew nearer, a young man further along pushed his call button, erasing Wang's bravado. She brushed on by him, spoke to the button pusher, then moved on forward to rush through a mundane safety routine. The daydream ended when a steward tapped on his shoulder, pointing at his still unfastened seatbelt. Push finally came to shove and Wang needed to know why McDowell acted the way he had. *We are playing both sides,* he thought, *but then, I have always been truthful with him.* He reached into his pocket, searched through the envelope McDowell gave him, inspected the Cathay Pacific ticket, and skimmed through the rest of the contents.

Stopped.

You are paranoid, you must stop thinking this way. McDowell can be trusted. He has a reason for acting the way he did. You should have called him. Maybe it had something to do with Slade.

*****

The plane touched down at twenty after five in the morning, twenty minutes ahead of schedule. He disembarked with his one carry-on and followed the crowd toward the baggage claim area, passed it by, stood on the curb and was quickly blocked by two men in gray suits. "Mr. Wang?" the smaller man asked. "Please accompany us, sir."

Wang considered his chances of out running them, the taller being around five feet six inches, and each extremely overweight. He looked around, saw police nearby, considered faking a collapse, a faint; just drop to the ground. Procrastination stalled the decision, and before he considered more options, the two men escorted him to a large black Mercedes and quickly sped from the airport, heading to Peking Road, slowing only when it hit heavy Hong Kong traffic, and eventually coming to a stop at the Langham Hotel. The man nearest the curb stepped from the car, held the door open and gestured to Wang to step from the vehicle and nodded a *'you're welcome'* gesture.

"Compliments of Mr. McDowell," the driver said. "He added I should pass on one thing."

"One thing?"

"You should've called me," the driver said in a mimicking way, adding, *"Don't fuck up again."*

Wang's demeanor wavered; his skin crept with a hot flush.

With confidence shaken he walked into the Langham. It was now seven thirty. He was on schedule.

"Ah yes, Mr. Wang. Your room is ready," the desk clerk said, smiling and passing a plastic card across the reception counter. "Just one key?" he asked.

Wang scratched his chin, waved a hand and looked around. The desk clerk took the hint.

"Yes, Mr. Wang, of course, just the one key."

He slid the card down the scanner, a small green light blinked and the door opened. He craned his head and looked inside, stepped in tentatively, gave the lavish suite a quick inspection and smiled. *Bless you, McDowell, very well done.* The bedroom was spacious, and well decorated. On the bed were four gift boxes. He inspected them from ten feet, had a feeling of discomfort; it was all too well orchestrated, too pre-meditated by McDowell. He glanced at the nearest box, sat on the edge of the bed, misgivings set aside, and carefully removed the wrapping. He found the box contained clothing in his size, three shirts, a suit, underwear. He took a deep breath, opened the next box, found two pairs of shoes, black loafers and brown lace ups, tried each pair on. Perfect fits. The third box was smaller. It contained a cellular phone with a charging unit. He flicked the cell open; it was fully charged and preprogrammed, its screen read, *Hello, Mr. Wang.* The third box contained night vision binoculars, a thirteen-mega pixel Olympus Pen camera, and a passport displaying a Hong Kong entry stamp. Entry was stamped with the current date, and the photograph of Wang was a duplicate of his genuine passport shot. A map of the surrounding Tsimshatsui shopping district and a few tourist pamphlets rounded it off, with addresses highlighted in bright yellow marker pen.

The final box, the smallest of the four, was the size of a shoebox. He allowed a few minutes to pass before opening it, his eyes widening as he recognized the Glock 9mm. He stared at the Glock, allowing a few more minutes to drag on by. He thought, *I need insurance*, and finally fondled the weapon, slipping the magazine from the butt, emptying it, slipping the slugs back in. It felt good, was heavy. *Heavy,* he thought, weighing it in his palm. *Heavy is good.*

He considered placing a call to McDowell's office. *Cannot call McDowell, need to keep him at arm's length.*

*****

It was eight o'clock on a fine Hong Kong morning, four in the afternoon in Los Angeles. Wang reached for the phone.

Dialed.

Played his ace card.

Bought insurance.

A woman answered. "SoCal Exports, this is Marcie."

His voice was quiet, subdued. "Let me speak with Sam Ridkin."

CHAPTER 20

BLAKE JAMMED A PILLOW over his head as the roar of a low flying jet stirred him. "Manuel," he groaned, "with his fuckin' leaf blower." He tugged at the cover, impatiently reached for the remote and flicked through channels just as the phone by the bed buzzed.

Dal still not quite awake, reached for the handset. "Yeah?"

"You guys up 'n about yet?"

"Jesus Christ, it should be illegal for the *sun* to be up this early. It's six o'clock!" Blake said, doing his best to sound somewhat polite.

"I'll be there this afternoon at four," Sam said, "I'll bring coffee and donuts. See you then."

While Dal was speaking with Sam, Blake groggily staggered off and requisitioned the shower. Dal cradled the phone and looked up as Blake disappeared into the bathroom, and called, "Breakfast?"

"Order in!"

They ordered in, watched a March Madness college game and two movies. Dal, pointing at the broadcaster, "The guys wearin' a wig."

"A hairpiece," Blake grinned.

"Yeah . . . whatever."

"Every guy ya see's wearin' a fuckin piece. What's with you and the hair?"

"Looks like a divot."

And so went the day's conversation.

At four o'clock there was a tapping at the door and Sam stepped in carrying two large bags. Adam McDowell followed close behind, precariously balancing a tray . . . five Starbucks cups and a box of . . .

"Krispy Kremes," Sam said. "I stopped by Crenshaw Boulevard especially for you boys, got plenty with pink icing and sprinkles. Enjoy."

Minutes later all four were scavenging through donuts.

"We're all set to go then," Sam said with his mouth full. "You boys will fly out of Van Nuys by private charter. I've got your papers here. There's been a change of plans. I've detailed your route through Nepal; it's all mapped out, memorize it and destroy it before reaching Hong Kong. Flush it down the john, whatever. From Hong Kong you'll fly to Tribhuvan International in Nepal. You'll be on Royal Nepalese, out of Hong Kong."

"You're right of course," McDowell said incoherently, nodding at Sam. "This *is* a far better plan."

Sam nodded agreement as he slid them each an envelope.

Blake reached across and asked, "What's this all about, Sam?"

"Change of plans. We've heard the Chinese are onto your Salesian priest guises; you're going in as trekking tourists. You'll shave off the beards, look like regular tourists," Sam said. "We've new luggage and clothing ready for you at the airport."

He peered at them, hoped the questions would be kept to a minimum. "Your new aliases are in the envelopes, memorize them. I have a barber coming in about an hour. He'll get you looking more like city slickers. Oh, and eh, don't worry. Your experience on Whitney won't be wasted. You'll need all the skills you can muster."

"I don't believe this shit," Dal sighed. "After all of that work?" He waved a hand at Sam. "What about all the Latin?"

"Yeah well," Sam said shaking his head, "shit happens."

He said it with peripheral awareness of McDowell's expression, of his demeanor. His cell phone played America the Beautiful, and Sam answered with the skill of a trained thespian. "What? When? Yeah, yeah, right, he's in Hong Kong? Okay, okay. Thanks, Marcie. Oops, another call coming in, darn, I missed it."

The replies were well orchestrated, and Sam was pleased with his performance, keeping a serious face as he flicked the phone shut. "Marcie says Wang just called in, had a family emergency, brother's been hospitalized in Hong Kong. He had to fly back on no notice, tried to call in but his cell was dead, says he'll contact me in a few days."

He flicked his eyes across McDowell's face, read his expression. McDowell seemed to be playing along, and Sam, turning his back to Dal and Blake, gave a quick wink to McDowell.

Another phone buzzed and McDowell reached into his pocket, flicked *his* cell open. "This is McDowell. Yeah, yeah, okay, hold on a second." He pressed the mute button, spoke to Sam. "Dunno what's going on, some kind of problem back at the Division, want me back there. They tried your cell but got call waiting."

Sam faked a concerned face. "Must be that call I just missed, it came in when I was speaking with Marcie."

"Guess I'll head back to Wilshire then," McDowell grunted, "if that's okay with you?"

"Not a problem, you're up to date on all that's going on. I'll finish the briefing and get the boys tidied up, get them off to the plane."

"Stay warm, guys," McDowell said, as he shook

hands with the two agents. "And don't drink the water."

He made his way to the elevator, stopped at the door of the lift, turned to Sam who'd hung back in the doorway, gave a thumbs up, and a final nod as the elevator doors closed. Back in the room, Sam picked up the envelopes, opened his brief case, and placed them back in.

"Whatcha doin', Sam?" Dal asked with a look of confusion. "We ain't looked through 'em yet."

Sam took three new envelopes from his case, handed one to Dal, another to Blake.

Blake inspected the passport in the envelope marked, Father Bond. He gave an approving grin. *Hmm*, he thought, *very excellent.*

Dal opened his envelope and smiled saying, "I sure do look reverent."

"Who's this other one for?" Blake asked.

"Take a look."

"Father Sung, huh," Blake said, pulling the passport from the envelope and flipping it open. "Not bad, not bad at all. When will we be seein' him?"

"Anytime now, he's due around five."

Dal took charge of the donut box and shrugged, "Shame we have to change the plan."

Sam looked away from the two agents for a few moments, then delivered his reply, a mix of contempt and relief. "We don't."

A soft tapping on the door had an apprehensive quality, a reluctantly gentle knuckle rap. Sam opened the door. "Father Sung, welcome, you look splendid."

Blake's eyebrows went up. "Good to see ya again, Mr. Sung."

Dal contemplated a wise-ass remark, but it was displaced somewhere in the brevity of Sung's entrance.

Blake asked, "How'd ya make out on the mountain?"

"Very well," he replied, dropping his voice, a little embarrassed to share his good fortune. "I received a five thousand dollar reward for holding that man; Father Paul too, five thousand. He asked me to thank you both."

"Murphy's Law," Dal squirmed.

"Yeah," Blake chuckled. "That fuckin' Irishman got us again."

Sam quickly dispensed with the welcoming barrage and began to lay out his strategy. "Firstly, let me say we're proceeding as originally planned, with a few minor changes. I'm gonna run through this just one time so stay with me. Keep all questions until I'm done. I've no doubt you'll have plenty of questions."

He nodded at Blake as he leaned on *you'll*. He looked directly into the face of each as he spoke, distributing equal eye contact time. "You're gonna hear shit you wished you weren't hearing, but it has to be said." He stopped, took a large gulp from his half-full coffee cup, words playing in his head. "There's a reason Adam was called away from our briefing. From the start I've suspected a mole in the Division, someone who's been dealing with the other side. Call it a gut feeling, whatever, but it made me wary. So I only let him hear what I wanted him to hear. Stuff I know he'd pass on to Beijing."

"Goddamnit, Sam," Blake said irritably. "Like we ain't already been through enough shit, what with the mountain and the fuckin' Latin, and now you're throwin' in espionage. Who are ya talkin' about?"

Sam held up both hands, gave Blake a long frustrated look. "Whoa, whoa, whoa! Hold it right there mister. The plans I discussed with you at the Radisson meeting were bogus for a reason. The plans just discussed in front of McDowell were also bogus. There isn't a Himalayan crossing planned. That shit was for the benefit of McDowell, and for his comrade, Mr. Wang."

219

There was a long silence as Sam took a short stroll around the hotel room, looked in a mirror, straightened his tie, and without turning said, "We just weren't totally sure about you, Mr. Sung." He moved his eyes to Sung's reflection. "But we are now."

Sung lowered his head in disbelief, resting it in his hands, unable to respond. The room fell silent, and after allowing time for the three to accept what he'd said, Sam turned and returned to the table, moving the box away from Dal, and picking out a donut. "Not only is Wang a bad seed, we've an even bigger dilemma. McDowell's accepted a large sum of money for information. We're aware of his bank balance, definitely not savings from Uncle Sam's pay checks." He paused, looked directly at Sung. "We received intelligence ahead of Wang's arrival, telling us for sure he was supplying information to the commies."

He filled his mouth with a half donut, swallowing hard. "You get one question each," he said in a relieved way and relaxing a little. "Anyone?"

He finished the last of his cold coffee, allowing a few more seconds to pass. Blake coughed. Sam switched his eyes to his number one man. "Okay, I can tell when you've got a bug up your ass, what's up?"

"Sorry to hear 'bout Wang." And he made a con-solatory head nod at Sung.

Sung accepted the sympathetic nod and lowered his gaze.

"Sorry, man," Blake said. "I know you two guys were tight." He switched back to Sam. "I sense there's more to McDowell's involvement than you're tellin' us. And Sam, that's the fuckin' bug that's up my ass."

Sam took in a long breath, pouting his lips. He rolled his eyes toward the ceiling and exhaled making a farting sound, closed the lid on the Krispy Kremes, gave a warning scowl to Dal who leaned toward the box, stood, and paced the room, searching for the most appropriate response.

"Don't pull any punches," Blake said, with an expression that suggested attack mode. "We need it straight, none of that politically correct bullshit. Ya said McDowell's supplyin' intelligence to the commies, you didn't say Beijing. So, ya know . . . the way ya said it, well, I smell a rat right there. Give it to us straight, Chief. What commies are you talkin' about?"

Sam sought subterfuge.

Subterfuge denied him.

He interlocked his fingers, cracked his knuckles, and decided it best to show all of his cards. "Adam's playing both sides. Beijing believes he's giving China the latest information, but we have it from one of our guys inside the Kremlin that the sonofabitch is selling the more advanced stuff to Moscow. Beijing's getting the Wal-Mart shit, while Moscow's being hand-fed Saks Fifth Avenue.

"If Beijing ever gets their hands on this, McDowell won't be safe anyplace on the planet. Wang, on the other hand, believes the information he receives from McDowell is being given to him exclusively. He passes the information from McDowell on to Beijing, so, unbeknownst to him, Wang's balls are on the chopping block as well."

He paused, read their faces, asked, "Questions?"

Blake took a few moments to eyeball Sam. "If McDowell's still in Los Angeles," he said. "Why not pick him up and fry his ass?"

Sam snorted, allowing contempt time enough to play its part. "He's more valuable out there. We'll use him to feed contrived information to his Russian cronies. We know there'll be a Chinese division waiting on your arrival, possibly Cheng's 13th Group Army."

"What exactly do you mean," Blake snapped, "that we're bein' set up?"

"Of course you're not being *set up*. What kind of

stupidity's that?"

Dal and Blake exchanged glances, as Sung, feeling the tension in the air, feigned interest in his passport.

"Set up! Can't believe you'd come out with shit like that," Sam growled. "They'll tail you, follow you to Slade. They have to believe you guys'll be in touch with him, think that you know where he's hiding out. You can be sure of one thing, they'll be waiting for you to enter through northwest China." He tapped his index finger on the envelope containing the map. "Adam has a copy of this map. He knows exactly the route you guys are supposedly taking."

Blake raised an eyebrow.

Sam said, "We believe Wang's been recalled to Beijing to head up their mission. Wang's an expert at the Himalayan crossing, isn't that right, Mr. Sung?"

Sung's eyes dimmed. "Yes, that is correct. Wang has made the crossing many times. He knows the passage like his own neighborhood, I am now sorry to say."

Sam's eyes crinkled as though feeling the discomfort. "Another bit of information we fed McDowell," he said. "He believes we're trying to get you three guys into Beijing, then on to Penghu and the Pescadore Island region. He knows if there's any way you manage to slip on by the Chinese, you'll continue on to Penghu. They've been leaked information that a sub will rendezvous with you guys off Penghu."

"Okay, Chief," Blake said, giving Dal and Sung a quick look. "So that's what *they've* been told. Tell us about the real deal."

"You're flying from Van Nuys on a Gulfstream G550. You'll re-fuel in Hawaii; continue on to Zhengzhou Xinzheng International in Henan Province. Your jet will taxi to a private hangar to avoid the usual formalities. Fortunately, money also talks in China. We greased the appropriate palms. You'll take a bus to Zhengzhou city, about twenty-six miles off."

Sung showed a flicker of confusion. "Do we need to know any of your people upon our arrival?"

"I can't disclose names," Sam said. "Let's just say we've people in place. We only utilize them when necessary, and they're very well compensated. One'll be your contact in an antiquities store, just outside of Beijing; another contact is in the Xishiku Cathedral."

He stayed silent for several seconds, then looked beyond Blake, looked at Sung. "Once in Zhengzhou you'll check in at the Crowne Plaza on Jinshui Road. Reservations are made for Fathers Bond, Sung and Dominic. Any intervention planned by Wang or McDowell will focus on the Himalayan route. General Cheng's Chinese 13th Army guys'll be waiting in the shadows. And we're certain the Chinese have orders not to apprehend you until you've hooked up with Slade."

Blake asked, "Can you tell us anythin' at all, ya know, about why the Chinese want Slade so bad?"

"Yeah, now we've got our ducks in a row, I guess I can do that. He was responsible for the death of General Cheng's son. Prior to that, he was on assignment gathering intelligence on Beijing's inevitable plans to move into Taiwan. The goings on in the South China Sea had him snooping around Penghu; he'd received intelligence that Beijing had some type of base established on the islets.

"This base is researching weather pattern manipulation and laser satellite guidance systems. We've been aware for some time of a research establishment operating on the Pescadores; one of our earlier sources led us to believe the Chinese were developing laser weapons technology supposedly to destroy any asteroid or meteor approaching earth."

"A meteor headed for earth?" Dal asked.

"Yes, a comet, same thing, more often called an asteroid or meteor. The West was cautious about Beijing's development of such a powerful weapon, yet to a certain point, thankful that Beijing was spending the big bucks in its development. If you took all the people working within the U.S.A on this potentially deadly asteroid collision threat, you wouldn't have enough to staff one Starbucks. So we kind of appreciate the Chinese making themselves galactic watchdogs. In fact, in 1995 a comet was on a dangerously close trajectory toward Earth, and then something unexpected happened."

Sam cleared his throat and continued, "For no logical reason, the comet's nucleus broke into at least three pieces, continuing single file off into space, closest fragment was about six million miles away, or twenty-five times further than the moon, but close enough without being a serious threat. Those in the know believe Beijing tracked the approaching comet, took a shot at it and possibly avoided a catastrophic collision with our planet.

"Beijing won't admit to it," Sam said shaking his head, "they won't even discuss it. But something blasted that comet, and it wasn't anything our guys did. We believe it was Beijing doing a little target practice."

"Jesus, that's a scary thought," Blake said, "Knowin' they're so far ahead of us. Is there anythin' more recent on record?"

"In 2004, the asteroid Toutatis passed within just four earth-moon distances, just nine hundred and sixty thousand miles from scoring a direct hit, not a lot of miles universally speaking. This thing was three miles long and weighs an estimated five thousand five hundred million pounds, the biggest rock to pass so close to earth in a hundred years, the asteroid that wiped out eighty-five percent of the earths species was twice its size.

"A 270-meter asteroid known as Apophis was first discovered in 2004. Its chances of smashing into earth in 2029 are as high as 1-in-37. Further studies ruled out the possibility of an impact in 2029, when the asteroid is expected to come within 29,450 kilometers of earth on its first fly by. A recalculation of the asteroid's path has shown the possibility of a subsequent fly by in 2036 by Apophis to be much closer. In fact, it may hit the planet. Taking all of the information into account, it seems it could hit the earth as early as 2032."

"So the Chinese are actin' as sentinels?" Dal asked.

"As long as they use their technology for shooting at asteroids, but maybe that's just target practice. If a rock the size of Apophis hit the earth's atmosphere, that atmosphere would barely slow the asteroid before it slammed into us. The impact would destroy an area the size of Texas, creating an enormous crater. There'd be so much dust and mineral vaporization blown up into the air it'd block out the sun, throw our planet into darkness. Waves created by the explosion'd generate tsunamis, earthquakes. Red-hot rocks falling back to earth would ignite forest fires. Apophis could alter its orbit around the sun, get knocked off course, anything could happen. The world may be forced to look to China or even Russia to move this thing off its collision course."

"I got the picture," Blake said. "Are there any predictions of future orbits?"

"The asteroid Toutatis last flew close by us in '92 then again in '96, but this is the nearest it's come to us since 1353. It won't be this close again until 2562; its orbit around the sun is so eccentric it can't be predicted with any degree of accuracy for much past three hundred years time. Scary thing is this, the experts can't say with any certainty that it'll hit us, they just have it on the '*Potentially Hazardous Asteroid*' list"

"That one that hit Russia," Blake asked, "How'd this compare to it?"

"That Tunguska meteorite annihilated seven hundred square miles of Siberian forest. The thing was less than a hundred yards in diameter. There're currently an estimated three hundred thousand small asteroids that can statistically hit us at least once every thousand years. UFO supporters believe the Russia incident was actually an exploding alien spacecraft. Some folks believe it could've been a nuclear-powered spacecraft, seeking fresh water from Lake Baikal. It encountered some malfunction and exploded in mid-air. Not a single grain of meteorite's ever been found at the crater site, and that adds strong credibility to the exploding UFO theory. They've since found a chunk of metal buried in the Tunguska region; it's believed to be a section of an alien craft. Makes you think about why none of the UFOs chased by Air Force jets each year are ever fired on."

"And your point is?" Dal asked.

"Major powers around the world send their best jets off on UFO pursuit, but they won't fire on 'em for fear of another explosion the size of Tunguska. Imagine if our guys fired on an unidentified craft off the coast of Los Angeles, just out from Palos Verdes where there've been plenty of sightings."

There was a long silence.

"Goodbye Trump National," Dal said, making a golf swing. "Makes sense, Jesus! UFO or big rock, whatever, seems like Beijing should be allowed to just go on with whatever the fuck they're doin'."

"The trade off's far too great," Sam replied. "To cut through the details, this development resulted in Slade stumbling across something far more sinister than a laser defense system. Once we got wind of the development of this 'star wars' technology, this laser satellite system, Slade was sent to infiltrate their base and secure data. Not only can they redirect or destroy asteroids and meteors, they're developing the technology to control weather patterns, as well as take out any US base or even a destroyer, sub, you name it. A Beijing system satellite would have the world at its feet. But rather than blatantly attack our military, they can just play God with our weather."

Blake coughed, a cue to interrupt. "You mean like move clouds about, create rain. How . . ." Sam gave a cold glare, not appreciating the interruption.

"They've given it the code name, 'Operation Compass.' The Chinese are focusing their attention not only on Taiwan, but also on the North Koreans, who've fully developed their intercontinental missile program as well as successfully testing nuclear devices, and we know for a fact they can reach the West Coast of the U.S.A. with these nuclear missiles. It's worrying a lot of people; the Japanese are steaming, especially as North Korean missiles are being test-fired over Japan. Tokyo and Beijing both see the North Koreans as a definite threat in the region, a kind of power struggle should one of these nations raise its militaristic head higher than the other.

"These countries, as well as the Philippines, are all making claims on regions in the South China Sea. Common belief is that there're tremendous natural gas fields beneath those waters, but we know China's reasons are deeper than natural gas fields. Five days of recent talks between the two Koreas, Japan, China, Russia and the U.S. ended with North Korea failing to even agree on a date for further meetings.

"After North Korea's recent nuclear tests, the UN imposed sanctions against them. The North Korean envoy focused solely on getting U.S. financial embargos removed. Their envoy over here said North Korea would continue rejecting U.S. pressure to discontinue tests. He said North Korea won't even tolerate the slightest bit of infringement on their sovereignty, says North Korea isn't afraid of war."

"So what this is leadin' up to, Sam," Blake postulated, "is a shoot out between 'em, to figure which of the fuckers," and he nodded toward the file sitting on the desk, "which of these motherfuckers, China, North Korea, or Russia, will claim salvage rights to the West, ya know, which of 'em beats up on us, and moves on in."

"That's an ugly scenario. There're Chinese who'll tell you they won't see the move into Taiwan happening in *their* lifetime. That's a load of bullshit of course, 'cause in most cases they're mostly the very old Chinese who're saying it. But the younger ones, they're *planning* on it, and the Red Army's primed for its eventual outcome."

Blake felt the goose bumps slowly move up his legs, traveling all the way to his neck.

"Is our government protestin'?" Dal asked, almost in a guilty *dare I even ask* tone.

"Our people growl a bit, but when our leaders try to bark, they do a mime job, know their attempts to rally support from allies is a virtual death knell for the leader of any of those nations. They'd get voted out next election, never fails, happened in Australia, Britain, France, and the U.S. Look at the figures, you go supporting unilateral military action, you lose your job. Mandate any continuation of multinational unilateral policy and watch your popularity figures go down the crapper. You won't see too many leaders committing troops, not one of our Democrats you won't." Then he thought for a few moments. "Maybe a Kennedy, but that'd be it.

"Look at how our government's support in the Middle East collapsed as nations withdrew their support. Those remaining are pretty much doing it as a sign of allegiance more than support. Great Britain being *the* most notable exception, they need us and'll always jump into bed with the U.S. Subsequently the British Prime Minister, Tony Blair, hung up his apron alongside Australia's Prime Minister, John Howard. Look at the plunge in popularity of our president. Supporting U.S. policy is the kiss of death to any world leader."

Dal gesticulated, "Jesus, Sam, I thought you were the

consummate Republican?"

"This goes way beyond party allegiance. The GOP has no obvious heir apparent to Bush. They'll inherit a deeply recessed economy with a record deficit, and a White House needing a cleaning crew to get rid of the mess left by the previous administration. Whoever they run, the candidate doesn't stand much of a chance if they head into a war we can't win. But the Democrats, well now, those guys can move right on in, they're used to manipulating bullshit, so they probably won't even *notice* the quagmire. They'll just solve problems by running the printing presses," and Sam grinned, obviously enjoying his side excursion into Washington politics, an arena he at one time considered entering, but he valued a *clear* conscience and doubted the chance of an African American such as himself winning the nomination. Besides, the two things *he* hated most came into political role play, kissing babies, and kissing ass. Sam did neither. He continued explaining the incursion into the Penghu facility, detailing Slade's part.

Fifteen minutes later, "So Beijing's stymied without this flash drive?" Dal asked.

"Exactly, their satellite program's in a hold pattern, but they can still play about with the weather."

"Ya mean to say they can orchestrate natural dis-asters?" Blake asked.

"Bingo. Simulations, copies, an art form the Chinese are masters at. They're mastering weather manipulation. But while our man has the flash drive, Beijing's well and truly screwed. If we can get a duplicate hard drive into their hands, one that they believe is the original from Penghu, we can shut down their system long enough to give us the upper hand. I hate to get into dirty warfare but that's what's necessary in these times. Like Einstein said, 'The pioneers of a warless world are the youth who refuse military service.' Unfortunately this isn't the case with China. Those guys are out there marching as we speak."

*****

LATER THAT DAY
AMERICAN INTERPOL DIVISION
WILSHIRE BOULEVARD
LOS ANGELES

"It should be obvious to you all by now," Sam said, "that with all of this uncertainty over McDowell and Wang, well, we couldn't disclose any meeting places until the last minute. There are plenty of Westerners in China, so Slade's no rarity, but he's unfamiliar with the territory, has never been an Asian operative. The original plan was to have him back within days, but once he got deeper, getting him back to the States as scheduled was no longer an option." He paused, looked at the group. "You guys following me here?"

They each nodded.

"The flash drive our man's acquired is less than one inch square and quite thin. You're all familiar with what I'm talking about. Anyway, it's fitted inside the heel of his boot." Sam placed his two index fingers an inch apart. "It's inscribed with the code name Compass 008. He can't risk being captured by Beijing for many reasons, the foremost being they'll locate the drive within minutes. Once you've hooked up with our man, and the worst scenario occurs, say you or Slade fall into Chinese hands, your mission will change from rescuing him to terminating him."

"Jesus!" Dal snapped in disbelief. "Ya want us to kill him?"

"If we can't get him out alive, yes, you'll terminate him."

"Why kill the guy?" Blake asked.

"If Beijing gets him under Sodium Pentothal, or

230

MK-ULTRA, there's no saying what repercussions could eventuate, could have a Francis Gary Powers incident all over again, don't want any part of that."

"Okay, Sam," Dal said looking at him with confusion. "So how do we spot him?"

"He'll be dressed as a priest. He'll be with one other guy, Father Lee, an actual priest. They'll both be sitting in a park by Nanhai Lake, alongside the Forbidden City. You'll spot 'em easily. They'll be there on April 17, or at least we're shooting for April 17, at ten o'clock. If they're not there, you'll need to move on to Tiantan Park. Be by the Hall of Prayer at the Temple of Heaven. You'll find 'em there around eleven thirty. They're the two locations, whichever of the two appears the safer at the time, well, that'll be the place you'll find them. Check out the military presence, you see troops, go to the second location. If you don't hook up with them on the 17th, you try again the following day."

"How long ago was this plan put together?" Blake asked.

"Weeks back."

"The guys we're meetin'," Dal asked, "any easy way to spot 'em, like, will they each have a hibiscus over one ear?

Blake grinned, but Sam remained emotionless. "Our two guys'll be sitting on the grass with a small statue in front of 'em. Two priests, pretty hard to miss."

"A statue . . ." Dal asked, "anythin' special about it?"

"It's a golden Tara. The flash drive from our guy's boot is been sealed inside its base. It'll be undetectable. If it stayed in the heel of his boot, you could all be at risk. It'd be far too easily found, and not easy to move from one person to another if necessary, unless you wear his shoe size." Sam forced a poor grin, and cleared his throat. "The statue's about eight inches high, and it must get to the States. Seeing as how you'll all be wearing Salesian robes, you'll have no problem spotting each other. He'll know who you guys are. Y'all clear on that?"

"Sounds a bit mercenary," Blake said, "all of that *killin' if necessary* shit."

Sam maintained a cool demeanor, but smiled apologetically, turning his face away. "Each of you is valuable to the Division, but sad to say, not indispensable."

"This ain't like you," said Dal. "This shit is comin' from someone else, ain't it?"

The answer was dismissive, almost flippant. "You got it, but don't bother going there. If you have to make sacrifices to get the Tara out of China, you do it. Understand?"

He hesitated, anticipated objection.

Got none.

"Hunter and Bellinger will fly with you as far as Hawaii," he said addressing Blake. "They'll go on to Beijing, arriving early April to prepare for the Beijing Open. They'll be on standby during each round. I'll have cell communication with 'em but prefer to reach 'em at their hotel. I'll leave a message if I miss 'em. They can call me easily enough. I'll call you and Dal at your hotel around April 16. Stay tuned to the phone around that time."

He nodded at Hunter. "How ready are you for this golf match?"

"I'm ready," and he looked at Bellinger. "Aren't I?"

"Well, is he, Patrice?"

"I'd put my money on him, Sam."

"I have," Hunter added. "I found great odds, got 500 to 1 with Ladbrokes. Put a grand on myself to finish in the top three, that's a cool half million."

"Christ, I'd like some of that action," Blake said.

Hunter shrugged.

"Action's still there, but only 100 to 1. Guess I scared 'em a bit."

"I'll take those odds," Dal said. "You sure you're shootin' good?"

"Fuck yeah I'm sure!" Hunter added assertively. "I shot a sixty-three down in Riverside County, at Oak Quarry. That good enough?"

"Christ yeah," Dal said. "Best I've ever shot there was a sixty-nine, and I was in a zone that day."

"But are you certain you can string four solid days together?" Blake asked.

"My golf game is like vintage fuckin' wine," Hunter said smiling, "each day it gets a little better."

"You might not be playing through to the end," Sam said with an apologetic frown. "Not because of missing the cut. If anything goes off kilter with our boys here," and he nodded to Sung, Blake, and Dal, "you guys might have to make a move prior to April 16th. If that's necessary, you'll need to drop out and miss playing the last day of The Open."

There was no reply from either Hunter or Bellinger, both choosing to ignore the possibility.

"We estimate that by mid-April, you three . . ." He paused, again nodding at Sung, Blake and Dal, "By then, you three will be pretty close to moving our man out of China."

Bell fidgeted in her seat, unhappy at the suggestion they might not complete their four-day golf stint.

Again, Sam gestured at Blake, Sung, and Dal. "You'll check into the Crowne Plaza, travel the 300 miles north to Beijing and meet up with the bishop at the Xishiku. The guy's name is Bishop Bolin."

At twenty minutes after ten, they sat in the limousine. The day was cool and bright, a strong breeze coming in from the west, a hint of salt air reaching Van Nuys from the coast. The limo pulled alongside the Gulfstream, and the six stepped from the Lincoln, walking single file toward the jet as Dal began whistling the theme from Bridge on The River

Kwai.

"Give me a break," Bell laughed. "You've got me marching in step."

The laughter became contagious. *One of the last laughs you'll be having for a while,* Sam thought as he joined the merriment.

"Hey, Chief," Dal said, turning and nodding appreciably. "Thanks for leavin' out the hair colorin'. I was sweatin' blood over that one."

Sam returned the smile. "Well, initially I figured a makeover was in order, but you guys looked so weathered after Whitney." He scrubbed at his own stubble. "Drew's beard's come through so gray, he doesn't need additional aging."

Blake turned to Dal, rubbing the side of his nose with his middle finger. Sam picked up on it, and smiled, ignoring the gesture.

The flight to Hawaii was routine, magazines, movie, a nap. Refueling gave the four time enough to change into comfortable tracksuits for the next leg of the flight. On arrival in Hawaii, Hunter flung his golf bag over his shoulder, and walked from the plane, while Bell carried luggage.

"Well, what can I say?" Blake said smiling. "Go hit 'em straight."

"Yeah, I'll see you guys in Beijing, or maybe not. Who knows? But I know this much, by the time I get to the first tee, I'll have planned on how I'm gonna spend that cool half mill."

Bell nodded to the group, "He's going to do well, believe me."

"Ah shit, gotta call Ladbrokes, I want some of this action," Dal said squinting at Blake. "Did ya lay the big odds? Come on man, what'd ya get, a hundred to one?"

The conversation continued along that line for three minutes, Dal badgering Blake, and Blake reveling at keeping

Dal in suspense. An hour passed. The Gulfstream sat in an enclosed private hangar. Blake strolled around the G550, showing an uneasy demeanor, making out as though he was inspecting the fuselage. He preferred any way to travel other than in a plane.

"So tell me what's goin' through your mind?" Dal asked. "Ya got that pre-occupied look on your face."

"Yeah, yeah, yeah, I'm thinkin' about McDowell and Wang. Got a feelin' we'll be seein' 'em soon, and I don't mean stateside."

"But you feel okay about workin' with Sung, right?" Dal asked.

"Workin' with Sung? Absolutely!" Blake said with a reassuring nod. "Sung's solid. Yeah, I feel good about Sung."

Dal took in his expression, thought he detected a little uncertainty. Blake saw the analytical gaze and reiterated, "Sung's cool. I'd stake my life on it."

Dal looked at him with a wry grin, and whispered, "Ya might be."

*****

"All set and ready to go," the pilot called. "All aboard, next stop's the land of stir fry."

Sung had already begun watching a monitor featuring U.S. mainland news. Dal and Blake were both readjusting their seatbelts as the news broadcast ended and a movie began. After a few hours sleep, Sung woke, tuned the monitor into a news broadcast that appeared to be a satellite channel out of Los Angeles. The subject being discussed immediately caught his attention.

"Wake up, look at this!" Sung snapped pointing at the screen. Dal and Blake woke abruptly, sat upright, and adjusted their focus.

"What's goin' on?" they asked in perfect sync.

"The body was discovered in the early hours of this morning," the news anchor said. "The victim is believed to be a member of a government unit; Washington has made no comment on the incident." The anchor gave a robotic smile. "The victim's name has not yet been released."

A police composite flashed onto the screen; it was unmistakably . . . Adam McDowell.

The talking head continued, his voice adding a dramatic touch. "A police spokesman told this reporter that an organization believed to represent a covert group has been operating from a private suite at a location on Wilshire Boulevard for the past two years."

"Jesus Christ!" Blake groaned. "That's McDowell."

"What the . . .?" Dal said staring in disbelief and shaking his head repeatedly.

Sung observed the monitor as the coverage switched from the police photograph to a wide-angle view of the Radisson from across Wilshire Boulevard. The camera panned the front of the hotel until it reached the twelfth floor, and zoomed in on a window.

"That's our office," Dal said staring at the monitor.

Sung muttered under his breath, "Could it be Wang, could he and Mr. McDowell have had a disagreement?"

"Can't be," Blake groaned, ruffling his hair in frustration. "Sam had that call, the one that come in from Wang, the call from Hong Kong." He unbuckled and began sliding from his seat, started a move toward the cabin, but was forced back as the Gulfstream banked left. "Hey!" he called to the pilot. "Can you get me a number in Los Angeles?"

Within minutes, Sam Ridkin was on the line. "Sam, what's goin' on with McDowell? You heard anythin'?"

"What, you know already?" Sam said incredulously. "Aren't you still in the air?"

"It's all over the fuckin' news. What's goin' on?"

"I'm on it," Sam replied. "Two guys, could be Russian, seen leaving the building. Doorman gave a description; big guys, he says, wearing dark suits. They left the suite around lunch time. He said the door lock had been forced. I won't go near the place until this settles down. I called Washington, and head office is briefed on the incident, but they say they've no likely suspects at this time."

"Jesus, Sam, why'd . . .?"

"Washington confirmed McDowell was playing both sides, like I said, selling the good stuff to Moscow." Sam's voice was monotone. "The way we see it, the Chinese figured they'd prefer cutting off the supply of information to the Kremlin. So McDowell was dispensable. We're just not onto which side took him out, maybe Moscow, the eh, two big guys in the suits, or maybe Beijing."

Blake's mood was indignant. "Gimme your best fuckin' guess."

"I'd put my money on Beijing," Sam replied. "Where exactly are you right now? How'd Sung react to the news?" A few moments of silence. "Can you talk?"

"Pilot says we're about two hours from Zhengzhou," Blake said glancing at Sung, turning his face away, moving his mouth nearer the phone. "Sam wha'dya mean, *can I talk?*"

"Forget it. Call me when you check in at the hotel."

"Got it. So eh, there's no change in plans?"

"Not from me, but there could be, need to know if McDowell passed our final meeting on to Beijing, or Moscow. Could determine if you guys go in over the Himalayas, or directly down through mainland China. By the time you check in I should have more."

Blake was peripherally aware of Dal's pleading eyes. He leaned into the cockpit, passed the phone back to the pilot, gave an inquiring look at Dal, and said, "Hey Dallas, did you pack those long johns?"

JASON DENARO

*****

They arrived at the Crowne Plaza ready to call it a day. The desk clerk eyed the three priests for a few moments. "Fathers, welcome to the Crowne Plaza," he said in English. "Please leave your passports and visas with me for safe keeping; you may collect them as you exit the hotel."

Blake's hood hung casually around his broad shoulders. He nudged Sung with his foot, pulled a face, clearly uncomfortable with the passport arrangement. Another guest asked the receptionist about the strong presence of armed security outside the hotel.

"Sir, it is in your interest that the highest level of security is maintained. If a guest raises suspicion, our security personnel may, at any time, place that person under surveillance. All communication may be monitored, and personal possessions in that guest's hotel room may be subject to random search. Also, be aware that photography can be perceived as a security breach, and may result in conflict with authorities." He paused for a moment, gesturing at their robes. "Unfortunately, Fathers, your being priests does not preclude you from an inconvenience such as this." His face slid into a facetious grin as he added with unabashed sincerity, "In China, we do not discriminate."

"Aw Jesus," Dal whispered as they moved away, "ya see the way that motherfucker eyeballed me?"

"Yes, I noticed," Sung said grinning. "It seems a darker beard may have been a good suggestion after all."

Blake looked ahead.

Whistled, *Hotel California*.

238

CHAPTER 21

HER MOUTH WAS SOFT, moist, with a smile that set Wang back. He walked in a confident stride toward the solitary figure sitting at the table, by the fountain.

"Lisa Ling?"

"Mr. Wang," she said, smiling up at him, "please, have a seat."

No coaxing required.

He stumbled clumsily as he reached to pull the chair. She was attractive, dark haired, a thirty-something year old with large brown almond eyes giving her a sleepy demeanor, as though she'd just woken, a woman with a look recognizable by most men who possessed a birth given ability to recognize that sensual *come-fuck-me* look. He slid the chair from under the table, sat, waved a hand toward the waiter, ordered a coffee, and allowed himself a few moments to absorb the beauty of the girl seated across from him.

"Miss Ling, our mutual friend, Mr. McDowell, says you have an item for me."

She reached across to the empty chair alongside of her, and placed the box in front of Wang. He reached across and her hand touched his and for an instant the touch gave him a blood rush like a hot flowing volcano and he smiled at her hand and thought, *hmm, a toucher too* and made a mental note of it.

She caught the smile, and quickly pulled back, realizing she had sent the wrong signal. He removed the lid, took a red velvet bundle from the box, and unwrapped an exquisite golden statue. He allowed himself to float blissfully in the fantasy world of this pseudo date. Lisa cleared her throat, uncomfortable with his hard, long stare, and he redirected his attention to the statue.

"Yes," he said, "it is a Tara." Again, his eyes locked on hers. "And a most beautiful one, I must say. Mr. McDowell said it is most important that I guard it." He studied her body language with interest. "I must assume the statue's intrinsic value is not his prime concern." He played naïve. "Can you enlighten me as to why this particular Tara is of such importance?"

He was fishing.

She didn't bite.

She gave him a quizzical glance. "I can't say," she said with asperity, still slightly embarrassed by his gaze. "Mr. McDowell is quite succinct. I've worked with him in the past and have learned not to question him, or expect him to expand on his orders. I was told to deliver the box to you, nothing more."

He ran his eyes across her, lingering too long on her firm, perky breasts pressed hard against the pink v-neck angora sweater. She could feel those eyes; could feel them circling her nipples, and it made her wish she'd dressed less provocatively. He felt the blood rush surging through his veins, shooting from the top of his head, a lightning bolt zapping at warp-speed, culminating at the tip of his penis, causing an uncontrollable erection. He slid the chair a little further under the table, shielding his embarrassment. The feeling was one of satisfaction, fully believing his meeting with this stunning girl was a result of fate, and even more hopefully, one of romantic persuasion. He was unable to quell his predatory desire, like an animal, subsequently gaining acuity, his sexual platitude all but served in one way, his ciphering eyes observing her mouth as she sipped on the

240

coffee.

She knew what he was thinking, knew his type, what was running through his debauched mind. She gazed up and he stared into his eyes. Unable to hold back, he said with a sigh of satisfaction, "Miss Ling, I hope you do not think I am speaking with disrespect, but I find you to be an extremely attractive woman."

She moved her eyes to the Tara with a look of consternation. "Please, Mr. Wang."

He felt her retract, and he switched to business mode. "This American in question, I hear you know him rather well."

"You could say that," she said, slightly flustered, hanging on for a second, two seconds. "We had a brief affair. I suppose one could consider this *knowing him well.*"

He realized their meeting had started on the wrong foot, searched for a way to swing it around. Before he found the words, she said, "You're out of line, Mr. Wang, you know that."

Surprised by her impetuous tone, he lowered his eyes respectfully, blushed slightly and said, "My deepest apology, Miss Ling."

They sat for an uncomfortable ten seconds, and then Lisa Ling's eyes grew thin. She said with a razor-edge delivery, "I don't need an intrusion into my private life."

The erection died.

Disliking her tone, he shook his head and scratched nervously at the side of his neck. "Tell me all you know."

"At this time, I'll tell you only what you *need* to know. His name's Slade."

"Very well then, describe him."

"He's like all other good looking Caucasian men, they all look the same to me." A slight grin raised one corner of her mouth - a sexual grin. And it plucked at Wang's chest.

"Is this your attempt at humor?"

"I'm not laughing," she said, trying to sound tentative. "It's the same way Asian people appear so alike to Caucasians."

"But that is different."

"Different? That sounds discriminatory, racist."

"You seem to have acquired . . ." and he paused as the waiter arrived with coffee, waited, watched as the man moved away. "You have acquired some Western attitude, no doubt from your American lover." Several minutes of silence ensued as perplexity clouded his mind. He worked on his coffee, searching, searching.

Lisa stared at him, gave her *impatient look.* "Mr. Wang, although money has been deposited in my account, it's only half of what was originally agreed upon."

He reached across and placed a solicitous hand on her forearm. "Miss Ling, I do not handle that side of the transaction."

She glared at the hand, allowing it to remain in place as she asked, "Can I assume you're going to do nothing to rectify the shortfall?"

"Did you not follow what I said?"

"Yes I understood, and you need to understand this, for half the amount, you'll get half the information," and her hand began sliding from beneath his.

He placed his coffee cup on the table and grabbed a hold of her wrist, the cup tumbling across the table, crashing to the floor, causing several guests to stare in their direction. Over his shoulder she could see two hotel employees looking toward the disturbance, as a security guard at a nearby table stood and hurried toward Wang who was now half standing, brushing coffee from his lap.

The guard spoke softly, with an air of authority. "Is there a problem, miss?"

"Yes there's a problem. This person is harassing me."

Wang's eyes seared through her. She finally smiled and whispered, "Half the amount, half of the information."

He took a few seconds to regain composure, to disperse what little vestige of sexual intent may have survived to that point. His immediate reaction was to grab this woman and give her a sound thrashing, but the urge disappeared in a wash of authoritarian demand as the security guard gave a dismissive grunt, placed a hand on Wang's shoulder, and nodded toward the exit.

Wang quickly wrapped the golden statue, placed it in its box, and was briskly escorted from the café. After some time in the manager's office apologizing, he made his way back to the to where he'd met with Lisa.

But she was gone.

*****

It seemed a punishment he didn't deserve. He faced an uncertain future in China without the comfort of support, even if that support came from McDowell and his connections. To affirm the immediacy of his predicament, he recalled McDowell's admonition should either fall from grace with Beijing. A few minutes later he stared at his image in the bathroom mirror, ran the tap, leaned over the basin and scooped handfuls of cold water onto his face. He unfolded a hand towel and began drying off.

After a drink from the mini-bar, he considered his options, thought he should place another call to Sam Ridkin. *Perhaps I should cut my losses. Too many unanswered questions, unanswerable questions. Have I made a mistake, should I have called McDowell as instructed?* He feared this moment, knew it would come, felt the insecurity as he eyed the Tara on the bedside table. Reluctance gave way to impulse. He reached for the cell phone, punched in the Los Angeles number.

"SoCal Exports."

"Is that you, Marcie?"

There was a long silence. The woman replied, "Marcie isn't working today. Who may I say is calling?"

"I am a friend of Mr. Ridkin, may I speak with him?"

The voice hesitated, the woman waving frantically to men in white shirts and loosened ties, signaling them to trace the call. A ginger headed man made a *keep talking* motion with his hand as two others worked furiously over a monitor. Wang sensed the commotion behind the voice, visualized something was not quite right.

He flicked the cell phone shut.

The ginger bearded man's complexion reddened. "Did you get it? Tell me you fuckin' got it!"

The monitor man made a time out gesture, waited, waved the ginger man off, then in a self gratifying voice shouted, "Yeah! We got it, we got it. We fuckin' got it!"

The ginger man shook his head impatiently and asked, "Where?"

"Fuckin' China," monitor man replied with jubilation. "The motherfucker's in China!"

CHAPTER 22

WESTERN HILLS COMMAND CENTER
BEIJING, CHINA

Commanding Officer, Major General Zhu Cheng

THE SOLDIER AT THE computer raised his hand, while remaining focused on the monitor for several moments. He laced his fingers behind his head, ignoring the man standing across from him. The man hesitated, started to say something, and did, after eventually attracting the desk sergeant's gaze.

"Here are those papers you requested," and he extended a hand as the corporal saluted, turned, and quickly walked from the room.

The man behind the desk glanced at the top paper, scratched the side of his nose, appeared aggravated, and flicked over to the second paper. With burgeoning anxiety he picked up the phone and punched at numbers. The dial tone continued for several seconds. He placed a Marlboro between his lips, nervously lit the cigarette, inhaled deeply, coughed out a plume of smoke as he replied, "Sir, yes sir, yes. Yes, I have the report, General." He scanned the pages with one hand, stubbing the cigarette with the other, the phone precariously balancing between shoulder and ear. He took another long look at the paperwork, then in a voice galvanized with fear, choked out the words, "Yes General.

The train was going to Datong." He wavered. "Yes General, that is correct sir; a woman's body as well." The desk man stood, walked nervously to a water cooler, the phone cord fully stretched across the room. He stopped, held up an index finger. "Yes General. Immediately, I will see to it."

Click.

His forehead ejected beads of perspiration, and his top lip quivered uncontrollably. He called to his assistant, "The general has ordered a set of these prints run through the International Data Bank. I want . . ." He paused, re-phrased the words. "*The general* expects results within the hour."

The corporal exited, wasting no time carrying out the order. The desk man pushed back in his chair, sighed, and with the weight of responsibility lifted from his shoulders, lit up another Marlboro.

Cheng's eyes darted about the office, frustrated at his inability to proceed further due to the lack of information. He'd already dispatched a division to apprehend the party responsible for the train deaths, had issued orders to the effect that once apprehended, the person be taken alive; he made it quite clear that any soldier responsible for the death of the assailant would himself be severely dealt with. "Will be shot," were his actual words.

Twenty-five minutes later, the nervous man behind the desk drowned his fifth Marlboro in a near full teacup, and stared at the printout. After an inspection, and some time gazing about the room as though begging divine intervention and not finding it, the desk man pressed the yellow button on the handset.

A gruff voice answered, "Cheng!"

"General, I have the results of the prints."

"And?"

"It is confirmed. He is an American."

Silence.

Nervous listening.

"No sir, he is *not* military. His name is Paul Slade."

More sweat glistened on the captain's forehead, his eyes closed as he absorbed the verbal beating. The look of fear subsided slightly and he allowed a nervous smile to creep onto his face, sensing a lessening in the anger. *Perhaps a reprieve,* he thought*. No need for fear*. In the next instant, the smile dissipated. "No sir, there is no photograph on file. I am sorry General, but there is nothing on file."

His eyes strayed about the room as though in search of a strategy. When the general was done with venting his anger, the captain said, "It seems the data bank was cleaned of all photographs, only a name remained by the fingerprints."

The man's voice struggled to produce any audible sound, his saliva glands deserting him as he made a frugal attempt to sound efficient. "Sir? The ear identification?"

A deadly quiet.

He shook off the tremor, tried for a more confident reply. "It was also missing, General."

There was no arguing with Cheng, and the captain did not attempt to do so. His guileless effort at a switchover from fear to confidence was as fruitless as it was abrupt. His immediate priority was self-preservation, his silence doing little to achieve that end.

He swallowed heavily, but there was little to swallow. He fumbled for the teacup, gulped a mouthful, spluttered, spat out remnants of the Marlboro, and said in a wooden perfunctory way, "General?"

CHAPTER 23

THE 7203 YARD HONG Hua International Golf Club was hosting the Volvo China Open from April 13 through 16. The three hundred and thirty-three acre course, designed by England's Nick Faldo, had been open for less than three years. Its creation involved the importation of over three million cubic yards of earth, turning a very flat site into a spectacularly undulating eighteen-hole layout. Although Gardner Hunter was mentally zoned for the Open, he was not considered a serious contender. Consequently, his arrival in China, along with caddy, Patrice Bellinger, passed unceremoniously.

Bellinger brought in the usual necessities, first aid medication, gloves, candy bars for Hunter to snack on during each round, and the most important item of all, a bottle of eye drop medication. She'd planned well ahead, had brought the drops along as a kind of, hmm . . . insurance, in case the going got tough.

Like that.

On the evening of April 10th, it was a Monday, Bell and Hunter checked into the Grand Hyatt on East Chang An Avenue, and headed directly to their room.

Luggage and clubs followed behind.

The decision on whether or not to share a room had been left to Hunter and Bell to decide. With their past relationship, with the *hot and heavy days* being years behind them, they were comfortable with just being *good friends*.

A player, and his caddy.

The suite, larger than a regular apartment, was spectacular, offering two bedrooms, each with a king size bed featuring floor to ceiling mirrors on either side. It left nothing to be desired.

"I'll take that one," Hunter said pointing to the right. "It looks a little larger. I'll need the extra space for the trophy."

"The trophy?" Bell chuckled, feigning exasperation, "how about for your ego?"

A knock on the door announced the arrival of clubs and luggage.

"Sir?" the young man said with a tone of uncertainty, wheeling the cart into the room.

Hunter pointed to his room, aware Bellinger was monitoring his wishful thinking. She said in a soft tone, "You have an incorrigibly pornographic mind, Mr. Hunter. But you know that already, right? The Louis Vuitton goes in there," she added in a raised voice. "The Samsonite is his." She passed the young man a ten dollar bill and he wheeled the cart from the room. "So Gard, you take the shower," she said, "I'll check out the menu." After a half minute she called, "Hey, this Grand Café looks pretty good, the Peking duck, it sounds *hmm* . . ."

The Grand Café featured a restaurant revolving around an interactive kitchen, bringing the excitement of cooking from back stage to the forefront. The wait for Peking duck was as eventful as it was ultimately rewarding, watching the chefs create spectacular dishes in full view of patrons. When the main course was done, Hunter contemplated dessert, as Bellinger went through plans for the following day. "We'll need to be at the course by ten," she said, "to feel the greens, the breeze, to hit a few hundred balls."

The next morning at eight o'clock, a limousine drove Bell and Hunter to the Hong Hua, where a personable player's assistant greeted them, retrieved their bag and luggage from the limo, placed the unmarked bag on an extended six-seat golf cart, and drove to the clubhouse.

"Your name, sir?" the young man inquired from back of the desk.

"Hunter, Gardner Hunter, and this here's my caddy, Patrice Bellinger."

The man nodded with cool unconcern and entered the information into an IBM computer. "Ah yes, from the United States. Welcome to Beijing, Mr. Hunter, Miss Berr . . ."

He struggled pronouncing her name.

Gave up.

"Sir, you have been allocated locker fifty-six. You may leave your personal effects there, Miss Berringer will have locker forty-five, in the ladies wing. Shower utensils are supplied and you'll find all you need in each locker. Towels will be replaced as they are used. If there is any way we can make your stay more pleasurable, please let me know."

He touched the golden name badge on his vest. "I am Michael."

*****

Sunday April 16th, day four, final day of play. The four hundred and twenty-two yard par four, fifteenth hole, was a classic dogleg that veered to the right. It featured an anorexic bunker that awaited any morsel headed its way, and a smaller sand trap at the corner of the dogleg. Both needed to be avoided. Looking deliberate and methodical, Hunter teed off with his driver.

A large tiered green lay ahead, protected by trees on three sides and a huge bunker front left; a typical risk reward hole and he loved it. He could unleash three hundred and twenty yards, leaving his money shot, an inside one hundred yard lob. He played his drive with a gentle fade, avoiding the hungry bunker. The ball caught a favorable kick on landing, and came to rest eighty-two yards from the green. His playing companion, a Korean named P.C. Kang, was fifty yards back of him. Kang chatted with his caddy, needed to place his ball on the back tier, any place else would remove a birdie from the equation. Hunter stood aside and caught Bellinger flicking her eyes toward the treetops.

"Bit of a breeze kickin' up," Hunter said quietly. "You think Kang sees it?"

"Nope."

The reply was definite.

"His caddy hasn't looked up," Bell said softly. "Kang has the same club he had before the wind kicked up. He's looking down the fairway."

Kang addressed the ball, swung, sending the ball off the clubface on a perfect trajectory.

And the wind grabbed it, sending it drifting, gaining height, climbing in the stiff breeze. It hung to the right for more time than Kang had hoped, and when it came to ground, it thumped down into white powdery silica, burying itself in a sandy grave to the right of the green.

Spectators groaned.

Kang heard the reaction.

The Chinese lady smiled.

"Great," Bell said softly, trying not to show unsportsmanlike jubilation. "Gard, did you see that drift?"

"Yeah, I got it."

Hunter pulled his sixty-degree lob wedge.

Stared the pin down.

He called the play. "Okay, three feet past the pin . . . then spin on back, baby."

The roar from the gallery was deafening as Hunter's ball floated high, touched down three feet past the pin, and spun back into the cup.

The Chinese lady applauded loudly as she slipped Bellinger a quick, happy wave.

"Take it easy, Gard," Bell said. "We've a way to go."

Hunter leaned to her ear and whispered, "But we're looking pretty hot, pretty, pretty, pretty fuckin' hot."

He was three strokes back with three holes remaining. On the sixteenth hole, Kang lipped out on a six-foot putt and the difference was just two strokes. Hunter, smelling blood, walked off the green toward his and Kang's golf bags, as Bellinger took note of Kang as he hung back on the green.

The Chinese lady, standing behind the green, stared at Bellinger and nodded to her camera bag that lay at her feet.

She unzipped the bag . . . and set the gray cat loose.

The cat made a frenzied dash across the green, sighting the nearest tree. An elderly man standing nearby turned, winked at the woman, opened his jacket and released the dog.

Fucking turmoil!

The small black dog had one mission in life . . . devouring the cat.

All eyes followed the melee, as spectators and cameras alike turned in the direction of the chase.

Bell quickly exchanged the bottle of water in Kang's bag with an identical bottle she'd carefully prepared for the occasion.

The cat, hair on end, eventually found refuge in the small tree as the dog trampolined in futile attempts at reaching its meal. After being restrained by a security atten-dant, it continued yapping as its plaintive cries faded toward a distant hospitality tent.

Bell threw an appreciative nod at the Chinese woman. The Chinese woman gave a girlish wave, a giggle too. She took a hold of the elderly man's arm, and the pair quietly strolled from the course.

It was an old trick.

Never failed.

Great for constipation, she'd often told Blake.

Bellinger had added a hefty squirt of eye drops to the water, allowing ten minutes to pass from the time Kang drank, to the time uncontrollable diarrhea set in. She had reached into the bag, handed a bottle of Evian to Hunter. He looked at it, said, "Don't need a drink yet, sweetie."

"Wipe your forehead," Bell whispered nudging him. "Look sweaty, and then take a fucking drink."

He looked at her quizzically, and gave a smile to Kang, took the bottle, wiped his forehead, and made a toasting gesture. He took the long drink, and, just like a suggestive yawn, Bell waited for it to work its magic.

Kang glanced at Hunter as he drank. *Come on,* Bell thought. *Monkey see, monkey do. Take a drink!*

Theory is, the urge to drink will bypass the mirror neuron system, which would render taking a drink in response to someone else, a conscious and imitative act. The same manner in which the mirror neuron system causes yawning, it would stimulate Kang's desire to drink water. Bellinger had seen it all before. It had never failed. *Yawn,* she thought, then *no, no, no, I mean drink. Take a drink!*

Kang's conscious response to drinking should be, *I am thirsty.*

The response to another person yawning is a subconscious perception and suggests that there are brain sections responsible for one's perception of the need to copy. The same applies to yawning. It does not begin with the mirror neuron system but actually bypasses it. This mirror-neuron system contains special types of brain cells, or neurons, that become active both when their owner does something, and when he or she senses someone else doing the same thing. Mirror neurons typically become active when a person consciously imitates an action of someone else. Subsequently, Kang nodded at Hunter, then reached to his caddy. "Water please," he said, and she passed the water to her man and he took a gulp. Bell glanced at her watch, as Hunter and Kang stepped to the seventeenth tee. *Just thirty minutes before we reach the eighteenth green.*

Kang found himself with an almost impossible shot from the greenside bunker, after which they headed to the eighteenth tee, both players all square.

"All square, one to play," Hunter said. "You gotta like those odds."

Hunter played his tee shot, and stood aside. Kang's discomfort as he addressed his ball was noticeable.

"What's Kang doin'?" he whispered to Bell. "He's losin' his balance. Look at him."

Swaying a little, Kang leaned into his caddy like a drunken sailor. Ten seconds later, he dashed from the tee box, hurrying from the course as the official, looking somewhat confused as he conversed on his two-way, scampered along in an effort to keep up with the fleeing Kang. Spectators looked about in confusion, as television viewers watched Hunter and his caddy standing with Kang's caddy on the eighteenth tee. On his arrival at the clubhouse, Kang dashed to the restroom.

Bell looked at her watch, made a conspicuous head shake, and gestured disapproval at an official.

"We have contacted the rules committee," the official said. "It appears Mr. Kang is allowed some time in which to return to play, based on the circumstances. If he causes undue delay, he *will* be disqualified."

Bell maintained a straight face, whispering to Hunter, "How long is *some time?*"

Impatient spectators began chanting, "Kang! Kang! Kang!"

An official voice came across the public address

system, "Mr. Kang has been alerted to a five minute time extension."

Four minutes later he emerged from the clubhouse, bowed apologetically to the crowd, took the lob wedge from his caddy, and stepped into the bunker. He made brief eye contact with Hunter, set up over the ball, made a swing and watched as the ball settled softly ten feet from the cup.

"That was a great save," Bell said in a hushed voice. "Going to be a close one."

In a display of uncontrollable release, the rear of Kang's beige trousers began turning brown, the odor causing groans from nearby spectators. There was a push to move away from the shocked golfer, as people stumbled over one another in a rush to move away from the stench, from the embarrassment. Many agreed Hunter would have won regardless, but Kang's demise would be the subject of golf conversations for years to come. 'DOING A KANG', became as much a catch cry as, '*DOING A VAN DE VELDE.*' The headline announced: 'KANG MESSES UP, HUNTER CLEANS UP!'

The next day's sporting pages carried graphic descriptions of the final round, photographs of Kang dashing from the eighteenth green. Fortunately, the shots were not in color.

The celebration extended past midnight.

A hefty check sat on the table as Hunter and Bell made another toast. Several press members hung about, bathing in the glory of the moment. During toasts, and a chorus of *Born In The U.S.A.* from rowdy, very intoxicated ex-patriot supporters, a tall man approached Hunter. He reached inside his coat as Hunter began to stand. Another man stepped forward, gesturing at Hunter to remain seated.

"Mr. Hunter," the tall man said. "I believe we owe you a substantial amount of money."

Bell placed a restraining hand on Hunter's arm,

easing him back into his chair.

The nearer man said, "We represent Ladbrokes."

The tall man removed an envelope from his jacket, presented it to Hunter. "We were somewhat undecided, what with the unusual withdrawal of Mr. Kang; however the Tour representative assures us the result does stand. This check covers your wager. You laid the odds of five hundred to one."

Hunter opened the envelope and without so much as glancing at the check, passed it sideways to Bell.

"A cool half million," Bell sighed.

"All is correct then, Mr. Hunter?" the tall man asked.

"Yeah, very correct."

The surrounding crowd erupted into more cheers as Bell raised the check above her head. She did a three sixty, displaying it to the cheering crowd.

"Order up guys!" Gardner Hunter shouted. "Drinks are on me."

'Born In The U.S.A.' . . . never sounded so good.

Hunter's celebration was to be of short duration. The Grand Hyatt was holding messages.

Sam Ridkin had called.

Twice.

CHAPTER 24

SIRENS PULLED BLAKE FROM his nap. Rubbing his eyes, he focused on Dal who was impatiently flicking through channels. Blake put his hands behind his head and stared with an appraising look in his eyes. "Mother of God," he grumbled, "gimme that fuckin' thing."

"Hey, hey, hey, you're sharin' the bed with me," Dal groaned, "no one said nothin' about the remote."

Relieved to have the other bed to himself, Sung chuckled, "You two sound like you belong together."

"Ain't easy, depends on his time of the month," Dal replied with a sardonic smile.

"Hey," Blake said with ice blue eyes cutting into Dal, "some respect here, Father Dominic."

Dal tossed the remote over Blake's head and Sung made the catch.

"Knock yourself out," Dal said, feigning offense. "See what *you* can find."

Blake stretched out and yawned. "Try the news channels. See if ya can dig up anythin' on McDowell."

Sung and Dal remained silent.

"Sung, for Christ's sake, find the news," Blake repeated.

But Sung was feigning sleep, and the remote lay in the palm of his outstretched hand.

Dal stared at him for a few seconds, then said, "Jesus, take a look at this guy, a minute back he was jabberin', now

257

he's fuckin' comatose." He glanced at Blake, caught the prelude to a snoring match, and mumbled, "Ah jeez, what's a guy t' do?"

He rolled onto his side, wrapped the pillow around his head, and began counting sheep. When the sheep were done jumping, he reached for the remote and finally settled on a news channel. A Chinese army officer, with emotion bordering on tears, was being interviewed. Another camera cut to a head shot of a soldier. Dal pointed the remote at the screen, about to press buttons, to surf channels. But there was something that tweaked his curiosity. He paused as the interviewer went the route most interviewers travel, pushing emotional buttons, trying to bring meltdown to the afflicted party. *Ratings for the benefit of viewers,* Dal thought, squinting, intently focusing on the broadcast as subtitles streamed along the bottom of the monitor.

Captain David Cheng was the eldest son of General Cheng. David Cheng was an up and coming officer in the People's Liberation Army. It is believed he was the victim of a Westerner, possibly American. Officials suspect the assailant to be a serial killer traveling through China. Two other victims were found by the railroad track near the city of Datong. One victim, also a soldier, appeared to have been thrown from a train. The talking head had Dal's undivided attention. *"The body of a woman was also found by the railroad tracks. Police believe it also originated from the train."* He sat there for a moment, frozen with disbelief, then called quietly to Blake, "Hey, wake up. Come on, wake up. Look at this shit."

The interviewer continued, *"A substantial reward is offered by the People's Republic for information leading to the apprehension of the suspect or suspects. We are appealing to the people for any information relevant to foreigners currently traveling through China. Please contact this number with any information on foreigners seen on board the train traveling from Datong to Beijing. Persons harboring foreigners and not reporting their presence will be severely punished.*"

The phone buzzed and Dal hit the mute button. "F-f-f-fuckin' phone," he stammered. He gathered his thoughts, cleared his throat, allowed some moments to slide by, moments for his voice to become priestly. "Hello."

"Who is this?" the voice on the other end barked.

An involuntary twitch in Dal's eyebrow belayed his simulation of Father Dominic. "This is Father Dominic," he replied, then paused as he connected the voice to the caller's face. "Is that you, Sam?"

"Dal, glad I caught you. Drew there?"

"Yeah, what's goin' on?"

"You saw the stuff about McDowell, right?"

"Yeah, caught some of it on the plane."

"Is Sung there?"

"Yeah."

"Okay then, just listen and don't say a word. I've sent a message to Hunter and Bellinger, and contacted one of our guys in Beijing."

Blake couldn't suppress his curiosity. He made a '*what's goin' on*' gesture.

Dal placed a palm over the handset. "Long story," he whispered. "Guess we'll read about it in the press."

With a rising sense of dread, he placed the phone back to his mouth. "So what's *our* next move, Sam? Any word on Slade?"

"He had a problem with a soldier on the Datong train, a gun fight with a few guys. One was killed, he was one of General Cheng's men."

"Could get messy," Dal said, shaking his head. "Changes the plan a bit, right?" He waited for a reply.

None came.

"What the fuck's goin' on?" Blake grumbled as he

scurried across the room and gestured for the phone.

"Hold on, Sam. Drew wants ya."

"Hey Sam, fill me in."

And Blake listened as the situation was explained.

"The general's searching for our boy. He's tightened the net on your operation. We're sending Hunter and Bellinger after Wang, he's a loose cannon. Can't have you guys side tracked by Wang. You stay with Slade. Wang'll probably try to hook up with Cheng at Western Hills."

Blake covered the receiver. "Feel like the mouse in a lab test, a maze, a really bad feelin', too many players." He could've elaborated, but paused, his hand hard over the phone, thinking. He waggled the handset at Dal, "And we ain't all playin' the same game."

The voice on the phone grew loud, impatient. "Drew, Drew! You there?"

"Yeah Sam, had to sneeze, sorry."

"Give my salutations to Sung, say goodbye to Dal. I want you to get them out of the room, we need to talk. Just turn around and say, *Great, Sam, thanks for the call, speak with you tomorrow.*"

He whispered, "*Got it,*" and looked around at Dal and Sung, each glued to the news broadcast. He said, "Great, Sam, thanks for the call. I'll speak with you tomorrow." He put on a fake laugh, replaced the handset, and turned toward the inquisitive faces.

"Sammy bein' funny," Dal said. "Now there's an 'aha' fuckin' moment."

Blake made a blank expressionless gaze, then his eyes flickered across the room.

Search as he may, a response eluded him.

CHAPTER 25

THE PHONE IN WANG'S suite buzzed.

"Mr. Wang, this is Lisa Ling."

He switched sides with the handset, wiped the sleep from his eyes as he squinted at his watch with the realization he'd only slept for three hours. Gave a nod, a smile.

"What a pleasant surprise, Miss Ling."

"No need for niceties, Mr. Wang. I require a show of support, a good faith gesture if we're to proceed with your search for Slade."

"Very well, and what might that *show of support* be?"

"A half million dollars in one hundred dollar bills, within twenty-four hours. Bring the money and I'll provide you with a photograph."

There was a long silence as Wang digested her words. He thought, *I was told there were no photographs.*

"Miss Ling, that is quite a large sum. May we begin with less?"

Intuition flashed red warning lights in her mind, and the light flared as she surmised Wang's inability to deliver. "This isn't open to negotiation. Can you, or can't you do as I ask?"

"Let me see . . ." He raised an eyebrow, swallowed hard, played for time, found it disconcerting that a woman was giving him an ultimatum. His face turned grim. "Can you call back tomorrow, say around noon? I will need to make a call to have my superiors contact a nearby bank, to clear funds first thing in the morning. It is such a large amount, such little notice." He leaned on *it is*, left no doubt the amount itself was the immediate problem.

Roiled between distrust and the need to retain the upper hand, she replied in a terse voice, "Don't lose sleep over it."

He felt her sinister tone.

She knew he did.

Click.

He set about flicking through the Yellow Pages; his finger running down the column until it came to a listing for a nearby bank. An hour later he left the bank, carefully clutching his chest, one hand firmly over a large envelope containing ten thousand dollars in new one hundred dollar bills. His next stop was a business center where he picked out three reams of dove white paper, paid the cashier, moving to a quiet corner, out of view of two other patrons working at computer bays. He reached into his pocket, removed one of the hundred dollar bills and glanced sideways over his left shoulder. He raised his eyes to the ceiling, saw the security dome, but there was nothing he could do about the camera, other than hunch over the workbench. He placed the bank note onto the upper corner of one paper sheet and traced its outline, repeating this until he had four rectangles on the sheet of dove white. Each measured 52mm x 1220mm. After the first page, he moved into production mode, carefully measuring lines with a plastic ruler. He placed the measured sheet onto a small stack, each measuring 10mm in height and passed twelve stacks to the man at the service counter.

The salesman stared with rapt interest.

"I'm working on an art project," Wang explained. "Can you cut these as I've marked on the top sheets?"

The man placed the first ream on the guillotine, set the program, and in a few minutes handed Wang stacks of banknote sized bills. He took the stacks to the copy machine, reached into his pocket, took the envelope containing the one hundred bank notes, and carefully removed the paper bands showing the denomination. Opening the band, he pressed it flat, laid it on the copier, and ran off a single copy. After carefully studying it, he trimmed neatly around its perimeter, repeating the exercise until the band reproduced itself sufficient times to give him fifty currency wrappers, representing a half million dollars in one hundred dollar bills. He placed the neat stacks into a large paper bag and returned to the counter, where he paid twenty-three Hong Kong dollars for a small roll of Scotch tape. Back in his room, he sat at the writing desk, grinning to himself, content in his feeling of satisfaction. One genuine bank note sat neatly on top of each stack of dove-white paper. He wrapped a band around each stack, and placed each of the stacks in the attaché, and gave his handy-work an admiring glance.

Hmm, yes, looks just like a half million dollars.

He positioned the genuine bank notes in the center of the top layer of bundles, hoping this would be the only bundle Lisa Ling would handle. He thought, *looks like money, smells like money; have to act like it really is a large amount of money.*

He reached for a towel, wiped his forehead, and waiting for the call, glancing nervously at the bedside clock. It showed almost mid-day, April 16. He surfed through channels, eyes bouncing from the screen to his watch, from his watch to the bedside table, back to the screen. His mind racing, faster, the anticipation showing as his shirt clung to his body. *Nearly time, she must call soon.*

He finished a bottle of Dasani, realized his need to pee and made his way to the bathroom. He began peeing, and as is often the way, the phone by the bed came to life. He fumbled his fly, was unable to stop midstream and his trouser leg clung damply as he leaped onto the bed, got a hand on the phone, composed himself, tried to compose himself a little more, panted, "This is Wang."

"You sound out of breath, Mr. Wang. You *have* got my money?"

"Yes."

Her tone was skeptical. "You do, really? You have the half million?"

"Of course, as requested, hundred dollar bills. What is our next move?"

She replied as though reading from a teleprompter. "Meet me downstairs, in the foyer, fifteen minutes. We'll exchange items in public, no third party, agree?"

Her self assuredness served to aggravate him all the more.

"Yes, the foyer, fifteen minutes."

He breathed a sigh of relief, placed the phone back on its cradle. *Thank God she does not want to do this in her room, with a third party present. She cannot display the contents of the brief case with so many people in the lobby area. This could work. Excellent!*

Hmm . . .

CHAPTER 26

HE CLUTCHED THE LEATHER case with a python-like grip, the mere thought of it containing a half million dollars more than justified his behavior. And besides, the genuine ten thousand was reason enough to be aware of any snatch-and-grab antics from passers by. When he entered the foyer, Lisa slid a hand under his arm.

He jumped away.

"My goodness, you are a nervous cat," she said, placing a finger on the attaché case. "It must be all of this money you have for me?"

"Are you alone?"

He slid a sideways glance at the two men standing suspiciously in opposite corners of the reception lounge. After a minute, one of the men greeted a woman, chatted, and the couple left.

The remaining man concerned Wang.

He tightened his grip on the case, slid his eyes back toward the man, and repeated his question, "Are you alone?"

She looked across the foyer, saw the man, grinned, and said reassuringly, "We must have mutual trust. Of course I'm alone." She pointed to a settee. "Let's sit over there; I need to see the money."

The python-like grip increased. "You have the photograph?"

"Of course, you'll see it when I see the money." She

nodded to the case as she said *the money.*

Wang bowed toward a group passing nonchalantly through the foyer. His voice was dry and untrusting. "It does not concern you that this . . ." and he waved his free hand about the foyer, "that this is far too public a place to open the case?"

She leaned forward, held up a finger. "Just a quick peek," she said, smiling reassuringly. "Then we'll go to my bank." She nudged her head toward the hotel door. "It's just minutes away."

He took a few seconds to digest the proposal, then nodded toward a table across from a large weeping tree. "We can sit at that table."

A pile of magazines was neatly stacked in the center of the table and a recently cleaned ashtray sat by the magazines. Wang eased into a chair, placing the briefcase by a copy of Vogue, as Lisa opened her handbag, took out a fresh pack of Du Maurier, peeled off the cellophane wrap, passed her lighter to Wang and sensually placed a cigarette between her lips. She felt his eyes, knew her mouth was doing its job. When she slowly looked up, she caught his stare and made a point of embarrassing him. She moved her pouted lips nearer to him, "Do you mind, it's a Zippo, and the flint sticks."

His hand trembled as he took the lighter and clumsily flicked it open. She moved the cigarette to the flame, inhaled lightly, her eyes rising slowly from the Du Maurier, locking onto his. If it was an attempt to put Wang at ease, it failed. He wasn't ready to trust her. A fresh bead of sweat trickled from his hairline. Her eyes caught the trickle.

"My goodness, Mr. Wang, you're perspiring."

The words were hardly out of her mouth when Wang snapped back in a defensive tone, "I have a half million dollars on the table, of course I am perspiring. I will feel far better when I have the photograph and this is in a bank."

She blew out a perfect smoke ring that drifted

toward him, and as he pulled back, she said, "Open the case, Wang."

And she asserted absolute control. The *Mr.* was gone. Her tone, no longer one of request, had become one of demand.

He turned the tumblers, sliding the buttons toward the corners of the case.

The locks sprung open.

Raising the lid he fumbled nervously, dropping it shut as he wiped his forehead, looking about to be sure no one had caught his behavior. A boy ran toward the table, reached for a magazine, causing Wang to snap both hands onto the black leather case, peering defensively at the intruder as he snatched a copy of Vogue, pulled a face at Wang, and toddled off in the direction of a woman inconspicuously nursing an infant in a far corner of the foyer.

Wang breathed a sigh of relief; re-opened the lid sufficiently for Lisa to sneak a peek at the bundles. He reached for the genuine bundle, hesitating as Ling's hand raced his own toward the notes. He moved his hand to the right, to the fake bundle, sufficiently maneuvering her onto the genuine notes to the left.

His heart pounded.

More perspiration.

She removed the stack from the case, placed the notes under her nose and riffling through it, smelling the paper as it created a gentle breeze. "I smell, hmm, ten thousand," she said sniffing, "very nice, very nice indeed."

She replaced the stack. Wang hid his anxiety and quickly closed the case, subconsciously thanking his God for good fortune. With a look of self-satisfaction, he turned the tumblers, stroked his forehead, felt the wet, and forced a smile. "You have seen your money. The photograph, let me have it."

"I don't have it."

"What?" He raised his voice, anger growing in his tone, but kept a forced smile. Not shouting, but quite emphatic, he snarled, "What do you mean, you *do not have it?*"

She didn't return the smile. "Surely you don't think I'd have the photograph with me. What do you take me for?"

"We had an arrangement. What was all that nonsense about trust?"

"You'll see the photograph when the money is in my bank's safety deposit box, not any sooner."

The bank was a five-minute cab ride from the Langham. When they arrived, the manager opened a small divider and escorted the pair to a private booth.

"Lisa, my dear," he said, smiling warmly. "It is good to see you again."

Wang leaned to her ear. "He appears to know you rather well."

"A distant cousin, he opened an account here for me for, hmm . . ." She paused and gave a few long moments thought to her choice of words. "It's an account for my extra curricular savings, you might say."

She placed her arms around the manager, gave a quick hug, then said to Wang, "He takes very good care of family interests."

The manager left them in a private room, and returned in thirty seconds carrying a safety deposit box. All three sat at a faux marble top desk, and Wang reluctantly placed his attaché case on the desk just inches from Lisa Ling's hand. She reached for the case and placed it into the steel box, pausing, then looking at him steadily. "You were saying we must have *trust*, now I'm trusting you."

She held his stare and slid the security box to the manager.

Wang eyed the closed box. He thought, *got you*, but

said, "Yes of course, *trust*," and smiled triumphantly.

She grinned at the manager and flicked her long black tresses in a rehearsed way. "I'll contact you with instructions on transferring the funds to an overseas account, perhaps Swiss." She said it with an affirmative nod. "Is this acceptable?"

"Of course, there will be the usual small transaction fee, but so long as you sign this consent form, I will be able to take these funds and carry out your instructions."

She signed relevant paperwork, and the manager handed over the key. "Thank you," she said, reaching out a hand. "May I have the envelope please?" and chuckled at the Hollywood inference.

The manager reached into a drawer, placed a brown bank envelope in Lisa's palm. Wang was still feeling a slight euphoria for having pulled off the fake note ploy, and fought hard to retain a calm demeanor. He looked about the room, took in the security cameras, became uneasy and instinctively lowered his head.

Lisa emptied the contents of the envelope.

A gold locket slid onto the desktop.

"You can look at the photograph, but I'll keep the locket."

Her pause was timely, closing her eyes and using a saddened voice. "The locket . . . it has sentimental value."

She opened the golden heart, a center hinged pendant. The left side carried a faded photograph of a Chinese woman, the right side, a photograph of a man in his mid-thirties.

Wang reached for the locket, had to tug it from her. He made a pleasured sound as his eyes took in the two miniature photographs. "Hmm, so this is the man," he scoffed. "This man in the locket, he is Paul?"

The conversation took on a frigid tone. She longed for the sound of his name, but despised the use of it by Wang. *My Paul*, she thought glaring coldly at Wang. *Sonofabitch,* she thought, then answering, "Yes, he's Paul."

Wang did his best to disguise his distaste. He looked up, uncomfortable with her frigid eyes. He returned her cols stare, and his finger jabbed a hole in the air between them. He hung for a second, two seconds, and then pointed at the other photograph. "Who is the woman? I must know everything about the locket."

"That's not your concern," she replied, and gave a stubborn shrug. "I don't understand."

"Of course you do not. You, like most people, see only the big picture."

She reached a hand toward him. He looked down at her warm palm and when he placed the locket into that warm place, he held onto her hand, the locket sandwiched between.

He grinned, unsure of her gaze.

"Be careful, Mr. Wang, don't fall prey to your devious wishful thinking."

She untangled the gold chain, and repositioned it around her neck. The chain snagged on her hair, and she said, "Would you mind?" He reached for the catch, brushing her hair aside, securing the clasp.

"When do we leave?" he asked. "I believe your agreement was to accompany me to Beijing." He moved around to face her, nodding at the locket. "To assist me in locating the face that matches the one in this."

He pointed at the golden heart, watching her with the unease of a man who knew full well a woman was finding him grossly unattractive.

"Meet me at three," she said, in a thoughtful tone. "I need to get things together."

Wang hesitated. *She can double back to the bank, bring some of the cash along with her, but I will have to chance it.* He rolled his eyes, made a condescending shrug. "At three, in the foyer, I will see you then."

At three o'clock, they once again sat by the weeping tree.

"I have two air tickets to Zhengzhou," Wang said. "I was unable to secure a flight for the entire journey, so from there we will travel to Beijing by bus. I am sorry about that, the bus journey is three hundred miles." He paused, one hand holding the tickets aloft. "We will get underway in the morning."

Almost forlornly, with a puppy-like expression, he added, "I was wondering if you would like to join me for dinner this evening, to dine with a very good Oriental man?" The words came out with a sarcastic implication, unappreciated by Lisa.

"A very good Oriental man? I have known many good Oriental men, Mr. Wang. When they're good, they're very, very good, but when they're bad, they're . . .

He waited. But she left him hanging.

After a minute, she said, "Dinner? Yes, why not? I'll be pleased to. Say at seven thirty?"

There was a stunned hesitation. "Really? Oh! I so look forward to enjoying your company. Let us hope it is less dramatic than the first time we sat together at a table."

"We can only hope now, can't we?"

Wang's invitation reeked of subversive overtone, but she knew better than to refuse the offer, lest it jeopardize the mission.

*****

He threw down several glasses of wine while waiting for a table, his eyes blurred. Lisa was concerned he might not survive if the wait for the table were much longer. Fifteen minutes later they were escorted to a corner setting. He ran an index finger down one side of the menu, surprising her with a quiet statement. "Miss Ling, there is a group in China whose mission it is to terminate your friend. If you help me to locate him, it could very well save his life."

Time to think.

Wang lied poorly.

She paused for several moments, mulled over the implication of his statement. "Really, and why exactly does this *group* want to kill him?"

She avoided his stare, keeping her eyes on the menu.

"He is a rogue operator who has killed several people," Wang said, "including the son of a general."

Her eyes moved off the menu.

"A general?"

"Yes, General Cheng."

He raised the fourth glass of wine to his mouth, as his eyes flickered about the restaurant, searching, his round face glistening with sweat. "General Cheng's son, David, was shot during a street fight." He gave a long stare. "A soldier with the general's son reported a skirmish with an American. This person killed David Cheng." He pointed gingerly at her neck. "An artist's impression of the assailant is strikingly similar to the photograph in that locket." A smile tugged at the corner of his mouth. "David Cheng was, what is it they say, ear marked for high places?" Wang grinned at her, held the expression for three full seconds, his tongue flickering snake-like across his lower lip, his grin evolving into a more serious expression. "He was with the 13th Group Chuan Army. He was being groomed to follow in his father's footsteps."

Her mouth was open. She was frozen-faced, and realized how weak she must appear to him at that moment.

Vulnerable.

She glanced about the restaurant in search of a waiter.

"I am a personal friend of General Cheng," Wang

said. "I knew each of his sons, David and Peter." He took a long pull on the near-empty glass of wine. "They are a most highly esteemed family."

She caught the waiter's eye and after a few more seconds perusing the menu, she chose Szechwan Chicken Salad. Wang selected Gingered Pork and Cabbage Soup. Two minutes after commencing the meal, Wang propped himself clumsily onto one elbow. "Miss Ling. May I call you Lisa?"

She found his inebriated state somewhat amusing.

"Certainly," she said, and pointed at his mouth. "You have something stuck on your front tooth."

As is the case with most women, she enjoyed playing with a man's minds, and Wang was a prime candidate. Just when he believed he'd slotted into a comfort zone with her . . . bang! She shot him down.

As he wiped his front teeth with his napkin, a slight blush added color to the oval face. "So, I can call you Lisa?"

Another wipe.

And it was all spoken through the napkin.

"Yes," she said raising her eyebrows, "I thought we'd settled that."

He grinned, mouth covered. "Sorry, I am always nervous around beautiful women."

"Flattery, Mr. Wang," and she faked a girlish giggle, "will get you everywhere."

She flashed a smile, got his spirits sufficiently high that he lowered the napkin and beamed a confident grin, reached for the wine, and tapped his finger on the empty bottle

"Lisa, do you mind if I order another?"

His eyes didn't leave hers.

"I don't think that's a good idea," she said imperturbably. "We need to be sharp in the morning. You look as though you've had more than enough."

"The wine is for you my dear. Perhaps it will help you cooperate a little more easily, to think more clearly."

"Hmm, if I get a little light headed, I'm sure I can count on you to assist me back to my room."

He gave a shrewd grin, then raised a hand to signal the waiter.

The Black American Express card caught Lisa's eye.

"Black Amex, very impressive. That's a considerable amount of spending power."

He appreciated her acknowledging the status of the Centurion Card.

"Yes, I am rewarded well for my work."

"Obviously, and apparently you're very good at *your work*." She placed extra emphasis on '*your work*'.

"I am considered to be one of the best at, eh . . . at *my work*."

"And *your work* is?"

They sat through a long minute of silence and Lisa said, "Don't you just hate that?"

He looked about, saw nothing. "Hate what?"

"Uncomfortable silences."

One side of his mouth turned upward. "Yes I do. To answer your question, my *work* is . . . well, I find people. I take care of problems."

*****

Wang swayed as he passed his ticket to the valet who quickly headed off to retrieve the car. He placed a hand against the wall to steady himself. Then, feeling the moment was right, took a step forward, reached for her arm, squeezed it, lost his balance and pulled her against him. Her arm scraped against the wall and he saw the expression of pain flash across her face. The odor of cabbage soup lingered heavily on his breath and she pulled away from him with a look of revulsion. Sizzling with temper, she said, "Too rough, Mr. Wang, far too rough."

Wang slurred his speech. "Please forgive me. I thought I was picking up some signs from you. I must have been getting mixed signals. I thought we might spend more time together, perhaps this evening?"

"Don't humor me, Mr. Wang. I sent no such signals." She backed off a few paces, brushing herself off. "I'm also very good at what I do. And spending the evening with a man I've just met is not among them."

Silence.

CHAPTER 27

HE STUBBED THE MARLBORO and called to the corporal who was fastidiously operating a copy machine in a far corner of the office. He said in a hoarse dry voice, "You have any cigarettes?" Wanted to say, *the general has me doing your fucking job as well as mine,* but that would have been disrespectful. "I'm out of smokes and can't leave my station. The general expects me to stay at my desk until five."

General Zhu Cheng was off someplace annoying other people; the captain wallowed in the reprieve. The atmosphere in the Western Command building resembled a courtroom awaiting verdict from a hung jury, and the captain's office insulated him from the increased activity following the death of the general's son.

Again, "You have any cigarettes?"

The answer came as the corporal slipped a pack of Gauloises from his jacket, tossing them onto the captain's desk. "Comrade, this's a fresh pack, go ahead, help your-self."

Three hours later, outside of the Command Center, Cheng stood tall on the raised dais where he addressed his meticulously uniformed troops. He posed, hands clenched behind him.

Mussolini, or perhaps George Patton.

The 13th Group Army consisted of two divisions, as well as a field artillery brigade, an armored brigade, an anti-

BLACK SABBATH

aircraft artillery brigade, and a communications regiment. The unit's 'Category A' division indicated the 13th was fully trained and equipped with the very latest weapon technology. The Group had its roots in a military sub-district of T'aiyueh, and could be traced back as far as 1939. In September of 2003, Cheng headed up the 13th Group Army on a mission to relieve border guards along the Yunnan border with Myanmar. Their mission, to offset any instability in the event the Burmese government collapsed. The general's deceased son, Captain David Cheng, was a member of the group and was subsequently decorated for valor.

Reports indicated that an air defense, or AAA unit, had deployed near Mengzhi village. There were rumors that during the group's deployment to the region, the younger Cheng had a problem with a local woman in the area, a Burmese girl, the daughter of one of the better families. The girl claimed Cheng's son had raped her. Her parents insisted on a quick marriage to salvage their daughter's honor. The following day, the girl and her family disappeared. The incident was swept under the rug; General Cheng's dogged pursuit of his son's killer took precedence. He was not about to allow the assailant to slip through his fingers, and would use every man in the 13th to achieve such an end.

At eight o'clock on the morning of April 17, Cheng completed his briefing. He had four of his best men prepared to join him for a visit to the cathedral in Beijing.

Bishop Jean Pierre Bolin was about to meet the devil.

*****

The Xishiku Cathedral was located west of Zhongnanhai, at Canchikou. Cheng, together with his four men, was greeted inside the church entry by three novice priests. It took a while for the more experienced of the three

277

to realize just who this officer was. When he did, he turned to those standing precariously behind him and whispered, "Not a word." He constructed a smile, shifted into a higher gear, fighting back a twinge of fear as he bowed to the officer with the stars on his collar.

But Cheng had heard the remark, and pounded his fist across the priest's face and the priest sprawled forward and slid along the aisle and blood gushed freely from a gash to his temple as his head slammed into a pew. One of Cheng's men moved quickly to give assistance, dropping to his knees, rolling the priest onto his back, but the priest's eyes were glazed, and the soldier slipped a hand across, shutting the dead eyes.

"General, he's dead. His head, it struck the pew."

Totally frustrated, Cheng loudly berated the man for his show of sympathy, but the soldier ignored the ranting general and remained kneeling by the young priest. Cheng pulled his side arm from its holster, pointed it at the soldier's temple, and squeezed off a shot.

The young priest did not travel alone to meet his God.

The soldier slumped forward in the center aisle, coming to rest draped across the priest, both eyes open, blood trickling from his mouth.

He was a young man.

Twenty years young. Not ready to depart the world, another pawn, totally disposable, totally gone. Cheng placed his boot on the dead man's chest, gave a gentle push, rolling the dead man off the priest. The other three soldiers passed a few almost indiscernible comments, and Cheng, catching the murmur of dissent, reeled about, gun still drawn, and addressed them in an angry, hostile tone. "You are to act only on my orders. If any of you move without my ordering, you will be shot!"

They stood at rigid attention.

Three terra cotta warriors.

"Remove both bodies, drag them away," Cheng ordered. "Sergeant Qui, call back to the 13th. Have more men dispatched here immediately."

The sergeant scurried from the cathedral, taking the steps three at a time, reached into the jeep and began chattering on a cellular phone. Unable to pick up a clear signal, he moved a few yards away and pulled at the antenna, shook the cell phone, looked at the back of the unit, opened it, removed the battery, replaced the battery, tried to call out one more time.

Nothing.

He threw the phone to the ground, stomping on it a few times and shouting at the sky, "Fucking Korean phone!"

The driver of a passing car saw the stomping, slowed, and the soldier turned. He pulled his side arm, and pointed it. The vehicle stopped, and slowly reversed. The soldier shouted from twenty feet, saw the fear in the driver's eyes, thought about it, smiled, and made a *take it easy* gesture as he called out in a pleading tone, "Comrade, do you have a phone?"

The driver looked dubious, yet disguising his reluctance passed his phone. The soldier walked away from the vehicle, and hastily punched in numbers. Twenty painful seconds later, he returned the phone to its owner. The tires squealed as the driver sped away, relieved to place distance between himself and Cheng's man. Swerving uncontrollably, avoiding potholes, he failed to see the three hooded priests walking toward the cathedral.

During his dash back to the cathedral, the soldier gave a curious glance at the three scrambling priests as they leaped from the path of the speeding driver. The soldier scaled the steps, and arrived breathless, just feet from Cheng, who stood observing a young priest mopping blood from the center aisle tiles, and two others dragging both bodies to the

279

sacristy at the rear of the altar.

"When you have completed your cleaning," Cheng shouted, "we will make certain you cooperate with my request."

The floor mopping continued. One priest swished the mop, wiping blood that trailed from the bodies being dragged along, and a soldier's foot inched the bucket along the aisle, moving it toward the altar as the priest feverishly worked on the tiles. Another priest toweled off blood spray from a dozen or so pews.

"You . . ." Cheng grunted pointing to the taller priest, "where is your bishop?"

The mopping priest lowered his eyes, ignoring the question. Cheng pulled the side arm from its holster, pointed it at the priest's forehead, held his aim, didn't speak for a long moment, then growling dismissively, "I do not have time for this." He motioned to the rear of the cathedral. "Move to the back. I will shoot you where the other two are." He made a sinuous cackle as he passed a hand around the church. "It will save your friend the need to clean the area a second time."

The shorter of the two priests panicked and made a dash for the door, bumping into Cheng as he pushed on by, sending the general tumbling sideways, taking one of his soldiers along with him, both falling between pews. The running priest reached the entry doors, cleared the doors, saw daylight, and sprinted toward the steps, running, running . . .

The shot reverberated through the cathedral and struck the running man between the shoulder blades, jolting the running man sideways across the steps, eyes frozen, tumbling down the final steps, tumbling, coming to rest on the pavement.

Didn't move again.

Spectators stared for a minute, two minutes, three,

then panicked at the sight of the priest's bloodied fall, they scrambled in all directions to escape the scene. Three priests, alerted by the gunshot and still shaken from a near miss with some lunatic speeding driver, ran to the man's assistance, but their help was of no use to the priest. With smoking gun in hand, Cheng stepped from the cathedral and shouted at the three men, "Move on, this isn't your concern!"

Blake whispered to the blonde haired priest, "Your hood, cover your fuckin' head." Dal tugged his hood around his face, turning away from Cheng as the three quickly made their way to the side of the cathedral. Mentally questioning their presence, Cheng kept the pistol raised, watching with lingering suspicion until the three had disappeared from sight.

A cry rang out from one terrified spectator, "My God, that priest, that poor man."

Cheng scanned the gathering crowd, ignored the cry, waved his handgun in the direction of the voice, and shouted, "Go, this is military business, move on!"

In hindsight, he felt he should've apprehended the three strangers. His hesitation was laid to rest when one of his soldiers called aloud, "General, the bishop, he is here!"

He dismissed his concern over the three hooded priests, reeled about, took a dozen paces back inside the cathedral - and came face to face with Bolin. Bishop Jean Pierre Bolin was a stout man in his mid sixties. His flushed shiny face held an expression of shock, and its color indicated possible high blood pressure. His mouth hung open as words eluded him. When he finally did speak, the words choked their way from his larynx. "What is this travesty?" he shouted. "This is a sin of the worst kind," and he waved both hands about the cathedral, flapping about like a bird trying to take flight. Again, shouting, "This is the house of God!"

Cheng dismissed the bishop's reaction, pointing at the priest who lay spread eagled at the base of the steps. He spat, and said, "I am General Cheng. You harbored a fugitive, a killer, an American named Paul Slade. Is this so?"

A long moment of frozen silence as Bolin sought the required response. He backed off several steps, replying with trepidation, "Yes, we had an injured man seeking help. We simply tended his wound."

No one moved for several seconds.

Silence.

Bolin swallowed hard, saw the cold stare in Cheng's eyes, and had a shot at explaining. "Caring for lost souls is a kindness we extend to all people. I do not inquire into their nationality, or of their business in China."

With no affection for men of the cloth, Cheng brushed off Bolin's comment, balanced on one foot, raised his boot and wiped a blood spatter from it, feigning more concern for the loss of shine on the brown leather than of the bishop's nervous body language.

"Then I can assume you were aware that this man was an American?"

Bolin leaned against one of the carved doors. "And if I was aware?"

Cheng's look of satisfaction intensified. "Hmm . . . yes. You knew, and you will accompany us."

He snapped to his sergeant, "Take him!"

The sergeant raised his weapon, tilting his head in the direction of the cathedral doors. Bolin swallowed hard, and found an ounce of bravado. "I will not leave the house of God."

Cheng bustled the bishop through the doors and raised his weapon, pointing it at Bolin who stared with unwavering defiance. Sensing the futility of his move, the general redirected the weapon at the priest standing alongside of Bolin. He placed the muzzle on the priest's temple - held the man's eyes. Without so much as turning away from the priest, Cheng slid his eyes to meet Bolin's, who was confused as to why this lunatic was pointing the weapon at one of his young priests, rather than at him. The general took a step back from the trembling man, gun now at arm's length.

"I usually give three seconds before I squeeze the trigger, but in light of your blatant defiance . . ."

The young priest's heart pounded as Cheng squeezed the trigger and a significant chunk from the back of the man's head scattered across the cathedral steps.

Bolin screamed, "Oh my Jesus!" as the body tumbled down the steps, the bishop scrambling down the bloodied steps and falling to the priest's side.

Cheng sprinted down to the pavement, straddling the man, and shouting, "Get up. Get way from him!"

Ignoring the order, Bolin lowered his head to the bloodied man's chest, and administered last rites. Frustrated by the bishop's insolence, Cheng dropped to one knee, prodding Bolin with the muzzle of the smoking revolver. "Get up, there is nothing you can do for him."

Bolin continued with the Latin, as Cheng pointed the weapon, and shouted repeatedly, "Get up, get up, get up!"

Blake, Dal and Sung heard the gun shot, and quickly emerged from the rear of the Xishiku. The general was peripherally aware of their arrival as Blake came to a sudden halt immediately behind him. Cheng was not prepared for the words the new arrival priest delivered. He began to turn as the blow connected. The man behind him snarled, "Motherfucker," and slammed an elbow into the side of Cheng's turning head and the general went down. Dal snatched up the loose gun, and quickly got off a single shot, dropping the sergeant standing at the top of the cathedral steps, unprepared for such aggression from a priest.

The sound of a blaring horn caused temporary cessation in activity. A military truck pulled to a stop at the rear of the agitated crowd, and soldiers alighted from the rear and began beating a path through the onlookers.

Blake heard the commotion, then saw the panicking crowd, people stumbling, and screaming. He saw the uniformed men emerging. Closer. No place to hide.

"Quick, thith way, follow me quickly," the voice said as a stranger tugged on Blake's sleeve. With the crowd pressing closely, Blake, Dal and Sung hunched, staying below the heads of the scrambling crowd, and inconspicuously melted into the throng.

Dal leaned into Blake. "Who are we followin'?"

"I dunno, but I hope t' Christ he's got a plan."

With no idea of the identity of the person leading them, Blake turned back to Dal, said, "At this point, I'd follow the devil," and he reached a hand onto *the devil's* shoulder as they weaved a pathway between the melee, Blake quickly running the sequence through his mind, called to the person in front, "Who are you?"

"I am Lee, Father Lee."

"Lee?" Blake said, sprinting and drawing a sharp breath, *who the fuck's Lee?*

"You were thuppothed to meet me at Nanhai Lake, in the park thith morning, at ten o'clock. I waited but you were not there. I went to the Temple of Heaven and waited, then I came thith way and thaw the dithturbanth. You are very lucky I came along when I did. I am to take you to Thlade."

The name clicked, *Thlade . . . Slade!*"

"Where's Slade . . . with you?" Blake asked.

He sensed Lee's hesitation, the momentary pause, the apprehension, the smidgeon of uncertainty.

"Ya want the password, right?" he asked, his head half cocked. "Uncle Sam sent us."

Lee turned and smiled.

"Mr. Thlade ith three hourth from here, in a white houth north-eath of Beijing, in Gubeikoult. It ith in Myun County." He allowed the smile to widen, spreading in a childlike excited way. "The houth hath the number eight on a red door, it good Feng Thui . . . you know?"

"Yeah, good Feng Shui, I know," Blake said panting. "Why'd ya pick this particular area, this house with the red door?"

"That houth ith near the Great Wall, many touritht, you not be notithed, you will better blend."

Dal, running hard, pushed his hood back and whined, "If ya weren't sure who we were, why'd ya help us back there?"

"I am a prieth," he said, with a fixed grin. "That ith the differenth between you and me. Thaving people ith what I do."

"Were ya with Slade?" Dal huffed. "Were ya with him when the people on the train were killed?"

"Yeth, but it wath unavoidable. Thlade killed to thave uth, to get to meet with you. I am very thory and have begged Our Lord for forgiveneth for both of uth, for Thlade and for mythelf."

"Did ya get it?" Dal asked, nudging Blake who was sprinting alongside at a steady pace. "Did ya get Our Lord's forgiveness?"

Lee grinned, acknowledging Dal's sense of humor. "Yeth, and now I can move forward."

"Í see," Blake said, trusting his ability to read people. "Then you're takin' us to Slade?"

Lee glanced nervously back in the direction of Xishiku. "Yeth, follow me, we will cut through the back road. It ith three hourth from here by buth, one will come along very thoon."

They increased their pace, and an hour later, with no bus in sight, Blake began appreciating his Mount Whitney training. Dal hung a few yards behind the other three men, and called, "Hey, Father Bond, ya suppose we could stop for an EKG?"

Lee took another look back, shaking his head, "Not a

good idea, too many tholdierth in thith area." Then tapping on his hood, "Pleathe, you mutht keep your hood on." He pointed down the roadway. "The buth, it will come along any time now."

They walked in single file, each looking like a Grim Reaper understudy. As he brought up the rear, Dal kicked a Coca-Cola can along the roadside. On the fourth kick, his curiosity was aroused by the Chinese wording on the rattling container. He bent, scooped up the can.

As the bullet whistled by Dal's ear, he dropped and shouted, "Christ!" and all four dived into the ditch along the road's edge.

Blake shouted, "What the fuck!" and tumbled on top of Lee. An approaching military jeep became air born as the driver gunned it, careening over a crest some eighty meters off, its front seat passenger was standing, clutching the roll bar with one hand, while the other squeezed off rifle shots.

Blake could feel the rage building as he raised himself from the ditch and dusted off his robe. "Fuckin' answer's right there," he growled, averting his eyes from the jeep as it slid to a halt alongside the four priests. Sung, Dal, and Lee slowly rose to their feet, hands raised above their heads, each yielding in a friendly manner to the soldier with the rifle, all four remaining in character, totally Salesian priests. *Maybe our cover's blown,* Blake thought, *or maybe this is nothin'.*

Sung smiled, nodding at the soldier as Blake, Lee and Dal followed his lead, a respectful move, and for a few moments the soldier mentally absorbed the group, concluding that all was well. Dal, with just his nose and one eye visible beneath the hood, slipped a sideway grin at Blake, and then nodded toward the three soldiers chatting among themselves. He whispered, "D'ya think we can squeeze into those uniforms?"

Blake leaned into Sung. "What're they sayin'?"

"They have been searching for three priests, there are

no prizes for guessing why," Sung said, keeping his eyes respectfully lowered. "The only reason we are still breathing is because there are four of us, not three, a stroke of good fortune."

"Yeah well," Dal whispered, "they just took their best shot at makin' it three."

Sensing the resentment, the highest ranking soldier casually strolled to Dal, reaching out and flicking the hood back off the blonde priest's head. Dal instinctively grabbed at the man's wrist, twisted, quickly spun him around, reaching his other arm around the soldier's head.

A fresh stick of celery being snapping, that was the sound.

Blake reached inside his cloak, took the blade from his belt, flinging it through the air to its target, embedding the blade deep in the chest of the nearest soldier, a *thwap* sound as it struck the man's breastbone. Sung heaved himself onto the third man as the surprised soldier made a desperate effort to reach his weapon on the seat of the jeep.

"Aw man," Dal groaned, "what do we do now?"

"Stay calm," Blake said. "We're lucky no one's seein' this," and he visually scouted the immediate area. "Sung, help me load these guys into the back of the jeep."

Father Lee knelt alongside the nearest soldier and began administering extreme unction.

"Inappropriate, wouldn't ya say, Father?" Blake said as he and Dal struggled to lift the largest of the three men.

The soft spoken priest shook his head, "Latht ritht are for all, and I muth make their journey to nexth life a pleathant one."

Blake heaved the body unceremoniously forward, losing his balance and tumbling into the trench by the roadside. "Ah shit," he winced, "it's my football ankle, think I've sprained the sonofabitch again."

Drew Blake had three memorable seasons with the

Minnesota Vikings. His days as a wide receiver left him with more than his share of memories, including torpedo like catches from Brad Johnson. The Vikings made the '96 playoffs. Blake tracked the ball, it torpedoed toward the far end of the field, he had it, just needed to run, began to run, running, running, stretching. Dived for the catch - had it. A perfect spiral from Johnson. Then, just as the ball nestled safely between Blake's hands, the defensive back, the safety and a line backer took it upon themselves to register their discontent with the great catch. Blake felt the ankle snap. All three slammed into the wide receiver. The pain would not have been as unbearable had they'd won the playoff. Fate was not with the Vikings in '96. Blake's legacy was a weakened right ankle.

Lee jumped into the driver's seat and Blake assumed he was familiar with the region. Sung and Dal, assuming the same, crammed into the rear, sitting uncomfortably on top of two deceased soldiers, with a third body crammed under their feet.

The sound of the jeep rattling along the road made for difficult conversation, made it necessary for Blake to shout, "Lee, get us someplace we can unload these guys!"

Driving with the confidence of a man familiar with the dusty narrow road, Lee flung the jeep around a sharp bend, drifting momentarily in the dust, narrowly avoiding a steep drop-off. Dal's hands were white to the bone as he gripped the roll bar, and with tears streaming back from his eyes, he shouted, "Goddamnit Lee, ya drive like a candidate for Le Mans. I'm glad ya know this road!"

"Yeah Lee," Blake shouted with the wind ripping through his hair, his hood flapping insanely about, as he leaned closer to the driver's ear, shouting even louder, "For a priest, ya handle this thing like a rally driver!" Then louder still, asking, "You've been around these parts a bit, huh?"

Lee flicked a disconcerting look, "Thorry, but thith

firtht time I am in thith area, I have never been on thith road before."

Dal groaned, "Aw thit!"

Lee screamed as he jammed a foot on the brake pedal, didn't see the approaching ox cart 'til he was on top of it. The jeep spun twice, began a slow out of control slide, and bounced heavily across a deep ditch, ejecting Blake and Sung. Two of the uniformed bodies tumbled across the dirt, tumbling, arms and legs flopping like rag dolls and coming to rest alongside a tall clump of dry brush. Dal, able to stay in the vehicle by clutching the roll bar with a death like grip, looked about for Lee, but Father Lee was no longer behind the wheel.

Standing tall, Dal shouted into the dust cloud, "Leeeeee! Leeeeee . . ."

Limping some fifty yards back from where the jeep had bounced across the ditch, Blake found Lee laying face up among a rock pile, his head misaligned with his body, eyes opening ever so briefly, a smile twitching one edge of his mouth. A droplet of blood leaked from the grinning edge as he motioned for Blake to come nearer. He slipped an arm around Lee, cradling his head, his free hand wiping blood from Lee's mouth as he made a groping vain effort to speak that only produced gibberish.

Blake turned to Dal, but Dal had looked away. He knew.

Then Lee whispered, "Number eight, eight, with red door . . ."

The child-like smile struggled to work its magic, and God allowed both edges of Lee's mouth to turn up ever so slightly. And God granted the priest one final emotion, allowing a tear to escape his eye, then Father Lee was gone.

"It's his neck," Blake said softly, then felt stupid for stating the obvious. With both hands on Lee's face, he whispered, "We gotta bury him, the others too."

Dal cupped his face in his hands, stayed that way for a long few minutes.

Blake walked away, and shed his tears in silence. When his eyes had dried, he turned to Sung. "We got four bodies and a slightly used jeep," he said, "and some place we know only as a white house with a red door, and the number eight." He gestured at the jeep, "Sung, take the jeep. You'll pass as one of the locals." He flicked a thumb at the nearest soldier. "Get out of those robes, get into that guy's uniform. You're drivin' this military thing. If anyone looks your way, act indifferent, act like one of the People's fuckin' Army." He took a water bottle from a bag in the rear compartment of the jeep, kneeled and poured the water into a dirt patch by the roadside, mixing until it became mud, spreading the mud over the rear license plate. "No point advertisin'," he said to Sung, who gave an approving nod. "They might start checkin' plates along the road. This could buy ya a bit more time, ya know, if you're spotted. At this point, Mr. Sung," he said, straightening up and shaking mud from his hands, "I'm ready to try any fuckin' thing."

Blake passed the water to Sung, who poured it into his cupped hands. He rinsed, dried them on his robe, then sensed a silence. He looked about and caught Dal squatting over Lee's body, and as much as Blake felt a need to comfort his friend, he didn't acknowledge his tears.

Blake slipped his hood back, forced a smile, said, "Come on, we gotta get movin' here. We need the uniform for Sung," and he pointed to one of the dead men. "Dal, come on man, snap out of it, give Sung a hand. Strip that guy's uniform."

Dal began removing trousers from the soldier, stopped, then sniffing the air, quickly turned away. "Aw shit . . . he's unloaded in 'em."

Sung began to comment but Blake cut him short. "The other guy's got blood all over, and that one over there's way too small. This's all ya got. Scrape 'em clean and put up with it. Take the jeep, drive a ways along this road, check out what's ahead for the next mile or two, see if ya can find some place out of sight where we can dump the bodies."

As Sung left the scene, Blake poked a thumb over his shoulder. "Dal, help me drag these two guys over there, behind that long grass. We'll wait here until Sung gets back."

When Sung was no longer in sight, the two cloaked men dragged all four bodies behind a rock formation, out of view of passing traffic. Dal checked his watch; Sung had now been gone ten minutes, twenty minutes, then thirty minutes. He squinted off into the distance. "I'm gettin' a bad feelin' about this," he said, "he's been gone way too long."

*****

Backed up vehicles closed off the single lane, causing the bus to grind along at a snail's pace, the driver's head pounding as he thumped impatiently on the steering wheel.

Wang leaned into the aisle. "Driver!" he called aloud, "what is the problem?"

With escalating blood pressure, the driver turned back toward Wang. "A check point," he said. "I heard the military is looking for a foreigner. I heard he killed some soldiers."

The bus came to a stop, crawled along a few more yards and abruptly jerked to another stop, as the frustrated driver yanked on the handbrake. The stop became prolonged, and Wang, growing irritably, craned out the window, trying to spot the cause of the delay. The windshield had picked up a variety of insects, and the dust had crusted over bug-guts, greatly reducing visibility. As the bus resumed its slow move forward, Wang squinted at the snarled traffic, placing a shading hand above his eyes and focusing on an army vehicle on the roadside ahead. It was propped on a car jack and had partly blocked the roadway, a wheel with a blown tire lying to one side, a soldier pushing hard on a wheel brace, tightening lug nuts on the spare. As the bus slowly maneuvered around the jeep, Wang looked directly down at the man.

The soldier continued working on the lug nuts, and without turning, raised a hand to acknowledge the driver's caution. Wang called aloud, "Bad place for a flat!"

Wiping his forehead of sweat, the soldier turned, flashing a smile at the bus passenger.

He froze mid smile.

Their eyes locked.

Impatient drivers began sounding horns behind the bus, and the driver happily increased its speed, as Wang began shouting, "Stop the bus! Stop the bus!"

Lisa Ling grabbed a hold of his shoulder. "Wang, what the hell's wrong with you?"

"That man back there, he is Sung Chiao."

"You're paranoid," she said. "You know we all look alike."

"I tell you he is Sung Chiao. Stop the bus!"

He thrust her hand from his shoulder, jumped from his seat and moved toward the closed door, catching a snarl from the driver. "Cannot stop, please . . ." the driver snapped, "return to your seat."

"Wang," Lisa called aloud, "you're embarrassing me."

The soldier placed his right foot on the destroyed tire, pushed the wheel into the ditch, vaulted into the jeep, started the motor and glanced about nervously as he waited for a break in the stream of cars. When a gap did open, he gunned the jeep, screamed across the narrow road and headed back toward Blake and Dal.

Meanwhile, the two priests found a large hedge of bushes, a far better place to hide the bodies than behind the rocks. When the soldiers were disposed of, Blake returned to a spot nearer the road, while Dal added extra cover to the bodies, lingering back, hovering over Lee, a final few words, a few more tears. He wiped his face, took a deep breath, turned about and sought Blake's approval. "Wha'dya think? Does this look okay from over there. Ya can't see 'em from back there, can ya?"

But Blake was done with the issue of body disposal. "Have to be, we ain't gonna hang around here waitin' for Sung." He made a shrugging move toward the bushes. "That'll have to do." He inched his way forward, glaring at a pair of dogs some distance along the road. "Ain't no way anyone's gonna spot 'em from the road," and he gave another concerned glance at the dogs, pointing at them. "Unless those fuckin' dogs come sniffin' around."

CHAPTER 28

BLAKE SCOUTED THE SURROUNDING area on a day that had quickly become overcast, then he and Dal moved humbly along the edge of the road, traveling some two hundred yards when the sound of a blasting horn grabbed their attention, causing them both to dive for the cover of roadside scrub, moments before the screeching jeep skidded toward them, kicking up dust and stones in its wake. With his face half submerged in a mud puddle, and one eye squinting at Blake, Dal agonized over the many ways the Chinese might entertain themselves during this blonde priest's interrogation. The vehicle left the road, heading in their direction, screeching to a halt just yards from the two mud covered priests. Sung looked frenzied, confused, as he leaped from the jeep.

"Goddamnit, Sung," Dal said wiping mud from his face, "what the fuck happened?"

It was a full ten seconds before Sung was able to catch his breath. "You are not going to believe this," he gasped, "it's Wang . . . he is here!"

"What the fuck are ya talkin' about?" Blake said angrily. "Wang's here? Impossible."

Sung drew a breath, trying to calm to a slower panic. There was so much he needed to weigh up, but he had little to do the weighing. "No, I tell you," he repeated diligently, "Wang is here, I saw him on a bus. I was as close to him as I am to you. He is here, I tell you."

Six miles further along the road, the bus came to a regular stop, and Wang quickly stepped out. Ling, carrying both bags, and in a more composed state of mind than her infuriated traveling companion, followed a minute behind, glaring in disbelief as Wang scurried back in the direction of the jeep. After a fifty yard sprint, he realized the futility of his action. He turned back and cursed the driver for not allowing him off sooner.

"What do we do now?" she asked, her head spinning with confusion.

It took him a few seconds to register her question, then instinctively replying in Cantonese, and he caught the confused look on her face. "I have got to think," he said. "I have to get back that way," and he pointed in the direction of the jeep. "Sung cannot be far back."

"You've got to think!" Lisa said angrily. "Thinking clearly seems to be the one thing you're totally incapable of." She dropped the luggage, kicked at one bag, and stormed off a few paces. "We've no car," she called with her back to Wang, "and no idea where we are." She waved her arms about, gesturing at the surroundings. "You've dragged me off the bus in the middle of nowhere." She moved nearer, her face inches from his. "We've a mission to complete, and my agreement is only to take you to Paul. Do you understand what I am saying?"

He turned and in the blink of an eye thrust a hand on her throat, glaring at her with crazed eyes, choking off any additional verbiage as a look of bewilderment spread across her face, her head pounding as she struggled to break free. He relaxed his grip enough for her to splutter, "You're choking me . . ."

There were so many things he wanted to say, so many scenarios to contemplate, but the combination of confusion and stress overwhelmed him, so much so that his need to acquiesce was the only sensible decision. His immediate natural desire to slap this indignant woman up and down the roadside would not serve him well. Momentarily raising his free hand, as though about to strike a blow to her face, he froze, caught himself, reeled back his emotions, knowing full well that alienating her at this point was something he couldn't allow himself to do.

Not now.

Not here by the roadside.

A more appropriate time would arise for his indulgence with Miss Ling.

"You just do not understand," he said, "do you, Ling?"

It was the first time she wasn't *Lisa*, or even *Miss Ling*. He tightened the grip on her throat. "We are here to get this person, but if in the course of events we come into contact with parties who represent a threat to the success of my mission, if this should occur, then I will deviate from my course and do whatever is in my power to destroy the intruder."

She gave him a frigid stare . . . held it for several moments as she recalled his roughness at the hotel parking lot.

"You're insane. Get your hand off me, I can't breathe."

He released his grip, his right eye flashing a nervous twitch. "That man by the roadside," he said, ". . . is no soldier. He is with our Intelligence Bureau. He was my associate. His name is Sung Chiao."

He gazed at her, turned, spat to his right.

Appeared to settle.

Just a little.

"I was led to believe that Blake would be on his way over the mountains with the Americans. If Sung is here, so close to Beijing, then Blake and his friends cannot be far off."

A military truck rumbled by, and Wang released the choke hold. For a brief moment he considered waving the truck down.

It was moving too fast.

Angry and confused he spluttered almost to himself, "They have arrived here quickly . . . interesting. We were to observe their journey across the Himalayas. This is most strange." Looking thoughtful, he eyed the approaching vehicles. "We were expecting them to cross from the west, hmm."

As the stream of traffic drew near, his waving failed to slow the flow as the approaching drivers instinctively swerved, bypassing the man with the flapping arms. Wang shouted abuse, gave the speeding traffic the international gesture of displeasure, a raised middle finger. Lisa, still reeling from Wang's stranglehold, gave a look of disbelief. "What's with the finger?" she coughed. "That's really rich, Wang. Yeah, that'll get us a ride."

She took off a sneaker, shaking out dust and pebbles, her hair disheveled and her face flushed as she bounced about on one foot while trying to balance. The prepubescent man behind the wheel of an approaching military truck slowed to a crawl.

Smiled.

Stopped the truck.

He grinned at the attractive young woman hopping by the roadside. "What are you doing out here? There is a dangerous foreigner at large. This is not a safe place."

She shrugged and allowed Wang to respond. He stepped to the truck, resting an elbow on the window edge and spoke quietly to the young soldier. "Do you know General Cheng?"

"I am with his 13th Group Army," he said, his eyes on Lisa, "at the Western Hills Command Center."

Wang beamed, "From Western Hills?"

The soldier forced his eyes to Wang, swung an arm across the rear of the seat and rummaged about in a bag, pulled a pack of cigarettes. He placed one between his lips, lighting it in a sensual way, his eyes switching back to Lisa as he inhaled. "Yes, Western Hills, do you know the general?"

Time to think, needed to think fast. "Yes, in fact I do, he is an old friend. You must take me to him, he is expecting me."

"That is quite impossible," and the smile died as the driver took on a serious tone.

Wang peered through the window, focusing sharply, leaving no doubt as to his intent. "This is a matter of national security. If you do not take me to General Cheng, I will see you are reprimanded for non-cooperation." They locked eyes for a long while, neither flinching. The driver looked away, and Wang growled, "You will see very soon that my request is legitimate."

A few more long moments passed as they held each other's stare, then the soldier reluctantly leaned across to the passenger's door, flicked the cigarette, and released the lock. "Get in, if you are lying, you will be a guest of the general in ways you cannot begin to imagine."

Wang turned to Ling, smiled. "So you see, even out here, *in the middle of nowhere* as you said, the righteous do get that which they justly deserve.

She was unable to catch much of the discussion between the two, but the body language clearly showed Wang had won the day. "So tell me," she said leaning close to Wang's ear, "what's your connection with this general?"

"I studied military strategy under him at Western Hills. Taiwan knew it was happening, but it suited them as much as it suited the general," Wang said with a smile. "He received information and Taiwan received information."

"So it's détente?"

"Yes, détente, neither is deprived nor cheated . . .

each is happy with détente."

"You're a double agent?"

"Interesting conclusion, however I would rather consider myself a capitalistic free agent. I believe that is somewhat different. Each side is comfortable with the arrangement, knowing who I am, and what it is that I provide. The arrangement is far better than my being an undercover agent whom no one can trust, an agent who is always under suspicion. Am I eh, making myself clear?"

The truck pulled alongside a tall white building as ten men in military attire, carrying M16s, greeted them. Roman numerals, representing the number '*two*', were clearly displayed on the entry walls of an insignificant looking building, a building unnoticed by thousands of tourists passing by en route to the Great Wall at Badaling. It was a full thirty seconds before Lisa stepped from the truck, preferring to remain in the vehicle, taking in the strong military presence. Wang, feeling her discomfort, stood back, held the door ajar, and with a smug look of self fulfillment, motioned for her to step out.

Insolence.

She spoke softly, her hand covering her mouth, "What are you getting us into?"

"Stay calm. The general will be glad to see me. Be patient, you will see."

Wang clutched his travel bag; unzipping it and checking that the contents were intact, that the Tara was safely wrapped in its red velvet cloth. The escort eyed them with suspicion as he opened the carry bags, rifling through each, removing the red velvet bundle, unwinding it, recognizing the statue.

"A gift for a friend?" he asked.

"Yes . . . my friend is a collector."

The escort rewrapped the statue and slowly patted Lisa down, his eyes on hers as he lowered himself, his hands running along each leg. His search of Wang took considerably less time, and was obviously far less satisfying. The most superior of the group, a handsome young officer, smiled and nodded to Lisa as he reached out to shake Wang's hand.

The officer said, "*Ni Hao*, Wang."

They spoke briefly in Mandarin as Wang went through a brief interrogation. Lisa smiled at the handsome soldier, letting out a sigh of relief as the conversation between the two took on a lighter mood. With eyes locked on the officer, she tilted her head toward Wang.

"You appear to know him rather well."

"This is Captain Peter Cheng," Wang announced with a touch of envy, sensing the signals between the two. "He is General Cheng's youngest son. His brother, David, was the soldier killed by your American friend." His next words were delivered with apprehension. "Captain Cheng led the group that recovered the bodies by the railway track, a soldier and a woman."

Again, the envy. "If it is of any interest to you, Peter commented to me on how attractive you are. He eh, asked if you are . . ." and he hesitated as though embarrassed, ". . . if you are my wife."

"And you said?" she asked, a corner of her lip twitching as she locked eyes with Peter Cheng. Wang grinned, said nothing. Lisa raised a hand, touched her cheek in a blushing way, and left the young officer no doubt that he was indeed the subject of their discussion.

Peter Cheng led them on a journey through the white building, into the nerve center of this Chinese Pentagon consisting of a myriad of passages. Lisa thought it a rabbit's warren, with one locked white door after another; each guarded by stone a faced sentry, each saluting the officer as he passed on by. They arrived at a pair of large double doors, and the captain knocked twice, and waited a few moments. A gruff, deep voice said, "Enter."

It was a palace sized room, with Puccini's Madame Butterfly playing softly, adding to the renaissance décor. Studded leather furnishings, beautifully gilt framed artwork, and a floor to ceiling mirror reflected the size of the room, summarily doubling its depth. A red leather chair faced away from them, the only indication of an occupant was a smoke pall wafting from its vicinity.

The chair slowly turned.

The man in the seat lowered a morning newspaper. He beamed a smile toward Wang, stubbed out his cigarette, stood and extended a hand. "My friend," he grinned, "welcome."

"It has been a long time, General," Wang said. "I would like you to meet an acquaintance, Miss Ling."

She put on a friendly face as Wang made the introduction.

The general gestured toward the young officer. "Of course you remember my son, Peter."

The officer clicked his heels as his eyes minimally brushed past Wang en route to Lisa. Once there, they lingered.

"My sincere condolences," Wang said, lowering his eyes. "The death of David was a terrible thing, such a fine young man, a credit to the People's Liberation Army."

The general's reply was swift. "Not all people value human life as we in China."

There was a long silence. *Would have been wiser had I not mentioned David's passing,* Wang thought, his face swiftly adopting a look of self admonishment, but quickly breathing a sigh of relief when the general said, "Thank you. He will be sadly missed," and he nodded at the captain. "Peter has quite large shoes to fill. I will have him accompany you to the mountains. He will be a fine leader of my 13th Chuan when we track the Americans, when they cross the Himalayas. We are, in fact, preparing to leave for the region first thing tomorrow."

He turned away from Wang who was struggling with a suitable way of telling Cheng that Ridkin's group was in fact, already in Beijing. He was about to speak when Cheng faced Ling, and took her hand. "And you, Miss Ling," he said, "are obviously not from Beijing."

Lisa hoped she'd correctly understood the question. She glanced at Wang, paused momentarily, then responded in her limited Chinese. "General, I was born in China."

"You have quite an accent, I can detect the American. Your family, are they still living in China?"

She paused, slowly shifted her eyes back toward Wang who jumped in and saved her.

"If I may, Comrade General, Miss Ling has been living in the United States for most of her life. Her Chinese is eh . . ." he chuckled, made light of it, "her Chinese is limited. She attempts a few Cantonese phrases, but has difficulty following conversation."

Cheng didn't speak for a few long moments. "Accept my apology, Miss Ling," and he nodded graciously to Wang. "Tell her I am sorry," and he gave Lisa a warm smile. "I spoke far too quickly."

She returned the smile, his hand still firmly grasping hers. After lingering a little too long with the gesture, he cleared his throat, straightening up, released her hand and turned to Peter. He nudged his head back toward Lisa and winked at his son. Any discomfort Lisa Ling brought into the room dissipated when tea and biscuits arrived, and all four sat about the table as though they'd known one another their entire lives.

"That is a splendid portrait of the Chairman," Wang said gesturing across the room.

The general smiled to himself and picked up a biscuit. "Yes, there are very few pictures on display now." He took a sip of his tea. "But I feel good about the Chairman; he did many great things for us."

He chewed for a half minute, washing down the biscuit with another sip of tea, then using the remaining piece of biscuit to point at the portrait, said, "His philosophy of having faith in the masses, faith in the Party, stands the test of time. These are two cardinal principles, if we doubt these principles, we in China shall accomplish nothing."

"True, so very true, General," Wang said reverently, knowing better than disagree with Cheng's party beliefs. Staying with the discussion, he mentally searched for a way to break the news that the Himalayan crossing never eventuated, that in fact, he had seen Sung Chiao that very day. But the window of opportunity was too brief as Wang, deep in thought, stared at Mao's portrait with less than convincing admiration. Another *window* was quite a problem, the more time passed by, the more difficult it became to break the news.

He remained fixated on the portrait of the Chairman as his misconstrued interest in the general's theological banter spurred a further patriotic outburst from Cheng. "Wang," he said, "we in China have an arduous task to ensure a better life for the near one and a half billion people in this great land. We have a destiny to build our once economically and culturally backward country into one that is prosperous and powerful, into a nation with a high level of modern culture. Do you not agree?"

Wang remained silent, still staring at the portrait as if it were alive, eyes analyzing the face as though Mao were communicating.

"Wang?"

"Yes, yes! Of course, General, I agree totally."

"A self-reliant defense system, Wang, a strong space program; we strive at all times to conduct rectification movements, both now and in the future. Our goal is to constantly rid ourselves of whatever is wrong. It is with this in mind that I have availed myself of a special visitor. He is in the guest quarters," and he chuckled in a sinister way, his eyes rising to the ceiling as he chuckled. "He is right above us."

"A visitor . . . someone I know?"

"When you were assigned to attend the meeting in Los Angeles, your bureau made the mistake of lowering security. Subsequently, with the use of a little deception, we discovered the identity of their man in Beijing." He rubbed his hands together briskly, a gesture of satisfaction, and pointed in quick jabs toward the ceiling. "He is now in my custody. Up there."

There was a few seconds of silence as both stood with eyes toward the ceiling. "Would you like to see him?"

Wang was stunned, couldn't guess who the general was holding. The possibilities scared him. He put on a nonchalant air. "Why, of course, but eh . . . need your guest *see me*?"

He left no doubt that he preferred any connection with Cheng remain discreet.

Cheng shrugged dismissingly, "Of course, we have a viewing room."

He turned to the captain and motioned to Lisa. "Peter, please remain here. Entertain our beautiful guest."

Peter Cheng grinned and passed the tray of biscuits to Lisa. She was attracted to this handsome officer. He intrigued her, causing her heart to step up its beat. And Captain Peter Cheng sensed the vibration.

"Your friend, Sung," Cheng said as they walked. "I have heard he is still working with Sam Ridkin's team." He took a moment to let the revelation sink in, analyzing Wang's reaction. "In fact, one of my sources heard a ridiculous rumor that Ridkin's team may be in China at this very moment. Perhaps they have deceptive skills of their own," and he made a failed attempt to lighten the moment by chuckling the words *deceptive skills.*

Wang's heart sunk to his stomach, and he felt a sudden weakness in his knees. The time had come, the window was wide open. "Comrade General," he said with a mouth depleted of saliva. "I have been waiting for the most opportune moment to discuss that very *rumor*." As hard as he tried, the words got stuck somewhere between his larynx and the tip of his tongue. Cheng picked up on '*opportune moment*.'

"*Opportune moment*, what are you saying?"

"Comrade General, in order to better serve the proletariat state, I try to practice my deception as often as possible, and, eh . . ."

Cheng grinned, "Along with all of your other Bourgeoisie qualities, no doubt?"

"Comrade General, sir, please allow me to explain. Forgive me if I appear to have caused undue delay." And he bit the bullet. "I now believe Ridkin's group is already here."

The walking stopped.

"What do you mean . . . *already here*?"

"Here, General . . . in Beijing."

Cheng's jaw tightened.

"Earlier today I came across Sung Chiao. He was changing a tire by the roadside. I was unable to get the bus driver to stop. By the time I was off the bus, Sung was gone." He swallowed hard, his body temperature rising. Then, a little shakier, "If Sung is here, so are the other men, probably the two agents, Blake and Dallas, perhaps even others."

"What!" Cheng spat the word. "Why did you not give me this information sooner?"

"Forgive me, Comrade General, the course of events since my arrival in China has allowed me no opportunity to pass this information on to you. You had so much to tell me and, and, and I waited for the most opportune time to pass the information on."

"How long ago, where did you see him?"

"Two hours back. I tried to have the bus stop but . . ."

"Idiot, you've allowed an opportunity to escape us!"

Is this a death sentence? Wang thought, head bowed.

"I have great concern over the death of my son," Cheng said. "My need to capture this American is greater than ever. It is not solely for the People's Republic; this man has turned it into a personal issue. He has information that must never leave China. You, Wang, will assist in his apprehension."

A momentary reprieve.

The general placed a firm hand on Wang's shoulder. "I've heard from Sellers."

The momentary reprieve dwindled at the mention of the name, Sellers. Wang felt one of his nine lives slipping away.

"Your brother has been released from hospital," Cheng said. "He is waiting for your call."

Interesting, Wang thought, *he still mentions Sellers, not McDowell*, and he felt privileged, felt privy knowing McDowell's double identity, something only he knew, something the general didn't. *Interesting.*

Cheng gave a sinister grin. "Your meeting back in Hong Kong with Miss Ling was very well orchestrated by Sellers. Unfortunately, Sellers, whose real identity was Adam McDowell, one of Ridkin's people, was caught out by our intelligence."

Wang's *privilege* died a quick death. He feigned ignorance and made a confused shrug, said, "McDowell?"

"Yes, he supplied us with information that proved to be suspect, while at the same time selling information to Moscow, information we considered accurate. We no longer need be concerned with the late Adam McDowell, for both he and his pseudonym, *Sellers,* are no more."

Wang swallowed deeply. *So much for feeling privileged . . . misassumption.* He shook his head in disbelief. "You are saying that Sellers, huh, McDowell, you are saying that he is . . . dead?"

Cheng shrugged, "How foolish of him to underestimate us."

They resumed the walk for one minute, two minutes, eventually arriving at a large door. Cheng removed a key from his pocket, slipped it into the lock. They entered a small room, sparsely furnished; warm, with mixed scent of wool carpet and lemon furniture polish. A large mirror hung ninety degrees to his right, and Wang's eye drifted to it, pulled by the glow emanating from behind it.

The general smiled, "Allow me to show you my ace card."

This is going to hurt, Wang thought. *What if it is someone I know, someone I cannot openly recognize . . .*

Cheng raised a hand, pointing at the two-way mirror. "Wait, first I must dim the lights."

He returned to the switch.

Killed the room's cold overhead fluorescent.

The glow from the mirror increased, changing the reflective surface into a large window. Wang pulled at his lip, a nervous habit he developed at a very early age. He felt the hairs stand on the back of his neck. Sitting forlornly in an equally small room on the reverse side of the mirror sat the general's *ace card* . . . Bishop Jean Pierre Bolin.

Wang stared hard, moved closer to the mirror, pointing in disbelief, "The bishop . . . *he* is your ace card?"

"In my deck, Wang, there's no better card. He gave assistance to the killer of my son. It's most unfortunate, however, that we have not been able to come up with a photograph of the American."

Wang wanted so badly to please Cheng, wanted to say, "*Well, actually, I do have a photograph; let me get it for you.*" But the words eluded him. He pondered, allowing time to pass, four seconds, ten seconds.

Wham! Another window of opportunity slammed shut.

"Wang, in your opinion, should we continue to extract information from the bishop, or move forward with our original plan to apprehend Ridkin's people?"

"In my opinion, General? I humbly suggest the Comrade General's ace card is more valuable than he realizes, perhaps better suited as bait with which to reel in the Ridkin team."

"And you are prepared to stake your life on *your opinion?*"

Wang swallowed hard.

CHAPTER 29

A SLIGHTLY INEBRIATED GARDNER Hunter waved a hand over the cheering crowd, "Order up guys, drinks on me!"

Hunter was a happy man. The celebration was short lived. The Grand Hyatt was holding two messages from Sam Ridkin. He and Bellinger were about to swing into action.

The desk clerk greeted them with a congratulatory salute, "Well done sir, congratulations."

Hunter swayed, belched, held up a finger and raised his trophy, and bowed to the desk clerk. The clerk, showing little genuine concern, said in an unaffected way, "I am holding two messages for you, Mr. Hunter."

He passed two note papers to Bell. She read the messages as she placed a steadying hand on Hunter's arm. "It's four o'clock, and eh, you might want to catch forty winks before this call comes in," and she gave a comforting squeeze. "You'll need a clear head for what's coming up. We're on our way to hook up with the boys." She ran her eyes over the notes one more time, as though the news might get better on the re-read.

It didn't.

She said, shaking her head in self reproach, "Don't wanna tell you this, but things are heating up. Sam's calling tonight."

Wordlessly, the couple made their way to their suite, placing the notes on Hunter's bedside table. It'd been a long day, and the best she could manage was a dutiful smile as she left the inebriated Hunter sitting and smiling stupidly at the silver trophy.

His shower began warm and ended cold. He liked it that way. Stepping from the bathroom, with his brain yet to fully recover from the day's excitement, he slipped into a pair of black Calvin Klein's, readjusted his balls, tousled his hair, and returned to sitting on the edge of the bed. After making a further testicle adjustment, he groaned, "Ah fuck, a half million bucks and no time to spend it."

Grinning, still a little stupidly, he reached for the notes. *Be in your room at seven along with Bellinger. I'll call.*

The dream had ended.

He called to Bell, "Dinner at six . . . that okay?"

"Sure . . . I can look respectable by then." She poked her head into his room. "Did you use all of the shampoo?"

"Nah, I used the soap."

She giggled, "Peasant!"

He got half dressed, beige slacks, brown loafers, hadn't decided on a shirt. Standing bare-chested, he stared into the bathroom mirror, hated the five o' clock shadow. *It's only Bell, not like it's a real date.* While staring into the steamed mirror, he reached to the glass with his right index finger, wrote the name *Wang*, ran his finger down the glass, making an arrow, then wrote *McDowell*. A second arrow trailed across to the name *Sung*. He traced a third arrow that ended on a large question mark, mulled it over for a few long moments but couldn't make the connection. With a querulous gaze he smeared the mirror clean with a face towel, and dismissed his bullshit scenario.

Once dressed, Hunter called toward the shower, "We're set to roll. I'll meet you in the restaurant. Oh, and Bell, might be a good idea to get packed before we eat, I got this gut feelin' we're gonna be movin' fast."

*****

Bell arrived at the elegant Redmoon Restaurant and found Hunter sitting at the bar. A band was playing The Beatles '*Yesterday*' on traditional Chinese instruments. When the piece was over, Hunter signaled a waiter who escorted the couple to a nearby table where they sat over two Cokes until the musicians had completed their set. They picked through a light salad, neither ordering alcohol, each aware of the importance of keeping a sharp mind for Ridkin's call. The call was twenty minutes off.

Toying with his food, Hunter said, "You feel there's more to all of this than meets the eye, don'tcha?"

"Do you?"

"I was thinkin' our time at the Open kinda dropped us both outa the loop, feel kinda bad." He looked up from his plate. "I hope the guys are okay. I know that's probably what Sam's callin' about, but maybe he's got a shit load of other bad news he's gonna dump on us."

It sounded like empty rhetoric, like Hunter laying his golfing guilt on the table.

"Listen Gard, that's the ninety percent of shit that people worry about, the ninety percent that never happens. Give me a break. If things were going that badly we'd have heard sooner. It's only been a few days, what can go so wrong in a few days?"

They stared at one another, neither speaking for awhile, both realizing maybe the answer was one neither was prepared to throw on out there.

"What can go so wrong in a few days?" he asked.

She assumed it was rhetorical, didn't answer.

Wanted to answer but stayed silent.

"Hmm . . . lemme hypothesize here," Hunter said.

Her stare evolved into a smile. She loved it when he

used big words.

"Hypothesize . . . hmm . . . you know what your using big words does to me?"

Hunter lifted his eyes to the ceiling, and moved his head from side to side. "What can go so wrong in a few days? Lemme see, The Ides of March, Caesar's dead. Pearl Harbor's hit, Hiroshima's wiped off the face of the planet, three days later Roosevelt says wipe out Nagasaki; ya know, just to drive home a point, just in case Hiroshima didn't strike a fuckin' nerve. The fuckin' Arabs wipe out the World Trade Center. A president is assassinated. Fuck, I dunno, Bell. Maybe I'm just a worry-monger. I'll have to work on that one darlin' now, won't I?" He gave an exasperated shrug. "Finish your coffee, then we'll go take the call. No more speculation. I'm done fuckin' around with hypotheticals."

"There you go, doing it again," she shuddered, "you teaser, you!"

*****

The phone by Hunter's bed buzzed at seven sharp. He swallowed hard, threw a nervous glance at Bellinger, who tried maintaining a dispassionate expression, visualizing Sam's imminent delivery. Hunter closed his eyes for a moment, moved near the phone, hesitantly placed a hand toward it, paused, eyed Bell, made a self admonishing face. Breathed in deeply, and exhaled. He picked up. "Sam?"

"I hear congratulations are in order, you did well. Picked up a small bonus too, good work. Don't spend my cut, okay?"

Good start, Hunter thought, throwing an assuring smile to Bellinger. She read his body language, relaxed a little.

"Thanks Sam. We'll celebrate when we get home; go to your favorite restaurant."

There was silence; Hunter tilted his head sideways, phone still pressed to his ear, looking at Bellinger, waiting.

Silence

"Sam . . . Sam . . . Ya there?"

Sam spent the next few minutes explaining McDowell's demise, and once he'd dropped that bombshell, he said, "Haven't heard from our team, but I do know that Bolin's been taken by Cheng's men, and he was your contact. It's a long, very long story, and the way things are shaping up, we look like we might need to ad-lib some of our moves."

"Fuck! Where do Bell and me fit into the *ad-lib* plan?"

"I want you to check out first thing tomorrow, find less conspicuous accommodation. There're a few loose cannons out there."

Hunter blinked, "Loose cannons?"

Bell caught the negative vibes and threw herself on Hunter's bed, laying face down with her feet kicking. She jammed her face into a pillow, and shouted into the goose down. When satisfied with her release, she rolled onto her back and stared mindlessly at the ceiling.

"We feel a more low key location is best," Sam said. "A few days in one spot is a couple too many. With your golf celebrity status the media could present a problem, what with interviews and recognition. We need you to keep a low profile."

Hunter's head was pounding and he struggled to moderate his thinking.

"We need to get our hands on the bishop," Sam said.

"Have you heard where this Bishop Bolin's bein' held?" Hunter asked, shaking his head at Bell's antics. "I mean, how do we know he's even alive?"

"He's been taken to the Western Hills Command Center," Sam replied. "Is he alive? Yes, we believe he is."

"How tough is it to crack this place?"

"They say it's impenetrable," Sam said, and added a disingenuous smile to his voice, "And rightly so; we don't get invitations to tour the site." He exhaled loud enough for Hunter to hear. "In comparison, our guys have given the Chinese carte blanche. They've ridden in our jets, been aboard our nuclear subs, joined in on classes at West Point, they even visited the strategic command center at Cheyenne Mountain. But to this day, none of our military or government people, including Rumsfeld, have been allowed to visit Western Hills. You just don't get in there."

"And your point is?"

"Your immediate priority is getting Bolin out of Cheng's clutches."

"Where exactly is this Command Center?"

"In Xishan, a suburb of Beijing, it's considered the Chinese equivalent of the Pentagon. Getting into it is gonna be a ten on a difficulty scale, but I can't think of a better candidate to do it."

After a lengthy pause, Hunter replied with a grin in his voice, "Flattery won't cut it, Chief."

There was a faint chuckle, followed by a distinct, *click.*

"Tough break about McDowell," Bell said with her eyes down. "What do you make of it all?"

"Yeah, poor Adam, huh," Hunter said. "I dunno. All sounds kinda fishy to me, very fuckin' fishy."

CHAPTER 30

THE BLACK 325i BLENDED into the moonlit night.

"What time have you got, Bell?"

"Two twenty."

"You ready for this?"

"Nuh uh," she said shaking her head. "I've a really bad feeling, just want to . . ."

He placed a finger on her lips, stopped her. "This is what I want, and don't argue with me." He nodded slowly to drive his point home. "Stay back here in the Beamer, keep the motor runnin'."

"But, but . . ."

"No buts, no reason for us both goin' in. I've got the layout up here," and he tapped on his forehead. "If they're holdin' the bishop where our people say, then that'll place him . . ." and he paused, shining a pencil beam onto a mapped floor plan. "That'll place him right here." He tapped on the map, fingering a room on the second floor, then leaning into the rear view mirror, said, "How's my make up?"

She smeared her fingers across his cheek, spreading the black paint closer to his ear. "Gard, please be careful. Stay alive long enough to cash the check," she pleaded, giving his arm a gentle thump. "Besides, you might have a future in golf."

"Yeah right, as long as *you* spike the water. I signed the back of the check, it's in your carry on." He nudged her.

"Just in case anythin' happens to . . ."

She stopped him mid-sentence, and asked in a surprised tone, "You *knew* about the water?"

"Yep, the dog and cat shit was fun, but you know, I really did have him beat. You should've had more faith in me, kiddo." Leaning forward, he kissed her gently on the cheek, then remembered his black face paint was quite communicable, and he pulled back. "Oops," he laughed, "smudged you, lemme wipe it off."

He reached to wipe the smear from her cheek but she turned away, placing her hand over the smudge. "No. Leave it," she said. "Get it when you get back." She gave a comforting grin. "And by the way, I won't be cashing any fucking check, so . . ."

"Sure you won't. See you in a bit."

And he was gone, blending into the night.

A phantom.

Perhaps it was psychological comfort having Bell waiting for him back in the Beamer. *Was great sharing showers with her*, he thought, keeping his mind off reality. He moved low to the ground, between bushes, but the ground cover decreased as he drew nearer the building.

Hmm, those showers.

And this led to another thought. Another visit to Carmel. Same hotel. Same foreplay. It dangled before him, that carrot did. *Priorities*, he thought jerking his mind back. *Let's get this guy out . . . there'll be time enough to have another crack at laying Patrice Bellinger.*

He reached the first window, spotted the wires running between double paned glass, acoustic glass with omni-directional microphones that would pick up the sound of breaking glass. He knew the type. They'd draw electrical energy from the very motion of him breaking the glass. Any shockwave would surely be detected. He thought *fuckin' sensors all around this place. I gotta connect a trigger to the window, attach a switch right by the side of the trigger on the frame of the window.* He reached into his kit, felt about, then paused, thought, *not right, feels wrong, too easy.*

He ran a laser-like beam around the edge, was tempted.

If I open the window, which in itself ain't difficult, that trigger will pull from the switch; cause a break in the electrical circuit. He scratched at his chin, pushed the hood back a little from his forehead. *Something, I'm missing something.* He mumbled beneath his breath, "I'm missing somethin' here."

The light.

The beam was wrong. *Fuckin' beam's refracting,* he thought, and then whispered, "Fuck me, you elaborate little buggers. They've got sensors embedded in the glass. Hmm . . . plan 'B'."

There really was no plan 'B'. *Plan 'B',* for want of a better reference involved hands on, involved waiting for Chinese personnel to access the building, but just one person . . . God willing.

He checked the time. *Bell will be getting' impatient.* He made his way to the main entrance. *Too much light.* Then the sound of voices. Three uniformed men. *Can I take the three? I can die here. Jesus, I really might die here in fuckin' China. If I take on all three, and one of 'em gets off a shot and she hears it and comes runnin', they'll have Bell. Fuck!*

The realization of having no *plan 'B'* brought a plethora of negative thoughts, but then a stroke of luck. The three soldiers pulled cigarettes from a pack, lit up, chatted awhile, and two of the three bid farewell, moved toward a nearby jeep, and left the third, a thinly built officer, leaning against the entry door stargazing like a man with not a care in the world. And the vehicle moved off.

Bingo!

Hunter slid the thin shining wire from his rear pocket.

317

The garrote was not his favorite means of killing, but on rare occasions he employed it. Aside from the blood spray, it had proven to be a silent, efficient killing machine, simple, portable . . . terminal.

The night air was heavy, a fine mist, or fog, moving across the ground. Eerie, reminded him of the English moors, the Hounds of the Baskervilles. *This could be okay. Just need to get closer, get behind the guy, slip this over his head, pull.* He glanced about, checking the surroundings. *Don't feel comfortable, I'm too exposed. Need to create a diversion, get the guy to move this way. Get him as he passes by.* He licked his lips, lowered the hood down his forehead, down to his eyebrows. Readied himself.

Hesitated.

Sweat ran into his eyes and he rubbed at it, smudging the black face paint, stinging, blurring his vision. He dropped lower to the ground, tried to regain focus, his mind not as sharp as it should be. He heard a vehicle approaching from his right. *Shit! Those two have come back.* He'd blown his window of opportunity. It was there and now it was gone, while he'd fucked about with indecision.

Aw fuck . . . aw man! He pulled the Sig, quickly attached the Coeur D' Lene, raised the weapon and the three shots struck like silent wasps, one for each man, dropping them right there, right at the entry of . . . With a look of satisfaction he lowered the Sig, as one soldier got to his knees, groping, and trying to scream. He was the largest of the three and he fumbled for his holstered sidearm as blood sprayed from a head wound.

"Come on, don't bust my balls," Hunter pleaded in an apologetic way. "Stay down, for Christ's sake!" But the soldier persisted as Hunter dashed the fifty meters to where the man was flailing about, disorientated, in shock, one bloodied hand clawing at the holstered weapon, unable to deal with the speed of the attack, and Hunter whipped the butt of the Sig hard across his skull, hearing the crunch . . . and then the dead eyes.

"Christ, what a fuckin' mess."

He placed all three in the jeep and drove the vehicle to a designated parking area, returned to the bloodied entry and began wiping the red pool, smearing it, rubbing with panicked strokes.

"Jesus, aw sweet Jesus, what a mess, what a mess," and he repeated it over and over.

It wasn't the best of clean up jobs, but it would suffice. Besides, he'd be gone before first light . . . with the bishop.

And he was in.

He moved along a lengthy corridor, heard distant laughter. Stopped. Moved back into the darkness of a doorway, the Sig against the side of his face, readied himself, leaned forward, just one eye sneaking a glance, catching the soldier sitting by a door accessing stairs, and the sound of lighthearted laughter filtered from the stairwell and Hunter pulled back into the shadows, not sure of what to make of the girlish giggle, and he bit hard on his lower lip and . . .

*****

Lisa brushed her hair aside, flicking it over Peter's face, lying in a frozen embrace for a long time until he whispered in her ear. She began a slow move, sliding her body down, working her way to his navel, pausing momentarily, teasing, descending. He let out an indiscernible gasp, held his breath, and gazed down on her beauty. This special girl had come into his life from nowhere. His eyes followed her every move as he drifted, savoring the ecstasy.

He sighed, "You are truly my beautiful butterfly."

"And you . . . my Captain Pinkerton."

She began a slow journey back toward his chest, running her tongue around one nipple, across his hairless body, reaching the opposite nipple, his sweat giving her a sense of excitement, his saltiness tasting magnificent.

"You know," Lisa said, "back in the days of Rome, the sweat from a gladiator would be scraped from his chest and bottled as an aphrodisiac. Hmm, you taste good, Peter Cheng."

She was unsure how much he'd understood. It didn't matter, the expression on his chiseled face indicated he was indeed, a happy man. As she moved further upward, her hair snagged in the locket swinging freely about her neck. When she tried to untangle the snag, he reached for the locket, pushing the catch and it sprang open. He gazed at it and considered the two small photographs. His voice hardened, more an army officer than a lover, "Who is this woman?"

Lisa was taken aback. *Why ask about the woman, why not 'who's this man?*

"She's my mother. She died a long time ago," she said pressing her hand over the locket. "Why do you ask?"

"I recognize this photograph," he said, his eyes fixed on the locket. "I am certain this woman is my mother's sister. This is my aunt."

"That's utter nonsense," Lisa said with a disingenuous smile. "It's ridiculous, how can you be sure?"

"I am very sure. We have the same photograph in a family album, the very same picture, same place. Look, she has a heart around her neck, look here." He pointed at the small photograph, touched the gold heart that hung around the woman's neck. "You see," he said. "This is the very same locket."

Lisa looked up at him, moved his hands back to her face and his dark eyes closed. When they opened they were no longer loving eyes. He took three slow, deep breaths, and the prolonged silence gave both he and Lisa Ling time to analyze the situation.

"When I was a boy, I was told my aunt gave birth to

a child, a girl. My aunt died after the baby arrived."

"What happened to the girl?" Lisa asked, fearing the answer. "Peter, please, I must dress. I need time; this is all so very confusing, it's too much too soon, please."

"Give me the locket. I need my father to see it."

"Your father, why does he need to see it? It's all that I have of my mother. I really hate to part with it."

She raised her knees, coiled into a fetal position and pulled the sheet around her shoulders, as if her nakedness suddenly caused discomfort.

Peter stood, walked around the bed, half sitting, and half leaning into her. "Please, Lisa, no questions. Allow me to show my father. It is most important that he see it." He focused more sharply at the picture on the opposite half of the locket. "This man," he said with disdain. "He is he your American lover?"

The cell phone in Peter's pocket buzzed. He opened it and spoke quietly for a half-minute. She was relieved. It gave her time to mull over her response.

He snapped the phone shut.

Smiled.

Waited.

She took in his inquiring gaze. "Yes," she said nodding, "he's a former friend."

She avoided further explanation. "You *will* give the locket back immediately after your father's seen it, yes?"

"Of course I will return it to you. You have my word."

At two-thirty on a cold morning, General Cheng sat by an open fire in the foyer of the Hyatt, as he and Wang talked over old times. An occasional tourist passed by, oblivious to the power of the uniformed man staring into the flames. Even though their bond was a strong, and went back many years, Wang was aware Cheng had a cruel streak, knew he couldn't fall back on the comfort of old friendship as a safety-net. Carefully thinking through the course of events, he wondered how he would explain the existence of the photograph.

Nothing came to mind.

Not yet.

"It's been a hard road, Wang. It's been difficult losing David, but this intruder, this Paul Slade, has the flash drive from the facility in Penghu, and mustn't take it out of China. We believe Ridkin's team will meet up with Slade, and from there they'll be trying to reach the Pescadores for the obvious exit to Taiwan. This mustn't be allowed to happen."

Like a rabbit mesmerized by a rattler, Wang sat unmoving. A few seconds passed, then a minute. Cheng stirred his teacup, and each raised their cups and drank as Cheng waited for Wang to begin some line of conversation. "You're very quiet," Cheng said. "I know you're thinking of what I have said. Please, share your thoughts with me."

"I'm sorry General. I can't understand how you've not obtained a photograph of this man, this Slade person. You have so many resources."

And Wang dug the hole a little deeper.

There was no question Cheng was annoyed at the inference of inefficiency. He grunted at Wang. "Our files were pillaged. But we will find the American. We're this close." He held up his hand, thumb and index finger almost touching. "So close that I can feel it."

Wang slipped a sly look at his watch and Cheng picked up on the not too subtle hint. There was another grunt, followed by a wave of his hand. "It's getting toward three o'clock, time to get back to the base," the general said. "It's been a long time since I've stayed out this late. I'll send a car for you later today."

He began a forced smile, but failed to pull it off. Turning away, he said, "Ten o'clock."

En route to his room, Wang hesitated as he passed

Lisa Ling's door. He paused, placed an ear to the door, wishful thinking. When he realized he was loitering, and also realized the security cameras gave full view of the hallways, he moved on.

A lovesick schoolboy.

It was at that point Wang dismissed any hope of a romantic connection.

That point.

That point in time when a chill scrambles up a man's spine and he thinks, *what the fuck am I doing?*

Two guests stepped from the elevator, strolling hand in hand toward him, giving a curious look as they passed. It appeared the man had brought a boyfriend back for what remained of the evening. Wang shrugged, sniggered. Harboring disappointment, he continued to his room, barely able to handle the anxiety now plucking at his chest.

CHAPTER 31

HUNTER LOOMED IN THE shadow of the doorway, turning his better ear to the sound of laughter, listening as it filtered from a nearby room. The soldier sat with his head resting on his chest, and one hand instinctively on his sidearm. As Hunter made a slight move forward, the soldier stood and took a long lazy stretch.

Hunter caught a glimpse of the sentry as he was momentarily jerked awake by a more intense laugh, that of a male. There was a cry of pleasure and the sentry's eyes lit up, thought he could hear heavy breathing, but then, after listening more intently decided his imagination had gotten the better of him, the highlight of a routinely dull evening. He stretched, looked to his left, to his right, stretched again, yawned, shrugged, then nonchalantly left the area.

Hunter moved with stealth, quietly, up the stairs, his back to the wall as he moved crab-like, the Sig-Sauer P228 clutched in both hands. He counted the doors, "Five, six, seven . . ."

It was the eighth door, the interrogation quarters.

Then, footsteps. *Soldiers,* he thought. *Gotta be soldiers, maybe a change of guard? Is there more than one? Maybe they found the guys in the jeep . . . shit!* He pushed hard against the wall, his eyes closed, listening as the pace quickened, then slowed, the footsteps coming to a halt at the door. He dropped to one knee, assumed a shooting posture.

"General?" an inquiring voice said. Then moments

later, "Oh, it *is* you, sir."

"Why've you left your post?" Cheng growled. "There's no one watching the bishop."

"The lavatory, I had to go," the sentry said. "I was expecting . . ." and he paused, not wanting to report his comrade's tardiness. "I looked in on the bishop just minutes ago. He's sleeping comfortably. The doctor will be tending to him in the morning."

The footsteps moved away and Hunter heard a chair being dragged across the floor, then a grunt as the sentry dropped into the seat, relaxing, letting out a sigh of relief. Hunter pushed a button on his Casio, ran the time frame through his mind, *five o'clock. I've got an hour of darkness, gotta get the guy out before sunup.*

Bell had been waiting in the BMW for over an hour, wondering why Hunter hadn't returned with Bolin. *Worst scenario,* she thought, *I'll leave the car and try to reach the bishop myself.*

The dozing sentry was a large man; he didn't feel the blow coming. In a split second Hunter's Sig connected with the man's skull, making a cracking sound, an almost echoing *thwhack*, leaving the soldier slumped in the chair. He strained to pull the man into the room, struggling with his weight as the big man slid across the small step of the doorway. He looked at the big man with a sympathetic eye, and said, "You're one fuckin' big Chinaman."

He reached back in the hallway, retrieved the chair, the rifle, pulled them into the room and flicked the flashlight back into action, running the beam toward the sound of heavy breathing. The light found a large lump of a man sleeping on a narrow bunk, his gray hair matted with blood. A deep red cassock and white under garments lay on a chair by the bed. Hunter moved slowly, untrusting, toward the sleeping man. *Could be a set up,* he thought, *they know I'm here.* He stopped, backed away.

Killed the light, stayed frozen for what seemed an eternity. *Can't go back, if they're onto me, they'll already have Bell.* He gave a quick wipe to his forehead, then switching the flashlight back on, moved toward the sleeping figure, following the beam as it traced a pathway across the room.

The odor of rancid sweat rose from the sleeping man.

Hunter placed his mouth to the man's ear, "Wake up," he whispered, shaking the man by the shoulder. "Shhh, wake up."

The sleeping man turned, raised a hand, and shielded his eyes from the flashlight.

"Wake up," Hunter repeated. "I'm here to get you out. Your guy, Broski, the cardinal," and he raised his voice, "Broski, he sent me to getcha out."

The man shielded his eyes. "Do I know you?"

"Shhh, depends," replied Hunter. "D'ya follow golf?"

"Golf?"

"Don't matter, gotta getcha outa here." And he flicked the beam across the room, motioning at the unconscious sentry. "Help me get the uniform off of this guy."

Bolin's nod conflicted with his ideology, but the rationale was unquestionable. He'd do whatever was necessary to be set free. He stared at the guard, asked, "Is this man dead?"

"Nah, he's fine, get into his clothes, ya look about the same size. Gimme a hand here, we gotta get this fucker onto the bed."

The pallid face of the unconscious sentry did little to ease the bishop's guilt as he and Hunter removed the man's uniform.

"His boots," Bolin grunted, pointing at the man's boots, "they are far too small."

"Use your own, ya look fine. Your head's been bleedin', ya look like crap."

The idiom didn't translate.

"They beat me, wanted information. I told them nothing," and he began weeping. "I cannot return to my cathedral. They have destroyed my beautiful church, my young priests."

"You'll be fine," Hunter whispered. "There's plenty of flock out there needin' a shepherd."

"A shepherd?" he said aloud, his voice hollow in the sparsely furnished room.

"Never mind, we got us a ride waitin' outside, so we need to move our asses."

He considered taking the jeep, still sitting forlornly with its three deceased occupants, but that'd be too much a deviation from 'plan 'A'.'

Fuckin' plan 'A', he thought, flashing a glance back at the jeep. Plan 'A' was a wash, and there was no point bringing another vehicle into play. They'd get to the Beamer.

They were almost at the car when Hunter realized Bolin was panting heavily, wheezing, trying to draw breath. The Beamer's motor was silent, and as Hunter made the dash, he thought, *can't hear nothin', the motor should be runnin', can't hear a thing.* He looked around for Bolin, saw the bishop making heavy weather of the two hundred yard sprint. He slowed, came to a stop, waited. When the bishop eventually closed the gap, Hunter said, "A little out of shape, aren't we? Stay here, rest a spell. I'm goin' ahead to check out somethin'," and he motioned toward the car. "I'll be back in a flash."

He moved toward the BMW, stopping some ten feet off, feeling uneasy. He called, "Bell? Bell?"

No answer.

He reached the car, found Bellinger sitting with both hands on the wheel, staring ahead, eyes closed, head precariously supported by the headrest.

"Bell? You okay?"

The muzzle rammed deep and sharp into Hunter's lower back, causing him to stand upright.

"Ah shit," he mumbled, half turning. The soldier was alone, perhaps lucky to have stumbled on the intruder, but on the other hand, perhaps extremely unlucky.

"Take it easy, take it easy," Hunter groaned, forcing a grin, his white teeth beaming from the nugget black face.

The soldier had no knowledge of Bolin's presence, as the bishop caught a glimpse of Hunter standing with arms above his head, a glimpse of the soldier with his back toward him. In tune with the gravity of the situation, Bolin continued moving forward. Hunter held his grin, and cast his eyes beyond the soldier, looking at the approaching man, sliding his eyes back, nodding and indicating to the soldier that there was, actually, someone standing behind him. The soldier grinned, called Hunter's bluff, ignoring what he believed to be a ploy. He smiled and shook his head from side to side.

"Yeah, there's someone behind ya," Hunter said, nodding at Bolin. "Take a peek."

He gave it momentary consideration, scowled, and spat in Hunter's direction, just as the full weight of Bolin heaved the soldier forward, sending him sprawling into the black faced man's arms. Hunter shoved him off, reached back for the Sig, pulled it from his belt, and fired three shots into the rear of the man's skull.

A muffled bap . . . followed by bap bap, and a gasp from the bishop.

Hunter jammed a hand over Bolin's gaping mouth. "Goddamnit! I'm sorry your eminence, it was him or us. Ain't like he won't have company tonight, plenty where he's goin'. Come on, settle down, we gotta move."

With an eye still on the bishop, Hunter reached in

the car, placed a hand on Bell's shoulder, said, "Bell, Bell, what's up?"

She slumped forward.

Please God, he thought, *not dead, just unconscious.*

He cradled her against his chest, touched her throat.

"Gotta be a pulse," he said in a pleading voice. "Please, be alive."

Found the pulse.

He kissed her cheek, and raised his eyes toward Heaven. "Sweet Jesus, thank you, please take care of her."

His discussion with Jesus was brief. He leaned forward, wiped the smudge from her cheek, turned, raised the Sig-Sauer, pointed it at the body lying beside the BMW, and pumped two more shots into the uniformed man.

"Help me with her," he said, not turning to Bolin, "gently, into the back seat, gently."

The bishop slid in the rear and carefully placed a restrainer around Bell as Hunter pulled a small piece of paper from his inside pocket, about the size of a postage stamp, and passed it back to Bolin. "Make sure it ain't too tight. This address, ya know where it's at?"

The bishop leaned forward, closer to the stamp. "Yes."

"Good," Hunter said with a propitious nod. "Direct me there."

He pulled up his hood and gave himself a warming hug, the pre-dawn wind snapping at his already numb ear lobes. They placed Bellinger's limp body onto the rear seat, and Hunter reversed the Beamer, and in a final display of anger . . . ran the car over the man's body.

The bishop cringed and blessed himself. Hunter caught him in the rear view mirror as the car squished across the soldier, two bumps that passed in less than two seconds. Insufficient time for a prayer, way too little for a quick blessing, but time enough for several million candlepower of security lighting to illuminate the area, turning it into Wrigley Field, a Red Sox World Series. Hunter squinted into the blinding glare, light zapping into him from every direction. In that instant he anticipated a hoard of charging militia, but none came. *Maybe we got us some time*, he thought. *The lights are automated, they don't mean nothin'.*

His sense of security was short lived.

He rubbed his eyes wearily, settling behind the wheel with just a shred more confidence. *Ain't no one comin', we're fine.* Then his eyes were drawn to the flashing light bars in his rear view mirror. Two pursuit cars sped from the Western Hills building, closing fast on the Beamer as Hunter threw it into a hard right turn. It all happened in slow motion and Hunter shouted, "Motherfuckers," and Bolin screamed, "Oh my God! Oh my God!"

Hunter called back, "Can he drive?"

"Who?"

"Your God. Can your God drive?"

"What are you talking about?" Bolin screamed in a confused tone as the Beamer increased speed to the sound of squealing tires.

"If your God can't handle this Beamer, if he ain't able to move its ass along any better than I'm doin', then callin' him ain't gonna do us any fuckin' good now, is it?"

Torn between panic and philosophizing with this blasphemous non-believer, Bolin allowed the profanity to go unnoticed. *There will be time to save this wretched soul,* he thought, his eyes raised in silent prayer. Hunter turned, threw a quick glance at Bellinger, and asked the bishop, "How's she doin?"

For a brief moment he thought he'd heard a moan, but she didn't stir. Bolin unbuckled, leaned back and felt her forehead. "She is unconscious, we need to get her to a doctor."

"Not yet. We need to get us the hell away from these

guys."

The Beamer increased the gap between the pursuing cars and themselves.

"Reach in back," Hunter said aloud. "On the floor - get my bag."

Bolin turned, pulled the canvas carry bag into the front seat, a Lufthansa carry on.

Heavy.

Damp.

Hunter threw the Beamer around a sharp bend, saw Bellinger tumble sideways.

"Come on, they're gainin' on us. Open the bag, but open it carefully."

Bolin's hand trembled as he slowly unzipped the bag and Hunter reached in with his eyes still on the road, feeling about, finding it, taking out the large bun shaped roll.

To the untrained eye, it would pass as modeling clay.

"Here, hold this," Hunter said. "You'll find some caps with wires attached. Take one of the caps, pass it to me."

Bolin followed the instructions and fumbled as Hunter drifted the Beamer into a left bend and the bishop dropped the detonation cap and . . .

He stayed silent, eyes picking up Hunter's glare in the rear view.

"What's up? Come on, gimme the cap."

"I, I, it fell, under the seat."

"Fell! What the f . . ."

The Beamer was on a straight stretch of road, no other vehicles in sight. *Lost the cocksuckers*, Hunter thought, pulling the BMW to the curb. He jumped from the car, scrambled about, feeling under the seat. Found the cap. He quickly slipped two wires into the clay, messed with the cap device, slipped back behind the wheel, and gunned the motor.

Again, flashing light bars, sirens screaming like banshees. He cussed, "Clever motherfuckers."

Two hundred meters and closing.

The C4 sat snugly in his lap, one hand fondling the apparatus, the other gripping the wheel.

He let go of the wheel, slid the sunroof open and slowed, allowing the gap to close. When the pursuers were within fifty yards, Hunter clicked the device, and hurled it skyward through the opening.

He caught the questioning look in Bolin's eye.

"A Hail Mary," he said, grinning broadly, eyes ahead.

The blast sent one car careening on its side, as the other bounced off a wall and burst into flames, shattering windows of buildings on either side of the road. Bolin turned, raised his eyes skyward and said, "Holy Mother of God."

"Nah, His mom ain't gonna help either. Good ol' C4, now she'll definitely help."

The bishop turned his attention back to the small piece of paper, squinting at the miniature directions. "Did you not have larger paper?" he asked. "This is most difficult to read."

"Ever tried chewin' a foolscap sheet, your Eminence, havin' to swallow it in a hurry?"

Bolin got the picture, read the street names, then pointed the way.

Hunter zigzagged up narrow laneways, down darkened streets; saw nothing but an occasional pedestrian and a few drunks staggering about here and there. No signs of intervention.

"Jesus, we're *too* lucky, huh?"

"You think?" came the soft voice from the back seat.

He whipped his head around. "Bell? Thank God. Are ya feelin' okay?"

"My head, it's pounding. I was slugged hard. I saw him coming, but he was right on top of me with . . . I think it was his rifle butt." She squinted, rubbing her eyes, trying to recognize the man in the passenger's seat, the large man wearing the military uniform.

Hunter saw her inquisitive look. "Say hello to Bishop Bolin."

"Whoa, I thought you were a soldier," Bell said. "That uniform."

Bolin stared as Hunter wiped at the black paint covering his face, hints of white now beginning to show on his cheeks, on the bridge of his nose. He took a few seconds before sensing the question hanging over the bishop's head.

"What's up?"

"I thought you were a black man."

"Nah, we couldn't get one," Hunter said, sniggering. "Those guys were all too busy jumpin' on quarterbacks." He wiped a little more of the paint from his cheek. "They sent me instead."

"I am sorry," Bolin said in a confused tone, "I do not understand."

"Gard," Bell winced, "What was that explosion I heard, did you . . .?"

"Did too, need to dump this car, get us cleaned up. It'll be light soon, how much further, Bishop?"

Bolin leaned forward, and pointed to an approaching intersection, "Turn at the next cross street, the address is just ahead. Do you know the person at this location?"

Hunter didn't respond, stayed focused on the road ahead. The Beamer rounded a corner, and rolled to a halt facing a green building where Hunter sounded the horn twice, waited a few seconds, then gave it three more sharp blasts.

A ground-level light flickered and a weary faced man peeked from the window. Hunter squinted at the face, then flicked his lights three times. A minute later a solidly built man pushed a small garage door open and waved them in. Hunter quickly pulled the BMW into the narrow space and killed the motor.

"Mr. Hunter, it is good to see you. Mr. Ridkin was able to get a message through, but I was not sure you would come before first light."

The man bowed reverently to the fat man in the soldier's uniform. "Your Eminence," the weary man said. "You are bleeding. Quickly, inside."

Looking like a Ninja warrior, Hunter stepped from the car and smiled, "Good to see ya again, Billie."

The weary man pulled the garage door closed, his eyes not leaving Hunter as he moved crab-like along the side of the car. When Bellinger stepped from the rear of the Beamer, the weary man nodded. "Please, come this way," and he led them into an antiquated and dilapidated house with layers of paint peeling from its walls. At the end of a small flight of steps they walked into a reasonably comfortable living area with awards and photographs of gymnasts displayed in random positions, perhaps hiding the worst of the damaged walls. He gestured to the bishop, "Make yourself comfortable, I wil fetch water and ointment for your wound."

"Bishop, this is Billie," Hunter said. "He's got quite a story to tell."

"It is good to meet you, thank you for your help." He motioned to Bell and Hunter. "These two Americans; they took a great risk to save me tonight."

Billie kneeled and kissed the ring on Bolin's hand. The bishop raised Billie to his feet. "What is your given name, my son?"

"Your Eminence, call me Billie." He shrugged in a self-conscious snicker. "I am known as Beijing Billie."

Billie smiled at Hunter, and said, "You have acquired a different complexion since we last met."

Hunter grinned; he had momentarily forgotten the black paint. "Yeah, gotta clean this shit off, don't wanna be mistaken for minstrel material."

"May I ask," Bolin said, "How you came by the name Beijing Billie?"

"I am the leading Olympic gold medalist for The People's Republic. I was six months in America on an exchange program, assisting junior gymnasts in their preparation for Olympic competition. My protégés gave me the name Beijing Billie. It was a good time in my life. I admire the United States greatly, especially the lifestyle. It was only the constant surveillance by our team managers that kept me from seeking asylum."

He moved to Hunter, gave a two handed shake, squeezed hard on Hunter's hand.

"You've one heck of a handshake, Billie," Hunter said.

"Yes, Mr. Hunter, the rings and parallel bars will do that. However, I no longer participate in gymnastics. China has younger men for that task."

Billie's rhetoric and speech amused Hunter as he told the bishop about his incredible time in America, how the barrier that prevented his staying remained with him, how it ate at his very soul. When his venting was over, the three relaxed for the first time in hours. Hunter placed the Sig on the table, removed the silencer and ejected the clip, as Billie inspected the bishop's wound.

"How d'ya feel, Bell?" Hunter asked.

"Got one hell of a headache, otherwise I'll be as good as new. Just need a good night's rest."

Billie glanced sideways, heard the comment. "I have aspirin. Please allow me, Miss Bell." He reached into a cabinet, removed a bottle, shaking four tablets into her palm.

"Billie, d'ya have a shower, one with hot water?"

Hunter asked touching his face. "We could use showers all round, gotta clean this shit off."

"There is not too much hot water. If you make it a quick shower, you could get two minutes each. I have laid out towels and robes for each of you."

"How about it, Bell, just like the good ol' days, you wanna share?"

The bishop pretended not to hear the comment. Bell smiled and Hunter began feeling lucky.

Resembling a symbol of solemnity, Bell said, "You're such a dreamer."

"Glad to have you back, kiddo. You had me scared there for a bit." He nodded to one side. "You go on ahead, leave me some *agua caliente*. I hate cold showers."

Billie walked to a small chest that doubled as a tea table, raised the lid, took out a folder, opened it, and pulled out some maps. He and Bolin huddled over a large map of Western China as Billie traced his finger west, west and further west, not stopping until it nudged the Himalayas. He reached back into the chest, took out two cellular phones, flicked one open, and pressed the contact button. "Yidui, our friends have arrived safely. Yes, they have the bishop."

Bellinger, toweling her hair dry, and wearing a white terry toweling robe, walked from the shower in time to hear Billie's comment.

"Yes. Yes. Yes," he nodded repeatedly into the phone. "Mr. Hunter and Miss Bellinger, yes. The bishop has injuries but nothing serious. They are in all need of rest. We will be there tomorrow evening."

He snapped the cellular closed, turned and smiled at the three people now staring at him, each with the same unspoken question.

"Yes my friends, many questions, I can see them in your eyes. All will be answered in due time, all will be answered."

"So Billie, whatcha been doin' since you were replaced with younger men?" Hunter asked, smiling as he gestured at the larger of the photographs hanging above a dilapidated sofa, the words, *younger men,* being a possible touchy point.

Billie raised his eyes from the map. "I climb mountains," he said, passing a hand over the map. "Many of these mountains."

There was a long silence.

Time to absorb the implications.

The possibilities.

He took in their expressions, grinned, and turned his attention back to the bishop's wound.

Bell shook her head and tapped on the map. "Oh my God," she exclaimed, "you climb *these* mountains?" She looked at Hunter. "So he's in, right?"

"Absolutely, if he wants to be in. Ya wanna be in Billie? Ya want another crack at the good ol' US of A, land of the free, home of the brave, all that shit?"

"You know I have always wanted to live in your country. If I can get you safely home to America, can Mr. Ridkin arrange asylum? My brother Paul might also like to come along."

"Billie my boy, if you can help us get over the mountains and into whatever the fuck's on the other side," and he looked at Bolin and nodded apologetically, then, back to Billie, "Billie old son, if ya can do that, well yeah, welcome to America."

The bishop smiled and spoke to Billie in Chinese. After a minute of chatting, agitation began to show on Billie's face. He shook his head in a *no* gesture as the bishop's voice had a pleading tone.

"What's goin' on?" Hunter asked abruptly.

"The bishop, he says he is concerned at crossing the mountains. He thought you would have a less strenuous means by which to get him out. He says he cannot stay here because the general will have him killed. He says he understands you have your orders."

"Christ, Gard," Bell said, with one hand on Hunter's knee. "Getting *him* over the mountains will slow us way down. Look at him; he's three hundred pounds if he's an ounce."

Billie said, "Your man Slade is with your compatriots, Blake, Dallas and a Taiwanese man. They are in a village a short distance from Beijing. An elderly woman is our contact in the house. Her name is Whea Chung. She is expecting our team to meet there."

"Sam has all his ducks in a row," Hunter said, shaking his head from side to side. Bellinger, now sitting on an old wooden bench across from the table, nodded, agreeing appreciably with Hunter.

"Billie, this guy we're gonna see," Hunter mused, "he ain't someone in our organization, right?"

"No, not in any way connected to the military, or to your Interpol people," Billie said, swallowing deeply. "I have a younger brother, his name is Lee. He is a priest. He was assigned as a watchdog at the Xishiku. It was he who kept a silent watch on His Eminence." Tears began to swell in Billie's eyes, and it was a long ten seconds before the silence ended.

"Lee?" Hunter asked, unfamiliar with the name.

Billie tried to regain composure. "Lee was sent by us to guide Mr. Blake and Mr. Dallas safely to meet you. I received word that an accident has claimed his life. He was a fine young man, a perfect brother. I loved him dearly."

"I'm very sorry, I'd like to have met him," Hunter said softly, feeling Billie's grief.

Bolin was clearly shocked. "Billie my friend, I am so sorry, I did not know. Father Lee was the finest of my young priests. May God rest his soul, I must pray for him, I've now lost three of my fine young men."

Hunter dared ask the question, "How'd your brother, Father Lee, well, how'd he die?" You said he was sent to guide our guys out, right?"

"He was with the Ridkin team, that's how we were told they were to be referred to, *the Ridkin team.* They were involved with a problem at the cathedral, with General Cheng in his effort to arrest our dear friend here." He motioned toward Bolin. "The general came face to face with Mr. Blake and his friends. Fortunately, my brother was on hand to guide your men safely away, but too late to save the young priests. We heard one was shot inside the cathedral, the other on the steps. My brother's timing was most fortuitous."

Minutes later, Billie began to prepare food, moving him away from the sadness that filled the room. Hunter had questions, but realized the need to place his curiosity on hold, the need for sympathy, allow a little time to pass. Billie broke the silence and spoke as he stirred the pot.

"While I prepare some dinner, you should take that shower. He pointed with a wooden spoon, pointed at Hunter's face. "That paint may become permanent."

"Yeah sure . . . in a bit."

"I know you want to hear about your friends," Billie said, his eyes staying on the pot as he stirred, "about how my brother died." He voice became hushed, monotone.

"I was hopin' it was all a bad dream."

"A nightmare," Billie said sadly. "There is a town on the other side of the city. Some children were playing with their dogs. They stumbled onto four bodies hidden under bushes. Whoever placed them there was in a rush, no serious attempt was made at concealment. My brother's neck, it was broken." He stopped stirring, looked across at Hunter, "The other three were soldiers, and this is very strange, one had been stripped of his uniform."

Bell had changed back into her track suit, her blonde

hair tied back in a stubby ponytail, a look that sparked a certain desire in Hunter. He had a few wild thoughts, but fought off the testosterone surge, switching channels back to Beijing Billie, visualizing a possible scenario. "What might've happened is this. Our guys had a confrontation with Cheng's men, and one of our guys is now wearin' the soldier's missin' uniform. That's a possibility. Your brother was the unlucky one in the group. Earlier, you said our guys are in a town on the other side of the city. If that's the case, how soon can we join 'em?"

"Whea Chung's house has a red door," Billie said. "On the door you will see the number, eight. Your team will meet you there."

"You're sayin' they're all there now?" Hunter asked.

"My informants tell me they are." His mind drifted back to his brother, and he made a hard swallow before resuming, "My brother, Lee, was meant to take you to the house to join them. But now, with him gone, there is another man who will take you. We have a very secure network in China, we keep it that way by having a backup plan."

"You have one now?"

Billie raised his eyebrows. "Yes, we were well aware of two operatives who entered China a few days back. They are meeting at the Western Hills Headquarters of General Cheng. Our observers have confirmed they were there at the time you were removing the bishop from that very building. One of our informants was actually the unfortunate guard you left with a very bad headache. Thank you for not disposing of him, it's taken a long time to arrange his infiltration. The three men in the jeep, they were not . . ."

"Listen to me. I avoid leavin' a paper trail," Hunter said, cutting Billie off. "You know, leavin' people to talk about me after the fact. The guys in the jeep, well . . . wrong place, wrong time. And that other guy, the guard, well . . . he was one huge motherfucker." He tilted his head at the bishop. "And this's his uniform the bishop's wearin'." Hunter stopped, and picked up the coat. "It's a good fit. How about the one who tagged Bellinger? I had to take him out too. Sorry, hope *he* wasn't one of your *fine young undercover agents.*"

Billie grinned, showing a little jubilance in his reply, a spring in his verbal step. "Oh no, he was the real thing, and according to our man, the one you left with the headache, the soldier you eliminated was extremely disliked."

And Billie's grin cleared any possibility of dubious allegiance.

"The journey ahead will quickly erase your mind of the past few days," Billie said in a more serious tone. "Those days will seem very small compared to what lies ahead."

He was about to explain more about 'what lies ahead,' but, at that moment, Bell nudged Hunter, pinching her nose and nodding her head toward the shower.

"We will meet tomorrow evening," Billie said chuckling. "Meanwhile, I believe Miss Bellinger has left a little hot water, please avail yourself of the shower." He reached for the cell phone, opened it. "Please excuse me. I have a call to make. The road to freedom, Mr. Hunter, is not without its toll," and he gave Hunter a strange look.

The look stayed with Hunter as he showered.

CHAPTER 32

THE ANTIQUITIES SHOP STOCKED the usual gamut of tourist knickknacks, jade statuary, jade jewelry, jade chess sets, and the far too saddening ivory equivalents. Yidui haggled with a couple of British travelers over the cost of a 'priceless' artifact. It had recently been unearthed, after a mandatory six months burial at the rear of the maker's foundry, and, as is customary, the artifact remained caked in a fine layer of verdigris and dirt, giving a weathered appearance, one that was most pleasing to the collector's eye. Even though the prospective buyer realized it couldn't be more than a few years old, they enjoyed the experience of the haggle, and invariably purchased the artifact.

Always did.

The telephone buzzed and Yidui excused himself from the counter.

"Hello Billie . . . yes . . . yes. Yes, our guests are ready to be moved to number eight."

"Is everything arranged?"

"Yes, I will collect them this evening at Whea Chung's. I hear the general has dispatched several of his 13th Army to the passes at the northwestern foothills. If that is the case, any exit west will be too perilous."

"East is also out. We have been informed the general has blocked all roads to the coast. Any journey toward the Pescadores will be far too risky."

Billie pondered his next words, considered how much

he could share with Yidui. Not only had he been alerted to Yidui's suspected treachery, he'd had previous dealings with the man, and preferred to work strictly on a *need to know* basis.

Yidui coughed, cleared his throat, and quietly whispered into the hand piece, as though fearing someone might overhear. "Billie, are they still dressed as priests?"

Hesitation.

Something about the way the words came out, as though Yidui hadn't been privy to the plan, as though he were fishing, trying to extract information. "Yidui, the bishop was the contact for you, correct?"

"Of course, why do you ask?"

"The bishop, he sent the American to you for the statue, for the Tara?"

"Yes, it is not the first time I have assisted with goods dispatched in statues, and yes, it is generally a Tara. I shipped a duplicate as part of this assignment to a woman in Hong Kong." He paused and during the deafening silence allowed his mind to hear the suspicion in Billie's inquisition. He let the name slip out. "I sent the statue to Hong Kong, as instructed by eh, by Mr. Sellers."

The name surprised Billie and he kicked it about for a few seconds. "But if you're as informed as you should be," Billie said in an apprehensive way, "why then are you asking how the Americans are dressed?"

"Am I sensing distrust in your voice, Billie? Am I being cross-examined? I do not have time for this. I must go, there are customers in the store. I will come to your house when they have left. Have our guests ready to move when I arrive. We will proceed without delay to Whea Chung's."

With that, Yidui placed the handset back on its base and returned to his tourists. They were smiling, an American Express traveler's check in hand, ready to be signed. Yidui carefully wrapped the artifact for his buyer, and when they'd left the store, he flipped the sign over.

Closed.

He moved to the rear of the store, weaving his way between urns and statuary, passing on by a writing bureau covered with invoices and small boxes overflowing with jewelry, stopping at an ivory tusk in an unfinished shape. It stood like a sentinel at one end of the bureau. He reached for the phone, punched in a number, said, "Mr. Sellers, this is Yidui."

"I've told you never to call me at this number during daylight hours, call only between eight and ten at night. I assume you're using the safe phone, the one I sent you?"

"Yes, the cell phone, of course, and I am sorry, it is an urgent matter that made the call necessary."

"Did you place the item inside the Tara?"

"Of course, just as instructed. When will I meet with you? There are . . ."

"Calling me like this can jeopardize our arrangement; it can place both our lives in danger. Cheng has the bishop, and this fucks with our plans. Without my flow of information, and with our mutual buddy, Wang, being in China, Beijing most likely knows more than they should about the mission. Moscow is very fuckin' pissed with Beijing for exterminating their prime source of intelligence, and Beijing's trying to pin the death of the Interpol guy, McDowell, on the fuckin' Ruskies."

And McDowell grinned at his role play, was enjoying being Sellers, enjoyed announcing his demise.

Was loving "being dead."

Well . . . *officially* dead.

"Mr. Sellers," Yidui whispered, jutting his round chin at the ceiling, "The reason I am calling you is to inform you that Bishop Bolin is in the hands of Ridkin's people. After his arrest, they were able to get him out of Western Hills. I am meeting with them tonight and taking them, and the bishop, to Whea Chung."

McDowell took several seconds to ponder the news, then slipped back into his Sellers role. *Hunter, it's gotta be fuckin' Hunter*, he thought. *Sam's given him and Bellinger the go-ahead.* He strung it together on the fly, hoping Yidui was lost in the rambled delivery. *Fuckin' Sam,* he thought, *and his 'don't contact me' bullshit.* He nervously drummed the eraser end of the pencil on the table as he considered breaking with procedure, considered placing a call through to SoCal Exports. The thought scurried through his mind. Got no further.

"Yidui," McDowell said, "go on ahead and pick 'em up as planned. I need to stay low. My face's all over the fuckin' news here in L.A."

It wasn't as though McDowell, while in his Sellers role, was consulting with Yidui, more like he was thinking out aloud, and he realized Yidui knew better than to reply.

CHAPTER 33

THE VILLAGE WAS NO more than a few dozen shacks with only a sprinkling of inhabitants staring at the four priests striding, hoods over their heads, and bearded faces resembling mountain men more so than priests.

"I am guessing it might be the smaller one down that gully," Sung said, pointing ahead with a glimmer of hope. "It matches the description, and it has a red door." A little nearer, he said, "I do not see a number, perhaps it has fallen off." He turned and gestured at the door with a flick of his thumb. "I have heard this old woman is a marvelous healer. I recall Wang speaking of her amazing healing powers."

"I wish Lee were here," Slade said. "Things'd be so much easier. I don't like all this guessing." He called ahead to Sung, "You say she's some kind of healer?"

The word *healer* had an immediate psychological effect on Blake, who immediately began limping more noticeably.

"Hang in there," Slade said with a compassionate face, "it's nearly rest time."

"This woman, she'd better be as good as ya say," Blake said softly. "I can't handle this hurt much longer."

Sung raised his staff and rapped on the door, pausing as his eye caught the faded outline of a figure eight. "Look right here," and he ran his finger across the impression of the number. "You see the different color of the paint? It is an eight."

The door creaked open and a white haired woman smiled at the four priests, opening the door wide, beckoning them in, and bowing as they entered. Light beams filtered through the thatch roof and small puddles had yet to drain from the previous evening's showers. The shack consisted of two rooms, a single windowless main living room with a rammed earth floor and a sunken fire pit in the center. An adjoining smaller room was in total darkness, except for a few more rays of light leaking through the aged roof. The meager furnishings were rickety, consisting of aged bamboo strung together with twine and surprisingly, an abundance of gray duct tape. The small bunks, table, and scattering of chairs, all appeared to be made from whatever could be salvaged from discarded trash.

"She says welcome," Sung translated. "She says she was expecting us sooner. Her name is Whea Chung, the one I have heard about. Her father was a Taiwanese resistance fighter who held out in the caves, a folk hero back in the days of Chiang Kai-shek."

Sung explained Blake's ankle injury to the woman. Although no more than a nasty sprain, it had caused his ankle to swell to twice its size. The old woman led him to a bunk where she removed his sandals, carefully bathing his feet in a large bowl of warm water, and manipulating the badly swollen ankle. She motioned toward the door, explained to Sung she needed to go to a neighbor's house to retrieve a special cream for treating the injury.

Slade stretched out on a makeshift bamboo bunk, looking as though he'd fall into a heavy sleep at any moment, while Dal, sitting across from him at a small table, gazed about the room like a kid in strange surroundings, his eyes mischievously searching for anything of interest. He reached for an old metal number, held it up to Blake. "Look at this," he said, his fingers inspecting the casting. "It's our missin' door number. If she's got nails, I'll bang it back up on the door for her."

The number had rusted, and the nails that once held it had long ago perished. Having received no reply from Blake, he placed it back on the table, and his searching eyes settled on a red porcelain bowl half filled with nuts. Guiltily, he took a few and began snacking.

"Cannot see her," Sung said, peeking through the door. "She is still in the house down the way."

Dal scooped a larger handful of nuts, threw them in his mouth. "It's manna from Heaven, Father Sung, manna from fuckin' Heaven." Within minutes, he'd chomped his way through a pound of the delicacy.

Fifteen minutes later the old woman returned. Dal smiled appreciably, nodding at the empty bowl with both cheeks still bulging. *A chipmunk-like impersonation*, Blake thought, shaking his head in dismay. Whea Chung glared at him and he felt the guilt, but she said nothing, only serving to worsen his guilt. She pulled the small table nearer to Blake, making what little was left of the nuts beyond Dal's reach. She began massaging the ankle with a pungent smelling cream, sparingly applying it from a jade jar.

"Hey Sung, ask her if she's got any more of those nuts," Dal ordered, in a self deprecating tone. "They were really good. I kinda feel bad, ya know, eatin' 'em all."

Sung made an apologetic shrug to the woman, and the two entered into a lengthy conversation. The animated discussion was apparently highly amusing as both Sung and Whea laughed uncontrollably. Dal and Blake became party to the contagious laughter unaware of the cause of the outbreak; Slade eavesdropped on Sung's whispering to Blake, and he too began a deep belly laugh.

"What's so funny?" Dal asked. "Aw, I get it, she's pissed because I ate the nuts, ain't she?"

Sung wiped tears from his eyes, and chuckled, "She has plenty more of the nuts in that room." He nodded to the smaller room. "But they are all chocolate coated." He fought back more tears, continued, "She says that since she lost her teeth, she, she . . ." and he let out another burst of laughter, "she says she sucks off the chocolate, and leaves the nuts in that red bowl."

As Dal gagged, Blake said, "Class man, show some fuckin' class."

When the laughing subsided, Blake stretched out, placed his interlocked fingers under his head and dozed off. Slade cracked the door an inch, peeked up and down the small row of shacks. "We gotta to get our ass's outa here," he said. "Gotta link up with Hunter and Bell. Christ, if only we had Lee . . ." He held the words, still feeling the loss of his traveling companion. "I miss him and his lisp. It took me awhile, but I finally was able to understand *most* of what he was saying." He opened the door a little wider, craning his neck to look farther to the right. "We gotta to do a recon of the cathedral. Maybe Hunter'll show up there, eventually."

"He *could* go there," Dal said speaking to Slade's back. "But Hunter doesn't know about David Leung's place. If he doesn't go to the cathedral, how about the park, ya know, the one where we were supposed to hook up with you . . . and Lee?"

Slade closed the door, backed into the room, rubbed his chin, making a face as he felt the roughness of several days beard growth. He leaned toward Blake who was in a light sleep as the old woman continued massaging his ankle.

"You know," Slade said, "I really think we need to get in touch with whoever's running that cathedral."

Dal shook his head. "I'm sure Sam has a plan to get the bishop outa Chinese hands." He pointed to Blake. "That guy back there. . ." and he flicked a thumb, "the guy you slugged when the tank showed up, well, he seemed pretty serious about keepin' the bishop. Lucky for him ya were outa

349

slugs. His uniform looked like he was a pretty high rankin' officer, maybe a captain."

He stretched for the red bowl, caught himself and quickly backed off.

"He didn't get a good look at our faces," Dal said. "But if he puts one and one together, he ain't gettin' three. The shot that whistled by us back there, it wasn't firin' practice, that sonofabitch just about fuckin' nailed me."

Blake stirred, yawned, and groaned, "Gotta move forward, that's for sure. The six of us need to get the fuck outa Dodge; gotta head to Leung's place. He's the best contact we got."

"Consider where we're at right now," Slade said. "We can't go east; they've got those routes covered."

"Why's that?" Blake asked, with absolutely no idea why Slade sounded so emphatic.

"When eh, when I was in Penghu, they came on pretty strong, I got most of the stuff I was after, but there was more. I was this close, Drew, this close," and he held his thumb and index finger half inch apart, repeating, "this fuckin' close, man."

Dal gave a quizzical look, cocked his head to the side. "I don't get it. Ya got the flash drive, and it's in this statue." He pointed at the small bag Slade had on the nearby table.

"Well, yeah, but when I was in the control room getting the stuff, two of their guys burst in on me, and eh, in the struggle one of those guys was, well, he was killed."

Blake stared at him quizzically, unsure of where Slade was headed.

"Not my style really, but becoming a habit," Slade said with a shrug. "Anyway, the other guy was wounded. I was kinda surprised during the fight when I got the upper hand and was about to finish him with my blade."

"Surprised? How so?"

"Well, he pleaded for his life."

"Yeah well," Blake said, "that's nothin' unusual, right?"

"Not really, except, well, this guy spoke near perfect English."

"No shit," said Dal, with a look of surprise. "That's a rarity, not too many of the fuckers here speak English. Not like it's a tourist attraction."

Slade paused, placed his fingers on his head and ruffled his hair. "I'm still putting it together, but at the time I had to do some quick thinking, so to speak. I knew there'd be a plan to get me out of China, and I needed to point the chasers in the wrong direction, to lead the hounds away from my exit route."

Blake's interest piqued, he sat up, leaned toward Slade, said, "So you . . .?" He lingered, then impatient for more, made a *come on* gesture with his hands.

"Well, the guy pleaded *so* badly," Slade said, "and he was sobbing, said his name was Lao, or something like that. Anyway he says he's an only child and his elderly parents counted on him to get by. Tells me if I spare his life he'd play dead long enough that I could get the hell out of the area. I guess I trusted the guy, couldn't cut him; it's like, ya know, when you've got a pet cow. You give the thing a name, killing it suddenly gets real hard. I'd rather be a vegetarian than kill Betsy."

Dal began to laugh, the laugh rolling into a coughing spate, spreading through the room.

Blake turned to Sung, "Ask Yum Yum here to get the boy some more nuts."

Slade went on, "So, I tell this guy, who by now is shaking uncontrollably, I tell him there're three other guys with me, and they're covering the perimeter and if he so much as raises his head, one of them will pop his ass."

Blake chuckled, "Really?"

"Yeah, really. So just then a siren starts blaring and I

need to high tail it out of there with the information I already have. So I say to this guy, who's now crying like a baby, I say to him I'll be back to take care of unfinished business. I say, *see you in a few days*. That's what I said; *see you in a few days*."

"Ya think he bought that shit?" Blake asked grinning.

"Yeah, he bought *that shit*. Well, I think he bought it."

Blake thought for a while. Dal held back, familiar with Blake's body language, waited for his delivery. "Okay then, lemme see if I've got this straight," Blake said. "You're sayin' that any move east toward the South China Sea is anticipated. Great, that's just fuckin' great, looks like we got us three choices, north, south or west."

"North and south are out," Slade said. "North we hit Russia, and south we need to go through too much Chinese territory."

"We must go west to the Himalayas," Sung said. "We must go to Myanmar."

"It was meant to be," Dal grunted in a disgusted tone. "Always was."

And Sung nodded in agreement.

"Yeah, yeah, yeah," Blake groaned. "So Mount fuckin' Whitney wasn't a waste after all."

"Right," Dal chipped in. "But, the Latin, I mean, did we really need the Latin?"

"Maybe, maybe not, it did get us off the mountain. Confession *was* good for the soul, remember."

"Yeah, but this guy," and he nodded at Sung, "he got the fuckin' reward."

"Are you still upset over that?" Sung said in a jovial voice. "When we get back to America I will treat you to the best vacation you have ever had. How would you like to heli-ski from the top of Whitney?"

Dal shrugged, reached for a newspaper that lay on the table, and jokingly tossed it toward Sung. He called aloud, "Hey, grandma, how about some more nuts? The ones *with* the fuckin' chocolate."

The newspaper scattered across the muddied floor and as Blake reached to collect the pages his eye was attracted to the loose page from the sporting section. He stopped, stared at the photograph. "Sonofabitch, take a look at this."

He placed the paper on the table. Dal gave a bewildered look, and both he and Sung said nothing. The sports page carried a photograph of Gardner Hunter kissing a large trophy. The caption below the picture was quickly translated by Sung. "It says American golfer, Gardner Hunter, wins Beijing Open. Oh, and look here, it says he was unavailable for interviews, says he checked out of his hotel unexpectedly, that his clubs remained in the hotel room. It says officials fear foul play, that Hunter was carrying a large amount of cash and checks. It says he was accompanied by his American caddy whose name is Bellinger."

Blake, favoring one leg, moved closer, a frown on his face.

"The writer says Hunter won in unusual circumstances," Sung read. "It says here that his nearest competitor, some person named Kang, from Korea, was last seen heading off toward the rest rooms, that he had a medical emergency and was unable to complete the final hole."

Blake grunted as Dal, shaking his head in a bemused way, grinned at him. "Sounds like the old eye-drop trick. Wha'dya think?"

"Yeah, Bell at her best, good for them. I got a hundred to one," Dal grinned. "Nice little surprise, hope we live to collect it."

"Wha'dya mean *hope*? Ain't like you to be negative. What's up, ya got bad vibes about this?"

"Yeah sorta," Dal said with a shrug. "What with us

353

draggin' our asses over the Himalayas, ya know, although it was in the original plan, it sorta got passed over. I guess I mentally softened up, and besides, that bad ankle of yours wasn't an issue back then."

"My ankle will be fine," Blake snapped defensively, annoyed at the inference he'd be a liability during a mountain crossing. He sneered at Dal, "Get used to the idea of cold, very fuckin' cold. Wear your long johns this time, genius. And do us both a favor, don't question my fitness again."

Sung grinned at Dal, shrugging and making a palms up *'what's his problem'* gesture.

"Wha . . . wha . . . what?" Dal said in a mock snarl at Sung.

The next morning at six o'clock, Blake gingerly tested the ankle. The pain was gone. *Jesus, how'd I recover so quickly? Back home it takes me days to recover.* He called, "Dal, wake up man, the ankle's healed. It's a miracle."

Dal groaned, dragged one hand across his mouth, a morning routine blending the saliva with his chin whiskers. "Thank Christ, I thought you were wakin' me with some inconsequential piece of useless fuckin' trivia. But no, this makes an early start to my day really worthwhile."

"Aw, come on Dal, my ankle was killin' me, gotta find out what that shit was the old woman rubbed on. I can corner the market with it back home, what with all those sportin' injuries. Can see it now, Blake's Miracle Cure, gotta find out about this stuff."

Blake's jubilation woke Sung, now propped on an elbow, staring in disbelief as Blake hopped about the room on one foot.

"Look at me, it's a miracle, I'm back to normal. Fuckin' Himalayas, bring 'em on, I'm there!"

The door opened and the sleepy woman entered the room and took in the scene. Sung, Slade and Dal were all laughing as Blake continued hopping about on the injured ankle.

"Hey, just the lady I wanna see, look at this." He motioned at his ankle. "I'm all better, thank you; tell her for me, Mr. Sung. Thank her for me."

Sung began speaking with Whea, explaining Blake's desire to buy the formula. The woman chatted back and fro with him, then broke into a fierce coughing spate. She grabbed at her chest and became faint. Sung flung his arms around her as she collapsed to the floor. He looked about, and said to Blake, "Give her mouth to mouth." He stared down at the gasping woman, then again to Blake, this time, in a more impassioned tone. "Please, Mr. Blake, if you want the formula, you must give her mouth to mouth."

"Sweet Jesus!" Blake shouted, brushing Sung aside, "Lemme in there."

He dropped to both knees, and began pumping on the woman's chest. Dal and Slade moved in closer, readying themselves to assist Blake. Sung placed a hand on Dal's shoulder, whispered in his ear. Dal grinned, placed a hand across his mouth, held back the laugh, and shared Sung's words with Slade, who'd been feeling bad for the woman. Blake was furiously massaging the woman's chest area as Dal leaned forward. He said, "Christ Almighty, the kiss of life, give her the kiss of life."

He continued pushing and gasping as his breath quickened, not taking his eyes off the woman. At this point the ripple of panic increased as Blake attempted to revive his cash cow. "Why don't I just use some of that Latin, short cut this shit, give her the last rites?" He pressed down more vigorously on the woman's chest, his fingers intertwined, his palms pressing downward. He raised her shirt, had both hands on her exposed breast. And as he applied pressure, he mumbled beneath his breath, "Push, count, push, count."

"Wait a minute," Dal said, "she's turnin' blue."

Slade winked at Sung, and Dal strained to retain a semblance of seriousness.

"Man it's a cryin' shame," Dal said, "your comin' so close to that miracle formula and all. If she croaks, you miss the gravy train."

"Jesus Christ," Blake grunted aloud. In a moment of despair he dropped his face over the old woman and began blowing desperately into her mouth, fingers pinching her nose closed as he administered the most important mouth-to-mouth ever performed by one human upon another. After minutes of feverish huffing and puffing, Sung, Slade and Dal could not hold back, all three burst into uncontrollable laughter. Totally out of breath, Blake kneeled upright, stared at the three hyenas rolling about on the dirt behind him. The woman sat up, threw her arms around Blake's neck and planted an impassioned kiss on the exhausted *priest's* mouth, the look in her eyes, one of sheer pleasure, her smile displaying four unequally spaced teeth.

"Aw shit, aw shit, aw shit!" Blake screamed as he sprung to his feet. "What the fuck. I'm a priest, for Christ's sake!"

"I think Father Bond has saved yet another soul, would you not say, Father Dominic?" Sung said amidst irrepressible laughter that continued for several minutes.

"Motherfuckers! I owe ya all," Blake spluttered. "I won't let this slide without gettin' back at you guys."

Dal's laughter slowed to a painful whimper as he held his aching sides, tears streaming down his face. "Sure you will dude. I'll think about this one the next time you forget to remind me to put on my long johns."

Blake continued wiping his lips; spat a few times into an empty bowl, gargled a cup of cold tea, and spat it too into the bowl.

Dal grinned and chuckled, "Class dude, show some fuckin' class."

*****

Dal pounded nails into the red door, returning the old rusted number eight to its original position. To Blake's dismay, Sung took the jar of ointment and worked the white lotion into his shoulders, grinning at Blake's disapproval. The atmosphere in the house with the red door weighed heavy with foreboding, light shimmering about the living area as the old woman stoked a struggling fire. As comforting as the glow appeared, it emitted very little warmth.

Blake shook his head vigorously at Sung and grumbled. "Sonofabitch, don't use it all." He paused a few moments then said, "Hey Sung. How do ya feel about makin' a visit to the cathedral? Scopin' it out, seein' how things stack up out there."

Sung nodded and rubbed his eyes wearily. "Sounds safe enough, later tonight should be a good time." He looked across at the flames, gesturing at Whea Chung, "I'll ask her to bring clothing from the village. It should not be a problem."

He yawned.

The lack of sleep had drained all four men, and after a few minutes had passed, the sound of snoring rumbled from Dal's corner of the room.

CHAPTER 34

AT SIX O'CLOCK THAT evening, Sung slipped into Dal's robe and sandals. He quietly moved to Blake and shook him by the shoulder. "Father Bond, time to move. Wake up."

"Damn!" Blake said squinting at the hooded man. "I thought I'd fuckin' died."

Sung raised a finger to his lips, "Shhh, I had to take Dal's robe; we need to get going to the cathedral."

Blake was hesitant. "We, what's this *we* shit, and shouldn't you be wearin' street clothes?"

"I thought it would be safer dressed as a priest, and seeing how a Salesian priest does not travel alone, I am hoping you will accompany me also as a priest." He nodded toward Dal. "Not the blonde. Your darker complexion will attract less attention."

Blake looked at Dal and mumbled, "Why should *you* sleep?" He nudged Dal's shoulder. "Dude, wake up, we're movin'. Sung and me are gonna check the cathedral out; see if we can find a contact there. Maybe find somethin' on Hunter and Bell."

What the . . .? Dal thought through his agitation. "How long do ya want us to wait back here?"

"Give us 'til mornin'. If we're not back by seven, you and Paul go ahead to this Leung guys place. It's close to the cathedral. We'll meet up with ya there. This guy, he's your best chance if the shit hits the fan."

Blake scratched at his head, screwing up his face enough to catch Dal's attention. "Another thought crossed my mind while you guys were sleepin'. Maybe this Leung guy's got some news on Bell and Hunter. That's all the more reason we need to get to him, if lookin' in the cathedral doesn't pan out, ya know?"

Ah shit, Dal thought, and gave a questioning look to Blake.

Sung and Blake set off in the direction of the Xishiku, looking like two priests on their way to the cathedral. They passed two drunken soldiers, got a cursory glance as the uniformed men passed on by. *That ain't a bad test,* Blake thought.

An approaching car slowed, and a young man leaned from the window. "Going to the special mass, Fathers?"

Blake lowered his eyes, looked away, as a sudden feeling of foreboding swept through him.

"Yes, we're headed to the cathedral," Sung replied. "You say it's *a special mass?*"

"Yes, the service is for the deceased priests, and for the safe return of Bishop Bolin." He pulled the car to a stop, stepped out as Blake took a few short steps away. "Fathers, can I offer you a ride?" He nodded repeatedly, scurried back to the car, and opened the rear door, smiled, gesturing for them to step in. The driver chatted away to Sung, who made certain he kept the conversation between himself and the driver, leaving no room for questions directed at Blake.

Parishioners streamed into the Xishiku as the young man pulled to the curb. He stepped from the car, opened the rear door, and made a waving motion with his hand toward the steps leading to the towering arched doors. A priest, standing atop the steps, saw the two priests leaving the car. He gave a relieved shrug, and skipped happily down the steps, taking them two at a time. He reminded Blake of a thin Friar Tuck, a man with not a care in the world, jovial, welcoming. He said, "I am so glad you have arrived early, Fathers. We received word you had been delayed. Since we lost three of our priests and the bishop . . ." he paused, choked a little, during which the joviality slipped away. "We have no one to perform the mass this evening. Our regular mass is early morning. This is the first time we have held an evening service." He made a half bowing gesture. "I am Father Chieu."

Sung turned to Blake, tried to smile but his face didn't cooperate.

"What's up?" Blake whispered.

"That Latin you thought would be wasted. I have some bad news."

Young Friar Tuck escorted the two men to the sacristy at the rear of the cathedral, the room in which Cheng had earlier placed the bodies. Tuck lowered his eyes and Sung saw his tears.

"What is it, why the tears?"

"This is where my three friends were found. Cheng's soldiers slaughtered them and dragged their bodies here." Looking away, he nudged his head to one corner of the small room. "We have been ordered not to discuss the incident." He paused, swallowed hard. "I must suffer in silence."

Blake whispered, "That's the shit that went down when we . . ."

Sung jabbed at his ribcage and whispered, "Do not say a word."

The young priest forced himself to control his emotions. "The Blessed Eucharist is eagerly awaiting your sermon, Fathers. It is very exciting to have you here. When we lost our three priests we requested three replacements. It is most gratifying to see our prayers have been answered." He opened a closet, passed a white chasuble to Sung, and another to Blake. He assisted pulling the robe over Blake's head, standing on his toes to clear his frame. Sung stood back, gave Blake an admiring once over.

Blake waited until the priest had moved away, then leaned to Sung's ear and whispered, "This is fuckin' great, Dal and his blonde hair. Thanks, Sung."

"Just look humble and follow my lead," Sung grinned. "You will be fine. I will give you the easy material."

The door to the altar opened, and four assistants wearing red cassocks and white robes entered the sacristy. Blake and Sung were each given two towering candles. The priest passed incense to the tallest of the four assistants who then placed it into the container and the priest lit the incense. The brass chain rattled on the container as the altar boy raised the small lid sufficiently to allow fumes to permeate the sacristy air. When the smaller of the boys spoke to the priest, Sung's knowledge of the Chinese dialect failed to kick in. He asked the priest about the boy's origin.

"Jei is Burmese. His family sent him here to practice the faith. They did not want him raised a Buddhist."

Sung turned his head to Blake, saw the inquisitive look, knew there was a question behind Blake's expression.

"He says the boy is from Myanmar. He came here to learn the religion."

"Why didn't you catch the language?"

"My Burmese is not good. It really was not a part of my upbringing, I stayed away from the place. It has far too many rebels and corrupt rulers. Myanmar is very dangerous, smart travelers avoid it."

Hmm, Blake thought, *all the more reason Beijing wouldn't be expectin' us to go that route.* He cringed as a horrendous electric organ began to grind away. *Last time I heard an organ sound like that was at a crematorium*, he thought. An over-reaching choir screeched a familiar tune. It almost resembled Ave Maria. Thankfully, the English words had been substituted with Latin. Blake and Sung hummed at first, then, as they walked from the sacristy, each of them comfortably joined in with the Latin. The mission-style oak benches were packed with parishioners noisily awaiting the priest's arrival. Overflow worshippers stood along the sides and at the rear of the pews. As the procession entered, the choir began singing the hymn, '*See the conquering hero comes.*' It took all of Sung's discipline to avoid Blake's demonic eyes. Father Chieu stepped to the pulpit and began speaking to the Chinese congregation. Blake waited for the Latin to come bubbling from the man's mouth. It didn't happen. He spoke in . . . Mandarin!

Blake felt his Adam's apple growing too large as he tried to swallow. "Sung, what the f . . ." he whispered through a bone-dry mouth.

"He is saying The Lord's Prayer in Mandarin, in honor of the three dead priests. I suspect the whole mass is going to be in Mandarin." He gave Blake a wry grin. "Lucky you."

Blake pushed his whisper to the next level, "Lucky me? What happened to the Latin, all that trainin', all that, and, and, and . . . ya mean to say the only thing we get to do in Latin is sing Ave fuckin' Maria?"

People kneeled and responded as the priest had his fifteen minutes of glory, accompanied by the screeching as it drifted from the rear of the cathedral. *A choir of young girls*, Blake thought as he compared the atmosphere to the formal mass he'd been subjected to during his youthful indoctrination.

Cell phones continually rang during the service, and some owners honored the correct procedure, stepping into the side aisle to take their call, the side aisle not being considered hallowed ground. When the young priest announced the word *peace*, each person turned and bowed to the nearest parishioner. *Just like fuckin' home,* Blake thought. But there was no hand shaking, no touching.

Feeling the need to contribute, and feeling somewhat

smug, Blake thought, *ain't gonna waste all that Latin.* He nudged Sung, nodded toward the pulpit. Sung tactfully shook his head, made several jerking moves, panic on his face. He flashed Blake a *'please no'* gesture. But Blake just gave a wink, smiled at the priest, and moved toward the pulpit. The congregation watched in silence, not knowing what the new, very tall priest could possibly have to say. He faced the packed house, tapped on the microphone, raised his right hand, then loudly and piously gave his best Latin blessing. When he was done with his very best Latin blessing, he added in English, "Peace be with you. Go with God."

Sung smiled, took a step forward and gave a blessing in Mandarin. Father Chieu, barely able to contain himself, raised his hands to God and smiled at the ceiling of the Xishiku. When the service had ended, the three moved to the rear of the altar, pushed through a door and entered the sacristy. They stood in silence for a few long moments, eyeing one another. It was a speechless acknowledgement of a job well done. When he did speak, Father Chieu chatted to Sung, complimenting him on Blake's surprise delivery. The room was a sanctuary, and within the confines of its surroundings, Blake pondered Dal's fortunate escape from the ordeal of the mass. *His turn will come,* Blake thought, *the little fuck!*

"So what's that all about?" he whispered to Sung, as the young priest bid goodnight to his four assistants.

"He says the general had the bishop at Western Hills Command Center."

"Aw, shit!"

"No, let me finish," Sung said. "The bishop escaped. They found one guard unconscious, another shot dead. There was a car chase, and those pursuing in military vehicles were also killed."

"Killed, how? What happened?"

"It was some kind of explosion."

"An explosion?"

"What are you thinking?"

"Anyone could have tried to get the bishop out," Blake said, rubbing his beard. "But I've a feelin' Sam's behind it, and if Sam sent anyone, it'd be Hunter."

"Mr. Hunter? You truly feel he has been sent in?"

"Yeah, he disappeared right after the golf tournament, that's gotta be a clue right there. Ain't like Gard not to stick around for a party. No one parties like him. If you were Hunter, and you were runnin' with the bishop, where would you take him?"

"Not sure. I will ask the priest if the bishop had any close friends. Perhaps he has relatives not too far from Western Hills."

When the priest had bid goodbye to the altar boys, Sung posed the question, "Father Chieu, if you were Bishop Bolin, and you needed a good place to go where the general could not find you, tell me, where would you go?"

Chieu hesitated, shrugged his shoulders, and shook his head in an '*I don't know*' gesture.

"He doesn't trust us," Blake mumbled to Sung.

"Father Chieu," Sung said, "would you like me to hear your confession?"

The young priest cleverly picked up on the opportunity and nodded. The confessional area was away from the pews, and Sung kissed the purple sash, placed it around his shoulders, genuflected, and entered the small booth.

"Tell me, my son," Sung intoned, "how long has it been since your last confession?"

"It has been two weeks, Father."

"Tell me your sins, so that our Savior can forgive them."

"Father, I have sins of lust and desire. Perhaps I am unworthy of the priesthood."

"We all have thoughts such as these. Have you prayed

for your brothers who were so mercilessly slain in this house of God?"

"Yes, Father, I have prayed several times each day."

"And for your bishop, have you prayed for his safe release?"

"Yes, Father. I have prayed for him to remain out of harm's way."

"My son, do you have any knowledge of where His Holy Eminence may be seeking safety?"

"He has a good friend, the brother of Father Lee."

"And this man, my son, what is his name?"

"Billie Hua."

"Do you believe this Billie Hua is the person with whom your bishop would seek shelter?"

"Yes, if I were the bishop, that is where I would seek refuge."

"Thank you my son. For penance say . . ."

Blake placed his hands in a pious praying position, smiled at Sung, bowed ever so slightly and whispered, "You, Father Sung, are one clever motherfucker."

The priest made a suggestion to Sung as they studied a map. "I can have our caretaker drive you to Mr. Hua's home. He has a motor car, and it's not unusual for him to travel to that area. There would be no suspicion raised if he was to go that way with two priests as passengers."

"Thank you, Father," Sung said. "That sounds very good. God bless you."

Father Chieu reached into his pocket, took out a cell phone, opened it, and pressed a button. Blake shot a look of uncertainty to Sung as the priest spoke for several long moments. As he placed the phone back into his pocket, he said with a smile, "My friend, Jinhai, will be here shortly. He will take you to Father Lee's brother."

"That will be good," Sung said with a generous smile.

Chieu rubbed at his eyes as he chatted, struggling with an occasional tear along the way.

"What's up?" Blake whispered behind Sung's head.

"He is telling me about the dead priests. They were very well liked. They helped many of the poorer people around the area, fed the elderly and took in the sick, the hungry.

"Tell him God will find a way to punish the guilty."

Footsteps echoed through the cathedral as a heavy-set man approached the sacristy. The priest opened the door and the heavy-set man entered. He was clean-shaven, well groomed. Chieu placed a hand on the heavy-set man's shoulder. "Fathers, this is my friend, Jinhai." Then to Jinhai, "These are the men you are to take to Billie."

Jinhai motioned for them to follow, speaking briefly to Sung as they walked down the steps. The two men thanked Father Chieu and waved goodbye as Blake peered through the car's rear window, still unsure of whom he could trust, still looking, always suspecting. His mind rambled, *Here we are, trustin' some guy we don't know, to drive us someplace unknown, to meet some guy we don't know, all the wrong ingredients.*

The drive took a little over thirty-five minutes, traveling through side streets, passing the same building three times. Blake noted the building, pointed the move out to Sung, who asked Jinhai why he was driving in circles.

"I prefer you do not memorize the route to the house," Jinhai said. "We do not place our people at risk."

The distrust was mutual.

Blake was still uneasy with the ploy. "Good move," he said with a shrug. "He doesn't know us, can't be too careful."

The car pulled up alongside of a small building. Jinhai sounded the horn three times, giving his high beam lights three clicks. The door of the garage opened and a smiling man waved them in. A black BMW and several cardboard boxes used all of the space from one wall to the other, leaving no space inside the garage for the car. Jinhai parked outside, and all three men quickly entered, and the smiling man closed the door behind them.

"Welcome my friends. I am Billie."

"Good t' meetcha. I'm Blake and this is Sung. Ya got the bishop here?"

He led them up the stairs and into his living room, where they were greeted by Hunter and Bellinger.

"Glad to see you guys," Hunter beamed. "Christ, we thought the worst, thought you might be dead."

"I heard ya played some awesome golf in Beijing," Blake beamed. "Won us some cash too, huh?"

"Yeah," Hunter said proudly. "Gonna have a big party when we get home. Bell here, well, she kinda upset Mr. Kang."

"Figured as much," Blake said. "Read the local paper. The old eye-drop trick, huh?"

"Our man here had it won anyway," Bell replied, smiling her best smile, "just needed insurance," and she placed her hands around her throat, making a choking gesture.

Blake cracked a smirk. "I forgot how good you look, Bell."

"Give it up Blake, you're a priest," Hunter groaned, an overprotective reaction.

A uniformed soldier strode in from the bathroom, catching Blake and Sung off guard.

"What the fuck!" Blake shouted, reaching for the handgun under his gown.

"It's okay, it's okay, this is Bishop Bolin," Hunter snapped, stepping between the three men as Blake held his pistol in a firing position.

"Jesus Christ, that uniform!" Blake said aggressively.

"Ya just took a year off of my life."

"Long story," Hunter said. "We need to get him some regular shit to wear. Billie, you got some stuff the bishop can change into?"

The introductions were made and the group sat down to a round of freshly brewed tea. Billie turned on some mellow elevator music. Blake recognized '*Puff the Magic Dragon.*'

"You said Slade and Dal are how far away?" Hunter asked Blake.

"At Whea Chung's place, we can be there pretty quick, but I think we should head on to David Leung's shop. Dal and Slade'll go to Leung's after seven in the mornin'. We said we'd meet 'em there if Sung and me didn't get back to the chocolate lady by seven."

"The chocolate lady?" Bell queried.

"Long story," Blake said winking at Sung. "Ask Dal about his nuts when ya see him."

"Oh yeah," Hunter grinned, "can hardly wait for this one."

CHAPTER 35

AT ONE O'CLOCK, YIDUI turned the "Open" sign to show "Closed," and set out from his antiquities store without calling ahead to Billie, his anticipated arrival time previously scheduled for eight o'clock. He wasn't up to another interrogation from the man harboring Hunter, Bellinger and the bishop.

Meanwhile, Dal and Slade waited at Whea Chung's home, expecting the return of Blake and Sung. Dal picked at some chocolate-coated nuts in a clean glass bowl, his mood melancholy. He said, "Wha'dya think, Paul, ya feel okay about what's goin' down?"

Slade stared at the gold statue, rubbed its crown with his thumb, and continued his staring for several long seconds. "Nothing we can do about it but wait." His eyes remained fixed on the Tara, and more long seconds passed by. "They said to give 'em until morning."

"I don't like it," Dal said, nervously scrubbing at his blonde hair, "somethin' ain't kosher."

Slade tapped on the base of the statue, thought about what was inside. He placed the Tara back on the red velvet cloth, rolled it a few times, and returned it to his back pack. He walked to the window in time to see movement in a car that was parked diagonally across from the house. At first it appeared to be empty, but as he was about to turn to Dal he saw the red glow, someone in the front seat, a cigarette in his mouth; a second or two later, another figure raised itself in the rear of the car.

"We got us some company," Slade said beneath his breath.

"What, who's out there?"

"I see two guys in a car," he replied, running his hands over his face, wiping his eyes hard and refocusing. "I think they're shadowing us."

"You're paranoid, it's just a coincidence; one way to find out." Dal stood and gestured at his clothing, "I'm dressed like a local. I'll go out there, walk by the car, see if they follow, wha'dya think?"

Slade gave it some thought. "I have to think they're waiting for the team to get back, they're after the whole enchilada, not just you and me. I don't think going out there is such a good idea. How about we go out back, circle around 'em, see if there are more of 'em back there. We can't let Blake and Sung come back to a welcoming committee."

"What about the old woman?"

"Whea, are you there?" Slade called.

No answer.

"Must be out," he said. "Getting some take-away."

"Can't wait for her to get back," Dal said. "But maybe, with those cronies out front, it's best she's not here."

"What if we leave, then Blake and Sung come back, find us gone?"

"Okay," Dal said. "Plan 'A': we go out back, get rid of the two guys stakin' out the house, take their car, and we go to the cathedral."

"What's plan 'B'?"

"Plan 'B' is we sneak out back, leave the two guys in the car watchin' the house, and we make our way to David Leung's place. After all, that's where we're gonna meet up if the guys didn't make it back here by seven."

"Is there a plan 'C'?" Slade asked.

"Ain't no plan 'C'," Dal grinned. "We'll need to

leave a message here in case the guys *do* make it back, some kind of message only they'll savvy."

"Wha'dya have in mind?"

"How about the words, *UCLA Professor*."

"Sounds good, they'll know exactly who we mean. Let's do it. Good plan."

Dal pulled a page from a note pad, wrote in large letters *UCLA Professor*, placed the note in the center of the table, clearly visible to anyone entering the room.

*****

At precisely eight fifteen, Yidui turned off his motor, walked to the door of Billie Hua's home, rapped on it and was warmly greeted by Beijing Billie, with one hand in an oven mitten, and looking every bit the perfect host.

"Yidui! Very well timed. Dinner is being served. Please, come in."

The antique dealer took an instinctive look up and down the street before cautiously stepping through the doorway.

"Eat up my friends, we have much to discuss, and much planning to do," Billie said, as he placed two bottles of Moutai in front of Hunter and Bell. The bishop poured a glass of the pungent local hooch, raising his glass in a toast to Hunter who quickly reciprocated, then quickly choked as the 120-proof-liquor burned his throat.

Billie laughed, "So you have never savored the national drink of China, Mr. Hunter?"

"What the fuck is this stuff?"

"Fermented distilled millet. Very good, is it not?"

"Jesus, no wonder you don't export it," Hunter gasped between breaths. After he'd thrown down a large cup of water, he squinted through tearing eyes at Yidui. "So, you say you can take us to David Leung's house?"

371

*****

When the meal had ended, Billie went to an adjoining room and returned with two carry bags. They contained clothing and personal effects for himself, as well as the bishop.

"Your Eminence," Billie said, "I have packed clothing in a size that may fit you, also some necessary personal goods. Please inspect the bag, any items I have omitted can be secured tomorrow at a nearby house. Meanwhile, there is a temporary change of clothing and a full-length coat in the room for you. Shoes are in the blue closet, please take whatever you need."

Bolin excused himself from the table, and carried his bag back to the adjoining room.

"It is nine o'clock," Yidui said. "We will be at David's house by eleven. Billie, have all the bags placed into the trunk of the car. Leave things messy, as though you will be returning in a day or so, like usual."

At ten they headed for Leung's house, all seven jammed into Yidui's five-seat sedan, with Bolin taking more than his share of the rear seat. When they arrived, David was alone. His two children and wife had retired early.

"It certainly is good to see you all safely together," David said as he went through a head count gesture. "But eh, Mr. Dallas, Mr. Slade, are they following?"

Blake explained the events of the evening, gave Leung the full gruesome rundown on the Mandarin mass. Leung looked at Sung, got a consoling nod back, followed by a sly grin. "He did very well," Sung said, nodding affirmatively.

"When do you expect the others to arrive?" David asked.

"Early tomorrow," Blake said in a hopeful tone. "They were still at Whea Chung's house when Sung and me left for the cathedral to eh," and he rolled his eyes, ". . . to do our fuckin' mass."

Sung grinned at Blake.

"Oh yes, Whea is such a delightful lady," David said. "Did you get to try her chocolate coated nuts? She coats them herself, quite popular with the children in the village."

"Yeah," Blake grinned. "Popular with Dal too."

"Yes," Leung replied. "She is particularly partial to the chocolate."

David Leung lit a cigarette. Exhaling slowly, speaking as the smoke streamed from his Ritz cracker thin lips, "We are preparing for a renewed plan for your exit from China. I expect a message to be delivered from one of our people some time in the next twenty-four hours. It will come directly from Mr. Ridkin. He is very aware of what's happening here. I have been informed Bishop Bolin must also leave China with your group. Mr. Ridkin is reassessing the situation, taking into account the Bishop's safety." He made a face, a gloomy expression. "All roads heading east to the coast are blocked by General Cheng's men."

Blake leaned toward David Leung. "Does Sam know the bishop ain't exactly iron-man material?"

"Mr. Ridkin says your time as priests has run its term. He says General Cheng is now stopping all priests. You are to destroy the priest's robes and dress as back packers, denim jeans and boots, climber's jackets. Be clean-shaven. He wants you traveling on American passports, which I will take care of in the morning."

"Ooo yeah!" Blake exhaled loudly. "Thank you, God! Where's that shower and razor?"

After Sung and Blake had showered and eagerly removed their beards, Blake pointed in the mirror and said in a narcissistic pose, "There you are my man; I thought I'd lost you. Welcome back."

"That's the Drew Blake we all know and love," Bell

said, smiling at him as he rejoined them.

"You got any scissors, David?" Blake asked. "I need to get rid of this hair hangin' over my ears."

"I'll take care of that," Bell said proudly. "I always did the grooming at home and I still have the knack. Get those scissors, David. Okay boys, the line starts here."

When Bell had completed the makeovers, Blake, Sung, and Hunter resembled college graduates. Billie and David gave the threesome the once over and nodded approval. "You most certainly look like city slickers," said David, "just like the professors at UCLA, quite a transformation."

Blake slipped into a black shirt with a slight dark green tartan effect and blue jeans. His feet thanked him for sliding them into comfortable Nike sneakers. Hunter stuffed his black tracksuit into a garbage bin, and was now wearing jeans and a deep blue roll-neck sweater. Bolin wore clothing that looked two sizes too small, but the outfit was a definite improvement on the military uniform he'd commandeered at Western Hills. His shoes were too large, and the big man didn't look ready for any kind of long haul.

Bell wore a tight top, her erect nipples clearly visible on her Beverly Hills implants, for which those in the room gave thanks to Beverly Hills. No one noticed the remainder of her outfit.

"Please, find a comfortable bunk, there are three in that room," David said pointing to a door to the right of the living room. "And there is another for you, Miss Bellinger, in that room over there where my children are sleeping. He nodded at Billie and Yidui. "You will have to use the lounge suite and sofa."

Hunter, Blake and the bishop disappeared into the room with the three bunks, and Bellinger quietly entered the children's room. Ten minutes later . . . the house fell silent.

374

CHAPTER 36

DAL AND SLADE SLIPPED through the door at the rear of Whea Chung's house. They made their way along a narrow track winding between small, dark dwellings. "Wha'dya think?" Slade whispered. "Feeling lucky so far?"

"Don't wanna be naïve enough to believe those two won't get tired of watchin' the house. They could be waitin' for Whea to get back. Hate to think she's gonna be in a shit load of grief on account of us. If we head on out now, we should be at Leung's house in about two or three hours."

Slade stopped, placed a hand on Dal's shoulder.

"What's up?"

"What you just said. I kinda feel bad leaving the old woman to face the music."

"Whatcha wanna do?"

"We have to check those guys out."

Dal sighed, scratched at his forehead. "Yeah, yeah, yeah, you're right. Check 'em out. Sure," and he nodded toward the car. "I'll go see."

The man at the wheel had his head resting on the center-pillar, appearing relaxed, blowing smoke at the moon, not a care in the world. The man in back didn't have a care in the world either, just lying in the back, with both feet hanging over the front seat. Slade moved into the rear of Whea's place, flicking on the lights as Dal moved along in shadows, making his way toward the car. The man at the wheel straightened up, shook the legs hanging from the rear, and both men slowly stepped from the car and made their way to Whea's door.

The smaller man, the one who'd been in the rear seat, peeked between the curtains. Then, pressing against the glass, realized the window wasn't locked. He raised the lower half of the window, placed one leg into the house, and two seconds later, was in. Paul Slade brought down a sharp blow to the man's neck. "One down," he groaned and slapped his hands together, a brief celebratory gesture. The man, the one who'd been at the wheel, raced to the door, put his shoulder into it, fell through, and bodily crashed into Paul Slade's arms. Dal had almost reached the car when the man who was at the wheel threw himself through Whea's door. He spun about and dashed across the narrow street, running, leaping, diving through the door. When he entered the room, he found Slade with one arm around the man who had been at the wheel; the man's eyes glazed, lifeless. Slade raised his eyes to Dal, lifting one shoulder in a shrug, releasing the death grip, and letting the man who had been at the wheel slide lifelessly to the floor.

"What kept you?" Slade asked. He gestured at the two still figures. "These boys must've heard about the chocolate. Wha'dya reckon?"

Dal shook his head at the two bodies, raised a hand, and said in a solemn tone, "In nominee Patris, et Filii, et Spiritus Sancti . . ." When he'd finished the blessing, he added, "What kept me? You try doin' a fifty yard dash dressed like Friar Tuck," and then added, "Amen!"

Slade, who hadn't been in on the Latin sessions, squinted, giving Dal a questioning frown.

"See if the keys are in that guy's pockets," Dal said. "We need to get 'em outa here. Gotta lose the car, can't leave it out front."

Slade felt through the driver's pockets, looked up at Dal, and shook his head, "No keys."

"I'll drag 'em out back," Dal said. "Key must still be in the car. You go bring it round and we'll get rid of these goons." He grabbed hold of the smaller man's armpits, dragged him through the house, getting him as far as the rear door. He went back for the larger man, took a hold of his ankles and thought, *heavy fucker*. Using all of his weight, Dal pulled, tugged, and jerked the two hundred pound dead weight to a position alongside his comrade.

Carson Dallas fell into a chair, cursed at the heavy robes then spotted the large barrel, its lid slightly askew.

Nuts.

He scooped a handful, soft chocolate melting in his hands. *So good,* he thought.

The sound of laughter stopped Slade as he stepped to the car. For a few frozen seconds he became a dark shadow, unmoving. The sound grew fainter, *moving away*. He dropped the hood from his head, his hair limp from sweat, sticking to his scalp as though he'd stepped from a shower.

As the car door opened, the interior light glowed, and Slade quickly reached in, covering the light and closing the door quietly behind him. He found the keys in the ignition, cranked the engine, and quietly rolled the car toward the house, steering it along the side alley and around back. At the rear of the house, he found Dal had propped one man by the door jamb, the other laying face down nearby.

Slade stepped over the door-jamb man, and took another large step across the second man.

Carson Dallas was as transparent as tracing paper. Slade saw through him, a chocolate junky. He sat with fists full of chocolate nuts, smiling widely. "We gotta take some of this stuff with us."

Slade shook his head, flicking a thumb over his shoulder. "What we gotta do," he said, "is get the hell out of here."

Dal hesitated a moment longer, threw a few handfuls

into a large paper bag, and tossed the bag to Slade who placed it on the dashboard of the car. Four long minutes later the two bodies were in the trunk and two sweat-soaked priests quietly drove away from chocolate heaven.

"That old lady sure makes great choc . . ."

Slade's grip on the wheel tightened, his eyes staying on the road ahead as he said through clenched teeth, "One more fuckin' word about chocolate and I'll fuckin' . . ."

"You're havin' a lot of fun at my expense, aren't you?"

"Not much."

When they'd driven a few moles, Slade swung the car off of the road, found a dirt track, stayed on it until it was too dangerous to go further. He killed the engine, looked about and asked, "Wha'dya think?"

"Looks okay in the dark," Dal snorted. "Best we move the stiffs someplace."

Dal opened the glove compartment, looked through some junk, a manual, receipts, and smiled when he found the small flashlight. He switched it on. "These two guys were doin' surveillance," he said. "Probably won't be missed until sun up. I'm gonna walk over toward those trees, see what's back there."

Twenty minutes later, the bodies were well hidden under a pile of branches and trash. They drove the car back to the roadway and moved it a further three miles.

"We gotta lose this car," Slade said, nodding to a dark side street opposite the cottage.

"You believe in miracles, Paul?"

Dal pointed toward a rack outside a small shop, a dim light glowing from its window. Four bicycles sat neatly parked in a rack alongside a wooden sidewall. Slade dumped the car out of sight of the roadway and jogged back the eighty meters where Dal stood looking at the selection. They chose two, and rolled them for fifty meters, far enough not to be heard from the house. They straddled the bikes and began furiously peddling. Slade pulled his robe up around his waist, annoyed with it continually snagging in the rear wheel of his bicycle. He wanted to cuss, but his '*cuss account*' was empty.

"Goddamn robe," Slade said, "I can't wait to get back into regular clothing."

"Stop whinin' and pedal. Maybe when we get to Leung's there'll be a change of clothin'."

"Wouldn't that be just too frickin' good?" Slade snarled, fighting the bicycle every inch of the way.

"Man, have you ever ridden a bike before?"

"Of course. But not wearin' a dress."

Pedaling along a side road, they heard an approaching vehicle, then saw the lights bouncing along a few hundred meters ahead. They steered the bikes off the road before the lights reached them, stood in a dark space between two small cottages, and watched as two trucks rumbled on by.

"Both military, possibly 13th Army Division," Slade said. "I've seen 'em before, something's happening for them to be out at this hour, and I'll wager it's something to do with us."

At three in the morning, they limped off the bikes and stood looking at the house they believed to be David Leung's home.

"Yeah this is it. There's the number over the door," Dal said. "Yep, see if you can see inside."

Slade pressed his nose to the glass window.

Dal repeated, "See if you can see inside."

"Wha d'ya think I'm doin' here, having a relationship with the frickin' window-pane?"

"Sorry dude, just anxious."

Slade pointed to a corner of the room. "I see some robes over a chair. Take a look."

"Yeah I see 'em, look like robes," Dal said. "Knock

on the door, see who comes out."

"Are you nuts? What if it's the wrong house?"

"We're priests. If it's someone we don't know, I can say I'm makin' a house call and I got the wrong place."

"Really? And wha'dya suggest you use to communicate that message, Mandarin, or fuckin' Klingon?"

Dal turned way, shrugged, sliding his hands in his pockets almost apologetically. Slade glancing sideways, sensing his hypothetical loneliness, said, "Aw . . . what the fuck!" And with that, he rapped on the door.

CHAPTER 37

AT A FEW MINUTES before six, the morning alert went out that Bolin had escaped. Wang met with General Cheng at ten o'clock and listened as Peter Cheng explained how he'd come by the golden locket. Cheng stared at the picture of the woman, raised his eyes toward his son, turned to Wang, and asked that he leave them in private for a few minutes.

"We have lost our ace-card. There was an intruder in the building during the night. The bishop's been taken. I need to speak with my son. Please excuse us. I will send for you shortly."

Cheng turned to a soldier standing by the door. "Escort our guest to the situation room." He opened the locket, tapped on the two photographs. "Peter, do you know who these people are?"

"I am told the man is a friend of Lisa Ling, the woman is her mother."

The general worked hard on distancing himself from the irritation, sat staring hard at the locket. "The man is eh, just her *friend*?" he said, doubting the connection was solely friendship.

"I suspect he's a former lover," Peter said.

Cheng called to the soldier, "Sergeant, bring me Wang."

When Wang entered, Cheng said, "I would like you to take a look at this locket, tell me if you recognize either of these people."

Wang took the locket, held it up a little closer as though better inspecting it. In reality he was stalling, but internally he realized the cat was out of the bag. He took a few long moments, swallowed hard, and said, "General, this man is Paul Slade." His tone was one of acquiescence, as though seeking mercy. "I am very sorry. He is the one who killed your son."

Cheng allowed a half minute to drag by, during which Wang stood in fearful silence. The general snapped, "And the flash drive, what of it?"

Wang's voice trembled. "I believe Slade has it."

"What other information do I need to drag from you about this person?"

"This is the man the American team is possibly travelling with. If they have not met up with him yet, I am sure they will very soon. I have information he has the flash drive inside a statue he is attempting to get back to the United States."

Cheng slipped a slight man-to-man smile to Wang, like a cat with a canary. "The drive, it is inside a statue?"

"Yes General, inside a Tara."

"How large is this Tara?"

"It is exactly the same as this." He reached into the carry bag, took the red velvet bundle and placed it on the table. Cheng unrolled the cloth, gently inspecting the statue, inverting it, tapping on its base, shaking it, and with his curiosity satisfied, stood it back on the red velvet.

Cheng felt the blood rise in his veins. He pointed at the locket, while holding Wang's frozen eyes, then said in a subdued tone, "Have these two photos enlarged, one of the woman, twenty of the man," and he pounded a fist on the table, causing Wang to flinch. Cheng's gaze moved back to the locket. "I want them within the hour. Give the locket to the guard. Have him carry out the task." He pointed at Wang

with a quick jabbing gesture. "Wait in the adjoining room. I
need to speak with my son once again."

Wang half-bowed, spoke with the soldier standing on
guard outside the door, and returned to the smaller room.

Peter whispered, "Why are you having a blow-up of
the woman?"

"Are you questioning me, Captain?"

There was no answer to that question.

Cheng walked to a window, hands in his pockets.
"There is something we need to discuss," he said in a solemn
tone.

"Am I free to speak, father?"

"Of course, what's on your mind?"

"I am very fond of Lisa. I am of a marriageable age;
I would like your consent to ask for her hand."

"This cannot be," Cheng said softly, without looking
at his son. "You see, Peter, the woman whose photograph is
in that locket first came into my life twenty-six years ago.
I met her after your mother passed away. We eh, we had a
relationship." He saddened, paused for a few long seconds,
and then cleared his throat. "We did not marry. There was a
political junta, I was sent off to the other side of the country,
and she took refuge aboard a ship that took her to Taiwan.
Last I heard, she gave birth to a child, a girl, in Taiwan. This
Lisa . . ." Again, the obligatory pause as he swallowed hard.
"Lisa Ling . . . this girl, she is your half-sister."

Stunned silence.

Peter leaned toward his father in disbelief. "Lisa is my
sister, my half-sister? We have never seen each other before
this week. We have already consummated our relationship."

"I am sorry, but you should not have *compromised*
this girl. Perhaps I should have Miss Ling escorted to another
location, one unknown to you. One in which I can control
her movement."

"Incarceration father, house arrest? Are you saying

you will have her placed under house arrest?"

"Call it what you will. I believe it is against your best interest at this time to prolong what can only be an impossible situation."

Peter found the whole story puzzling. He had no choice but to go along with the general, to obey his wishes. "I must see her, and return the locket. This is a promise I gave to her."

"What do you mean, *a promise*? I will not change my feelings on the subject based on you giving *a promise*. My position regarding your relationship with Miss Ling, with your sister, is non-negotiable."

"You have raised me to be honorable. I cannot break my word."

"Are you willing to give me your word that once you return the locket, you will never see this girl again?"

"Father, perhaps you can take a small measure of cheer in knowing she said you are *an impressive man*."

"She might not express such an opinion should you tell her I am her father, that you are her half-brother."

"No doubt," Peter said, "the general might prefer that *he* be the one to break the joyous news to his newly-found daughter."

"I cannot do that," the general said as returned to the window overlooking the road below. "The girl is your own flesh and blood. You are both my children, yet somehow she remains foreign to me. Her life has been molded by strangers, molded in a foreign culture. This is why she is just another girl to you, but in reality, as your sister . . ."

Peter began entertaining panicked thoughts. *What if I tell Lisa and she still agrees to accept me as her husband? What if we can get out of China, get away from the clutches of my father? He would not be the first father who refused a potential daughter-in- law, ostracizing a son in the process.* He dismissed the negative thoughts, lingered for a few long seconds in a cloak of confusion.

After a short pause, the general's voice brought Captain Peter Cheng back to reality. "If I agree to tell her of the situation and you personally return the locket," the general said, "will this mean you will comply with my request and will not see the girl again?"

Peter stalled for time, reaching across the desk and picking up the Tara, appearing to entertain the thought of never seeing Lisa again. His heart skipped the next few beats and the room temperature seemed to drop below freezing. A cold shiver encompassed his body. *I cannot do this,* he thought. *I have found the girl I want. I cannot comply with your wishes, Father.*

"Did you hear me?" General Cheng demanded, bringing Peter back to the present. He snapped the Tara from his hand and thrust it back onto the red velvet cloth.

"I am not surprised you have adopted such an attitude, father. You are far too accustomed to having orders obeyed."

Cheng stormed around the desk to confront his son. He grasped Peter by the shoulders, but instead of rage, his eyes were pleading. "Peter, we can turn the clock back, forget this ever happened." He squeezed hard, gave Peter's shoulders an assuring shake. "Forget this girl, or it will surely destroy your future. It is bad enough I have lost my eldest son to this American, now I risk losing my remaining son to a girl who has come into our lives *because* of this same man."

Peter felt his shoulders ache as the grip tightened.

"Peter, you are the most outstanding young officer in the Chuan Army. Do not jeopardize this for one girl, please. There will be others."

He pulled back from his father, snapped to attention and gave a crisp salute. The moment was broken by a tapping. The door opened and the guard handed the locket back to the general.

"The copies?" Cheng asked.

"They have been completed, General."

When the guard stepped back from the room, Peter let the salute die. "It is useless, you are Major General Cheng. How could I consider not complying with your request?"

Cheng took one hesitant step forward, both hands outstretched toward the young officer. "It would be most embarrassing for me to explain my son marrying his half-sister. It would end our careers."

"Yes, Father. You are absolutely correct. How could I be so . . ."

And he lied well.

Lisa wasn't a prize he was about to brush aside to comply with the wishes of his father; she wasn't about to become a sacrificial lamb, wasted for the good of the Cheng Dynasty, for the People's Liberation Army, for the Chuan 13th.

"If I may be excused, Father, I will return the locket and say my goodbyes to Lisa. However, I cannot tell her that you are her father. That good news will need come from you."

"I agree. That will come from me, when the time is appropriate. But for now my priority is locating the bishop, and this Paul Slade. I have a strong suspicion when I find one, I will find the other."

Peter stood emotionless. "What assignment do you wish me to attend after I conclude my visit to the girl?"

"First thing in the morning, you will head up a division and cut off all exits from Beijing. They cannot have gotten too far with Bolin. He is a large over-weight man, in no condition to move quickly. I want this city shut down, am I clear?"

"Yes, General," and he made a robotic salute, eyes glazed, staring through the man he faced. "I will have the division cover all roads. We will begin questioning the bishop's associates; he could very well be at one of their homes."

CHAPTER 38

AT ONE O'CLOCK, in her suite at the Tianlun Dynasty Hotel, Lisa Ling, feeling demure, lay in the embrace of Peter Cheng.

They kissed.

A long lingering kiss.

"Thank you Peter."

"For what?"

"For being here, for loving me."

He turned away.

"Peter, a famous writer, Charles Dickens, once said, 'In every life, no matter how full or empty is one's purse, there is tragedy. It is the one promise life always fulfills. Happiness is a gift, and the trick is not to expect it, but to delight in it and to add to other people's store of it. What happens, if too early we lose a parent, a party on whom we rely for nearly everything? What did people do when their family shrank? They cried their tears, but then they did the vital thing. They built a new family, person by person. They came to see that family be defined not only as those who share love, but as those for whom they would give their love.' The time has come to build that new family, Peter. Together we will share that love." She laid her lips on his ear, and whispered, "Tell me we'll always be together."

He had thought of the words a thousand times, but knew however they came out, they would seem inappropriate at best, most certainly inadequate. His heart fluttered and his tightening embrace almost pulled Lisa through his body and she admired him with wide unblinking brown eyes, as though the slightest hint of a blink might cause him to vanish.

Neither let up, each held the other as though they were one. She felt herself drifting, drifting, yet sleep eluded her. Sleep meandered through her head, but remained beyond reach.

She forced the question, "Peter, what is it? I sense something is worrying you."

"You speak of building a new family. Before that is possible, we have a decision to make. I know what my decision is; you need to let me hear yours. Only then will I undertake *the vital thing.*"

"What are you talking about, what vital thing, what's happening?"

"Lisa, the general, my father, he has told me I am not to see you again."

"What! Why, what have I done to offend him? Have I upset him in some way?"

"You are from America. He feels we are too different. He does not wish his remaining son to be corrupted by the ways of capitalism."

He forced a smile. She didn't buy it.

"Peter, I can't believe that. Let me speak with him. I know I can put him at ease."

"No!" He reached into his pocket and placed the locket in her hand, then squeezed her hand closed around the small heart, unable to hold back the solitary tear that ran down his face. She leaned her head into his, and with a soft turning of her face, wiped his tear with her cheek.

Her head rolled from side to side, finally coming to rest as she stared into his adoring eyes. "I love you Peter Cheng. It's destiny that's brought us together, brought me from the other side of the world. We can't allow your father to come between us. He has no right."

He gazed into her eyes, wanted to say, *"But you are my sister,"* but said, "I love you so much, my butterfly."

CHAPTER 39

SLADE COULD BARELY STAND upright following the grueling bike ride. He and Dal quietly placed their bikes against the front wall of the house, and Dal pushed Slade forward. "Try to look like a priest for Christ's sake," Dal said quietly, "in case it's the wrong house."

Slade felt the dampness building on his forehead. He tapped on the door, a dim light came on, and the voice from inside said, "Yes, who is it?"

"It's eh . . . it's me, Father Dominic from the cathedral. I need to speak with you".

"Father Dominic?"

"Yes," Slade answered, with a lack of conviction, as he slid a glance at Dal. "I'm Father Dominic, from the cathedral."

"Silence.

The silence lingered for ten, twenty seconds. Feeling insecure about who might be on the other side, Slade dragged the words from the depth of his soul. "Can you please open the door?"

A sliver of light escaped as the door opened. It fell onto Slade's face, caught the beard and hood that clearly defined him as a priest.

"Quickly," David Leung grinned opening the door wider, "come inside."

The two men scurried into the house.

"How did you get here," Leung asked, "on foot?"

"We took two bicycles," Dal replied. "Me and Slade here, we've been peddlin' like Lance fuckin' Armstrong!"

Leung stepped out front, dragging Dal along with him and retrieving the nearest bike. "You get the other, bring it into the house," he said. "Two bicycles will attract attention. They will have to be removed before daylight. I will arrange that. It will be light in about three hours."

"Are the other guys here?" Dal asked.

"Yes, they are sleeping like babies."

"Who's here?" asked Slade.

"Mr. Blake is here, along with Mr. Sung, Miss Bellinger, Mr. Hunter, Billie and Bishop Bolin."

"What are you doin', advertisin' group rates?" Dal quipped as he nudged Slade.

"What's the bishop doing here?" Slade asked.

"He was arrested by General Cheng. His cover's destroyed. Your man, Hunter, was sent to free him. He brought Bishop Bolin here. The bishop needs to flee China."

"Fuckin' lovely," said Dal. "How do you suppose we do that, stage some kind of religious procession? Just Hail Mary the guy out of the place?" He groaned, looked at Slade. "The thing is," he said with an enigmatic smile, "can ya see us takin' the bishop over mountains?"

"Nope," Slade shrugged. "Don't see that happening at all."

"Ah shit," Dal said exhaling. "Where's Blake sleepin'?"

David Leung led him to Blake's room. Dal reached beneath the shade of the small bunk-side lamp and switched on the light.

"Rise and shine, sleepy head," he said, squinting at Blake, who was now clean shaven. "Hey pretty boy, all clean shaven and lookin' very fuckin' cosmopolitan!"

Blake squinted, tried to focus on his watch as he groaned, "Jesus, I thought you were Sasquatch. What's that smell? Go take a shower and shave that fungus off your face. Ya smell like fuckin' road kill." Then, spotting Slade, "Hey Paul, glad to see you made it here safely. Has Dal been takin' good care of you?"

"Great to see you too," Dal threw in sarcastically, sniffing at his armpit.

David Leung figured there wasn't much sense going back to his bed. He brewed up fresh coffee as Dal and Slade chatted with Blake. "He did it in what?" Dal asked in disbelief, as Blake expounded the Latin mass experience.

"Fuckin' Mandarin," Blake groaned, with a shoulder shrug. "He did it in fuckin' Mandarin."

Dal smiled and said, "Sam's supposed to have all contingencies covered."

"Yeah well, he didn't cover that one. Fuckin' Mandarin I tell ya. Father Sung here . . ." and Blake pointed at Sung who was grinning at Blake's religious experience, "well, Father Sung and I did very well; we got to say a few lines. We're quite proud of ourselves, all things considered."

Dal slapped Blake on the shoulder, and said in a sarcastic tone, "Sorry I wasn't there to help out".

"Yeah, sure you are," Blake said, winking at Sung. "So am I, Dal. So am I."

David Leung brought the large coffee pot to the table and placed several cups by the pot.

"I'll go wake the others," Blake said. "We need to get movin' before first light."

Hunter and Bell came from their rooms, each of them giving a warm hug to Blake and Dal.

"Guys," Blake said, "like ya to meet Paul Slade."

"I hear you're quite the golfer," Slade said, shaking Hunter's hand.

"Got a great caddy, owe it all to her," Hunter admitted, as he draped one arm around Bell's shoulder and gave a squeeze.

"Yes, we read it in the paper," Sung chipped in. "Something about your nearest competitor needing an extended bathroom visit."

"Shouldn't drink the water," Hunter said, shaking his head. "What do they call it, Fujikura's revenge?"

"Yes indeed," Sung said grinning, "something like that."

"All right, all right," Blake said.

Bell coughed, throwing a quick smile at Blake and Dal.

Leung's tone was subdued. "Please, seat yourselves around the table. As soon as our other guests join us, I will brief you on what lies ahead."

Leung checked on his family who were still sleeping, then quietly closed their bedroom door just as Billie and Yidui joined the group around the table.

"This is my friend, Yidui, whom Mr. Slade is familiar with," Leung said, gesturing. "He operates an antiquities store in Datong, and has been assisting our cause for several years. He is a close confidant of Mr. Ridkin and eh, Mr. McDowell. He is responsible for the placement of Mr. Slade's valuable cargo inside this lovely lady."

Leung reached for the bag Slade had placed on the table, removed the red velvet bundle and unwrapped the Tara, placing it on the center of the table. All eyes focused on the statue as he tapped on the gold crown.

"I have found over the years that espionage is in many ways comparable to true love, it never runs smooth. Just when you are feeling comfortable with the course of events, a surprise springs up and bumps you off track, sending you on a different tangent. This mission has now been bumped onto a different tangent. Getting Mr. Slade and this golden lady back to the United States has added complexities. The death of General Cheng's son, as well as the involvement of our still sleeping guest, Bishop Bolin, has changed our plans immeasurably."

"Ain't there some other way for the bishop to get his ass out of China?" Blake asked. "We really aren't up to baby-sittin' some out of shape, middle-aged priest tryin' to cross the Himalayas, assumin' of course, the Himalayas are still a consideration."

"Hmm, yes, the Himalayas," Leung said, directing his reply at Blake. "General Cheng's expecting you to attempt one of three possible exit routes, the Himalayas, of course, into Nepal. Then we have east, toward the Yellow Sea, and finally southeast toward Hong Kong. Each of these directions currently has more than the normal number of military personnel on stand by."

He stirred his coffee, took a few moments to take a long gulp.

"Mr. Slade, I am afraid short of dressing you as a woman, your slipping through any of these routes is an absolute impossibility."

Blake and Dal grinned at Slade, who failed to appreciate the comment for fear David Leung might be the slightest bit serious about the masquerade. Dal couldn't resist the opportunity.

"We could travel as a couple, hey, Pauline?"

"Fuck you, Father Dominic," Slade said, looking at Leung with a contemptuous glare. "You *are* jerking my chain, aren't you?"

"I have given it consideration," Leung said grinning, "but it would most certainly be a last resort." And he winked at Blake.

Slade saw the wink.

"Jesus, don't do that," Paul Slade said, letting out a huge sigh of relief, "it's too darn early in the day."

"So what's the deal, David?" Blake asked, rubbing his eyes. "Why can't we split into two groups? One group takes the bishop the least difficult way, and the other guys can go with Paul, get the flash drive back home."

"That was a consideration," Leung said, "but Sam Ridkin did give me one final instruction."

"And that was?" asked Dal.

"He said to keep you all together for the remainder of the mission. He wants Mr. Hunter and Miss Bellinger to complete their time in China with yourself and Mr. Blake. He believes Mr. Slade's safety lies with strength in numbers." He stopped for a moment, gave a shrug, "I must I agree."

"Did Sam know about Bolin?" Blake asked, "about him bein' extra baggage?"

"Yes, of course. He had already assigned the rescue on the day following the golf tournament, as soon as he received word of the bishop's incarceration. He allowed Mr. Hunter time to complete the tournament. It appears Mr. Ridkin had a sizeable wager on the outcome of the golf game."

"Sonofabitch," Dal coughed, "and he didn't tell us!"

Blake said, "I'm sure he'll throw some of the winnings your way."

"Let's not go suckin' dick just yet," Dal sulked, "I'm the only fucker who *didn't* lay a bet on the game."

"It appears so," David grinned, "it also appears I have said more than I should," Leung sighed. "I thought you were already aware of the Division's big win on Mr. Hunter's golfing victory?"

"The Division," Dal snapped, "ya mean they were *all* bettin' on him?"

Blake grinned, a Kodak moment.

"Don't go lookin' at me like that," Dal said to Blake. "I can feel the look. Don't appreciate *the look*."

"Best we change the subject," Leung said, smiling. "It seems I'm getting in deeper with each word."

Blake flicked a thumb at Slade. "Okay, change the subject. What can you tell us about the contents of this flash drive?"

"Surely your boss briefed you guys on this?" Slade replied looking at Blake, then at Dal.

"Yeah, but I wanna hear it from you, hot shot."

"Comes down to some type of weather manipulation the Chinese have developed," Slade said. "A way to use their satellites to cause floods, tsunamis . . . like that."

Blake had heard this from Sam, but maybe, just maybe, Slade had heard a different story from Broski. *Ain't no harm in tryin'*, Blake thought. He waited ten seconds, fifteen, but it seemed Slade was done saying all he was going to say on the subject.

He surprised Blake, kicking in with, "I heard from reasonably reliable sources that Beijing has had a few dry runs with this technology. They call it Operation Compass. But you probably already have that from *your* boss, right?" He said it with a sarcastic touch. "What scares me the most are recent tsunamis off Hawaii and the Philippines; word is these were small shots taken by Beijing. They realized the power utilized was insufficient to cause major disasters, they wanted more, so they unleashed one mother of all zaps." He paused, realizing all eyes were staring at him.

"You got our attention," Dal said. "Where'd they unleash this *zap*?"

Slade swallowed hard, his eyes turned down. He said, "Gulf of Mexico."

Blake placed both hands on the table, slowly stood, and leaned toward Slade.

"The Gulf of fuckin' Mexico? You mean New Orleans?"

"So you know your geography, huh? Yep, you got it. New Orleans. The mother of all zaps. It's what happens when man plays God."

"Christ," Dal said. "This'd kick off World War Three if it ever got out."

"That's why we've gotta get this stuff back home,"

Slade said. "Beijing knows once we have the same technology, well, we'll have detente. Checkmate. They won't mess with it 'cause they know we'll zap a big one right back into the ocean off of Shanghai."

"That'd mess with Japan," Blake added.

"That's true, the ability to direct the tsunami has been taken into consideration; the scientists who perfected the workings of this are able to tabulate the angle of immersion. Once the beam zaps the ocean floor it forces the resultant wave in the direction tabulated from the satellite. China's also used powerful ground-based lasers to effectively blind our satellites that are over its territory."

A large groan interrupted the discussion as Bolin stretched and yawned loudly.

"Your Eminence, please join us," David Leung said. "We have fresh coffee."

"Thank you, but I would prefer tea if you do not mind."

"Of course, allow me," Leung said, stepping into the small kitchen area and quickly returning with a cup of green tea.

"I am sorry, Your Eminence. It is the American influence. Please allow me to introduce my guests."

Leung turned toward the group standing around the table and made introductions. The bishop nodded to each man as their names were announced.

"Good, we're all awake and I must assume quite alert. Right, Mr. Dallas?" Leung said. He stepped back into the kitchen and called to Yidui. "Can you help for a moment?"

After a brief side-bar in the cramped kitchen, they returned to the table where Leung began a conversation in Chinese, a conversation directed at Bolin and Sung, during which the four Americans chatted among themselves.

"Mr. Blake," Leung said, gesturing with a finger. "Can I have a minute of your time?"

Blake stepped into the kitchen. "Yeah David, what's up?"

"We need to clear the air on a very important issue. You can relay this to your three associates; however, we prefer that for the time being, you refrain from sharing it with Mr. Sung. Do you agree?"

"I've no idea where you're headin' with this, but sure, I can live without sharin' with Sung. What's on your mind?"

"Before you all set off for your training on Whitney, we received intelligence from our people that one or both of the Taiwanese agents had been bought by Beijing. Subsequently, we arranged to separate Sung and Wang. Mr. McDowell was assigned Wang, and we left Sung with you and Mr. Dallas."

"So you're sayin' Mc Dowell was testin' Wang?"

"Yes. He played along with Wang. Certain leaks were allowed, information that wasn't injurious to the United States. The Interpol Division had clearance from the FBI, CIA and Washington to play along. The plan was to sell information to Beijing and Moscow. The information appeared genuine and didn't place America's security at risk. However, when two Russian agents visited Adam McDowell's office and attempted to assassinate him, Mr. Ridkin decided the safest place for McDowell was for him to be dead, until this mission is completed."

"But he *is* dead, right?"

"Yes, he is dead to the entire world except a select few, of which you are now one."

Blake slumped into a small chair. "Adam's alive?"

"Correct, but he'll stay dead until this mission reaches a safe conclusion."

"Who else knows he's alive?"

"Sam of course, Yidui, myself . . . you. As far as your team is concerned, well, you can tell them at your discretion.

But it can't be shared with Sung Chiao."

"Sung is fine, he's been up front and in the thick of it since day one."

"None the less, until we are able to get Slade back to the United States with the information, we prefer Sung Chiao believes McDowell is dead."

Blake shook his head in disbelief. He moved back to the doorway, then turned about and added, "My understandin' is that Sung has top security clearance from both Taiwan and the FBI. They say his record is impeccable."

"True, but so too was Mr. Wang's. Please, you must agree to keep this among only those I have named."

Blake nodded acknowledgement. "So what's goin' on with Wang?"

"We're carefully monitoring the movements of Mr. Wang. We know he's in Beijing. We also know he's meeting with General Cheng. We arranged for one of our operatives to rendezvous with him. This person is taking a considerable risk and has been with Wang for the past week. She has now infiltrated the Western Hills building. You have heard of her, Lisa Ling."

"Heard the name once or twice back at the Division. Do the other guys know about her involvement?"

"Well, not your guys, not really, just Mr. Slade. You are aware he and Lisa had an hmm, let us say a strong friendship several years ago."

"So, they were an item?"

"An item?" Leung said, analyzing the question. "Yes, I suppose you could say that, an item."

Blake breathed in deeply, closing his eyes. "Does Slade know the girl's in Beijing, that she's on the case?"

"To the best of our knowledge there is no evidence of recent communication between the two. There has not been for quite some time. The department thought it best to assign them different continents. If all goes to plan, their paths will cross in China. Lisa Ling will meet with Wang in Hong Kong. She will give Wang a replica of the Tara; identical to the statue Mr. Slade is carrying. Wang will switch statues when the opportunity arises."

"Wang plans on meetin' up with us?"

"That is where the mystery deepens. We suspect Wang will have his associate, Sung, switch the statues."

"That's if your hunch about Sung pans out, and I think you're barkin' up the wrong tree."

There was a pause, as though a confrontational moment needed time to slide on by.

"It seems logical Mr. Sung would be the obvious choice to exchange Mr. Slade's Tara with that carried by Wang," Leung said, giving a hard stare to Blake. "After all, they are associates."

"Yeah, well, as logical as you wanna make it appear, I trust Sung. Your hypothesis ain't realistic, David. I'll bet my life on Sung."

"None the less, I am going to send Sung with Yidui to another associate's house to collect two carry bags containing clothing and provisions for your journey. While Mr. Sung is absent I will go over the plan for your exit route. I prefer he is not present at that time."

"One question, how'd McDowell escape the two thugs at his office?"

"He was lucky, very lucky. The shot grazed his forehead. The impact was severe enough to throw him from his chair. His head struck the corner of a cabinet as he went down. It looked convincing with the amount of blood that pooled around from laying unconscious for so long. First impression left little doubt the shot was fatal. Apparently, the cleaner knocked on the office door and disturbed the intruders. They made a hasty retreat, believing McDowell was indeed dead. Mr. Ridkin chose to allow that belief to stand, thus the news coverage."

"He could've fuckin' told us," Blake growled.

"Best you believed him dead. If you were apprehended by the Chinese they would have eventually extracted that information from you."

"Damnit!"

They returned to the larger room where the group was engaged in an argument over how Chinese men were getting taller, playing on American basketball teams, and winning most gymnastic and some diving events.

"Yeah, gotta be steroids I say, they've gotta have some new kind of super drug the West ain't able to detect," Dal said, snarling at Sung, who jovially waved him off. "Eight foot tall Chinese guys playin' in the NBA, gimme a fuckin' break."

As the discussion gained momentum, David Leung stepped in and motioned to Sung and Yidui. "Best you get underway and return promptly."

Yidui's eyes crinkled. He straightened up, leaned toward Sung and said, "Shall we?"

Sung and Yidui got up and gestured to Leung. Sung tipped his head to Blake, winked at Dal, and the pair stepped from the house.

Blake didn't like the game, didn't like alienating Sung.

As Leung prepared a fresh pot of coffee, his cell phone vibrated. He stepped into a quiet corner of the empty guest bedroom, spoke for a few minutes, jotting notes on a pad, and returned to the group. His mood appeared more somber. "I have just received a call from one of our operatives," he said. "He has been attempting to contact me, but it has been impossible because there has been severe jamming around the region where he is located. He has been in direct contact with a U.S. base, going through two other channels to reach that contact. It appears Sam is working in unison with Admiral Bates, and they have put together a plan for your route out of China." Leung's voice dropped to a whisper. "It involves a Navy SEAL rescue."

What the fuck, Blake thought. "Did Sam mention the name Wolf Brandt?"

"Yes, the name did come up. I believe he will lead the SEAL. However, it is far more involved. I can get a message through to him, as long as we link up with the two relay agents, but seeing as how there is no direct connection, it could take anywhere from an hour to eh, perhaps as long as several days."

"Just like back home," Dal said, grinning at Blake, "for English, press *numero uno*."

Blake asked, "So what's the plan?"

David Leung unfolded a large map showing China and Myanmar, placing a teacup on each corner so it wouldn't curl up. He pointed to Datong. "Sam and the admiral have arranged for a plane to be on standby right here, just outside Datong." He tapped on one location as Blake eyed the map. "There will be a truck waiting. You will drive it to Datong."

He passed the address to Blake. "I will contact the owner and inform him you are on your way." Leung placed a pencil mark on Datong. "From here you will fly to Mong Yu, on the Myanmar border," he paused, circled the name on the map. "Right . . . here." He ran the pencil in a straight line, ran it southwest toward the border. "The plane on which you will be traveling is a Chinese version of the Antonov An-2, known as the Y-5. It has a range well over nine hundred kilometers, which will get you halfway to the Myanmar border. The beauty of this plane is that it runs on automobile fuel and can land on a strip as short as two hundred meters. It has a passenger capacity of twelve travelers, enough room for your group, and a ceiling of nearly five thousand meters, fifteen thousand feet or thereabouts, making it more than suitable should you encounter eh, intervention."

"Whoa, whoa, whoa, David. What the fuck?

Intervention?"

"Its top speed of one hundred and sixty miles per hour is not as fast as most planes currently in service, Mr. Blake. But it will more than make up for it in its maneuverability," Leung said. "This particular plane carries the Chinese insignia and should serve you well as you fly over some very tight military areas."

"Wha'dya mean . . ." Blake repeated, ". . . *inter fuckin' vention?*"

"There is a possibility you could encounter ground-to-air missile batteries," and David Leung made an apologetic shrug. "The Chinese markings should prevent this from occurring, but the same markings also prevent the plane from crossing into Myanmar. It will necessitate your landing on the China side of the border. From there you will proceed on foot to Mandalay. We are hoping to have transport ready to meet you on your arrival."

"Fuckin' lovely," Dal groaned. "You're hopin', huh? Fuckin' lovely."

"So eh," Blake added, "we just need to hope the ground troops don't get trigger happy, or worse yet, get news that we're on that plane."

"Should the need arise, the pilot, who is well known to Chinese officers, will enter into friendly communication with the ground force. He will dissuade them from firing on his plane. Once you land, you will proceed by truck to Mandalay. We are hoping to have a rescue plan in motion to pick you up outside of Mandalay."

Slade groaned, "Hoping?"

Dal wiped the back of his hand across his mouth, mumbling, "There's that word again, hopin'. Uh-huh." He shook his head, "Don't like *hopin'*."

"We need to play it by ear," David Leung said. "Billie will communicate directly with me. I will relay your progress through the two connecting agents. It will be passed on to

Admiral Bates, then the whole procedure will be reversed and you will receive coordinates for a possible pick up."

"God Almighty," Dal said. "That sounds like a government disaster waitin' to happen. That *is* a real shaky chain of events." In disgust, he turned away from Leung and walked toward the door, with Hunter following close behind. They stepped through the door that led to the rear of the house, and Hunter gave it a little help in closing, the slam shaking the ceramic ducks now hanging crookedly on the wall by the doorway.

"I understand their annoyance, Mr. Blake," Leung said, straightening the ducks, "but you must appreciate this is a huge undertaking. The placement and timing of a rescue team depends on how you progress. If you encounter a day's delay, or even a few hours in reaching a coordinate, well, that could be a serious consequence for any rescue group waiting on ground or attempting a fly-in rescue.

"The troops in Myanmar are unsympathetic toward Americans. They are more than adequately armed to take on any invasion force. And please, believe me when I say, that is exactly the way the Burmese would report an incursion involving your group . . . it would be construed as an American invasion force. The media would dearly love to play that story along, especially as your president is openly condemning the junta for not recognizing the huge political victory of the imprisoned Aung San Suu Kyi. The Burmese would parade your bodies before the world press in a show of retaliatory contempt for United States meddling."

"Okay, so we go to this place right here outside of Datong," Blake said tapping on the map.

"Yes. When you arrive you will proceed west for two kilometers. You will come onto a field that is being irrigated. It is very dry, very arid land. There is a large storage shed on the eastern side of the field. The shed contains two planes, and the pilot is expecting you. His name is Harry Ching.

Communication will not be a problem, his English will surprise you."

"This is the route once we land?" Blake asked, leaning over the map.

"Yes, once you cross into Myanmar you will come across a village by the name of Mong Yu. There you will find a farmer whose property is about two kilometers past the town, on this road." He pointed at the road. "There are many flowers and fruit trees in his fields, very different from the sparse uncultivated adjoining land, making it easy to distinguish."

Leung placed a circle on the road running west of Mong Yu. "The farmer's helped us on several occasions. He's placed a yellow tractor at the gateway leading to the house so our people can readily find his property. They're supporters of Suu Kyi and her National League for Democracy.

"This farmer will supply you with the truck you'll use for the remainder of your journey to Mandalay. The truck will contain weapons, three side arms, compasses, several flares, some grenades, a length of rope with climbing gear, as well as first aid necessities. You will also find several containers of water; remember, do not drink the local water."

"Once we reach Mandalay," Blake asked, "we get a ride home. Right, David?"

"Of course, if all goes according to plan."

"And if it doesn't go to plan?" Bell asked.

"Miss Bellinger, if all does not go according to plan, well . . . Mr. Blake and Mr. Sung will be more than adequately trained for the crossing of the Arakan Yoma."

Bell gave David Leung a quizzical look. "And the Arakan Yoma is, umm, what exactly?"

"The Arakan Yoma is a mountain range, a most treacherous mountain range, of which the largest peak is Mt. Victoria. I heard that while your compatriots were in training for their possible mountain crossing, you and Mr.

Hunter were playing golf. Do either of you have climbing experience?'

A minute later, Hunter and Dal reentered the room, looking as though they'd each let off sufficient steam. Blake, in anticipation of Hunter's reaction, asked, "Hey, Gard, ya know all that time ya spent hittin' golf balls while we were bustin' our balls on Whitney . . .

"And your point is?"

"Aha, aha."

"What the fuck's that mean . . . *aha, aha?*"

"You're gonna be needin' some serious spikes, and I ain't talkin' golf spikes." He gestured at Bellinger. "And some for your cute caddy here as well."

Bellinger hadn't raised her head from her hands. She'd rested it there for the past four minutes. Eventually her eyes lifted to meet Hunter's, and her mouth hung open. "We're going over mountains, can you believe this?" she said. "Don't know if I can do that, Gard. We're going to die."

Hunter squeezed out a grin. "Sure ya can do it, honey. I'll carry ya if I have to. Don't you go worryin' yourself now, I'm here for ya."

"What about the bishop?" Dal asked. "Ain't no way he's gonna handle a mountain crossin'."

"I will personally see to the safety of His Eminence," Billie said.

"Billie, seriously now, how the fuck do you think the bishop can make that climb?" Blake asked. "Ya know the terrain."

Billie thought for a few seconds. "I have done many climbs. I will team up with him and Mr. Sung. Between the two of us, we should be able to get him through."

Just as the details had been hashed out, Sung and Yidui banged in, carrying two duffle bags filled with equipment.

"Looks like we're all set then," Blake said, exhaling

in an exasperated way. "I guess its photo time."

David Leung opened a cabinet and withdrew blank British, Italian, and Swiss passports, a Polaroid camera, a collection of rubber stamps and two ink pads, one blue and one red. "You will travel as Swiss nationals. Sung and Billie will have Chinese passports in the names of Mathew Kung, and Charlie Yee. Your Eminence, I will also give you a Chinese passport under the name of Lee Junjie."

"A very good name, it means handsome and outstanding," Bolin said, obliviously smiling at Blake.

Dal coughed and wriggled about on his chair just as Leung took the photo.

"Oh, Mr. Dallas, you moved. I may not have sufficient film to shoot another."

When the photographs were done, Blake reached over to the Polaroid and looked at Dal's shot.

"Ah jeez, Dal, it's nearly as bad as mine. We look like Joliet Jake and Elwood."

"This is awful, David," Dal whined, "haven't you got more film, dude?"

"They will be fine. No one expects studio quality photographs on a passport, Mr. Dallas."

David's wife came from her bedroom and bid good morning to the group, then lowered herself to her knees, kissing Bolin's ring. Dal gave Blake the '*we should've done the same*' look. Blake just made a sucking sound with his teeth, and ignored the gesture.

Mrs. Leung said, "I will prepare the children for school and be out of your way. I am sure you have much to take care of." She bustled about the small house; served cereal to the two children and all three were gone in the space of ten minutes.

"Nice family, David," Bell remarked.

"Yes, we returned here from California to raise them in our homeland. Maybe one day they too can visit UCLA, or even attend that college. They were most memorable times for me."

"We all set then?" Blake asked, ignoring the sentimentality.

"Yes, check your back packs and you can be underway. Billie, keep that cell phone where you can hear it. I have packed three charged batteries. Keep them all dry." He handed a folded map to Blake. "Here is the map with the route and villages marked out. Take good care of it. If you have to destroy it, burn it." He pulled his sleeve up, looked at his watch. "It is five minutes before nine. Synchronize watches."

They headed off from David Leung's home at seventeen minutes after nine, looking back at Leung and Yidui as they waved from the door, watching the group rounding the end of the street. Their journey toward the house with their ride to Datong had begun.

*****

The jeep appeared from nowhere, one man standing, peering through binoculars, a military jeep with four or five soldiers, all armed, speeding their way. Hunter jumped forward, pushing Bell behind a stack of pallets. He pulled his Sig and reeled off three shots. The driver swerved, and the vehicle spun sideways into a large electrical pole as Blake reeled off four shots from his Glock and Dal fired two quick rounds and two bullets ricocheted off a wall behind the bishop's head and four more whistled by Billie's ear.

"Stay down, for Christ's sake!" Blake shouted at Billie, who seemed more concerned with taking in the firefight than with his own safety. The sound of gunfire mixed with shouting added to the confusion, and the soldier wearing the officer's uniform continually barked orders at his men, two appearing severely wounded, maybe even deceased, lying motionless. Realizing he'd only one man backing him up, the soldier wearing the officer's uniform dived to one side, rolling once, twice, firing as he rolled, getting off three more shots.

Bolin tumbled sideways and Billie shouted, "The bishop is hit! He is down, he is . . ."

Bolin laid still, a neat hole through his cheek, the slug having exited the rear of his skull. Bell comforted Billie who was crying, his arms draped around Bolin's chest, refusing to release his hold.

"Leave him, Billie. We've gotta get out of here," she pleaded. "That guy might've called in. If he did, there're sure to be others on the way here."

"Jesus Christ, man!" Blake shouted at Hunter who'd stopped running. He'd turned back, dived for Bolin's backpack, pulling the bishop's passport. He flashed a terror filled glance to Blake, considered how little time he had, nodded, then both he and Dal scampered in opposite directions as the dogged Chinese officer fired more shots in each of their directions.

"Go, go, go!" Dal shouted, scrambling for cover behind a black sedan parked outside of a wooden shop front, as people peeked from windows and doorways, calling aloud as the officer shouted back at them.

"What the fuck is he sayin'?" Blake shouted to Sung.

"He told them to call through to the base at Western Hills, to get troops up here."

"Aw, that's great," Blake said turning. He shouted, "Gimme cover. On three!"

Hunter shouted back, "Good for go! Good for go!"

"One, two. . . " and Hunter and Dal opened a barrage of firepower that quickly dropped the young officer and his surviving soldier.

Blake ran directly toward the fallen men, hands outstretched; gun ready, firing three shots into the soldiers, then aiming at the officer, a young man with the rank of captain lying at Blake's feet. Blake looked into the officer's eyes, hesitating as he began to stir.

He aimed at the man's forehead, squeezed the trigger.

Nothing.

He looked at the hand-gun, a questioning look. *Fuckin' clip. It can't be empty.*

He moved his eyes from the gun to the officer, from the officer to the gun, then back at the pleading eyes staring up at him.

He placed the gun nearer, squeezed the trigger again, and again. The hammer snapped down . . . nothing. He kneeled, slipped the combat blade from his belt, placing the tip to the young man's throat, pressing down on the knife.

The handsome officer showed resolve, knew he was about to die. He spoke softly as he peered at the man with the blue eyes. "My dying with honor is far better than any life with dishonor. Do it."

Then Dal shouted, "Tank!"

Blake heard the rumbling. He looked to his right, to his left, then back at the handsome officer.

"Fuck! I gotta tell ya, this is definitely your lucky day."

Dal scrambled to Blake's side. "That tank's headin' this way, and it ain't George Patton. Are you gonna finish this guy, or give him your fuckin' phone number?"

The tank rattled over the hill, a mere two hundred meters off. Blake nudged his head in its direction, said, "That's a T99."

He allowed a faint man-to-man grin to slip onto his face. "Good news, bad news, comrade. You're one lucky motherfucker, but you're gonna have to get used to livin' *life with dishonor.*" Then with a slap across the officer's head,

Blake sheathed his blade and shouted, "Let's go, go, go!"

Slade slung the backpack over his shoulder, feeling for the Tara, reassuring himself that it had not dropped out in the confusion of the firefight. They scrambled between houses, dashing through a grove of short trees and hedges, running, running, running. *Almost there,* Blake thought, *maybe another hundred meters.* As the sound of the tank became a distant rumble, Dal panted between breaths. "They probably stopped to check out the bishop and the dude you were havin' a near fuckin' relationship with."

"The bishop, yeah," Blake replied, "too bad, but I doubt he'd have made the crossin'."

Billie sobbed as he ran, and Bell, feeling badly for him, slowed and ran by his side.

"He'll be fine, Bell," Hunter called, "just keep goin', it ain't far now."

The tank crew fussed around the young officer, shouting into their radio. Blake could hear sirens, knew it was an ambulance. *At least one of those guys is alive, lucky man. I had him right there.* He grabbed Billie by his shirt and pulled him along, and then spotted the house where the truck was waiting. They dashed into the garage and piled into the truck, Blake gunning the motor, kicking up dust and dirt as the truck scraped the side of the garage, shooting onto the narrow road outside the property. There was a cloud of dust . . . and they were gone.

Ten minutes out, Blake said, "We gotta get off this road. They're gonna be all over us like a cheap suit."

"Yeah, ya got that right," Dal added, repeatedly glancing out the rear window.

"Dal," Blake called over the rattles and ruptured exhaust noise, "take a look at that map. See if ya can find any other roads."

"Find any other roads? I'm worried about 'em usin' a chopper or plane or somethin' to spot us."

"Yeah, yeah, yeah, just didn't wanna throw that out there to worry the hell out of everyone. Thanks, Dallas!"

"Aw, Christ!"

CHAPTER 40

ALTHOUGH HE WAS TIRED, the salute was crisp. Fifty men stood at attention as General Cheng strode along the column, inspecting the troops as Captain Peter Cheng followed two paces back.

"You will return with the bishop," Cheng barked, with demonic eyes. "I do not want him harmed. Do I make myself clear? He must be returned safely."

He stopped, turned to the nearest man, stared at him for a moment, weighing his fear. The soldier twitched a nervous eye, and a tremor ran through his face as his neck tightened. The general ran his eyes across the man's face; saw the pulse in his neck, savoring the fear he instilled. He spun about, walked further along the line. "Those men," he barked, "they are to be taken alive." He pulled his peaked hat more firmly onto his head, looked at his son for a long moment, then grunted and tugged on his jacket. "Peter, you represent The Peoples Liberation Army." He made a half wave gesture at the troops, keeping his eyes on them as he directed his comment to his son. "Do not disappoint me." He placed a hand on the captain's shoulder. "This mission will be a success. However, should you fail, you will answer directly to me as your general, not as your father." His eye contact flicked back to Peter. "Do you understand, Captain?"

The young captain stood frozen, his right hand locked in a salute.

"Captain?"

"Yes of course, General, understood."

"When you return," the general added, with a twinge of doubt, "you will bid farewell to Miss Ling."

Peter's eyes caught his father's look of doubt, felt the peripheral frigidity.

"And Captain," the general said, "do not return without the bishop alive and well. Take four trucks to these locations." He slipped a map from a thin folder, pointed to exit routes around Beijing. "Bolin will be seeking refuge. Question the occupants at each of these locations. Have them returned here for interrogation. Do you have any questions?"

"No General, we will be underway immediately."

"It is seven o'clock," the general said glancing at his watch, "have two trucks patrol the city, three men in each. Better we show a strong presence rather than leave trucks stationary at checkpoints. Take four small vehicles and your best men."

"Will that be all?"

"Yes, you are dismissed."

In the silence following the general's departure, Peter Cheng harbored his anger. The words repeated again and again. *When you return you will bid farewell to Miss Ling.* An order? He didn't feel he could accept it as *an order*, better they were words of advice from an annoyed father to a disobedient son.

Peter Cheng rode with two officers in the lead jeep followed by four trucks, each carrying thirteen soldiers. His mind was elsewhere as he peered into the near setting sun. He reached the first of the checkpoints at the western perimeter of Beijing, pulled into a siding, and waited for the trucks to join him. He accepted a cigarette from the driver of the jeep, as an officer from the accompanying vehicle approached him, lit the cigarette.

"Peter, you and I have been in the service of The People's Army for many years now. I recognize when you are preoccupied. What is it that is troubling you?"

The captain smiled briefly, exhaling a puff of smoke. "I am having a minor family conflict, nothing to speak of."

The officer nodded understandingly and stepped away from the jeep.

"Can you have the men set up the barricade?" Peter asked as he watched a smoke ring melt into the windshield of the jeep. "I need time alone, time to think."

He swung his legs around as he exited the jeep, walked slowly to the side of the road. The moon was full, and he imagined himself with Lisa, standing under the same moon. But the image was not in China. He saw the Golden Gate Bridge, saw America, saw their future. *Can I do this? How can we get out of China? My father will be relentless in his efforts to find me. There must be a way.* He thought deeply, scheming as his mind created one scenario after another. He dropped the remains of the cigarette, swiveled his foot on it, strolled back to the jeep, and stretched out in the front seat, his feet hanging over the passenger's door, head on the driver's armrest. Sleep was badly needed, but his mind demanded he remain awake, if not for the sake of duty, then just to think of Lisa. He pulled another cigarette and the officer standing by him lit it. Tilting his head, he exhaled and gazed at the stars, smiling at a flock of birds as their silhouettes sharpened against the full moon.

Envied their freedom.

The two-way radio in the jeep crackled to life. He answered, "Captain Cheng."

"Captain, we have a report there are a group of suspicious back-packers walking west out of the city." The voice was excited, rushed. "One of the people fits the description of Bishop Bolin."

The caller gave his location.

"We are not too far from them," Peter said. "We will intercept them and get back to you if we need assistance.

How many in the group?"

"Five, sir."

"We have more than enough to cover them. Hold back and cover your current positions. This group may turn out to be nothing."

"Yes, Captain. We will monitor the situation and check back with you in an hour."

Peter replaced the hand piece, stepped from the jeep and stretched, thought about the group. *Surely the bishop is not about to walk into my open arms. That would be far too easy, it is probably just a group of back-packers.*

"Peter," the man with the lighter interrupted, "that call, was it anything?"

"Might be, I will take three men, check out a group traveling west from the city, probably back-packers. Best that you remain here."

He sat in the rear of the vehicle, looked about, smiled, waving to three children playing; running, trying to get a kite airborne in a windless sky. The smallest child, a girl no more than eight years of age, lagged behind the two boys. Peter's eyes stayed on her as he thought of Lisa. *She was like that, a beautiful little girl, a magnificent butterfly. Free.*

A horn blasted, snapping him back to reality, the driver shouting, pointing. Peter stared ahead through military glasses, reached forward, touched the driver on the shoulder, and shouted, "Stop, stop! Stop up ahead there, on the rise!"

There was a high spot on the road ahead, and the jeep pulled into the knoll. Peter stood in the rear, focused, said, "What a waste of time, just what I expected, back-packers, a waste of time." He lowered his internal alert level and instructed his driver, "Drive further along this road, I will interrogate them."

The jeep slowed as it pulled in front of the group, cutting them off as the uniformed men stepped from the vehicle. With one hand on his holster, Peter approached the tallest man who appeared to be the leader in the group.

"Your papers," he said, then with one hand out-stretched, "your passports, please."

Back-packs fell to the ground, and each kneeled, reached into his pack, and after some digging and nervous fumbling, handed a passport to the officer. Peter passed a cursory glance over each, looked at the travelers, and asked, "Scandinavian?"

They nodded yes.

"What is the purpose of your visit to China?"

"We are with a Scandinavian contingent visiting Beijing. We are gathering information for the Scandinavian Visitor's Bureau for their upcoming Beijing Olympics promotion."

"Information?"

"Accommodation, restaurants, places to visit; you know, the stuff in tourist brochures."

Peter again studied each passport, studied each face. "Thank you. I am sorry for the inconvenience, have a good visit."

He returned the passports, walked back to the jeep and sat in the rear. He reached into his jacket, slipped out the pack of cigarettes, and one of the soldiers reached across with a light. He moved his face toward the flame as it illuminated his chiseled features. *Have to get a lighter*, he thought inhaling.

The night had grown bitterly cold, with a thick almost engineered fog that came and went like a sheet slowly drawn across a frigid moon. They waited for sunrise in a covered check-point offering minimal protection from the chill, from the dampness. When the fog passed, Peter Cheng welcomed the weak morning sun, anticipating its warmth.

An hour later the driver pulled alongside a secluded teahouse and the five soldiers took a break from the morning mist as Peter folded his arms around his shoulders, embracing himself, shuddering, and trying to warm away the remnants of the early chill. Those under his command were grateful for Captain Peter. His reputation for fairness was a welcome change from his late brother. David Cheng had the general's genes, had a reputation as a troublemaker, an even more tarnished record following the incident involving the abduction of the farmer's daughter. The incident would have ruined David Cheng's career, but like a good father, the general saved the day.

The owner of the small teahouse was a timid man, perhaps even a little gun shy of the soldiers sitting at his tables. He looked about, as though fearful for his family. He called to the rear. Peter recognized the two children running toward him; they were the kite fliers.

"This is my youngest child," the man said, placing a hand on her head, "her name is Yuan."

Peter smiled widely. "Yuan means graceful young lady, and you are indeed that. I saw you running with the kite. You are indeed most graceful."

The radio in the jeep beeped, and one of the men hurried to pick up the call. He called from the jeep. "Captain, it is for you."

The voice was excited. "Captain, they are on the move, seven people, the Americans, with two Chinese men and a large man. We are certain the large man is Bishop Bolin."

The handsome captain looked about in a casual disbelieving way, thought of Lisa, thought of her even more when Yuan leaned in the doorway and wriggled three fingers at him. He grinned, winked back.

A voice said, "Captain, are you there, sir?"

He shook off the smile, lost the moment. "Yes, I heard," he snapped into the hand-piece. "Your description is very much like the last report you sent through. They were tourists. How can you be so sure?"

"One of the men is very large," the voice said. "He fits the description of Bishop Bolin."

He doubted the need to chase them down, *more Scandinavians, just another group of back packers*. But he'd check them out just the same, this was his mission. He didn't feel like doing anything, his mind was in other places, in America with Lisa. The word *asylum* loomed heavy in his mind. *I can't do this to my father; there must be another way. I need to leave China, but I can't dishonor him.*

"Goodbye, Yuan," he waved to the small girl. "I will bring you a really good kite next time I am by this way."

She looked around to her father, turned back to the handsome officer. "I will wait for you," she called, with a coy smile.

The captain nodded to his driver. "We are about ten minutes from where they were seen." He pointed east. "Head that way."

It was nearing nine thirty on what was now a sunny morning. Peter Cheng was ill prepared for what lay ahead.

CHAPTER 41

THE NEW LOCATION FOR Sam Ridkin's AID office was a lock-down facility situated on the ninth floor of a building off Wilshire Boulevard. Access was by way of an old style elevator that ascended at an insolent crawl, rattling and threatening its passengers with uncertainty.

The earlier Russian assault now resulted in overkill. A full body scan unit revealed the appendages of each arrival, showed each roll of fat, the crack in their ass, and how well they were hung. Sam's secretary, Marcie, lodged an immediate objection, her figure being somewhat fuller than she wanted exposed. But try as he may, Sam's diplomacy was of no use, and she sensed his satisfaction each time she passed by the unit.

She had a privacy adaptor available for visitors, mainly men. They would slip it over their crotch. The scan would show the solid cover rather than how well each male visitor was hung. Marcie found the scan unit fascinating . . . from her side of the screen.

The team had been in China for thirteen days. It was now April 28. At ten o'clock, the phone on Sam's desk buzzed and Marcie was there, her voice more excited than usual.

"Marcie, what's up?"

"On line one, it's, it's . . . Sam, you won't believe this."

"Jesus, Marcie."

"Try again, higher up."

Sam raised his voice a few octaves, repeating in a higher pitch, "Jesus, Marcie," and chuckled to himself.

"Sam, it's the president."

"President of what?"

"The president of us," Marcie whispered, as though the identity of the caller might be overheard.

Sam pressed the button to line one. "Yes sir, this is Sam Ridkin."

"Sam, it's been too long. We'll have to have ya visit the ranch soon, you and Sarah. Sam, I'm callin' ya about what's happenin' in China. We're very concerned about tests bein' conducted by Beijing over the past twenty-four hours. The Chinese are keepin' it hush-hush, and of course Beijing will keep on denyin' they took place. You with me so far, Sam?"

"Yes sir, I'm listening."

"There's been a whole lot of military movement on two fronts in China, the northern Myanmar border, and the South China Sea; it's all too goddamn close to Taiwan. We suspect Beijing could be makin' a unilateral move into one or both of those territories. They've several intelligence gatherin' satellites in position watchin' our naval movements, waitin' to see if we deploy in that direction. Quite frankly, Sam, we're not game to make a move without full knowledge of their laser technology. What we do know about their Operation Compass project is limited. This'll change when your team gets the flash drive back here. Beijing'll hammer us if we make a pre-emptive move, we'll come out lookin' like the aggressor."

"What about the United Nations, Mr. President?"

"Fuck the UN. Those cocksuckers will never back us up."

"Mr. President, I was under the impression our satellites were second to none. Sir, can I ask a question?"

"Fire away."

"Has Beijing tested out this weapon, this weather manipulation?"

"They did a small test run recently over Western Myanmar, usin' trade wind manipulation; they caused the biggest cyclone to hit the place since '68. It killed over two hundred people, left over twenty thousand homeless. Those fuckers are able to create winds in excess of two hundred miles an hour."

"You say that was a small test run? Have they done a stronger test, something more recent?"

"Yeah, they did one full strength test."

"And eh, that was where exactly?"

"New Orleans."

Silence.

"Sam?"

"Damnit, Mr. President. That's the kind of stuff that could start a major military conflict," Sam said, showing surprise. He'd already heard the rumor, but not from a source as high as the Commander in Chief.

"Right now, if it came down to a war, we'd come out second best. I'm sorry to be the one to tell you, it's been kept very hush, hush. If it leaks, we'll deny it, as will Beijing. We know the Chinese have acquired technology from former Soviet scientists. The Soviet assistance has moved their anti-satellite program dramatically forward. We've done our best at circumventin' the spread of former Soviet nuclear weapons, but this has been at the expense of us keepin' a watch on Beijing's anti-satellite technology. The fuckin' Chinese have their noses way ahead of our people in super satellite development."

"Mr. President, I thought our Miracl laser at White Sands was state of the art. Does Beijing have better than that?"

"They do. We've spent over a trillion developin'

423

Miracl. Our unit can focus over a million-watt energy stream into a beam just six feet wide, and this blowtorch effect can destroy satellites hundreds of miles in outer space. But fuckin' Beijing is perfecting a laser beam far finer. It's at least double the power of Miracl. They're able to pinpoint and destroy meteors and satellites farther out while we're still scratchin' the surface mere hundreds of miles from us, shit that's in our own backyard."

Sam suspected the president was searching for the least painful way to deliver the rest of his mid-game preamble. "Sam, gettin' the flash drive is paramount. We know for sure that Beijing's anti-satellite system is already aimed at the United States satellite fleet, we need to get one up on 'em, and we can do that when your guys get back with the flash drive. I'm sending a car to collect you. I'll join you there in around four hours. Call home; tell Sarah you'll be away for a few days on classified business. And tell her to keep it to herself. You can contact her from our final destination. Don't worry about packin', you'll find all you need at the other end."

"Mr. President, can you tell me where *the other end* is?"

"I can tell ya this much, it ain't outa the country."

"Thank you, sir. I'll be ready when your man arrives."

"I look forward to seein' you later today then."

The smartly uniformed officer entered the SoCal office. As he walked toward the front desk, Marcie stared at the monitor, felt her eyebrow twitch, but suppressed the smile.

"Ma'am, I'm here to collect Mr. Ridkin," he said in a Southern drawl.

"Certainly, he's been expecting you."

Sam's home phone rang four times before the answering machine picked up. "Honey, I've got to go away for a few days. I'll call you tonight, let you know all's fine. One of those last minute government things, the type I can't talk about. Don't you go losing sleep over it, things'll be fine. Love you, bye."

He placed the phone back on the handset as Marcie buzzed from the front desk. "Mr. Ridkin, there's a very well equipped officer here to see you." She said it blushing a little.

Sam grinned, knowing she was enjoying the new screening process. "Send him in, Marcie."

She smiled at the tall young man, nodding at his sidearm, "Is that a Glock you're carrying?"

The officer looked down at the holstered weapon. "No Ma'am, it's a Beretta."

The drive to Oxnard passed through a landscape partly desiccated by the Santa Ana wind and numerous small towns dispersed among occasional glimpses of rugged beauty. The journey allowed Sam time to ruminate, time to consider possible scenarios. *Why does the president want to personally meet with me? To avoid possible phone tapping, sure, that's gotta be it.* He watched as resinous scrub merged into new neighborhoods, and beaches flashed on by as the staff car moved toward Ventura County. He tried not over thinking the meeting. *Why?*

And the question repeated, *Why?*

"Nearly there sir, good thing the traffic's light. It's always a pleasant drive, this drive up the coast."

"Yeah," Sam replied from a million miles off, "isn't bad at all."

Sam's mind lingered in limbo, somewhere between confusion and fear, then the driver swung the car into Port Hueneme Naval Weapons Division Base. He slid the two side windows open, passed an envelope to the armed sentry who saluted saying, "Captain Manning, sir."

He peered into the rear of the vehicle, took another

close look at the contents of the envelope, nodded at Manning and waved him through. The captain pulled the car deep into the complex, moving it slowly into a large hangar, nosing it to an oval shaped door in a far wall. As the vehicle slowed, the door began to slide open and a large tunnel stretched out ahead of them.

"This is our route to the base," Manning said, smiling at Sam.

Sixty minutes later they exited the darkness of the tunnel, arriving in another hanger. Manning cruised to an office door, stopped, stepped out, tapped on Sam's window. Sam slipped out, straightened up, looked about, and turned to Manning, who closed the door and pointed ahead.

"Pretty secure location I'd assume," Sam said.

"Affirmative," Manning said gruffly. "Quite secure. Please follow me; the Commander in Chief should be here any minute."

Sam tried his ice breaker approach. "So eh, are you on his personal staff?"

"Yes sir, have been for six years. Good man for a Texan," Manning said, grinning. "Proud to be with him, sir."

"Captain Manning, is it?" Sam asked pointing a finger at the officer's nameplate.

"Affirmative."

They walked quickly through a maze of passageways, entered a large room that could only be a conference area.

"Please sir, have a seat, the president will join us shortly."

Sam took a seat, and began to browse through a coffee table book that showed the evolution of military air power in the U.S.A. He was soon fully immersed in the illustrations and lost track of time. He was about to let loose with a yawn when the officer stepped back into the room. The officer snapped to attention and announced in a loud voice that shocked Sam into full awareness, "The President of the United States."

Sam stood and smiled as the man himself strode toward him, one hand outstretched, and the other giving a short salute to the officer. "Captain Manning, how's it goin', son?"

"Fine thank you, Mr. President."

The captain left the room, closing the door quietly as he exited.

"How ya doin' Sam, how's Sarah?"

"We're both doing well, Mr. President, thank you. I trust Laura's doing well?"

"Yeah, Sam, she's doin' real well. She walks Barney every day. Take a seat, Sam; we need to get right down to business here. We'll be joined by a few of my people when I'm ready to call 'em on in, but I wanna bring you up to speed ahead of 'em gettin' here."

"This is all to do with my team in China, right?"

"Yeah, that, and a shit load more. Like I said, we gotta get that flash drive at any cost. We've been updated by our people handlin' satellite spy equipment. They're tellin' us there's been an unusually large amount of military activity goin' on in China over the past few days. We know your team's tryin' to make it out with the information, but I'm concerned their chances are quickly diminishin'. We believe their best chance of slippin' past the troop deployment is to head to Myanmar. This'll mean crossin' the Arakan Yoma Mountains in the southern Himalayas, means they'll be crossin' into Myanmar, into Burma. Ya think they're up to that?"

"Well, they trained for a mountain crossing," Sam said, then paused, shrugging in an apologetic way. "At least three of them did. They did a training camp on Mount Whitney. Yes sir, I'm confident they can handle a mountain crossing."

"Sam, I know ya don't need to hear this shit, but in the event they run into problems along the way . . ."

The pause was enough for Sam to say, "I know how that goes, sir."

"We'll say we know Jack shit, Sam. Even with my hand on a goddamn Bible, so help me God."

The president gave an assuring smile, more to press home the fact than apologize for bailing.

"Yes sir, standard operating procedure. My team's aware of how it works."

Sam played his cards close to his chest. He had an underlying sense that his first duty was to his team. His country always came in second, a distant second.

"Beijing's moved a number of its forces to the Myanmar border. The 13th Chuan Army has a large contingency based permanently at a place called Menghai, on the southern China-Myanmar border. A hard nut Chinese general named Cheng is headin' up the operation; our people say he's one mean motherfucker, Sam. Our latest report says there's in excess of a thousand troops based there, includin' one hundred officers. What we're proposin' is your team, Drew Blake isn't it?" Sam nodded *yes*, as the president poured water into two glasses, chuckling as he poured Sam's glass. "I used to throw in ice," he said tilting his head, winking at Sam. "And a shot of Jimmy Beam, but not these days, ain't done that since bein' governor. Jeb can have it to himself, until he takes my spot after those goddamn democrats are done fuckin' over the country, and they will, always have. Like a leopard changin' its spots, ain't gonna happen," and he gave a wink to Sam. "But I still like to use these whiskey glasses, ya know, they're old friends."

They touched glasses, and the president moved to a filing cabinet, pulled a drawer, and placed a map of China on the small table. "We need for Blake to lead your guys directly to a point right here," and he fingered a coordinate. "Right here north of Menghai." He took a pen, circled Menghai. "We feel Beijing'd think Menghai is the last place anyone'd use as an exit route, because the Chinese've got a strong military presence there." He hesitated, acknowledged the soft tapping on the door, called, "Yeah!"

Three suited men entered.

"Sam, these guys'll brief you up-to-the-minute on the situation in Beijing." He made the introductions and the five men focused on the attaché case being opened by the man wearing the bow tie.

"Mr. President, Mr. Ridkin, this is very disconcerting information."

The bow tie man placed a folder on the table, slid it across to the president who read it in silence for three or four minutes, closed the folder, and leaned back in his seat.

"I see they've beefed up their military detachments along the border again, Colin."

"Yes sir," bow tie man said. "The troop movement has doubled in the past twenty- four hours."

The other two men coughed simultaneously. Bow tie man picked up on the body language and appeared uncomfortable. He reached to the smaller of his two accomplices, took a red folder from the small man.

The president asked, "Is that the letter?"

"Yes sir, unfortunately," said Colin. He held the letter toward Sam, and continued, "Our man in China intercepted a courier en route from Beijing to a meetin' with an Iranian agent. The Iranian tipped our guy off to the meeting with the Arab. He suspected he was being set up, figured our man would be a good back up if eh, if things messed up."

"Go on, Colin," the president said. "Cut to the chase. Sam's okay. He can hear what's on the list."

"Thank you sir, I needed to hear that."

Colin reached into his jacket pocket, removed a pair

of reading spectacles snuggly folded in a two inch long case. He unfolded the glasses and waited just long enough for a bead of sweat to find the crease between his eyebrows. "Sir, this is a list giving a number of our top military installations, underground locations throughout the nation. Beijing's already got a copy of the list. They have satellites aimed at each location."

"Thanks, Colin, pass it here will ya?"

He read the list softly, stopping every so often, looking at the three men, searching for confirmation. "Not good," the president said. "Fort Huachuca, Arizona. Munds Park, Arizona. Page, Arizona. 29 Palms, California. Catalina Island, California. Chocolate Mountains, California. Panamint Mountains Death Valley, California. Deep Springs, California. Lancaster, California. Mt. Lassen, California. Mt. Shasta, California, and NORAD in the Cheyenne Mountains to name just a few of the facilities on the list. Sam, these are all secret military underground facilities usin' tunnels linked to other military locations. They specialize in stealth technology, missile defense systems, radar development, anti-gravity engineering, and space weaponry together with other stuff so far out there I'm not gonna mention. If these sites were targeted and destroyed, we'd be effectively shut down as a military force. If Beijing has these installations in the sights of their satellite lasers, it'd be good night and good luck America."

Sam was silent. He wanted to ask where the connection was between what he'd just heard and Operation Compass. The answer came in the Commander-in-Chief's next words. "Your team's our best hope of breathin' a sigh of relief over this situation. The flash drive'll enable us to block Operation Compass. With that technology in our hands, we'll stymie every satellite the Chinese, Russians, and any other nation has up there. We've considered dispatchin' a Navy SEAL unit to Myanmar to get your team out, but the Chinese situation made it far too risky."

Sam Ridkin, up to date with the Myanmar situation, said, "I understand Myanmar's a touchy issue right now."

"That's an understatement, Sam. The junta suspects a possible U.S. invasion. They feel we're gearin' up to ally with Thailand, that we're gonna cross into Myanmar. What's the latest with their military build up, Colin?" the president asked bow-tie man.

"Well sir, they've deployed air defense battalions right through Myanmar. They're fitted with a wide range of radar jammers, shoulder launched artillery, as well as short, medium, and long-range artillery and missiles. Procurement has included at least 100 Igla-1E low altitude surface-to-air missiles; they got these from Bulgaria and the air defense equipment from Sweden and Ukraine."

"Fuckin' Swedes, have to make a krona or two I guess," the president said grinning.

Bow tie man continued, "They created an Office of Chief of Air Defense, quickly followed by an expansion of forces. The equipment required for most of these units was supplied to Burma by Beijing."

"How 'bout our Russian friends? They're equal opportunist motherfuckers," the president smirked. "What did those Cossack bastards unload onto Myanmar?"

"Sir, Russia's supplied them with modern fighter jets including twenty MiG-29s and major artillery, as well as air defense systems. Their junta has also acquired missile technology as well as undisclosed military hardware from Moscow."

Colin slipped a finger back of the bow tie, loosened it, raised his eyes to meet the president's. The president interlocked his fingers, cracking his knuckles as he nodded to Sam. "Thanks Colin. So there it is. Your boys are probably in the middle of a goddamn hornet's nest that's developing into a real goddamn clusterfuck. Thing is, they don't know they're in it."

"But *my boys* are the best. Blake has sharp perception for what's going on around him. Dallas, Bellinger and Hunter, they are all skilled professionals."

"And I'm assured Paul Slade is pretty darn good at his job too," the president added. "But we feel they're in a situation that could blow out of all proportion at any time, and not just from the possible spyin' implication. If we go on in to get 'em out, well, it'd constitute a U.S. invasion of Myanmar and could drag Thailand into the conflict, bein' a strong ally of ours. Between you and me, Sam, the Thai already got themselves a nuclear weapon tucked away. China would be chompin' at the bit to get a piece of *that* action."

"Mr. President," bow tie man said, "we do need to keep in mind that Myanmar's armed forces, their Tatmadaw, are on continual alert in the case of a U.S. led foreign invasion. It was said a top-secret document was leaked to the Asia Times Online news. It stated a U.S.-Thai joint invasion was eminent, which only served to further step up their military strength." He mustered up a shrug, together with a dismissive roll of his eyes. "Stalinist North Korea and the junta in Yangon already have a military and trade relationship, so North Korea would be very quick to support the Burmese in an effort to strike at us." Colin took a deep swallow, loosened his collar a little. "The Burmese, the Myanmar regime, has also acquired a nuclear research reactor from Russia."

The president struggled to keep his anger under control. "Moscow sold 'em a fuckin' reactor!"

"Yes sir," bow tie man quivered. "You were, uh, you were informed at the time."

"Goddamnit Colin. I must've missed that one, must've been among the reports when I was at Camp David."

"Yes sir," bow tie man said. "The junta claims the reactor is for peaceful purposes. Mr. President, the military government in Yangon is in bed with the North Koreans. Our people tell us Myanmar has been stockpiling scuds."

"What's the latest diplomatic banter on all this?"

"The Thai are upset."

"No shit the Thai are upset!"

"Very upset, sir," Colin stammered. "We've received strongly worded complaints from them over the threats the Burmese are throwing at Bangkok."

"Fuck the Thai," the president groaned raising an interjecting hand, his palm facing bow tie man. "We imposed sanctions on Myanmar a few years back. What was it, an import ban?" He answered his own question. "Yeah, it was, and we seized assets and quit financial dealin's with the Burmese. That didn't seem to have much of an effect, they still do what they fuckin' well want. Until that woman they've locked away takes power, their whole fuckin' army's under the control of a bunch of thugs."

"Actually sir, it was in excess of thirteen million dollars in transactions. It messed up their financial system for a while, they stopped dealing in dollars."

A smirk crept across the president's face, and a chuckle spread through the group.

"Colin, have we lodged any recent requests regardin' Aung San Suu Kyi? I assume she's still under house arrest?"

"No and yes, sir," bow tie man replied. "The Secretary of State has lodged more requests than there are democratic objections in Congress. She's still being detained; they let her out every so often to appease the objectors. The monks lead the protestors, some of them get gunned down, then she's back under house arrest again. The U.N. is shouting about it, formal requests and all that stuff. U.N. envoy, Ibrahim Gambari, traveled over there, tried to convince them to stop gunning down demonstrators."

Those in the room nodded as bow tie man pressed home the point. "They've been attacking monasteries, and beating the monks. They've got troops stationed on every corner of the two biggest cities, Yangon and Mandalay."

The president raised two fingers, bow tie man paused. "What about the other guys around 'em, other nations, any cooperation, Colin?"

"China and Japan have joined forces to help end the problem," bow tie man replied. "Japanese Prime Minister, Yasuo Fukuda said he agreed in a phone conversation with his Chinese counterpart, Wen Jiabao, to work together on international efforts to solve the crisis."

The president kicked at the carpet, appeared annoyed. "Apparently, our demands for immediate and unconditional release of Suu Kyi keep fallin' on deaf ears. I wasn't surprised when the Burmese response was to tell us to mind our own fuckin' business." He looked at bow tie man, then pointed to the map. "Colin, if there's a flair-up with the Burmese or Beijing, how thin can we spread our boys?"

"Well sir, we've got thin, and we've got anorexic. Our forces are spread anorexic thin. We can't handle Beijing even with the forces we currently have on standby."

"Wha'dya think we should do, Colin, what's your opinion?"

"Well Mr. President, with things as they are with Afghanistan, not to mention North Korea doing its usual amount of saber rattling, the road to Myanmar would be a one-way street."

The meeting continued for another forty-five minutes. When it ended, the president dismissed the three men, and sat alone with Sam Ridkin.

"Sam, I want you on this until the team is outa that fuckin' place. You'll operate at our base under Catalina. This way you'll have hands on with our best military personnel. A SEAL unit will be on stand by. I got our best man, Wolf Brandt, up to date on the situation. We'll deploy one of our subs, the Texas, in the event of an offshore pickup in the Andaman Sea." He jabbed a finger at the carpet. "It's over three thousand meters deep, so we got plenty of room to maneuver. Go to the base, Sam. Steve Bates is expectin' you. He'll familiarize you with the facility, fill you in on one of our operatives in China, guy's name's Harry Ching, a brilliant flyer, flown quite a few missions for Bates, but he was unable to fly Slade out. The timin' just wasn't with us." He rolled his eyes as though annoyed that the timing *wasn't with us.* "Our man was takin' care of another assignment," he said semi-apologetically. "But he's back there now, prepped for a quick flight out. He's based outside of Datong and he'll be there, Sam. He'll be there for your team. I'll be in contact with you daily and we'll both be up to the minute with the situation. You'll be able to call home each day, ya know, to put Sarah at ease."

"Thanks. I assure you, Drew Blake and his team are as good as you'd want over there. If he can't get through, well, no one can."

The president called, "Captain!"

Manning stepped back into the room, reached a hand toward Sam. "Sir, if you'll accompany me."

Once in the staff car, Manning drove deeper into the hangar, then into a white tunnel with fluorescent strip lighting along each side.

"Captain, exactly where does this take us?"

"It exits under Catalina; it's one of our strategic control centers. The admiral and I have been instructed to consider you as having full clearance. We're aware you've an old SF-86 on file."

Sam was impressed. The researching of his security status had cleared his entry into this strange *non-existent* world, this subterranean Catalina fortress. *So much for confidentiality*, he thought.

*****

The captain led him through a dormitory area, arriving at a hallway, doors similar to any hotel hallway, each bearing a number.

"Interesting, Captain. Just like a hotel, huh? Do you have guests in each room?"

"Yes sir. The rooms are generally fully occupied on special occasions." He pointed at the ceiling and suppressed a grin. "Like when the regular tourist hotel up top is booked."

"Right," Sam grinned. "Thanks."

"Sir, dinner will be served at eighteen hundred hours. The dining area is straight along this hallway, door number twenty-one." Manning pointed off to the right. "All you require in the way of clothing and toiletries is in your room. Please call me by pushing button 'one' on your bedside phone. It's a direct line." He tapped on a small intercom unit attached to his left shoulder. "I'm always here."

Sam showered and lay on the king-size bed; flicked on the remote, surfed through channels. *Just like home,* he thought, *nothing different.* He watched the local Los Angeles news, and after a short time slipped into a sleep, one cut short by a knocking that came from a connecting door. He swung his legs off the bed, walked to the door, turned the lock.

"Sam, I hate being dead. It's a real fuckin' inconvenience."

CHAPTER 42

AT FIVE IN THE morning, General Cheng's voice was gruff. "Wang, stay at the hotel, I will send my driver. Bring Miss Ling along as well. Be ready in an hour."

Silence

"Wang?"

It took a several moments for his brain to focus. "Yes General. In one hour, out front of the hotel."

Two minutes later, on the phone to Lisa Ling, "We're being collected in one hour. General Cheng's sending his car."

She placed the phone on the handset, rolled to face Peter. "Your father's sending a car for Wang and me, wants us at Western Hills. Do you suppose there's something happening I should be concerned with?"

"My father wishes to separate us." He paused, swallowed hard, thought for a long few moments. "I am going on a mission this morning; I need to return to the barracks. There are reports that the American we've been searching for is in Beijing. This incident with the bishop means the report is probably correct. I must dress and return to my unit. The general will be expecting me to take my men out this morning."

She rolled away, laid her head on the pillow and stared at the ceiling. The words came out with reservation. "Have you ever wanted to leave this life behind, to live some other place?"

Peter maneuvered himself into a dominant position. He propped on one elbow, with hands turned palms up, and gave Lisa a curious look. "What are you saying, that I should desert the military?"

"Do you want to spend your life in that uniform?" she asked, moving a slow hand toward his clothing at the foot of the bed, "having your father ruling your every move?"

"Before I met you, I would never have considered being anything other than a soldier."

"And now?"

"You know how I feel about you; you know my answer."

"Come with me, Peter. Come away from all this."

"How can we, Lisa. How can I leave China? It's impossible."

The question hung between them for ten seconds. "I can make it happen if you being with me is what you truly want. I have the connections to get you asylum. You can come to America with me, through the embassy."

"The embassy, is that the only way?"

"Well there's one other, but that would depend on a question you'd need to ask me."

"A question?"

"Yes. I like the sound of the name, Lisa Cheng." She slipped the tip of her tongue between her teeth, ran it over her lower lip. "It has a ring to it, don't you think?"

He smiled widely, rolled closer to her warm body and said, "Sounds very good, Miss Ling." He raised her hand and pressed his lips into her palm, "Would you do me the honor?"

"Is that a proposal, Captain?" she replied in a coy way, teasing him, tilting her face back, her lips forming an inviting pout.

"You've already accepted, Miss Ling."

She stroked his hair, ran a finger along the contour

of his lips, and offered no resistance as Peter covered her mouth with his, her eyes closing as she locked in the feeling, the warmth.

"You've such warm lips," she said, "not like those of a hardened soldier."

She sucked gently on his lower lip, ran her red nails through his hair. A loud knock at the door cut the moment short. "Lisa!" Wang called. "Are you there, are you ready?"

She placed a hand on Peter's mouth, answered loudly as though calling from the bathroom, "Um . . . not quite, I'm in the shower. I'll meet you in the lobby, in around thirty minutes."

It was Peter's first shared shower and he treasured each moment, steam fogging the glass screen and the bath-room mirror. He smoothed soap along her body, her breasts pressed firmly against the glass screen.

"I have never felt so happy," he said, "so complete. I feel as though I have known you all of my life."

She took a deep breath, wondered, *am I his first? Does he have the moves?* She could taste him, feel his texture, his manliness. Firm. Erect. *The bed's fine,* she thought, *but this is the shower, shower sex is, hmm . . .*

Her skin was slippery, warm, the shower head directed away from them. He ran one hand around her shoulders, pulled her nearer. With a searching mouth and hands that no longer hesitated, he explored every curve, his eyes shut, a blind man imprinting her shape forever to memory. The perfume of the shampoo caused his nose to twitch, and he sneezed.

"Bless you," she said, in an routine way, yet with a tone of sincerity. He grinned at her *blessing*.

"I have not heard that before," he said, a questioning smile spreading across his face.

Then, in a rhythmic way, his body moved with hers, swaying, following her lead.

"Your fingers," she whispered, "wonderful."

Her hands moved slowly to his hair, and she gently applied pressure, moving his head down, slowly, her tongue lingering on his lips as their mouths passed. His tongue traced a descending path, moving slowly, between her breasts, down her upper abdomen, to her navel. He raised the feeling of intensity by lingering in that perfect navel, the perfect navel on the perfect flat stomach of his perfect woman. He listened as her breathing picked up pace, interrupted by the occasional groan. He felt empowered, felt the passion rising, slid his tongue lower, found her silky patch, slipping both hands to her inner thighs.

She trembled as his fingers slid along her skin, feeling the spot where her softness began to separate. Her moaning intensified and he hesitated.

"Don't you stop," she groaned, "not now."

He had never done it before, yet it felt instinctive, like it was meant to be. He pressed his mouth into her damp silky curls and drew it into his mouth. There was a little firmness, and the firmness increased as he sucked on whatever it was. *Different.* And a little further down, he found the warm opening, his tongue flickering like a snake, her groans intensifying.

"Oh Peter, oh Peter. Ohhh Peterrr." And her moaning brought them to the precipice. While she was somewhere between 'Oh' and 'Peter,' he spread her legs further apart, cupped his hands on her buttock, and thrust his rock hard erection into her body, a feeling such as no other in the universe. Again, a cry of, "Oh Peter," and her eyes rolled upward as uncontrollable spasms, accompanied by more intense moaning overtook her body. Their orgasms merged, neither aware of where one had begun and the other ended. If there was ever doubt as to the stress-ceiling of Lisa's brain, that doubt had now been well and truly removed.

The sensations were all foreign to Peter. *All of my*

life . . . no . . . all of our lives, my sister. It was a thought and remained just that, a thought. He would never tell her, never jeopardize their future. Lisa's arms felt so perfect wrapped around his waist, a moment to be treasured, a moment they each hoped to share for a lifetime. He wanted to stay there for eternity, engulfed in the sensation, the bliss. There were so many words to be said, but he held back lest he spoil the moment. He had her in his arms, and that was all that mattered.

When it had ended, she left the shower ahead of him; sat scribbling figures on a note pad, heard him slide the shower screen shut, staying under the hot water a minute longer. When the water stopped, she imagined him toweling off, heard the bristling as he toweled his hair. Peter entered the room expecting to find her in a romantic, maybe wistful mood.

She wasn't.

"What are you doing?"

"Looking at my cash flow," she replied, as she lay under the sheets. "We're going to make a plan to leave China. We'll need cash on hand. I can't use a credit card; it'd be too easy for your father to track our movements. He'll increase security at all airports looking for you. We need to find a way out other than airports, and that'll take cash, perhaps quite a great amount of cash."

He sat alongside and placed a hand on her thigh.

"You don't want to leave China, do you?" she asked.

"I want you, Lisa Ling."

"Oh."

He gave her a boyish smile. "What do you mean, oh?"

"Hmm, didn't mean anything really. Perhaps now that you've taken me, you're not so . . ."

He cut her off. "What do you have in mind?"

441

"How long will it be before your father suspects you're no longer at the base?"

"That is a difficult question."

Lisa continued her calculations on the note pad for ten more seconds, then raising her eyes from the pad, dropped her serious mode and gave him a loving look.

"It would depend on who replies to the general's inquiry," he said, "on how much time that person allows to pass while locating me." He moved the sheet off her legs, ran a finger along her calf. "We could have five, possibly six hours," he said shaking his head, "maybe seven or eight."

Tears swelled on her lower lids as she leaned forward and kissed his cheek. "That will be all the time we'll need my darling. We need to place as much distance as possible between your father and us. For that we'll need cash." She turned away, avoiding his curious gaze, catching one escaping tear. She asked, "Can you get cash?"

She ran a hand-towel across his brow as droplets of sweat trickled down his face. *Cash*, he thought, *how can I get cash?* His reply came in a dubious tone. "Not without raising suspicion, cash could take many days."

"Peter, this is something we need to do. I have a Swiss account; I'll make inquiries today to withdraw funds. After the meeting with your father, I'll go to the Beijing City Bank and arrange a cash transfer from Switzerland."

She reached into a small valise on the bedside table, took out a bank book, checked her account balance. *Three thousand dollars, but then I've got the other, the money in the safety deposit box, the cash that Wang paid me, a half million dollars.*

She dressed, placed two fingers on her lips and moved them to Peter's. "Hold this kiss, my love," she said. "I'll be back shortly."

She waited for the elevator and felt his eyes on her as he watched from the room. When the elevator door slid shut, he walked across the room to a window where he had a clear view of the Tianlun's entrance, watched as a staff car bearing red flags flapping from both front guards, moved slowly from the front of the hotel. He took the stairs to the foyer level, proceeding directly to his quarters where he changed into a fresh uniform. Once in his office, he went about the start of what was to be the worst day of his life.

*****

Although tired, the captain's salute to his division was as crisp as ever. His Chuan Army Division stood at attention as General Cheng strode along the line, pausing, and nodding to his son. "Captain, you're looking a little off color this morning. I expect you're ready to give your best effort in the search for the killer of your brother?"

"Of course, for the People's Army," Peter replied, "and for us, father."

His eyes averted his father's glare; he clicked his heels, and stared directly ahead.

Captain Peter felt good about himself. Although he'd not been able set aside savings during his time in the military, the satisfaction of manliness was adequate compensation. He'd often pondered how the men in the 13th Chuan despised his brother, the way that David could make them dance to his tune. Any respect he got was the result of fear, of intimidation, not admiration. He recalled how David would strut about like a man with a nine inch dick. In reality it was his nine-millimeter side arm that nurtured the respect.

It was twenty after nine when the captain and his men moved toward the second group of back packers. Somewhat complacent following the first interrogation of the earlier group of Scandinavians, these tourists were treated with far less caution. Perhaps it was the breakfast and the cigarettes; perhaps his feeling of helplessness, of not knowing how to fulfill his new dream, how to be with Lisa while not destroying his father's career. He raised his binoculars, focused on the hikers as they moved along in single file, steadied the binoculars, didn't believe what he was seeing. *The large one in the center of the group could be the bishop.*

The single line of walkers intrigued him, but he preferred to believe they were just *another annoying group of fucking Scandinavians.* "Go slower," he said, touching the driver's shoulder, "it is nothing."

Still standing, binoculars lowered to his chin and one hand on the roll bar of the jeep, his eyes caught a sudden move from the *fucking Scandinavians.* The man leading the group dived behind a row of wooden pallets, and the others in the group followed suit. Before Peter could react, the driver swerved off the road, ran sideways into a large electrical pole, the impact throwing Peter and the other two soldiers from the vehicle.

It was all a blur.

The noise.

The firefight.

The shouting as two of his men went down.

The feeling of pain.

He recalled the man with the blue eyes.

The man with the blue eyes pointed a weapon and Peter knew he was about to die. Then the man with the blue eyes cussed, checked his weapon. Had it jammed? Nothing happened. Peter recalled pleading as the man with the blue eyes kneeled, pulled a shiny blade, and pressed it against the captain's throat. Another blue eyed man appeared on the scene. Then there was the shouting, "Let's go, go, go!"

Peter Cheng tried focusing on the two military men that were yelling down at him. One, the larger of the two, propped Peter against his leg, then paused as the sound of a siren attracted his attention. There was a silence that lasted like a too-long anesthetic. Peter Cheng began spinning,

spinning, as a bilious feeling overcame him, and he drifted into unconsciousness.

*****

"Captain, Captain, can you hear me?"

Peter opened his eyes, saw the image and felt the hurt as he tried to draw breath, a white angel hovering over him, taking his hand, and gently holding his wrist.

"He is looking better, his pulse is normal," the angel said to another, standing alongside.

"Captain, can you hear me?"

He stared at the white sky, took half a minute to realize the sky was the ceiling of an all white room, *but there are light beams coming from the clouds above; the angels, they're so blurred.* After ten long seconds, he began to reel his brain back from the strange world it was visiting. He blinked several times and forced a smile at the two medical assistants standing by his bed.

"Captain, can you hear me?"

"Who are you, where am I?"

"You were wounded, you are in a hospital. You were most fortunate the tank came along, scaring off your attackers."

"Tank? I saw no tank. I remember seeing the Scandinavians, the big man, Bolin, I think. There was a man with blue eyes. They fired on us, then it, it, it is all . . . nothing."

He gripped the nurse's wrist, tried to lift himself, was too weak and slumped back onto the pillow.

"My men?" he asked. "How are my men?"

The angel seemed suddenly grave.

"I am sorry Captain, you are the only survivor."

Reality hit hard. He jerked his head off the pillow. "They are dead, all dead?"

"I am sorry Captain. We were told you were fortunate the patrol happened along when it did," the angel said shaking her head. "They arrived in time to ward off your assailants."

He delved deep, again the images of the two blue-eyed men looking down at him, had a fleeting memory of looking into the nose of a handgun, the repetitive clicking of the hammer, the look on the blue-eyed man's face as the weapon misfired. He moved a slow hand to his throat, recalled the cold steel, a voice, two voices, then nothing. Here he was in this white world, in the soft, safe hands of these angels.

Despite his anxiety, he faked a smile. "Thank you, you are very good angels."

"Angels?" the voice echoed, as his delirium persisted.

"Yes, angels, thank you. I need to sleep, my head is aching. Where am I wounded?"

"The bullet grazed your temple, a little more to the left and you would have joined your troops and the bishop. Your God was watching over you."

He shifted his weight from one side to the other as though the adjustment helped free up the words. "The bishop, where is the bishop?"

"I am afraid he was killed in the confrontation."

"The bishop is dead?"

Silence.

He repeated, "Bishop Bolin is dead?"

"We have his body in an adjoining room awaiting official identification from one of the Xishiku priests."

Again, in a disbelieving tone, "The bishop is dead?"

His father's words bounced about in his head. *Don't return without Bolin, alive and well.*

He feared the answer, but asked, "Has General Cheng been informed of the bishop's death?"

"Yes, we are expecting the general at any time."
Shit.

"How long have I been here, here in this room?"

"You have been unconscious for three hours. The general ordered military police assigned to your room." The nurse gestured toward the door. "There are two of his people outside waiting for you to regain consciousness."

The nurse studied Peter's face, saw the eyes widen, sensing his apprehension.

"We prefer they remain out of this room until you, eh, until you have had sufficient time to gather your thoughts." She leaned on *your thoughts.* It confirmed his worst fears. He needed to think, needed a feasible explanation as to how the confrontation had gone so horribly wrong.

"How long must I remain here?"

"Until the doctor releases you."

"How long will that be?"

"Maybe tomorrow."

He stared at overhead lighting with an almost trance-like demeanor. "I cannot wait that long."

"Captain?" the nurse said with a quizzical face. "You need to leave sooner?"

"It is nothing, nothing at all," he said, wishing he could retract the words. "I cannot think clearly, my head is spinning."

He had never felt so alone, so isolated, and he needed Lisa more than ever. He swallowed hard as he considered the inevitable confrontation with his father, the consequence of what lay ahead, with the bishop's body in the nearby room. He bit hard on his lip as blood from the head wound seeped through the dressing, all too warm on his forehead. Lifting a hand, he touched above his eye then lowered the finger, looked at the blood as tears swelled in his eyes.

At two forty-five, General Cheng strode into the room.

CHAPTER 43

THE DRIVE TO WESTERN Hills was slow; police detouring traffic around an accident, directing vehicles down back streets, and funneling the three lanes ahead into one. Growing impatient, the driver leaned on the vehicle's horn, gesturing to the nearest motorcycle cop. The cop mounted his bike, flicked on flashing lights, got his siren blaring and cut a wide swath through the quagmire. Three military trucks screamed on by headed in the opposite direction with flags flying on each fender, an officer's staff car leading the military entourage as it roared on by. Wang craned his neck to catch a glimpse of the passenger as their driver pulled to one side, making way for the trucks.

With his neck fully turned, Wang said, "That is General Cheng," and made several fast jabs at the passing convoy, shouting at his driver. "Turn about, follow him!"

"I am sorry," his driver replied, eyeing the fast moving parade in the rear view mirror. "I was ordered to take you to the general's office. Unless I hear otherwise, I must carry out that order."

Regardless of vehement protesting for the remainder of the drive to Western Hills, the driver was well schooled in obeying orders. Wang cussed at the man, but he remained doggedly tuned, he was someplace else. Once inside the building, the driver led them to a waiting area outside the general's office where they remained for more than an hour. An aide entered the room and sat by them as they thumbed through magazines on Chinese history and culture.

"There has been an incident," the aide said in a somber tone. "General Cheng has instructed that you remain here until his return." He pointed at a wall clock, "within an hour or so." He made a face, and shrugged, "Very congested traffic."

"Yes, the traffic," Wang replied in an annoyed tone. "You say there is an incident?"

"The general will answer any questions when he meets with you."

*****

Red-faced and showing lack of temperament, General Cheng strode into the waiting area, his eyes bulging with rage. He glared at Lisa, then glared even harder at Wang. He grabbed at the brass handle of his office door, turned it, pushing the door open and pointing in a sharp demanding way. The word was spat at him, abrupt and demanding, "Inside!"

Wang felt his knees weaken as the door slammed shut.

"This morning I lost several good young men." He stabbed a finger at Wang. "You are to blame for this. Had you been forthcoming with information on Sung's presence, we could have avoided this disaster."

"General, please . . ." Wang said in a consoling manner, which only served to push Cheng's blood pressure to a level some place between his pupils and the peak of his cap.

"Quiet!" Cheng shouted, pounding his fist on the mahogany desk. He stood silently, and took a few long moments to gather his thoughts. "This morning, a group of my men led by my son Peter, had a skirmish with your friend Sung and his murderous American associates. My soldiers were ambushed when they peaceably approached the group. They are dead, Wang." If the earlier pounding of his fist didn't shake the foundations, this revelation certainly did as Cheng slammed into the desk a second time, shouting, "Dead, Wang, dead!"

Lisa slumped into a chair. She turned white and mumbled incoherently, something about *my Peter*, while still maintaining an impassive expression. She asked in a weak voice, "Is Peter alive?"

The general hesitated, thought of replying *yes your brother survived,* but felt there would be a more appropriate time to break *that* piece of news. He nodded, removed his coat, and hung it on the rack. He replied without a backward glance, "He is wounded. I am going to interview him regarding the incident when he has regained consciousness. I have two officers at the hospital. They will call when my son is able to speak. We will locate these murderous Americans."

"Where is the hospital?" Lisa asked. "I need to see him."

The general's stone cold visage caused her to shudder. Cheng's immediate priority was maintaining the search for Slade, for the *murderous Americans.* Mumbling to himself, he opened a desk drawer, and removed a folder. After a half-minute of surreptitious browsing, he raised his eyes to meet Wang's.

Lisa wanted to repeat the question but sensed the anger in Cheng's eyes. She wisely chose to wait. He picked through the paperwork, pausing on one page, then reading through it slowly, pouring some drink from a decanter and throwing it down, blood pressure still off of the chart. After a long minute, his eyes found Lisa's, and he caught her questioning expression.

Between sips and snorts he grumbled, "Perhaps later today. I will need to speak with my son while his mind is clear. Your presence will only serve as a distraction; it could cloud his memory of the incident."

"Can I at least accompany you and wait until you've spoken with him?"

The reply was forced with a tinge of doubt, "I see no reason why that would be a problem."

Cheng's conversing with Lisa gave Wang a chance to draw breath, a reprieve, a chance to escape the wrath of the general's displeasure.

Wang cleared his throat. "General, may I inquire about the purpose of our original meeting this morning, prior to this eh, incident?"

"Wang, the magnitude of your mistake is unforgivable," Cheng said. "The purpose was to discuss a plan for you to work with my son, to pool your resources, locate the American, this person, Slade."

"And how was I to be a part of this plan?" Lisa asked, as her expression intensified. "What was the reason for *my* meeting with you?"

Cheng glanced at her, took a second before answering. "I was . . ." He considered his next words carefully. "I am requesting you no longer see my son," he said. "You and he are from opposite cultures, from different worlds. He has been raised in Beijing. Your blood is the same as his, but . . ." He paused, considered this an opportunity to break the news. "You are both Chinese but *your* upbringing is American. It cannot work between the two of you. It would be as foolish as . . ." Again, the pause. "As foolish as brother and sister marrying; the same blood, it's unacceptable, and so too are opposing destinies. You and Peter are not destined to procreate, you are not meant to be as one."

His desk phone cut into the discussion and Cheng listened intently to the voice on the line.

"What are you saying?" he asked, "that he is rambling, that he is incoherent?" He felt Lisa's inquiring gaze, and ignored it. "I will be there shortly. Do not permit entry to anyone other than medical staff."

He turned, strode to the window, his face red in the glow of the sunlight struggling to penetrate the Beijing smog. Reeling about, Cheng snatched up a paper from the stack on his desk, made out like he was reading, bought a little time, perhaps time to settle his anger, then thumped the paper back onto the pile, causing Lisa to close her eyes and force down a wave of nausea. *He's alive* she thought, *Peter's alive*.

"I trust my message is clear, Miss Ling."

She nodded.

"Very well," he grunted. "You will have the opportunity to bid farewell to him."

The words were delivered as though shot from a shredder, curt, succinct, yet with jagged edges and an unquestionable tone of finality, spoken without remorse and lacking empathy.

"You and Mr. Wang," Cheng said, turning away, "will both accompany me to the hospital."

They arrived at the ward at twenty after midday. The two men by the door stood at attention, their eyes intent as Cheng strode toward them. One reached for the door, opened it.

Peter's eyes found Lisa as she entered the room, one step behind his father.

Cheng forced a smile. "It is good to see you are conscious, Peter."

"You are not angered with me, General?"

"Why did you disobey my orders?"

"Disobey your orders?" he responded with surprise. "We attempted to apprehend the Americans, but they hit us with heavy fire. We were caught unaware."

"Unaware! I have been informed you had only three men with you, why not fifty men?"

"I did not feel the situation called for such a large force," the captain said. "I thought it wiser for the division to be spread, to be moved about to cover the city exits."

"Not one of your better decisions. What will the politicians in Beijing think of your bungling? You, the son of Major General Cheng, of you losing your men to a group of American rabble."

Peter shrugged apologetically and thought, *I have nothing to lose at this stage.*

"We have more politicians than officers," Peter said, with a forced half-grin. "Perhaps a few less will not be a bad thing. It is too easy for them to assume the world out there is safe." He tried to sit more erect, groaning as the pain intensified. "My men fought gallantly. I accept full responsibility for my decision to split the division, to take fewer men with me than you expected."

"And that is exactly where you disobeyed my directive!"

"Had the Americans chosen one of the expected exits," Peter said, shaking his head, "and I had left fewer men to guard that exit, then that too would have been one of my less than *better decisions.*"

"Do not assume the people in Beijing are any wiser than you or I. Conscience is not measured by the level of one's responsibilities." He turned to Wang. "Beijing has little conscience; they expect subordinates to react in a similar fashion." He tapped a few times on his chest. "They expect *this* general to react as a general, not as Captain Peter Cheng's father. Therefore, you will face charges for your actions. I have nothing more to say to you. I will bid you farewell, my son. When you have sufficiently recovered, you will be placed under arrest and face your superiors. Also, I have no doubt the church will have many questions regarding the death of the bishop." He motioned toward Lisa. "Miss Ling, please accompany Wang and myself to your hotel." His expression changed noticeably as he addressed Wang. "I will arrange to see you again at a later time, perhaps tomorrow.

I'll contact you."

"Miss Ling," Cheng said, "perhaps I am not determining the correct course, but difficult choices do not always determine the most ideal journey." He glanced briefly at Peter, nodded, and then diverted his stare back to Lisa.

My daughter, he thought, but said, "I will arrange for your earliest departure from China."

CHAPTER 44

STONES RICOCHETED FROM THE under-carriage of the truck as Blake squinted into the dust ahead. Hunter repeatedly checked his compass while Dal kept an occasional eye on the passing parade, simultaneously trying to follow along on the map as they moved in a westerly direction. Hunter named towns along the way, as best he could, his voice wavering as the rugged terrain rocked the truck from side to side and the water could be heard swishing about in the containers in the rear.

Dal's eyes locked onto workers busily repairing fallen houses. A strong earthquake had recently rumbled through a swath of western China's mountainous Xinjiang region. The carnage was evidenced by the number hard at work repairing old dwellings constructed in the 1960's and 1970's.

According to the Xinjiang Seismological Bureau, the 6.1-magnitude quake struck the sparsely populated region in the early morning, killing several people. Xinjiang, a seismically active area, remained of major concern to seismologists. China's deadliest earthquake struck the northeastern city of Tangshan in July of 1976. It killed an estimated 240,000 people. Its magnitude was measured at 7.7 to 8.3. China's western regions were well known for their earthquakes, and the number of fatal quakes in recent months, at least six on record, had Blake's attention.

Just weeks prior to their arrival, a strong quake had struck the southwestern province of Yunnan province, killing sixteen people. It was too close for comfort for Sam's team. Subsequently, they were cognizant of the slightest vibration. The lack of shock absorbers on the truck did little in the way of sharpening an acute sense of vibration.

Hunter read a name, an upcoming town. It was unpronounceable, with pastures as barren as Dal had seen in any mid-western drought. But in the mid-west there was calm, here there was a tension, an uneasiness he didn't like, an uneasiness that tightened the knot in his gut.

He closed his eyes for a moment, saw the haystacks, heard the kids playing, twenty-four, sixteen hut, hut. He visualized the ball spiraling through the sky, landing in the hands of a wide receiver. He wanted to be back home, but he was here in earthquake heaven, rattling through the barren landscape of western fucking China.

For three painful minutes he stayed silent, his mind overwhelmed by the dry panorama, by ruined cottages. Then, as he heard Hunter's voice, he jerked his head up and reality slammed him hard.

"Jesus Christ!" Hunter shouted, "the empty light's flashin'. David better be right about that extra gas."

Dal leaned across, reached past Blake and tapped on the gauge. He flicked a thumb over his shoulder at the dust billowing in their wake. "Hate to be hitchin' a ride out here," he groaned.

Blake made light of their predicament, "Seems we're headed in the right direction though. Keep your eyes open for a Shell. I'll top up and we can pick up some burgers and fries." He grinned back at Bell, faked an assuring smile, disguising the feeling of dread boiling deep in the pit of his gut.

Patrice Bellinger fantasized about a tri-tip, medium rare, and salivated at the thought. "I'd kill for a steak right now," she said, making a pleading face at Hunter.

Slade chipped in, bouncing about in the rear seat,

"Really, a steak?"

"A bowl of pasta," Dal said, and made a pained face. "Topped with red sauce and scampi," and he ran his tongue around his lips. "Now *that* would be much better!"

Bell glared at Dal, flipped a hand as if brushing him aside and said, "Pfhhht."

"Okay you guys, knock it off," Blake said, peering ahead at a fresh dust cloud. "There's somethin' ahead, and it's kickin' up this fuckin' dust cloud we're headin' into. I gotta slow down until we get around whatever the hell it is. Better pray it ain't military."

As Blake pulled the truck around the horse drawn cart, the man and woman waved at the truck. Billie hung from his window, and said in Mandarin, "Hello, do you know these roads?"

"Yes, we have a farm near Datong."

"Are you headed in that direction?"

"Not quite, we are returning from Beijing, our son works in the city."

"Does this road go to Datong?" Billie asked.

"Yes, but there is a shorter route you can take in that truck," he said, and pointed at the old horse. "Our horse cannot make that journey; it is far too treacherous for her old legs."

Blake slowed the truck, looked left and right, peered back behind, making sure no one was following.

Billie called to the man, "We will pay you to come along with us, to take us the shorter route. We will pay you well for going out of your way."

The woman smiled and nudged her husband as Billie filled Blake in on the conversation. Blake pulled the truck to a stop, his eyes raised in hope of having found a reliable navigator. The old man climbed from the cart and limped toward the truck, nodding a greeting to the occupants, and continuing to speak with Billie.

Interpreting as the man spoke, Sung said to Blake, "He is asking Billie how much he will be paid for taking us to Datong by using the shorter back route. He says it is not in his direction."

"Tell him we'll give him a hundred bucks in Yuan. That'll keep him in rice for a few years."

Sung passed the message on in Mandarin, which placed a wide grin on the old man's weathered face. His wide grin showed three teeth that hung precariously from his upper gum.

Blake avoided the man's grin as Sung explained, "He says he doesn't really want to deviate too much from his route, but for a little extra he says he'll come with us. His wife can continue on with the cart because she needs to get it back to their farm before dark."

Dal grinned, couldn't resist making a crack. "Didn't think she looked that fit, shame about the horse, what are they gonna do, leave it here? Long haul for the old girl."

"Yeah right," Blake snapped, not being quite up for Dal's poorly timed humor.

"Ah jeez, gotta get my kicks when I can," Dal whined. "Cut me a little slack here."

Blake said to Billie, "Ask him if he knows the farm we're lookin' for."

Billie and Sung set about describing the farm, its field and the large shed. The man gazed about wordlessly for some thirty seconds, chatted quietly to his wife, then came back at Billie, who listened, nodded and gestured to Blake, "He knows where it is, says the owner does some flying, taking tourists out over the Yangtze and the Great Wall. Sounds like our man. He helps the local farmers from time to time, flying provisions in from Beijing."

The old man chatted a little more. Then Billie added, "He says the owner of the plane allows his old horse to rest from heavy loads of seed and fertilizer."

"Ask him if there are any military posts or soldiers out this way."

Blake leaned back against the truck as the old man juggled the question for ten seconds. *Maybe not too cooperative,* Blake thought.

The man remained stubbornly silent.

Billie counted seven hundred Yuan into the farmer's hand, but he seemed unaffected.

The old fuck's workin' us, Blake thought. "You ain't on top of him, are ya Billie?" Blake said. "Tell him we'll double it if he tells us all he knows about troops up ahead. Tell him no one'll know he's given us any help."

Billie passed on the request, asking about troop deployment. The man took in the question as he mentally counted the notes being placed in his palm. When the neatly stacked bundle came to a halt, he spoke to Billie for several minutes. Blake tried to read his face, but his expression didn't change. After more chatting, the farmer pointed to the west, then to the south, as Billie and Sung took turns asking questions.

"Jesus Christ," Dal said. "That ain't an answer, that's a fuckin' oration. What did he say, Sung?"

"He says there have been a few trucks on the road south of here," and Sung pointed southward. "He says they are mostly troops from the city. I suspect they are the 13th Chuan soldiers. He says one of the trucks stopped by a farm and caused some problems with the occupants, namely the farmer's wife. Most of what he said was about the misfortune of the farmers here in this region, how much they dislike the military."

"That's good," Blake said. "How about bases, any troops near Datong?"

The old man's face turned hard, his black eyes skittering away from Billie. He withdrew for a minute, then in a cautious tone was reluctant in his reply.

Billie shook his head. "No, not yet, but he says there used to be. They all moved south to strengthen the border. They took over from the police who had been patrolling the border. He said a fleet of army trucks from Beijing passed through here recently. They numbered in the hundreds, he says. It took ten minutes for the column to pass by his farm."

"That's a lot of fuckin' soldiers," Dal groaned.

Blake said, "Ask him where they were headed."

After a few questions and some conversation, Billie said, "He says they were heading toward Yunnan's border with Myanmar. He says he has a cousin who is a policeman; says his cousin was surprised when he was not removed from border duty when the soldiers arrived. The cousin told him the police were being retrained by the soldiers."

"Sonofabitch," Dal said. "Why do they want civilian cops? They're a military unit. You'd expect they'd piss the cops off, send 'em packin'."

"He says the police were trained as a mobile unit," Billie said. "What's even worse, he says the locals around here see that as a sign of prewar preparations by the army."

"Lovely," Dal said quietly. "We sure can time our entrance. We miss the quake and get here ahead of a fuckin' civil war . . . hey!"

"There you go again," Blake said grinning, "Soundin' like a fuckin' Canuck."

The old man bid farewell to his wife, and the truck continued on its journey, driving a few more kilometers until the farmer pointed to a distant hill.

"What's he sayin'?" Blake asked Sung.

"He says you should cut around those trees ahead, and drive directly toward that rocky outcrop; he says you can just about make out Datong from up there, says it's way off in the distance, but you can see it. He says if there are any troop trucks, you might just be able to make them out from that hill top."

The drive to the high point pushed the truck's suspension to its limit. Blake and Dal stepped from the vehicle and the old man pointed west toward a hazy cloud. He said, "Datong."

"Fuckin' L.A.," Dal said, "just on a smaller scale."

Slade stepped from the truck, dusted off his shirt, and stared at the distant dust cloud.

"Ain't any way anyone can spot military shit from here," Blake said. "Ask him how much longer it'll take for us to reach the farm."

Billie questioned the man, and came back with, "Two hours."

Blake squinted at his watch, "Should get there around five."

At twenty minutes after five, the farmer pointed to the aviator's property, slowly stepped from the truck, and told Billie he would walk the rest of the way. Said his property was less than two kilometers farther on, limping as he moved away. Blake, feeling badly for him, said, "Billie, tell him ya can drive him to his place. We'll wait for ya to get back. He can't live more than forty minutes off."

Billie helped the old timer back into the truck, sat behind the wheel and accelerated in the direction of the man's property. The others remained by the roadside, watched the truck disappear into an ever-growing cloud of beige dust, then began walking across the small field; the ground was dry, more beige landscape. *Hard ground to make a livin' from*, Blake thought, kicking at loose stones in his path.

The barn was a monolith, sitting in a sparse moonscape, towering and rust colored with large doors that could accommodate a 767. Tire tracks led from it toward a noticeably cleared area about a hundred meters off to the east, with a windsock flapping at one end of the field the only indication that this could in fact, be an airstrip.

Hunter pointed at the windsock, queried, "Runway?"

"Yeah, a short one," Slade said. "I've never seen one that short."

They stepped into the barn and looked in amazement at the spectacular bi-plane. Another, in a somewhat less gracious state, sat farther off toward a corner of the structure.

"So this is the plane, huh?" Dal commented, strolling along the fuselage, looking up at it, its massive wing towering over him. The older, more neglected plane appeared to be a crop duster. *Now that one over there, that could be used for target practice,* Dal thought, doubting the crop duster's ability to survive one hard landing, its appearance far less impressive, the less pampered child of the two.

A solitary figure approached from a small door hidden away behind the older plane. He spoke from twenty meters, pointing to the plane as he approached. "I have three others like her; they're spread about the place, one in Myanmar, another in Russia, they're kind of on stand by, but this one, well, this one's my baby." He pointed to a second plane. "That old one's a duster. Bates said you guys'd be here about this time. You're right on the dot."

Blake was taken aback by the Chinese man's American accent.

"My name's Harry Ching, and you, I assume, are Agent Drew Blake."

"Yeah, I'm Blake."

"Yes, of course you are."

"Where the heck are you from? David said you'd communicate with us no problem, but 'til now I thought he was jerkin' my weenie."

"David likes surprising guys he sends through to me. Yidui enjoys playing the Chinese thing too, but Yidui's another story. We've been a darn good team; those guys,

Leung, and eh, Yidui too, I guess. They stick their necks out for their uncle."

Blake looked at Slade, who was shaking his head and smiling.

"So whereabouts are ya from in the States?" Blake asked.

"San Francisco, Chinatown actually, I was born there. Been here for a few years doing some work for you guys, on the quiet." He made a very definite wink. "You know."

Blake came straight out with the obvious question. "In that case, Harry, why didn't ya get Slade out of here instead of us goin' through all of this bullshit?"

"I was on another assignment with the U.S.A.F. and was redirected to Beijing. Slade here . . ." and he nodded at Slade, "well, his meeting with his contact should've gone smoothly, but eh, you know how plans sometimes get skewed." He looked beyond Blake, looked toward Sung who had hung back toward the nose of the plane, then asked Blake in a quiet voice, "That Chinese guy snooping around back there. Is he okay?"

"Yeah, no worries, Sung's with us. He's fine."

"How about these other guys?" and he nodded at Hunter, and smiled as he nodded toward Bell. "They all part of your original team or uh, have you picked up a straggler or two along the way?"

Blake called to the rest of his team still giving the plane the once over.

"This is . . ." and he made the introductions.

"We got one other guy. He's eh . . . like you said, *a straggler*, name's Beijing Billie; he's givin' one of your neighbors a lift back that-a-ways." He pointed westward as he spoke, and Harry glanced in the direction indicated.

Dal tipped his head at the plane. "It looks like it just came from the factory; you keep it lookin' good."

Harry stood back, admiring his baby, like a father

with a newborn; smiling and running a hand along the side of the fuselage. "This bi-plane is an Antonov. She can land on a strip of roadway just two hundred meters long, that's about six hundred and fifty feet," he said. "I can taxi her right up to a gas station, fill up on auto gas and fly on out. She has an auxiliary tank giving her a range of a bit over two thousand kilometers or just over thirteen hundred miles, enough to get you guys to the Burmese border with just one quick stop along the way to refuel."

He walked under the enormous dual wings, waving a slow hand like a car salesman showing off the latest model. "What other plane can do that? When I got her, the color was bland, so I restored her to original military colors. The Chinese think she's great, so I let them use her for their annual air show. She's one of their biggest attractions. They particularly appreciate the new interior. I had a friend in Beijing custom fit it. Reupholstered the seats with blue fabric, relined the cabin; I wanted blue carpet, but gray was the only color the guy had. I fly her cross country, so taking you guys south shouldn't raise suspicion. I've taken a few dignitaries up, a few generals, you know."

Blake nodded in amazement at this Chinese aviator with the California accent. As he spoke, Harry patted the Antonov's wing, stroking her as though she were a living thing, a pet.

"When can we get under way?" Blake asked.

"As soon as I do a final checklist."

"Checklist? She looks ready to me."

"Mr. Blake, there are four things a pilot can never retrieve when he needs them, firstly, the altitude above him, secondly, the airspeed he's bled off, and thirdly, the extra fuel in the truck that he didn't have time to take on."

"Okay, that's three. What's the fourth?"

"The unused checklist from the wreckage," Harry replied in a sardonic tone.

There was a symphony of mordant groans, and Dal said, "Let him do the fuckin' checklist."

It was a ten minute process, and the group was all smiles when Harry eventually gave a thumbs up gesture.

"Everything we need's loaded on board," he said. "Tanks are full, coffee is in the flasks, and I've provided reading material for your pleasure." He gave a snappy salute, clicking his heels.

Just what I need, Blake thought, *another fuckin' comedian.*

"It'll take us around eleven hours, including one stop to refuel in either Daguan or Jiulong," Harry said. "I'll let the people there know I'm coming in around two o'clock in the morning. They'll leave the lights on for me," He said it just like the commercial, with a slight twang, smiling at his Motel 6 inference. "If we get underway at eight o'clock, we could be at Wanding around seven in the morning. The best time to fly is at night; less chance of trouble should there be any suspicion." He pointed a finger skyward. "That's when there's no other traffic up there."

Blake suspected this pilot was a frustrated airline captain, excursions in the plane gratifying his desire to impress friends and guests. But fortunately, Harry lacked the one idiosyncrasy common to so many retired commercial pilots - *captainism.*

"Must cost you a bomb to fill this fucker," Hunter said, tapping on the wing.

"My rich uncle keeps me well subsidized, very well in fact."

"Your uncle?" Bellinger asked. "Is his name Sam?"

"You got that right, Miss."

"So we're related," Bellinger replied to a chuckling Harry Ching.

"Climb on board, I'll show you around. I'll taxi her out and we'll get under way as soon as your friend gets

465

here."

Bellinger held up a hand. "Harry, do you have a rest room on board?"

"Ouch, sorry Miss, no bathroom, but I do supply a large bucket."

"Charming!" she said making a face. "Entertainment for all. Do you have a bathroom I can use before we get under way?"

"Yeah me too," Slade chipped in, anticipating a *yes* from Harry. "I don't fancy using the bucket either."

"Then it's unanimous," Dal smirked, nudging Blake.

"You say you've been doin' some flyin' with the U.S.A.F." Blake said. "How many hours have you logged?"

Harry's tone belied suspicion, and the flyer seemed a little apprehensive in his response. "Hmm, not much these days . . . they've placed me on a . . . hmm, a kind of a retired status."

"Uh ha, why's that?" Dal asked.

"My last medical turned up a small problem."

"A problem huh, you mind sharin' that one with us?" Blake said.

They hung on Harry's answer. He put on a sad air, looked down to avoid eye contact then gingerly answered, "Narcolepsy."

A queue formed at the bathroom door as Harry boiled up water and made coffee. Sung sat and chatted with Harry, asked about Chinatown, asked how he managed to master such accent-free Chinese.

"My family history's pretty interesting. My grand-father was a Shaolin monk, way back in 1828, when Chiang Kai Shek's soldiers destroyed the temples. That's when he fled to Taiwan," Harry said, pointing to the south east. "From there he shipped out to the States. My ancestors have a lot to thank Chiang Kai Shek for. If it weren't for the commies taking over this place, I might never have been born in the U.S. Strange ain't it, the way destiny works."

It was ten minutes before six o'clock when Harry poured coffees and passed a tray of Oreos around. "I get them fresh from my uncle," he said with a grin. "When I was a kid, my father and grandfather both spoke only Chinese at home. I was raised speaking only Chinese. I started school in California at the age of five, so it wasn't too long before I was speaking American as well. When I enlisted in the U.S. Air Force, I put my Chinese to good use. Admiral Bates assigned me this mission over two years back, and the Navy funded the operation. I've flown out about a dozen of our guys since being stationed here. Don't expect to be here too much longer though, things are heating up in Beijing. Jintao is increasing the strength of his military." He paused, took on a worried look. "I got this thing about surface to air missiles."

"Just charmin'," Dal said, "just what I need to hear while readin' the in-flight magazines . . . *for my pleasure* of course, and enjoyin' that special flask of coffee. Not to mention usin' the fuckin' bucket."

"Aw, don't worry," Harry said, flicking a thumb toward the Antonov, "I've just enough chutes to go around . . . and a spare bucket."

467

CHAPTER 45

AT TWENTY MINUTES AFTER midday, Lisa sat in the rear of the general's staff car for the return drive to her hotel. Forty-eight minutes later she stepped from the vehicle. General Cheng spoke to her for the last time, his breath fogging the half-dropped window, his nose only just clearing the tinted glass.

"My dear girl, there is much I would like to say, but some things are best left unsaid. Had we met under less testing circumstances, I am sure weould have a different relationship."

Lisa frowned, her eyes momentarily shifting away, trying to read into the comment. Cheng caught the questioning expression, but disallowed her time to dissect what he'd said.

"Finalize your business at your earliest convenience. I do not wish to appear discourteous; however, due to the situation at hand it is best you leave Beijing within twenty-four hours. I trust I need not appoint a guard to see my request is carried out?"

"Request, General?"

He gave up a wry grin. "The word *request*, it is eh, more politically correct, is it not?" He grinned, raised the window, and the car drove off. She watched it shrink into the distance, waved down a cab and made her way to the Beijing City Bank, it was time to access that Swiss account. Inside the bank, she filled out a withdrawal slip, passed it to the teller, who gave a cursory glance and entered the account number into the bank's computer.

Her mind moved to Peter, how they'd slip out of China. *Plenty of cash*, she thought. *Maybe fly into Canada. Yes, Canada, safer for Peter. We'll go into Canada, rent a car, drive south.* She smiled at the teller. The man appeared removed, distant.

THREE MINUTES. The teller seemed less removed.

FOUR MINUTES. Lisa queried the teller, "Is there a problem?"

SIX MINUTES. The teller turned, signaled to the manager.

EIGHT MINUTES. The manager gave an apologetic look to Lisa. "I am so sorry, Miss Ling. This account has been closed."

"What?"

"There are no funds available."

"You've got the wrong account," Lisa stuttered. "Please re-enter the account number."

The manager gestured for the teller to move aside, personally punched in the numbers, and got the same result, account closed. He lifted his eyes, shook his head. "Miss Ling, I am afraid what you have been told is correct, the funds were withdrawn by another party over a week ago." He scrolled the monitor, smiled, gave her a brief glimmer of hope. "I see you have another account here, a personal account with this branch showing a balance of almost three thousand dollars." He tapped a finger on the monitor. "But this Swiss account . . . well, it is most definitely closed."

She exhaled with a trembling sound, her mouth

parchment dry. "Can you tell me who made the with-drawal?"

"I am afraid that is not possible, such information is confidential."

An older couple approached a nearby teller, the manager nodded, waving a greeting. Despite the fact her head was spinning and her mind was in a state of denial, Lisa thought quickly. She needed to play a bluff, needed to get around bank policy, needed to know who had taken the funds. The thought flashed through her mind. *Who knew about the funds in the account? Only those who deposited the money, but they wouldn't be taking it out. They need my cooperation; they depend on my loyalty, my silence. They don't need the money badly enough to cross me. Then there's Wang. He knew. He had an account at the same Swiss bank. It has to be Wang.*

"How forgetful of me," she said, putting on a brave face. "It's my cousin, Wang. How could I be so stupid? He and I discussed it over dinner. I asked him to shift funds to his account for a few weeks. You see, I'm negotiating a business purchase with my partner, Wang Jingwei. We decided it more prudent that our funds come from a single account, rather than mess with separate accounts, you understand." She smiled and nodded, hoping he'd swallow it. "It must have been the Sake; we did celebrate excessively that night." She let out another soft laugh. "How could I be so forgetful?" Flicking her hair back, she laid on a little more charm. "What date did Wang do our transfer?"

And he swallowed it, the hook, the line, and the . . .

Now totally swept up in the story, he glanced at the monitor. "Yes of course, here it is, a transaction on April 21. It shows right here, the morning of April 21."

"That's it," Lisa said clicking her fingers, her eyes opening in an '*I should have known*' expression. "April 21, that's it. We celebrated the deal the previous evening. Thank you so much. I'll have my cousin take care of finalizing the funds required from his account. I must be going. Thanks again for your understanding."

At fifteen minutes after one, Lisa struggled to walk calmly from the bank. She found placing one foot in front of the other an arduous task. Her emotions flared, her motor sensory perception all but deserting her. She felt the dizziness, considered fainting, but what then? *Police, questions? I can't pass out, I have to get Wang.* When she reached the door of the bank she leaned against the wall, placed one hand on a leather sofa and proceeded to slowly and inconspicuously slide into the chair, remaining slumped there for several minutes.

After ten minutes had passed, she managed to sit erect, but still in a vegetated state, her mind numb, staring back into the bank, unable to accept that her Swiss account now held a zero balance. At two fifteen, Lisa Ling walked into her hotel room, picked up the bedside phone and placed a call to her Hong Kong bank.

"I'd like to speak with the manager. Please tell him it's Lisa Ling calling, from Beijing."

She waited a minute, two minutes. After three, a familiar voice said, "Lisa, it's so nice to hear from you. How is everything going?"

"Not good. I need you to take the brief case from the safety deposit box. Transfer the funds to me at the Beijing City Bank. I'll give you my account number." She rattled off the numbers, snapping, "Please be quick, this is quite urgent."

"Of course, it is a good thing you signed the papers, or I would not be able to do this. It is firmly against bank policy to . . ."

She cut him off. "Yes, yes! Please, this is an emergency, let's not discuss bank policy. How soon will the funds arrive?"

His voice switched to business mode. "It will arrive as soon as the cash is counted, perhaps eh, within the hour. Let me have a number where I can reach you. I will call you when the funds transfer."

"Thank you. I'll wait for your call. I appreciate your assistance with this. I'll bring you something very special when I return."

Forty-five minutes later, her room phone buzzed. "Lisa, I do not know how to tell you this. The money in the brief case, it . . ."

"What's up? Is there a problem?"

"The cash, it is almost all blank paper. Only the outer note, and eh, and one bundle are real money, we counted just ten thousand dollars."

Silence.

He mustered up a pleading voice. "Lisa. Lisa . . . hello?"

"I'm here. It's paper? But . . . but . . . we, I mean, I . . ."

"There is only one banknote on the top of each bundle. On first inspection it appeared the brief case was full of genuine money, but Lisa, I opened the box in the presence of two clerks. I feel very badly about this. Do you want me to call in the police, perhaps fingerprints?"

"No. No police. I'll handle it myself. Can you transfer the ten thousand immediately?"

"Yes of course, it will be in your account within fifteen minutes. I am so sorry. I will place the case and paper back in the box. Perhaps there is some way you can use it to . . . I cannot think how . . . perhaps some way you can recoup some of the loss . . . this is something I have not previously encountered. I am so sorry that I cannot be of more help."

She steamed from the hotel with thoughts of Wang, *a dead man walking*. She went directly to a nearby store, found the menswear section, tried to settle her anxiety as she watched the salesman bidding farewell to another customer.

Hmm, she thought, *same size as Peter. Surely I can't be too far off.*

"Welcome to our store," the salesman nodded, "can I help you?"

"I'd like two pairs of trousers and three of these shirts." She pointed to flannel shirts hanging on a display rack. "I also need a few pairs of warm sox, three changes of underwear, a pair of shoes, a sweater, and a warm jacket. Make it two, yes two pairs of shoes, one pair for hiking."

The salesman stared at her, pondered such an extensive list, felt the need to write it down as a waiter would when taking a dinner order.

"Quite a list, what size would you like?"

She gave him a head to toe inspection. "Your size looks about what I'm after. It's for my brother, his luggage was misplaced. He's sleeping in my hotel." She gave a chuckle. "Poor devil only has the clothes on his back. I thought I'd surprise him when he wakes."

She picked through the selection of shirts, chose three, all a sedate gray flannel, very warm. She came across a red roll-neck sweater, pictured Peter skiing down a slope, smiling at her as she tried to stay ahead of him. *You can't catch me, Peter, can't catch me.* Images ran through her mind, images of them sharing their lives in America, of spending a day at Disneyland, another in New York, a lifetime of nights in bed.

The salesman stepped back into her life, and shut down the dream. "Miss, Miss? Will this be all?"

He placed the clothing in a large carry bag, and Lisa made her way to the street. She hailed a red cab and had the driver take her back to the Tianlun Dynasty Hotel. In her room, she emptied the clothing onto the bed, selected one outfit and placed it into the store's plastic bag, packing the remaining items in a carry bag, and then organized her own luggage. She took the hotel's bathroom samples, two towels, a roll of toilet paper, then checked her bag and the carry bag at the hotel luggage storage area, telling the desk girl she would return for the bags in an hour or so.

She placed a call to her bank.

"Yes, Miss Ling. Right here, hmm, yes, funds have just arrived, ten thousand dollars, less fees. It is in your account."

"Thank you. I'll be there shortly. Can you give me U.S. dollars?"

"Certainly, we will expect you shortly."

Lisa left the bank at ten minutes before four, making her next stop at a store specializing in fireworks for use in popular celebrations. They were proudly advertising their connection to the Beijing Olympics. She looked over the display, selected a string of large red firecrackers, fifty strung together, intertwined so that once lit, the explosive sounds would replicate gunfire. The young man working the store spoke sufficient English for the two to communicate.

"Can you make the fuse longer?" she asked.

"Well, we do not usually customize stock. That would be a special order."

Lisa placed a fifty-dollar bill on the counter top.

"How long would you like . . . before the noise begins?"

The fuse was eight feet in length, and, if he was correct, it allowed three minutes for Lisa to make her move. When she arrived at the hospital, she casually walked along the floor on which Peter's ward was located, peeked around the corner; one guard still sat by the door. She reversed along the hallway to a room with *Staff Only* displayed on the door; a storage area containing a few buckets, several large bottles of ammonia, and three mops. She placed the plastic bag inside the room, closed the door, and made her way to Peter's room.

"Hello, Corporal. May I visit Captain Cheng?" she asked the tired guard as he raised himself from the chair. He gave her a once over, gesturing for her to turn around, making a twirling motion with one hand. She turned about, expecting he'd pat her down. He didn't. He said, "I've been told no visitors."

She mustered an appealing smile. The guard stayed stone faced. Her smile held its ground. "You can go in for a few minutes," he said relenting. "Make it fast. My sergeant is taking a break." He nodded at the two chairs by the door. "I do not want him to hear that I allowed you to enter the room."

It was twenty minutes before six o'clock when Lisa smiled at the young corporal and slipped into the room. Peter was sleeping when she moved to his bedside, leaning over him, placing a gentle kiss on his cheek. His eyes opened slowly, a warm smile appeared, a smile she treasured.

"Oh Peter, how close we came to losing each other. Are you feeling well enough to travel?"

"I think so. I was able to use the bathroom, the pain has stopped. They have given me morphine."

"I can't believe your father would have you charged. We can't take that chance. We must get you out of here."

A long pause, then, "Lisa, were you able to get the money you spoke of?"

He sensed the uneasiness in her manner.

"Wang took the funds from the account," she said with eyes down. "He also gave me fake money as my fee for accompanying him here to China."

Anger pulsed in Peter's veins as Lisa explained the course of events. The anger gave him strength, spurring a desire within him to confront Wang.

"How do we get out of here?" he groaned, raising himself to one elbow.

She placed a finger on his lips. "Shush, I have a plan.

Trust me. When I get back in a few minutes, the guards should be gone. I'll have a change of clothing for you. But Peter, you'll need to be ready to move quickly, oh . . . and what size shoe do you wear?"

"Ten. Why?"

"Good. Listen to me, you'll hear noise, don't let it worry you. You must be prepared to move quickly. Three minutes."

She left the room, nodding her thanks to the guard and moving toward the staff door, opened it, took her bag, walked to the farthest end of the hallway and pressed the elevator button. When the elevator doors opened, an intern stood smiling at her. *Not part of my plan*, she thought. She stepped in, saw the number four glowing above the doors. She pressed five. When it reached the fourth floor, the intern stepped out. She moved on to the fifth floor, the doors sliding open, *no one waiting, good.* She punched the selector button, returning the elevator to the second floor, removed the string of fireworks from the plastic bag, and thought about the length of the fuse. *I've lost some time, fucking intern, now the fuse is too long. I need to shorten it.* She broke it halfway along, lit it, threw the firecrackers back into the elevator, pressed the button for the tenth floor, and leaped back into the passageway as the doors slid closed, the indicator showing it ascending.

Good.

She returned to the staff door, stepped inside, waited, listening to a barrage of what sounded like gunshots, accompanied a few seconds later by the sounds of people running, racing by the small room. She cracked open the door, saw the shouting and confusion, caught sight of the corporal's derriere as he sprinted on by, weapon drawn. She waited a few seconds, and then dashed from the storage room and into Peter's arms. "Quickly," she whispered, "change into these clothes."

At six o'clock they left the ward, went down two flights of stairs, through a side door marked *ambulance entry only*, and within minutes were walking among people making the early evening journey home from their day at work. She wrapped an arm around his waist, his face contorting as he strained to walk at a spritely pace. "We've done it," she said, squeezing his arm as he grimaced.

"Pain, there is so much pain," he groaned, his head aching with the dissipating reprieve of the morphine; the demon drums ever increasing, pounding away as the general's voice repeated and repeated and repeated, *Get the bishop back alive, back alive, back alive.* Peter's face bore an expression unfamiliar to Lisa, a vengeful glare, scowling and squeezing the words out between clenched teeth, "Wang," he seethed, "I must get Wang."

CHAPTER 46

SHE COLLECTED HER BAGGAGE that evening at fifteen minutes after six, while Peter waited in the cab. Twenty-five minutes later, she knocked on David Leung's door.

"Lisa, you should have called ahead," he said suspiciously, looking over her shoulder, simultaneously feeling the small .38 sitting snugly in his back pocket, allowing one hand to rest on the butt, and nudging his head toward the passenger waiting in the taxi.

"Who do you have with you?"

"A friend."

"A friend?"

"Please, David, I need help."

"Who is in the taxi?"

"I need to bring him in."

"But I must know. Who is he?"

"He's my friend, isn't that enough?"

"Of course, come."

Leung stepped to one side, motioned to the passenger in the taxi. Lisa returned to the car, paid the driver, and carried her bags to the house. Peter stepped from the cab, stumbled once, twice, moved forward and nodded appreciably to David Leung as he entered.

"You are wounded," David exclaimed as Peter passed, seeing the blood seeping through the bandage around the captain's head wound. David Leung slid the weapon from his pocket, kept it in a hand behind him, out of sight.

The cab that had been following them at a discreet distance had gone unnoticed. The driver parked in the shadows, and the passenger slipped him, and vanished into the shadows.

"David, this is Peter," Lisa said. "Please don't be alarmed. Peter is General Cheng's son."

Leung turned stone-faced, and there were no words for a few long moments. He thought about his cousin, who, just three years earlier, had taken in a refugee. Cheng's men traced the man's movements, located him and shot the cousin. Then there was his friend who'd also assisted two Taiwanese refugees, he too came to a quick death at the hands of General Cheng's men. David Leung firmly believed it was a fool who did the same thing over and over and expected a different result. He quashed images of a repeat, slipping the gun away, and looking intently at the young man with the bandaged head.

The fear of God entered his world, his mouth began to form words. None came.

In the awkward silence that followed, he could feel his eyes betray him, a death sentence if he became involved in whatever was afoot. Then Lisa spoke the words Leung wished he'd never heard, "I'm taking Peter back to America. We need your help," and the words bounced about in his mind like a pachinko ball. *Need your help - Need your help - Need your help!*

He sank into a chair, his head sagging. Then after a half-minute: "My help?"

"The usual things," Lisa said. "Passport, papers, whatever is necessary to get us out of China. If I could have linked up with the team, we could have joined them, but I know that's no longer possible."

Leung's eyebrows were raised as he replied affirmatively, "Yes, it is most definitely no longer a possibility," and he looked more closely at the young man with the bandaged head. "Lisa, this is a powder keg. Does General Cheng have any idea of your movements? Does he suspect what you are planning?"

"No, we didn't pre-plan this, David." She shrugged, took on a panicked look and shook her head. "It all went wrong, it just turned out this way."

"And what of Wang? Have you completed your assignment with him? Did you give him the Tara statue as planned?"

"Of course he has the statue. He's been seeing the general quite frequently. He was at the hospital just this morning when I visited Peter. He has the statue in his carry bag. He takes it everyplace."

"Is he still in the city?"

"Yes."

"Where?"

"He's still checked in at the Tianlun Dynasty Hotel. He closed off the Swiss account; I hope Uncle Sam doesn't have high hopes of those funds going back to the treasury."

"He took the funds?"

"Every penny."

"I have seen this type of thing before, but the money is almost always recovered."

"Recovered? How'll that happen?"

"The funds are monitored. Wang will not get away with the money, especially as he moved it into his own Swiss account."

"But the Swiss won't release information, right?"

"As independent as they are, our people have authorities tracking the entire situation. Wang can get the funds into, but not out of any account. They have a block on the account, and inform our people of any attempt to withdraw funds."

"You knew about the withdrawal?"

"We were informed the funds had been moved over a week back. I was surprised you had not called me on it sooner."

It was as though David Leung had contacted a case of verbal diarrhea, just rambling on as people do when they get on a roll.

She let him ramble.

"I have been in contact with our man here in Beijing about the funds," David said. "When the deal was struck to send ten million dollars into Wang's account, we quickly received consent from Washington."

"Consent?"

"Permission to proceed with the transfer," and Leung grinned, drawing a long breath. "It is American taxpayer's money. Wang most certainly wont be spending a penny of it."

Peter reached forward, extended his hand to Leung, gave a humble nod and spoke in English. Lisa appreciated his thoughtfulness. "I am most sorry I have intruded in your home," he said. "I thank you for any help you give."

David left the room to gather the necessary supplies from a medicine cabinet. Peter looked about nervously as he sat alongside Lisa on an old tapestry settee, could hear Leung rattling about in an adjoining room, could hear running water. He gently placed a hand on Lisa's thigh and looked despairingly toward the heavens, a faded ceiling with a rosette-framed light bulb. At some stage during the long painful silence, Lisa squeezed his hand and saw a solitary tear escape his eye.

"Did I hurt you?" she asked smiling, trying to make light of the moment.

His head turned, eyes hidden beneath their lids, another droplet escaping. She leaned into him, her lips stopping the tear from reaching his cheek.

"There's something worrying you," she said. "What is it?"

"Why did you not tell him about the money Wang gave you ... about the fake money?"

Lisa spread her hands, and leaned closer. "My reason for keeping it from you was a selfish one. If I'd told you I was worried, you would have delayed our leaving China. You would have gone after Wang. I don't want you putting yourself at risk . . ." She trailed off, waited for him to argue, even just a little, but he stayed silent. "If we're apprehended due to a skirmish with Wang," she said, "not only would it be very bad for us, but could lead the soldiers back here to David."

He allowed long moments to slip by as he analyzed her explanation, a protracted, pained silence. When he spoke, he did so without raising his eyes. "You are going to allow Wang to get away with what he has done?" and he gave a half wave, a quitting gesture, a defeatist shrug. "You will really allow him to keep what is rightfully yours?" It was a long, pained silence. He spoke without raising his eyes.

She whispered intensely, dramatically, "I'm thinking of a plan, but it doesn't involve you." She shook her head and said even more softly, "I must see Wang alone."

"That is unwise," he snapped. "You must stay here. I will find Wang."

"No Peter, you aren't in any condition."

He felt himself flush, unaccustomed to a woman assessing his ability. He responded defensively, "I will be fine. Do not . . ." then realizing he had snapped at her, he paused, took a deep breath, heard Leung intentionally rattling about as he tactlessly reminded them they were not alone.

Ignoring the rebuke, she replied with a sigh, "If you insist," and nodded toward the rattling noise, "perhaps David can have someone accompany with you."

"My love, there is much about me you do not know.

My training is at the highest level. Taking care of Wang will be a simple task. When I confront him, he will be the one disadvantaged, not me."

David Leung looked apologetically at the couple as he returned with a bowl of hot water and an array of medications, placing them on the table and removing Peter's dressing.

He addressed Peter in Mandarin, "Do you have a weapon with you?"

He frowned, answered softly, "No."

He redirected the question to Lisa, had expected her to say yes, but she sat upright, fidgeted a little, a glimmer of insecurity in her body language. "No, I've no weapon. I usually carry a small Beretta, but this was far too important a mission to risk being found in possession of a weapon. As it so happened, I was searched on arrival at Western Hills, if a weapon had been found in my possession, well, it would have been most unfortunate."

David reached into his rear pocket, placed the old Czech CZ 75 .38 caliber handgun on the table. It had seen better days, had lost its luster, had a patina of rust along the barrel.

"It is not much, but I will feel better if you carry this until you reach safety."

"Does it have ammunition?" Peter asked hesitantly, moving his face nearer, inspecting it with pessimistic caution. "What I should say is, in the event I need to use it, does it even function?"

"Thankfully, it has a safety lock," he said grinning. "I have fired it once, in the air of course. I cannot vouch for accuracy, my target was vast, as was my expectation of its reliability."

All three laughed and David began bathing the young captain's wound.

"I agree," Peter said cringing. "At this point, any

weapon will be of comfort."

It was near eight o'clock when the man waiting in the shadows had exhausted his patience. He moved to the front of David Leung's house, placed an ear to the window, heard their voices but couldn't make out the conversation. He looked about, spotted a trash can at the side of the house. He knew what he needed, found an empty pickle jar among the trash, wiped it clean and returned to the window. He placed the open end against the glass and pressed his ear to the butt of the jar.

The lights of a passing car silhouetted the man against the window. In the brevity of that moment, Peter's eye caught the silhouette, and he signaled to David, pointed, and placed a finger over his lips.

Lisa swiveled about, snatched the CZ 75 from the table, noticed the safety lock was on. She tried to remove the safety, but it had jammed. She dropped to one knee, both arms fully outstretched - a bluff - a firing position. *Better than no gun at all*. Peter momentarily flashed his eyes at her, surprised by the speed of her reaction.

David Leung took three paces toward the door as Lisa squatted below the table. He glanced across at her, then lowered his eyes to the door handle. She nodded, mouthed, *go ahead.* He slipped the lock into the open position, backing ever so quietly into the adjoining kitchenette.

Wang pressed his ear harder to the glass jar.

Heard nothing.

They've gone, he thought. *They have slipped out back.*

He stepped lightly.

Cat-like.

He placed a hand on the door knob, applied pressure, expected resistance, got none. He turned the handle and thrust the door open and shot into the room with the Glock in one hand and his ever-present carry bag in the other, his eyes scanning, scanning, sweeping the interior, not seeing Lisa crouched below knee level. With a false sense of security he lowered the weapon as David Leung leaped from the kitchenette, a clumsy effort at best, tripping forward and pushing Wang off balance. As Wang fell, he got off two quick shots, a deafening sound that shook the small room, reverberating off the walls, rattling the window. The first shot ricocheted as Peter made a feeble attempt to stand, then jerked back, looked stunned, and slumped to a kneeling posture.

The odor of cordite spread about, and a hazy mist clouded the ceiling rosette. As the captain fell, Wang continued his own sideways tumble, reeling off two more shots along the way. Lisa, finally able to release the safety, took a bead on Wang, fired once; hit him as he was halfway to the floor. Peter rolled behind the table as David Leung threw himself, football style, fully outstretched, coming to rest on top of Wang. He ripped the gun from Wang's hand as Wang jerked violently, pushing David off, his body heaving, jerking, kicking.

Stopping.

Ling was still crouching. She saw Wang was down, and directed her eyes to Peter, couldn't locate his position, thought she'd heard moaning but her ears were ringing from the blasts, her eyes not sharp after the muzzle flashes.

Again, the moan, it came from across the room.

She scrambled around the upended table, found Peter lying on his side, blood bubbling from his chest. She screamed, began sobbing uncontrollably and David was there in an instant, pressing both hands firmly on the wound and . . . and . . .

The small entry at the rear of Wang's skull left little doubt he'd died moments after the single shot left Lisa's CZ.

Lisa laid her head on Peter's chest as he strained,

and whispered, "The short time we have shared must last an eternity. You are the sister I have never had, the love I have always prayed for, the angel I will await in the next world." A blood bubble formed on his lips. It grew, burst, accompanied by a gurgling sound as a final breath escaped his lips, his lifeless eyes staring at the rosette.

Captain Peter had left her life.

CHAPTER 47

THE BI-PLANE WEAVED, veering sideways in the black sky as Harry pulled into a steep climb, struggling with the controls, the Antonov heavy when asked to perform steep turns and quick maneuvers. The chopper was now less than three thousand feet off their tail.

Harry Ching and Paul Slade instinctively lowered their heads as the chopper sent another burst of gunfire into the Antonov's fuselage. Drew Blake shouted as he stormed into the cockpit, the impact of the hits exploding along the plane's rear. His shouts were wasted on the those in the cockpit as their intercom headsets blocked external sound because of the positioning of the plane's exhaust, just two feet from Slade's right foot; conversation was impossible unless through the headsets. Blake shouted again, but Paul Slade and Harry Ching couldn't hear a word. He reached forward, grabbed at Harry's headset, ripped it off, shouted directly into the aviator's ear, "Come on Harry for Christ's sake, do somethin' different, think outside the fuckin' box!"

Ignoring Blake, the aviator continued pushing the Antonov to a height of thirty-eight hundred meters. "We're over twelve thousand feet and that chopper can't go much higher!" he yelled, his message barely audible above the noise of the engine as smoke billowed along the length of the fuselage and Harry shouted even louder with a terrifying tenacity, "I'm gonna try pushing her a bit higher!" and he pointed at the gauges and leaned forward and tapped on one in an unnerving way while attempting to appear in control. "We've lost some of our horses," he said. "This little girl has a thousand of 'em; right now she feels more like eight hundred. If we can maintain this ceiling, that chopper can't stay with us. If I'm right, that chopper's ceiling has gotta be around thirteen thousand feet, that's just over four thousand meters." He looked about, strained to see the chopper, and when he spotted it he flipped a thumb in its direction. "He can make one ninety miles an hour." Then, pointing straight up, "We gotta go higher, get above those clouds. If we can get to fourteen thousand, enough to stay above him, we can give him the slip." He waved a hand at the clouds and said with a pessimistic shrug, "If those cloud layers don't break."

Gardner Hunter thought about joining Blake in the cockpit; felt he needed to be where the controls were being worked, but like a flame to a moth, the chopper held his gaze. The muzzle flash from the chopper's automatic sprayed from beneath the Antonov hitting the tail, and taking a section off the tip of one wing.

Hunter stared down, subconsciously questioning the sudden glow. *What the fuck, their faces are so clear, like their bein' lit up.* The chopper's gunner made panicked *take it down gestures* with his hands. Over and over, the panic worsened with each passing moment, while the glow illuminated the gunner's features, his face now contorted as he shouted. He repeatedly jabbed the pilot as the chopper began to invert. And then, in the nanosecond that it took Gardner Hunter to figure what was going on, in that nanosecond that it took him to blink, to focus, in that absolutely miniscule nanosecond, the chopper ignited in a blinding ball of flame, lighting the night sky with an eerie orange glow that gave Hunter flashbacks of a most splendid Tahitian sunset.

Shielding his eyes, Harry shouted, "They've blown the fucking tip off of the starboard wing!"

Slade twisted in the direction Harry pointed, and saw

the meter long section missing from the wingtip. He shouted a jumble of panicked words, then realizing he had headset communication, continued in a normal tone, "That's what took the chopper out. Saw it getting blown off with the last hit we took, blew it clean down into their rotor. Lucky we were above 'em or it would've missed."

The Antonov shuddered and Slade gave Harry a worried look.

"Can ya still control her, Harry?"

"Yeah, but it doesn't feel good. The motor's been hit, were losing oil pressure fast. Air speed's dropped to one forty, if we drop to ninety, she'll stall."

Harry Ching tapped on the gauge showing one twenty-five and dropping.

Blake shouted, "How far to the border town?"

"Thirty minutes."

Blake's eyes took on a viscosity of hope. He squatted behind Harry, raised the pilot's headset, and shouted even louder, "We are gonna make it, right Harry?"

The aviator stared at the array of gauges. "Look at this," and he tapped on the fuel gauge, and shouted over the engine's roar, "This should be showing three quarters full. It's dropped below half in a few minutes." He flicked a thumb. "Go aft, see if you can smell gas."

Blake scrambled into the cabin area, was greeted by Dal wind milling his arms about and shouting, "What the fuck's this smell back here!"

Hunter and Slade followed Blake to the rear of the Antonov, all three peering from the windows at the gasoline spray in the plane's wake as Harry rolled his girl to the left and began a vertical descent; an uncomfortable feeling with only stars showing which way was up. Blake stumbled back into the cockpit as the plane refused to respond to her master's effort, regardless of several procedures to get her back on track. Accepting the inevitable, Harry decided it was time to share with his passengers.

"Go back again," the pilot shouted, leaning into Blake, "and have the guys hand out the chutes!"

"Hand out the fuckin' chutes?"

The last time Drew Blake had reason to jump from a plane was on a mission over South America. This was déjà vu. He let out a deep breath, moved into the cabin and made demonic eye contact with Dal.

Sung waved at Blake, made finger jabbing motions at the tail and then placed his hands around his mouth to form a megaphone, and yelled, "The tail, it's been hit!"

Blake shouted to Dal and pointed to the parachutes. Dal, being absolutely reluctant to jump from a solid aircraft, called, "Are you sure Harry's correctly assessed the fuckin' situation?"

Blake nodded *yes*. He was a good liar, always had been. He moved closer to Dal, and placing a reassuring hand on his shoulder, said, "Where's that calm demeanor you show in stressful situations?"

"Fuck you, I ain't seein' you in no rush to jump out."

Harry considered his options, fly the aircraft over a possible safe area and parachute out, or attempt to land the disabled Antonov. Slade shrugged, a *'what are we gonna do?'* gesture.

"I can do one of two things," Harry called aloud, "try to land a plane that's broke, or jump, and I got no yearning to do the latter."

Blake re-entered the cockpit, his parachute strapped on, and gave Harry his *what the fuck's happening* shrug as he squatted between him and Slade. He gestured for Slade's headset, took it, slipped it on, was about to speak when Harry said, "I guess it's my call whether we all jump or I try to land this baby."

In the next minute, the Antonov dropped another

hundred meters, with Harry again tapping on the gas gauge now showing empty.

"We're running on fumes. But if we can stay up here a little longer, until first light, I might be able to put her down," he said lowering the starboard wing and looking toward the ground. "Down there someplace," and he pointed. "It'd be guesswork in this darkness, can't risk it."

The silent passengers sensed each vibration, near gagging at the odor of gasoline. Billie and Sung strained to catch a glimpse of anything, as Patrice Bellinger reached across the aisle, tightly grasping Gardner Hunter's hand.

The aviator waved across at Blake, who'd commandeered the co-pilot's seat. "Shit man," Harry said perspiring, "don't recall being this wet since I ditched a Cessna on the Hoover Dam."

"Gimme it straight," Blake exclaimed with a nervous tremor. "What're our chances? It's your call, no one's gonna hold you to blame for the outcome. Wha'dya say?"

"There's plan 'A'," Harry replied, "I could stay up here long enough to see what's down there. My money says I can put her down."

"And plan 'B'?"

"If we run out of gas and it's still dark, we jump."

"Fuck! That's it? That's plan 'B'? I say we keep flyin' until she splutters."

"Splutters?"

"Come on Harry, fuckin' humor me here."

"Don't know what to tell you," and he gave another quick look at the gauge. "What can I say to give you a little hope?"

"Well, lemme see. Can you glide her?"

"Oh yeah, she'll glide. She'll glide like a rock." He made a diving motion with his hand, didn't look at Blake. "Yeah, she'll glide . . . straight down. If you hear me yell, jump, jump, jump, the last two will be echoes. If you stop to ask why, you'll be talking to yourself. At that point, you'll be the pilot."

Blake, wet and white, returned to the bullet riddled cabin and discussed what he and Harry had figured to be their best chance.

"So, we wait until the gas goes and jump?" Dal muttered. "It's pitch fuckin' black out there. Nothin but jungle."

"Yeah well," Blake said putting on bravado, "helps to break your fall. Harry'll keep her as high as possible. When the gas runs dry he'll see if he can make out the horizon. If he can see the ground, he'll figure our chances. If not . . . we jump. So, with that in mind let's all be clear on how we fuckin' jump."

Slade offered to go through the jump procedure and Bell began sobbing.

"Hey . . . hey . . . hey! What the fuck? Come on, take it like a man," Dal said, and gave her a thumbs up.

"Yeah sweetie, I'll take care of ya," Hunter said, reaching over his seat and squeezing her shoulder.

Ten minutes later the Antonov was still airborne.

"Get ready to go!" Harry shouted, straining to be heard above the scream of the engine. "We're losing altitude fast!" And in the next breath he shouted, "Go! Go! Go!"

Wind screamed into the Antonov as Slade pulled back from the opened door, giving an extra tug to the buckle securing his backpack containing the Tara. Magazines and Styrofoam cups shot about the cabin as the cold night air ripped into their faces. Slade gave a thumbs-up to those in the cabin, hesitated, stared into the blackness, and leaped into the night.

Blake placed a hand on Patrice Bellinger's arm as she gave Hunter a final hug. She didn't procrastinate. She glanced in the direction Slade had fallen, thought she spotted the faint shape of a chute, and she was gone. Hunter stepped to the door, grinned at Blake, and in the blink of an eye, disappeared from sight. Billie came around and half-stood, half-kneeled by Sung, gave Sung Chiao a nod, pointed down toward terra firma and within seconds they too had left the Antonov.

Blake and Dal hung back.

"Harry, get your ass out here," Blake called to the cockpit.

"Be out in a minute, you guys go on ahead, get out of here now!"

Blake had a bad feeling about Harry, thought he might have a *go down with the ship* mentality, *doesn't wanna lose the fuckin' plane.*

"Harry, get your ass out here!" Dal shouted, tugging at the aviator's shoulder.

Squinting ahead, Harry shouted, "I think I can land her, just need to hold at twelve hundred feet, just until I see the light on the horizon, could be any minute now."

"We'll stay with you!" Blake shouted.

"'Kay, okay. I'll jump with you guys, Jesus Christ, let me get out of this seat."

He shunted them back into the cabin, slipped into his chute, stood alongside them, and pointed at the opening. "We're getting too low!" he shouted. Then a short half minute later, he held both thumbs up, nodding repeatedly, reassuringly pointing *at what must be the ground*, Blake thought, and the aviator shouted with a furious roar, "Goooo! You gotta goooo. Now, go, go, goooo!"

They leaped from the plane and the moment they'd jumped, Harry pulled back from the opening, slammed the door shut and scrambled back to the controls.

As chutes billowed in the black sky, the Antonov disappeared from view.

CHAPTER 48

DAVID LEUNG WHISPERED INTO the phone, speaking with his sister, "Millie, this is David, are they still there?"

"Why are you whispering? You sound worried. What is it?"

"I need them to stay with you for the night, and I want the children to stay with you tomorrow. Do not send them to school."

"What has happened, David?"

"There is a problem, a slight problem here at the house. I will explain later."

Lisa was still dazed. Her heart hadn't stopped palpitating, a persistent drum beat at her temples accompanied by a ringing that reverberated in her ears. She placed a hand over each ear and pressed several times, throwing an inquisitive look to David, speaking her first words since the encounter with Wang.

"Who are you calling?"

"My family is at my sister's home. They cannot come here until this mess has been cleaned, until all of the danger has gone."

"I'm sorry, David," she sobbed. "I'm so sorry. I can't think straight. I've caused this horrible mess for you."

"Do not worry," he said turning away, feeling her tears. "I will take care of this. It is of far more importance that we get you out of China immediately. The general will

494

close all roads and airports when he finds his son is no longer at the hospital. He will be expecting you to be planning an escape route." He put up his palms, shifting his head slightly, looking directly into Lisa's closed eyes. "I have a plan. It is a little different, but it is the best I can come up with . . . and it has worked once before."

"Just once before?" Lisa sobbed, raising her red eyes at him. She smiled skeptically, pushed by him and quickly walked to the bathroom where she shut the door and broke into a crying spate. He could hear her throwing up, her head hanging over the small enamel basin. She looked at the face in the mirror, looked at blood-shot eyes, windows to her soul that now resembled the stained-glass in a church. Her throat was parched, a result of all the dry retching, of stomach acid. She cupped both hands under the tap, pooled water and gargled, careful not to swallow.

David heard the gargle. "Are you all right in there? Do not drink from the tap, I have drinking water."

Her reply was muffled. She tried again, found her voice, said with false confidence, "The water's the least of my concerns. I'm ready to try anything. What do you have in mind?"

David had moved to the window during her gargle, his eyes darting nervously at the street. He flicked the cell phone open, placed another call.

"Yidui? Thank goodness you are still here. I was worried you had already set off for Datong. We have a problem. Can you be here in thirty minutes?"

He listened for a few seconds, then nodded positively as Lisa, dabbing at her lips, stepped from the bathroom.

"You can, in twenty? Yes, thank you, and bring your two cousins with their van. Yes, yes, absolutely, we need the van."

He placed a hand over the phone, and leaned toward Lisa.

495

"It is all fine, do not worry, I am taking care of this." But his concern showed, and his voice rose. "Damn it, Yidui. I cannot say why right now, get the van, you will see when you arrive." He shut the cell, shut it with conviction, and stepped from the room.

Lisa forced herself to move back to where Peter lay. She slid back the sheet that David had placed over the body, looked at his face, gazed down on him and fingered the golden locket still around her neck. *Peter held this in his hands*, she thought closing her fingers warmly around it, closing her eyes around the memory, avoiding the growing red stain seeping through the sheet, spreading across the floor. She lowered herself to his face, placed a soft kiss on his cheek. "Sleep, my love," she whispered, "sleep."

She was running on fumes and David sensed it as he stepped back into the room. He righted the table, placed a small shoe-sized box on it, and helped Lisa into a chair. As she sat head in hands, he removed a plastic cape from the box and placed it around her shoulders. "I know this is a most difficult time for you, but what I am about to do must be done."

Her eyes remained tightly shut as he focused on her face. Fifteen minutes later she looked down at long black tresses strewn about the chair.

With the bulk of her hair gone, David took clippers from the box and set about buzzing her nape to ear level. He sprayed water onto her crown and combed the short sleek hair. He stood back, admired his work, and gestured toward the bathroom. She walked in, and stared into the mirror.

David removed his glasses, wiped them on the corner of his jacket, and slid them back on, then searched about in the small box, found it, and beckoned Lisa back to the room.

"Here, close your eyes and raise your chin."

She felt the dampness of something being pressed

above her upper lip. David stepped back as a self-gratifying smile spread across his face. "I think you would fool your own mother. Place these spectacles on." He waved a hand back toward the bathroom. "Go, take a look. What do you think?"

She faced the mirror and gazed in amazement at the image of a young man with sleekly styled hair and a moustache. David Leung had transformed her into quite a handsome figure. *The glasses add a touch of respectability and worldliness. Except for the red eyes, I really look good.*

David cleaned up the hair and brought out men's clothing in her size. "Quickly, get into this outfit while I prepare documents."

When she had changed into gray trousers and a white shirt, David cocked a curious eyebrow, slipped a tie around her collar and tied it in a neat Windsor knot, then answered her unasked questions. "I have always cut my family's hair. The moustache is standard equipment in my business, along with the passports and aliases."

She faced the Polaroid. As David was about to take the photograph, she thought about Peter's laugh, how she'd imagined their visit to Disneyland, thought of all they'd planned. She wondered if the heartache would stay this way, if he would remain with her forever.

David was anxious, repeatedly turning, throwing sharp uneasy glances toward the window. When Lisa had composed herself, she looked at the lens and he snapped her picture.

A few minutes later the Polaroid image magically appeared and he attached the photograph to a passport.

"Welcome, Michael Long. This is an American passport, little point in you having a Chinese one. You are an American businessman returning home from a meeting in Beijing. I will stamp your entry date. Be sure you familiarize yourself with your itinerary for the past few days of your visit. I will arrange your ticket to San Francisco. I have a man who will have it ready for you at the airport; the first flight out will be an early one, the red eye. I will let you know shortly, after I call him. You will need to throw some luggage together with the usual travel goods, men's of course. No female cosmetics or medical paraphernalia, understood?"

It was rhetorical but Lisa nodded her head. "What's happening next? That phone call? Peter?"

"Nothing," he said. "At least nothing that will involve you. Help will arrive shortly." He gestured at a closet. "You will need a briefcase with initials M.L. I have a few to choose from, each with a removable base in which I will seal your American passport," and he smiled in a comforting way, "in the name of Lisa Ling of course, we cannot overlook the finer details." He pointed and said, "Select a briefcase from that closet. I can place initials on one. Be sure to add business papers from the pile in the drawer, scribble some notes, a few signatures, the initials M.L. Include a few men's magazines, Golf Digest, G.Q. I will seal your American passport in the lining of the case. Do not remove it until your plane begins its descent into San Francisco."

Wang's body lay on its back, a plastic drop-sheet obscuring it from view. Lisa averted her eyes from that area of the room, crossing her legs, thinking of how men sat, *different than women*. She uncrossed them, sat with knees apart and began riffling through a small pile of magazines. She pulled a Golf Digest and a Horse and Hound, found business papers, memorandums of meetings, scribbled a few notations along the top of randomly chosen pages, a few initials here and there, and threw in some detritus . . . staples, clips . . . stuff like that.

"This attaché case is yours, the passport is right here," David said gesturing at the concealed section. *Looks good, no one will find it,* she thought. He placed the magazines and papers in the case, and closed it.

"I will not set the tumblers. It only raises suspicion if it is locked. Remember to change back to Lisa Ling when you disembark. Once aboard you can remove the shirt, the tie, and put on the black roll neck sweater."

She gave a quizzical glance. "Why?"

"Your neck, your throat, you cannot take a chance on a missing Adam's apple, now can you?"

A car pulled to a stop and brought silence to the room. Lisa threw a questioning look at David as he peered out the window. He turned back, smiled. "It is fine, do not be alarmed. Yidui has arrived."

David greeted Yidui outside the house, briefing him on what had happened.

"They are both dead?" Lisa heard Yidui exclaim in a shocked tone.

"It all happened so fast," Leung said surreptitiously. "Wang burst in and began firing."

Yidui stepped into the house, his eyes immediately fixing on the well-groomed young man across from him. Lisa nodded. He returned the nod to the stranger with the moustache and glasses, hesitating, mindlessly questioning this person's identity, then moved nearer to the bodies.

"What a mess, David," he said, quickly returning to the front door and signaling two men who were waiting in the shadows. They entered, gave a bow of respect to David as he quickly locked the door behind them.

"Where is Lisa?" Yidui asked, waving a hand toward the bedroom door. "Is she resting?"

David grinned at the well-groomed young man and gave a slow nod. "This is Michael Long. We need to get him out tonight."

Yidui glanced curiously. David took on a look of self-satisfaction as he gave a reassuring nod to Lisa. "I've worked some magic," he chuckled. "This *is* Lisa."

Yidui stared in disbelief. "You are a woman? Brilliant

work, just brilliant!"

She rolled her eyes and her mouth took on a whimsical pout. She held Yidui's stare for a few long moments, after which reality returned and she waved a hand over the scene. "This should never have happened," she said. "I am very sorry."

Yidui shifted his attention back to Lisa, passing a hand from her head to toe. "This will work. I would never have suspected you to be a woman."

"Need to get them both in the van, clean this mess," David said, squatting by Peter's body. "We need to be sure there is not a trace of what has happened this evening." He placed a hand on Peter as he spoke, was silent for half a minute, and then walked the few paces to Wang. With disdain, he scowled down at him, put one hard kick into the rib cage of the body, and cussed in Mandarin.

One of the men moved to Peter and looked at the young man covered to the chin with the blood-soaked sheet. David was ready for the reaction, saw it, knew it as their eyes widened upon recognizing the deceased.

"You recognize him huh, yes, it is General Cheng's son."

The man quickly stepped back from the body, let out a long breath and shook his head and began speaking to Yidui and David, his voice sounding as though he'd sucked on helium.

"What's he saying?" Lisa inquired.

David reluctantly translated. "He said if he had known who the body was, he would not have come. He says the general will not rest until he has found the persons responsible, as well as any who have helped along the way."

David Leung searched through Wang's bag, took out the red bundle, un-wrapped the statue. It had done a three-sixty, ended up in the hands of Yidui, where it had started.

500

After all the effort, all the planning, they were standing there with the statue containing the replacement flash drive.

"Waste of a good plan," David said to Yidui. "There must be a way to salvage it. It was too good."

Yidui gave it some thought as his men wrapped Wang in a large black plastic sheet.

Lisa gazed at her new passport, liked the way she looked, wondered how long it would take for her hair to vaguely resemble a woman's. But for now, she was Michael Long. *Not bad*, she thought, *I can do this*. She looked at Peter and kicked back into crying mode.

"We believe we have a plan," David said, ignoring the tears. "We are going to take Peter and Wang to an area on the way to Datong. From there we will place a call to the Western Hills building and tell the person taking the call that there has been a gunfight with the Americans. We will say the caller witnessed a confrontation and two of the Americans were wounded. In the scuffle, Peter bravely secured a backpack from one of the wounded Americans, was hit by gunfire in the struggle, and the Americans took the bag and fled, forcing you to accompany them." He said it all in one breath, with a touch of pride.

Lisa visualized the scenario, running it through her mind like an old black and white movie. She moved across to the window as David and Yidui continued discussing the plan. The sound of raindrops distracted her momentarily. It had been a strange evening; the moon had freed itself from the clouds, adding a touch of silver to the tiled rooftops along the narrow street. Once again, thoughts of Peter came thundering into her head, the wrath of his father, how he'd be enraged at his son's death, retribution would be merciless. The general would be passionate in his efforts to capture Slade and the others. If only he knew it was Wang who had fired the fatal shot.

She looked confused, shook her head. "How will

Wang's death fit into the plan?"

David broke off his chatting with Yidui. "Wang was last seen in pursuit of the Americans. His body will be found along the road. Ironically, he will be considered quite the hero, dying in the gunfight, attempting to apprehend the Americans. You will be assumed a hostage."

"And Peter?" she asked.

"I will open the base of Wang's statue, remove the corrupted flash drive, and place it in Peter's clenched fist. It will be assumed Peter had successfully regained possession of the original drive, the one Slade removed from Penghu. No one will suspect that it is not the original drive. It will appear as though Peter took it from the American's bag. If all goes to plan, the drive will be returned to Beijing's satellite mother computer and hurriedly re-installed. Black Sabbath will infect the entire program and Operation Compass will shut down."

She stared at David, said nothing.

Yidui rubbed his chin, looked up at David. "It sounds feasible. I wish we could have . . ." He stopped, and his eyes widened. "Of course, whoever takes the call at Western Hills will not be able to definitely recognize the captain's voice, especially if the line is crackling and the voice has a rushed, panicked tone. We will make out the captain himself is leaving the message for his father."

"That can work," David chimed in. "He can say he has recovered the flash drive from Slade, and has been wounded in the process. He can give the location, and ask that an ambulance be rushed to his aide. He can also say Wang has gone off in pursuit of the fleeing Americans."

"That is it," Yidui said. "That will work. I will have a very reliable person familiarize himself with the plan. He will make a credible witness to the entire event. But do you think they will be suspicious of Peter Cheng being out of uniform?"

"No. It is common for civilian clothing to be worn when the need to blend in is necessary. I have seen the general wearing a suit on one occasion, a clandestine meeting with a young lady no doubt." He placed a hand over his mouth, raised his eyebrows and sniggered. "Peter being out of uniform will not be an issue."

*****

On Monday, May 21, at ten in the morning, Michael Long stood at the ticketing counter at Beijing airport, ticket and passport in hand, spectacles on the bridge of his nose. He made a screwed up face, sneezed and noisily blew into a Kleenex, and was unceremoniously waved on through. He walked along the aisle and dropped into seat 8C.

*****

A shocked General Cheng stared for a several long minutes, while the unfortunate officer who had delivered the news stood at attention. "I am very sorry, General. They are bringing the captain in right now."

Cheng lowered his eyes to the small item on the desk. "You say this was found in his hand?"

"Yes sir, clenched in the captain's fist."

"And where was his weapon?"

"By his side, the magazine was empty. Witnesses say he fought bravely to the end."

"Where was Wang found?

"We were told he pursued the attackers, was shot a kilometer from where the captain was found."

Cheng let out a long shaky breath, his stoic demeanor on the verge of collapse. "Was a Chinese girl seen during the confrontation?"

"Yes General. The witness says the girl was taken at

gunpoint."

Cheng muttered the words to himself, "Hostage, they have her as a hostage." His voice quivered, "Lisa Ling, my only surviving child."

The soldier missed the hushed comment. "I'm sorry General, I did not hear."

"It is nothing, Captain. It really does not matter." He picked up the flash drive, rubbed his thumb on its smooth surface, slipped on a pair of strong bi-focal glasses, and read the inscription, *Compass 008*.

"Take this immediately to Taiyuan. Give it to Major General Siang. No one but Siang, understand? He will be most pleased for its safe return. Peter has done well."

When the soldier left the room, Cheng opened the drawer of his desk, stared at the OSZ-92 service pistol, and considered taking the weapon from the drawer. He placed a hand on the snug grip, and slowly moved the weapon upward, placing it beneath his chin. He meditated on his children, David, Peter . . . and Lisa Ling.

All gone.

His finger tightened on the trigger.

CHAPTER 49

THE JUMP FROM THE Antonov shocked Blake's system, as sub zero temperature ripped into his face, stinging as he strained to look for signs of the other jumpers, of more chutes. Wind whistled by his ears, ballooning his cheeks, as the descent filled his mouth with icy air, and tears streamed back from his reddened eyes as they crinkled in the corners. He placed his hands to his mouth, shouted into the blackness, "Hey guys. Can ya hear me?"

"I'm freezin," Dal shouted back. "Got some serious shrinkage goin' on."

"Can ya see the others?"

Dal tugged at the hang straps, looked down, and shouted, "Slade, ya down there?"

"I'm here," came the faint reply from Slade. "Can see two chutes under me, could be Sung, Billie. I can't see Harry."

"You up there, Harry?" Blake called.

No reply.

"Harry, ya hear me?"

Blake sucked in a breath of freezing night air, waited for a reply, but the only sounds were the wind and the riffling noise of the chute flapping as he fell earthward. He tried opening his eyes, but the frigid air ripped at his face and the best he could manage was a thin squint. Each time he tried to spot one of the other chutes, the wind flapped under his eyelids, causing him to cover them as tears shot up the edges of his forehead. He closed his eyes tight, felt the sting of the salt.

Prayed.

Blake wasn't an overly religious person. His Catholic upbringing sold him on the belief that it was a clever man who invented God. But here he was, asking God's help. He turned his head and thought about Harry, of how he'd hesitated. *Goddamn - the fucker didn't jump.* He twisted about, faced the direction the plane had been traveling, saw the thin orange crescent on the horizon. *Fuckin' Harry, he's tryin' to land her, had me jump from a perfectly good plane.* He blocked the fear, placed his mind in an amusement park, a pretend parachute drop. *I'm not really fallin', not really thousands of feet above solid ground. I'll keep my eyes closed, pretend I'm at Disneyland. Make it believable, gotta keep 'em closed. Ride will be over soon, then I'll get a hot dog, load it with mustard, relish too. Have a Pepsi.*

But reality can be cruel. Blake heard the sound of the Antonov as it drew nearer. *Jesus! Harry's turned her around. He's above me someplace.* Trying to turn his harness, trying to pinpoint the direction of the plane, trying to spot something, trying to...

In a fleeting moment it was there, the roar of engine noise accompanied by a neck jerking sideways drag as the Antonov roared over him, the bi-plane swerving as the aviator reefed it to starboard, missing the chute but dragging it along in its wake, a flapping tangle of straps and white nylon and a body and . . .

The body grimaced, tugging at the hang straps, eyes shut tight, unable to control the canopy as it lost its shape, twisting, twirling, dragging along parallel to wherever the ground below was, was, was . . .

Consciousness left him.

Harry fought to correct the bird, snapping his head around, thought he'd taken out the jumper. He rarely cussed, but shouted, "Oh fuck, oh fuck!" Then to himself, "I see it, goddamnit, I see it. Come on baby, get up, get up! Get the fuck up!" He raised the flaps, nudging the nose upward as the old plane recognized the request. It was more a case of positive thinking on Harry's part, he was sure she'd gained a few feet; sure she did it just to appease him. Then, after a heavy sigh, his eyes flashed back to where he'd seen the chute. "Jesus, I hit one of 'em," he snorted, his eyes searching, a sensation of panic taking over his senses. He had that glimmer on the horizon, but then he had the need to turn the big bird, to know he hadn't hit, hadn't hit . . .

And his eyes searched with resolve.

The Antonov swung about in a slow heavy loop, the engine groaning as though asking its master to just let it die in peace. Harry ignored the whine, could feel the vibration as the imbalanced wings showed disapproval of his aerobatics. He strained his vision, peering this way and that, had to find the chute, saw a faint white dot dropping quickly toward the treetops. "That's gotta be him," and he shouted at the flapping chute, "I missed you, slow down, your canopy isn't full," then groaning, "get it open; deploy the back-up chute. Please, get the fucking thing open."

He turned the Antonov to the east, saw the orange crescent growing larger, its glow silhouetting the horizon. He circled the plane over the jump area, dropping it to a lower altitude, nursing it, squeezing every drop of gas into the engine. *I gotta be on fumes,* he thought as the landscape came more into view. *Please God, any clearing'll do, only need six hundred feet, you can spare that, six hundred feet, just six hundred, six hundred, just six hundred, six hundred . . . .*

When his mind was done running the words, he bellowed at the instrument panel, "Give me six hundred fucking feet, just six hundred!"

The looming treetops reminded him of a broccoli

display on a produce counter. *It's too close cropped*, he thought, *it's too tight*. He looked to the left, to the right. *She's dropping too fast*.

"Christ Almighty, give me an opening!" he shouted at the topography. Then in a quieter monotone, "Where's that jumper, where's the jumper, did it open, come on, where are you, where's the fucking jumper?" No one heard, his comments passing between him and Miss Antonov. But she had eyes and she spotted the small road. It was no more than a track running east to west. "Only thirty feet wide, " he said, "but we can make it, baby, thirty feet, thirty feet, just thirty fucking feet".

He aligned Miss Antonov's nose with the narrow road and she began her final descent. He spoke to her with warmth, with appreciation, as though a harsh tone would be disadvantageous at such a crucial moment. "Come on baby, sorry I shouted at you. But I didn't jump, couldn't do that to you, honey. So come on, just one last time for Uncle Harry, nice 'n easy now. Down we go, easy peezee."

And just as all seemed to be going well. . . the engine died.

*****

Carson Dallas pulled his knees into a fetal position, bracing, treetops smashing into his legs just after he'd said a brief prayer, his mind feeling each of the cracking sounds. *Snapping branches, not my bones*. His body weight swathed a path through the sixty foot birch, his descent speeding, not slowing, the chute shredding its way through jagged branches. *Has to be close, gonna hit*. He sensed the nearness of the jungle floor, pulled his head into his chest, prepared for impact. He hit with the velocity of a free fall from thirty feet, rolled and lay unmoving in stunned disbelief. The sound from above was as though the tree was about to crash down as Blake plummeted through the thick canopy, landing a short distance from Dal.

"Drew!" Dal called aloud, "S'that you?"

Blake's voice reflected the hurt. "My ankle, fuckin' chute got, I dunno, Harry came right onto me, the back-up chute opened when I was almost right on the fuckin' treetops." He doubled over, grabbed at his ankle. "Goddamn ankle, I think it's busted!"

It was an expensive catch on that sunny day with the Minnesota Vikings.

"Guess Harry went for plan 'A'," Dal said, releasing his harness. "How bad are ya?"

"Pretty bad," Blake groaned, applying pressure to the pain. "Can you get the cream out of my pack?"

Dal dug about in the backpack and opened the jar of Whea Chung's miracle cure as Blake unlaced his boot, grimacing as pain shot through him and the ankle swelled.

"Looks worse than before," Dal said, twisting his face. "You won't be gettin' the boot back on if this swellin' don't go down."

"Aw Christ, shoot me why don'tcha?" He looked skyward. "Hey, if Harry lands that fuckin' thing, please put my body in the plane where the critters can't get at me."

"Yeah, yeah, yeah . . . fuckin' hero," Dal said, slipping the cream back into the pack.

*****

The aviator pulled on the pneumatic brakes using every drop of energy he could muster as the Antonov screamed onto the roadway. Stopping the beast proved far more difficult than planes utilizing hydraulics. To further exacerbate the stopping problem, the braking handle was on the left side of the control wheel. The Antonov had one rudder bar for the plane's full right rudder and another operating the plane's full left rudder brake. Harry always disliked the braking system; the use of the pneumatic brakes was an acquired skill he was yet to master. He had the skill, but with such a rapid descent, that skill level was being fully tested. *Need to apply equal pressure*, he thought. Difficult enough, but the degree of difficulty was increased ten-fold with death staring the pilot in the face as he attempted stopping the plane with trembling hands rather than shaking feet.

"I should be on top of this," he said in a cold sweat as the plane fought the turbulence. The wind shear effect was very slight at first, but could botch the landing if it intensified. A quick look at the altimeter showed eighty feet, the next thing Harry knew there were the treetops, ripping at the undercarriage. There were no flames and he assumed that the initial impact could be fire free due to the empty fuel tank. He was thankful for the empty tanks. *Bitter irony*, he thought. Higher branches tore a section from the port wing, giving a kind of balance to the wingspan, hardly of use at this point as the pilot fought to keep the visual descent going in a straight line, concerned the trees would grab his girl and fling her sideways.

Can't happen, he thought, *it'd be fatal*.

Then there was nothing but fear.

Fifteen noisy seconds later, when she finally came to a halt, the aviator, too shaken to stand, slid from the plane, fell to his knees and slapped both hands on the dirt road. His shoulder ached. *Dislocated*, he thought as he wrapped an arm around the twisted wheel strut for support and raising himself from beneath the fuselage. He placed both arms against the undercarriage and shouted into the early morning air, "I love this lady!"

The sound of an approaching runner cut his jubilation short. He limped into the thick ground cover alongside the road as the runner pushed his way across the makeshift landing strip.

"Harry, Harry! You okay?"

"Dal? Jesus am I glad to see you! I clipped one of the chutes. Where are the others, did you see any of the other guys?"

"Just Blake, he's back there a ways, banged up his ankle comin' through the trees. Think he's a bit pissed with you though. You look kinda beige, you okay?"

"Bad landing, trainee pilot," he replied trying to make light of it. "Thank God Blake's okay. Is he really okay?"

"Gimme a minute, I'll go get him, help him back here."

Dal returned a few minutes later with an arm around Blake's waist.

"For somethin' we all jumped out of," Blake snarled angrily, nodding at the Antonov, "that fuckin' plane ain't lookin' too bad." He used an accusing tone. "Thanks for that, Harry. And eh, thanks for the fuckin' thrill on the way down."

"Hey, what can I say? She made it. No other plane could've done it. Well, maybe a Harrier, but not on regular gas. The little lady here got us further than I planned."

"Fuckin backup chute . . ." Blake grumbled.

"But it worked," Harry chuckled. "You're here."

"*Here*, Harry? Oh that's rich," Blake growled, "and where the fuck is *here*?"

He shook his head, pointing to his right. "I think we're on the Myanmar side of the line."

"Whoa, whoa, whoa, hold on!" a confused Blake said. "You're tellin' me we're out of China?"

Harry raised his good arm, pointing into the distance. "See that high land to the east, I believe it's the border. As I brought her down, I caught a glimpse of a few landmarks." He pulled a face and shrugged, "Guess I was a little out with my coordinates."

"A little out," Blake groaned, "...a little

fuckin'out!"

"It was the strong wind and you guys bitching about having to jump. If you'd all jumped sooner instead of procrastinating, we'd all be in China. I wanted to keep her in the air, kept heading west, toward Myanmar, to Burma."

"Burma huh, that's good news, right?" Dal asked.

"Yeah," Harry said with a pained voice, limping away a little dazed, looking ahead along the track. "The others, where are the other guys? It's gonna take some muscle to hide the plane away before we head south."

"Hide the plane," Dal sighed. "Hide the fuckin' plane. You can't be serious? You think they'll spot it and target in on us?"

"Something like that. If the Burmese find her, they'll be all over us. They'll have no problems trading us back to the Chinese. Their sympathies are with Beijing, especially since our guys placed sanctions on 'em."

"You sayin' the Burmese are as bad as the Chinese?" asked Dal.

As Harry was about to elaborate, a voice called from further down the road.

"Hey, you guys!"

Bell, Hunter, Sung, and Billie limped slowly toward the plane.

"Y'all made it down okay then?" asked Dal.

"It was freezing," Bellinger whined, rubbing her cheeks. "I'm still numb."

"The triumph of feminism," Blake groaned, "equal opportunity jumpers. Glad ya made it, missy."

"Was a little rough going for a while there," Bell groaned in a pained way.

"Really," Harry grinned. "I'll pass your complaint onto customer services." He cleared his throat. "I thought maybe you'd all be a little more thankful of my . . .

But there was a round of coughs and groans and a,

"You're fuckin' kiddin'," from Blake.

"I could get a fire going," Harry said, feeling somewhat unappreciated, "but we'd only attract attention. We still have flasks on board, maybe there's still some coffee." He clambered back aboard the Antonov, and a minute later called, "Yeah, we got coffee . . . and a few Oreos." He pointed over their heads. "How about we push her over toward that canopy of trees? We can rest up a bit, get the blood circulating."

They managed to get the plane sufficiently off the road to avoid aerial surveillance, but travelers using the road would most certainly spot the Antonov.

"If they're doing satellite surveillance they'll see her on this road, but they're gonna need to be really good to spot her under this canopy," Harry said, passing coffee flasks among the group, staring at Blake who was gingerly rubbing his ankle. "So, how bad is it?"

Dal looked at Blake, then at Harry. "Well, what we gotta decide is this," Dal said. "Which of us gets to shoot the Minnesota Viking here?" Then . . . nudging Blake, "How's about we draw straws?"

Blake ignored the quip.

"I rubbed some cream into it. Should be okay soon," he said pointing at the treetops. "I think I blacked out for a few seconds, I remember openin' my eyes, seein' the backup chute openin'. Then I caught a hard branch, kind of knocked the wind out of me, wasn't expectin' the ground to be so close, twisted the ankle when I hit."

"Fucks up any plan involvin' mountains," Dal said. "Wha'dya think Billie?"

"Mount Victoria is ten thousand feet high, cannot see you doing it, Mr. Blake. The journey as far as the Arakan Mountains alone would be too much for a sprained ankle." He gave a consoling look, adding, "You cannot possibly make the climb."

Dal recognized Blake's body language. He withdrew for a long minute, closed his eyes, and hoped the situation would go away. Two minutes later he opened them, only to find Blake's stubborn look of determination still lingered.

Dal and Hunter sat by the Antonov while Bell chatted with Slade and Sung, allowing Blake time to languish in self-pity, staring at the swollen ankle.

"The ankle's still swollen huh, Drew?" Bell asked in a compassionate voice. "How long did you say that stuff takes to work?"

Before he could reply, a loud clap shook the ground and torrential rain began belting down from the sky and they scrambled for the shelter of the wings and Blake grumbled, "Fuckin' great, just what we need."

"It'll blow over," Harry said. "The jungle gets these rain-showers every day," and added a self-ingratiating smirk, "that's why it's called monsoonal jungle."

"Right," Blake responded, looking at Dal who fought to hide a smirk. "Fuckin' jungle," Blake snorted with a pained face of his own.

An hour later, with the narrow road under water, the sound of a horn had them all turn, facing west as an truck rattled toward them, finally panting to a halt. The driver strained to roll down the window, giving the scene a curious once over, then raising his eyes toward the heavens, pulling a face and pointing at the clouds. "Wet," he called from the truck.

Billie hurried across to the truck and spoke to the driver for a minute or two. The driver eased the vehicle to the side of the road, tentatively stepped from the cabin, and hobbled to the shelter of the huge wing.

"This plane, it is yours?" he asked, looking from one to the other.

"Yeah, plane is mine," Harry replied.

"You leave plane here?"

"No," Dal scoffed, "he's gonna dismantle the mother-fucker and we're all gonna carry it home."

Billie tried translating the reply but couldn't quite deliver it with the same sarcastic touch. The man chatted with Billie for several minutes.

"You look like the cat that swallowed the canary," Dal said to Billie. "So what's the deal with the trucker?"

"Says he can help us reach Mandalay, says we are in the Shan State and that he is a Karen. His people, the Karen, they are pro-American. They fight against the Burmese troops who are controlled by the junta. He says that he has a friend in a village just an hour or so from here. If the roads are not flooded he is willing to take us there in this truck," and Billie nodded at the ancient wreck. "Once there, he says his friend will take us to Mandalay in *his* truck."

"God help us if it's like this," Hunter said, eyeing the rusted body work.

Blake gazed at the cargo. "Jesus, he's haulin' pigs."

"A baker's dozen," Dal said, quickly counting heads.

Blake peered in the rear of the truck, peered at the bed riddled with rust holes, its squealing cargo lucky to avoid their feet from slipping and sliding on a proliferation of pig shit, straw, and a thin layer of rust that one might believe could very likely be the only thing holding the wreck together. Blake's highly developed faculty of judgment alerted him to the reality of his immediate future. He flashed a pleading eye to Dal and snapped, "I ain't ridin' in back of this fucker!"

But the seat in the cabin could only fit three people.

The driver moved around to the rear and gestured at his cargo.

"He says two of us can ride in front, the rest will have to climb in back. He is taking the pigs to a market outside of Mandalay." One side of Billie's mouth edged up as he nodded to Harry. "He also says if you are leaving the plane, he would like it as payment for our passage to Mandalay."

Dal picked up the frown on Harry's face.

"You don't seem too keen to trade your girl, and uh . . ." and he flicked a thumb at the bi-plane, "she uh, she ain't exactly barterin' material no more."

*****

For the next fifteen minutes they were entertained by the driver singing as he drove along the wet, narrow track. He came into a clearing, pointed to people working a nearby field, rambled on for a few minutes, and gestured at the field workers. Billie passed on his comment. "Those people are Karen," he says, "good people, true Burmese."

The truck arrived at a sprinkling of huts, hissed, panted, and the motor was laid to rest for the day. Dal hung from the window, turned an ear toward the hood and gestured with a groan, "Yeah, don't that sound just fuckin' great."

Amidst the squealing swine, Drew Blake laid back, his ankle resting on Hunter's lap. He raised his head, dragged his sleeve across his mouth, tried to ignore the foul stench. Dal and Bell stepped from the cabin as the driver moved around the front of the smoking radiator where he stood for a sad minute, hands on his hips, shaking his head at the hissing relic.

The sound of a stringed instrument, accompanied by a man singing a melodic chant, caught their attention. The truck driver moved toward the source, a nearby hut, signaling for the others to wait by the truck. He returned a few minutes later and invited the group to enter. The musician sat alone in deep concentration, adjusting the tuning key of the instrument. He was neatly groomed and quite regal, with black almond shaped eyes that didn't move off the strings as he said to Billie, "This is a bad time for foreigners to pass through Shan State. We are in bitter conflict with the junta." He gave the group a quick once over. "Are they well enough armed to pass through this region?"

Billie, using some type of large leaf, scraped away at his legs, removing what could only be pig shit, keeping the cleaning process going as he passed on the question.

"Tell him we're okay," Blake replied. "Let him know we're more than tourists. Tell him we're American freedom fighters."

The man nodded, grinned, eyes not moving from the instrument. The truck driver turned, gestured toward the door leading from the hut.

"He says we should bathe," Billie said, making a face. "There is a well."

*****

Thirty minutes later the rain dissipated, the skies were once again blue, a rainbow painted the western horizon and children began playing and splashing about in mud puddles. One group ran to Bellinger, fascinated by her long blonde hair. Although matted, it bore a resemblance to strands of gold and they began laughing and speaking to her in Burmese.

"What are they saying?" she asked Billie.

But Billie began laughing and Sung stepped in. "They are saying you remind them of a Christian missionary who once passed this way. She did some Bible work and sang a song the children liked."

"Oh, that's cute," Bell said squatting to their eye level and holding the smallest child's hand. "Do they remember the song?"

Billie asked the children and they broke into giggles, then nudging the smallest of the children forward. She began to sing. "Doe, a deer, a female deer, ray a drop of golden sun, me a name I call myself, far a long, long way to run . . ."

517

And all the children joined in the remainder of the song.

"Mr. Rodgers and Mr. Hammerstein would be very proud of you all," Bell said laughing. "Well done." She held her smile at the children while asking Billie, "Where are their mothers? I'd love to meet them and talk about these kids."

Billie asked the musician and a minute later his reply came in a solemn tone. "He says the military raided their village, killing most of the men. The women were raped and executed. Fortunately, these children were away at the time. When they returned, they found only bodies."

Blake looked at Bell, who was standing mouth agape, hands on either side of her face in horror. She forced the words, "What's being done about it?"

Billie asked the man and then translated his reply. "Some international observers," Billie said, "have called this campaign against the Karen ethnic-cleansing, genocide, a crime against humanity. He says there was a meeting of the United Nations, but three nations refused to discuss the crisis."

Hunter leaned forward and asked, "Can we guess who?"

"He says Japan, Russia, and China feel the Burmese situation does not threaten regional security and peace. Japan says it will not enter into discussions over the Burmese situation."

"You know," Dal said, leaning toward Blake, "there's always some country gettin' kicked in the nuts by a bunch of thugs who assume power. What a mess. Wish we could help these people."

Blake angrily shook his head and Hunter frustrated, kicked at the ground, causing mud to splatter his boots. The truck driver pointed at the workers in the field and spoke again to Billie, who listened intently. "He says things have gotten even worse in the past weeks. The junta's generals have mounted a strong assault on all the Karen people. He says that more than two hundred thousand Karen villagers are now sheltering in temporary camps along the Myanmar-Thai border."

"Wish we could help," Blake said dismissingly, "but we ain't gonna get involved."

Billie told the man what Blake had said and relayed the man's reply. "He says that is what the rest of the world is saying, *we cannot get involved.* He says the Burmese military is destroying all opposition, and the international community is sitting back and ignoring the atrocities."

Dal spat, wiped his mouth. "Welcome to beautiful Burma," he snarled in disgust. "Such a fuckin' relief ya know, bein' out of China and all."

Blake tried to walk, but the ankle was far worse than first suspected. Bell kneeled at his feet and gently squeezed the base of his leg as Blake groaned, unable to conceal the pain.

"You guys need to get Slade's information back home," Bellinger said. "You can't stay here, and Drew can't do any long hauls. I think I should stay with him and you guys go on ahead to Mandalay. We'll catch up in a day or so."

The suggestion didn't sit well with Dal. "Fuck that. I go nowhere without Drew. If he stays, I stay."

Hunter threw in his two cents worth. "Yeah, me and Bell, we're a matched set too, where she goes . . . so go I."

"Okay you guys," Blake mumbled. "Enough with the buddy buddy bullshit. I'll be fine back here for a bit, Bell can stay. Dal, you hold Hunter's fuckin' hand and both of you be good boys, and don't go playin' with each other's weenies."

Billie made quiet conversation with the truck driver, and after a few minutes, turned to Slade and said, "His name is Chakra Khan, we can call him Chakra. He says his family was executed in this village two months ago. The soldiers raped his wife and two daughters, and then shot each of them in the back of the head. He was forced to watch the atrocities. They threw him a shovel and made him bury his family. He says none of the soldiers were older than twenty years of age. He was left to tell others what to expect from the junta. The Karen hunted them down, killed all fifteen rapists."

"Tell Chakra we feel bad for him. If we could help in any way . . ." Blake dropped his head as an exploding clap of thunder signaled a further downpour.

At two o'clock, Chakra sat eating with the group as another Burmese villager entered the shack and chatted, pointing this way and that.

"What's goin' on, Billie?" Hunter asked.

"He says you should get going right away, there are soldiers just a few kilometers east of here. He has his truck ready to go, you must all leave. He says there is a safe place in Mingun, not far from Mandalay. His uncle has a small fishing boat he uses to take tourists on river cruises." Billie listened intently as Chakra described their destination. "He says Mingun is a small town eleven kilometers up the Ayeyawady River from Mandalay. There we will find the ruins of a Buddhist temple; it is called the Mingun Paya. You are to signal the boat. It will be waiting off the beach by the Paya, three days from now."

The meal quickly ended and the group stepped from the cover and warmth of the hut, and stepped out into the steamy aftermath of the storm, each stopping in their tracks at the site of their transportation, a truck with a large canvas canopy on which a rear flap was loosely secured by rope tie downs. Although there were no animals onboard, the single seat was split by the gear shift, leaving just one spot for a passenger.

"I ain't bumpin' about in the back of another fuckin' truck," Blake said in a non-negotiable way.

"Okay, so *we'll* go on the truck," Hunter said reluctantly. "You and Bell follow when you're able to travel. We'll meet you both three days from now, at midday, at Mingun."

"You guys have all the bags," Bell replied. "Just leave a couple of Glocks and a full magazine for each. The lighter we travel the better." She said it while placing Blake's foot into a bowl of cold water. "Let's soak this for awhile. Wish we had some ice."

Hunter looked back at Blake and reached into his backpack. "Here are two trackers, only good for a hundred feet or so, batteries are weak. Leave the Glock and take this, there's a spare clip, it gives you plenty of rounds." He passed the Sig with a spare magazine of fifteen shots. "Take this as well, ya never know," and he handed over the Coeur D' Lene suppressor.

"Thanks, I like the silencer. Don't know that we'll be talkin' to each other on these gizmos." He clicked the speak switch on the matchbox size unit, and made a face at the static. "Don't sound too good. But I'm sure my ankle will be okay in a day or two. I'll keep the cream on it, and my weight off." He winked at Bellinger and passed her the second unit. "Bell can nursemaid me until then."

Like sardines in a can, they sat jammed on board the truck, waving back to Bellinger and Blake and moving off in a southerly direction. Hunter had a death grip on the rear tray, a similar hold as Dal, Harry, Slade, Chakra and Sung. Billie travelled first class, sweating it out in the cabin with the driver, a young man in his mid-twenties who'd never been introduced to body deodorant. The air in the cabin was made up of a fine blend of odors, consisting of more pig shit, human shit, stale breath and the too often foul fart that arrived with great fanfare as the young driver happily cheered his uncontrollable flatulence. Billie rolled his eyes as the young man jovially burst into lengthy verbiage.

This is hard to take, Billie thought as he tried to get the window down. But try as he may, it stayed firmly closed.

Three minutes passed, as well as a lot of wind, Billie was feeling the need for fresh air, held up a hand, stopped the driver's verbal diarrhea, and pleaded, "I must pee, pull over! Pull over!"

Slade stepped from the rear, and asked, "Billie, what's he been saying?"

Billie's inhaling of fresh air nearly resulted in hyperventilation, propping himself against a tree, and fumbling with his zipper. While he peed, he said, "He says his family lives in Mandalay and they will be pleased if we choose to stay overnight at their home."

"That might work," Slade said, as he too took advantage of the bathroom break.

"Yes, if they are not afflicted with *his* problem," Billie said, touching his nose.

"Tell him we appreciate his offer," Slade said shaking off. "Ask him how far the place is from Mingun."

"He says it is along the Ayeyawady, a kilometer south of Mingun, along the river bank. If Buddha is on our side, we will be there in two days."

Slade turned away, cupped a hand over his nose and stared toward the mist now engulfing the mountains ahead. "And if he ain't?" he grumbled.

CHAPTER 50

SAM HAD RETURNED home following a call from Manning, the change in plans having necessitated his early return from Catalina. It was good being in his own bed, but his repose was short lived. The phone by the bed buzzed incessantly. He rolled to face the bedside clock. Squinted. *Twenty minutes after midnight.*

"Hello?"

"Mr. Ridkin, I do apologize for this poorly timed call."

Jerking his body upright, Sam glanced sideways at his wife. She groaned, almost ignoring the disturbance, gave a hint of a snore and fell back to sleep.

"Yidui," Sam growled. "What the fuck are you doing calling me, and how'd you get my home number?"

"You do underestimate me, Mr. Ridkin," Yidui chuckled, "I've always had *your* number."

There was a pause. Sam waited for the voice to continue, his mind racing as the silence became elongated. *Oh shit*! He heard the clicking as Yidui punched at the digits and the Ridkin bedroom exploded in a ball of flames and the incendiary device consumed the two figures that lay on the bed. In an instant Sam was no more than a blackened corpse, tumbling forward, rolling off the bed as the fireball spread throughout the house.

*****

523

Her arms wrapped around him, pulling him out of the horror, clutching him tight, his head resting on her shoulder, trembling, wet with sweat. "Sam! You're having a nightmare!"

"Oh sweet Jesus!" and he laid his head on her shoulder, his dark face a lather.

"I'm sorry. I've gotta get outside, have a smoke, gotta settle down. You try getting back to sleep. It's okay."

"Are you sure you're . . ."

"Yes, yes. I'm fine," he said making his way to the extensively stocked minibar and selecting a bottle of Jim Beam. He poured a full glass, stepped into the cool night air and lit up a Marlboro. He sighed, "Fuckin' Yidui!"

*****

It was raining in the predawn hour of this Los Angeles morning. The street sweeper was scurrying along an empty road ahead of morning traffic, along a silent Wilshire Boulevard. Sam cracked open the window, listening to the brushes as they spun furiously, scraping the curb as the sweeper turned the corner, his mind lingering on his nightmare. *Yidui*, he thought, *goddamn the man!*

The knock on the door came early. He opened it and gave his best-forced smile as Adam McDowell entered.

"Adam, you're eh, you're early, wasn't expecting you until after seven. Keeping a low profile, huh?" He stepped back, looked at McDowell's suave attire. "Playing dead, it seems to agree with you."

"Yeah, yeah, yeah, don't want those Russkies coming back, getting another crack at doing their job, real nice guys, Grigori and Aleksei." He let out a sly grin that left Sam wondering. "So Sam, what's the status on the team?"

Sam moved to the desk, didn't feel good about sitting in the chair, needed to be in a more readied position,

524

unsure what to expect in view of the earlier phone call. He sat sidesaddle on the desktop, stalling, staring at the family Christmas picture, appearing preoccupied, an attempt to avoid McDowell's inquisitive gaze. Once again he thought about the pre-dawn phone call from the CIA Director, *unlike those guys to break with procedure.*

McDowell said, "Sam?"

"Ah yeah, Adam, not too promising at present I'm afraid." He placed the photograph down, met McDowell's eyes, tried to read into him, sneaking a peripheral glimpse at the wall clock, knowing he needed to buy time, that he had to stall for around an hour. The clock said six forty-five.

McDowell reached across, picked up the framed family picture as Sam analyzed his body language, sensing McDowell's tenuous attitude. "Family looks happy, Sam. I can remember when I had a family," and he nodded at the portrait. "Had a picture just like this, very nice."

Sam had heard about McDowell's family. Most of what he'd heard was open to conjecture. Perhaps this was an opportunity to lay conjecture to rest. *Dare I push it? I need to stall for time.* "What happened, Adam? I never really looked into your loss. It was classified and . . ." He got no further. McDowell quickly returned the picture to its place on the desk and walked to the window.

"You see this view? I heard of a man thrown from a window just like this one, Sam."

Sam's blood ran cold as he stared down on Wilshire.

"It was in Manhattan," McDowell continued. "I'd just started with the agency, met this guy there, he was set to retire. They sent him and another guy along to eh - to take care of a problem the motherfuckers at the agency were having."

He wasn't comfortable with the start of McDowell's story. "This isn't classified material," he said faking a smile. "Is it, Adam?"

"Fuck classified. Those manipulators at the agency have fucked up more times than I've jerked off. You know how they get away with it? Yeah, *you* know. You've seen enough of it. They call it classified; bury it under a shit-load of departmental crap. Assassinations, murders, conspiracy theories, whatever they want. They've got the original license to kill."

"I hear a lot of stuff, Adam, but obviously not everything," and he pointed at the window. "And what's this about a guy going out the window?"

"Long time ago, back in '53, a guy named Frank Olson, part of a team working on mind control drugs."

Sam frowned. "MK-ULTRA, yeah, I've heard the story. I've done some reading up on the Olson incident. It was called suicide. He supposedly jumped. They said he was on LSD."

"He didn't fuckin' jump, Sam. He was smacked on the head with the butt end of a pistol. Next thing, he was on the pavement thirteen stories down. Back in '75 there was a commission set up by the president, by Ford; they said the CIA slipped Olson a lethal dose of LSD. Now-a-days they're using water boarding. Different flavor, same smell. There're no rules with the CIA. They write their own goddamn rules."

Feeling the sweat forming on his brow, Sam reached in his pocket for a tissue, made out he was wiping his nose; turning away from McDowell and making a quick wipe of his forehead. "So what's your involvement in all of this, Adam?"

"No direct involvement. After the recent attempt on my life, I kinda withdrew, just like you told me. Did the whole bullshit thing with Wang, then like a good little boy, I went to ground. You know you've ruined it for me in Chinatown, I can't show my face at that fuckin' restaurant."

"Where's this heading, Adam?"

"Patience, Sam, patience." He walked to the window, unlocked it, cracked it an inch and lit a cigarette. "One night, I had a few too many drinks with one of the CIA guys who'd been in that Manhattan room with Olson. He tells me how he met with Bill Colby, the agency director at the time."

"Yeah, Colby," Sam nodded, letting McDowell continue on.

"They asked Congress to pay off Olson's family, gave 'em close to a million bucks." He took a long hard pull on the cigarette, exhaled at the cracked window. "Oh yeah, and gave the family an apology too, called it a private humanitarian relief bill. A crock of shit is what it was, Sam. They were even invited to the White House and got an apology from fuckin' Ford himself. You know how clever those bastards are. Frank Olson's son was presented with a nicely abridged CIA file on his father's work. Fuckin' abridged, can you believe that? How the fuck do you abridge an official file? If they can pull that off, then Jesus, I got no chance. They aren't Grigori and Aleksei. If they come to see me, I don't resurrect from *that* visit."

Sam repeated his question, "And your involvement is . . . what exactly?"

"I was wearing a wire, recorded my conversation with the guy, I got the whole meeting on tape."

"You know that stuff's inadmissible, right?"

"It's admissible to the people I contacted."

Sam shook his head. "Tell me," he groaned with a look of disbelief. "Tell me you didn't try to sell the goddamn tape."

"I'm not getting any younger, have to get the fuckin' Rubles where I can."

McDowell was borderline irrational, and Sam had difficulty disguising his uneasiness. The manner in which he was pouring his heart out left little doubt in Sam's mind he wouldn't have the opportunity to share the story. He moved

527

around back of the desk, placing a hand on the edge of the drawer as he recalled another incident, a time when a CIA operative attempted to extort the agency. A poison tipped pin fitted to the end of a golf umbrella turned his round at Pebble Beach into his final visit to the links. His body was discovered floating by the eighteenth fairway, heart attack they said. It was later found he had over eight million dollars of unaccountable income sitting in an offshore account. The pin had been developed at great expense by the CIA, developed for Francis Gary Powers. A quick painless end Powers opted not to take, a subsequent waste of millions of taxpayer dollars; but maybe not, at least it had found its way into the everyday marketplace.

Sam played a dangerous card. "Adam, tell me, do you have an offshore account?"

McDowell blinked. It was sufficient, an affirmative reply. "You asked me to play the bad apple," he said. "I didn't need to act out the role. How'd you guess?"

"Your family. We researched your history before you joined the Division."

"It was classified!"

"We twisted a few arms. You know how it goes. A few bucks here, a few there."

"So you knew they were being held by the agency?"

"Took us some time to get it, but yeah . . . we knew."

"Those cocksuckers sent me into a hornet's nest. Said my family would have a nasty accident if I didn't play along. Why me, Sam? Why the fuck did they choose me? There were other guys far more dispensable than poor old Adam McDowell."

"What was the mission?"

"Wanted to blow the whole Israeli thing sky high, agency figured the fastest way was by demolishing the Wailing Wall, the Western Wall. Hit it the week before the

Jewish festival of Shavouot, early June; blame it on the other guys. Figured there'd be a fast reaction by the Israeli Army. No inquiry, just retaliation."

Sam shook his head in disbelief. "That makes Operation Compass look like small change." He felt stupid after saying it, but kept his eyes on the drawer, couldn't allow McDowell to see his expression, see distrust.

McDowell drew hard on the cigarette. "I told them I didn't want any part of it, but they had my kids, had my wife. They were smug fuckers, knew they had me, had me by the balls."

"The Wailing Wall," Sam said, "it's still standing."

"It goes deeper. Back in 1993, before I left the agency, I was approached by this guy, a Russian, name was Sergeievich Dostoevsky, with the KGB you know. It was before Yeltsin disbanded it in '95. Sergei was playing both teams, got pretty pissed off when the agency folded. We did a lot of trading, you know the shit I'm talking about. They were after information we had on mind-bending shit, not the old MK-ULTRA, that stuff's passé. They had their mitts on the newer poison tips, shit like that. It all seemed pretty harmless at the time." He stubbed the cigarette out, pulled another, lit it. "We felt we were doing the world a service. When the KGB folded I resigned from the CIA, then Sergei and me, you know, we kind of hooked up."

"A service, how so?"

"Keeping things even, a balance of technology, but you know what? The deeper I dug for tid-bits, the dirtier it got. I couldn't trade all of the shit I dug up, not with Moscow, but I could see the value if eh, if the agency wanted it kept hush-hush."

"Dirty? Like what?"

"You don't need to hear this shit, Sam," and he flipped a thumb toward the door. "I know they're after me; I'm as good as dead, as dead as Frank fuckin' Olson. The agency, they don't have a three strike rule. I got no place to hide. Got those fuckers, got Moscow, got Beijing too. What would you do in my place?" They sat in silence for a few long moments and Sam wondered if McDowell was actually waiting on a reply. "I needed insurance, Sam. Well guess what, insurance don't always pay. I'm between a goddamn rock and a hard place."

Sam could hear the elevator door opening, just needed to keep McDowell's mind preoccupied. *Could be the agency heavies, could be anyone, just need to keep McDowell talking.* He posed the question, "What've you done?" It was rhetorical, a stall, he knew of McDowell's betrayal, of the accounts, of the double dealing, of his collusion with Yidui. And in McDowell's state-of-mind, perhaps it was interpreted as a good question, appropriate, deserving of a less perfunctory response.

A good question.

Unfortunately, McDowell, totally irrational, gave a crazed look to Sam. "You think I'm crazy, right Sam?"

"I've never thought that," he said, avoiding provocation.

"I had to do it, no choice. Had no help. Not from you guys, not from the agency, no one had my back."

Sam's eyes flickered to the wall clock, watched the second hand, thought of the gun in the nearby drawer. The elevator hadn't gone his way, no heavies, nothing. *Maybe all that I have is the gun in my desk. I need to make a move.* "We can get you into a safe-house," he said. "You can start over again."

"Yeah, really Sam, like start a new family?" McDowell made a forced grin in spite of himself. "My family is ashes, fuckin' gas explosion and fire. Fuckin' bullshit, Sam. Those guys at the agency, they turned the gas on, set up a fuse. You know how it works, jam a bagel in the toaster, turn the gas on full, a minute later, boom! Fuckin' house burns to the ground." His teeth clenched as his fist pounded onto the desktop. "Fuck 'em all!"

"Don't know what to say, where were you when this happened?"

"They sent me on some bullshit assignment just to get me out of the way. Took me awhile to figure who the guys were, ya know, the ones who were in my home, the guys who last saw my family breathing. There was four of 'em."

"And?"

"They each met with nasty fuckin' accidents."

"When?"

McDowell grinned. It was a Jack Nicholson smile, like he was going to announce . . . here's Johnny!

Sam heard his heart rate speed up and said with reluctance, "So then, you eh . . . gave them the tape?"

"Yeah, and I got a nice retirement egg for it too. They didn't want to break up their little team, guess they had a McDowell family file they needed to put closure to. I eventually gave them the tape, just a week back, after the funds were in my account of course. Two days back I get the ex-CIA guy's wife calling me having a fuckin' conniption on the phone. She says her husband's missing. It was his eighty-fourth birthday. Well, ya don't have to be a rocket scientist. He's down a mine shaft out in the desert, won't be finding *him* in a hurry." He slid a worried look at Sam. "I figured they'd be paying me a visit, so fuckin' predictable."

"You knew they'd come for you."

"Of course I knew. They sent their foursome to my place yesterday. But I was ready for 'em Sam. Two at the rear door, two out front. They came in two at a time, easy pickings, too easy."

He's lost it, Sam thought. His mind shifted to the nine-millimeter sitting in the drawer, wondering if McDowell knew about the gun.

"That's a hell of a confession. Now I know what a priest feels like."

"Speaking of priests, where are the guys at in China?"

Sam's eyes dropped to the desktop, thinking fast. He quickly checked the time, just after seven thirty, knew the door would soon be opening.

"Don't do it," McDowell snarled. "Move away from the fuckin' drawer."

Sam spun about, scrambled under the desk, reaching up for the drawer handle. In that moment, in the panic, he recalled his safety procedure. *The gun's not loaded. The clip, have gotta get the clip.*

Better late than never, his two men arrived, heard the commotion and burst through the door, each dropping behind a sofa as one shouted, "Give it up Adam! We know about the Russians, we know you were set up."

McDowell dropped into a shooting position, then seeing Sam fumbling about for the clip, rolled to the desk, reached up, slamming the drawer shut on Sam's fingers.

Sam screeched, "What the hell are they talking about, set up?"

"You disappoint me, if only you weren't so tied up in your fuckin' Chinese mission. Those guys who supposedly hit me in the office, Grigori and Aleksei, they were on the take. Moscow didn't want me dead; they wanted Beijing to think I was dead. I had to go along with it."

He's rambling, Sam thought, *totally irrational.*

McDowell looked about with crazed eyes. "They found I was selling the same playbook to each team. Well, almost the same." He paused for a long fifteen seconds. "The blow to my head, it was hard to take but served its purpose, served your purpose too. Wang was easy to fool; I was fooling him for you and me both. Seeing as how I'm gonna finish you right here, it doesn't matter much if you know a bit more."

Their eye contact remained locked, as Sam groaned at the delayed pain from the slammed drawer, his knuckles screaming, maybe a broken finger or two. McDowell moved quickly, spun about, and dropped into a firing position. He reeled off three shoots at the sofa, heard a groan, hit one of the agents, shouted, "Motherfucker!" and then dropped back and held the Glock at Sam's head.

"I can't believe this is happening!" Sam hollered. "There's gotta be a way to help you."

"There you go, thinking about yourself again. What do you want, Sam, rights to the story? You wanna sell it to the highest bidder? It's too late to help me, the fuckin' CIA! Government mafia is what they are, home grown fuckin' Gestapo. I was just like you when they recruited me, Sam. But they . . ."

The man behind the sofa called aloud, "Give it up, Adam! There're more guys on their way up. You can't get out!"

"What the fuck? What are you gonna do, throw me out the fuckin' window like you did Olson?"

His mind chewed on itself as the sound of a two-way crackled and the man behind the sofa shouted, "Go! Go! Go!" and Sam stood with both hands waving and he was shouting, "Noooo!" and the two agents dived through the splintered opening and they were firing a volley, a series of bap, bap, bap and bap, bap. McDowell danced like a puppet on invisible strings, his body jerking, gyrating, as each slug bounced him backwards, shunting him toward the window. Two nine millimeter slugs speared through him and rocketed on through the double paned glass, McDowell stumbling backward, eyes glazed, his Glock landing on the carpet by Sam's feet, the whole scene playing out as though in super-slow motion as McDowell's backward stumbling motion continued, another rally of shots plucking at his coat.

"What the fuck are you people doing?" Sam shouted. "Stop firing!"

The window blew out, sucking cordite from the room and showering glass onto the pavement several stories below. When the mayhem ceased, Adam McDowell was gone and the floor of the room was covered in glass.

Glittering.

Shards.

Silence.

CHAPTER 51

THE OFFICER GAVE AN informal salute, unnecessary of course, but none the less appreciated by Sam. "All systems go," he snapped. "Please follow me."

He accompanied the snappy young man who ushered him to a large conference room where an ominous looking guard stood to one side of double doors. The guard snapped to attention, eyes sideways, almost fearful as he peripherally observed the president and Admiral Bates moving toward him from farther along the passageway. The officer returned the salute, opened one door, and stepped aside as the president led the way through.

Each took up a position at an oval carved ebony table.

"Sam," the president said in a somber mood. "We're deeply saddened by the incident with McDowell, and, eh, I don't wanna appear callous, but we're quite concerned about the amount of information he might've passed on to Beijing and Moscow. We know McDowell and Sellers crossed paths some years back, at the CIA. We uncovered his liaison with the former KGB Agent, guy named Sergeievich Dostoevsky. We've good reason to suspect they had quite a sideline goin', clandestine sales to Moscow and Beijing. This Sergei character's quite an operator. The CIA's considerin' acquirin' his services."

Sam half raised a hand.

"Go ahead, Sam."

"Sir, it's been a really bad week and there's nothing I can do to change what's happened and I don't believe it's gonna get any better." All in one breath. "No doubt there'll be an inquiry, but I'll face that when it happens."

"You've got that right, there's gonna be an inquiry. Your position with the Division might be in jeopardy. We can't cover for you, Sam."

Silence.

"Mr. President, I'll face the music when the time comes, but right now I'm concerned for my guys. Have you had word on Blake and the team?"

The president nodded at Bates, who said, "Our satellite picked up a plane flying out of Datong; we assume it's our man, Harry Ching. He's taken your team and flown toward Burma."

"I assume that's good news, Mr. President?"

"Might be," the president said. "Plane went down intact I'm told. We picked it up in a remote location in Myanmar, saw some chutes. One of our satellites sensed people movin' around. It picked up a vehicle arrivin' at the site. Dunno if the guys boarded it voluntarily or by force. Could be a military truck, we've no way of tellin'. The junta is hostile toward us, so if they've got our guys they could use them as a bargainin' tool for us liftin' sanctions. If it comes to that, Sam, I'm gonna have to deny knowledge. God knows what those fuckers'll do from there. The general runnin' the military junta is in bed with the Chinese, so I gotta think if I don't go their way with the sanctions, they'll take the easy route, they'll just hand our guys back over the border."

"With the travel drive, I'd suspect?"

"Yeah Sam, unless the Burmese are into souvenir collectin', can't imagine the junta's men re-packin' backpacks. They'll just knock our guys about and kick their asses back to Beijing."

"Any idea where the truck took them?"

Steve Bates spread a map on the table and pointed to a location northeast of Mandalay. "We have them somewhere near the town of Lashio, at the end of the Burma Road, around three hundred miles south of the Chinese border. They could be en route to Mandalay. That's good in my opinion. They could have hooked up with Karen freedom fighters. If Karen were driving the truck, that's as good as our guys having a marine team linking up with them. They hate the junta militia, they'll support our team all the way."

"Admiral," Sam queried. "Did the exchange of statues go through? I mean, did Wang get to make the switch before the plane left Datong?"

"We know there was a skirmish before our guys reached Datong. Our satellite tracked some tank movements in that area, there was a bunch of activity. Several vehicles converged on the scene, and then quickly left. We know that two vehicles went directly to a hospital in Beijing. We also know a small group left the scene before the vehicles arrived; they then traveled by truck to Datong. The satellite was able to clearly follow their movement. If Wang was at the scene, I'm hopeful Slade somehow allowed the changeover of the statues to take place. But I can't know for sure, not yet, sir. There seemed to be some unexplained movement or what appeared to be collateral damage . . . bodies, but we're not sure. It could have something to do with Wang, hard to say. McDowell could have leaked information through."

Ridkin gave a cursory wave, as though apologizing for his right-hand man's traitorous behavior.

Steve Bates made a similar gesture. "We're trying to reach Yidui, but we've not been able to contact him to this point. We'll keep trying. If Beijing doesn't upload Black Sabbath, our guys will need to re-think its entire post 2020 space architecture."

Sam avoided the Yidui reference, his eyes remaining focused on the tip of a cigarette he repeatedly tapped on the rim of the ashtray. "Mr. President, may I?"

"Sure Sam, go ahead."

"Do we have a possible pick up planned for Mandalay?"

"We're trying to get help into Mandalay," Bates replied. "But the Burmese junta recently carried out ethnic cleansing in a few of the outlying villages. They slaughtered two hundred inhabitants, kids as well. Not the time to organize anything that could be misconstrued by the junta as retaliation."

"Mr. President, isn't there anything we can do to help these people?" Sam asked, clearly upset at Bates.

"We sent Connie over there to lodge our objection to the situation regardin' Aung San Suu Kyi. It apparently fell on deaf ears. The first lady put in her buck's worth too. But that fuckin' junta plays by its own rules, knows it has Beijing, North Korea, and Russia standin' on the sidelines. And they're all encouragin' the junta to keep givin' us the bird. If we can get Suu Kyi's National League into office, Myanmar might get back to some normality." He shook his head. "Sam, this is Myanmar's fuckin' holocaust. It's unbelievable that acts of atrocity like these are goin' on as we speak, but even more unbelievable that we haven't been able to stop 'em."

Bates walked around the table, and the president sensed his discomfort. "Spill it, Steve. What's on your mind? We need to know. I'd rather discuss it here in front of Sam. If it doesn't sound too good, I'll know not to bring it up at an official fuckin' meetin'."

"Mr. President, the Chinese are moving forward aggressively with their Operation Compass satellite navigation system. They're doing to our GPS 3 and Europe's Galileo systems exactly what the French leadership tried to do to our system two years back. Under France's guidance, Europe originally planned to neutralize the military advantage of our system by putting their own signal on a frequency so close to our M-code that any attempt we made to jam their signal would interfere with our own system's operation. It was a typical French underhanded move aimed at giving them a de facto veto over our military operations." Bates made a shrugging gesture. "The rest of Europe forced France into acquiescence by refusing to follow them into a possible conflict with us. But the Chinese, Mr. President, well they're not a part of anything like the ESA or the EU. Beijing's not subject to any of the pressures that led the French to *reconsider*. Europe isn't about to figure out the implications of this for their system for quite some time, but it's obvious that China's made good use of its role in Galileo. Beijing's gained experience as well as know-how in military satellite navigation technology from Europe. Those lessons won't be wasted by Beijing; they'll definitely use them to advantage."

"Steve, is Europe sharin' their offensive technology with China?"

"No sir. Europe said it would only share the non-offensive parts of their technology with the Chinese, seeing as how Europe had figured out how to separate the military technology from the civil uses; a huge mistake by the Europeans."

Sam nodded to Bates, cleared his throat before asking the one question he least wanted to ask. "Admiral, I know in the past, Beijing used their rather primitive Beidou navigation network with limited military application. With that in mind, how much farther advanced is the Compass system?"

"Mr. Ridkin, Mr. President, as primitive as Beidou is, it's already provided Beijing with a substantial number of ICBMs, and they're all aimed at U.S. targets. Thanks to the technology they've collected from Europe, they're now in a position to further expand their own military satellite navigation system far beyond ours. In fact, Japan, India and Australia can thank the EU and the ESA for the increased Chinese satellite threat to their regions. Beijing's Compass system will be operational much sooner if we're unable to get the corrupted flash drive back into their computer. We need to set their program back a few years so we've time to implement our technology, to prevent Beijing's Compass system from being capable of striking U.S. military facilities. Our newer GPS satellites will need to feature far more advanced technology, enabling the system to overcome any attempts by Beijing or any enemy to interfere. Not only should this technology include pseudo-random burst transmissions and frequency hopping, we should also further develop space to earth laser communications. I believe our guys are already working on navigation information being embedded into regular military communications."

The president held up a hand. "Whoa there, I get the picture, sounds like our next battle will be with Darth Vader," and he chuckled, a futile attempt to introduce lightheartedness into the somber mood in the room.

"Mr. President, if I may sir," Bates said. "At times, I feel the magnitude of the situation isn't being passed on to you by your more eh, official people." He leaned on the words *official people*, at the same time making a feeble effort to carry an apologetic expression. "Sir, the gate is closing. It's time to grab the cow by the tail and yank it back into the corral." He paused momentarily, reached for a glass, took a quick gulp of water, running his eyes across the faces. No one in the room took up the opportunity to speak. Bates continued, "The best move for us would be to proceed directly from the GPS 3 to a GPS 4 system. We need to move on to a system with the highest achievable signal strength, with more applications and far greater durability. This will not only keep us ahead in satellite and space based navigation technology, it also prevents both China and Europe from even coming close to matching our timing, navigation, and positioning capability. We need to become more realistic; we need to look beyond the moon. Outer space is the new frontier Mr. President. The Chinese know this and are working feverishly at getting their satellites out there ahead of ours. Our earth-based installations are sitting ducks. The days of operating vulnerable earth-based installations that are so easily targeted will go the way of the dodo."

"Admiral," Sam said, "surely the U.S. has contingencies in the event of an attack on our satellite system?"

"Our intelligence," Bates said, "has informed us the Chinese are already preparing to place super satellites in outer space, far surpassing orbital reserves. Their Operation Compass will implement this move. In space warfare, when satellites are destroyed, it's plain common sense to have reserves in place. We're going to have to start planning to hide reserve satellites in outer space, outside of the earth-moon system. Re-establishing a satellite system following an attack would be far speedier when spare satellites are orbiting and can be immediately shifted to a position where they can continue on with the task of the destroyed unit. This, therefore, would be our contingency."

The president stood and stretched his legs, paced around the room to the sound of silence. He turned and postulated with one finger directed at Sam. "So, all of this can be weighted heavily our way if your team successfully gets the flash drive back home and Beijing gets their missin' unit back, the one carryin' Black Sabbath." He nodded. "Einstein was on the button, what was it he said? Somethin' like, *it's appallingly obvious when our technology exceeds our humanity.*"

"Mr. President, as Drew Blake would say in a word, if he were here, *abso-fuckin'-lutely.*"

CHAPTER 52

THEY RESTED THROUGH THE day, and as evening approached, the sound of shouting stirred them both from their light sleep. Chakra stormed into the hut, placing a hand near Bellinger's mouth, shaking her by the shoulder, and pointing toward two trucks a few hundred meters from the village. "Soldier come," he whispered in broken English. "You go quickly. I speak with them. Maybe they just pass through."

Blake tried to stand on the ankle, but the pain was bad and he toppled onto Bellinger's arm. She balanced him, then quickly reached for the Springfield XD 357. Their backpacks had gone off with the rest of the group, which made for light traveling. Chakra pointed to a rear door, and Blake, hobbling along with Bell's help, stumbled through the door and sought refuge in nearby undergrowth just moments before two trucks came to an abrupt halt nearby and a group of soldiers scampered from beneath canopies. There was a great deal of shouting and the officer doing the shouting had two of his men subdue Chakra, dragging him off to a nearby tree.

"He is wearing a very nice cross," one man said, eyeing the gold cross. " I can take it, Sergeant Quiang?"

"Leave it. Secure him to the tree," Quiang said in a superior, gruff tone.

Blake grabbed hold of Bellinger's arm, pulling her back into the lower foliage. "The fuckers've got Chakra, don't have a good feelin' about this, I ain't about to let him die." They each attached sound suppressors, crawled closer to the edge of the clearing, and Blake said, "I can't move. You go on over the other side of the trucks," and he tipped his head toward the second truck, the nearest of the two. "There's enough cover for you to make it. We'll get 'em in the crossfire. I count seven of 'em; you take the three nearest you, I'll handle the others. Sync our watches." He squinted at his watch, looked at Bell's. "Mine says ten after five, at twelve after, we open up," and he counted down, "three, two, one, set."

"Got it."

Chakra wept as Quiang unbuttoned his shirt, reached for the gold crucifix, and tore it from the crying man's neck. The sergeant looked down at the cross, bit into it and smiled through clenched teeth at the crying man, slid the cross into his pocket, then twisted the crying man's arm from behind his back, and spotted the gold wedding band.

Another wide smile.

More gold.

The ring was snug, wouldn't budge. Quiang slid a long blade from his boot, placed the point of the blade at the base of Chakra's finger and pressed down.

Bell, who had quickly positioned herself at the rear of the nearest truck, let loose with a volley of shots, dropping the three men nearest the larger vehicle. Quiang reeled about, couldn't see where the shots were coming from. He dropped the blade and dived for cover as five more shots ripped through the two men to his right. The remaining soldier dashed toward the truck, not realizing Bellinger had a position behind the vehicle. She slid the Springfield into the rear of her belt, waited until the running soldier was close, closer, right there, was on top of her, and she stiff-armed the running man at throat level.

He fell to the ground, tried swiveling about in the

mud, turning, groping, went for his M16, and swung it toward Bell. She kicked out and teeth shattered in his mouth as his head swung away and blood splattered into the muddy water that had pooled about him and, and, and . . .

And it happened at warp speed.

Bellinger pulled the blade from her boot and in one fast move plunged it into the man's neck, held it there, stared down into his eyes, ripped the blade upward and spat the words, "For Chakra's family."

Blake had remained hidden during Bell's 'call to action.' He saw her stiff arm, saw her drop the runner. *Gotta love a woman who puts out the trash*, he thought, amazed at Bellinger's rapid reaction. He'd kept the Sig trained on the man lying at Bell's feet, *in case she ain't as sharp as she should be*, he thought sarcastically. His attention swung back to the man with Chakra's cross, the sergeant, on Quiang as he began a frenzied dash away from the scene, running, running, thrashing, a panicked sprint to place distance between him and the two shooters.

He's movin' too fast!" Blake shouted. "I can't chase after him."

Bellinger raced to Chakra, slipped the bloodied blade under his bindings, cutting him free and he slid to his knees as she tried to comfort him.

"Da blu, da blu," he repeated through a flock of tears, his face on Bell's shoulder.

"It's okay, it's okay."

But the tears were there and his emotions let them flow for several long minutes.

Bell could hear Blake messing with the clip of his Sig. She patted Chakra on the head a few comforting times, said, "Stay here," and raced across the narrow mud roadway to where Blake was kneeling. "What do we do?" she said pointing in the direction Quiang had run. "He's sure to raise the alarm."

Blake kept a sharp eye on the thicket; nodding at Chakra who was sitting by the tree, quietly sobbing. "Can't leave him here, they'll be back; they'll butcher anyone they find in the village."

"How about the truck?" Bell said, squinting toward the truck. "We can put some distance between us and them. How's the ankle feeling?"

"Strange that you should ask, amazin' how a few hours can make a difference. Maybe it's that cream."

But he grimaced and she squatted alongside, half sitting on the running board of the truck, placing a hand on the ankle and applying a little pressure as he balked and she asked, "You think you can handle a few miles in the truck?"

"Have to do it; stayin' here's a moot point."

She moved back to Chakra, raised him to his feet and motioned at the truck. "We go in truck, okay?" she said, nodding. He understood and nodded back, pointing in a southerly direction, similar to that taken hours earlier by the rest of their party.

"I'm sorry you have to travel on that ankle, but you know what they say, the best laid plans of mice and . . ."

"Fuck what they say," Blake said, waving her off. "Get me into the truck, and eh, I'm really impressed how you handled that guy. Guess that's another thing Hunter taught you, huh?"

She sensed a touch of macho competitiveness in his tone. "Gard taught me lots of things," she said, grinning as she avoided Blake's searching gaze.

"Yeah, I'll bet he did. Just get me into the fuckin' truck."

*****

Chakra drove ten kilometers before the truck began coughing. He checked the temperature gauge, realized the

545

motor was at seizure stage, pointed to the dashboard, and pulled off the road into a thick overhang of foliage. Vines draped either side of the truck making it a tight squeeze as they struggled to open the doors. Chakra moved to the hood, stood back shaking his head in dismay at the spread of holes ventilating the radiator. "Truck dead," he said to Bell as he pointed to the damage.

Blake grinned at the choice of words. "Truck not dead, truck fucked," he grunted, looking around at the dense rain forest. "So where do we go from here?" and he answered his own question. "Only way out is to walk. Oh, sweet Jesus!"

Chakra reached into the rear, dug about, found three flashlights and a large machete, passed the machete to Bell. He reached back in, dug a little more, grabbing another for himself. The heavy growth was mostly thick healthy vines draped from low hanging branches, and Chakra began cutting a narrow passageway into the fringe of the green chasm. Their progress through the thicket was at a snail's pace.

"How's the ankle?" Bell asked, taking a break from her hacking duty.

Blake placed a hand on her shoulder, took over the machete, tried not to show the pain. "It's my ankle, not my arm. I can hack away for a while."

Three hours of hacking brought them to a small river, fast flowing, muddy. The flashlights had exhausted most of their battery power, and the weak beam made it difficult to see the opposite bank. To conserve what little battery life remained, they shut two of the lights down, making slow progress with the use of a single unit. Wading downstream, Blake thought how clever it was of Chakra to take their trail well away from their point of entry. *Can't be too cautious* he thought. *If the soldiers are followin' our machete trail, the river'll stop 'em dead.*

Chakra found a shallow crossing, and the three made their way to the far bank.

"I've a feelin' he knows his way around these parts," Blake said. "Wha'dya think?"

"One can only hope, huh?" Bell said, swatting hopelessly at the cloud of mosquitoes swarming around them, the jungle heat now quite unbearable.

Chakra stopped, gave a half-smile and pointed to a secluded clearing on the river's edge. "Must rest now," he said, "too hot to travel."

Blake gingerly lowered himself under a grove of monstrous leaves; leaves that anyone would be forgiven for believing could only have come directly from the set of Jurassic Park. He filled the air with more than his usual eloquent outbursts of *'fuck this'*, and *'fuckin' mosquitoes.'* In fact, Drew Blake spent the next few minutes in self-talk, denigrating everything from Sam Ridkin, to Carson Dallas, to Jesus Christ Himself. When he was done, when he'd exhausted his list of profanities, he pulled a small Swiss Army knife and hacked away at his heavy trouser. Chakra raised his eyebrows and gave a knowing grin, shaking his head in disapproval. Blake ignored him, and when he was done, passed the knife to Bell and said, "Here, cut those things down, it'll be cooler."

When Bell had removed the lower portion of her trouser legs, Blake cut off both of his shirt sleeves above the elbows, and Chakra continued shaking his head in abject disapproval. Three hours later they both appreciated his disapproval of the tailoring alterations, their accessible skin absolutely delighting the mosquito population, together with the leeches that were now quite attached to them. By midnight the temperature had dropped appreciably, a slow drizzle adding further to their discomfort. They huddled under the cover of a large rhododendron as Chakra tried to light a freshly rolled cigarette. It remained unlit, soggy, eventually drooping onto his chin. He carefully removed its remains, placed it into his military-style vest pocket, and smiled sadly at Blake.

They huddled in silence, aware of the sounds of the jungle now magnified by the darkness, as distant rumblings of thunder accompanied fluorescent flashes and Bellinger huddled a little closer to Blake. He squinted, raised his eyes toward the illuminated treetops, and grinned, squeezing her in closer, thanking the weather Gods. She looked about and frowned, pulled her raised collar around her ears, trying to stay dry as she fought off wave after wave of mosquitoes. Water ran from the rhododendron as Blake wiped her face with a remnant of his shirt sleeve. With each flash, each accompanying rumbling, she snuggled a little closer into his chest, and he hugged a little tighter, and thanked the weather Gods. Sensing a window of opportunity, he asked, "So, I hear you and Hunter were an item once, huh?" he said with a disconcerted look.

She cocked her head to one side.

Stared at him.

"Why are you bringing that up, is it my alluring looks, the cutaway fashion?" She dropped her eyes to her forearms. "Is it all this mosquito ravished skin?"

Blake liked her smile, her perfect teeth, and most of all, those lips. Oh, and of course, her sense of humor. He grinned and replied, "Nah, ain't any of those things, more like a dyin' man's last wish."

"Well, you do know how to dash a girl's hopes, which, may I add, were up there for just a moment, but only just hanging by a thread. Ah well, one can only dream."

"Ain't all that's up," Blake mumbled.

The discussion was abruptly stopped by a rumbling sound. "What the fuck was that?" Blake snapped, turning to Chakra.

"That tiger, there are many tigers in jungle, many tigers."

Bellinger reached for the Springfield, placing it on

her lap.

"But it is not a problem," Chakra said smiling at Bell. "Tigers scared; tigers not eat woman."

"That's really fuckin' reassurin'," Blake said. "So you stay awake while we catch some sleep, yes?"

Twenty-five minutes later the rain had intensified and the temperature of the cool night air plummeted. Blake grinned peering through the canopy. *Feels kind of good,* he thought. But what he appreciated most about the inclement conditions was Patrice Bellinger wrapped more tightly around him.

"Fuckin' rain, wish it'd stop," he said to her quietly, not meaning a word of it.

"Me too, I'm cold."

A loud thunderclap caused her to flinch, made her increase her hold around his chest. He flashed a momentary glance at the clouds, screwing his face as the storm intensified overhead. *Excellent,* he thought, but said in a concerned voice, "Fuckin' weather. Don't look good. You try to get some sleep. I'm gonna look for anythin' that'll burn. Get us a fire goin'."

Bell and Chakra managed a light sleep in spite of the rain, the cold, and her entertaining the thought of passing through some large cat's intestinal system. Blake was almost done with gathering small branches and damp leaves. *Might burn,* he thought. *Better than nothin'.* Then he heard static.

"Bell? That you?"

Nothing

Static

"Yeah, it's me, there's someone out there, and they're getting nearer, and nearer," Bell's voice garbled. "And I can hear screams, and their coming from someplace not too far from us. There is screaming and . . ."

Blake whispered into his transmitter, "Bell, stay down, stay quiet. I'm comin' back."

"Drew, I'm scared."

Static

"Drew?"

Static

"Drew! Whatever it is, it's thrashing at the branches, the leaves. Drew?"

A voice came through.

Faint.

Fading.

More static

"Bell, lay flat. Stop speaking. I'm not far off. Be there soon."

"Kay."

"Bell?"

"Yes, I said okay."

"Oh Drew! Drew, it's right on top of me. Drew . . ."

She sprang to her feet, legs apart.

A shooter's pose.

She faced the sound of the runners, her Springfield fully extended. Three young men broke through the thick reeds, falling exhausted in front of Bellinger, her Springfield leveled squarely at the nearest man's torso.

"What the fuck's goin' on?" Blake called aloud as he stumbled into Chakra, his Sig outstretched in a firing position.

"Stop, stop, do not shoot," Chakra pleaded. "These men are good, these are Karen villagers."

Blake lowered the weapon. "Who are they runnin' from?"

"I speak English," the younger man said as he cautiously raised himself onto one knee.

"This kid," Bellinger said looking closely at his face, "he can't be more than sixteen."

The youngest of the three, still gasping for breath, held up a hand, shook his head, his eyes remaining respectfully downward. "My name is Kaloo."

"Okay, okay, relax. We ain't gonna hurt you," Blake said. "What's happenin' with you guys?"

"Soldiers, maybe one hundred, maybe two, they attack village, burn all, burn clinic and mission school. They capture villagers. Some escape in the jungle, they hiding."

"Are soldiers following you now?" Bell asked, staring off into the darkness.

"I think not. We try to reach Karen village, beyond river."

"How far's the village?" Blake asked.

"I not sure; think three, four hour toward hills."

Kaloo raised a bleeding arm, pointing in a southerly direction.

"Whatever," Blake grunted in dismay. "Four hours? Great! Let's get these guys cleaned up and get goin'. It's almost sun up."

One of the other two spoke to Kaloo, his voice nervous, a trembling gibberish. The tone was one of concern at the direction Kaloo had pointed.

"What's he sayin'?" Blake asked.

"He says he knows the jungle very well, says soldier hide fire in ground."

Blake gave Chakra an inquisitive expression, cocked an eyebrow and said, "Fire in ground - what's he talkin' about?"

Chakra questioned Kaloo, then relaying the conversation, said, "He says fire, but he means land mines. Many buried in jungle, best we travel in river. No land mines in water."

"Just great," Blake grumbled to Bellinger. "Back to the fuckin' leeches."

More chattering between Kaloo and his two friends, and Chakra shifted his eyes to Blake. "He says soldiers take eight hundred Karen people, force them carry many things used to attack villages. Those who say no . . . they shot. They kill fifteen women, eight children, made men bury them by road."

"This is true," Kaloo said. "I have seen with my eyes." He raised his hand to his face. "I see soldiers beat, kill our people because they will not carry supplies. Many thousands run from Burma."

Two hours and twenty minutes later, the sound of women's voices drifted from the opposite bank. Kaloo stopped, placed a finger over his mouth, turned to the group and whispered, "I think Karen villagers hide near here. You wait, I come back." He motioned for them to stay back, moved through the monstrous rhododendron leaves, then disappeared for several minutes. He reappeared to the delight of Bellinger and Blake, calling from across the water, "It safe, they are Karen, they friends. Come, come."

The Karen were gathered in a makeshift commune, at least one hundred and fifty displaced villagers. Some had set up shelters using bamboo and striped shade cloth. *Could double as a Sunday bazaar,* Bell thought, *perhaps a flea market.*

Even though the women and children greeted them with smiles, their faces carried the scars of fear. They were on the brink of exhaustion, many of the women clutching crying babies, all grossly undernourished, huddling about, their food supply exhausted or abandoned in their hasty escape from the junta's men. Kaloo spoke with some of the refugees, then returned to Blake, his eyes down as tears ran freely. He turned and pointed back at a young mother lying beside a small girl, stroking her hair, humming to the child. And the child was lifeless.

Kaloo kneeled by Bell. "Little girl, she has been dead for three days. Woman will not let men bury body."

Tears flocked down Bell's cheeks, heart-broken as she watched the crying children. She saw the look of bewilderment in their eyes, the hopelessness on the faces of the young mothers. Many of the women were beyond the breaking point, and the children sensed this, and they cried all the more. Some of the men had gathered firewood, mostly green, all wet. Groups huddled around small burning piles, no more than dwindling embers. Bellinger and Blake joined them, hands lowered over the faint glow, imagining it was warming, hoping they were drying off. But there was little warmth.

Just psychological comfort.

Blake gave a reassuring smile to those curiously nodding to him and Bellinger. If nothing else, he felt their presence had given the people a level of encouragement. One woman chatted at length with Chakra, and every minute or so she would begin to cry. Chakra slipped a glance to Bellinger, shook his head, lowering his eyes as he poked at the embers. Every few minutes new tears escaped his eyes, but he continued poking the embers, let the tears flow, hoping no one noticed. She told stories of rape, of murder, and other atrocities committed by the Burmese Army, describing how she'd fled with only the possessions on her back, spoke of how the army had blocked off their regular roads, forcing the Karen to revert to jungle travel to reach their farms.

One woman broke into tears as she nursed her baby. She told of how the Burmese soldiers had hunted her and her family through the jungle. She was unable to continue, the atrocities committed by the soldiers on her and her daughters had reduced her to a shell. An older man sat by Kaloo. He knew the boy, patted him several times on the back as he spoke. He had reasonable English skills and struck up a conversation with Bellinger.

"It is good to see you," the old man said. "Are you English?"

"American," she replied.

"American people, they are very good. To be like

America is good for Burma. We pray for democracy, have dreams for our country," and he began shaking Bellinger's hand as though he were pumping water.

She grinned broadly, more at his pumping handshake than his verbiage. "I hope your dreams will come true."

When she managed to free her hand from his grip, she asked about his experience with the Burmese soldiers.

"I worked at a Mission in Toungoo District," he replied. "We give medicine and teeth care. We teach Karen and English language to children, have Bibles and toys. The people of Burma live in hope that our leader, Aung San Suu Kyi, will be set free so we can live in a democracy. Burma Army soldiers forced many villagers from our district. Many killed by mines, many lose legs, arms. The soldiers, they attacked the mission, bury many land mines around mission so we cannot return to our homes."

"Where'd they get the land mines?" Blake asked.

Before an answer could be given, a man on the perimeter shouted a warning. In the next moment a spray of gunfire dropped him as four Burmese militia burst through the trees, taking aim at the gathering. Blake and Bellinger reeled about and in the millisecond it took for the soldiers to realize they'd stumbled into more than a group of helpless refugees, all four were dropped by a volley of shots from Blake and Bell. Bellinger pumped two more shots from the Springfield into one of the soldiers. *He's surely dead this time*, Blake thought, momentarily stunned by Bellinger's fast and ruthless response.

They swung their weapons toward the jungle, listened, heard nothing. The four had come alone. The villagers began running toward Bellinger and Blake, shouting, "Da blu! Da blu!"

"They are thanking you," Kaloo said smiling, as four of the Karen men dragged the soldiers into a thicket and quickly hid their valuable weapons under blankets in the shelters. "Guns very good, we need guns," he said, his smile now wider.

One young girl latched onto Bellinger's hand. Another came up and asked if she wanted a warm drink, nodding at a pan hanging over one of the fires. An elderly woman sat by Bell, offering her a food platter. She'd been rehearsing a few words of English and was excited at the opportunity to use them. She smiled, said, "Thank you, thank you."

Bellinger pulled a blanket over her legs, looked at Blake with tear filled eyes. She whispered, "Why?" Her voice was choked, strained. "How can we just walk away from this? How can we possibly go home like none of this happened?"

Blake avoided her gaze, said nothing, let the question hang there.

After an uncomfortable silence, he tipped his head toward her. "You know what this is, Bell?"

Her eyes stayed down. She replied, "Genocide."

"Nah. Evolution is what it is, writin' history. This is their American Revolution, their Civil War, their War of Independence." He said it with disguised inadequacy. "Only way we'll be dragged into this mess is if China or Russia starts sendin' in troops, or if the regime here develops a nuclear weapon. Then, just maybe, our guys might be sent in. But that's it. Other than that, Uncle Sam ain't gettin' involved. You see Bell, these people, they ain't ever gonna give up. We can't do much to help 'em right now, but their determination isn't driven by greed or hate, it's in their blood. This is their homeland, their Burma."

That evening, Bell again snuggled close to Blake. He liked it, gave serious thought to making a move, but the need of a good hot shower had him place the advance on hold.

"What?" she whispered, sensing his eyes. "What are you thinking?" She snuggled closer, her eyes fixed on his. He laid back, fingers interlocked behind his head, his mind drifting as he shifted his attention to the stars barely visible between treetops. *I could kiss her,* he thought. *We could . . .*

But he didn't. He looked on either side, at the spread of sleeping refugees huddled about. There were no barriers, not physical nor mental. They were all equal in each other's eyes, and in the eyes of their God. The following morning, Bellinger and Blake ate a meager breakfast, mostly roots of some kind or other that were boiled in a large pot.

"I've eaten worse with Dal," Blake said quietly to Bellinger, "near Mount Whitney, when we were learnin' Latin." He paused, looked around at the huddled villagers. "Fat fuckin' good that's gonna do us now."

She gave a smile, and Blake caught the smile. He took it in, realizing it carried a certain element of intimacy, different to previous smiles.

Hmm, I like that, he thought

As they headed off in a southerly direction, Blake again felt remorse for the people he'd grown to admire, felt sorrow as they placed physical and emotional distance between themselves and the villagers, daring not to look back; knowing too well it would be that final farewell wave that would truly test his emotions.

CHAPTER 53

THE JUNGLE GAVE NO quarters, no thanks for their kindness, treated all with equal contempt. Chakra and Kaloo swung the machetes like men possessed, with Blake and Bellinger following close behind.

Blake called to Kaloo, "What about the land mines?"

"Not where jungle is thick . . . they are only where pathways go."

"Makes sense," Blake said. "Don't make for fast travel, but it makes sense."

Two hours later Kaloo turned, signaling for those following to step back. "Do not move," he said with a deathly expression, slowly pointing to his foot. "I am on mine."

Chakra had Blake and Bell slowly, carefully, back away, had them retracing their tracks.

"What's he going to do?" Bellinger called to Chakra as he spoke softly to a trembling Kaloo.

"We cannot help him," Chakra said with a definite head shake. "Mine will go . . . he is dead for certain."

Kaloo looked at a nearby branch and called to Chakra.

"What did he say?" Blake asked.

"He says he will leap to branch, get away from mine."

"No chance," Blake said, and waved Bell to move back. "Back up, this is gonna get awful fuckin' messy."

Kaloo signaled for them to move further back, his concern serving to elevate Blake's level of guilt over his inability to help. Then, as Kaloo began to slightly squat, as he prepared to spring toward the branch, the mine detonated. The force of the explosion flung him ten feet through the air, his mauled body landing just feet from where Blake huddled. Dazed and barely conscious from the concussion, Blake raised himself on one knee, as amorphous shreds of brain matter and pieces of flesh rained down around him. He found himself amidst an array of blood soaked clothing, the wreckage that once was the effervescent Kaloo.

Bell hurried to Blake with total disregard for the possibility of additional mines. He staggered to his feet, somewhat disoriented, waving at her to stop running. She froze, redirected her attention to Kaloo, but there was nothing that could be done for the boy. The impact had destroyed his body, his neck broken as the blast propelled him upward into low hanging branches. Chakra studied the remains of the body for several minutes, dragged it into a thickly brushed area, and covered it with leaves and grass. It was more than Bell could take. She swiveled about and leaned into nearby brush and vomited and didn't stop until the dry retching turned to spasms and her throat burned from bile. Three minutes passed and she turned to face Blake, her face pale, eyes reddened. He gave her a comforting hug, led her away, retrieved the machete and resumed hacking duty. She moved away from him, a flock of tears running down her face, not wanting Blake to see her sadness. He moved past Chakra, caught up to Bell. "Hey, hey," he called, taking a firm hold of her shoulder. "Slow down, it ain't a fuckin' sprint. Let Chakra take the helm, he's better at spottin' mines."

She didn't turn to face him; he sensed her avoidance and placed a hand lightly on her shoulder. She turned, kept her head down, stayed that way for just a few seconds, then raised her eyes. Along with the eye contact came the trembling lower lip. She burst into tears again and Blake wrapped his arms around her as she howled uncontrollably into his chest, "Kaloo, Oh my God, Kaloo."

After a very long minute of consoling, he coaxed her along by the hand, and the journey continued.

At four o'clock, he tried to figure how much territory they'd covered. The possibility of meeting up with the rest of the team in Mandalay seemed remote at best. He'd become so pre-occupied with the carnage and plight of the Karen that he'd lost his sense of priorities. Chakra had moved fifty meters ahead, and Blake, seeing the clearing not too far off, called for Chakra to fall back, but he had already come to an abrupt halt, staring at what lay ahead.

"What's up?" Blake called to Chakra. "Land mines?"

"Yes."

"Ya think we can cross?"

He didn't need to wait for an answer. A young woman carrying a small child walked from the opposite side of the clearing, stopping in her tracks as she spotted the three strangers across from her. Her face showed momentary fear, but Chakra's smile eased her suspicion. He slowly walked to the woman with the child, stepping warily, feeling his way, moving slowly, one foot after the other, gently, feeling the soft soil, waiting for a click, for . . . he reached half way across the cleared area, realizing the soil had recently been disturbed, not for land mines . . . he was atop a mass burial site. Chakra stood frozen. He turned to Blake and Bell, and passed a hand over the area around them, holding the woman's hand amongst her barrage of tears. He pointed to Blake and Bell, nodding his head at the woman and assuring her that his two companions were not to be feared.

"She says soldier killed whole village." He waved a hand across the mounds. "These are all Karen people; soldier made men dig, then kill all. They are buried here. Soldiers burn rice field, shoot all people. She says she went to old rice field, needed to find rice, says she will not run away, this her home, she will die here."

The woman sat with the child on her lap, tears flowing as she rambled on in a shaky voice.

"She says husband buried here. Soldiers forced village men walk in front of them to find land mines. Many die so soldiers not in danger."

The explanation continued for several minutes. It appeared the villagers were being forced to act as human mine detectors, made to walk along the tracks so the soldiers could safely follow behind. She explained to Chakra how the men were made to act as human shields, forced at gunpoint to walk ahead of construction bulldozers, to clear the roadway of mines, human minesweepers. The Burmese Army shot the injured to avoid slowing the construction process.

"Let's get movin'" Blake said. "We can't stop to help, gotta get to Mandalay."

Although he said the words, his heart wasn't in it. He wanted to turn back, to fight, but the mission came first. He thought of possible ways of returning to Burma, ways he could organize a group of mercenary freedom fighters. The thinking gave him optimism, something to work toward, a pressure-relief valve.

It made it all feel just a little better.

Just a little.

I'll discuss it with Sam, off the record of course, fuckin' butchers.

They moved ahead, travelling several miles through monsoonal jungle alive with mosquitoes, spiders of every imaginable species, leaches and squawking bird life, then at four o'clock they heard the sound of running water.

"River near," Chakra called with a look of excitement. Blake and Bellinger immediately thought of bathing.

When they reached the riverbank, they were surprised

to find a bamboo bridge spanning the water, and several villagers carrying their worldly possessions made their way across the bridge. Blake took notice of how rapidly the water was flowing, not still, not like the river they'd waded through earlier.

"Hey, Chakra, where's this river go?"

"This very small river, it goes to Irrawaddy, goes to big river."

"The Irrawaddy?" Bell repeated, in a confused tone. "Doesn't it flow through Mandalay?"

"Got it," Blake said. "We need to follow this and we'll be right there, right where we need to be to meet the guys." He placed a firm hand on Chakra's shoulder. "Can we get a boat, can we go downriver?"

"There are many boats in village nearby. We go . . . find boat."

They arrived at the site of the village and came across six children, the eldest being no more than sixteen years of age. He spoke to Chakra, told him how the Burmese soldiers had burned the village and shot fifteen of the inhabitants, said both parents were among the dead. Their house lay in ruins, no more than a few posts and twisted tin roofing remaining. He said how he'd stay behind to take care of his five siblings, how he'd fight the soldiers, if only he had a weapon.

"Ask if they've a boat someplace," Blake prompted.

Chakra spoke with the boy for several minutes. "He says big house down river has a boat, if soldiers not take it."

They said farewell to the six children, and again Bellinger felt useless. Blake thought of how he'd approach Sam Ridkin when he got back to Los Angeles. How he'd ask permission to get back to Myanmar to help these people.

"Bell, if I ever complain about a hotel room, or an over-done steak, just smack me over the head, okay?"

The comment was meant to lighten her torment, but

her mood required far more than words, and Drew Blake was doing his best not to allow his emotions to spill over. They walked another mile, reached a large three-story dwelling, one of the few to survive torching.

"If there was a boat here," Blake mumbled. "It ain't here now."

Chakra moved off toward a figure hovering back in the shadows, spent a few long minutes in animated conversation.

"What do you suppose they're talking about?" Bell asked.

"Search me," Blake said. "Ain't much good stuff to talk about."

"Do you think we could get a mercenary task force together to help these people, you know, some SEALs?"

"Thought never crossed my mind," Blake replied smiling.

The man in the shadows was wary of Chakra. His leg was bleeding and he appeared to be in shock as he hobbled toward him.

"My name, Saw Mu, my family all gone," he sobbed. "Soldiers take my sons to carry for them, my daughter taken. They beat me, burn boat dock." He pointed to the smoldering remains. "My father, he very old, he stay behind, think soldier no harm old man. They find him in beetle-nut grove at edge of village . . . shoot him. Me hide, feel shame, I could give no help," and he broke into tears and began tearing at his hair.

Bell swallowed hard, wanted to hug him, to tell him help would be on its way, but knew it'd be a lie. There'd be no help, not from the UN, not from the U.S. *No reason for them to send help. No oil fields, no gas fields, no territorial advantages. These people have no collateral the West wants, so they'll be left at the mercy of the junta and its thugs.*

Blake kicked hard at the ground, his frustration now beyond boiling point. They both understood too well why these people were insignificant in the scheme of things. Bellinger looked into Blake's eyes, saw the anger, saw his sky-blue eyes more icy than she had ever seen, his jaw more angular.

"You do not have a boat?" Chakra asked, assuming the soldiers had taken it.

"My boat down river, not leave boat here, too dangerous."

"You can take us to Mingun?" Chakra asked.

"Yes, me no stay here, can do nothing to help my family. Have friends in Mandalay. Me return, bring friends, me find family, me fight."

Blake stared at the man, admiring his resolve. Bell's emotions were drained, she didn't need this as the man openly sobbed in distress and Chakra tried to comfort him. When his tears tailed off, he led the three to his boat, an old blue fishing trawler. Blake stood back with his hands forming a frame, looking through the frame, staring at the blue boat.

"African Queen, that's what she is, African fuckin' Queen." He turned and gave a half-cocked squint to Bellinger, grinned and flicked his thumb at the old boat. He cackled, "Climb aboard, Rosie."

The day had been hot and the temperature had soared above eighty degrees. Bell pondered the women bathing their children along the riverbank, wanting to join them, wanting to be with people, with children playing and splashing about as children do. *This is the Burma the tourist books promote. If it only were true.*

"You see Bell," Blake said with an arm around her shoulder, "they're resilient, they'll move on, they'll put all this shit behind 'em, make new lives."

"How can you say that?"

"It's what people do, history goes on."

She didn't buy it, just waved and smiled at the

beautiful children, and they returned her wave.

"Soap?" she called in desperation, but the women just waved and smiled.

The blue boat continued downstream with Chakra comfortable at the helm. He raised his head, gesturing ahead of the boat's bow. "We will see Mingun in maybe three hours."

"Should give the guns a check over," Blake said. "Ya know, what with the rain and stuff, gotta be ready, just in case."

He and Bell returned to the cover of the cabin, went through a clean-up on the Sig and the Springfield, emptied the spare magazine clips, wiped the cartridges dry and reloaded each clip. Chakra kept a sharp eye out for Burmese soldiers, renowned for sniping on passing boat people as the jungle closed in on them, and the river bank on either side drew nearer.

For a while, there was no sound, no movement along the shoreline. Blake nodded with an air of concern, peeking through the cabin window, Bell resting by his side, her head on his shoulder.

"Stay low in cabin," Chakra called, spotting a small fire several hundred meters ahead. "There are people on bank."

"Who are they?" Bell whispered. "What are they?"

"I am not sure," he said shaking his head, "Maybe soldiers, maybe Karen, I am not sure."

He killed the small light on the boat's bow, stopped the motor, and allowed the blue boat to drift along slowly in the current, the four passengers squatting motionless in the cabin. The night air felt like God had switched on the air conditioner as Bellinger and Blake huddled on the floor, Blake staring at the cabin ceiling, with a comforting hold of Bell's hand.

Bell muttered, "You feel that?"

"What?"

"That dull thud."

"Wha'dya mean?"

"We've stopped moving."

Chakra glanced at Saw Mu, gave him a look that made Blake shudder. "We on sand bar," he said.

"All right, and that means?" Blake asked in an *I-need-to-know-how-fuckin'-bad-this-is* kind of way.

"Boat stuck, tide low. We not move."

"We're fucked," Blake sighed. "We're stuck out here in the middle of the river like sittin' ducks."

So this is how it ends, he thought. Then Chakra and Saw Mu moved to the bow of the boat and began pushing on two long poles, trying to set the boat free. He quickly made his way to the bow, crouched low, aware of the activity by the campfire on the riverbank, the fire no more than two hundred meters from their position with the sound of voices carrying across the water to the blue boat.

"How bad is it?" he whispered to Chakra.

"Much silt in river, we not move, we stuck very bad."

"Just fuckin' lovely," Blake muttered. "Can't we push her off?"

"We try; you look at moon, big moon, make much light. Men at fire are soldiers. They will see us, you must stay down. Saw Mu will say we fishing. If lucky, they not trouble us."

Blake squinted toward the shore, didn't like the words, '*if we lucky.*' He scurried back to Bellinger, the chill in the air plummeting the temperature and leaving him wishing he'd never cut the sleeves from his shirt.

"What's happening?" she asked without raising her head from her knees.

"Can ya believe it, we're fuckin' stuck. They're tryin' to push us free, Chakra says we might get lucky. Fuckin' lucky, can ya believe that?

A few minutes passed and Bell began sobbing. She tried to keep it to herself but Blake knew, just pretended not to. He ran his fingers through his hair, stretching his neck from one side to the other, hearing the usual sounds as vertebrae clicked into place.

"Did ya hear that?"

"What was it?"

"Old war wound. The bullet's still in there. Every so often it grinds against the bone, makes that clickin' sound."

"And eh . . . which war was that, the Crimean?"

She giggled a little, just enough to bring her back, as Blake eased her head onto his shoulder, stroking her forehead and whispering, "Hang in there, missy. I know it's tough, but try not to let it get to you too much; think of it like this, when we get that flash drive back home, we'll have done our bit to fight these motherfuckers. When the Chinese lose their ability to play God with their satellites, it'll affect the regime that's takin' over Burma; they all feed off of each other. Break one link and their chain's weakened. What we're doin' here is goin' to break that link. We just need to get Slade's Operation Compass shit back home."

Chakra scurried back to the cabin, out of breath from his attempts at pushing the boat free of the sand bar.

"What's up?" Blake asked.

"Boat stuck tight, cannot push off, must wait for river to rise."

"Fuck! How long will that be?"

"Yes, fuck. Saw Mu say tide move boat in one hour, maybe two."

"Aw shit, how long'll it take us to get to Mingun?"

"It six-thirty now, if we stay here, maybe one, maybe two hour, maybe we in Mingun midnight, maybe later."

A voice called from the riverbank. Chakra listened, and then called softly to Saw Mu.

Blake whispered, "What's goin' on?"

"Soldier . . . he ask what we do in boat."

As Chakra spoke, Saw Mu called back to the shore.

"What'd he say?" Blake asked.

"He says we fishing. Say we stuck on sand."

There was silence for a few minutes. Again the voice called from the riverbank.

"What?" Blake asked.

"Soldier ask why we on river with no light on back of boat. Saw mu, he say light dead. Say we get another in Mandalay."

More shouting from the riverbank.

"What's happenin' now?" Blake whispered.

"Soldier asks why we no have light on front of boat."

*****

The moon began to rise in the night sky, appearing as a sphere, climbing and illuminating the river, giving the soldiers clear vision of Saw Mu and Chakra. Blake peered from the cabin window as Bell covered the small interior globe. They could see the campfire, could make out the silhouettes around it.

"I can see guys over there," Blake whispered, "looks like there are four, maybe five of 'em around a campfire. I smell food and it sure smells good. You feel like some take away?"

"Yeah sure, and don't forget the Pepsi," Bell said sarcastically. Blake chuckled. Bellinger remained squatting in the corner of the cabin, head resting on her knees in a fetal position, fending off the chilly night air.

"How about this," Blake said, "when we get home, I'll take ya to the best little Japanese restaurant in town. It's a little spot called . . ."

567

Three shots echoed in the still night air, two shattering the glass side window of the cabin, the third barely missing the boat and Blake heard a splash and four more shots zapped on by and Chakra scrambled into the cabin, dived across the floor, rolled once, twice, and struck his temple on a table leg. When he cleared his glazed eyes he stared at Blake, and shook his head. Bellinger saw the look in his eyes, saw him reliving memories of what he'd gone through the previous day; the shots brought it all back, his village, his family. He relived the massacre.

"Don't lose it now, man," Blake pleaded. "We need ya, what's goin' on?"

"They kill Saw Mu, he fall in river."

The splash, Blake thought moving to the doorway of the cabin, saw the soldier looking in the direction of the boat. *He could be usin' binoculars, but I doubt it. If he's just tryin' to count heads and thinks the boat's crewless, maybe we can wait until they're done eatin', lay low until the tide just floats us off.*

"That food those guys are cookin' sure smells good, wha d'ya think they're eatin'?"

Chakra looked at him as though he were crazy and didn't reply. Blake let out a long, slow breath, turned to Bell and slid back to the floor, placing an arm around her and squeezing gently. "Okay missy. Just how hungry are ya?" he whispered to her as he screwed the sound suppressor onto the threaded barrel of the Sig. "I'll be back in a few, okay? Do ya want boiled or fried rice with that order?"

Her look began as one of amazement, but turned to a lighthearted chuckle. "You're serious, aren't you?" she said. "You're really going for the food. I know anything I say won't change your mind so just be careful."

She felt bad that she was remaining in the boat, but as Blake had said, it only takes one to do the job, and it was best she remain in the boat and double the chances of someone getting back to the team in Mingun.

"I gotta do it; it'll make me feel a damn site better." He flicked a thumb over his shoulder. "Kinda even the score for those people back there."

He slid into the water, surprised to find it so warm, the cool night air having made his skin goose bumped. He swam away from the boat, the slow current moving him downstream, allowing him to avoid splashing as he breast stroked toward the shore, the Sig snuggly tucked into his belt. He realized just how low the tide was when the sand touched his feet, and he was just eighty or so meters from the blue boat, he thought, *I can wade the rest of the way.*

Staying low, moving along on his knees, with just his eyes above water level, he made his way to a heavily overgrown bank some fifty meters from the fire's glow, slipping ashore, more like an alligator than a man. He felt the side of his boot, removed his blade. It wasn't his weapon of choice, Gardner Hunter was the blade specialist, and apparently some of Hunter's skills had rubbed off on Bellinger. He had a flash of how well she'd taken out the guy at Chakra's place. Slit him open from belly to bow tie with one quick upward move. *Ah well, the lady was pissed, what can one expect? He thought, I hope she likes the food.*

He edged his way nearer the campsite as another two shots ripped through the night air as the soldier with the itchy trigger took pot shots at the helpless boat. *Sonofabitch,* Blake thought. *If he keeps that up he can hit Bell. That cabin's thin enough. He'll blow holes clean through it. She'll be clingin' to a fuckin' surfboard by sunrise.*

The shooting helped cover any sound from Blake's forward movement, the shots echoing in his ears, and in the ears of the soldiers. He peered between the undergrowth, counted four men, three around the fire, the fourth was the shooter, aiming menacingly at the blue boat stuck motionless in the middle of the river.

The second soldier stood and walked toward Blake, stopping within a few feet of his position, unzipped his trousers, and began peeing into the bushes just feet from where Blake kneeled, steam drifting by his face, and he closed his nostrils to the rancid odor of urine, staying that way until the man shook himself off, the last drops flipping onto Blake's cheek.

Go, Blake thought, *just go*. But the man stood there staring ahead, ten meters from the other three men. He turned to face the river and in that second, the soldier with the trigger finger, the fourth man, reeled off three more shots. In that ever-so-brief window of opportunity, Blake grabbed the soldier, placed one hand around his mouth, and buried the blade deep into the man's neck and lowered him to the ground.

His comrades heard nothing, their ears still ringing from the gunfire. When they did look around and called his name, there was no reply. One began walking, calling, looking about, and Blake stayed low as he drew nearer. *Unarmed, good. Left his shooter by the fire, back with the fourth man who's stirrin' our dinner.* As the soldier stepped into the bushes, Blake made a quick upward move, thrusting the blade under the man's rib cage, grunting as he bore the weight of the body as it fell limp into his arms. *Two down,* he thought, stealthily moving from his cover, carefully aiming the Sig at the shooter standing on the river bank.

The cook sat contentedly stirring the pot; tasting the food, happy with his efforts. For Blake, the aroma created flashbacks of Chinatown's best, made him even more cognizant of not messing up dinner. *Can't have him fall on the fuckin' food, can't spill it.*

He waited until the cook placed the pot on the ground, then took his shot at the man with the trigger finger. One carefully placed slug and the shooter slumped to his knees, posed as though in prayer, then fell face first onto the river's edge, a neat hole in the back of his skull. The cook hadn't turned back, had assumed the shot came from the boat. He picked up his rifle and let out a flurry of wayward automatic fire. Blake squeezed off one shot and it was all too easy. He moved forward and gazed down at the dead cook. "Just kids," he mumbled. "They're no more than fuckin' kids!"

The pot was hot and extremely difficult to handle, making the return to the boat the most difficult part of the evening. The river quickly cooled the metal as he waded to where the water was chest high, then realizing the pot could actually float, swam the remainder of the way nudging the thing along with his forehead. At times, the current tried to lay claim to their supper, but he quickly redirected it toward the boat.

"Lucy, I'm home," he called. "They eh . . . they were out of Pepsi."

CHAPTER 54

THE INCOMING TIDE RAISED the blue boat, allowing it to escape the sandbar. At twenty minutes after one in the morning, amidst a scattering of fishing boats that carried the aroma of cooked fish, cheap alcohol and what one could only hope was rice, cooked in a variety of unimaginable ways, the blue boat weighed anchor opposite the temple at the Mingun Paya, as the sound of men shouting along the riverbank caught the attention of all three.

"Anyone we know?" Blake groaned

"Don't think so," Bell said, peering through the cabin window. "They all look alike."

She placed her arms around his neck, smiled, and Blake backed off a little. She felt his body stiffen, and tilting her head she thought for a moment, and said with a smile in her voice, "Oh, what's with that - rejection? Must be my breath."

"Nah, last thing on my mind, I gotta back off a bit. When you're this close . . . you're a bit blurry."

She studied him for a few long moments, then pulling him back said, "My Lord, you *are* getting old, Mr. Blake!"

"Just a number," he said grinning. "I left my readin' glasses back at the office, but gimme a rain-check. You can test this *old* man out when we get back home."

"You've got it, and the Japanese dinner too. I'll hold you to that."

He'd been here before; in fact, one of his fondest

memories of Patrice Bellinger was a week the pair shared in Lagos. It was doomed, however, once Gardner Hunter entered the fray. From that point forward, Blake had taken a back seat. *Fuck Hunter,* he thought, and savored Bell's warm embrace.

It was nothing sexual. He and Bell were just friends, the best kind of relationship; genuine, with no reciprocal expectations from either, each knowing the other would be there when the need arose.

He allowed the mood to build, then in a timely fashion said, "So eh, tell me, missy, there ain't nothin' goin' on between you and Hunter, right?"

It was rhetorical, but she eased the embrace, placing her hands on his chest, and moving him to arm's length. "Me and Gard?" she said with an elevated voice, cocking her head and making a disapproving face. "It's not someplace I need to go right now, and besides, what we had was a lifetime ago and in any case . . ."

"Yeah, a lifetime ago."

"Hmm, do I detect sour grapes, Mr. Blake? It sounds like there's something missing in your life."

Long moments slipped by. She persisted. "Well, am I right?"

"Sweetie, the most important thing missin' in my life is a reason to wake up each morning. That single moment after I open my eyes, and there's that someone to turn to who loves me, who loves me even more and holds me even tighter through tough times . . . and through good. I don't wanna spend what's left of my fuckin' life trying to regain that moment."

The moment was cut short as a distant voice called toward them. Chakra, sitting with feet dangling in the water, replied to the approaching boat and the person aboard responded in a succinct, friendly voice. Blake scrambled to the cabin window, listening to the voice, backing out of sight as Bell sidled up to him on all fours, giving him an inquisitive look, squeezing his arm.

"Chakra," Blake said in a hushed voice. "Who is it?"

"He says he is looking for friend he is meeting here."

The pause allowed the boat to draw nearer. Blake's voice strained a little higher. "Ask him who the friend is he's meetin'."

A minute of friendly conversation dragged by as Blake sat against the wheel housing, drumming his fingers nervously until Bell, unable to take any more of his drumming, placed a firm hand on his, cracking a knuckle or two and causing Blake to go, "Ouch!"

Chakra popped his head in the cabin and broke the tension. "He says he is looking for Uncle Sam."

*****

It was five o'clock when the blue boat moored by the small ramp. Harry and Billie were waiting on shore, both dressed in tattered village clothing, allowing them to blend nicely with the locals.

"Where are Dal and the other guys?" Blake asked not directing the question at anyone in particular.

Restrained from painting too gloomy a picture, Harry gave as many details as he thought necessary. "We couldn't take a chance on them being seen," he said, "Too many stories about soldiers passing through these parts and shooting at the locals. We've been laying low waiting for you guys. Good timing, we were leaving today." He made an apologetic shrug and flipped a thumb over his shoulder. "I guess you're all hungry, we've got food."

"Chakra tells me your experiences back on the river were not good," Sung said, stepping up to Blake. "We were fortunate; our truck came along the back roads." And he turned, giving Bell a '*sorry it happened*' look.

"Let's get back to the other guys," Blake said. "They're waitin' at a house backaways."

Bell gave Chakra a farewell hug, and Blake said, "Appreciate all you've done. Keep your eyes open and your ass down. Good luck, man."

Chakra untied the blue boat. His eleven-kilometer journey to Mandalay had begun.

*****

The Mingun Paya was peaceful. A nun dressed in a robe, with traditional orange sash, and carrying a black umbrella walked toward them, appearing oblivious to the atrocities taking place outside of her immediate surroundings. They passed her by with nods all around and a warm smile from Bell. As they drew nearer the house, a familiar voice called, "How's the ankle?"

"What a fuckin' nightmare," Blake replied with a deep sigh of relief. "Good to see you guys at last!"

Harry closed the door as all seven exchanged greetings and a mish mash of rushed horror stories.

"Well," Blake said, flashing Slade a nodding smile, "ya got that statue ready for its ride home?"

"Got it," Slade replied. "Billie spoke with Yidui two days back. We were lucky to get the call, batteries got wet, had just enough life for the cell to work."

"What's the plan then?" Blake asked. "Their people in Mandalay, are they ready for us?"

"Good news, bad news," Harry said.

"Don't gimme that shit. I've had more than my share of bad fuckin' news. Where's our guy?"

Aware Blake was in no mood to be messed with, Harry threw a pleading look to Dal.

"Hang with me here," Dal said with an air of self-doubt. "Lemme finish before ya go jumpin' all over me." He had Blake's simmering attention. "How many people get a chance to be a Catholic priest?" He paused, not expecting any kind of reply. The pause heightened Blake's attention . . . along with his blood pressure. "And . . . and . . . and how many people get to be a Buddhist monk as well as a Catholic fuckin' priest?"

Blake held the stare as Dal rolled his eyes and gave it another pathetic shot. "It's like this," he said in a pleading way that drew no sympathy from Blake. "We spoke with Yidui and he wants us to head onto Bagan by ferry. Once we get there, we're meetin' up with an American guy who's a Buddhist monk." He pursed his lips, could feel the chill from Blake's eyes. "He's studyin' here . . . here in Burma. Gonna take us to a monastery, he's gonna set us up to head out overland."

"Overland! Where the fuck is *overland*?"

"Bay of Bengal . . ."

This time the roll of the eyes came from Blake. "You're jerkin' my weenie," he said shifting his glare to Harry, to Slade, back to Dal, then to Sung. After a tense pause, he let out a grumbling chuckle and made a dismissive gesture. "You fuckers, you're all good, really good, straight faces 'n all. You had me fooled for a bit."

Bell sniggered as Dal looked at Slade, whose eyes remained lowered. Harry stepped away from the group, and with his back to Blake, said, "It isn't so bad. Beats what you guys went through on Mount Whitney."

"Jesus Christ, you really *are* serious," Blake said, shaking his head, and staring at Harry's back. "That's it then?" he asked. "That's the best you guys can come up with?"

"For now," Dal said in a subdued voice. "We're gonna take the ferry to Bagan where we'll meet with the monk."

Harry's eyes narrowed. He looked over at Blake, then sneaked a relieved look at Dal, and passed him an appreciative wink.

The ferry was a short walk from the house. On arrival, they were relieved to discover they were not the only tourists making the journey. Blake gave the ancient vessel a quick once over. "She ain't exactly the African fuckin' Queen," he said, "but Jesus . . . she ain't far off."

"Could do with a coat of paint," Harry shrugged, "but we either get aboard, or we swim."

"Ah well," Blake shrugged.

They paid the equivalent of sixteen dollars per head and boarded by way of a narrow plank that required reasonable balancing skills. At six o'clock, the ferry began its scheduled morning departure from the riverbank, a journey that was not too unpleasant, as there were no bullets flying and no burned villages to be seen. It stopped along the way for supplies and to collect extra crewmembers. Blake, nervous about the stops, cast a suspicious look on newly arriving passengers. As they set off on the next leg of the journey, two men standing on the bow of the dilapidated vessel pushed with long red and white striped poles, digging the poles down into the riverbed, using the red stripes to test the depth of the murky water. *Great, just what I need,* Blake thought, *more sand banks.* But the way was clear and the ferry made steady, slow progress, passing through scenery that was far from noteworthy.

The lack of river traffic concerned Blake. He had difficulty shaking off thoughts of soldiers around each bend, and was suspicious of occasional stares from passengers. But what made him most uneasy was the lack of river traffic. He called to Billie, "Not much river traffic. Don't like it, busy is good Billie, I've a bad gut feelin'." But as they moved along, and as he dissected the shoreline, he could see that there were no soldiers. A little farther on, the river widened,

577

and Blake turned to Slade, who was leaning on the railing looking concerned. "The bank's too far away," he said in a hushed voice. "I don't like it." He pointed at the bank. "I don't see much happenin' on shore. Too fuckin' quiet"

The occasional stop provided the group with an alternative to worrying, sleeping, and eating. The 'barbers' pole came out frequently, the bowmen pushing into the riverbed, measuring depth, providing Blake with ugly memories of the blue boat stuck on the sandbar. They arrived at Bagan at five o'clock, just ahead of sunset, and the ferry edged its way into a sandy beach. Blake and Billie discreetly observed three monks gathered some fifteen meters away. After an appropriate time, scouring the gathering of food sellers and family members happily greeting departing travelers, Blake said, "Stroll on over, check 'em out."

Billie approached the three, spoke for a minute, walked back to Blake. "Not ours," he said.

A young man approached Sung. "Are you with Uncle Sam's group?"

Sung smiled, spoke for a few moments, nodded back to Blake and the group with noticeable reluctance, followed the stranger to an abandoned Paya, one of over two thousand remaining from over thirteen thousand original temples in Bagan. Blake hesitated before entering, looking about with a nagging discomfort, and took a final step into the Paya as the young man closed the door behind them.

"Welcome my friends. My name's Michael. We received word of your harrowing journey. I'm sorry your time in Myanmar has been less than the tourist brochures convey," and he passed a hand around the ancient walls of the crypt-like enclosure. "This is a safe place in which I'll prepare you for the remainder of your journey. There's water and clothing in the chest, over there." He pointed to a large chest. "I'm sorry this seems so unprepared. The original plan was for you to proceed to the monastery," he said in a remorseful tone. "But the soldiers have been more active than usual." He lowered his eyes, blinking a few times, shedding a tear. "A few days back, two of our monks were taken because they protested the burning of their village. Some of our people have fled to Thailand. I've been here six months, from San Diego, from the Hsi Fang Temple, a Chinese Ch'an and Pure Land Buddhist temple. I've worked with our Taiwanese brothers, and have been briefed on your movements since your departure from Datong."

Dal placed a hand over his mouth and mumbled to Hunter, "Too much information."

"I was hoping to return to Hsi Fang in a year's time, but now that you've been rerouted through Bagan, I've had a request from my superiors to escort you safely to the Bay." He pointed to a chest. "When you're adequately prepared, we'll proceed to the monastery where you can clean up, eat, and sleep. In the morning, there'll be a group of monks leaving on the bus. We'll join them."

"Tell me, Michael," Hunter said. "Do you really believe you can free this land, you know, with the junta in control?"

"You must be Burmese to fully appreciate the blood we spill."

"Enlighten me," Hunter said.

"We are people of a different breed, conceived in desolation and loneliness, born with the smell of freedom in our nostrils. If freedom means dying, then we are bred to seek out death as lesser men seek out women. And if need be, we will remain infatuated all of our lives with dreams of the tomb."

"Sounds like ya go though life with a serious anger management issue," Dal said.

"It is a rage, not anger."

"Same difference."

"One must understand the rage, Mr. Dallas, the

beauty . . . the craving to set our Burma free."

There was a long silence, and when Michael allowed some time for the concessionary looks and nods to pass, he went about heating water over a gas burner. "Please step behind that screen," he said nodding. "Change into the robes in the chest. You'll find all you require in there."

He passed Dal and Bellinger a bottle of dark liquid. "Rub this into your faces and arms. When I've shaved your heads, you'll need to rub it on your scalp. Be sure to cover your legs from the knees down, plenty on the feet and on the backs of your hands."

Dal gazed at the bottle, looked back at the monk and groaned, "Must we?"

"Just fuckin' do it, Dallas," Blake snapped angrily from back of the screen, as Sung reluctantly stripped off.

"It's all bullshit," Blake groaned angrily, just as his eyes caught a glimpse of the charm swinging around Sung's neck. He flicked a thumb at the gold pendant. "So tell me, Mr. Sung. What is that? I ain't seen one like it. Not that I'm some kind of voyeur, you know, it just caught my eye. I know it ain't a holy medal. So what is it?"

"It is a Chi Lin and Tortoise," he said, giving Blake an assuring smile while at the same time feeling embarrassed by his near nudity. "It is regarded as two of the most important symbols in feng shui. It wards off negative energy, and has protective capabilities to overcome the effect of bad flying stars."

"Flying stars?"

"Yes, the combination of Chi Lin with a tortoise will protect me from bad feng shui. My father gave this to me many years back. I have never removed it."

"Right," Blake scoffed. "Flyin' fuckin' stars, whatever works for ya, Mr. Sung. Different, but it sure is pretty."

"On my return I will send you one from Taiwan."

"Yeah, I'd like that. Feng shui, huh? Thanks Sung.

Ya know, I'd really like that."

*****

It took less than an hour to complete the trans-
formations, except for Blake, who was Michael's final victim,
his look of sufferance providing entertainment as they stood
sniggering at the final shave customer.

Dal resembled a young Gandhi, the shaved head and
dark complexion was quite becoming, and Bell commented
favorably on his new look. Blake, on the other hand, awaited
approval, he made a full three sixty in a model-like slow
turn. Facing the gathering of the bald, Dal, about to make a
cutting remark, pointed at him, but Blake threw a piercing
stare that stopped him open mouthed.

"Not a fuckin' word!" Blake snapped. "Not one!"

At a little past seven o'clock, Harry, Sung, and Billie,
stuffed the discarded clothing into two bags as Michael
removed hair from the Paya.

"This Paya has been used many times as a halfway
house, when families need rest on their exodus to Thailand,"
Michael said. "The soldiers check everywhere, but we receive
warning from our monk's chanting. Our people understand
the signals. We move the families very quickly. We have
saved many Karen in this manner."

At seven-thirty, they headed off on a short ten-minute
walk to the monastery where the group passed their first
test. Michael walked them through heavy wooden doors,
passing by other monks who nodded at the new group. Blake
wondered if Michael had given advance notice of their
arrival.

He didn't ask.

Just rolled with the blows.

The young monk led them to a small room. The focal
point was a scattering of bunks positioned beneath windows

covered with bamboo blinds. Michael said, "This is your sleeping area."

"Ain't exactly the Radisson," Blake grumbled as he stared up at the towering stone Buddha at the end of the room.

Bell tilted her head toward him. "You remember what you told me to do the next time you complained about anything?"

He leaned in close and whispered, "Right," and remained silent for several long moments.

Early the next morning, near the Gawdawpalin Temple, the monks congregated at the entrance to the Bagan Hotel, a popular spot where they routinely begged for donations of food. Michael led Drew Blake, Carson Dallas, and company into the blue bus, where they all blended in with the large group of saffron robed monks, Michael's grin showing that he was extremely pleased with his handiwork.

Blake grinned at Dal, murmuring in his ear, "Ya really look good, dude; maybe I'll get ya a season pass to a tannin' salon when we get home."

Dal didn't respond. He knew better. Blake recognized the familiar *fuck you* look on Dal's face, and relished the moment.

The bus ride was hot, stinky, with rank humidity creating a need for body deodorant, the monks moaning a monotone hum, the gentle swaying of the bus and the chanting having an anesthetizing affect prompting Bell into a light sleep, her mind immersed in the faint cries of villagers, children, and wailing women. She jerked herself awake, deciding she didn't want the nightmare. Straightening up, she was surprised to see only a handful of the original number of monks remaining onboard.

"Good nap?" Hunter asked.

"How long did I sleep?"

"Long time, slept like a baby, drooled too."

"Oh, shut up," she said laughing, hoping he was kidding.

They'd been on the bus for three and a half hours, and Blake could see the mountain range in the distance. He nudged Dal. "Remember our Whitney trainin' in the monks robes; ya know, all that shit we thought was a waste of time?"

Dal was dozing, eyes shut tight, too tight to open for Blake's query. He grunted, arms folded, his chin buried deep in his chest.

"Dal, wake up."

"Wha . . . wha . . . what's up?"

"Take a look out there," he said pointing at the mountains ahead. "Hey Sung," he called, "What's that up ahead?"

"Southern tip of the Himalayas, the Arakan Yoma Mountains."

"We goin' over 'em?"

"Yes we must, if we are to get to Sittwe."

Dal moved his head to the left, to the right, heard the cracking, rubbed his neck, then stared at the snow-capped terrain. "Christ Almighty, will this bus make it over those mountains?"

"Only if it's got wings tucked away," Harry answered, chuckling as he moved across to sit by Blake. "It wasn't providence that led you guys to my place," he said in a more somber tone. "And it wasn't a four-leaf clover that placed Michael at Bagan. You know how things work."

Blake opened his mouth . . . said nothing.

"Admiral Bates and a few of the guys at the control center have been your guardian angels on most of this mission."

Blake gave a surprised look. "Hate when I'm outa the loop."

"Best you weren't expecting the world, in case things

broke down."

"Broke down? Ya mean to say things *went well*? Thank Christ for that, I thought we were makin' heavy weather of it, hate to think those people back in the villages thought it was eh . . . *goin' fuckin' well*. I hope Bates and the other guys are gettin' their jollies, ya know, what with 'em playin' God, danglin' us on the end of their strings like so many fuckin' puppets. We were dyin' out there, man. That ain't considered *'goin' well'* in my books. Fuck Bates, and fuck his desk jockeys."

The oration brought a round of applause, and a few calls of, "Here, here," from Slade and Dal.

"Well done m' man," Dal quipped. "Can we get that on tape for the chief? Like him to hear it, a most noble summation." Dal slapped his hands on his knees and gave Blake two thumbs up.

"And ya were sayin', Harry . . ." Blake grunted insincerely.

"What I was getting around to . . ." and he pointed to the west, "If you look in that direction, you'll see exactly what I'm talking about."

Blake imagined he caught a glimpse of a small plane sitting by a few broken down carts off in the distance, but lost view of the plane as the bus turned a slight bend. He brushed it off, thought he'd imagined it. There was a sprinkling of small, neatly kept bungalows spread about the perimeter of green farmland. It had been carved from dense jungle that formed an immense green frame around the harvested fields. Slade walked by Harry's side as he moved toward a large barn, with Billie, Sung, Hunter, Blake, Dal, Bell and Michael falling behind, their eyes uneasy, scouting the surrounding fields.

Harry dragged hard on the huge door, scrapping as it cut along the muddied ground, its resistance suggesting it had not allowed access in quite some time.

"Been awhile," Harry groaned.

"How long?" Slade inquired.

"Hmm, about eight months. Last time I was here was . . ."

"Don't like it, Harry. Things that don't get used tend to fuck up, know what I mean?"

"Nah, not this one, she's an old faithful. I can smell her from here. Can you smell her, the fuel, the oil? "

There was no sign of a plane. If there had been an Antonov, it was now nowhere to be seen.

"What the fuck's goin' on?" Blake groaned in disappointment. "What the fuck's goin' on?"

Dal found a spot to sit. He sat and kicked with frustration at the ground.

Harry Ching found humor in the scene. He tipped the hood back on his saffron gown, and said, "Well, don't you all look like a lot of disgruntled monks, thee of little faith," and he played with their emotions for a half minute. "Come on, get your asses up. Follow me."

He led them out of the barn, circling around rear, and stood staring at two nearly indistinguishable doors. He ran a hand along the lower edge, found the lever, and dragged it outward, and grunting, "Open sesame."

It was their ticket out of jail, another Antonov.

"Isn't she a sight for sore eyes?"

It wasn't quite in the restored condition of its twin, but would do the job. Excited to get it out and running, Harry clambered up into the cabin, wasting no time checking her over. "You're a bit dusty, baby," he called out, winking to Blake. "We had her tucked away in here eighteen months back, used her for three missions into Thailand." He nodded to the rear of the plane. "She's still got the scars to show." He pointed to a scattering of holes, rays of light streaming through the fuselage like a hundred mini-beams from a projectionist's camera in a darkened movie theater.

"Eight months huh," Dal said, "like ya didn't have time to patch the holes!"

"Burmese border guys took a few shots, nothing some duct tape can't fix, but I rather like the way the light filters through, adds ambience, don'tcha think?"

Dal walked to the nearest hole, plugging his finger through. "Fuck ambience. You sure it's okay? It's riddled."

Blake gave Dal *the look,* and said, "It's a plane, not a fuckin' horse!"

The nose of the Antonov faced inward, its tail nearly touching the doors of the shed. Harry hooked the wheel struts to a rope, had the farmer bring two oxen to the barn, and within minutes the Antonov was looking resplendent as it stood in bright sunlight. Harry was thrilled as he passed a hand over the bi-plane, glad to be back in something over which he had control.

"Ladies and gentlemen, boarding passes please," and he clicked his heels. "Today's feature movie will be Castaway, starring Tom Hanks."

"What if you hadn't made it this far?" Dal asked. "What if we all made it here but you were fuckin' dead back there someplace . . . what if we had no fuckin' pilot?"

"Then you'd miss a good movie."

There were no laughs.

"You'd have Sung and Billie, and those mountains over there . . ." and he pointed at the towering snow-capped peaks. "They'd be a great challenge. You guys were prepared for that contingency, correct?"

"Just what we would've needed," Blake grumbled, "another challenge."

The nine monks climbed into the plane and Blake assumed the co-pilot seat, watching as Harry started the bullet riddled Antonov. He turned the engine over, it spluttered, and died.

He cranked it again.

Nothing.

"What's up, Harry, why ain't we goin' someplace?"

"Technical hiccup, gimme a minute."

He climbed from the plane, walked out of the barn, returning minutes later with a crude looking instrument that could have been a hammer in a previous life. He opened the engine access, gave something a hard whap, whap, threw the implement to one side and clambered back onboard.

"Fuel pump sticks when it isn't used for a spell."

"Aw, jeez," Blake groaned from the cabin. Dal and Hunter were stoic.

"Okay passengers, this is your captain, please return your seats to an upright position and fasten seat belts."

Harry laughed aloud, and placed his headset on, with Blake following suit. He asked Harry the burning question, "If we get up there, Harry, where are we comin' down?"

He turned the key, the engine spluttered, shook the plane a few times, continued to splutter, more splutters than Harry would have liked. He had his head tilted as though listening for a familiar melody, then smiled as the engine produced a steady roar that brought a loud cheer from the cabin that neither Harry nor Blake heard. The plane left the ground two hundred meters from its starting point, and Harry swung it off to the west as it began climbing over the Himalayas. He pointed north, slipping off the headset, shouting aloud back into the cabin, "Up ahead, Mount Victoria." Then to Blake as he replaced his headset, "You think you could've made it over if you had to walk?"

"Never know, hey."

Once past the Arakan Yoma, and at thirteen thousand feet, Harry began a slow descent.

"I'm going to put her down in a safe spot, about a mile off Sittwe. There's a private plane strip there, the guy has another Antonov he's been restoring. He serviced this baby twice, so he'll take care of the engine."

The Antonov banked sharply to starboard as Harry struggled with the controls, realizing the tail control wasn't responding as it should.

"What's the problem?" Blake shouted.

"Don't know, I thought I felt a loud thud, a bump."

Harry leaned across, looking back toward the tail. "Jesus, we've lost half of the fucking tail." Then another explosion and he realized they were being targeted from the ground.

"Goddamn Burmese Army. They've got all this new shit from the Russians."

"New shit?"

"Surface to air," he said, wiping sweat from his forehead. "We're in some deep kimchi."

It was the first time Blake had heard Harry Ching sounding worried as he jerked the Antonov into a steep climb, the tail shuddering badly.

"If I can get higher we'll have cloud cover. As long as they don't use heat-seeking shit, we might stand a chance."

"Might stand a chance?" Blake shouted. "Might!"

"Think we need some serious prayers. Go check on the others; let 'em know what's going on."

Blake unbuckled, stepped into the cabin. The rest of the team struggled to unbuckle their belts, buckles that were sticking from lack of use.

Bell shouted, "Slade and Sung, they've been hit, Sung's bad!"

Air ripped through a hole the size of a bowling ball alongside Sung's seat. Shrapnel had passed through him, one small piece impacting Paul Slade's head.

"Get something over here!" Bell screamed. "He's bleeding really badly from his side," and she placed a gentle arm around Sung's shoulder.

Blake and Dal moved Sung to the aisle, tying a splint around his waist then quickly wrapping a bandage around

Slade's head, covering a deep cut that ran down his forehead and across his eyes.

"Can't stop the bleedin' on Sung," Blake said. "Gotta get him to a hospital."

"No hospital," Sung groaned. "I am not staying here. I must go with you."

Blake looked at Dal, and Dal looked away. They comforted the two wounded men for the remaining ninety minutes until Harry began the descent, nursing the plane down on a neat strip just off the Bay of Bengal, taxiing to a hangar where two SUV's sat in an area off to one side, and a mechanic worked on the engine of a Cessna. Harry eased the Antonov to a halt and was first out of the plane as the mechanic raised his head from under the hood, and waved a screwdriver.

"Harry, good to see you. I was told you might be comin' in this week, glad you made it safely. I wouldn't have your job for the world, man."

Cutting the man off, Harry shouted, "Got two wounded guys, get a doctor here, fast!"

The mechanic dropped the smile, flicked his cell phone open and placed the call. Another man grabbed a stretcher, ran to the plane, and Dal, Hunter, and Billie carefully moved Sung along the fuselage and placed him on the stretcher.

"Get him out here quickly!" Blake snapped. "But careful, be careful."

Dal moved to the rear of the stretcher, guiding Sung's head from the doorway of the plane, then assisted Slade, now completely blinded by the bandage swathed around the upper half of his head. Within minutes, a white van arrived and Blake spun around, realized he had no weapon, and just stood there in a defensive pose . . . looking quite ridiculous in his monk's robe.

"It's okay, it's okay," Harry shouted. "It's the doctor."

The man rushed to Sung's side, took one look and flashed a glance at Harry. "Bad," he said. "Have to get him to emergency, can't stay here, needs surgery."

Blake asked, "What're his chances?"

"None if he stays here. You know the authorities; they'll have questions, probably keep him here . . . if he survives. He's already lost a lot of blood." He raised Sung's robe. "Look here, he has a sliver of metal in his abdomen," then whispering to Blake, "don't like his chances."

He looked across at Slade's injury, but stayed by Sung, the whole time applying pressure to the wound.

"He needs surgery too. That gash across his head looks bad," and he nodded to Slade. "Could need an ophthalmologist, I can't tell without cleaning him up." But he stayed with Sung, pressing on the wound.

"We'll take 'em both with us," Blake said, looking at Harry. "Wha'dya think, Harry?"

"If Sung's going to go, he's going to go," the aviator said. "He's going to go among friends, not in some Burmese army hospital." He leaned into Sung's ear and asked, "Sung, you hear me?"

Sung nodded slowly, appealing directly into Harry Ching's eyes. "Take me with you, Harry. I do not want to stay here."

It was a silent unanimous vote.

They placed Sung and Slade in the rear of an SUV, and loaded their packs.

"Okay guys," Harry called out. "Mount up!"

The *monks* squeezed into the vehicle and Blake removed the red velvet bundle, preferring to carry it rather than have it out of reach. Hunter glanced quickly at Blake, and said quietly, "Good idea."

The fishing port had scores of boats moored along its docks. Harry waited a moment, looking over the boats, a concerned look, said, "Just checking, could be a navy vessel among 'em. But maybe not, I'm getting a little paranoid. Guess they're all fishing boats, it's the main industries here in Sittwe."

Blake gave the fleet a cursory glance and thought, *fuck 'em.* He was out of niceties, even mentally.

When the SUV came to a stop, Harry looked across at a tall man working on an enormous fishing net onboard one of the larger boats. He leaned from the passenger's window, and called, "Hey, you're as ugly as ever, you old bastard."

"Harry, is that you?"

Blake, Hunter, and Billie slid the stretcher from the truck and carried Sung to a cabin, as Bell and Billie assisted Slade.

"Christ, Harry, what is this, a Buddhist convention?"

"Yeah, we're trying to make a fashion statement. Listen, we've got two of our guys seriously injured here. Any chance of a medic or a nurse coming along to help out with them?"

"I'm on it. Didn't recognize you without the hair, don't look too bad." He pulled a cell phone, stayed on it for a minute. "Nurse's on the way."

"Thanks for that, and thanks for the styling critique too. I don't recommend it for cold nights. When can we get underway?"

The fisherman stepped into his marina office, looked about, opened a panel that appeared to be a filing cabinet but concealed a fancy array of satellite communication equipment. He stepped into the waiting area, said, "All systems go. We've a rendezvous in two hours, dead west from here. Let's get onboard."

A vehicle whipped into the parking lot alongside, coming to a stop by the cabin door.

"Nurse's here," the fisherman said. "Good timing, let's go."

Slade and Sung laid in front of the boat, while the nurse

sat by Sung's side, continually monitoring his condition. A few minutes later she glanced at Blake, gave a slight shake of her head, lowering her eyes to Sung, then glancing away. She caught Blake's eyes, and mouthed, "Not good."

CHAPTER 55

THEY HUDDLED IN SILENCE, this small group of monks with their saffron robes clinging to them like wetsuits, as the East China Sea whipped about with the fury of a thousand lashes. The small group relived memories of Myanmar, bitter memories of its ruthless junta. The man at the helm looked below, saw the silence, and secured the wheel. He stepped down, joined them, opened a cabinet, reached in and passed Dal a silver flask. "Here, take a little of this. It will help."

"Yeah, thanks. What is it?"

"Medicinal brandy, it will take the chill out of your bones, especially with your head shaved that way."

Bell shivered, her head and face totally wrapped in the dark orange shawl, her attention distracted by the deep groan coming from the passenger curled beneath the blanket.

"You okay?" Blake asked, placing a hand on Sung's shoulder.

"My legs, I cannot feel my legs."

Bell felt a wave of inadequacy. She shook her head as a tear escaped one eye. She turned her face away, not wanting Blake to see. Hunter placed a finger on her cheek, touching her softly.

And the tear was gone.

She raised her eyes slowly to meet his, forcing a smile, whispering, "Thanks, Gard."

"For what?"

"Being here."

Blake shouted, his voice struggling to be heard above the fury of the sea mercilessly thrashing at the keel, "Hey, hey, hey, hey! What's that up ahead? I see a light."

He repeatedly jabbed an excited finger aft, as Dal and Hunter stood shielding their eyes from the spray, each focusing in the direction Blake was pointing.

"Don't see nothin'!" Hunter shouted.

"No, no! Wait until we rise on the crest," and he pointed to the east. "There, over that way!"

The boat slid sideways, falling into another trough, the sea either side of the boat closing in, swallowing the small craft.

In an effort to talk the boat up the wall of the trough, Blake shouted, "Come on you sonofabitch, get on up!" The climb seemed to take an eternity. Blake thought, *whatever it was I saw, could be gone by the time we get out of this fuckin' trough.* When the boat reached the top, Blake saw nothing.

Sung groaned as Bell carefully placed his head in her lap, stroking his hair, but it didn't help his pain.

"Hey, Father Dominic," Sung whispered in a gravely voice, motioning with his head for Dal to come nearer.

"Hang in their partner," Dal said, forcing a smile. "Don't want me to hear your confession, do ya?"

"That would be bitter irony," Sung said, his voice faint. "Dal, it hurts, it really hurts. I do not think . . ."

"Hey, hey, I don't wanna hear any of that *can't make it* shit, okay?"

"Sure," Sung groaned, sitting a little more erect. "Sure, but there is something I want to say. The reward I collected for handing over the man on the mountain, back in the sheds, you remember?"

"Yeah sure," Dal replied. "Ya diddled me out of that one." But his smile was far from convincing.

"When we get back," Sung groaned, "I am going to

take . . ." He paused, took a painful breath. "I am going to take us all on the best vacation to Mount Whitney . . ."

"It'll be summer," Dal said, smiling at Sung. "But we can do a rain-check. Anyhow, we'll be needin' a few months to get over this," and he rubbed on his shaved scalp. "I'll need time to grow my hair back. By then the slopes'll be white powder, but yeah, sounds great. We'll all be there."

Dal turned to Blake who was still peering into the dark eastern sky, still searching for the elusive light, still hoping his imagination was not playing games. He reluctantly glanced back in Dal's direction, throwing him a *how's he doin'* look, and getting a quick head shake. Dal screwed his face up, shook his head and grimaced, mouthing the words, '*not good*' and held Blake's stare. The boat raised itself above the boiling sea one more time, and there, right in front, no more than two hundred meters astern . . . the strange light reappeared.

It materialized like a huge whale, white, pearlescent, a testament to Melville's memory, the conning tower rising into the moonlit sky like a tall building, gray, shining, and reflecting the coldness of the moon's glow. The monster was four hundred feet in length, and as it drew closer, men could be seen scurrying about on deck. They were dressed in dark gray uniforms, and each wore a bright green flotation vest. *What if they're Chinese*, Blake thought, *or even Russian*?

As they drew nearer, he noticed three men frantically signaling two others who appeared to be bobbing about above the waves. When the bobbing men peaked on a crest, Blake could see they were wearing scuba gear, but couldn't figure how this could be possible, how it was they could be above the waves while suited up in scuba gear, and then as they drew nearer he realized they were in a Zodiac, waving as they drew alongside.

A rope came from the Zodiac and Dal secured it to a handrail along the running board. The man in front of the

Zodiac pulled the rubber dinghy alongside.

"Hey you monkeys," the man called, "You looking for your uncle?"

Blake grinned at the American voice, feeling safe for the first time in weeks, feeling relieved. He shouted, "My uncle? Maybe, what's his name?"

"Sam!"

"I don't believe it, is that you, Wolf Brandt?"

He reached out and the navy SEAL grabbed his old friend's arm.

"What's the name of this behemoth, Mr. Brandt?" Dal shouted, nodding toward the gray monster.

"USS Texas, but you guys can call her home for the next few days, your first leg back to the home of the brave."

Brandt did a quick recon of the soaked passengers. "How many heads you got here, Mr. Blake?"

Blake turned to the shivering group huddling in the cabin, and noticed the nurse had her face turned away from Sung.

Blake called, "Nine."

Bell raised her hands and showed him eight fingers, then placed her palm on Sung's face, running her fingers across his eyes.

Closing them.

She leaned over, kissing the top of his head.

For a moment, Blake was silent, then drawing a deep breath he let out a saddened, "Fuck!"

In the cold night, in the light of a silvery moon, Blake and God shared some silent words, a prayer for his friend, Sung Chiao.

Dal swallowed hard, squeezing Bell's shoulder as he comforted her.

Blake quickly moved to where Sung lay, and took his friend's hand. He placed his face against Sung's cheek and whispered, "It was an adventure, Father Sung. Ain't ever gonna forget ya."

He thought about it, knew his friend would want him to have it. *It is a Chi Lin and Tortoise. It is regarded as two of the most important symbols in feng shui. It wards off negative energy, and has protective capabilities that can overcome the effect of bad flying stars. The combination of a Chi Lin with a tortoise will protect me from bad feng shui. I have never removed it.*

Blake reached inside the saffron gown, felt for it, had it, and respectfully slipped the chain over Sung's head. A salt water spray whipped his face as a stream of tears let loose and Blake raised his head and allowed the spray to wet him down.

And he welcomed the subterfuge.

Dal glanced back toward Slade, his blood-soaked bandage tightly wrapped around his eyes, hands doggedly clutching the velvet bundle.

"Blake, Blake?" he called, turning his face into the wind.

"Yeah Paul, I'm here. Calm down."

"What's goin' on? Are they our guys?"

CHAPTER 56

IT WAS A COOL San Diego evening when the Ridkin team stepped off the USS Ronald Reagan, the carrier having rendezvoused with the USS Texas, and safely transported the group the remainder of their journey. Another of the Interpol operatives, Pete Pirelli, joined them as they sat around a table in The Fish Market Restaurant. Sam had requested Pirelli bring Blake's Porsche along, knowing the gesture would be a comforting touch.

A waiter approached with two trays of fresh sour dough and a bottle of Pinot. It seemed a lifetime since Drew Blake and Carson Dallas had visited San Diego, and being guests of Harry Ching gave it an added touch. The waiter showed the bottle to Harry, who said, "Just open it, we've waited long enough."

"Here's to the Texas and the Reagan," Blake said raising the first glass. "They made the journey home, well . . ." he choked momentarily, then, a little maudlin, "they made it a true home-comin'."

With glasses raised, a soft bout of *here, here* spread around the table.

Michael was glad to be home. His excursion in Myanmar had been quite sufficient. And, being the only genuine monk in the group, being the only person among the shaved headed party still garbed in a saffron robe, he attracted more than his usual plethora of inquiring glances from passers-by.

"You must all come to one of our meditation services," he said, making a knowing smile. "You'll benefit
greatly from it."

There was another round of *hear, hear,* and Blake
toasted, "Thanks, Michael, job well done. Can't say I'll be
back for my next haircut, but you saved the day." He choked
for a few moments, then added, "Here's to missin' friends."
He tilted his head and his blue eyes caught the light as he
slipped a quick wink to Dal. Bell and Hunter each moved
their glasses toward the center of the table and the rims
clinked.

Slade, wearing an eye patch, smiled and turned to
Lisa Ling, reaching toward her and placing one hand on her
arm. "You went through a lot, Lisa," he said. "I'm sorry it
turned out the way it did."

"Thank you," she sniffed, struggling to quell the
tears. "We gave it our best shot," and she lowered her head,
adding in a shaky voice, "I'll miss my Peter."

"There'll be another Peter," Sam said, placing a
gentle hand on her arm, "another special man, give it time."

She dismissed his condolence in a trance-like way as
she stared at nothing, and said in a melancholy voice, "There
was something about Peter, something . . . I don't know . . .
I can't quite describe it."

Sam passed her a tissue.

She trembled, dabbed at her eyes.

"Eh, Drew," Sam said, in an effort to change the
mood. "I had Pirelli bring your Porsche, it's out back," and
he did a short head-tilt toward the car lot, "in the car lot."

The Tara sat in the center of the table alongside the
Sunday copy of the Los Angeles Times. Blazoned across
the front page was the headline, "*MYSTERY VIRUS SHUTS
DOWN RED SATELLITES.*"

"Black fuckin' Sabbath," Blake said. "The motherfucker actually worked."

Beijing Billie reached for the statue, staring at the hole in its base, shaking his head and saying in a resolute way, "If only the world knew what this small statue has been through."

"Well Billie," Blake said, breaking off a large chunk of warm sough-dough. "I gotta believe that one day," and he paused, took a bite, "that one day the world *will* know."

"Not from us they won't," Sam mumbled.

"Not from fuckin' Beijing either," Dal added, making a face.

"Another toast," Blake said aloud, feeling somberness creeping into the group. They raised their glasses as a smiling Drew Blake positioned his head in a familiar Michael Madsen tilt, his fluorescent blue eyes raised to the stars as he searched for words. After several long moments he smiled at Beijing Billie. "Welcome to America, Billie, where dreams once came true."

Engrossed in a world of his own, Sam slipped a hand into his jacket and pulled his cell phone, mumbling to himself, "Seven o'clock here, ten at night in Beijing." He punched a preset number, waited on Yidui to pick up.

*****

Renee Fleming's rendition of Puccini's Madam Butterfly held Yidui's attention, his sleepy, arrogant face absorbing the performance, his eyes filling with tears as he wallowed in the soprano's superb delivery of *Un Bel Di Vedremo*.

Stretched out on the antique chaise lounge, he reached for a fresh tissue, continually wiping away tears. An emotional man was Yidui. When he'd dispensed with the tears, he reached for a box of caramelized popcorn, throwing down a few handfuls, allowing his head to settle deeper in the goose down pillow, and he began drifting into a light sleep.

The brilliance of the aria was shattered by the buzzing of the cellular phone. Yidui jerked his head, causing the popcorn box to slip from his chest, spilling the contents on the ornate rug. Annoyed, he brushed himself off, glanced at the caller's name, Sellers.

"Mr. Sellers?" he answered, a question in his voice. "Is that you?"

Sam smirked, "Evening, Yidui," and switched the phone to speaker mode.

The sound of Fleming's brilliant voice reverberated about the table as Sam gazed at those seated around, their eyes focused on his cell phone, yet each clearly appreciating the soprano's brilliance . . . all the way from China.

"Let her go, Sam, wait until she hits the high note," Blake said. "Ya know, just after the butterfly leaves her hand."

"Yeah," Sam grinned, "I know Madam Butterfly well. I've got it."

The world slipped into thirty frame-per-second slow mo speed, the soprano pouring her heart into the aria as Puccini backed up the waiter's arrival with fresh sourdough, then the pace of Sam's world accelerated to warp speed and a cameo of all that had transpired shot by, faster, faster, snippets of the journey as described to him by Blake, and Slade; faces, villages, the land mines, the mangled bodies, the crying children, all to the accompaniment of Puccini's aria.

The aria.

Those butchers of Burma.

The Interpol chief could only imagine what they'd been through, and it was the rage within that sweetened this moment of revenge. His eyes locked on Blake's as he spoke into the phone, taking on an indifferent tone. "Yidui," Sam said, "turn the music down." He paused, listening as the soprano dropped a few decibels, then said, "Why'd you do it? We paid you well."

Fleming hit the high note . . . and Sam *punched in the numbers.*

Static!

"Now *that* was a fuckin' blast," Pirelli sniggered, "Franco would be proud."

"Peace in our time," Sam said, savoring the silence. "A great president once said those words, looks like we might stay on track just a little longer."

"Yeah, peace in our fuckin' time," Dal said with a slow nod to Sam.

*****

Drew Blake left the restaurant and made his way to the parking lot. He slid a hand inside his shirt, felt the Chi Lin and Tortoise charm. "Wards off negative energy," he muttered, "and protects me from flyin' fuckin' stars. Sure." He gave the sky a cursory glance. Thought, *Asteroids . . . hmm, flyin' stars.*

"Ain't ever takin' it off, Mr. Sung," he sighed, and his tear filled eyes searched the heavens. He caught sight of a shooting star, and gave the silvery streak a friendly nod.

He paused, watched as it vanished, raised the collar of his jacket as the cool evening breeze chilled his shaved head.

He shuddered.

Embraced the discomfort.

About the Author

JASON DENARO is an American author/artist with in excess of 200 published works. He is ranked among the world's top 100 wildlife artists by the U.S. publication, "Wildlife Art News." His works are also recorded in Max Germaine's "Encyclopedia of Australian Artists & Galleries." As an international selling author of the Drew Blake series of novels, Vortex, Fiddler, Vatican FileSS, and Shades of Gray, Jason Denaro has travelled through many of his researched locations, including France, Switzerland, China, Italy, England, the Philippines, Taiwan, Japan, Australia, and the USA. The author is also the recipient of the 2009 United States Commerce Association Award."

OTHER WORKS FROM THIS AUTHOR

(EXCERPT)

VORTEX

HER EYES WERE THE color of the moon in a daylight sky.

Chateau La Mouliniere Bordeaux Blanc sparkled as it snaked its way along spaces between terra-cotta tiles, slithering toward the lower level of the floor, and merging into hot, dark blood that pooled alongside the charred body lying crumpled on the floor, a body that only minutes earlier had beamed life.

She had been a stunning girl, a temptress whom most men could only dream of having, and had spent the previous evening with two of those dreamers, Ramone Flourette and Philippe Bouvier.

"Michelle, you are more radiant than ever," the first man said as entered her apartment, passing her a red rose as his slightly smaller friend followed two paces behind.

The smaller man nodded energetically as he steadied his breathing. "Mon dieu, she's more stunning than you described," he said. "Her eyes, they are so beautiful." *He said . . . bee-you-tee full.*

Philippe flashed a near perfect grin; too perfect a row of teeth for a Frenchman, a smile from which a hint of garlic tinged with mint freshener made an ever so brief escape. He glanced at Ramone, caught the look of expectation in his friend's eyes, let out a chuckle. He started to comment, then thought better of it for a few brief moments, then went with it anyway. "Philippe, please," he grinned, "she will want more than we have brought along."

The girl with eyes the color of the moon in a daylight sky overheard the comment. She shook her head, and giggled in a girlish way, "Oh, you two," she said, placing a hand on the taller man's arm, "it has been a long time." She continued to giggle, closing the door behind them with a nudge of her bare foot, moving to a liquor cabinet, opening the heavy carved oak doors, and placing a hand on an ice-bucket. "I have Chateaux Bordeaux, and uh," she said nodding, "as I recall, it is your favorite, Ramone."

She popped the cork, poured the champagne into a fine fluted glass and placed the red rose alongside. "It is a beautiful rose," she said. "So very thoughtful of you, you are such a romanticist." She reached for the flower, raised it in a sensual way, stroking it against her cheek, repeating the words with closed eyes, "Such a romanticist."

The Frenchman blushed, his eyes remaining on his forearm, lingering on the warmth of her touch. "Thank you. Just a small glass, you would not be trying to tire me early now, would you?"

The two men removed their coats and followed the

girl to the one bedroom.

"That perfume," Ramone said, "it has such an alluring aroma. What is it? Is it new?"

"It is Jean Patou's Amour Amour," and she leaned into him. "The same as the last time you visited."

Ramone sniffed her neck, then slowly, moving back, nodded, in an acquiescing way, "Of course, I should have remembered. It is the aroma of well . . . it is the aroma of you. It is Michelle."

Ramone resembled a caricature of Dagwood, lanky, awkward. For him, finding willing women had long been a task necessitating payment for services. He wiped saliva from his lower lip and looked about the room, his eyes protruding sufficiently to add a Jackie Gleeson touch to his Dagwood-like appearance. He was a man who had been short changed by the good-looks Gods, at the end of the queue when chiseled features were dished out. But he tried to appear cool, and to a miniscule degree, he succeeded. His eyes scanned the apartment as he said in a suave voice, "You have redecorated since I was last here. It appears even more comfortable than I recall."

"You noticed," she said coyly. "Yes, it is comfortable. I do not need a great deal of space, after all, there is just myself and the cat, and of course . . ." She smiled and tilted her head at Philippe, "my occasional very *special* guests," and she leaned on *special*. She didn't need to tell him, her eye contact sufficed, but she passed a slow hand in the direction of the bed and sighed, as though excited, "Do not be shy. Make yourselves comfortable. I will take a quick shower and slip into . . ." She hesitated, blushed just a little, and then threw in with a well timed giggle, "I will slip into something a little easier to umm, to slip out of." She pressed a button as she passed by the music system, letting loose Ravel's Boléro. It drifted about the room with a repetitive haunting melody that triggered fond memories for Ramone.

He knew the routine.

"Yes, yes," he said enthusiastically unlacing his boots and humming along with Boléro, not needing a prompt to sit on the edge of the bed. He had spent many evenings with Michelle, each better than the previous. Her exquisite sounds, her purring so catlike, as her lips let out soft puffs in his ear, her tongue running around his lobe, her lips sucking until he felt his ear had grown in length. And each time, she had left him wondering if her orgasms were staged. He gave her the benefit of the doubt, believing he had indeed, worked his *special magic. After all,* he thought, as he jutted a proud chin forward, *I am a Frenchman!*

Her cries to God were indelibly etched in his mind, along with Ravel's Boléro, cries that kept him returning to the girl with eyes the color of the moon in a daylight sky. Her multiple orgasms, staged as they may very well have been, had given him a feeling of manliness, a sensation of being needed, being appreciated.

Ramone was reticent in telling others of this spectacular girl, he wanted to keep her to himself, but on this occasion, he had brought along another man, and this left him wondering if the additional partner would dilute Michelle's affections. But then she knew she would be well rewarded, as had always been the case. Another man would hardly change her modus operandi. As the night progressed she found herself immersed in the many pleasures of a *ménage à trois.*

Her hair fell freely, one man's fingers stroking it, another finding pleasure elsewhere on her soft body. She pulled on Ramone's head, pressed him down harder, moving him from side to side, up and down. Her guidance didn't hinder his motion, didn't break his tempo one bit, and then, as though a flutist played a hypnotic melody, the three began to sway, their hearts beating as one, swaying to Ravel's haunting melody, erections impatiently seeking her out as her breast swayed slowly left to right, right to left, swaying, swaying, her eyes facing the ceiling, her breath coming in short gasps. Boléro never sounded so good.

Ramone tasted her essence, feeling the sensation of being a better lover than he had ever been. And as an exhausted Philippe fell to one side, Michelle turned her attention to the man who had brought the lilies, wrapping her legs around him. Now she was on fire, arching her throat, losing herself in whatever orgasm it was, perhaps her ninth, maybe her tenth as she moved in sync to Ravel's Boléro.

Ramone had long ceased counting.

She gave in to him completely, opening her heart, her soul, her arms, her lips. His erection, now noticeably raw skinned became a minor aggravation he easily set aside with no thought of consequence, and he entered her for what could only be a record time. Pain was set aside right now, well, he was aware of his diminishing layers of skin, of the rash that was quickly developing, but then there were those sounds.

She made *those* sounds.

Sounds of appreciation, of sheer ecstasy and it made him feel a special sensation, made him feel appreciated.

At last Ramone took a break and all three laid back, their eyes staring at the ornate ceiling. Time to recuperate, time *she* didn't need. Moving from one to the other was an enjoyable challenge, and she experienced quite a buzz from the inventiveness. *Hmm*, she thought, *what shall I do next?*

"And so?" Ramone shrugged.

And all three began laughing.

"And so, hmm, let me see. . ." Michelle said, smiling, "and so thank God I have nothing planned for today. You have worn me out, you naughty boys."

And the three drifted into a deep sleep, until the sound of the phone woke them.

She raised herself from the bed as Philippe's arm

dropped from her waist. "Certainly," she said softly into the handset. "I will look forward to it. I will call you back, say . . ." and she glanced at the clock, "say in an hour or so." She placed the phone on its base, and slipped into a white negligee.

Ramone stood, stretched, moved from the bed, and made his way toward the bathroom, from where he called, "Good morning, Michelle."

"Sorry for the early wake up call," she replied, her face slack with sleep. "That was my sister, Susanna. She is an early riser." She glanced across at him, lowered her eyes. "Hmm, you seem to be an early riser as well."

"Forgive me, but eh . . ." he said placing both hands over his crotch, "I have no control over it."

"Oh," she grinned, "so it has a mind of its own?" She turned away, and moved to the kitchen where she went about brewing fresh coffee.

Following a short breakfast, Ramone reached into his pocket, removed a small object, and outstretched his closed fist toward the girl. "Here," he said, "this is for you."

Her blue eyes widened. "For me?" she beamed. "My goodness, you are far too generous."

It was an exquisite diamond of at least three karats, worth far more than the girl with the beautiful eyes could earn in a year of *entertainment*. He raised it between his thumb and index finger and allowed the light to form a spectrum through its perfect facets.

"In appreciation of your warmth, and for. . ." he nodded and searched for the words, "and for your beauty. A night neither of us will soon forget." He was about to say something different, perhaps tell her that in retrospect, the stone was easily worth several return visits, a batch of credits maybe, but he said, "I can only hope we are welcome back." Then lowering his eyes, he blushed just a little, and his voice quivered, "Of course, when we have regained sufficient energy. Perhaps then we can add further to your jewelry collection?"

Such was not the fate of the girl with eyes the color of the moon in a daylight sky.

Ramone and Philippe hugged her, neither passing up the opportunity to press against her firm, perky breasts. The two men limped to the sidewalk and surveyed the small terraced cottage as thoughts of the evening's eroticism replayed in their minds. Such an innocent cottage, its blue window boxes with overflowing geraniums and quaint louvers painted a matching faded eggshell. Who could ever imagine?

Philippe: "You look a little tired."

Ramone: "Me, tired? My God, I have never felt so young, have never felt so. . ." He hesitated, and glancing back at the window with the geranium smile, added, "so . . . so . . . so alive."

They were talking at the same time, chattering away like two excited children as they moved with some difficulty toward the Peugeot parked at the curb.

The two men were the last to see the girl alive.

The magnitude of their involvement far outweighed the pleasures of the evening. The girl with eyes the color of the moon in a daylight sky did not die alone. The Persian cat lay by her side, that pet upon which she had lavished countless hours of grooming, the burned feline resembling a rabbit on a spit. The girl too, burned to a crisp, her form wrapped in what resembled overcooked pig rind more so than skin. Surprisingly though, the odor was inoffensive. It was, in fact, not unlike barbequed pork, almost tempting if one were a little hungry, until the source of the aroma was revealed. But until then, the appealing bouquet hung suspended, suspended in the innocent cottage with the pretty geranium filled window boxes.

After the fourth buzz, the answer machine kicked in.

"Hello, this is Michelle. I am unable to take your call at the moment. Please leave a message and I will call you back shortly."

She never would.

*****

EXCERPT

FIDDLER

August 16, dog day of summer, feast of Saint Roch the patron saint of dogs. At the University of California, San Diego, the day is hot, stagnant and marked by a dull lack of progress for the fiddler. Leaves glisten as a gentle warm drifting mist creates a silvery glow, enough of a mist to generate discomfort for the solitary figure squatting on the hilltop beneath sparsely spread branches of an aged eucalyptus. In a velvet-lined case by his knee lay a finely handcrafted violin by the Romanian master, Virgil Boda. He pauses, senses movement, reaches into a Nike sports bag and removes a pair of binoculars.

The UCSD athletes are about to hit the track. He focuses . . . no one out there yet. The binoculars pick up a moist spray and he wipes off the lenses, places them back in the bag. He takes the violin from its case, raises it and begins his haunting piece, plays Pyotr Ilyich Tchaikovsky's Concerto, one of the most highly praised violin concertos. He passes an angry scowl at the drizzle, hangs over the Boda trying to protect the impeccable finish from the moisture. The bow, made of Pernambuco with Mongolian horsehair, gently caresses the strings, and the haunting sound of the vivacissimo meanders through the treetops, the humid breeze betraying him and carrying his concerto down the slope to the red track of the UCSD field.

610

The pretty one . . . the blonde. The chosen one. Ah yes, like clockwork the pretty one is there.

*****

EXCERPT

VATICAN FILESS

The wheels spun as the Testarossa resumed its journey. Blake hadn't driven but three minutes when a white Mercedes drew dangerously close to their rear. He eyed the 500SL but the tinted glass made it impossible to see the occupant's faces. As he dropped the Ferrari to fourth gear and increased the gap between the two vehicles, Zan sensed Blake's concern and adjusted the passenger's rear view mirror, giving him a better view.

"Sorry," he said swallowing hard and turning to Blake. "Bad news, Mr. Blake."

"What's goin' on kid?" he said as the Benz quickly closed the gap. "These guys are really pushin' me along. I can push her more, but don't want to scratch your baby."

"Push her," Zan said. "Push her, it's a long story and I'll explain later, you just need to lose 'em, and I seriously mean lose 'em fast."

Blake sensed the urgency in the kid's voice. "Don't fuck about kid, put me in the picture, is this a matter of life and death or . . . you know . . . or should I just should casually lose 'em?"

Blake's eyes flashed to the speedometer as Zan turned back to focus more clearly on the pursuer. Blake lowered the window and the draught, together with the roar of the engine was immediately deafening. Zan leaned toward Blake and shouted, "Definitely a matter of life and death. It goes back quite a way. Family vendetta shit. You gotta lose that Benz."

Zan wanted to share more but this was neither the time nor the place. He would find out soon enough why Zan Fiorelli had entered his life.

Blake sat erect, and sneaked a peek at the speedometer; two hundred and ten kilometers-per-hour. He adjusted his rear view mirror and for the first time in weeks felt adrenalin surging through his body, his hands no longer trembled and he shouted at Zan, "In my backpack, get my gun!"

"You got a gun, how the hell . . ."

"Just get it. I've got connections, okay!"

He suspected Blake could be armed, but such an aggressive counter move? He assumed the Mercedes would give them a hair-raising chase, and definitely scare Blake a little. But a firefight was not expected. He tentatively passed the Sig Saur to Blake.

Blake called aloud, "In the side pack, get the clip."

He eased off of the gas pedal and allowed the SL to edge alongside, then in a quick moment thought he recognized the gaunt faced man who shouted from the passengers seat, "Pull over, stop your car."

Blake nodded, smiled and gave a friendly wave, then realized the passenger was the tourist who had taken their photo back at the Piazza.

He nudged Zan. "Hey, that's the guy who took our . . ."

Surprised by the returned wave, the passenger half-heartedly raised one hand in a reciprocal way, then realizing what he was doing - leaned from the window and pointed the M16 at the Ferrari.

"Jesus!" Blake shouted, slamming his foot onto the brake and causing the massive discs on the Ferrari to lock, and smoke to billow from the screaming Pirellis. As a spray of automatic fire shot across the hood of the Testarossa, Zan dropped his head and braced both hands on the dashboard. The Mercedes shot past the stationary Ferrari and Blake accelerated in short time and dropped onto the rear bumper of the Benz.

He shouted, "motherfuckers!" as Zan, now devoid of color and amazed at Blake's rapid reaction, cringed in his seat, astonished at his driver's metamorphosis from a reluctant quasi-drunken bum to a stereotypical James Bond. He'd been expecting Blake to handle the situation differently, expected him to shake off the Benz.

With one hand on the wheel and the other fully extended toward the SL, Blake drew bead on the back tire of the Benz and fired off a single shot. They watched the 500SL as it hurtled through the steel guard rail and became airborne. Blake waved the Sig Saur at the disappearing Mercedes, shouted, "Have a nice flight, you should've bought the gull-wing model you sonofabitch!"

He slowed the red car and pulled to the shoulder, slipped the Sig into the rear of his belt and casually walked to the edge of the road to catch the fireball as the Benz impacted rocks several hundred of feet below.

He pulled a pack of Marlboro, lit one with a steady hand, exhaled and passed the pack to Zan. "What a blast, huh kid? Waste of a nice fuckin' car though." Then his demeanor took on a more serious tone. "A family vendetta, huh? You got some explainin' to do."

Zan thought about the vendetta for a moment as he stared into the ebony abyss. He muttered three words as smoke rose from the wreck. "I don't smoke," and passed the Marlboro back.

Zan lowered his voice. "They picked the wrong guy to fuck with, that's for damn sure. Jesus Christ, that was unexpected." He flicked Blake a momentary glance, just a brief movement of his eyes, his head didn't turn, his eyes tracking slowly back to the rising smoke, following it to its source. As he craned his neck for a better view, he said in a quivering voice, "Jesus Christ, I don't believe it!"

*****

EXCERPT

SHADES OF GRAY

"Recent discoveries in quantum physics have revealed there are many universes. Our Libra facility in Zurich is actively involved in sub-atomic particle transference." He paused and took in the looks of confusion. "To put this simply, we've already moved subjects to a parallel universe, successfully transporting people through time, proving we can go back – that we can, in fact, visit the past."

Sam placed his cup noisily on the table as the three agents sitting around him grunted, sighed, and shuffled about in disbelief. Blake looked across at Danzig and shook his head. Danzig was quick to respond. "I agree, Mr. Blake. Believing in man's ability to travel to parallel universes has until recently been considered by most to be a ludicrous theory – nothing more than pure science fiction."

"Rightfully so," Sam groaned, again scrubbing at his head.

"The philosophy of a single universe is similar to a driver thinking he can only move his car along a single road," Danzig said. "One from which he cannot detour."

He illustrated his point by imitating a driver's hands maneuvering a steering wheel. "He feels he cannot make a sudden turn onto a service road," and he pointed as though about to turn. "We've proven the driver can in fact take an alternative road, one running parallel to the road he's traveling on. This new road, running parallel to the original, allows him to feel the same sensations, and he therefore arrives at the same destination as he would if he'd driven on the freeway."

Dal nudged Patrice Bellinger and made an under-the-table jerking motion with one hand. Bell grinned, stifling a laugh, turning away in an effort to recompose. No longer having her attention, Dal gave a glance to Blake who'd caught the jerking hand movement and mouthed the word, *practicing?*

"Parallel universes, huh?" Sam queried with a wry smile. "Really now – this all seems totally unrealistic. Too much like science fiction. Describe it to me – what exactly is a *parallel universe?*"

"It's a duplicate image of our own world. Just as a document transmitted by a facsimile is an exact copy of the original."

"You sayin'," Blake said leaning forward, "that you've already sent people back?"

"As difficult as it is for you to believe, we have in fact transferred two of our people, Dominic Falceaux and Denis Morbeque, into a parallel universe. They had a specific assignment resulting in significant advantages for today's world." This statement produced a round of dubious eye rolling. "Our physicists," Danzig continued, "have made significant progress since Galileo, Copernicus and Newton. In their time they believed our universe to be similar to a huge clock with each of its hands marked with a dot indicating that planets moved around the sun. Back then many imagined the universe to be infinite in all directions, with space having no end. The great thinkers prior to the year 1009 believed the universe occupied every corner of the heavens. Then along came Einstein and his theory of relativity and much of that early thinking died a quick death." Danzig stood, twitched, paced the room, paused, spiraled and gestured with one palm

615

outstretched,

"Mr. Ridkin, there are so many promising and bizarre theories subjectively studied by our group of Zurich based physicists."

Dal flipped out a fourth finger, followed by, "Your people – they *were* involved with the Eldridge experiment? Now you're sayin' you've sent those two guys someplace to another time, in another universe? Let's cut to the chase here. What's the *specific assignment* your guys were seein' to?"

"In due time, Mr. Dallas – in due time, you've heard of the Black Death, the plague of the 14th century? Do you realize the percentile reduction in the world's population in the mid-14th century due to the bubonic plague? It *was* between twenty-five and fifty percent of the population. That's around two hundred million people. Today it continues to kill about three thousand people annually. Long ago, our scientists decoded the genome of the bubonic bacterium also known as Black Death. You must realize our planet cannot support a burgeoning population and that we've already reduced our world's size on one occasion. Our intervention is not a simple matter of black or white. For survival we must think in shades of gray."

*****

REVIEWS OF THE AUTHOR'S PREVIOUS WORKS

VORTEX

First in the Drew Blake series of novels

"A fast paced sci-fi thriller set in Paris. Packed with action, French ambience, romance, and a villain

readers will ultimately be rooting for. Tears, laughter, chills and thrills, "VORTEX" has it all, a movie between the covers."

FIDDLER

Second in the Drew Blake series of novels

Is the boy next-door a killer?
Suspense, suspense, suspense!

The portrayal of a serial killer is often seen as an "unusual freak" that looks and sounds visibly different to the "norm." Not so, Andy Fillard, a musical prodigy who plays a violin, and eventually becomes a sought after teacher. Events cause him to turn his back on his musical talent. He keeps his hand in with the instrument he loves, creates the finest silent killing weapon, the garrote, a violin string stretched between wooden handles,

The FIDDLER is an ordinary insignificant man, the kind that blends into any background, melts into any crowd. Those who pass him in the street never look at him twice. For a short time he is a happily married. When that fails, he becomes a stalker, a hunter of attractive blonds, but not just women, Andy Fillard has his boys.

*****

"FIDDLER is a spine chilling read that travels along at warp speed, taking the reader on a police chase through Europe, into the monastery of Montecassino, and culminating in a surprise anti climax in Albuquerque,

New Mexico. Brilliantly written, with masterly character development, that leaves the reader wanting more."

R. Gene Heinrich

Editor: www.WritingRaw.com

*****

VATICAN FILESS

Third in the Drew Blake series of novels

As World War two drew to an end, there were in excess of seven hundred million ounces of gold in Fort Knox. This represented seventy-five percent of the world's gold inventory. Today there is no record of the amount of gold in the National Depository. A physical annual audit is federal law, but to the present day the treasury refuses to conduct one. In fact, an audit has not been conducted since 1953, not since ordered by President Eisenhower. Vatican File*SS* addresses the question - where is the missing bullion from Fort Knox? Common belief is that by the end of 1971, President Johnson consented to the Fort Knox gold being secretly removed and drained to London, supposedly to finance the war in Vietnam.

In 1982, President Ronald Regan appointed a group of men known as the Gold Commission. Their task - report to Congress on the gold reserve. The following is their final report to Congress.

"The U.S. treasury possesses no gold. The Federal Reserve now owns all of the gold that was left in Fort Knox, holding it against the national debt. This money has been stolen from the American citizens and placed into the hands of a small group of private investors in the Federal Reserve, the money changers."

A subsequent visit by world media was merely a staged event for the cameras. The strong belief is that the rear stacks within the vaults were nothing more than plated silver bullion.

"Vatican File*SS* takes the reader on a thought provoking journey that explores the origin of Nazi and Ustasha gold hoards. It exposes the ruthless killings by Ustasha Catholic priests in their routing of gold to Rome's Vatican and Swiss Banks. The search for Mussolini's dumped gold is accurately documented in this deeply researched work. Exciting and revealing – Vatican File*SS* is a hard to put down novel. Find a comfortable seat, and buckle up."

SHADES OF GRAY

Fourth in the Drew Blake series of novels

"Jason Denaro jet-propels the reader into the historic 1356 Battle of Poitiers in which King John of France struggles against the superior forces of England's Prince Edward, the Black Prince.

Shades of Gray delivers the fury and splendor of medieval times, of knights on chargers, of bitter rivalries, of vividly described blood chilling battles, and ruthless plunder.

It is a no holds barred superbly researched work based on correct time frames and events, yet delivered with a sci-fi touch. The horrific factual accounting of

619

the pandemic known as the Black Death, sets the stage for this epic adventure.

Just as the reader believes "Shades of Gray" to be a work of fiction - the modern world is confronted with a new pandemic. And another story line initially based on fiction - becomes fact. As with Fiddler, Vatican File*SS*, and Black Sabbath, Jason Denaro hits a home run and beats history to the punch. Shades is a spellbinding read from beginning to end, one that will satisfy a broad spectrum of readers, from historical to science fiction to adventure to thriller - Shades of Gray delivers."

Stephen S. Martino

Harvard

*****

Visit the author's website at www.JasonDenaro.com

Breinigsville, PA USA
10 December 2010
250945BV00001BA/10/P